T0315281

THE
DRYAD
STORM

Also by Laurie Forest

The Black Witch Chronicles
The Black Witch
The Iron Flower
The Shadow Wand
The Demon Tide
Wandfasted (ebook novel)*
Light Mage (ebook novel)*
*Also available in print in the anthology *The Rebel Mages*

LAURIE FOREST

THE
DRYAD
STORM

HARPER
An Imprint of HarperCollins*Publishers*

To the ever growing
Worldwide Environmental Movement
Rise up, Dryad'khin

Your time has come.

Icelandic Mountains

Northern Forest

ALFSIGROTH

Northern Caledonian Mountains

GARDNERIA

GARDNERIA

•VONOR

Agolith Desert

WESTERN OCEAN

Eastern Pass

Southern Caledonian Moun

Wastelands

WESTERN REALM

North

CONTINENT OF THE REALMS

SOUTHERN OCEAN

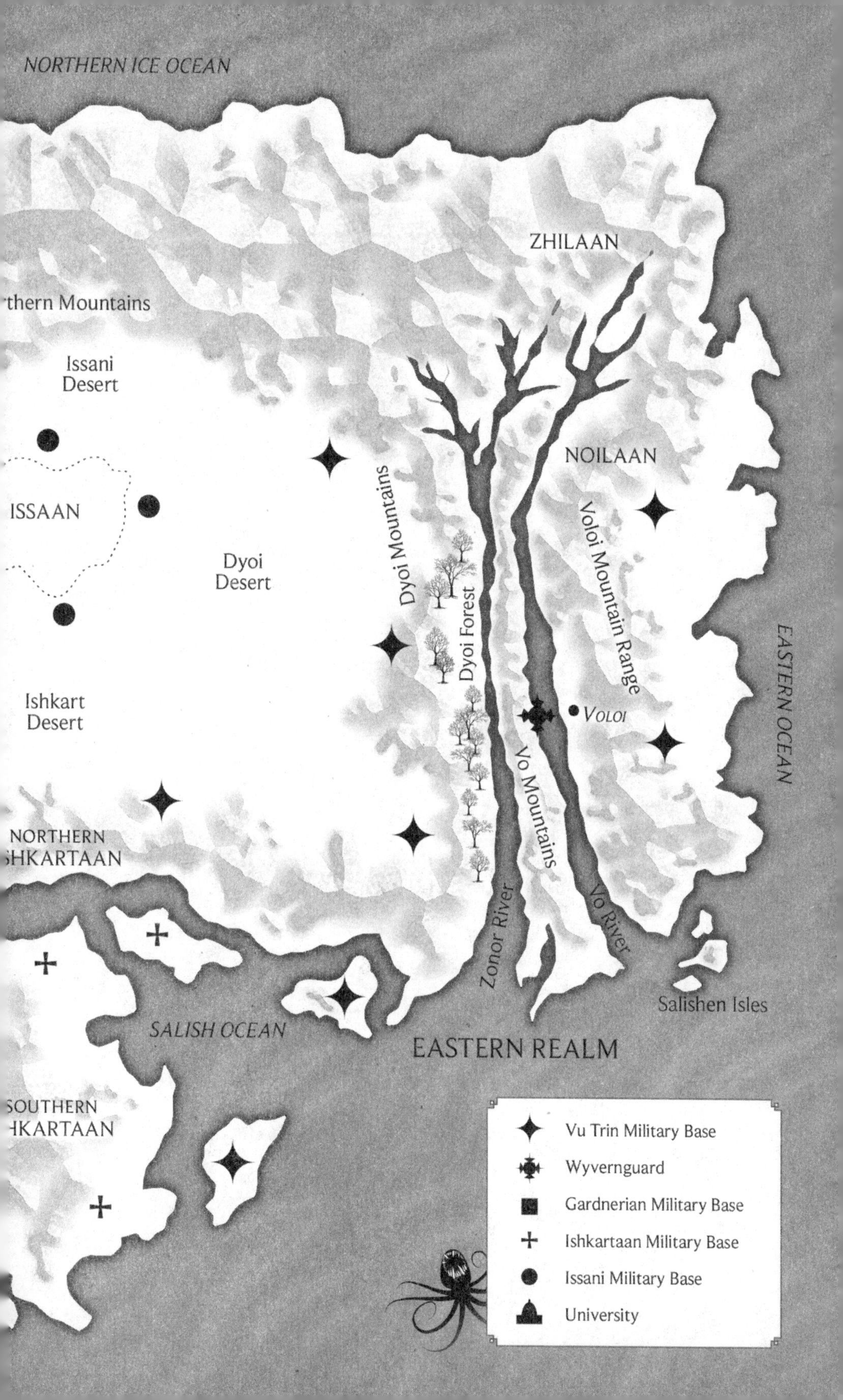
NORTHERN ICE OCEAN
ZHILAAN
rthern Mountains
Issani Desert
NOILAAN
ISSAAN
Dyoi Desert
Dyoi Mountains
Dyoi Forest
Voloi Mountain Range
Ishkart Desert
VOLOI
EASTERN OCEAN
Vo Mountains
NORTHERN
SHKARTAAN
Zonor River
Vo River
Salishen Isles
SALISH OCEAN
EASTERN REALM
SOUTHERN
HKARTAAN
Vu Trin Military Base
Wyvernguard
Gardnerian Military Base
Ishkartaan Military Base
Issani Military Base
University

PROLOGUE

Forest Prophecy
Alder Xanthos

City of Cyme, Amazakaraan
Two days before Xishlon

A primal scream tears from Alder Xanthos's throat. Explosions sound on all sides, hammering her ears as Mages soar down into Amazakaraan on their broken, shrieking dragons, laying waste to the city of Cyme.

Alder raises the living branch in her hand, her heartbeat thundering against her ribs, readying herself for battle inside the translucent green dome-shield she and her soldier friend, Vestylle Oona'rin, cast around the Queenhall to protect the fleeing Amaz.

A closer explosion sends a burst of pain through Alder's head as the Mages throw down bolt after bolt of Shadowfire, leveling the remaining buildings surrounding the Queenhall. Monstrous gray Shadow trees rise from each explosion, high as the clouds, the grotesque forest rapidly overtaking Cyme's valley under its nightmare canopy-prison.

Azion! Alder screams through her mind-link to her eagle kindred as she curses herself for sending Azion out to survey the incoming attack. Desperation rakes her throat. At any moment, Azion *has* to soar out of the Shadow chaos and through the verdant, wavering dome. She can sense his frantic heartbeats and desperation to reach her growing closer by the moment.

A powerful explosion booms from Cyme's forested periphery. Alder's lungs contract, the ground beneath her feet shuddering. The screams of trees rip through her mind, and pain streaks through her Dryad rootlines, nearly whiting out her vision. Blinking hard, she's just able to make out the wall of steely flame bursting up from the tree line edging the great valley's northern edge.

Alder watches, frozen in shock and pain, as the wall of gray flame roars north, a gigantic swath of the Caledonian Forest igniting with Shadowfire, the death of so many trees gouging a growing portion of her Forest-melded power from her lines. As she realizes, with soul-shredding horror, that the Mages on their shrieking, broken dragons aren't just bent on destroying her beloved Cyme.

They're going to raze her entire kindred *Forest*.

A stronger sense of Azion blasts through Alder, her heart-bonded bird's rasping cry of terror lashing through the back of her mind along with the screams of her dying Forest.

"Azion!" Alder bellows, launching herself toward the shield, ready to hurl herself clear through it.

A strong hand clamps around her shoulder, and she skids to a stop.

Alder whips her head around to find Vestylle holding her with a viselike grip, fierceness marking the young Smaragdalfar sorceress's emerald-patterned face, a rune stylus glowing green in Vestylle's hand.

"Let me go!" Alder growls, yanking herself away from Vestylle. She moves to launch herself at the shield, her mind pounding with combined terror for Azion and her Forest as her kindred eagle draws closer.

"No!" Vestylle snaps as she takes hold of Alder once more. "They'll *kill you* like they killed our queen! We've got to get East *now*!"

Wild desperation overtaking her, Alder struggles against Vestylle's grip. *"Azion!"* she screams, kicking and flailing as Vestylle drags her toward the Queenhall's Subland entrance.

Alder's anguish turns feral. Because she knows what Vestylle is doing, pulling her through an arching doorway, down spiraling stairs cut into the valley's pale stone, then through a crimson-torchlit cavern. She's being dragged toward the emergency portals in the Sublands below the Queenhall—portals through which almost all the surviving Amaz have already escaped to the East, save for the portal guards, Alder, and Vestylle, their small group the last of the rearguard soldiers reinforcing the failing shield with their combined Dryad and Smaragdalfar magic.

The only types of magic able to tenuously hold their power against the Magedom's incoming Shadow.

Azion's and the Forest's terror burgeons, blazing through Alder's weakening rootlines, as she's hit with the growing awareness that her kindred bird is just outside the shield. With a snarl, she breaks free of Vestylle's grip and launches into a run back toward the stairs.

THE DRYAD STORM

"Alder!" Vestylle cries.

Alder barely registers the panic in her friend's voice as she sprints up the stairs, multiple explosions rattling the very earth.

Rattling her *Forest*.

"Don't be a *fool!*" Vestylle bellows, thumping up the stairs behind her. "Our shield is about to fall!"

Ignoring her, Alder sprints toward the top of the stairs, agony piercing her chest as Azion's frantic call blasts through their bond along with the horrified screams of her tree kindreds.

Azion! My Forest! I'm coming!

Her eagle kindred's squawking cries tear through Alder's mind with slingshot force as she reaches the top of the newly deserted stairs and races toward the door, her whole being distilled into the desire to save her kindred bird and Forest. Her beautiful feathered one . . . her *trees* . . .

"Alder!" Vestylle yells again.

Alder's magic plummets as the Shadowfire spreads through her Forest. Certain of her narrowing window of time, Alder spins, rasps out a Dryadin spell, and thrusts her branch toward Vestylle, hurling out magic.

A green, glass-like shield rises from the ground before Vestylle, her friend's silver eyes widening as she's forced to a halt at the top of the staircase.

Emboldened, Alder turns and throws the Queenhall's door open, bursts through it . . . and skids to a stop.

High Mage Marcus Vogel sits on dragonback just past the rapidly decaying dome-shield, his dark cloak flowing behind him, Fallon Bane on dragonback beside him. There's a dark gray wand in Vogel's hand.

Shadow curling from its tip.

Vogel narrows his pale green eyes, a vicious glint in them as his lip ticks up. "Dryad," he croons. "We've been searching for you."

Pulse quickening, Alder pivots her gaze to Fallon Bane, who gloats at her from astride her multi-eyed dragon, a dark wand in her hand. Fallon and Vogel are surrounded by an army, spectral fingers of Shadow mist rising around them from the plaza's stone floor.

Alder looks around frantically as her sense of her kindred eagle's proximity intensifies. The heat in her rootlines turns agonizing, her trees crying out to her as they burn, the giant Shadow trees the Mages cast over Cyme looming mockingly above.

Rage blasting through her, Alder raises her living branch and aims it straight at Vogel.

"Go ahead, greenling," Fallon Bane chides, a smug smile overtaking her mouth as she raises her dark wand toward the distant sky.

Roaring wind powers to life over Alder's flaming Forest, forming churning clouds rife with black lightning. Two tornadoes descend from the unnatural clouds, and Alder watches, wide-eyed, as they funnel toward the flaming trees.

An explosion detonates, and Alder flinches, her rootlines contracting painfully as the gray Shadowfire whips into the tornadoes, then bursts over a huge expanse of her Forest. A vision slashes through Alder's mind's eye, overtaking her sight—her beloved animals futilely trying to flee from the terrifying Shadowfire as her miraculous Forest, more complex than any human city, burns. Color is stripped away from the Forest as it falls to the unnatural fire, the Shadow leaving behind only gray waste just as it has in the city, consuming all color except for the green of the Mages' skin, the Forest green hue of her own skin, and the emerald green of Vestylle's.

And the green glow of her and Vestylle's magic.

Warrior fury sizzles through Alder, and she glares daggers at the evil forces before her. A spell snarling from her throat, she raises her branch once more, tenses her rootlines, and pulls on her power . . .

. . . only to find it depleting to char as her kindred Forest is murdered, tree by tree.

"It's working," Vogel observes to Fallon, all the Mages' eyes focused on Alder with glittering looks of anticipation.

Panic rising, Alder glances down to find the hue of her hands and lower arms graying as her power is siphoned out of her. In some small recess of her grief-razed mind, realization hits. They're *experimenting* on her. Her gaze slides to the Shadow Wand in Vogel's hand, and she can *feel* it. Feel the Wand eating her Forest's magical aura and siphoning away both her power and the elemental magic of the trees as her Forest burns, its magic morphing into twisted Void power . . .

"*Azion!*" Alder screams again, the name torn from her heart.

Time is running out. Her shield is wavering along with her diminishing power, and Vestylle will have to seal the portals in a matter of minutes. But in this moment, she doesn't care. She can sense Azion, her beloved winged one, *right here.*

Commander Damion Bane emerges from the Shadow mist, gliding into view on dragonback, a bright, wicked smile on his face as his dragon halts beside his sister's.

His green eyes narrow on Alder with delight. "Is this what you're looking for?"

THE DRYAD STORM

He raises a limp golden eagle in the air, the bird's talons gripped in his fist.

The ground seems to shift beneath Alder's feet, and she almost drops to her knees.

All the gold and russet hues have been stripped from Azion's beautiful form, only pale gray remaining, one of his wings nearly torn off. Black blood cakes his feathers, his injured wing hanging limply from his body. His powerful beak is tied with dark Shadow vine, and his once golden eyes . . . they're ash-hued as they meet Alder's gaze with a misery so acute that Alder fears she might come undone.

In that split second as their eyes meet, a thousand memories flash through Alder's mind. Countless sunsets with Azion on her shoulder. The two of them nestled high in the trees of their Forest. Watching Azion's first hatchlings emerge, proud joy in both their breasts . . .

Damion hoists the eagle and shakes him like one might shake a sack of millet. "It was crawling toward your shield," he sneers. "Was it looking for you? Put up an impressive fight, I'll admit. I enjoyed breaking it. It flopped around so pathetically after I smashed its wing."

Wrath surges through Alder's veins. With a growl, she leaps toward Damion Bane, ready to hurl herself through her sputtering shield, even as every military instinct within her blares out *Stop! It's a trap!* and Vogel raises his Wand . . .

The door behind her bangs open, and a cord whips around her ankles and wrists, then gives a violent backward tug.

A protest bursts from Alder as her legs are pulled out from under her just as Vogel's bolt of Shadow hits her shield, the decaying barrier punching inward, its green hue turning gray.

"Stop!" Alder growls as the side of her shoulder and face collide with the tiled ground and she's slid backward. She glances behind her, finding herself tethered by glowing emerald Varg cords, Vestylle dragging her toward the Queenhall's Subland entrance as Azion lets out another soul-breaking squawk of distress.

Clawing futilely for purchase, Alder looks toward the Mages just as Vestylle blasts out green rays of light from her stylus. Several suspended Varg runes, big as wagon wheels, flash into existence and hurtle toward the Queenhall's dome-shield.

The runes slam into the shield and are absorbed, Vestylle's Varg power racing over the translucent green barrier and overtaking the gray just as Vogel levels another blast of Shadow power at their barrier. Its surface punches in farther this time, Alder's desperation skyrocketing.

Azion is *so close.*

"*Let me GO!*" Alder rages at Vestylle.

"*NO!*" Vestylle snarls back at her, just as Alcippe Feyir races out of the Queen-hall and takes hold of one of Alder's tethers, the huge rose-hued Amaz warrior aiding Vestylle in dragging Alder backward.

"The Mages want to trap you and take hold of you!" Vestylle grinds out. "Just like they took Wynter and Valasca as their prisoners!"

"*Azion!*" Alder cries, half hearing Vestylle as she struggles against her bonds and is towed by both Vestylle and Alcippe toward the doorway.

"You will *live*, Dryad'kin!" Vestylle insists as they near the door, the sorceress's voice breaking with emotion. "You will live to avenge Azion!"

"*No . . . NO!*" Alder screams as she's pulled through the open door and Vogel's viperlike expression turns venomous.

"We'll track you down, tree filth," Vogel promises, giving Damion Bane a quick, prodding look.

Damion shoots Alder a smile and grips Azion's head, then wrenches it around so hard Alder can hear the crunching break.

"*No!*" she screams again, her whole world caving in around her as she senses Azion's pulse cease. "*NO!*"

Damion Bane's amused chuckle is the last thing Alder hears before she's hauled down the stone stairs, screaming, the entire world reduced to the shattering of her heart. She continues to scream, barely noticing herself being yanked through a winding tunnel and thrown through the shimmering gold interior of the last remaining charged portal, set for the East.

Alder hurtles out of the portal's golden maw and is thrust into a purple Forest with gray-tinged leaves, her stomach heaving.

Her grayed hands slap down on violet grass, and she gasps for breath. She looks around frantically, not knowing how long she's been caught in the portal's lag.

Has it been days? Weeks? She's certain the lag was significant, with so many people traveling such a vast distance through the portal, the lag longer still for the last ones through.

Beyond the trees' purple canopy, she can just make out a decimated mountain range. Its upper half looks like it's been blasted away, tendrils of Shadow rising from it, the sight increasing her alarm.

Alder's bonds dissolve, and she springs up, whirls around, and leaps back toward the portal only to find herself stumbling straight through its fading form.

"Azion!" she cries with such force she almost vomits, her legs buckling as the last of her magic shreds inside her, the remaining traces of her green glimmer turning full gray.

Overcome by despair and the soul-crushing sensation of her dying distant Forest, she falls to her knees. The heartbreaking image of the tortured Azion and the sound of his last pained cry tear through her devastated mind again and again and *again*.

Alder throws back her head and wails, dropping her now lifeless branch to the ground, her kindred gone, her Forest gone.

Her Dryad heart destroyed.

She remains there, gutted by grief, knowing the only reason she survived the murder of her kindred Forest is that her lineage is not full Dryad.

She rises shakily from the purple brush as Vestylle, Alcippe, and a clutch of Amaz soldiers step toward her, their faces as grave as the overcast sky.

Growling, Alder springs at Vestylle and shoves her with the last of her strength.

Vestylle stumbles backward, looking distraught. "I'm sorry," she chokes out, tears glazing her silver eyes. "Alder, I'm so sorry—"

"Leave. Me. *Be*," Alder snarls back in Dryadin, not caring that Vestylle doesn't understand the language. Not caring about *anything*.

Lips trembling, Vestylle holds up her palms in surrender.

Alder turns and stumbles away from them all, shambling toward the edge of the purple clearing, before her legs give way and she crumples into a magic-depleted heap.

"Leave me alone!" she hisses at any Amaz who tries to come near, knowing she's now a destroyed thing, *none* of them understanding. *None* of them of Dryad blood. With Azion and her kindred Forest, she was never broken, never alone, even though it was often a lonely path, being the sole Dryad'kin amongst the Amaz. But *now* . . . now she is truly alone and broken, despite her bonds to her adopted people. She's forever forsaken without her Forest, like an animal whose habitat and sustenance has been annihilated, her rootlines stripped bare.

Shattered, Alder sits for a long time and watches the Amaz soldiers come and go, until dusk descends and thunder rolls across the bleak gray sky.

"When she gets hold of herself, we're going to need her," Alcippe says to Vestylle.

Alder looks on listlessly as the warriors turn toward where she's still bunched up on the ground at the edge of the clearing in the gloomy twilight. Alder can practically feel the grief spitting off her own grayed skin, her rootlines stripped raw. Killed off, like her Forest.

Like Azion.

"She needs time," Vestylle insists, face tense. "She just lost her Forest. Her *kindred*—"

"There is no *time!*" Alcippe snaps back, her tattooed features twisting. "The Mages used their attack on Noilaan as *practice*. The destruction of Amazakaraan was *practice*. And killing the greatest queen who ever lived, more *practice!*" Alcippe shakes her head, seeming too choked up to continue.

Grief for Queen Alkaia knifes through Alder, followed by a welling of rancid misery for her friend Valasca and the gentle Icaral Wynter Eirllyn, both taken prisoner by the Mages.

Alcippe drags her hand across her eyes, swiping away tears. "Apparently, while we were all caught in the portal lag, the Mage Roaches annexed the entirety of Issaan. Refugees are streaming into Noilaan. The Issani brought the last surviving flock of their giant Saffron Eagles with them, but the birds are going to die. They won't eat. They need their natural habitat, but it's gone. The Mages razed Issaan's entire Olneya Forest."

Vestylle glances at Alder with concern, and Alder knows her friend is worried about the mention of eagles and forests. And she's right to be. It's like a knife strike straight through Alder's chest to hear of yet more displaced eagles and their destroyed habitat. She also knows that the destruction of the giant Saffron Eagles and their Forest is a chilling omen written about in the Issani religious texts, signaling the triumph of the incoming Shadow evil.

Stricken, Alder looks toward the decimated Vo Mountain Range. She overheard that they're in Noilaan's Vo Forest, about a league north of Voloi. But even this far from the city, the purple trees carpeting the mountain's slope are tinged gray, a remnant of Vogel's Shadow attack on Voloi.

The Magedom's Shadow poison entrenched here in the East just as it is in the West.

Alcippe gestures toward her. "We're going to need Alder's forest-empath abilities to read where Elloren Gardner Grey is through the trees."

Alder startles. Through her morass of grief, her every last Dryad sense pricks up. The recesses of her mind light with memories of her moments in Verpacia with

THE DRYAD STORM

Elloren Gardner Grey, a Dryad-lineage one. An untethered Mage, like all Mages, shunned by the Forest.

But Elloren . . . she was different from so many Mages. So much so that Alder and Valasca allied with her to rescue trafficked Selkies as well as to free the Icaral Ariel Haven and the Icaral child Pyrgo from Valgard's prison.

Every nerve on alert, Alder listens as Alcippe and Vestylle converse in low tones. Alcippe conveys what they've learned of the Magedom's attack on the Eastern Realm—Voloi and its Wyvernguard are in ruins. And a freak explosion took out the top half of the Vo Mountain Range and Vogel's hidden Shadow forces within it, that explosion responsible for saving the rest of Noilaan from Mage invasion and complete Shadow destruction.

"I was right about the Crow Witch," Alcippe says, her tone as weighty as the huge axe strapped to her back. "Elloren Gardner Grey is Vogel's witch now. She conjured a great Shadow tree over the Vo River. Almost destroyed the entirety of Voloi and beyond until the Icaral male Yvan Guryev struck her down, as *I should have* when I had the chance."

Urgency lights in Alder, her mother's blood swelling in her veins with its mix of Wyvern, Urisk, and Ishkart heritage. Alder remembers her Wyvern senses picking up the fire churning in Yvan Guryev, back when she thought him Yvan Guriel, part Fire Fae, never suspecting the wings he was hiding. She also remembers how his fire *burned* for Elloren Gardner Grey.

And Elloren . . . her desire to fight against the Magedom and for her allies and loved ones was true.

And she burned for Yvan Guryev in return.

Alder chews over this information, shocked that Yvan was the one to bring the Black Witch down. Then shocked again as she listens, with her Wyvern hearing, to learn that Elloren escaped the Eastern Realm, Vogel having taken over her body and mind.

Alder's grief implodes into an abyss, scouring her out fully.

Because things are truly over for every Forest on Erthia.

It's only a matter of time.

With his captive Black Witch and growing Shadow power, Vogel will be *unstoppable.*

So, a few hours later, when Alcippe calls to her in a stilted attempt at a gentle voice, "Alder, Queen Freyja has summoned you to her," instead of heeding the call to any queen, Alder gets up on unsteady legs and walks away from Alcippe and Vestylle.

Because it's all over.

"Let her go," she hears Vestylle urge as Alder stumbles into the unfamiliar purple woods, not caring about the tears blurring her vision, not caring if she walks through this foreign wilderness until she passes out. Wanting to die with the last remnants of living Forest.

As the purple trees close in around her and thunder drums in the distance, this Forest's unfamiliar birdsong wrenches her heart anew.

Eventually, Alder falls to her knees, wave upon wave of sorrow swamping her. She presses her palms to the dark purple trunk before her, hangs her head and weeps.

She senses the Forest waking up to her. Senses the settling of its gentle aura around her shoulders like a soft cloak. And then, its rippling wave of connection, Tree'kin to Tree'kin.

The love and complex beauty in this purple Forest's enfolding energy shatters Alder's heart anew, because she knows what's coming—the Magedom's Shadow magic is going to consume this Forest *whole*, along with every other surviving Forest.

And a world without Forest, without trees, is *finished*.

Alcippe's voice invades her mind—

We're going to need Alder to read where the Black Witch is through the trees.

Her throat clenches with bark-hard defiance. She won't scry the Forest in front of any Amaz, not even her new queen. No, she'll read how her Forest will end *alone* and spare her people this horror. That will be her final gift to them. Her late mother, a Great Seer for the Amaz, inherited the divination power of every group in her Ishkart, Urisk, and Wyvern lineage, and Alder has inherited these scrying abilities in turn, along with her mother's power empathy. But unlike her mother and other seers, Alder has no need for scrying cards made from stiff leaves, or for sticks for casting. She needs no candle or incense smoke to coax meaning from wood. She can read the trees directly.

For, like her father, she is most essentially Dryad'kin, through and through.

And so, bracing herself to face the incoming horror, Alder pushes both palms hard against the deep-purple trunk before her and slides her fingertips over the crenelated bark, letting splinters pierce the skin under her grayed nails, blood to sap for the deepest of readings.

THE DRYAD STORM

For this final, world-upending reading.

Alder shudders as the Forest's consciousness links with her mind and blasts Elloren Gardner Grey's face into her thoughts.

Alder pulls in a hard, rasping breath, her world tilting once more. Because Elloren . . .

. . . she's deeply altered, her ears now gentle points, her hue a deeper forest green.

A full *Dryad* green, with a new moss-green streak running through her midnight-black hair.

Alder's back arches, every muscle stiffening as she's flooded with the astonishing sense of Elloren's link to III, the Great Northern Source Tree. The Third Sacred Tree of Erthia. Elloren has been utterly transformed into something new, completely free of Vogel's Shadow grip.

No longer the Black Witch but a *Dryad* Witch.

Aligned with the Forest and with Erthia's rejuvenating power.

Alder digs in deeper, nails biting into bark, blood flowing into wood. Confusion wells as she reads the prophecy still flowing through the Forest's sap, the Black Witch still destined to fight the Great Icaral. A remembrance of the twin tornadoes Fallon Bane so easily conjured to rip apart Alder's Forest assaults her, and the blood drains from her face.

Could Fallon be the true Black Witch instead of Elloren? Destined to fight Yvan Guryev? While Elloren is now a weapon aligned with the Forest.

A weapon who could turn the tide of that prophesied battle.

Alder's heartbeat quickens, gooseflesh rushing over her skin.

Once Vogel finds out Elloren has become a Dryad Fae, he will want her dead. And Alder overheard Alcippe telling Freyja that the Vu Trin are bent on slaying Elloren, as well. *Everyone* will want to slay her, including the Amaz. Alder knows there will be no convincing her people to align with Elloren based on her reading from the trees, not after the destruction Elloren came close to raining down on Voloi.

Alder's heart beats faster.

Vogel knows what it takes to kill a Dryad. A chill races down her spine. She looks at her grayed hands and tenses her withered rootlines. Vogel *knows* that he can deplete Dryad power by killing the wilds.

And he's not just targeting the Forest.

She can feel, in the trees' consciousness, that Vogel's Shadow power is massing against the waterways and oceans too. Even the skies above.

A multipronged attack of Shadow, brewing against the entire Natural World.

It's true, what Alcippe conveyed, Alder considers as she grips the tree. *His attack on Amazakaraan and the East was just the beginning.*

Practice.

Which means the Dryad Tree'kin are going to need everyone united in this fight if they're going to save Erthia.

But . . . it's *impossible.*

The threat too huge, the people who might fight it too beaten down and divided, even though the trees now have Elloren on their side.

"Show me what to do," Alder rasps to the Forest, quivering with despair.

The image of a Wand-Stylus, glowing green and edged with prismatic light, shimmers into Alder's mind.

A rush of connection to that Wand-Stylus whips around her, coursing through her with chest-expanding force, the palm of her right hand tingling. Alder pulls her hand away from the trunk and draws in a shocked breath as she finds the image of III—the Great Tree and Heart of the Forest—imprinted on her palm. She peers up at the purple canopy, tears in her eyes, as she realizes what this purple Vo Forest is doing.

Marking her as its Guardian.

"I can't be Guardian to you," she chokes out. "My kindred has been *murdered.* I cannot be Guardian without a kindred."

A crackling of twigs sounds, and Alder turns as an emaciated, horse-size eagle staggers toward her. Its singed feathers are a wash of grays, its eyes dulled by devastation, burn marks on its taloned feet.

"Oh," Alder says, compassion tightening her chest as fresh tears well. As she realizes this damaged Forest is bringing her a fellow orphan.

And this giant winged one isn't a gray eagle at all.

This is one of the Saffron Eagles from the decimated Central Desert lands, stripped of her color by Shadow and torn from her home. Alder can sense the bird's grief over this strange new place. Over the *wrongness* of this habitat.

"Both of us," she says to the eagle, her voice breaking, "both of us have lost our habitat."

Alder holds out a shaking hand, and the eagle nears cautiously, then lowers her great head, Alder's palm meeting grayed feathers. They touch, forehead to forehead, and Alder is flooded with the bird's heartbreak, her hands trembling against feathers and bark.

And as much as her own heart is broken in this moment, as much as her kindred's death feels like it destroyed her very soul, a remaining shard of Alder's heart knows that this new Forest, a Forest that has just weathered its own devastating blow . . .

It's calling to her.

Calling her to take this equally battered bird as kindred. To bind with this Forest as Guardian, even with the unstoppable Shadow bearing down. To find the allies of the Dryad Witch—her fellow Forest Guardian—so they can save Elloren Gardner Grey. And to find the Forest's Wand of Power—the Verdyllion, the Great Wand of Myth.

And so, even though her body quivers with grief, Alder summons her last remnant of courage and answers the Dryad call.

"I accept you," she says in Dryadin to the bird, voice breaking as she caresses the side of the eagle's great head. "In the name of Azion, my beloved, I accept you as kindred." She looks to the gray-tinged purple canopy above, pressing her free palm to bark. "And I accept you, Vo Forest, as Guardian'kin. I will fight for you. I will die for you. I pledge myself to you, Forest kindred."

Silence descends, even the chirring of insects momentarily ceasing.

And then, the Forest's aura loosens in a great rumble and flows in, a huge sigh pushed through Alder's chest as the trees' Life-giving energy rushes through her rootlines, restoring her Dryad magic, the tingling energy passing from her into her eagle, who shivers, as well. Alder's eyes widen as the deep-green glimmer of her skin returns and a violet branching pattern spreads over it, even as a smattering of the great eagle's grayed feathers morph into the color of flame, the eagle's eyes brightening to orange.

Fireling. The Saffron Eagle's Issani name lights in Alder's mind.

"Well met, Fireling," Alder says, her heart swelling. "We will fight together, Great One, for what's left of our Forest."

More rustling echoes in the woods, and Alder gasps as six more emaciated gray eagles move toward her, then three more. Forest power rushes through the root-rich ground toward the eagles, and they stiffen, smatterings of gray feathers turning flame-hued, their dulled eyes lighting into sunburnt orange.

"My flock," Alder whispers, realizing in one monumental sweep of emotion that no one is ever truly lost, truly alone.

Not while there are trees still rooted and breathing on Erthia's soil.

The Shadow is coming for the land, she thinks to her displaced flock and battered Forest. *It's coming for you. But it's also coming for the Air and the Life-giving Waters.*

It's coming.

She looks at each of the eagles in turn. "Who here will fight with me for the Forest?"

The eagles fan out their wings as one and lower themselves to the ground, wings to roots, as pride bursts through Alder's breast.

"We fight then, kindreds," she vows, Dryad and Amaz steel rising.

Forest steel rising.

"In the name of Azion, free eagle of the Caledonian Mountains," Alder vows, "we fight for the surviving Forest."

Purple branches from every nearby tree drop down around her, one landing in Alder's lap. Tears mist her eyes, and power from the ground rushes into her and thrums through her Dryad rootlines.

A sense of the momentous building, Alder picks up one of the purple branches. The Forest's power surges through her and into it, connecting the branch to her rootlines and filling it with life. Tightening her grip around the living branch, Alder sheathes it at her side . . . and rises.

✳

PRELUDE

✳

CHAPTER ONE

SELKIE MAGE

Gareth Keeler

Salishen Isles, Eastern Realm
Xishlon night

Gareth glances up at the purple moon through Noilaan's translucent dome-shield, unsure he'll be able to get through this Xishlon night without his heart breaking completely apart.

This love-amplifying purple moonlight . . . he knows it's a source of festivity for the Noi'khin. His fellow Vu Trin soldiers are excitedly streaming off *The Water Viper*—the naval ship they're all stationed on. Several other Vu Trin naval ships are docked here, just below where the huge Vo River meets the Salish Ocean, but the ship Gareth is stationed on is unique in that the majority of its naval soldiers are Sylphan Air Fae. His fellow Vu Trin barely spare him a glance as they disembark, having been granted a Xishlon-evening's leave by their tough but fair-minded commander, the young Sylphan Air Fae Zephyr Quillen.

Gareth ties off one of the ship's dock lines to a steel hitch and pauses, drawn in by the rippling violet water before him, the Xishlon moon a wavy reflection in it. As if the moon's location is not in the lavender-star-splashed sky above but in the ocean world below.

The moon's thrall is a mounting torment, filling his heart with a ceaseless, serrated longing for a Selkie who is oceans away, living in the waters' great depths.

Where he can never follow.

Gareth fights the urge to jump through that shimmering violet moon straight into the Salish Ocean's waters. To submerge himself and swim west without ceasing.

Until he finds Marina.

The bond they formed in Verpacia is always at the forefront of his mind, as is the kiss they shared in the foyer of the North Tower, not long before she regained her skin and power.

It was like all the tides of Erthia had broken free.

One kiss led to another and another, the two of them not able to bear being parted that evening. And so, they snuck out, and he let her lead him through the nighttime woods under a full moon like this one. The two of them journeyed through the dark toward the lake they could both sense, the body of water nestled deep within the Verpacian wilds.

Standing on the lake's bank as wildlife softly chirred around them, Marina sinuously drew off his tunic and kissed the skin over his thrumming heart. She pulled off her own clothing, Gareth's pulse quickening as desire raced through his veins in response to the sight of Marina's moon-washed, naked form. And then, she took his hand in hers and, together, they walked into the water. Not into the sweet kiss of salt water that Gareth knew they both craved, but still, being in water of any type was always so much better than bearing the harsh desiccation of land.

Far under the water they pulled each other close and kissed unreservedly, giving in to the powerful draw they'd both felt building for some time. A draw Gareth had forcibly held himself removed from, especially given the particular cruelties Marina had endured on land.

That most female Selkies endured on land.

They stopped short of taking each other to mate that evening, even though it had felt right in a soul-deep way. Because they also knew that a life mated to each other would forever turn her into a cursed creature like him—trapped between two worlds.

Yes, if he remains very still, he can stay underwater for an unnaturally long time, but not long enough to make a life beneath the waves, his half-Selkie lungs cursedly dependent on air.

"If you were Selkie . . ." Marina had ventured, her melodic voice tight with anguish, "I'd take you as my ooo'ohn'uuniahohn'."

The vibration of her language through the dark water shivered through Gareth, his neck arching slightly as his bones resonated with its low frequency.

And Gareth knew, without Marina needing to translate, the meaning of her words.

The one you join your tides to.

But the terrible fact remained—he's not full Selkie.

And he's not fully a Mage either.

He's always been able to sense the water power that flows through his affinity lines with the strength of an oceanic tide. But every time he was wandtested, he found himself unable to manifest even a drop of it.

His magic completely trapped inside him.

Strangled.

After Marina left that night, he remained on the lake's bottom for a long time, alone in the dark, never wanting to emerge. Close to an hour later, he surfaced, raging and gulping for air. Cursing his very lungs over the need for it.

Cursing the very air he needed to keep living this trapped life.

"Do you even feel it, Crow?"

The familiar, taunting female voice hits like a hammer, shattering Gareth's thoughts, hurtling him back to the present. He focuses on tying off one final line before rising to meet the Sylphan Fae soldier Xylo Skye's confrontational storm-gray stare. There's an unkind smile on her pewter lips, her slender form bracketed by a knot of other naval Vu Trin, their black uniforms, like Gareth's own, marked with a blue dragon—the Goddess Vo's water manifestation.

Xylo Skye points toward the violet moon above. "I bet the Xishlon moon doesn't affect you."

"Of course it doesn't," blue-hued Thym'ellia Vyyr bites out from beside her. The Urisk soldier tosses Gareth an unfriendly grin. "Mages don't have hearts, you know that."

Gareth inwardly flinches as, laughing, they saunter off, making their way toward the purple-glittering port city of Salish. A cacophony of music dances in the air, sensual drumbeats resonating through Gareth as he stares after the soldiers. Stares over the bustling city as the moon's thrall scours out his heart anew.

"Pay them no heed."

Unable to swallow the ache in his throat, Gareth turns toward Commander Quillen and meets her steady gaze.

His young commander's stance is strong, radiating her ever-present intensity, like a typhoon about to be unleashed. Her puffed hair is the mottled-steel hues of storm clouds, her skin the ashen black of a hurricane's eye, her ears curving to sharp points.

He's heard stories of his commander's childhood years—taken in by the siblings Lucretia and Fain Quillen after Zephyr's parents were murdered by Gardnerians. Lucretia and Fain were almost killed themselves by the tornado that six-year-old

THE DRYAD STORM

Zephyr summoned as her parents were cut down, the screaming, raging child raining down hail the size of boulders as Lucretia and Fain battled back her magic and got her off the Spine's apex before the Gardnerians could murder her too.

"Did they give you a hard time about your hair in the West?" Zephyr Quillen asks Gareth in that succinct way of hers.

She doesn't need to specify what she means. Gareth knows she's asking if he was tormented for his Selkie silver-tipped black hair back in Gardneria.

"They did," he replies, his words clipped and devoid of emotion. But he can remember the taunts as if it were yesterday. His ostracism in Valgard.

And the danger.

He was beaten more than once by other Mage teens, his only solace escaping by boat to the ocean. Or visiting with Elloren, Trystan, and Rafe Gardner. Especially Trystan, Gareth's closest friend in all the world prior to meeting Marina, perhaps the only Mage Gareth knows who completely understands what it means to live on the reviled outside of things. And Trystan always seemed to comprehend, in his quiet, deep way, Gareth's constant pain over being kept forever from the ocean's depths. Forever skimming its surface.

Gareth can sense Commander Quillen's understanding as well. It never fails to touch him, since her own life was ripped apart by Mages, a group he's firmly slotted into here in the East. Yet, here she is, pausing with him instead of frolicking with the others under this cursedly beckoning moon.

"Many years ago," Zephyr says as she squints up at the violet orb, the metal hoops rimming her ears catching its jeweled light, "my people terrorized both the Kelts and what they called at the time the 'Lesser Fae.' Summoned wind swirls to slam them into distant targets for sport." She lets out a disdainful breath through her teeth. "Basically scared them into paying a land tax. I read about it in some Keltish history books in the Voloi University archives. The Sylphan aristocracy was *monstrous.*"

She sets her piercing gaze back on Gareth. "About three generations later, after a stormy revolution, the Sylphan monarchy was ousted and, over time, the Air Fae Court became a Sidhe voice for the oppressed—a true light in this world." Her lips thin. "But I keep my people's cruel ancient history in my thoughts. A cautionary tale, if you will." She tilts her head, bringing her hands to her hips. "None of it defines me, Noi'khin. Neither the cruelty, nor the light. Nor should being a Mage define you. We make our own way in this world." A heartfelt note steals into her tone. "I see it in you, Selkie'kin. I see how land is not your true home."

Gareth stiffens and looks away, his jaw tensing as the truth of her words prompts an upswell of yearning in his chest.

"Here," Commander Quillen says gruffly. Gareth turns to find her thrusting a small black cloth pouch toward him. "Your holiday pay." Her lips tilt up. "And a small stash of Sanjire root." She swipes her hand toward the city, her usual brusque manner returning. "Go. Take the evening off. 'Find the moon.'" She cocks a brow at him, an amused glint in her eyes. "Or find some good wine, at least." Her gaze hardens. "Tomorrow, we sail."

To war.

A chill runs down Gareth's spine.

But he's ready. Ready to use his uncanny sense of ocean tides and incoming weather to aid the Vu Trin navy.

To fight the Magedom.

Gareth accepts the pouch, and Commander Quillen gives him a curt nod then strides off. When he glances down at the pouch once more, his gaze slides to the green glimmer of his Mage skin. A glimmer even the purple Xishlon moon can't tint away.

The ache in his heart resurging, he thrusts the pouch into his pants' pocket and strides off the dock and onto the large boardwalk that edges the beach. But not across it and into the festive city.

Instead, Gareth walks away from the city, ignoring the curious looks and glares cast his way by revelers he passes as he follows a pull on his heart that's stronger than the Xishlon moon's.

Some boisterous Noi children race in front of him, gripping streamers of linked violet runic orbs and sparklers crackling with lavender light, and Gareth's gaze lands on a Wanted poster affixed to the boardwalk piling beside him. His steps slow then stop as he pauses before it.

Elloren.

He's seen these postings before, and he fears for his friend. The news that Elloren has Black Witch power was shocking in the extreme. He's sure she never knew it. Sure that someone tampered with her wandtestings. Made her a pawn in some hidden game.

Yes, someone knew.

That whole time they were at Verpax University, someone *had* to have known what she was. He remembers how he and Elloren promised to fast to each other if it came to it, when the threat of forced wandfastings loomed over everyone. How they were always there for each other, their friendship a solid, sure comfort in an increasingly cruel world.

Gareth tears his gaze from the posting and resumes walking, striding off the boardwalk and across the moonlit beach. Certain the Vu Trin are making a mistake. Because it's clear from Elloren's evil depiction on the postings that they're not simply searching for her. They're *hunting* her.

He's spoken to Commander Quillen about it. Openly voiced his support for Elloren. Refuted the slurs aimed at her by his fellow Vu Trin mariners, which only reinforced his outcast status on his ship and in this land. Before his advocacy for Elloren, some of his fellow mariners were willing to give him a chance, but now they've stated that his "Mage blood" is rising to the surface and "polluting" the "slim bit of Selkie good." His life so oddly flipped. Reviled in the West for his silver-tipped hair and his host of odd aquatic abilities, and now, reviled in the East for the green glimmer of his skin.

Gareth pauses, finding himself alone on a blessedly isolated stretch of beach, his trapped water magic tingling with anticipation as he looks out over the water toward the forest of deep-purple mangroves in the far distance. The forest that is tugging on his Magelines. The ocean-loving trees are bunched near a narrow peninsula jutting out from the coastline, their roots arcing down into the water like curving stilts, tethered to the ocean's floor.

Trees caught in the middle—half on land, half on sea.

Just like him.

The first time he encountered Salishen's famed mangroves, he was mesmerized by them in an instant, sensing a soul-deep kinship that affected him profoundly and still does, to the point where his trapped water magic thrums to life and eddies through his lines whenever he makes contact with a mangrove tree's slick bark.

The grove wakes up to his nearness, its enthralling energy swirling around him, prompting Gareth to draw off his naval tunic. Then his boots. His socks. He piles his garb on a rocky outcropping and, dressed only in his dark uniform pants, wades into the water.

The ocean laps over his feet and ankles, warm and embracing, and Gareth pulls in a euphoric breath, entranced by the ocean's liquid beauty. Feeling like he's coming home, he keeps advancing until he's up to his neck. Then drops under.

As he launches himself into a smooth stroke, everything in Gareth yearns to inhale a deep breath of salt water. Iridescent silver fish close in around him in joyful welcome, and he swims toward the mangrove forest as if born in the ocean's depths. He darts into the grove's tangle of underwater roots, gliding just above the ocean floor.

Never wanting to surface.

His sense of homecoming increases as purple crabs scuttle boisterously around him and a violet manatee swims near to eye him with curious, affectionate interest. A school of translucent jellyfish ghost by, their ethereal beauty striking a chord deep in Gareth's Selkie soul, and he lingers amidst the Noi Mangroves' roots for a long stretch, everything in him blessedly merged with both water and grove and the kindred life they support.

But then, a tight pain in Gareth's lungs pricks to life. At first, he ignores it, his usual outrage rearing, everything in him revolting against this merciless biological need of his cursed form. But the pain intensifies, and soon his lungs are burning, hot tears warming his eyes as he's forced to swim toward the Xishlon moon's shimmering, luminous form overhead.

He bursts through the water's surface and gulps in air, raging against the moon, against every last thing keeping him away from Marina and the ocean's deepest depths, the cruel moon's light a merciless *torture*.

"Gareth!"

Caught off guard by Commander Quillen's urgent, distant voice, he turns to finds her racing toward him over the shore. A naked, blue-hued, silver-haired Selkie strides just behind her, a silver seal pelt tied around her shoulders.

Gareth's lungs seize, the whole world contracting. The crowd forming on the shore seems to blur as a child's cry of "Mamma, look! A seal woman!" cuts through the murmurs of amazement.

Commander Quillen slows, but Marina breaks into a sprint toward Gareth. He launches himself toward her in a rapid stroke, aching with gladness at how strong and sleek Marina looks splashing into the distant water.

"Gareth!" Marina cries, and Gareth is swept into a powerful tide of love. A rasping bark escaping her lips, Marina dives into the water and swims toward him. They near each other rapidly, then meet in the waves.

Capsized by emotion, Gareth catches Marina in a desperate embrace before she draws him under the water in a swirl of crystalline purple, the sealskin tied around her shoulders flashing silver as it ripples behind her like a cloak.

Overcome, Gareth sweeps her into a passionate kiss that she enthusiastically returns, the two of them embracing until Gareth's lungs begin to ache, then burn, and he has to make for the surface again.

Breaking through into the purple Xishlon world, he gasps in air as Marina surfaces beside him. She pulls him into another besotted embrace, his hand tangling in her waterfall of hair, his lips pressing a kiss to her temple, the Xishlon moon's heart-opening lull intensifying his passion for her. "Marina, *my love.*"

"My *tide,*" she manages against his cheek, her gills ruffling like feathers against his neck, her fractured, flutelike tones rife with feeling. "My ever-flowing tide."

Tears warming his eyes, Gareth takes hold of her arms, wanting to draw her under the water and never surface. "How did you get past Noilaan's dome-shield?" he wonders.

She turns one arm over, revealing the small scarlet Amaz shield-safe rune emblazoned there. Gareth nods, remembering the measures the Amaz took when they helped the freed Selkies get back to their ocean home.

"Why did you risk coming here?" Gareth implores, concerned even as his heart thuds with joy.

Marina's ocean eyes darken with urgency. "To warn you, and to gain your help." She glances toward the shore where Commander Quillen stands, a crowd of Noi'khin surrounding her. "Vogel is coming for the Waters, Gareth," she cautions. "He wants to wipe out my people along with our ocean kindreds. He's conjured a Shadow sea."

Shock eddies through Gareth. "What do you mean?"

"The Mages," Marina continues, "they're infecting the Western oceans with a mass of Shadow power that rolls over the waters like a tide and siphons up the oceans' elemental power. I've warned your Commander Quillen of this. It's only a matter of time before the Mages send their corrupted Shadow sea east. They're going to consume the whole Natural Matrix of Erthia's Waters with it. We *need* you, Gareth. Your Selkie'kin need you."

"Come," Gareth says, motioning toward the mangroves. "Tell me everything."

Gareth spares one more glance toward the crowd on the shore. Commander Quillen is now surrounded by a small contingent of Vu Trin, the knot of dark-clad soldiers standing out in sharp relief amidst the purple-garbed revelers.

He and Marina duck underwater and swim to the grove, gliding around arcing roots into the heart of the grove's embrace before emerging inside a private, sheltered space above the water's calm surface, the salt water inside the grove a gentle, lapping tide. They climb onto a partially submerged root and face each other. Jewel-toned dragonflies flit around them, the water skimming Marina's full blue breasts, and Gareth ignores the rush of desire that sparks to life at the sight.

"Tell me what Vogel's done," Gareth prods, taking hold of her smooth hand.

Marina's face twists with anguish. "His Shadow sea is corrupting the Waters. Blotting out color and creating unnatural tides. It's killing our kindreds. The seals. The octopuses and fish. All underwater life. He's turning more and more of them into twisted multi-eyed creatures. Creating Shadow kraken. Gareth, he's creating a weapon out of our ocean."

Our ocean. Gareth's heart tightens over her phrasing. As if he's Selkie'kin. It guts him, her futile insistence on his inclusion.

Gareth motions north. "We received word that the Vo River has been marked by Death Fae runes filled with Asrai magic to ward off Shadow incursion. Could the same be done to the ocean waters?"

Marina shakes her head. "Shadow power can break through most runic wards."

Alarm ripples through Gareth. "But . . . that could bring down the entire East."

"That's why your Selkie'kin need you. We need your power. Sheer might is needed."

"Marina, whatever water power I have is trapped inside me."

Her ocean-hued eyes narrow with blistering intensity. "Have you ever used a wand underwater?"

"I have. But nothing came of it."

"Did you ever try water wood, instead of a wand?" Marina waves a graceful blue hand toward the mangroves surrounding them. "Wood that thrives in salt water." Her gaze warms with affection. "Like you, my Selkie'kin."

Gareth looks to the mangroves. Trees he can sense reaching out to him. Trees he never encountered until coming to the East . . . trees that stir the magic trapped inside him.

"I tried to access my power using a mangrove branch once," he admits, his lines burgeoning with bound-up water magic, achingly tight. "I thought . . . because I feel such a strong rise in my magic around these trees . . . I thought they could enable me to send my power through a branch instead of a wand's layered wood, even though that's something only the most powerful Mages can do." He shakes his head, the shard of longing cutting deep. "But my magic remained trapped."

Marina is undaunted. "Did you try an underwater root? And did you use the words of Selkie'kin?"

Gareth's heart quickens, the two of them exchanging a look of momentous import. "No," he admits.

"Give me the words to one of your Mage spells," Marina commands, tension mounting in the air.

Gareth sounds out a water spell in the Ancient Tongue. "It means 'funnel up the waters,'" he tells her, pulse thrumming.

Marina breaks off a dark purple mangrove root from under the water, then sinks below the waves. Gareth dives with her, swimming down amongst the arcing roots to the ocean's sandy floor. Pausing there, Marina sounds out a few flutelike words, then gives him a prodding look.

Gareth tries to mimic her intonation, struggling to draw the tones from low in his throat, the words almost impossible to form. Marina frowns but seems resigned that this is the best he can manage. She hands him the root with a look of encouragement.

Gareth sounds out the spell in the Selkie language.

Energy sizzles through his lines, and his lungs tighten with shock as a sliver of his water magic breaks free and flows through his lines and arm into the root. A slender, swirling funnel of water bursts from the root's tip and twirls up through the purple water.

Gareth gasps, drawing in too much salt water.

Choking, he makes for the surface, grasping hold of a large root to propel himself faster. He breaks through, coughing and sputtering as Marina bursts up beside him. Stunned, he looks at the mangrove root in his grip, his wand hand thrumming with elemental energy, the conjured funnel's expanding ripples spreading out around them in concentric circles.

Gareth's astonished gaze locks with Marina's as he clings to one of the mangrove's massive roots, his magic alight and streaming through his lines, his skin tingling at every point of contact with the tree. "I thought . . ." he gasps, his heart in his throat. "I thought I was forever powerless. How could you possibly know this?"

"There's a Mage," Marina begins, lips trembling. "A Light Mage. His name is Alaric Fynnes. He and his shunned Selkie mate, Nerissa, sought me out to tell me their story, which sparked ideas concerning your magic. Alaric was cast overboard several years ago, when Vogel obtained the Shadow Wand . . ."

Gareth listens as Marina tells the tale. How this young Gardnerian priest-apprentice, Alaric, was thrown overboard by Vogel's Shadow-corrupted magic and rescued by a Selkie, Nerissa. And how Nerissa helped Alaric survive on a small, deserted island, the two of them eventually falling in love and Nerissa being cast out of her Selkie enclave when she refused to forsake him.

"And then Alaric and Nerissa joined their tides," Marina says with a look of great significance at the mention of the Selkie mating bond, passion flaring in her eyes, an unmistakable invitation there. The very air seems to shift between them, Gareth's heart skipping a beat. It's a struggle not to be swept into an unfightable storm of wanting her, the purple moon above only amplifying the draw.

"Gareth," Marina says, gills flaring, "when Selkie'kin join their tides in a love bond, they link their abilities and *merge* them. That happened with Alaric and Nerissa, even though Alaric is not Selkie'kin. He gained water power and the ability to wield it through the roots of water-bound trees instead of a wand made from the branch of a land-bound tree. And Nerissa gained a thread of his light power. An actual Mageline of it." Marina pulls in a deep breath, gills ruffling with emotion. "My love, I believe there's a chance we might free even more of your magic if we joined our tides as they did."

A hard pulse of want surges through Gareth, the two of them poised on a precipice. But he holds back, the painful awareness that taking her to mate would inflict on her an inescapable reality. Marina would likely be shunned, like Nerissa. Forever cut off from her close-knit family. Her beloved sister. Gareth knows how much Marina loves her underwater home. Her life as a linguist and diplomat and musician. And her kindreds—she's told him of her close relationship with several octopuses, the intelligent, color-shifter creatures enamored of her, as well. It's a rich life she has, under the ocean's waters. A joyous life.

A life he *cannot* rip her away from.

"We spoke of this back in Verpacia," he says, voice rough, his want for her like a straining tidal wave caught in his center. "Mating for you—and for me, as well—it's for life. You'd be forever trapped between two worlds. Like I am."

"Gareth," she presses, eyes storming, "Alaric can *breathe underwater* now."

They stare at each other for a protracted moment, and Gareth feels as if the entire world has paused.

He swallows. "If we mate . . ." he begins, barely aware of the buzz of dragonflies and the gentle lapping of the water ". . . our abilities may not manifest the way we would hope." Their eyes lock. "It's a risk," he finally manages.

"Worth taking," she insists without hesitation, and he can tell from the passion firing in her eyes that she's already decided. "I don't want anyone else," she breathes out, adamant, gills flaring. "I'm already caught in the middle. So let me be caught there. With you."

Gareth's heart leaps, then expands, his love for her a powerful, surging tide.

He sets down the mangrove root and reaches into his wet pants pocket for the damp money pouch, then fishes out the vial within. "We were all given this," he says, swallowing thickly as he hands her the vial, letting his gaze briefly wander over Marina's form, his pulse thudding. "For Xishlon. It's Sanjire root."

Marina nods and draws closer, giving him a heated look as she unstoppers the vial and takes out some of the root, then places it on her blue tongue.

Gareth's gaze skims over her full breasts. Her blue nipples. Her cascading silver hair. His cresting desire surges as he takes in the curves that lie below the shimmering purple water. And then Marina pulls him into an embrace and kisses him, the warm press of her body and the salt water on her lips sparking a heat that quickly intensifies to storming heights in the Xishlon moonlight.

Gareth groans and gives in to it fully, gives in to his bottomless love for her, as they pull each other under the waves, the mangrove roots twisting and arcing around them. Marina tugging at his pants. Then tearing at them. Shredding them off, her eyes bright with a want that further fires up Gareth's own.

She presses her body against his, skin to skin, and he eagerly returns her feverish caresses, his arms encircling her as he captures her mouth with his. And then she wraps her legs around his waist, and his hard want surges as he kisses her ravenously, heatedly aware of how her thighs are open to him. She draws him closer, angling her hips in invitation, sliding against him.

Unable to hold back any longer, Gareth fully joins with her, a cry torn from his throat, the rush of ecstasy an unstoppable tide. Love and pleasure eddy through him in an ever-swelling current, and then . . . a series of stings blooms along the sides of his neck.

He pulls in a deep breath of water.

Stunned, he pulls in another breath, holding Marina tight, the salt water flooding his lungs, magic exploding to life within him as the entirety of the Waters links to his lines. He catches Marina up in another kiss and senses her awareness of the change in him from the new urgency in her touch. The two of them passionately joined, they float down until he's pressing her into the ocean's floor, deep inside her and shot through with unbearable excitement. She pushes up against him, the two of them falling into a rapidly cresting rhythm until pleasure and love overtake them both in a hot rush and he cries out as their tides fully merge.

They stay like that for a long moment, wrapped tight around each other amidst the mangrove roots as a multitude of fish joyfully encircle them.

And Gareth pulls in breath after breath of glorious, salty Ocean.

"I can breathe," he finally murmurs against Marina's warm skin, stunned to find the words coming out of him in the Selkie tongue. He reaches up to find gills newly formed on the sides of his neck, his underwater voice incredibly clear. All the Ocean sounds around him incredibly clear, distant whale song resonating through him, sparking a reflexive ecstasy. "I never want to touch land again," he huffs out in Selkie, overcome as tears heat his eyes and mingle with the cooler water. He takes hold of Marina's hands, drawing back slightly to take her in, feeling wonderstruck. "My mate," he says, the tears flowing. "My forever love."

Marina is crying as well, a look of Ocean-deep love in her eyes.

"Do you feel the merging of our powers?" Gareth asks Marina, anticipation brimming.

She nods. "A line of tingling energy, forming inside me. I can both feel and see our combined magic flashing through it in the back of my mind . . ."

The purple light of the moon above the waves snuffs out, startling them both into silence, the underwater world snapping to gray. Gareth's pull toward the mangroves intensifies with the energy of alarm.

Gareth meets Marina's gaze, the shock racing through him mirrored in her eyes. They swim toward the water's grayed surface and break through to find the moon turned to shadowy steel.

A sudden disturbance in the water has them glancing down. Another wave of surprise eddies through Gareth to see schools of fish and other Ocean animals rapidly fleeing north.

He exchanges a fraught look with Marina, fighting off the grove's mounting, almost grappling, draw toward its center. The two of them launch into a fast stroke away from the grove, the Salish Ocean's vast, gray-tinted expanse now spread out before them. Vu Trin alarm horns pierce the air, all the distant shore music and revelry extinguished.

THE DRYAD STORM

Peering west toward the horizon, Gareth gives an inward start. There's a rapidly enlarging mass of dark gray advancing over the water like a demonic tide.

"The Shadow sea," Marina breathes out, gazing at the mass with wide-eyed dread.

Defiance churns to life inside Gareth's lines. He dives below the water's surface just as one of the larger mangroves releases a stout purple root and the Waters float it toward him, the power of the entire Ocean roaring through him once he grabs hold of it.

Gareth thrusts his wand arm upward as he launches himself back toward the surface while murmuring a wand spell in the Selkie language, the low tones flowing smoothly from the base of his throat, the translation effortless.

Power shoots through him with such force that it rattles his wrist. Energy blasts from the root and breaks through the water's steel gray surface just before Gareth emerges, his huge waterspout bolting high into the air.

A blaring Selkie battle sign.

"We'll fight Vogel's Mages with all the magic we can summon," Gareth says to Marina as they exchange a look of determination . . . and launch themselves toward the Shadow sea.

CHAPTER TWO

THE REAPING TIMES

Gwynnifer Croft Sykes

Valgard, Gardneria
Ten days after Xishlon

Gwynnifer Croft Sykes hurries along the green-torchlit periphery of Valgard's huge, crowded Cathedral Plaza, night closing in on all sides. Fear tightens her chest in a constricting ache, but she holds fast against it, her jaw stiff with defiance.

Because she's all too clear on the monster the Magedom has become.

And so, Gwynn beats back the fear and anguish threatening to tear her apart and scans the vast throngs of black-clad Mages, intent on finding her parents amidst the sea of zealous Gardnerians eagerly drinking in High Mage Marcus Vogel's every last syllable. She knows it's vital that she make an appearance with her kin on this night.

As cover.

But the surrounding *color* . . . she can't let her mounting draw to it reveal her rebellious nature or her awakening light power, her wand hand increasingly gleaming with any hue her trapped light magery is drawn to. And so, Gwynn clenches it, struggling to ignore the brilliant green of the torchlight and the golden luminescence of the fiery Blessing Stars suspended around the plaza. A speckling of green-and-gold sparks flits through Gwynn's vision and affinity lines, the glow from the torchlight and stars mingling to produce a heady chartreuse luminescence that bathes the mob's enraptured faces and the plaza's central statue depicting the Great Black Witch killing the Cursed Icaral.

A chill races down Gwynn's spine as she takes in the martial statue. Because the Magedom has found its next Black Witch—Elloren Gardner Grey.

A Black Witch who could finish bringing the Reaping Times to all of Erthia.

A Black Witch who is now fasted to Vogel, as evidenced by the gray fastlines marking the High Mage's hands as well as the dark military uniform he now wears instead of his former priestly garb.

"My Blessed Holy Mages . . ." Vogel's rune-amplified voice thunders out over the packed plaza.

Bile rises in Gwynnifer's throat, and she quickens her stride even as her knees tremble. She casts a glance toward where Vogel stands on the landing atop Valgard Cathedral's huge sweeping staircase. A forest green amplification rune hovers just below his chin, and rows of Mage soldiers line the stairs before him.

A shiver races through Gwynn as she takes in the four glamoured pyrr-demons bracketing Vogel. She can spot their true natures through the veil of their Mage glamour quite clearly. As a former Bearer of the Wand of Myth, she can detect the simmering red points of their eyes and their twisted Shadow-smoke horns, as well as the Shadow rising from Vogel's Wand of Power, the gray tendrils twining around the High Mage's form . . .

The Wand of Myth pulses hard in the back of Gwynn's mind, its spiraling green form flashing with chromatic light, a vision of herself and six other Bearers with multihued light power shimmering to life around the Wand. A vision that's ocur-ring more and more frequently, along with a sense of the direction the Wand lies in. Like a migratory pull on Gwynn's very center. North. And down. Below the ground, drawing ever closer . . .

One of the demons pivots its head in her direction, as if it's scented something in the air. Fear igniting, Gwynn ducks her head slightly and averts her eyes, her breathing carefully measured, every nerve in her body primed for flight. Because she knows that if she meets the demon's sulfuric eyes, even for a blink of a moment, it will sense the Wand of Myth in her very thoughts.

And mark her as one of its former Bearers.

"We have dealt a staggering blow against the heathens of the East," Vogel states as Gwynn resumes searching for her parents. "Our Blessed Black Witch and Mage forces have struck down Noilaan's Wyvernguard and their unholy cesspit-city of Voloi."

A rousing wave of cheers and applause swells, unity crackling in the air as Gwynn keeps her eyes averted from the demons.

"But be warned, Holy Mages," Vogel intones, his amplified voice a bone-deep vibration resonating through her, "the Icaral demon and his Dryad beasts have taken hold of our Black Witch."

Thunderous outrage crashes through the plaza, Gwynn's shock momentarily skidding her to a halt.

"The Dryad beasts are portalling our Black Witch to their warded Northern Forest," Vogel warns. "Bent on slaying her. She is caught in a portal lag as we speak. And the surviving Vu Trin forces are mobilizing, ready to advance upon both our Black Witch and our most Holy Magedom."

He pauses, and Gwynn can feel the righteous fury of the crowd rising around her, her pulse ratcheting up to a gallop.

"We are nothing but Crows and Roaches to them," Vogel seethes. "They live to see us cower before them. They live to blot out the Ancient One's own Holy Light. But the Reaping Times, my Blessed brethren, are *here*."

Vogel thrusts up the Shadow Wand, and the crowd's fury explodes, their roar of vicious support battering through Gwynn's ears. She stiffens, horror streaking through her lines. Because there's no protection from this nightmare. Or from Vogel's Shadow Wand.

But she'll go down fighting the Magedom with *everything* in her.

"We will use their own heathen power to smite them," Vogel snarls, raising the smoking gray Wand. "And make use of our sanctified Shadow power to slay the Great Icaral demon and his Dryad Fae beasts, then *free our Black Witch!*"

The crowd goes wild just as Gwynn spots her parents at the edge of the mob. A surge of agony almost buckles her legs as she takes in the way her stout, jovial mother and wandmaster father are cheering.

"Pray with me, Mages," Vogel croons, and the crowd settles. "Let us pray for our Blessed fallen in the East."

Gwynn slides in beside her parents as they bow their heads, close their eyes, and bring fists to their chests. The zealous tension that tightens their beloved faces strikes like a blade through Gwynn's heart.

Hand quivering, Gwynn reaches out to touch her father's arm, her gut twisting anew at the sight of the white armbands wrapped around his and her mother's arms. White bird pins are affixed to their shoulders, depicting the Ancient One's holy messenger clutching a bouquet of Ironflowers, the decorations a tribute to Gardneria's "Blessed fallen Mages," so "cruelly cut down" by the Eastern Realm's "heathen" forces.

Lies, Gwynn wants to scream at her parents while she shakes them until they *see*. *You're being fed lies upon lies upon lies!*

THE DRYAD STORM

But Gwynn knows from the beatific reverence in her parents' expressions that they're hopelessly immersed in their collective sacred story like the rest of the crowd—like she, herself, once was. Certain they're living in the Reaping Times that will cleanse Erthia of all Evil Ones and usher in a perfect Magedom.

Her father opens his eyes and turns to her, just as a tear streams down Gwynn's face. A look of kind concern tightens his gray-bearded, bespectacled face, and he brings one hand to her shoulder, gutting Gwynn anew.

Heart constricting with misery, Gwynn gives her father a false, wavering smile and reverently makes the sign of the Blessing Star on her chest. His expression relaxes into relieved approval, and Gwynn knows he imagines her to be emotionally caught up in Vogel's holy words, his daughter securely on the One True Path.

The prayer concluded, Gwynn's mother opens her eyes, spots Gwynn and breaks into a warm, happy smile, which sends another clutch of agony shuddering through Gwynn's chest. She forces a happy return smile, her heart fracturing over her wildly traitorous path.

But what she's set in motion this evening *must* be brought to completion.

Gwynn remembers the moment everything changed for her, the horror of it branded on her soul. Her family is Styvian, part of the very strictest sect of Gard-nerians, and they never mingle with non-Mages. But one night several months ago, at a rally much like this one, her connection to the Wand of Myth revealed the true nature of Vogel's Shadow magic. She fled the rally and took a wrong turn in her panic, accidentally venturing outside of her sheltered Styvian world.

Halted in her tracks by the sound of children screaming, she shifted course and ran toward the screams, certain that Evil Ones had taken hold of Mage children, as all the stories warned they were wont to do. Full of the Ancient One's own fury, Gwynn swiped a rock from the ground then raced into the dark alley . . .

. . . and the sight she was met with exploded her entire world view.

A mob of six Gardnerian men, some wearing strict Styvian garb, were hold-ing down two Urisk girls—a blue-hued child who looked no more than six years old, and a pale rose-hued child with pink braids who was, at most, eleven. Horror speared through Gwynn as she registered the men digging knives into the tops of the screaming children's ears and swiping off the points, blood streaking down the girls' terrified faces.

At that moment, something in Gwynn broke, like glass shattering.

Screaming, she leaped at the Mages and, with her stone, beat whichever of their heads she could reach, so full of outrage she barely heard their snarls of "Get back, you staen'en bitch!" and barely felt it when they shoved her to the ground and fled, yelling parting threats—"Your family will hear of this, heathen lover!"

Her heart thundering, Gwynn scrabbled toward the sobbing children. They screamed and recoiled from her at first before fearfully allowing her ministrations, the little one vomiting all over Gwynn's tunic as she ripped cloth from her underskirts and bandaged their bloody ears the best she could with shaking hands, then rushed the children back to the non-Styvian home where they worked as indentured maids. In hushed tones, she vowed to help them get out of Gardneria, the translucent image of two Watcher birds of the Ancient One briefly shimmering into view, perched on the girls' shoulders, the sight streaking a bolt of religious upheaval through her.

"Rise up, Holy Mages," Vogel charges, yanking Gwynn from the horrific, life-changing memory. "We will break through the Dryad Fae wards surrounding the Northern Forest," Vogel seethes, "and burn the wilds there to ash for the Magedom's reaping *plow!*"

Rigorous cheers rise, fists thrust into the air, her parents enthusiastically looking at Gwynn as bile rises in her throat. She forces another emotional smile, close to retching all over the plaza's polished tile.

She's tried—*tried*—to make her parents and fastmate, Geoffrey, see the horrific truth.

That night, after she aided the Urisk girls, she ran home and told her parents and fastmate *everything* in a tangled rush, desperate to keep Geoffrey from deploying to be part of something so monstrous. Desperate to enlist her family's help in fighting this nightmare. She breathlessly revealed to them how the Gardnerians were torturing children, and how Vogel had aligned himself with something wicked and Erthia-destroying.

And she told them that she saw the Ancient One's Watcher birds perched on the Urisk children's shoulders.

Geoffrey and her parents exchanged dire looks and listened intently as Gwynn pleaded with them to turn against the Magedom. Geoffrey embraced her tenderly, and Gwynn burst into relieved tears, hope swelling in her rattled heart. Her mother warmed up a bowl of her favorite chicken dumpling soup and her father handed her a mug of soothing honeyed tea, and they all murmured words of comfort and support, promising to carefully consider her revelations.

THE DRYAD STORM

The next morning, Gwynn entered the kitchen with a spark of hope burning in her chest. The spark was immediately snuffed out when she found not only her parents and Geoffrey there, but her family's stern-faced religious leader, Priest Orioth, bracketed by several church acolytes, who glowered at her just as condemningly as the Styvian priest.

The acolytes' wands drawn.

Panic surging, Gwynn launched into breathless pleas, imploring her fastmate and parents not to send her away, only to be met with their stoic, agonized refusals and her mother bursting into tears. And then, both Geoffrey and her father exchanged pained, knowing looks with Priest Orioth, who nodded solemnly, and Gwynn felt the abyss opening beneath her.

When Gwynn moved to flee the kitchen, wands flicked out, and her wrists were quickly tethered together and leashed to the acolytes.

"Didn't you hear anything I told you?" she implored Geoffrey as she struggled against her bonds, tears streaming down her face. "They're attacking *children!*"

"*Heathen* children!" Geoffrey snarled back at her, the level of zealous anger in his tone something new, the anguished look of agreement her parents gave him like a lance through her soul.

In that moment, as Gwynn was led away for "purification," she realized that her parents and Geoffrey were irretrievably lost to her.

And so, during her church imprisonment, she read *The Book of the Ancients* without ceasing. Nodded in emphatic agreement to every last thing the priests and their acolytes said. After a month, it was determined that she had been saved from the grip of Heathen Evil by the Ancient One's Holy Grace, and her parents and Geoffrey joyously welcomed her back into the fold.

And Gwynnifer began planning her own strike against Vogel's nightmare.

She began with whispered comments murmured near Urisk laborers in various shops, revealing her access to the Valgard armory and a whole host of grimoires and magical tools. One thing led to another, and when the Resistance connection flowed in like a stealthy tide, Gwynn opened her arms wide and dove in.

"I . . . I need to find Geoffrey," Gwynn whispers to her parents as Vogel's voice continues to sound out over the plaza and what she longs to say balls up in her throat.

I love you, Pappa and Mamma. I love you so much.

But this has to be fought.

Her father gives her hand another warm, approving squeeze, which she returns, lips trembling. She reaches out and grasps her mother's hand one last time, tears flowing, certain her parents are once more mistaking her show of emotion for zealous love of their Great High Mage.

Their *monster*.

"The heathens will fall, and the Magedom will *rise!*" Vogel booms.

Another thunderous roar bursts from the crowd as Gwynn turns her back on her parents . . . on her entire life.

She strides toward the rear of the plaza, her heart striking into a harder rhythm against her ribs as she spots her fastmate standing stiffly on duty amongst the soldiers lining the plaza, their uniforms all marked with the Ancient One's Holy Bird, one of the flaming Blessing Stars encircling the plaza suspended in the air above Geoffrey.

Cold dread shivers through Gwynn, something she never thought she'd feel when faced with her formerly beloved fastmate.

When Geoffrey returned from clearing heathens from the forests of Northern Gardneria, there was an off-kilter harshness to him that was never there before as well as an odd gray glow ringing his eyes that only Gwynnifer can see. It made her retch into their privy's washbasin, cementing the realization that her longtime love had given himself over to the monstrous.

Becoming a soldier of the Gardnerian nightmare.

Geoffrey turns his head and catches sight of Gwynn. She gives an inward jolt, the gray glow around his irises catapulting her out of her memories. Dread slithers through her as she takes in the animalistic way his nostrils flare, as if he's scenting her approach. She fights the urge to recoil.

His stare eerily unblinking, Geoffrey lifts his lips in a slight smile, as if with emotion half-remembered. "What's the matter?" he asks as she nears.

She takes his offered hands and kisses him on both cheeks, gutted anew by the familiarity of the intimacy and his warm scent. "It's just . . ." She struggles to find the lie.

Geoffrey's gaze turns piercing, as if he's rooting for impurities the way the priest and his acolytes did that terrible morn she was taken away.

Forcing her lips into a quavering smile, Gwynn gestures all around. "It's just so *beautiful* to see the Magedom so united."

The hard planes of Geoffrey's face relax as Gwynn's pulse hammers in her neck.

"I'm going to find Echo and a few others," she enthuses brightly, "to go hear the Valgard Choir straight after this. I might not see you until much later."

Geoffrey nods, a more genuine smile now on his lips. "I'll see you later, then," he says, sounding so much like the old Geoffrey that a sob almost rips out of Gwynn's throat. "I'll volunteer for night guard."

She struggles not to nod too enthusiastically. "Yes. You should. It's a blessing to guard our most holy cathedral."

Another genuine smile breaks through on Geoffrey's face, and Gwynn has to beat back her anguish as he leans his tall frame down and kisses her.

Sure she'll come apart at the seams if she hesitates a second longer, she forces one last smile, lets go of his familiar hands and walks away, leaving her devastated heart on the tiled ground behind her. Forgetting herself, she chances one sidelong look toward Vogel and his demons.

To find the sulfuric red-eyed gaze of one of them pinned directly on her.

Panic breaks through her lightlines like a crimson tide. The image of the Wand of Myth blasts through her mind and strobes there, as if in blaring warning. Gwynn darts off the plaza and into the shadows of an alley, then down a side street. Reaching into her tunic's pocket with a shaking hand, she grabs hold of one of the Issani demon-diversion rune stones she's pilfered from the Valgard armory's cache of magical tools from all the lands, the golden-rune-marked Issani stones able to draw off a pyrr-demon's sight tracking. She presses its center, activating the rune, then hurls the stone into a side alley before swerving down another street, inwardly flinching as an intimidating mob of male Mages pass by. Their gazes slide over her strict Styvian garb and white armband as they pass, nodding with looks of approval.

Every nerve blazing, Gwynn purposefully bumps into a Mage at the mob's rear, murmuring her apologies as she surreptitiously slips another activated stone into the stern young man's pocket before she turns around a corner.

Her gaze alights on a Wanted poster tacked on the storefront window beside her, and she skids to a halt before it. There are identical postings tacked up all over the city, a drawing of a young, wickedly striking Mage printed on them. He glares at her with a conniving expression, his feral green eyes seeming to peer straight into Gwynn's soul, a dark wand raised menacingly in his hand.

Wandmaster Mavrik Glass.

Traitor to the Magedom. Wanted by the Mage Guard.

Gwynnifer's eyes slide toward the Wanted poster to the right of Mavrik Glass's, a posting Gwynn *hasn't* seen before. Paling, she takes in the female emblazoned on it, a sinister Alfsigr Icaral demon with evil silver eyes, her black wings fanned out threateningly, a green Wand-Stylus with a spiraling handle in the Icaral demon's bone-pale hand.

Wynter Eirllyn, the posting says. *Icaral beast and runic sorceress. The Icaral and her Wand of Power wanted by the Mage Guard.*

Gwynn's gaze zeroes in on the Wand, the whole world receding as the image of the verdant Wand pulses through her mind once more and an astonishing realization punches into her.

The Wand of Myth . . . it's in the possession of an Icaral demon.

The sulfuric red gaze of Vogel's pyrr-demons invades Gwynn's mind. She remembers how those same demons relentlessly tracked the Wand so many years ago, before she sent it away with Sage Gaffney. Demons aboveground and demons below, all wanting the Great Wand of Myth. And now, one of them has it.

But this Icaral demon . . . Gwynn's been assured by the Resistance that Wynter Eirllyn is an ally.

Bent on trusting the Resistance, Gwynn lurches back into motion. She rounds another corner and finds a bonfire aflame in a small plaza's center. The bonfire's heat licks over her as she cautiously passes and takes in the great pile of Gardnerian women's clothing being eaten by the flames. Four conservatively garbed Mage women stand beside the fire, slim torches gripped in their hands. Their searching gazes look over Gwynn, and they nod at her equally strict garb, devoid of the forbidden Fae colors Gwynn spots on the burning fabric—vivid purple embroidery edging the hem of one; saffron daisies fashioned from delicate ribbon scattered over another.

The forbidden hues sizzle through Gwynn's Level One lightlines, and she tenses her wand hand against their pull, shuddering to think of what might have become of the owners of that garb since wearing Fae colors became an imprisonable crime.

Her own attraction to Fae colors now an imprisonable crime.

Every night, mobs with torches stalk the streets, rooting out the "impurities" of the city, burning books and other "blasphemous" items. Ransacking stores thought to be impure and setting them alight with Blessing Stars. And every night, Urisk are at risk of being beaten and having the points of their ears viciously cropped.

In the narrow alley that leads to her home, Gwynn slows and focuses on two small cloaked figures huddled there. Relief floods her—the two Urisk girls are waiting just where she told them to be.

THE DRYAD STORM

Ten-year-old Bloom'ilya and skinny six-year-old Ee'vee fearfully meet her gaze. Little Ee'vee is pulling in stacatto breaths, the blue-hued child's large sapphire eyes glancing repeatedly at the alley's ends, her threadbare cloth toy fawn clutched in one arm. Bloom'ilya looks wan and equally frightened, hunched low and holding on to Ee'vee's hand.

Gwynn's heart twists at the sight of the girls' mutilated ears, her own pain forced away as she's faced with the nightmare bearing down on these two children.

"Are you ready?" Gwynn whispers, and the girls respond with jerky nods. "Wait here," Gwynn directs, summoning a hard edge of courage on their behalf, hating to leave them, but certain that they're safe here for the moment.

When she exits the dark alley, Gwynn's home comes into view.

Her emotions seize at the sight of the beloved, charmingly vertical house, sandwiched between Valgard's sprawling armory and Mage Council offices, one room to each story. All Gwynn's happy childhood memories are wrapped up in this wedged-in space. All her happy adult memories, too, the one-room apartment she shares with Geoffrey located high up on the dwelling's fifth floor.

Gwynn's gaze sweeps toward the armory, determination firing as she takes in the threadbare force of two Level Five soldiers standing sentry before it, the six additional soldiers who are usually stationed there attending Vogel's rally. The soldiers nod to her in greeting as she approaches her home's Ironwood front door, Ironflowers carved into the door's dark wood to convey a protective blessing.

Forcing measured breaths, Gwynn retrieves her keys from her tunic pocket, unlocks the door with a trembling hand and slips inside. She shuts the door firmly and relocks it, glancing toward the unlocked kitchen window across from her that Wandmaster Mavrik Glass is supposed to slip through any moment now, the window's forest green curtains slid open.

Leaning against the front door, her palms to the polished Ironwood, Gwynn forces measured breaths and closes her eyes as she summons every last sliver of will. Doggedly setting back into motion, she opens her eyes and races up and up and up her home's spiraling staircase, until she reaches the tower bedroom of her childhood at its apex.

She pauses, struck hard by grief.

Her mother has kept the space frozen in time. White birds and Blessing Stars Gwynn fashioned from paper years ago in a rush of religious zeal hang from slim strings throughout the room in happy flocks and constellations. As they are on every floor, dead Ironwood trees are set into the walls, their leafless branches tangling overhead, the dead trees symbolic of Mage dominion over the Fae wilds. Countless religious books and pious journals line the shelves set below the tower's ring of windows, which afford a panoramic view of nighttime Valgard. Gwynn pivots to her craft table, pushed up against one of the windows, the surface still littered with multiple replicas she carved, so many years ago, of the Wand of Myth.

The Wand now in the hands of an Alfsigr Icaral demon.

Her pulse a steady, pounding rhythm, Gwynn lowers herself to the Ironwood floor and searches under her broad bed. Her breath catches as she finds all her forged and stolen grimoires gone, smuggled away as she was told they would be, her sacks of carefully fashioned and pilfered rune stones taken, as well.

She straightens and peers out the windows at the unimpeded view. The Ironflower trees that used to stand around the tower were mercilessly cut down, as were all the living trees in Valgard, to cleanse the city of their "Fae stain." For a moment, she's overcome by the bittersweet memory of how, for years before she and Geoffry were Sealed, he would climb those trees and visit her on the sly.

Swallowing back a suffocating swell of misery, Gwynn grabs her stuffed travel sack and moves to throw its strap over her shoulder.

"Leave it," a harsh, masculine voice orders from behind her.

Startled, Gwynn drops the bag and whirls around, heart thundering as she meets the piercing green eyes of the young Mage poised at the top of the stairs, his skin glimmering a brooding forest green in the tower's dim light.

"Mage Glass?" Gwynn can barely breathe out the Resistance wandmaster's name.

His eyes narrow in appraisal. "Call me Mavrik," he drawls.

As he saunters toward her, her trapped light magery breaks into a fitful shimmer, and Gwynn wonders if she's made a terrible mistake. Moving with controlled ferocity, Mavrik Glass gives her a cool smirk that doesn't reach his assessing eyes—eyes that are taking in every last inch of her as if evaluating the fitness of a horse for a long, rigorous journey through hell and back. He tosses the edge of his dark cloak over one shoulder in a fluid motion, revealing multiple wands sheathed at his side.

"I know what you're thinking," he croons, eyes glinting with battle-hardened mischief. He leans in, as if confiding a delicious secret, her magic sparking unsettlingly toward him. "'He's *so much* better looking than his picture on the Wanted posters.'" He draws back, scrutinizing her. "That's because the Magedom can't seem to help itself." He gestures toward his face. "Making me look so pointy-featured and evil on the posters." He cocks a brow. "I *am* evil. Make no mistake about it. But a conundrum for the Magedom, as they like to picture their villains as vile looking."

Gwynn gapes at him, a knot caught in her throat. Thrown by his blithe banter at a time like this.

Mavrik Glass glances at the paper Watchers hanging from her ceiling. The Blessing Stars suspended on slim threads. "Interesting base of military-level operations you have here." He cocks an amused brow as his gaze swings back to hers. "Ready to become a renegade, Princess?"

It takes Gwynn a moment to summon the courage to answer, her entire world about to be torn apart. "There are two servant girls," she reminds him, emphatic. "They're coming with us."

"It's sorted," he states. That intimidating glint returns to his eyes, and Gwynn is filled with the impression that Mavrik Glass does things his own way, no questions asked. She moves to pick up her dropped bag, and he halts her with a raised palm. "*Leave it.* We need to travel fast."

"But . . ." She glances around, suddenly unable to bear the course she's set herself on, her breath coming in forced shudders as defiance rears and she moves to pick up the bag once more.

Mavrik's hand closes around her upper arm, his expression shot through with intensity, and her trapped magic gives a confusingly strong surge toward him. "Gwynn, I said *leave* it."

She startles at his use of her familiar name. "You don't understand." She yanks her arm out of his grip, trembling. "I'm leaving my fastmate. My family. *Everything.*"

Mavrik's eyes flash. "I *do* understand." He holds up a hand, fastmarks looped around it and his wrist too. And Gwynn can tell, from the sudden streak of pain blazing in his eyes, that at some point, he left everything behind, as well.

"I loved him," she admits, voice splintering. "I loved my fastmate."

"He's lost to you," Mavrik says, harsh as an axe through her heart. She winces, tears pooling in her eyes, then shuts them tight, struggling not to shatter over what she's about to do.

"Gwynnifer," Mavrik says, his hand coming around her arm once more, both his voice and touch gentler now, her magic sizzling toward him as if it wants to stream straight into his hand. She opens her tear-soaked eyes to find his gaze locked on her with a look of vast compassion. "Have your moment of grief," he says, low and measured. "*One* moment. I did, as well. Your path just became impossibly hard and harsh. Like mine has been. But it's *just*."

Gwynn thinks of Bloom'ilya and Ee'vee huddled in the alley—of *everyone* who is being brutally abused by the Magedom.

"I *believed*. I believed *all* of it," she blurts out, voice breaking. "I was *wrong*."

His lips give a bitter twist. "Welcome to the circle of Mage unbelievers." His eyes take on a conspiratorial glint as he leans in. "Trust me—once you get used to us, we're a lot more fun. That's the upside." Stepping back, he holds his hand out to her, serious once more, his eyes flicking toward her bag. "Your old life is dead to you, Gwynnifer. Let it go. We need to leave."

There's a strong note of alliance in his tone. Gwynn pulls in a deep breath and rallies her courage. Leaving her bag on the floor, she takes Mavrik Glass's hand.

Prismatic sparks flash through her vision, and her lines seize. She gasps, every last shred of her trapped magic contracting toward his hand while she's blasted by a sense of *his* magic straining toward *her*—a hot stream of fire, a tempestuous whoosh of air, a black dart of vining earth and a roiling rush of water.

Mavrik flinches, his breathing going as uneven as hers. He gives her an intense look as their invisible combined power swirls together with grasping potency. But there's no time to wonder at any of it as he pulls her into motion, and she descends with him into the shadows of the night.

CHAPTER THREE

SHADOW HIVE

Sparrow Trillium

Unknown location
Unknown time after Xishlon

"Thierren!" Sparrow screams as she's dragged away in a net of vines by her tormentor from the Fae Islands—the vile Mage Tilor—into a wall of silvery mist surrounded by an arch of Shadow runes.

As the silver closes in around her, she cries out, overtaken by the sensation of her Shadow-grayed body being sped through the mist so fast she might come apart, before she just as abruptly slows and Tilor yanks her into an alabaster cave. Her gut clenches in terror, and her back scrapes against the cave's rough stone as she clings to a sliver of hope that Thierren, her Level Five Mage love, survived Vogel's destruction of Noilaan and will come after her.

"Thierren!" she screams again, and Tilor spits out a jeering laugh. He turns and slides his glowing gray-eyed gaze over her bound form, his strength seeming enhanced as he pulls her forward.

Sparrow looks frantically around the torchlit tunnel, her pulse jumping in her throat as she's hauled into an impossibly gigantic alabaster cavern. Its pale reaches seem to stretch up forever, and horrifying masses of multi-eyed, gigantic wraith bats hang from its walls.

Tilor drags her into another tunnel cut into the cavern's white stone, its walls lined with rows of nightmarish multi-eyed scorpios as big as men. The mantis-scorpion creatures' gray bodies are stretched out and distorted, smoking runes marked on their thoraxes, their lethal-looking stingers quivering at the ends of raised segmented tails. With pulse-quickening uniformity, the scorpios' grotesque masses of eyes snap toward Sparrow, their chilling gazes full of predatory interest, and her panicked mind turns over why the stone of this mountainous interior is the alabaster hue of Spine stone . . .

Her lungs seize as certainty slams through her.

They're in the Western Realm. That arch of Shadow runes Tilor dragged her through that made her feel as if her body was about to be pulled apart into a million particles of static . . .

. . . *it was a runic portal.*

A strangled cry bursts from Sparrow's throat as she realizes that Thierren is leagues upon leagues away in the Eastern Realm, if he's even alive. As she's being forced through the interior of one of the *Western* Realm's Spines. The Northern Spine or the Southern Spine, she doesn't know which.

Fearing she'll retch, she takes in the full nightmare as they emerge into another mammoth cavern.

A gigantic hive lines the walls, like a magnified hornet's nest. Men are emerging from the hive cells, the Mage soldiers amongst them moving freely, their irises ringed with Shadow, their fastlines emitting tendrils of Shadow corruption. Keltish, Alfsigr, and Urisk men seem to be contained in one area, the non-Mages tethered to their hive cells via chains made of Shadow runes attached to the runic collars encircling their necks, their expressions deadened, their eyes fully gray. *Slaves to the Magedom,* Sparrow intuits, her alarm mounting. *Slaves to Vogel's Shadow power.*

Sparrow's last image of Thierren invades her mind—Thierren in his Vu Trin uniform, surrounded by dead dragons and slain Mage soldiers, screaming her name as Tilor flew her away on dragonback.

Desperation storming through her thoughts, Sparrow's mind careens about.

Is Thierren even still alive? And Effrey . . . did the child get to safety? Or is the entire East now in Vogel's grip? Even Elloren Gardner with her Black Witch power was easily bested by Vogel's Shadow, her mind consumed by it. And the portal Sparrow was dragged through . . . was there a time lag like most portals have? How many days have passed since Xishlon?

Sparrow's thoughts shut off as she's yanked sideways, a cry of protest erupting from her throat as she's towed into yet another curving tunnel then dumped in front of a small, Shadow-barred cavern, two Mage soldiers with gray-rimmed eyes bracketing the entrance.

"I'm housing her *here,*" Tilor tells the soldiers, motioning toward the cavern, his tone shot through with arrogance. The soldiers stare at Sparrow's bound form with leers so chilling, her skin crawls.

"She's *mine*," Tilor snarls. "Vogel gave her to *me*."

The guards' hungry looks turn to ones of resignation, and Tilor's aggression recedes, his expression morphing to smugness. "I'd like some privacy," he gloats, glancing pointedly at Sparrow, his teeth bared in an excited smile.

Sparrow clenches her fists, desperate for the dagger Tilor confiscated from her with a chiding laugh.

The soldiers dip their heads deferentially, casting quick looks of envy toward Sparrow before they stride away from the cell.

"One more thing," Tilor calls after them, and they pause and turn, the tunnel's silvery torchlight flickering over them all. "If you hear her scream, ignore it." The words slide from Tilor's tongue like he's tasting them.

Sparrow grows light-headed as another wave of fear sweeps through her. Smiling, Tilor lifts his wand and murmurs a spell, and the cell's Shadow bars turn to mist.

Sparrow breaks into futile revolt, kicking and struggling against her vine bindings. Tilor strikes with frightening speed, his booted foot slamming into her side with brutal force, the wind propelled from her lungs as she contracts with agony.

Vicious anger streaks across Tilor's face as he drags her into the cell and dumps her in a corner. He lifts his wand, and gray vines spring from its tip and tether her to the floor.

Sparrow begins to sob. *Thierren*, is all she can think, screaming his name in her mind. *Thierren!*

Murmuring a spell, Tilor points his wand at Sparrow's torso, and her bindings dissolve.

He steps back, expression excited, and a harder slash of terror knifes through her as she realizes he *wants* her to try to flee. *Wants* her to fight him.

Shivering with both rage and fear, she rises on unsteady legs and readies herself to do just that, balling her fists, clear she's about to be horrifically abused but determined to inflict at least some small measure of pain in return.

With a growling cry, she launches herself at Tilor, going straight for his eyes. He anticipates her and counters in a blur, a gasp tearing from her throat when she's grabbed and effortlessly hurled at the wall behind her. Her back collides with stone, and she plummets to the floor in an aching heap.

"You little. Urisk. *Whore*," Tilor growls as he paces in front of her, then raises his wand and murmurs a spell that sends an uncomfortable tingle over Sparrow's skin.

"You don't deserve to be covered in Mage-sanctified Shadow," he sneers.

Sparrow glances down to find tendrils of smoke rising from every speck of her exposed skin, her Shadow-gray coloration morphing back to its natural lavender. Trembling, she readies herself once more to claw his face.

He stares her down, his gaze flicking lasciviously over her from head to toe. "I wanted to be the first to fully possess you," he drawls, a ripple of outrage crossing his features before his green lips inch up into a lewd smile. "But I imagine Thierren Stone has already broken you in."

A snarl rises in Sparrow's throat, but she swallows it back, noticing Tilor has not replaced the prison cavern's bars. Seizing her chance, she bolts toward him, knocks the wand from his hand, and dives toward the exit.

Tilor's unnaturally strong hand clamps around her arm, her trajectory painfully halted as the world swings sideways. Crying out, she's hurtled back into the cell, her back and head slamming against stone once more, stars exploding in her vision.

Tilor levels his wand at her.

Shadow vines burst from its tip, netting her to the cavern wall. Murmuring a spell, he flicks his wand, and the netting wrapped around her wrists and ankles spreads out, splaying her arms and legs apart.

Her breath comes in short, desperate gasps. Tilor's eyes spark with glee as he sheathes his wand and saunters forward, his leer slithering over Sparrow's beautiful Xishlon dress. Her rageful tears come faster as she chokes on the memory of how she fashioned this dress for her Xishlon night with Thierren, handcrafting every one of its multitude of violet-silk flowers.

Tilor reaches toward Sparrow's chest, and she lets out a growl of protest, her skin crawling as he fondles the petals of one of the small violets, then yanks the flower from the fabric and tosses it to the floor before running his hand territorially over her breast and squeezing tight.

White-hot fury shocks through Sparrow. She sucks saliva into the center of her mouth and spits at Tilor's face, her heart pounding with rage as she drowns in the certainty that her life is over. But she'll go down fighting.

Tilor's eyes ignite with rage. In a blur, he raises his fist.

Sparrow jerks her head back against the stone, sure she's about to be punched with bone-smashing force, just as a hooded figure darts into the cavern and launches at them both.

Blood explodes from Tilor's neck, a knifepoint appearing through his throat's center, and he lets out a gurgling groan. His eyes bulge and his body shudders, more blood spraying over Sparrow. A flash of blue light detonates from the blade, exploding Tilor's neck in a larger splash of blood and gore, and his head falls off as his decapitated body crumples to the ground.

Sparrow blinks away blood and spits gore from her lips as she stares, in dazed shock, at the gray-hued, point-eared, sharp-featured young woman before her. Amaz runic tattoos mark the woman's face, her garb that of a Mage soldier, a dark Gardnerian military cloak fastened over her shoulders, hood raised. There's a charged blade in her fist, its runes glowing bright emerald green.

"Who are you?" Sparrow rasps as the Amaz raises her blade and deftly slices through Sparrow's bindings, freeing her.

"Valasca Xanthrir, at your service," the Amaz answers before she sheathes her blade and lowers herself to Tilor's decapitated, bloody corpse. All business, she yanks off his cloak, weapons, and clothing and hands his garb to Sparrow. "Put these on," she directs with warrior calm, narrowing her dark blue eyes on Sparrow. "Be quick about it."

"H-h-how did you get free of the Mages?" Sparrow sputters as she yanks off her dress and throws Tilor's tunic and pants on with quavering hands.

Valasca cocks a rakish brow as she gathers Tilor's wand and weapons. "I'm the former head of the Amaz Queen's Guard. It's not a position given to the untalented." She shoots Tilor's corpse a disgusted look. "I saw him drag you past."

Sparrow gapes at her. "But . . . but all the soldiers . . . their *magic* . . ."

Valasca's eyes fill with a sly light as she pats her sheathed blade. "Ah, well, it seems the Crows made a rather large mistake. They dumped this Amaz Ash'rion blade they stole from Elloren Gardner within my sight." She lifts a palm marked with a gray rune. "Varg-infused retrieval rune. I spelled down its green glow so it would look vanquished." She grins at Sparrow, who notices a multitude of Mage blades sheathed in Valasca's belt and another pushed into the side of her boot, along with two wands. "And, turns out," Valasca continues, "Mage wands can be used as runic styluses with some spell modifications. And I happen to be a rune sorceress." She winks at Sparrow. "I've a few tricks up my sleeve."

Sparrow's mind whirls. "You know Elloren?"

Valasca spits out a laugh as she finds places to sheathe Tilor's weapons and hands one of the blades to Sparrow. "It's a bit of an involved story."

"I was with her in Valgard," Sparrow confides as she takes hold of the weapon.

Valasca looks at her closely, one brow cocked. "She told me about you. Sparrow Trillium, is it? The seamstress?"

Sparrow nods and sheathes the blade through her belt, then pulls Thierren's bloodied cloak over her shoulders.

"Well, Sparrow Trillium," Valasca says in an overly polite cadence, "would you like to stand here and continue these introductions, or would you rather get the hells out of here and kill a few Mages while we're at it?"

Sparrow gives her a grim look. "There's a huge army out there . . ."

Valasca huffs out a breath, rolling her eyes. "Yes, we've terrible odds. I'd say the whole of Erthia has terrible odds at the moment." Her dark eyes take on a battle-fierce light, her lips lifting. "I believe in being ridiculously feisty in the face of impending doom. Are you with me?"

Rebellion coalesces inside Sparrow, sparking hot. "I'm with you," she vows.

Valasca shoots her a more lethal grin. "Well, then, I suspect we'll get on just fine."

"I need to get back East," Sparrow blurts out. "There's a child there who's family to me . . . Effrey. I don't know what happened to him. And I need to find Thierren Stone. He's joined the Vu Trin."

Valasca cocks a black brow, obviously catching both Thierren's blaringly Gardnerian name as well as the ardent emotion Sparrow can't keep from her tone when speaking of him.

"Well, Sparrow Trillium," Valasca says. "I wouldn't mind getting back to my Great Love, Ni Vin, either, but our allies and all of our loved ones are currently clear across a desert from us." Valasca gives her a pointed look. "It's you and me, Urisk."

An icy wind blasts into the cavern, hurling both Sparrow and Valasca off their feet and slamming their bodies into the wall beside them, groans forced from both their throats. Icy cages slam down around them, the cold stinging Sparrow's skin as their wrists are pinned to the wall with frigid ice shackles.

Fallon Bane sweeps into the cavern, her black cloak flowing behind her, and Sparrow's lungs seize. There's a thick commander's stripe marking Fallon's Level Five tunic, and she has a black dragon talon pushed through her long tied-back tresses.

Fallon's green eyes glare hate at Valasca before she casts Sparrow an incredulous glare, recognition lighting her features. "*You* again?" She spits out a disgusted sound before turning back to Valasca. She jabs her wand into Valasca's throat, forcing her chin up. "I've been keeping an eye on you, Amaz," Fallon hisses. "Did you really think I'd let such a valuable runic sorceress escape?" She leans closer, baring her teeth. "Especially one who killed my *brother?*"

Valasca's mouth tilts into a chiding grin. "Truth told, Sylus proved to be a bit of a lightweight."

Painfully cold hoarfrost forms all over the cave as Fallon jabs her wand harder. "Well, I'm *not*," she snarls. "Don't underestimate me, *Amaz*."

"Oh, I wouldn't dream of it, *Crow*," Valasca bites back before swiftly murmuring a spell under her breath.

Glowing emerald runes flash to life on Valasca's forehead and the center of her neck, and Fallon's eyes widen. An explosion of raying, green power detonates from the runes, and Fallon is punched from the cave cell by an invisible pulse of magic, her wand blasting from her hand, all the ice in the room instantly shattering, including Sparrow's and Valasca's frigid shackles. Sparrow teeters and almost loses her footing while Valasca unsheathes her Ash'rion blade in a blur and slides her fingers over its rune-marked hilt.

A thin bolt of green spears toward Fallon's wand, and it explodes in a flash of verdant fire just as bootheels sound and a wand is tossed to Fallon from the hallway's side. Fallon deftly catches it before casting Valasca a look that's so malicious, Sparrow's skin breaks into gooseflesh.

Mages run into view, wands raised, as Fallon growls out a spell along with them and Valasca points her blade toward them, rapidly conjuring a translucent emerald shield-wall into existence before herself and Sparrow.

Multiple blasts of gray Mage power slam against the shield, and Sparrow flinches, Fallon's wintry blast punching a frosty concavity into Valasca's barrier that Sparrow fears will break clear through it. But the barrier holds, icy fractures spiderwebbing over the shield's expanse.

Growling out a curse, Valasca points her blade downward. A bolt of green light blasts from it and smashes a sizable hole straight through the stone floor in a spray of rocks that Sparrow has to shield her face from.

"C'mon!" Valasca cries as she grabs Sparrow's arm and hurls her into the hole.

Sparrow tumbles into its darkness and lands on another stone floor in a painful heap.

Valasca drops down beside her, the small, rocky space instantly lit up by the glowing green runes on Valasca's blade, revealing a tunnel before them. Valasca angles her blade upward and murmurs another spell. In a burst of jade light, green-crystalline stone forms across the hole above, sealing it shut.

Fallon's muffled roar of fury sounds through the stone as Valasca lifts her blade once more and murmurs another spell. Large Varg runes spring to life on every surface of the cave, just as an explosion detonates above them, shaking the ground beneath their feet.

Sparrow frantically takes in the icy spiderwebbing cracks forming all over the barrier above them.

"Might be a good time to make a run for it," Valasca prods.

They break into a sprint through the narrow tunnel and round a bend, where Valasca pauses to conjure another green glass barrier behind them. At the same moment, a larger ground-shaking explosion sounds from the direction they came from.

"Where are we?" Sparrow pants as they launch into another sprint.

"Welcome to the Smaragdalfar Resistance's Sublands," Valasca jauntily replies, the two of them racing through another curving, Varg-rune-marked tunnel and into a larger cave. "We're just below the Northern Spine. And we need to get to the Resistance's Subland base of operations under Valgard. We don't have much time."

Another explosion sounds, and Sparrow raises her hands to shield her face from a spray of rocks and stones. Spitting out a string of curses, Valasca grabs firm hold of Sparrow's arm and yanks her sideways, veering them down a side tunnel.

Sparrow turns her head, and fear constricts her throat as Fallon Bane drops down behind them, ice blasting into being on the cave walls surrounding her and swiftly rippling in their direction. Fallon's murderous green eyes zero in on them, and she raises her wand.

TRAITOR TO THE MAGEDOM

Gwynnifer Croft Sykes

Valgard, Gardneria
Ten days after Xishlon

"Give me your wand hand," Mavrik Glass orders, coolly dominant.

The golden light from the small, suspended fire-orb he's conjured flickers over his arresting features as he and Gwynn pause in the cramped kitchen of Gwynn's family home.

Near the curtained back window they're about to flee through.

"Why?" Gwynn asks, the forest green of Mavrik's penetrating gaze playing havoc with her lightlines. Verdant sparks crackle across her vision, a shimmer of the rich color racing over her wand hand as her power strains toward his with unsettling force.

"I need to link our fasting spells," he clarifies, jaw ticking, body tense, as if he's steeling himself against their disquieting magical draw, as well.

"But . . . I'm not fasted to you," Gwynn sputters through their magical thrall. How can he possibly link their fasting spells?

Rapid-fire, her mind scours over every page of every grimoire she's ever laid eyes on, searching for a spell that can connect unrelated fastlines, her trapped light magery giving her a picture-perfect memory.

Mavrik rolls his eyes and gives her a look of exasperation as he holds up a hand, his fastmarks a markedly different design than hers. "I'm quite clear we're not fasted," he says. He turns his hand, palm up, thrusting it toward her. "Gwynn, we're *really* short of time. Give me your hand."

His tone is brusque, and Gwynn's chest tightens with apprehension. His intense, domineering energy is nothing like Geoffrey's mild-mannered congeniality . . .

A pang of turmoil twists her heart.

That's how Geoffrey used to be. Before he stopped caring if children are tortured.

Seeming cognizant of her flare of anguish, Mavrik tenses his brow. He unsheathes one of his wands and holds it up for her perusal, and Gwynn takes in the charged sapphire Noi runes marked on the wand's slim, dark surface, stunned by his display of blatant—and thoroughly forbidden—magical mixing.

"I'm going to connect a combined Noi-and-Mage tracking spell and a Mage vine spell to our fastlines," he explains, "and weave Noi barrier-breaking and linking spells around it. That way, if we get separated, I can track your location and reel you in."

Gwynn's mind whirls as she mentally connects the elemental building blocks of the spells he's proposing, the puzzle pieces falling into their slots. "Oh," she breathes. "That's clever."

Mavrik smirks, mischief dancing in his green eyes. "Wandmaster. Remember?"

Gwynn's light power gives another sparkling surge toward him, and she catches his slight shiver and the sudden tightening around his eyes, magical tension thick in the air.

"Our magic . . ." she manages, fighting its pull to move toward him. "There's some type of thrall between us."

"I know," he stiffly agrees. "But there's no time to parse it out. We have to think past it."

Struggling to focus through the captivating thrall, Gwynn places her wand hand in his.

Her trapped light power spangles through her lines toward their linked hands in a heady, multicolored rush as she's overcome by the sensation of his power sizzling toward her in turn. His eyes widen as he takes in her suddenly green-glowing hand, heat sizzling across her face.

"What's triggering the green?" Mavrik asks, swallowing thickly.

She bites her lip. "Your eyes," she admits.

"I was told you're a Level One Light Mage," he presses, a skeptical edge to his tone.

"I am," she insists, a tremble kicking up in the hand she has in his. "I can't access any of the magic in my lines."

Mavrik's grip firms around her, as if to help her quell her tremors. He peers closely at her. Her cheeks heat further in response to their sustained, forbidden hand-holding, the women of her sect *never* allowed to touch the skin of a man who is not their fastmate.

Mavrik gently pivots her palm up, and another rush of multihued sparks flash through her lines and vision. Her breathing suspends. He presses his wand's tip to the center of her palm and murmurs a stream of spells, low in his throat, his eyes narrowing in concentration.

He has fastlines around his wrists, Gwynn notes. *He's fully Sealed like me . . .*

A sting lights along Gwynn's fastlines, and she flinches as thin blue and green lines crackle out of the wand tip. The magic forks around their hands like threads of lighting, encasing them in a fizzing net. Gwynn pulls in a surprised breath as the lightning net draws into their fastlines, their dark, looping fastmarks briefly pulsing blue and green before their normal black hue returns and the sting recedes.

Mavrik releases her hand and resheathes his wand, his magic-sparking eyes meeting hers. "Did you mark the runes around the armory and place the anchoring rune like we directed?"

"I did," she affirms, lowering herself to pull up a floor tile, revealing a circular disc of black lumenstone she stole from the armory, the disc marked with a glowing forest green Mage anchoring rune.

Mavrik lowers himself beside her, and draws a thicker black wand emblazoned with emerald Varg runes. He points the wand's tip at the rune stone and meets Gwynn's gaze with lightning-rod intensity. "Are you ready?"

Her throat unbearably tight, she nods.

Murmuring a spell, Mavrik touches the wand's tip to the anchoring rune.

The rune shifts to a brighter green. A magical tang bursts to life, and a light-headed sense of diving off a cliff sweeps through Gwynn as the anchoring rune sends its charge out to every complementary rune she marked around the armory.

"Let's go," Mavrik urges.

They spring up and stride to the kitchen's back window . . . and catch sight of a Mage soldier just beyond it.

Gwynn's heart flies into her throat as they both draw sharply back, past the window's sides, then peer out through the slim gaps at the curtains' edges.

The Mage is just outside the window, down on one knee, silver Level Five stripes marking his uniform and cloak. He's unsheathed his wand and is pressing its tip to the rune now visible on the cobbled ground, the overturned flowerpot it was hidden under pushed aside, four more Level Five soldiers closing in around him.

"The cobbler stumbled into the pot and found the rune," the soldier explains to the others.

Gwynn's pulse explodes as she turns back to the flashing anchor rune at their feet, glowing *brighter and brighter* . . .

A lethal resolve entering his gaze, Mavrik grabs hold of her wrist, their magics spearing toward each other as he pulls her toward the front door.

Gwynn plants her feet, *hard*, resisting his pull.

Mavrik's eyes snap to hers, a demand in them. "Gwynnifer," he hisses, his eyes flicking toward the anchor rune. "We are literally *out of time*."

"The armory guards," Gwynn cautions in a vehement whisper as the anchor rune gains potency. "We can't just stride out this door."

Mavrik grins dangerously at her. "*Watch* me."

He kicks the door open and pulls her onto the landing beside him, the two Level Five guards bracketing the adjacent armory's entrance immediately turning toward them.

"Good evening, gentlemen," Mavrik taunts.

Gwynn's alarm skyrockets as the guards' eyes widen. Their expressions turn murderous, and they unsheathe their wands at the same time that Mavrik levels his Varg-rune-marked wand at them, viper swift, while murmuring a spell.

Two thin bolts of emerald flame flash from Mavrik's wand toward the wands of the guards and explode the weapons in verdant flame. Releasing Gwynn's wrist, Mavrik sweeps his wand in a wide arc over the entire thoroughfare before them, intoning Smaragdalfar spells with single-minded fluency.

Gwynn flinches back against the doorframe as a multitude of thick black columns of vine explode up through the cobbled street before them, one column blasting from beneath the guards' feet and hurling them into the air. People scream as carts and carriages are upended and the columns rise, branching out into dense tree shapes.

Gwynn gapes at the scene, frozen in place by the potency of Mavrik's earth magery, as the armory's guards right themselves, draw fresh wands, and launch themselves toward them.

With focused calm, Mavrik levels his wand at them once more, his finger sliding over one of its runes.

Wind bursts from his wand and slams into the guards, punching them backward, their wands blown from their hands. Mavrik's conjured vine trees enlarge further as people flee. Mavrik thrusts his wand forward and blasts wind around his conjured vine forest, lifting street debris into his turbulent storm.

Earth and wind, Gwynn considers as her hair whips against her face. *Mavrik has Level Five earth and wind.*

"C'mon," Mavrik urges, stepping toward the street, but Gwynn remains frozen in place.

Wind buffeting them both, he rounds on her, taking in her frozen stance with a look of sheer incredulity. "Do you need an engraved invitation?" he asks, his tone glass-sharp as he thrusts his hand toward her.

Gwynn grabs his hand, and they sprint into the fleeing crowds and whipping winds and are quickly enveloped in the chaos of the destroyed street as they skirt rubble and the huge vine tree forms.

Green light flashes over the world as they reach the thoroughfare's other side.

They both turn and see a huge Mage rune sizzling to life on the armory, covering two of its stories.

Runic firebomb, Gwynn notes, before the huge explosion she enabled detonates in an earsplitting *BOOM.*

A cry tears from her throat as the armory, her family's home, and the Mage Council building on her home's other side burst into green flames, the explosion ringing in her ears, her legs almost buckling beneath her.

Traitor to the Magedom. Staen'en blasphemer.

The names for what she has just become strike through her with devastating force, her course irrevocably set.

Mavrik tugs on her arm, and Gwynn stumbles into a sprint, tears burning her eyes even as renewed purpose grips hold, the two of them dashing toward the dark alley where she prays Bloom'ilya and Ee'vee are still waiting.

Please be there, please Ancient One let them be there, Gwynn petitions as she and Mavrik bolt into the long alley and her eyes adjust to the dark.

A soft emerald glow flashes into being from the tip of Mavrik's wand, and relief lashes through Gwynn to find the girls still huddled there, backs pressed to the alley's dark wall.

Bloom'ilya's pale rose face and little Ee'vee's sky blue expression morph into startled looks at the sight of Gwynn and Mavrik barreling down the narrow alley toward them. The girls' gazes snap toward the Wanted poster affixed on the wall across from where they're huddled, Mavrik's evilly rendered face glaring from it.

Gwynn catches Mavrik's horrified look as they slow and his gaze passes over the girls' mutilated ears. He drops to one knee before them, and they recoil, eyes flicking from him to the poster and back to him again as Ee'vee hugs her threadbare fawn toy and begins to cry.

"I'm Mavrik Glass," he tells them in a tone so compassionate it catches Gwynn off guard. "You've probably seen my picture—" he glances over his shoulder at the poster "—well, pretty much everywhere." He dips his head in a gesture of apology. "*Not* a flattering one, I'll give you that. But I'm certainly *not* on the side of the Mages." His gaze turns fierce. "I'm on *your* side. And I think you should come with us. *Quickly.*"

For a split second, the girls hold his intense stare. They look to each other, then to Gwynn as if seeking reassurance, little Ee'vee's lip quivering as she hugs her toy.

Pulse thrumming, Gwynn nods encouragingly and holds out a hand, and the girls leap to their feet.

Wasting no time, Mavrik sweeps skinny little Ee'vee up in one arm, while Gwynn grasps quick hold of Bloom'ilya's trembling hand. Multiple bootheels pound at their rear, men's voices shouting to each other. They all turn, Ee'vee letting out a fearful shriek as several Mage soldiers run into view, wands drawn.

"They're here!" one of the Mages bellows.

Mavrik points his wand at the soldiers and hurls a spell at them before the Mages can get one out. Glowing green vines lash from his wand's tip and fly forward several feet before expanding into a tightly woven shield that spans the alley's width, walling them off.

"*Go, go, GO!*" Mavrik urges, and they launch into a run toward the alley's far end.

An explosion sounds behind them, and a galvanizing jolt of fear races down Gwynn's spine as they dart into a faster sprint and Gwynn glances over her shoulder to find Mavrik's vine wall igniting with silver gray flame, the strange fire burrowing into the ground instead of flaring up like normal fire.

Dread fires through Gwynn. *Demonic Shadowfire.*

The dark fire is streaking through the ground toward them, two Mages with glowing red eyes and Shadow horns appearing through the smoke where Mavrik's barrier just was.

Their sulfurous eyes lock with Gwynn's, and recognition shocks through her as she sights them through their glamoured forms—it's the same pyrr-demons she and Sage encountered, so many years ago . . .

The demons bare their teeth in predatory smiles, and the taller of the two raises a hand.

Before Gwynn can cry out a warning to Mavrik, pain strafes through her lines, and she's frozen in place. Invisible bonds seem to be hooked into her lightlines, holding her captive. The scene around her blinks out, save for the two glamoured demons, the taller demon's terrifyingly multitoned voice searing through her mind.

WHERE IS THE WAND, MAGE WHORE! WE KNOW YOU CAN TRACK IT!

KILL HER! the other snarls. *BEFORE SHE CAN JOIN WITH OTHER LIGHT BEARERS!*

NO! the taller demon shrieks. *LET HER LEAD US TO THE SECOND WAND OF POWER! THEN WE DEVOUR HER!*

Then they're palpably rooting through Gwynn's thoughts, burrowing through her mind, their power scorching around the image of the Wand of Myth pulsing there, and her resurgent sense of the Wand drawing ever closer . . .

"Gwynnifer!"

Mavrik's sudden grip around her hand and the potent flash of his Level Five power around hers cuts through the demons' thrall. The world snaps back into focus, her free will flooding in just as a blast of the demons' steely fire explodes against a translucent green shield Mavrik must have conjured while she was enthralled, the shield's Varg-emerald color shimmering to gray.

Panic shoots through Gwynn's veins as she tightens her hold on Bloom'ilya's hand and Mavrik pulls them both into a run, Ee'vee still gripped in his arm. "They're glamoured pyrr-demons!" Gwynn cries

"I know!" Mavrik fires back before leading Gwynn and the terrified girls toward another alley the moment his shield falls, twin bolts of silver gray fire narrowly missing them as they duck into the alley. Mavrik lets go of Gwynn's hand, redraws his Varg wand, and aims it over his shoulder while growling out a spell, blasting another shield into being, this one a wall of emerald flame.

A ground-shaking *boom* crashes against the shield, and its green flame pulses gray.

"That's *not strong enough* to hold them off!" Gwynn yells as she parses through her knowledge of demonic magic with rapid-fire speed.

Not waiting for his response, Gwynn lets go of Bloom'ilya and grips Mavrik's wrist, ignoring the rush of prismatic sparks racing through her lines while wresting hold of the demon-spell-blocking rune stone in her pocket. Drawing it out, she thrusts the stone against Mavrik's wand. "Draw this rune's power through your shield *now!*" she cries.

Their eyes lock in a flash of alliance, comprehension igniting in Mavrik's gaze. He snarls out a spell, and a second wall of roiling green power bursts out of his wand to form a second shield, this one translucent emerald, against his wall of graying fire.

Another booming punch slams against the first shield, wiping out its flame, but the second shield remains standing.

Launching back into motion, Mavrik leads Gwynn and the children toward the alley's end, all of them skidding to a halt before a pile of broken-down crates.

After setting down a sobbing Ee'vee, Mavrik hurls aside the crates and levels his wand at the ground as Gwynn draws both girls close.

A shattering explosion sounds to their side, all of them flinching as the translucent shield Mavrik cast erupts into gray flame at the same moment that a wheel-size emerald Varg rune appears at their feet. The rune rapidly sizzles away to reveal a hole with a metal ladder leading into eerily greenlit depths.

The Sublands, Gwynn registers, heart pounding. The supposedly hellish lair of the vicious Smaragdalfar Elves. Are they about to trade one hell for another?

"*Go!*" Mavrik growls at Gwynn as their shield falls and the glamoured pyrr-demons, backed by countless Mage soldiers, launch themselves forward.

Clear out of options, Gwynn reaches in her tunic pocket and thrusts her last Varg rune stone into Mavrik's grip before prodding a shivering Bloom'ilya down the ladder.

Mavrik presses the stone to his wand and conjures another shield, the demons' and Mages' magic punching hard against it as Gwynn grabs a hysterical Ee'vee and swiftly follows Bloom'ilya down the ladder, her legs shaking, the ball of her foot almost slipping off a metal rung.

Gwynn and the girls touch down inside a narrow tunnel around the ladder's base, and she quickly scans her surroundings. Black rough-cut stone encircles them, lit sporadically with luminous Varg runes, a second tunnel's entrance before them.

Scared for Mavrik, Gwynn turns just as he lands beside them with a heavy *thud*, springs up, and points his wand toward the hole above them. An emerald rune shimmers to life over the circular entrance and sizzles into a barrier of crystalline green stone.

"We need to *move*," Mavrik urges as he scoops up Ee'vee and urges Gwynn and Bloom'ilya forward.

Taking hold of Bloom'ilya's trembling hand, Gwynn sprints into the tunnel and down a sharp, rocky incline, Mavrik's bootheels thudding behind her. He prods her down a series of ladders, then through two curving tunnels, muffled explosions booming to their rear, louder and louder . . .

They spill into a huge cavern, and Gwynn skids to a halt, her breath seizing in her chest. It's like they've been shrunk down and set inside the center of a giant green geode. Huge, jutting crystals surround them, their glittering majesty overtaking Gwynnifer's trapped light magery, large tree roots above them winding around the geode's mammoth crystals along with a net of Varg runes. The crystals' verdant color flashes into Gwynn's vision and races through her lightlines, surprise sparking as her vision clears and she takes in the Smaragdalfar army standing before them. Lethal Varg swords made from interlocking emerald runes are gripped in every Smaragdalfar Elf's hand, and three Noi portals pulse a short distance behind the army.

All the swords are raised and leveled in their direction.

Gwynn's shock is a war hammer to her chest. Because there, in the center of the Smaragdalfar Elf army between two male Alfsigr Elf archers, stands the Icaral Elf demon from the Wanted posters—Wynter Eirllyn.

There's a Watcher perched on the Icaral's shoulder, and her dark wings are fanned out behind her, silver fire burning in her eyes.

The image of the huge Ironwood tree made of starlight bursts into Gwynnifer's mind, and she gasps, the tree-vision's glow fracturing into prismatic light as Gwynn's whole world contracts toward the spiraling, green-glowing Wand gripped in Wynter Eirllyn's hand.

CHAPTER FIVE

MANGROVE BOND

Marina Song Spinner

Salish Ocean, Salishen Isles, Noilaan
Xishlon night

Marina steels herself, battling back the undertow of horror as she takes in Vogel's incoming wall of Shadow sea. Her arms arc through the salty water in rapid, rhythmic strokes, her sealskin tied firmly around her shoulders, as she and Gareth swim toward the Vu Trin navy's ships moving toward the dark mass. Gareth's mangrove root is clenched in his teeth, both of them ready to join with the Vu Trin to do battle with the Shadow sea. Above them, the purple moon has morphed to gray, its loving light snuffed out.

A sense of the mangroves trying to draw her back to them tugs at Marina's newly forming energy lines, the strange feeling like phantom tethers struggling to reel her in.

Thrown by the sensation, Marina resists the mangroves' pull as her thoughts storm.

Vogel's mass of corruption got here so *quickly*, the incoming tidal wave of gray chaos roaring straight toward Southern Noilaan's translucent dome-shield. Marina's thoughts careen to her people. The last time she was allowed in their territory, there was talk of all of them fleeing East to escape the Shadow sea's killing path.

Panic grips hold.

Where are they? Were they overtaken by the Shadow sea?

She was shunned by her people when she professed her love for Gareth and refused to forsake him, but even so, nearly everyone she loves was potentially in the path of that Shadow sea.

"Our Selkie'kin," Marina cries out to Gareth as they swim, her gills so tense with fear she's unable to get the words out clearly. But she can tell, by the stark look Gareth flashes toward her, that he understands.

Marina's stream of dread turns into a swifter current of alarm as the incoming Shadow tide comes to a roaring halt before Noilaan's shield. A net of Shadow flows up and over the huge dome-shield, and Marina and Gareth slow, treading water, as the Shadow net dims the world to a darker shade of steel and Gareth takes his mangrove root in hand.

"Gareth," Marina manages, gills flaring, "the Noi runes on the East's shield . . . they won't be strong enough to hold back the Shadow. The Mage, Alaric—he told of its rune-destroying abilities."

"Is anything strong enough to hold it back?" he presses.

She nods. "Alaric and the Selkie Nerissa went to a Shadow-destroyed continent in the West. They read the journals of a Death Fae who witnessed the Shadow's destruction there and learned that Varg magic can fight against Shadow. And—" her eyes widen with the spark of an idea "—so can *Dryad magic.*"

Marina's attention is snagged once more by the mangrove's pull, her new lines of energy crackling to brighter life throughout her body. Gareth's head jerks toward the mangroves. "Do you feel that?" he asks.

"They're pulling on the lines forming in me," she affirms, her gills ruffling as she meets his stare. "The Mage affinity lines I gained when we joined our tides and merged our powers."

Gareth's ocean green eyes narrow on hers. "I think the mangroves are trying to tell us something, and I think we should follow their pull. When I'm close to the center of the grove, my magic amplifies. If I send out magic from there, my Dryad power might be strong enough to strengthen Noilaan's shielding."

Exchanging a blazing look of agreement, they launch themselves back toward the purple saltwater trees at a fast stroke.

Darting underwater, they glide through the mangroves' arcing roots and slow before the huge roots of the grove's central, largest tree. The pull of the tree on Marina's new lines of energy tingles under her skin and through her hands, urging her closer. Surrendering to the pull, they both press their palms to one of the tree's roots.

All the power of the grove swoops in around them in a whirling tide, and the scene around Marina cuts out as both she and Gareth are drawn into the purple-shimmering darkness of the huge mangrove trunk's center.

They reach for each other at the same time, pulling each other into a protective embrace as Marina is filled with a vision of a huge tree made of prismatic starlight and covered in ethereal birds *linking* to them, its stunningly potent energy intimately connected to the mangroves, feeding Life and Balance into them through a continent-spanning network of roots.

The trees of the continent all connected.

The huge tree's name—III—resonating through her mind.

But then, nightmare images assault Marina—scenes of Erthia's every tree being consumed by a Shadow storm, the gray-roiling skies siphoning up the Natural World's land power to rain poison down on Erthia's previously pure, Life-giving Waters, choking the life and color out of them.

Marina lets out a strangled cry as she's overcome by a fuller sense of how the land and Ocean are connected in their vulnerability.

The visions of Erthia's destruction dissipate, and a new vision emerges—the suspended, pulsing image of a spiraling Wand-Stylus glowing with prismatic light. The name of this magical tool reverberates through her mind.

Verdyllion.

Urgency shivers through Marina, the lines of energy in her hand pulling toward the Wand-Stylus, the sense of an invitation to join with the power of the Forest through the Verdyllion burbling up.

"I will help you fight the Shadow power," Marina murmurs to the Verdyllion, and she's instantly swept up in an escalating sense of *rightness* as she reaches out at the same time Gareth does, and they bring their hands to the Wand-Stylus.

The image of the Verdyllion flares into rays of chromatic light, sending both Marina and Gareth spiraling down through the Great Tree's dark center. They grab hold of each other, another flash of color bursting through both Marina's sight and lines as color and sound pour back into the world and the mangrove forest around her snaps back into clarity.

Her gills and lungs struggling to pull in an even breath, Marina finds herself wrapped around Gareth and just above the grove's sloshing waterline, her back to the huge mangrove's trunk. He draws slightly back from her, astonishment rippling through Marina as she blinks at an equally astonished Gareth, amazed by his transformation.

There's a deeper forest green hue and shimmer to his skin, a purple mangrove branching pattern overlaying it, his previously naked form now garbed with purple armor made from fused mangrove leaves. She reaches up to run her fingers over the Dryad Fae points now gracing both of Gareth's ears, noting the broader streaks of Selkie-silver and a new streak of mangrove-purple that now color his tousled black hair.

Marina glances down and is amazed to find herself garbed in the same armor, her sealskin secure around her shoulders, an identical deep purple pattern branching over her own dark blue skin. A sting crackles against her palm, and her gaze slides to it. Astonishment wells as she takes in the image imprinted there of the Great Tree from the vision she had in the mangrove, a sense of Erthia's entire Forest network joining to her sense of Erthia's Waters.

Marina holds her palm up to Gareth, and he responds by raising his identically marked palm. "I saw the Great Tree in a vision," he hastily imparts.

"I saw it too—"

Marina's words break off as something slick slides around her arm and gently hugs her. She looks down to find it's an octopus tentacle, a prism of hues rippling over the color-shifter's hide. Other tentacles embrace her calf, her waist, and the water around them lights up with swirls of the octopuses' glowing color as Marina is hit by a palpable wave of the creatures' joyous affection.

One tentacle tip twirls gently around her finger, the octopuses' energy suddenly rippling through Marina's newfound lines in a rush of prismatic light as their magic connects not only with her but with the energy of the surrounding mangrove forest.

My kindred ones, Marina thinks, as a multitude of bonds to these beautiful, bioluminescent creatures lock into place.

A pang of affection tightens Marina's heart as Salish Electric Eels swim in to join the octopuses, their dark purple bodies pulsing with multicolored lightning. Bioluminescent cat sharks, dragonfish, firefly squid and jellyfish emerge into view, all of them pulsing chromatic light through the water, as if summoned there by their own mangrove call.

"The Great Tree," Marina shakily says to Gareth as her bond to her octopuses swells in her breast, "it bound me to both the mangroves and all these kindreds."

Urgency overtakes Gareth's expression. "I feel a connection to an incoming kindred. Marina, it's *strong*—"

Above them, the dome-shield's Noi runes flash out rays of sapphire, cutting off Gareth as they both startle. They jerk their heads up, gray light rippling through the dome's runes.

Marina's octopuses retreat toward the Ocean floor, and she swims out of the grove with Gareth just as the Eastern Realm's protective dome blinks out of being.

Marina's gills flare in a hard gasp as the runes marking every runic vessel and every runic supported structure on the heavily populated distant coast go dark.

A chorus of screams rises and Marina stiffens in horror. She grabs Gareth's slick arm as every runic airship falls and every rune-supported structure collapses, their great, shuddering crashes sending shock waves through the water.

An earsplitting *CRACK* sounds to the south, followed by a rumbling roar.

A surge of shock tightens Marina's gills as a churning barrier of storm rises, spitting white lightning.

"The Sylphan Fae," Gareth says, "they're trying to wall off the Shadow sea."

Another Ocean-jostling *BOOM* streaks pain through Marina's sensitive ears as the Shadow sea crashes into the Sylphan wall of storm. The world flashes bright white then dark gray as the Sylphan stormwall is rapidly consumed by the Shadow sea.

The Vu Trin naval ships launch themselves backward in a swirl of Fae wind power, rapidly retreating toward Marina and Gareth as the Shadow sea slowly advances.

Marina climbs onto a broad root with Gareth, and he breaks off and readies a mangrove root at the same moment that a winged swarm blasts out of the incoming wall of Shadow sea, soaring toward the retreating Vu Trin vessels.

"What is this evil?" Marina growls, terrified for her kindreds, for the mangroves, for every living thing in the path of this advancing abomination, the feral instinct to fight rising.

The leading winged beast soars toward the ship closest to Marina and Gareth, easily dodging Vu Trin arrows and bolts of power.

Marina flicks out her blue claws and readies her sharpening teeth as she surveys the beast. It's the size and shape of a man, with a gray body and bat-like wings. It swoops toward them before arcing back toward the nearest ship, and Marina gets a glimpse of the creature's four bulbous, gray eyes, bony ridged head, two telescoping mouths, and six insectile limbs. It darts toward the side of the ship and hovers there, soon joined by its swarm, their wings beating the air. Long, black tongues flick out of their mouths, along with a spray of what looks like Shadow liquid, the gray spray splashing against the ship from all directions.

The ship explodes in an inferno of silvery fire, its wood seeming to melt instantaneously.

"Holy gods, Marina," Gareth rasps out as disbelief strikes through Marina, all of the Vu Trin on that ship, murdered.

Her emotions slip into chaos.

If these Shadow-sea demons can take down an entire naval ship so quickly, then she and Gareth, her octopus kindreds, and the mangroves . . . as well as all of Southern Noilaan . . . none of them stand a *chance* . . .

"The kindred I sensed," Gareth chokes out, "it's still coming toward me . . . its energy is flowing around my *lines*."

A huge gray whale suddenly breaches the water's surface nearby, and Marina's eyes widen, the whale's trajectory an arrow straight toward them. Before Marina or Gareth can get a word out, several other whales—a whole pod of them—surface in dramatic sprays and glide toward the mangrove forest.

Static sizzles through Marina's mating bond to Gareth, and she's filled with the overwhelming sense of the pod's energy clicking into Gareth's lines like a lock engaging, as strong as Erthia's axis.

The portentous realization hits—*these are Gareth's kindred.*

Incredulity leaps through their bond as Gareth dives into the water and launches himself toward the lead whale, the gigantic kindred sliding through the waves to reach him as another Vu Trin ship explodes.

The whale and Gareth make contact, and he slides aboard his kindred's back then turns to Marina, his mangrove root in hand.

"Go!" she calls to him, sensing this kindred bond fused to Gareth and Gareth alone, the link clearly enabling him to withstand the whales' monumental stores of power, which she can feel spitting static through the very air.

Stores of electric power that no whale should have . . .

What are they? Marina marvels as Gareth and his pod of whales turn and start for the swarm of Shadow demons and the incoming Shadow sea in the distance, lightning crackling to life all over the whales' skin.

Marina's gills flare with awe as realization detonates through her.

Storm Whales.

The Great Blessed Ones of her people's religious fables, fated to return when the Great Unbalancing comes for Erthia's Life-giving Waters.

Heart in her throat, Marina watches as Gareth lifts his mangrove root, his body now covered in crackling lightning. An explosion of lightning blasts from Gareth's root at the same time that the whales shoot great bolts of it from their blowholes, the bolts of power forking toward Vogel's Shadow demons.

The demons explode in bursts of starlight white, and Marina's heart thunders as Gareth and his pod dive underwater. They soon resurface past the Vu Trin naval ships and blast out a huge wall of crackling lightning toward Vogel's Shadow sea.

The lightning wall collides with the Shadow sea's leading edge in a seismic *CRACK*.

The Shadow sea skids backward as a sheet of storm clouds shot through with lightning rises before it, rapidly forming a dome that encases a huge expanse of Ocean and the entirety of Southern Noilaan.

Walling out the Shadow sea.

Gareth and the entire pod of whales dive underwater, disappearing beneath the waves. Marina waits, pulse pounding, knowing she's witnessing a myth come to life. That the foretold fight against the Great Unbalancing is *here*.

Now.

Marina absently grips the slim mangrove root under the water beside her, and it breaks off in her hand. Her eyes snap toward it as she's flooded by a sense of the mangroves flowing their collective power into her via the root, which feels so *alive* . . . as if, through her lines, it maintains its living connection to the trees. As if she's become an extension of the grove itself.

Show me what to do, she implores the mangroves, opening herself up to them like she opens herself up to her beloved Ocean's tides.

Her octopuses, some jellyfish, and a whole riot of other bioluminescent animals are suddenly swimming around her in urgent swirls, prisms of color pulsing over their surfaces.

Astonishment streaks through Marina as all her color-shifting octopuses and other luminous creatures morph to a glowing mangrove purple.

Marina can feel the mangroves' underwater roots drawing energy from the burst of color. They take on a violet glow, newly luminous with magic, the sea surrounding them illuminated by the bright purple light.

Power crackles through Marina's lines toward the living root in her hand, the mangroves' elemental energy coursing through it.

I can draw on my kindreds' light power, Marina realizes in a shocked rush. Following the mangroves' pull on her lines, she thrusts her root toward the sky.

Beams of purple light burst from it, raying up and over the grove's canopy to form a translucent purple dome, like the inside of a jellyfish's mantle, that soon encases the entire mangrove forest.

Euphoria rising, Marina glances at her bioluminescent allies—Ocean life and land life united against the Shadow.

I'm a bridge, Marina realizes in a world-upending wave. *Linking the light power of the Ocean to Land power. Just like Gareth is a bridge from Forest to Water.*

A conch shell horn sounds, powerfully loud, and Marina's gaze jerks toward it, the sound coming from the surviving Vu Trin naval ships.

Before she can react to the distant figures leaping from the water to scale their way onto the ships, tethers of silvery power fly toward her from the direction of the vessels and slap around her wrists, ankles, and waist.

Marina snarls in protest as her living mangrove root falls from her hand and she's yanked into the Ocean, then sped away from her octopuses toward the ship, streaming past the two ships that were reduced to scattered, flaming debris. Her invisible bindings tighten, and a breath is forced from her gills as she's yanked into the air, flown through the sky in an arc then thrown down onto a surviving ship's black-lacquered deck.

She doesn't quite believe the sight she's met with.

Selkie soldiers in blue-shell armor surround her, deadly cone-snail spears raised and fury in their eyes as they circle Marina's bound form.

CHAPTER
SIX

VERDYLLION

Gwynnifer Croft Sykes

Western Sublands
Ten days after Xishlon

Gwynn's stunned gaze rivets onto the Icaral Elf staring at her. Wynter Eirrlyn's hair is like newly fallen snow, her sleek black wings fanned out, her eyes alight with silver fire, a translucent Watcher perched on her shoulder.

A Smaragdalfar army surrounds the Icaral, about a hundred strong, but Gwynn's shock is so great, the martial threat and the green-geode Subland world surrounding them seem to blur into pure, verdant light.

Gwynn focuses on the glowing Wand of Myth in Wynter's pale hand—the Wand the glamoured pyrr-demons so desperately want. A familiar image flashes into the back of Gwynn's mind—the Wand of Myth superimposed over a Great Ironwood Tree made of multihued starlight.

Heart thrumming, Gwynn meets the Icaral's gaze once more, and a riot of prismatic light energy detonates in Gwynn's vision, an echoing energy spangling across the Icaral's eyes. Chromatic threads of lightning burst to life through Wynter's wings and around the Wand in her hand, both her wings and the Wand spitting sparks of energy toward Gwynn that her lines spit back, as if their magics are *calling* to each other.

As if the *Wand of Myth* is calling them to each other . . .

A harsh, Subland-rattling *BOOM* shakes the earth beneath them and their magic-thrall breaks, Bloom'ilya's grip tightening on Gwynn's hand while Ee'vee lets out a terrified shriek against Mavrik's shoulder.

"We've got a Mage army and glamoured pyrr-demons on our tail!" Mavrik yells to Wynter and the Subland army. "We've got to get these children to the *East!*"

Gwynn's gaze snaps to Mavrik, and she's stunned by how unintimidated he seems by all the blades leveled at them. Urgency burns in Mavrik's eyes, one hand tight around his wand, his other arm hugging a whimpering Ee'vee close to his chest.

As the Smaragdalfar Elves take in the children's cropped ears, Gwynnifer sees their expressions heat to outrage, which immediately slips Gwynn into alliance with them, weapons be damned.

"The demons are after the Wand!" Gywnn blurts out, pointing at it emphatically as the trapped light magic in her lines strains toward it. "We can't let them get hold of it!"

A severe-looking Smaragdalfar soldier with a half-shaved head and glowing emerald Varg runes marking half her face thrusts up a palm and barks out a command in the Subland Elf tongue. Her flinty tone is one of military authority, her merciless silver eyes pinned on Gwynn with withering force.

All the blades leveled at them lower as one, and the soldiers leap into action, along with the Icaral. Close to half of them run toward the tunnel Gwynn and her companions emerged from, one of several tunnels that empty into this geode-cavern. The soldiers fan out in front of the tunnel's mouth to form a line of defense, then drop to one knee and aim their weapons, Wynter Eirllyn in the center of their line, the Wand of Myth raised.

Another, closer *BOOM* sounds, and Gwynn startles, her heartbeat accelerating as she realizes Mavrik's last barrier has fallen and the pyrr-demons and Mages are barreling toward them.

Toward the *Wand*.

A powerful bolt of silver energy blasts from the Wand of Myth, and Gwynn flinches. Lines of emerald energy erupt from the soldiers' Varg blades, and the combined power quickly forms a thick pane of translucent, rippling green to wall off the tunnel, a huge silver Alfsigr rune forming in the pane's center, flashing color at its edges.

A *CRACK* hits the shield, the sound knifing through Gwynn's ears, and Bloom'ilya cries out in terror. Mavrik darts in front of her and raises his wand, the shield raying out green and silver light as Wynter and the soldiers continue to feed lines of power into it.

A more powerful, bone-shuddering *BOOM* sounds, and Gwynn reflexively hugs a shivering Bloom'ilya, Wynter's huge silver rune pulsing an ominous gray.

"The demons," Gwynn calls out, voice tight with dread, "they're *here*."

She exchanges a dire look with Mavrik, her magic leaping toward him, before Mavrik pivots toward the cavern's other side, where more Subland soldiers are guarding what appear to be three runic portals.

Noi military portals, Gwynn surmises, recognizing the runes from the countless grimoires she's pilfered from her father's armory. From eavesdropping on her father's hushed military conversations, she's certain that these Noi portals are part of an underground Resistance network of portals and corridors the Mages have only recently discovered.

And are methodically searching out and destroying.

"Portal these children East," Mavrik yells to the guards. *"Now!"*

Ee'vee lets out a howl of protest, her skinny arms tightening around Mavrik's neck as a willowy female Smaragdalfar soldier with long emerald hair rushes toward them. She's armed with a Varg-marked bow and quiver and several Varg blades. The two Alfsigr Elf archers run over with her, and Gwynn notices that the taller Alfsigr soldier with the intense stare bears a striking resemblance to Wynter Eirllyn. The second man is slender with a quiet, compassionate air, his silver eyes taking in the terrified children with an expression of great concern.

"We'll portal them to the East," the willowy woman promises.

Gwynn latches on to the kindness in the woman's melodic voice as she struggles against her light magery's hypnotic pull toward the mesmerizing emerald pattern of the woman's skin. The Subland woman and the slender Alfsigr male reach out to take the children in hand.

A tenuous trust crystallizes in Gwynn. "Go with them," she encourages the girls, desperate to get Bloom'ilya and Ee'vee away from the incoming battle's front line.

Ee'vee screams and scrabbles to keep hold of Mavrik while he gently but firmly pries off her grasping fingers, murmuring comfortingly to her, "Shhh, it's all right. Ee'vee, look at me. *Look at me,* love."

Another floor-shaking *BOOM* slams against the shield as Wynter and the Smaragdalfar blast more power into it.

Choking back sobs, Ee'vee stops fighting and meets Mavrik's intense gaze, still clutching hold of him and her threadbare fawn toy for dear life.

"Do you trust me?" he asks, his demeanor so solid, so sure in this moment that Gwynn's throat knots against an unbidden upswell of emotion, her power sparking even more intensely toward him.

Ee'vee gives Mavrik one, quick nod.

Seizing his chance, Mavrik assures Ee'vee, "Mynx and Rhys will keep you safe, love," before quickly handing her off to the willowy Smaragdalfar woman.

"Are you and your friend ready to take a portal ride?" the woman, Mynx, asks Ee'vee, forcing brightness into her tone and smiling as she hugs the child close.

Weeping, Ee'vee burrows her head against Mynx's chest. The Subland woman briefly meets the intense silver gaze of the tall Alfsigr archer, and Gwynn catches the impassioned look that crosses his chiseled features, the bow gripped in his pale hand at the ready.

The slender Alfsigr archer, Rhys, holds his hand out to Bloom'ilya. "We will not hurt you, child."

Breaking into heaving sobs, Bloom'ilya gives in and takes Rhys's hand, Watchers briefly shimmering to life on both girls' shoulders as they're guided to the geode-cavern's far end. Bloom'ilya turns to give Gwynn one last, heartbreaking look, and Gwynn's own heart twists as she takes in the glimmering gold interiors of the three sapphire-rune-bracketed portals.

A fierce reluctance to send the girls into an unknown world rises in Gwynn, chokingly tight, but she holds fast against it as they're passed to two female Subland soldiers. Gwynn's breath catches as the children and the soldiers disappear into the portals' golden depths, her conflict soon overtaken by a tenuous surge of relief.

They're free of Gardneria, she assures herself. *And once they clear the portal lag, they'll be in the East.* Gwynn blinks back tears, instinctively *sure* that these Smaragdalfar Elves she's been taught to hate and fear her whole life are Bloom'ilya and Ee'vee's best shot at survival.

A soldier runs to Mavrik. The two of them exchange a few words in rapid-fire Smaragdalfarin, and surprise darts through Gwynn over Mavrik's fluency. The soldier hands Mavrik a Varg-rune-marked charging stone that Mavrik places on his Varg wand's faintly glowing runes. The runes instantly brighten.

Another cave jostling *BOOM* detonates, but Wynter's rune holds fast this time, its brightness undimmed, the shield secure.

"When are we portaling East?" Gwynn asks Mavrik. Before he can answer, a woman's distant voice yells something in Smaragdalfarin, her voice echoing out from a separate, unshielded tunnel to the right of the tunnel they arrived through.

In her mind, Gwynn briskly rifles through the Smaragdalfarin translation dictionary she embedded there, along with multiple other language dictionaries, thankful again that her light magery, even trapped as it is, gives her the ability to remember in exacting detail anything she sees. She quickly parses out some of the meaning.

Children . . . portals . . . Alfsigr soldiers . . .

The woman's urgent words continue to echo off the tunnel's stone along with what sounds like a strengthening sea of thudding bootheels shot through with children's scattered cries.

An elderly Smaragdalfar woman bursts from the tunnel and runs toward them, an emerald-glowing rune stylus gripped in her hand. There's a battle-hardened expression on her weathered, emerald-patterned face. A large number of terrified-looking Smaragdalfar children rush in behind her in panicked flight, three younger, heavily armed Smaragdalfar women bringing up the rear.

A little boy, not more than five years old, shrieks in horror and skids to a halt when he catches sight of Gwynn and Mavrik as well as Wynter, Rhys, and the taller Alfsigr Elf male. The elderly runic sorceress scoops up the child and gives Mavrik and the Alfsigr Elves grim nods that they return. Gesturing toward them, the elderly woman calls out to the children a string of words in Smaragdalfarin that Gwynn recognizes as *friends* and *will not hurt you.* Other Smaragdalfar soldiers close in around the children and usher them and their caretakers toward the portals.

"Where are these children from?" Gwynn asks Mavrik, a sick guilt over their fear clenching her gut as translucent Watchers flash into view once more, a single Watcher perched on each child's shoulder.

"They're escapees from the Alfsigr lumenstone mines," Mavrik explains.

Shock overtakes Gwynn, and she meets his gaze. The eye contact triggers a stronger pull on her lines toward him that she knows he feels too as they both shiver against it, but even the mind-scattering effect of their magical draw isn't enough to distract from this horror.

Mavrik's brow knots, his gaze turning searching, as if he recognizes something in her that he's felt himself. "Gwynn," he says, "the Smaragdalfar people have been imprisoned in the Sublands by the Alfsigr military for *decades*, adults and children alike. All of it abetted by the Mage Council and military."

Gwynn's gut heaves and she fears she might retch. She's heard of the lumenstone mines, but she had no idea the Alfsigr were imprisoning people who are not depraved criminals there, much less *children*.

The elderly Smaragdalfar sorceress yells something to Mavrik, too fast for Gwynn to translate, the woman motioning toward the tunnel the children ran in from.

THE DRYAD STORM

Mavrik nods at the woman before turning back to Gwynn. "Now that my wand is fully charged, I'm going to help them wall off the open tunnels while the children and others evacuate." He glances toward the large crowd of children bottlenecked in front of the three portals. "In a matter of moments, we're going to break down the West's entire underground network of Noi military portals so that the Mages and the Alfsigr military can't make use of them."

Their magical pull surges, and Mavrik hesitates, his jaw flexing as if he's fighting to concentrate around their mutual thrall as Gwynn fights off the almost gravitational urge to move toward him.

"There's only so much charge in those portals, and they're slow to recharge," he forces out, then swallows, his gaze softening into something akin to real affection. "You should go with them, Gwynnifer. Your work for us is done."

Gwynn pulls in a shaky breath, her heart inexplicably tightening due to the intimate tone he's wrapped around her name. Reluctance to be parted from him rises.

"My light magery gives me a perfect memory of any image I've ever seen," she confides, her voice quavering as her magic strains toward his. "And I've read multitudes of high-level military grimoires from my father's armory. Which means I have an encyclopedia of spells in my mind that you might have need of, including knowledge of primordial Shadow magic from a demonic grimoire. I want to stay and help you fight the Magedom."

"No," Mavrik counters. He sounds firm, but the word is tight in his throat, as if refuting her is going against his every magical instinct. "The Mages and the Alfsigr will likely find a way to attack while we're holding the line. Gwynn, you've done your part, just *go*."

The pained look overtaking his expression steals Gwynn's breath. She knows—just *knows* from the intensity of that look—that if she touched him right now, she'd find his Level Five magic straining as relentlessly toward her lines as her trapped light magic is flashing toward his.

The image of the Great Tree pulses in the back of Gwynn's mind, and she's overwhelmed by a sense of life-altering crossroads dividing before her. Her choice in this moment will be irrevocable.

"*I'm staying*," she states. She glances toward the rapidly diminishing bottleneck of children being led through the portals, the will to fight for them—and for the Wand—intensifying as she meets Mavrik's gaze once more. "I'm staying, and I'm going East with you."

The tension in Mavrik's expression doesn't lessen. "If we survive holding this line, we're not portaling to the East," he warns. "We're portaling to the Northern Forest. To take down the Black Witch."

Thrown, Gwynn gives him a questioning look.

"Elloren Gardner Grey used to possess Wynter's Wand of Power," Mavrik explains. "Because of that, Wynter can sense her location through it. Right now, Elloren's caught in a Dryad portal lag. The portal's trajectory is set for the Northern Forest, so we're going to portal there and use the Wand to break through the forest's Dryad warding and get to Elloren before Vogel does." Mavrik's expression turns steely. "Then we're going to strike her down."

Gwynn gapes at him, acid-yellow alarm blazing through her lines. "You should be portaling that Wand to the East *right now*," she protests. "You need to get it as far away from Vogel as you possibly can. There's a reason he and his demons are after it. You can't let them get hold of it!"

"It's a risk we have to take," Mavrik shoots back. "The Northern Forest's wards have stood unbroken for generations." He glances at Wynter. "That Wand of Power can break through locks and wards like nothing I've ever seen."

Gwynn's alarm turns incandescent as she levels her finger toward the Wand in Wynter's hand. "If Vogel gets hold of that Wand and the Shadow Wand both . . ." Gwynn casts about for a way to express the vast danger that she can sense, deep in her core, as the image of the Wand pulses hard against her mind, a renewed line-tugging draw toward Wynter taking hold as the last of the children disappear through the portals' golden depths.

Her decision to remain here set, Gwynn meets Wynter's silver-fire gaze. The graceful Icaral lowers the Wand and strides toward her with an air of purpose, as if Wynter is swept up in the same pull toward Gwynnifer, the Wand of Myth casting the Icaral's pale form in a penumbra of green light.

The crystalline cavern seems to contract around them both as Wynter stops before her.

"I am Wynter Eirllyn, Ealaiontora Empath of Alfsigroth," Wynter states, her black wings drawing in behind her, threads of silvery lightning crackling through them. Her pale hand glows with the Wand's verdant light as she lifts it. "I saw your face in my dreams, fellow Bearer of the Verdyllion."

Gwynn pulls in a deep breath, the Wand of Myth's true name resonating through her, a stronger draw to both the Verdyllion and to this Elfin Icaral tugging on her trapped power—on her very soul—Bearer to Bearer.

A vision overtakes Gwynn's mind—branches twining out from the Verdyllion Wand of Myth to form a Great Ironwood Tree wreathed in verdant mist, the Tree filling this entire geode-cavern. Watchers shiver into being, perched all over the Great Tree's branches, one appearing on Wynter's shoulder.

A flash of prismatic shimmer sparkles through both the Tree and Gwynn's lines, every color flashing through her gaze as her confusing pull toward Mavrik intensifies, as well. Gwynn looks at him and knows, from his equally thrown expression and tense stance, that he's also aware of their strange, mounting draw toward each other's power. A pull that the Verdyllion seems to be *amplifying*.

Gwynn turns back to Wynter, everything impressed on her in church cast into upheaval, the Sacred Wand in the hands of a "Cursed Winged One." But Wynter Eirllyn radiates the very opposite of evil. Her silvery eyes gleam with compassion, and all the Watchers, including the one on Wynter's shoulder, keep their starlight eyes trained on Gwynnifer.

Waiting.

Decided, Gwynn surrenders to the Wand's pull, hurtling recklessly toward alliance not only with Mavrik, but with this Icaral Wand Bearer.

The Tree-vision dissipates, save for the single Watcher perched on Wynter's shoulder.

"I saw the Verdyllion in dreams," Gwynn shakily tells Wynter. "And a vision just hit me . . . a vision I've seen again and again. A Great Tree wreathed in green mist and filled with multihued light. And . . ." She glances pointedly at the Watcher on Wynter's shoulder.

Wynter gives her a knowing look, and as the Watcher shivers out of sight, Gwynn can tell that Wynter sees them, as well.

"The Verdyllion," Gwynn says, her eyes flicking toward the Wand, "it's still linked to me. I can feel it."

Wynter nods in solemn agreement. "The Verdyllion is calling on all of its Bearers to unite. To fight the Shadow with light power. I've seen visions of us gathered around the Verdyllion."

Gwynn's astonished mind spins as a memory hits from when she was thirteen years old—giving Sagellyn Gaffney the Verdyllion Wand that fateful, blue-lit morning in Valgard, so that the Wand could escape to Halfix and be hidden from the Mages and glamoured pyrr-demons . . .

"Sagellyn . . ." Gwynn stammers, "she was a Bearer of the Verdyllion. Do you think she's feeling this call, as well?"

"I do," Wynter responds, and the Wand's glow takes on a beckoning, chromatic pulse. "We are the Blessed Bearers spoken about in my people's *Elliontorin* holy book. To the Noi, we're known as the Vhion, and to the Smaragdalfar as the Oo'nour'iel—Oo'na's Seven Light Bearers. Our light power, amplified by the Verdyllion, is a weapon against the Shadow."

A memory of the pyrr-demon's words assaults Gwynn's mind—

KILL HER! BEFORE SHE CAN JOIN WITH THE OTHER LIGHT BEARERS!

Gwynn's brow furrows. "But . . . I have no access to my light power. I'm a Level One Mage—"

Running boot steps sound from a small, unshielded tunnel near their side, cutting into Gwynn's turbulent thoughts, a woman's urgent shouting in the Common Tongue drawing everyone's attention.

"Incoming storm spiders!"

Wynter and Mavrik raise their wands and slide protectively in front of Gwynn as a contingent of soldiers level weapons at the tunnel.

A young woman with the tattoos of the Amaz surges out of it with a slender, lavender-hued Urisk woman tight on her heels, both of them dressed incongruously in Mage-soldier garb. The Amaz woman is gray-hued with short, spiky black hair, a barely charged Varg blade raised in her hand, a look of urgency burning in her dark eyes.

"Valasca!" both Mavrik and Wynter exclaim as one, stepping forward.

The Amaz woman—Valasca—snaps her gaze to them, her eyes widening with a look of recognition before she regains her air of ferocity. "Portal out of here *now*!" she growls.

"We *can't*!" the commanding Smaragdalfar woman with the Varg-rune-marked face and half-shaved head growls back at her, the woman's runic sword flashing a threatening emerald light. "We're recharging these portals and recalibrating their trajectory to the Northern Forest!"

Valasca curses, jabbing her thumb toward the tunnel behind her. "*Fallon Bane* is on our tail! And she's sent a swarm of corrupted storm spiders ahead of her! They'll throw cyclones that will smash *right through* any barriers you can conjure, as well as your portals!"

"We can take out storm spiders," Mavrik snarls.

Valasca's gaze pierces into him. "Not ones corrupted with Shadow and covered in deflection runes, you can't!"

Now it's Mavrik's turn to curse before his gaze turns unfocused, as if he's rooting through his mind for some magical option. Gwynn battles back a spike of terror. Everything she's read about storm spiders and deflection runes in the armory's grimoires flashes through her mind, along with images of detailed ink renderings of the horrifying beasts.

"How long till they get here?" Mavrik demands as the Smaragdalfar woman orders her army to form a defensive line in front of the portals.

"Not long," Valasca answers. She holds up her blade. "I threw up a few barriers before I exhausted most of my weapon's charge. But my shields aren't strong enough to hold off those spiders and Fallon for long."

Gwynn's light mage mind swiftly riffles through all the runes in a huge Alfsigr military grimoire she scanned over a year ago and zeroes in on an obscure silver rune, one of the few that can defend against storm spiders.

"There's an Alfsigr arachnid-defense rune," she blurts out, just as Mavrik's eyes glint with what looks like an idea.

"And an Alfsigr storm-shield rune," he adds, eyes meeting hers in a flash of such intense urgency, a frisson of tingling energy shoots through her lines. Both of them eagerly look to Wynter.

Because Gwynn and Mavrik might not be able to create Alfsigr runes, but the Alfsigr Icaral *runic sorceress* before them can.

Unspoken agreement lighting her gaze, Wynter holds out the Verdyllion to them. "Concentrate on the defensive runes and touch my hand," she prods. "I'll empathically read your combined knowledge and create the runes with the Verdyllion."

Wasting no time, they grab Wynter's hand, Mavrik's fingers wrapping around Gwynn's hand, as well. An explosion of invisible sparks sizzles out from Mavrik's touch as the tips of Gwynn's and Mavrik's fingers slide forward over Wynter's hand and they both make contact with the Verdyllion.

The Great Tree image bursts through Gwynn's vision, raying out prismatic light of every hue as Gwynn's lines pull hard toward Mavrik's and abruptly *open*.

Gwynn gasps as she's filled with the sudden, line-expanding sense of Mavrik's every Level Five line—fire, air, wind and earth—a shudder passing through them both as their eyes lock in a burst of snapping energy and Gwynn's light magery burgeons to life. It's like a floodgate being blasted wide-open, Gwynn's power coursing, flashing and sparking, toward Mavrik's lines, their magic melding into what feels like one Balanced system of interconnected lines channeling all five elemental powers.

Wynter lifts the Verdyllion, and they follow her motion as Wynter moves its tip in a sweeping arc to form two huge, bright silver Alfsigr runes in the air between them and the tunnel Valasca and her Urisk companion ran through. One rune is the arachnid-defense rune Gwynn is struggling to hold in the forefront of her mind, and the other is Mavrik's storm-shield rune.

A chorus of loud clacks sounds through the tunnel, followed by a tinny, echoing insectile shriek that sends a powerful chill through Gwynnifer's veins. She, Mavrik, and Wynter keep tight hold of the Verdyllion.

A giant spider scuttles into view, big as a horse, and terror crackles down Gwynn's spine as more spiders swarm in behind the creature, chittering and clacking and gnashing chitinous jaws. For several seconds, Gwynn can't breathe, the spiders' nightmarish heads distorted with a multitude of glowing gray eyes, and their rune-marked thoraxes fitted with two raised holes just behind their heads, seemingly endless numbers of them scuttling into the cavern . . .

It's not enough, Gwynn's thoughts and heart pound out. *Our two runes are not enough for an attack this large.*

Forcing herself to focus, Gwynn sends her thoughts flying desperately through grimoires and swiftly locates a possible spell.

"What is this rune you've found?" Wynter asks, gaze stark as she empathically senses Gwynn's thoughts.

"An Issani multiplication spell!" Gwynn cries. "But you can't cast it, and neither can Mavrik—it's not an Alfsigr or Mage spell!"

"But *you* can," Wynter fiercely returns.

Gwynn's eyes widen, what Wynter is insinuating explosively clear—Light Mages are able to cast runic spells from *every* magical system, not just their own. And Gwynn's light magery is now *unblocked.*

Gwynn murmurs the spell, and Mavrik's hand tightens around both hers and Wynter's, Gwynn's heart thundering against her chest.

As her light magery breaks *free.*

It rushes through Mavrik's power with such intensity that her lungs contract and her vision sparks Issani gold, her magic shimmering through his wand hand and into the Verdyllion.

Gilded light bursts from the Wand and rays through the suspended runes before them.

The silver runes flash gold then miraculously multiply, countless identical silver runes springing out from them to form a huge interlocking barrier wall just as the spiders rear back and blast out bolts of roaring gray storm from their raised thorax holes, dark Shadow lightning arcing through it.

The Shadow storm slams into their silvery runic barrier, the sheer force of the Shadow assault driving their barrier back a few paces as the Subland soldiers closing in around their sides fire uncharged arrows and blades through the runic shield, the insects' furious shrieks echoing against the cavern's crystalline walls as they're struck.

A flash of sapphire light rays out from the portals behind them, and a Subland soldier yells something in Smaragdalfarin, too fast for Gwynn to translate. She looks at Mavrik in urgent question as the Alfsigr runes continue to multiply, Gwynn's light magery rushing through the Verdyllion and into the thickening runic barrier, the magic in her lines and Wynter's rapidly depleting.

"Only a few minutes before the portals are charged," Mavrik translates.

Relief surges through Gwynn but it's immediately punched down as another echoing, earsplitting shriek rattles the cave. A gigantic, insectile mass squeezes into the geode-cavern, its upper head covered with a riot of gray-glowing eyes. The creature pushes the rest of its body into the cavern and unfolds into a barn-size spider. Black, chitinous half-moon horns rise from its head, and Shadow-tainted Mage deflection runes are marked all over its body. Four extra pairs of legs made of what looks like dark lightning bolts sizzle out over its eight limbs.

"Goddess help us," Valasca murmurs from beside them. "Fallon bound a queen."

The queen spider slams its lightning legs onto the floor with a thunderous CRACK.

Dark lightning buzzes out over the floor's flat expanse and forks toward and against their runic barrier, the barrier's runes whirring into a solid silvery blur that spits reactive threads of lightning.

"My light magery," Gwynn rasps to Mavrik and Wynter as the magic flowing out of her sputters. "I can feel it depleting . . ."

A tide of dark mist billows from the queen spider's underside and slithers toward their barrier and then over its expanse, their barrier's silver coloration pulsing away in strobing fits of storm gray.

Mavrik yanks his hand from theirs, and Gwynn's light magic contracts into its trapped state with such slingshot force that she sways on her feet, her hand dropping from Wynter's.

Drawing his Varg-marked wand, Mavrik grits out a spell and throws a bolt of glowing emerald energy that quickly expands into a huge half-orb shield of shimmering, emerald light in front of them, walling off their side of the geode-cavern, the soldiers beside them blasting their emerald magic into it.

The queen spider lunges forward, the very air gaining a stinging charge as the beast hurls out a prone, whirling tornado.

The tornado slams into their original rune shield and shatters it in an explosion of bright silver light, the spider's storm rushing forward to pummel against Mavrik's green orb barrier.

Gwynn's heart slams against her ribs as another flash of sapphire light rays out from behind them.

"The portals are charged!" a woman's voice rings out in the Common Tongue, her words barely cutting through the roar of the attacking storm as Mavrik feeds power into his half-dome barrier, leaning into it but skidding back alarmingly as the Subland soldiers make for the charged portals.

Mavrik grunts, muscles tensing as he jabs his wand arm harder toward his orb shield, slapping his free hand around his wrist to steady his wand hand, the bolt of power he's feeding into his shield brightening its forest green glow as Shadow wind gusts and dark lightning cracks against it. The queen spider lets out a floor-rattling shriek and intensifies her onslaught of storm.

"Go! Go!" Mavrik urges Gwynn and Wynter, Valasca and the purple Urisk woman hugging Valasca's side as he keeps tenuous hold of his orb shield. "Get that Wand out of here!"

Valasca grips both the purple woman's and Wynter's arms and tugs them into motion. Wynter casts Mavrik a tortured look before the three of them sprint toward the charged portal while Gwynn finds herself frozen as she realizes what Mavrik is doing.

Sacrificing himself so they can escape.

The image of Mavrik's look of horror when he took in Bloom'ilya's and Ee'vee's cropped ears burns through Gwynn's mind. He's the only Mage she's ever encountered, in her closed Styvian Mage world, who actually *cared*.

Who saw the cruelty and responded with full-on rebellion.

A visceral panic strikes through her, over the possibility of losing both their confusing magical connection and *him*.

Through Mavrik's green orb shield, Gwynn can just make out a new swarm of spiders pouring into the geode-cavern, scuttling over and clinging to every surface, their queen's dark lightning scything into Mavrik's weakening shield with mounting force. The air grows more charged, all the spiders' bodies seeming to swell and take on a steely glow. A static sting courses through the air, setting Gwynn's teeth on edge, her hair lifting along her scalp as her terror rises.

"Mavrik!" she cries.

He turns and spots her, and his eyes ignite with fury. Snarling out an epithet, he launches himself toward her, the urgency in his gaze sending a bolt of resolve straight through Gwynn's center, static rising in the air.

Mavrik grabs her arms and tries to push her toward the portal, and an explosion of multicolored sparks races through her lines from the contact. She grabs hold of his wrists in turn, the skin-to-skin contact abruptly unblocking the remaining shreds of her light power. Her magic rushes into his lines, and their eyes meet in a flash of intensity as they're hit by a violent blast of energy.

A fiery, forking sting assaults Gwynn's sides, and she cries out in pain as Mavrik's body is blasted against hers and they're blown straight across the cavern's floor toward the portal's golden maw, a chill sweeping over her skin.

Fallon Bane sweeps into the cavern, ice shimmering over the cave's stone. Her wand is raised, her vicious gaze pinned on Gwynn.

Fallon's cry of *"Nooooo!"* is the last thing Gwynn hears before she and Mavrik are blasted into the portal's golden depths.

SELKIE WAR

Marina Song Spinner

Salish Ocean, Salishen Isles, Noilaan
Xishlon night

Marina struggles against her invisible bindings, the ship's black lacquered deck hard under her knees, her shock like a harpoon to the gut. Alarmed, she takes in the furious Selkie soldiers surrounding her with their lethal cone-snail spears— venom-coated weapons that could fell her in a heartbeat—the Selkie soldiers' blue-shell-hewn battle armor muted to navy hues by the East's Shadowed moon- light, their silver sealskins secured around their shoulders.

Marina's gaze snaps toward the naval ship's Vu Trin crew, the soldiers all being restrained by Selkies, spears to their throats, magic-dampening bull kelp fronds binding the wrists of Vu Trin naval commander Zephyr Quillen. The young, dark- hued commander's steel gray eyes warily take in the situation as Vogel's Shadow sea distantly roars against the huge, lightning-spitting dome-shield made of storm magic that Gareth and his whale kindreds conjured.

Marina's gaze darts toward the scores of Selkie soldiers streaming onto the coast- line, more soldiers invading every ship in sight, a line of them ringing the periphery of each naval vessel's deck.

Her mind whirls.

My people's Ocean army must have been amassing underwater here long before Noilaan's dome-shield fell. How did they get through that shield?

Marina looks over the ship rail's edge toward the water, the origin point of her invisible bindings, and meets the ferocious gaze of a Naiad witch.

The blue-scaled witch is treading water close to the ship's side. Her glowing cerulean blue eyes are fixed on Marina, one web-fingered hand raised and holding a charged rune stone. The stone's looping rune glows a vivid scarlet interspersed with bright pinpricks of emerald Varg light.

Marina's gaze sharpens with recognition—it's one of the Amaz rune stones given to Marina and the other land-trapped Selkies by Queen Alkaia and her Council of Sorceresses. The rune stone holds enough magic to break the spells that snared groups of Selkie women on shore during the full moon.

A split-second realization hits home—the Naiad witch must have found a way to reconfigure the powerful Amaz magic so that the Ocean army could break down shield spells as well as snare spells, allowing them to traverse Noilaan's border shield, come to land, and wage war.

As if sensing Marina's comprehension, the Naiad witch smiles, black teeth gleaming, her scaled skin and long, lashing fishtail glittering a vivid blue even in the Shadowed moon's grayed light, her tentacle hair writhing.

Marina turns, and surprise floods her when she finds her combative soldier brother, Storm Tide, shouldering his way through the ranks toward her, his gills flared in anger. Outrage slashes through Marina, and she growls, wrestling against her bindings as she boldly meets her brother's cleaving stare. Storm Tide's hand flashes out mariner sign-language commands to the surrounding soldiers with staccato emphasis, even as his livid ocean-hued eyes remain locked on hers.

"Let me *go!*" Marina snarls at him. "You're fighting the *wrong war!*" She's certain her brother won't understand her air-speech words but knows he'll grasp her tone.

Storm Tide's expression practically spits spears as he turns toward the Naiad witch and signs, *"Release Song Spinner!"*

Glaring murderously at Marina, the witch raises her webbed palm, and Marina's bindings abruptly dissolve. She springs to her feet, ready to face her brother down.

"Where are the rest of our people?" Marina signs at her brother, desperate for news of their family and loved ones, fearing the worst.

"Here!" Storm Tide signs back, gesturing toward the northern waters inside the shielding. He bares his teeth at Commander Zephyr Quillen. *"Well protected from these Ocean killers!"*

"Ocean dweller," Commander Quillen both says and manages to sign to Storm Tide, the Vu Trin commander's expression fierce as she ignores the lethal spear at her throat. "We are *not* your enemies!"

"She speaks the truth!" Marina says and signs to her brother, hands flying.

Marina's gaze darts back toward the Selkie land invasion, a chill racing through her as line upon line of Ocean-shifter soldiers march out of the water and onto the coast, spears in hand. And not just Selkie'kin. Marina spots the black-shell armor of a contingent of shark-shifters, their necklaces of teeth allowing them to return to their shark forms. There's also a distant unit of gray shell-armored whale-shifters who hold their whale forms in a resonant song.

All the armies of the Ocean, suddenly aligned and able to come on land.

Vu Trin forces are moving toward the beach, including a line of archers spreading across the entire boardwalk, arrows nocked. But Marina knows the Vu Trin are no match for her people—not with their weapons stripped of Noi runes from Vogel's Shadow attack and every Ocean spear holding enough cone-snail venom to fell scores of Eastern Realm soldiers. Marina's gaze swings to Erthia's real enemy, the distant Shadow sea, then back to her brother, urgency churning in her core.

"My brother," she signs. *"Please hear me out! You are attacking the wrong people!"*

Storm Tide bares his teeth at her. *"You are ensorcelled by the land parasites!"* he emphatically signs back, his hands moving like they're weapons, his gills flaring. Storm Tide pauses, his gaze raking over the purple branching pattern newly emblazoned on Marina's deep-blue form, a look of open disgust twisting his features. *"You need to be forcibly cleansed of this land corruption!"* he signs. *"We will deal with the Ocean killers."*

"We do not seek to harm your ocean," Zephyr Quillen both states and signs, lightning crackling in her eyes.

"Silence, lying one!" Storm Tide signs back with the full wrath of a storming Sea. *"We know the full extent of your corruption. You land filth killed off an entire distant continent! Sent Shadow over it and into its surrounding Ocean! Killed every last reef! Sucked the breath clear out of those Waters! I've seen the seas around this dead continent with my own eyes. And I've seen how your Shadow power rains down poison from the skies into the Oceans of the Western Realm. And now, you land filth are poised to rain down this corruption over the East to kill off the remaining Ocean!"* Storm Tide swings his tempest-spitting gaze back at Marina. *"They must ALL DIE to save our Waters!"*

Marina stares her brother down as purple light explodes through her lines, the full might of the mangrove forest and her octopus kindreds rising within her. The power of her mating bond to her beloved rising.

"These land dwellers are our *allies*," she growls and signs, pointing a finger toward the armies facing off along the coast. *"That* is what will kill our entire Ocean. Us fighting each other. Instead of banding together to fight *that*!" She swings her finger toward the distant Shadow sea. "My brother, please hear me out—our division is what the Shadow *wants*."

Her brother's face ignites with a look of unmitigated anger.

"*We all know of your unnatural love for a Mage,*" he signs, letting out a low snarl. "*A Mage!*" He sniffs at Marina, nostrils flaring with obvious revulsion. "*I can* smell *him on you. I can scent that you actually* mated *with this land filth. Where is he? I will run a spear through him with my own hands!*"

A *SNAP* of electricity discharges, startling them all, the dome-shield Gareth and the Storm Whales cast over Southern Noilaan flashing bright white. Explosive sprays burst from the nearby water as the entire pod of lightning-coated whales breaches the waves.

The lead whale swims straight toward them, Gareth on its back, lightning pulsing over his mangrove-leaf-armored form.

Storm Tide and the Selkie and Vu Trin soldiers all gape at Gareth and the Storm Whales. A resolute expression hardens Gareth's features before he leaps off the back of one of the Ocean Goddess's own prophesied whales and swims to the ship. He's momentarily cut from Marina's sight, and her heart thuds as she hears him climbing the ship's rope ladder before reappearing to land deftly on his feet before them. He takes hold of the mangrove root clenched in his teeth, his intense eyes meeting Marina's, his gaze blazing with bright lightning.

"My tide," Marina manages, an ache of love for him welling in her chest, strong as the Ocean.

Storm Tide and Marina's other Selkie'kin survey Gareth's green-glimmering, gilled, and point-eared form with expressions of vast confusion. She catches their nostrils flaring as they breathe in his Selkie scent, watches their astonishment intensify as their gazes rake over Gareth's Selkie-silver- and mangrove-purple-streaked hair. Even her famously unyielding brother seems utterly thrown.

Gareth holds out his hand to Marina, and she takes it, her heart soaring as she thrills to the electricity sizzling over his skin.

"*This,*" Marina says and signs to her brother, to them all, "is Gareth Keeler, my chosen mate." She gestures to the lightning-flashing whales now encircling the ship. "He has been called to be a Storm Whale Warrior for Erthia's Waters. And both of us are being called to bind both land and sea peoples to the mangrove trees—to link the power of both our dominions."

"It cannot be," Storm Tide signs with a look of confusion as he gapes at the huge whale pod, then at Gareth, before his gaze swings back to Marina. *"He is not full Selkie, and we are Ocean'kin. We do not bond with trees . . ."*

"All the myths are converging," Gareth signs and says to Storm Tide. "So that all the Peoples of Erthia can come together and fight *that."* Gareth points his root at the distant Shadow sea pressing up against the southern side of his lightning dome, an echoing lightning crackling over his own skin, defiance in his gaze.

"Forge a new myth," Marina implores the Selkies and Vu Trin both. "Erthia needs all of us to set down our differences and come to the Forest. As *one."* Marina lets go of Gareth's hand, and they both raise their palms, displaying the image of the Great Ironwood Tree, III.

But even with mythical whales surrounding them, no one budges.

Storm Tide's gaze turns explosive as it bores into Marina's. *"Have you lost your mind? You are asking us to trust* landlings? *You are an apprenticed Selkie* bard. *You* know *our songs. When in the* entirety of history *has it been a good idea to 'set down our differences' with* them?"

Marina meets her brother's gaze without flinching. "When in the entirety of history have we seen a threat that could undo the *entire Natural World*?" She points, once more, at the black mass of Shadow. "Something that will kill *everything."*

"We stand together as one, or we fall together with all of Erthia," Gareth signs and states. "And every last person and thing we love, above sea and below, will be *destroyed."*

"Please, my brother," Marina says and signs, her tones fracturing. *"Stop fighting.* And come with us to our Forest. To build a bridge between Land and Water to save Erthia."

Silence. Weapons still raised.

The whales grow agitated, circling the ship before forming a rigid line, all of them turned toward the north.

Gareth inclines his head toward the pod, lightning pulsing over his skin with the same staccato urgency as the light power forking over the whales' huge bodies.

"What are they sensing?" Zephyr presses Gareth.

Gareth's gaze swings to his Vu Trin commander, his expression stark. Before he can get a word out, a huge dark wave ripples up from the Shadow sea and flows over the lightning dome like a malignant tide.

Feeling like a trapped animal, Marina glances around as the world darkens to blackish-gray, the gray moon muting to a Void. Only the lightning coursing over the Storm Whales' bodies and striking over Gareth's skin and through his eyes illuminates the ship's deck and surrounding Ocean with pulsing white light.

Gareth meets Marina's eyes, and Marina swears she can feel a jolt of the whales' power in his gaze. "Vogel has trapped us here," Gareth states and signs. "Which means he's trapped the bulk of those on Erthia who possess strong water magic—the Ocean Peoples of Erthia and the Sylphan Vu Trin—"

"There are others," Commander Quillen cuts in.

Gareth turns his gray-green eyes on her. "Yes. The Asrai Vu Trin. Who are sure to deploy south once they hear of this attack on Noilaan's southern Waters. But this Shadow sea we've walled off from the Vo isn't the main line of attack on Erthia's Waters. That's what my whale kindreds are sensing."

"Lies!" Storm Tide militantly signs out.

"What line of attack do they sense?" Zephyr challenges Gareth, ignoring Storm Tide's outburst and the spear still pointed at her throat.

A dire look overtakes Gareth's expression, and Marina's gills tighten. "The northern Vo River Cypress trees are sending my whales a vision," he says and signs. "There's a monstrous Shadow force coming for the Waters of the East. But it's massing in the far north." Gareth swallows, a terrifying look of foreboding crossing his features as he glances toward the mangroves then sets his gaze back on Zephyr, Storm Tide, and then Marina, a chill coursing over her skin.

"Vogel is attacking the Vo River at its northern origin," Gareth says and signs, his lightning-flashing eyes like two warning beacons in the darkness, "to entrench and flow Shadow pollution through the East via the river's waters, to bring down Noilaan's entire Natural World with Shadow power." Gareth's gaze swings back to Storm Tide, a martial steadiness in it. "And that Shadow power will be flowing *right toward us.*"

CHAPTER EIGHT

CHROMATIC POWER

Gwynnifer Croft Sykes

Agolith Desert
Eleven days after Xishlon

Gwynn hurtles out of the portal's golden depths and lands front-first against the stone floor of a green-torchlit cavern, its crimson walls marked with glowing emerald Varg and blue Noi runes.

Her palms smack down on cold rock, and then Mavrik's hard body slams against her back as he's thrown from the portal behind her. The collision of their bodies forces the breath from Gwynn's throat, Mavrik's palms slapping down on either side of hers, the edge of his wand hand brushing her own.

Invisible sparks race up Gwynn's arm from that point of skin-to-skin contact, and they both shudder, her light magic once more unleashed and flowing into Mavrik's lines in a spangled, prismatic rush.

Her eyes flick toward her wand hand, and she's shocked to find it alight with pulsing color until Mavrik hauls his body off hers, breaking all contact. Gwynn's light magery snaps painfully back to its trapped state, her lines *straining* to relink to his.

Heart skidding, Gwynn pushes herself to her knees, looks at Mavrik, and freezes, transfixed by the wavering lines of glowing color pulsing over his hand, as well. The cavern and Subland soldiers surrounding them fade to a blur, the forbidden Fae color hypnotic. Like sunrays diffracting through a bottle of oil . . .

Breathing hard, Mavrik lifts his wand hand and views the color rippling over it with wide eyes, his brow lined with sweat.

"What just happened to us?" Gwynn rasps, holding up her own, color-infused wand hand.

He shakes his head, swallowing. "I don't know. Wynter's Wand . . . it linked our lines somehow. When we touch." He looks at her, awe blazing in his green eyes. "Gwynnifer, your light magic just protected us both from a direct lightning strike."

Gwynn blinks at him, his words triggering a recollection from one of the Valgard armory's countless books on magery—it outlined that Level Five Light Mages can't be killed by light power, including a direct lightning strike.

"I've never been able to access even a spark of my power," she says, confused.

"But *I* can," he counters, seeming dazed. "When you grabbed hold of me, you flooded my lines with your magic and turned me into a Light Mage. Gwynn, you just saved my life as well as your own."

Gwynn gapes at him, speechless. She crinkles her eyes to try to clear away the sparks of color flashing through them. "This thrall between us," she finally manages, "it's difficult to think past."

"I know," he admits, giving her an intense look.

The image of the Verdyllion is suddenly flashing in Gwynn's mind, the desperate need to locate it surging. Forcing herself to focus, Gwynn scans the wan, battered-looking Smaragdalfar soldiers scattered throughout the torchlit cavern and zeroes in on Wynter's pale winged form. Relief and alarm ignite—relief over the sight of the Verdyllion grasped in Wynter's hand, and alarm over the way Wynter is slumped on the ground.

"Are you hurt, Wyn'terlyn?" the slender Elf, Rhys, asks her in Alfsigr, Gwynn parsing the translation from the Alfsigr language dictionary imprinted in her mind.

"I am unhurt, Rhysindor," Wynter assures him, her black wings fluttering weakly. "My magic is simply depleted from creating so many runes." Rhys and the Amaz warrior Valasca help Wynter to her feet, Valasca's Urisk companion beside them.

And then, as if drawn by the force of Gwynn's gaze on her, Wynter's silver eyes meet Gwynnifer's.

The second their eyes meet, the Verdyllion's spiraling length pulses with prismatic light, and a sizzling sting washes over Gwynn's wand hand, kindling light power through her lines in raying, prismatic flashes. Gwynn gulps as Wynter's eyes flutter then roll back as she falls sideways. Rhys and Valasca catch her in a flurry of concern. The taller, fierce-eyed Alfsigr archer who resembles Wynter, the lavender Urisk woman, and a knot of Subland soldiers close in around them and, together, they lead Wynter away through one of the cavern's rune-lit corridors.

Drawing in a ragged breath, Gwynn glances down at her color-pulsing wand hand once more, swept up in the feeling that what's happening between herself, Mavrik, Wynter, and the Verdyllion is like a maelstrom of light power brewing on the horizon. She turns to the disappearing triad of portals, only traces of their runic arches still wavering in the air.

An upswell of urgency tightens Gwynn's chest as she meets the belligerent silver gaze of the domineering, female Smaragdalfar soldier with the half-shaved head who seems to be the Subland army's commander. Lines of dark green metallic hoops pierce the woman's pointed ears, glowing Varg tattoos blaze on half her emerald-patterned face. The cylindrical hilts of several collapsed Varg swords are sheathed at her sides, and a necklace with pendants depicting the emerald-hued Subland Goddess Oo'na and her white messenger birds hangs around her neck. She's bracketed by two young Smaragdalfar Elf soldiers also wearing religious Oo'na necklaces, one of the soldiers a broad-shouldered, muscular young man with a furious expression; the other a refined-looking, lean man possessing a blade-sharp calm that feels dangerous.

"The children I came here with," Gwynn calls to the woman in a frayed voice, "where in the East were they portaled to?"

The Smaragdalfar woman's eyes flash with a look of outrage. "Somewhere surrounded by *armed Smaragdalfar guards*," she bites out. "Away from Mages who crop the ears of *children*."

Gwynn recoils from the woman's brutal tone, as if it were Gwynn herself who sliced the tips from the children's ears.

Disorientation and remorse spinning through her, Gwynn absently grasps her tingling wand hand, hyperaware of the reverberating effect of Mavrik's touch. "Where are we?" she implores, turning to him.

"The Sublands under the Agolith Desert," he answers as he rises to his feet, voice strained.

Gwynn freezes, his answer like a fist to the gut.

The Agolith Desert. Leagues and leagues and leagues away from home.

Her gut clenches tighter. *The home I destroyed.*

Bile burns Gwynn's throat, and she struggles to swallow it back, swept up in the memory of her parents' home being blown up by runes she, herself, marked.

Light-headed, she staggers to her feet, her attention yanked to her clothing as one of her sleeves falls away. Her gaze jerks toward the lines of charred, puckered fabric running down both sides of her sacred Mage blacks. Remnants of the storm spiders' electrified Shadow power is still forking over the charred fabric in muted flashes of gray, her garb's black threads fraying and gradually crumbling to ash as the remnants of Shadow power course outward, consuming the fabric. A sliver of Gwynn's naked side appears, her body increasingly exposed . . .

Mortification explodes as she grabs at the fraying garb, her gaze snapping toward Mavrik as the side of his tunic's collar drops, exposing his collarbone. Seeming surprised, Mavrik glances at it, then over his shoulder. Cursing under his breath, he grips his tunic's front and tugs it forward, a few threads audibly snapping. The black silk tears away from his body, the entire back of his tunic destroyed.

Gwynn's pulse skyrockets at the forbidden sight of his naked chest, all taut muscle with a trace of dark hair in its center, his deep green nipples exposed.

She meets his eyes in a flash of unsettling heat. Shame surging, she looks away, desperately clutching at the sides of her clothing to keep it from falling open or, even worse, *off*. A raw panic grips hold . . . being so exposed . . . seeing Mavrik so exposed . . . it makes her feel as if her center is coming unmoored.

Mavrik calls to someone in Smaragdalfarin, and she winces, her gaze now riveted to the stone floor as her heart races, her emotions too turbulent for her to focus on a translation. A melodic female voice answers him as Gwynn struggles to control her panicked breathing, her new reality crashing down with cyclonic force.

It's over.

An irrevocable line has been crossed, leaving her unanchored and splayed open, body and soul. She's an enemy of the Magedom now, an enemy to her own family, in unknown terrain. Surrounded by non-Gardnerians—people she was taught, her whole life, to view as Evil Ones, her recent contact with Bloom'ilya and little Ee'vee her first real connection to people outside of her closed Styvian Mage circle.

Is this how Sage felt? Gwynn agonizes, remorse knifing through her as she considers how she left her good friend to fend for herself when the Gardnerian wolves closed in around her in Verpacia. Without aid, without alliance . . .

"Gwynnifer." Mavrik's deep voice jolts her from her tortured thoughts. His tone is forceful, but there's an underlying note of compassion in it that has Gwynn raising her tear-burning eyes to meet his intent stare.

She blinks, thrown off-kilter again by the sight of him, his chest now blessedly covered, but by a vivid emerald Smaragdalfar tunic.

Gwynn inhales, the sight of a Gardnerian male dressed in forbidden Fae color a shock to her system . . . a shock to her *lightlines*. A tingle races straight through her lines, the verdant hue of Mavrik's eyes intensifying the sensation.

"Here, Gwynnifer," a heavily accented and melodic female voice chimes in.

Gwynn turns to the willowy Smaragdalfar archer, Mynx, who helped Ee'vee through the portal, surprised to find the striking woman there. Mynx is holding out bright emerald Smaragdalfar garb to Gwynn, her gaze suffused with concern.

"I . . . I *can't* . . ." Gwynn's face burns as she makes no move to accept the taboo clothing, afraid that if she stops clutching the edges of her long black tunic and underlying skirt, her sacred black garb will completely give way.

Mynx turns and calls out something toward a knot of male soldiers. One strides forward, casting a quick, wary look toward Gwynn before he unfastens his cloak and hands it to her. Mynx flicks her graceful hand at the soldier in a shooing motion, and he steps away. Gwynn catches a quick, unreadable look from Mavrik before Mynx sets the Smaragdalfar clothing down on the red stone floor before Gwynn, then straightens and holds the cloak out to its full expanse, walling Gwynn off from the rest of the cavern.

"Go ahead and change," she prods.

Her heart pattering hummingbird-fast, Gwynn releases her hold on the sides of her garb, her mortified flush turning scorching as both her tunic and long skirt give way, along with her undergarments. The cavern's cool air skims her sides, raising an uncomfortable sweep of gooseflesh.

Hands trembling, Gwynn hastily tugs off the remnants of her destroyed garb and, for the first time in her life, puts on nonblack clothing. She pulls the bright emerald tunic over her head and slides on pants of an equally vivid-green hue, forcing back a remembrance of the lines in *The Book of the Ancients* that condemn garb like this, and her for wearing it.

The image of the piles of color-edged Gardnerian garb being burned in Valgard assaults her mind as she glances down at the Shadow lightning–singed pile at her feet, feeling as if she's drowning in the sudden culture shock of wearing pants— something Mage women are forbidden to do—her thighs encircled by fabric, the shape of her legs so brazenly on display.

She tenses, lacking the headspace to rapidly process this transgression, but she also knows she can't stay hidden behind this cloak forever.

"All right, I'm done," she manages.

Mynx lowers the cloak, and her eyes make a swift sweep over Gwynn's emerald-garbed frame. Gwynn hugs herself tight. Cheeks and neck burning, she meets Mavrik's eyes across the cavern's expanse. A flash of what looks like under-standing lights in his, bringing the sting of tears to her own. But still, she can't bring herself to approach him dressed like this, feeling as if her legs are naked before him.

Mavrik looks away and she knows, from the stiffening of his stance, that, unlike the others here, he truly comprehends the suffocating morass of cultural and religious upheaval she's fallen into.

"Mavrik Glass," a sharp, Noi-accented female voice calls out, as several heavily armed Vu Trin soldiers enter the space from a side tunnel.

Noi soldiers, covertly active in the Western Realm Resistance, Gwynn surmises.

The Vu Trin glance briefly at Gwynn before launching into a stream of conversation in Noi with Mavrik.

Gwynn translates bits and pieces—"Summoned by Commander Fi Suur . . ." and Mavrik's response ". . . destroyed Mage armory"—before Mavrik is being led toward one of the cavern's tunnels.

"I'll be back soon," he calls to her, and Gwynn latches ahold of his promise like a lifeline as he disappears with the Vu Trin into the stone corridor's rune-lit depths.

Shaken, Gwynn looks at Mynx. "Where did they portal the children to?" she asks, hoping she'll get an answer this time.

"I *told you,*" the commanding soldier with the half-shaved head snaps in heavily accented Common Tongue as she knifes a withering glare at both Gwynn and Mynx, "they're somewhere *safe.* Away from Crows and Maggots."

Mynx stiffens and levels a scalding look at the soldier. "You don't have to be wretched to her, Yyzz'ra," she bites out. "She helped destroy *thousands* of Mage weapons."

"*We don't need the Crows' help!*" Yyzz'ra seethes back before hurling out what sounds like a series of Subland expletives. Yyzz'ra's outburst is met with a biting reply in Smaragdalfarin from Mynx that's too fast for Gwynn to translate.

Yyzz'ra narrows her silver gaze on Mynx, her mouth twisting in an unkind smile. "You have sympathy toward the Crows and Maggots because you're *rutting* with the Icaral's brother."

Spots of color form on Mynx's cheeks, and she turns away, seeming cast into utter humiliation as Yyzz'ra barks out a mocking laugh and takes her leave down the tunnel with a number of Subland soldiers.

Mynx stiffens her jaw and visibly gathers herself, then meets Gwynn's gaze. "I'm Mynx'lia'luure," she says, her tone shot through with real kindness. "You may call me Mynx, as the others do."

They stare at each other for a protracted moment as Gwynn desperately tries to quell the slight tremble that's kicked up all over her body. "Have you . . . shut down the Western portal system?" Gwynn asks, motioning toward the portals' blue tracings, only mist remaining.

Mynx's silver eyes glint like battle-hardened steel. "We did." Gwynn catches a quick flash of anguish in her expression. "We got everyone out that we could."

Gwynn can read the unspoken in Mynx's splintered tone.

Everyone we could get out before the Mages cut off the escape routes, making life a living hell for those left behind. The Western Realm completely fallen.

A different sort of shame swamps Gwynn, filling her with rancid guilt—she's broken free of the Magedom physically, but her mind and emotions are still ensnared by it, when she should be casting *all of it* aside. But she can't help it. Just the act of wearing bright emerald garb—and *pants*—feels unmooring to the extreme.

"Come," Mynx says to Gwynn, a searching light in her eyes that feels like an undeserved port in a storm. "Let's get you settled in for the night, and get you some food."

"Eat, Roachling," Yyzz'ra orders in the Western Common Tongue.

Feeling the inward sting of the slur, Gwynn looks warily to where Yyzz'ra sits amidst a circle of Subland soldiers around one of the large cavern's multiple emerald-flamed bonfires. The bowls in their laps are filled with the strange, wormlike food in Gwynn's own bowl, the fragrant steam wafting up from it smelling of rich spice and mushroom.

After a trek through several long, circuitous tunnels, they reached this heavily Varg-warded gathering cavern, and Gwynn immediately retreated into a solitary alcove just behind Mynx'lia'luure and her circle of soldiers.

Her emotions a storm, Gwynn glances up at the huge tree roots woven along the cavern ceiling, as they were throughout Valgard's Sublands, a protective net of Varg runes covering the ceiling's expanse.

Lowering her gaze, Gwynn focuses on parsing out the Subland Elf conversation, rapidly ascertaining that they're positioned in an incredibly sheltered spot with the Agolith Desert's thickest, most violently powerful storm bands surrounding the land above them—storm bands set down by the Zhilon'ile weather Wyverns of the East during the last Realm War.

To wall off the Magedom's forces.

Awe overtakes her at the thought of the huge, deadly storm bands she's only read about protecting the land above them.

"You still haven't taken a bite," Yyzz'ra chides, breaking into Gwynn's thoughts. There's an unkind glint in Yyzz'ra's eyes as she narrows them on Gwynn, a mocking smile on her lips as her eyes flick toward the bowl of food cradled in Gwynn's lap. "Don't fret, Roachling. It's not a bowl of *worms*."

"*Stop*, Yyzz'ra," Mynx'lia'luure retorts in Smaragdalfarin, her gaze flickering with censure. "She's not calling you 'Snake Elf.' So leave off with the slurs and accusations."

Yyzz'ra snorts a laugh, her gaze remaining fixed on Gwynn with a damning light. Gwynn tenses, a sting of shame racing over her neck for ever having countenanced slurs like Snake Elf, her past ignorance further cementing her outsider status in this new world she's found herself in. A world the Verdyllion and the Watchers have led her to.

Yyzz'ra's penetrating gaze swings to Mynx. "You just love the Crows and Maggots, don't you? How many cups of tea have you given the Icaral's brother? A full thirty?"

Anger fair crackles off Mynx as she gives Yyzz'ra a confrontational smile. "And what if I have, Yyzz'ra? What if I want to give Cael *all the tea in the world*?"

Yyzz'ra lets out a contemptuous snort. "Oh, it's clear you've already given him 'all the tea in the world.'"

Mynx snaps something emotional in Smaragdalfarin that's too fast for Gwynn to translate, then rises, fists balled.

Anger sparks in Yyzz'ra's eyes. "Don't you have first watch, soldier?"

Mynx shoots Yyzz'ra a glare before turning to Gwynn. "You did a brave thing, Gwynnifer, when you destroyed that armory and got those children out of Valgard. I, for one, am grateful for it." She casts the Subland Elves then Gwynn a worried look, obviously reluctant to leave Gwynn alone with them, before she walks off, her gait tight with tension.

Yyzz'ra launches into furtive conversation with the Elves in Smaragdalfarin, their gazes sliding toward Gwynn with wariness every so often. Gwynn tenses each time, her mind a haze of stress as she averts her gaze, not wanting them to surmise her ability to translate in her eyes.

"We need to take Oo'na's Eyil'lynorin Shard away from the Icaral as soon as she breaks through the Northern Forest's warding," Yyzz'ra says, her tone covert, Gwynn's every sense prickling to sharper life over mention of the Subland name for the Verdyllion.

One of the soldiers shakes his head. "The Shard won't allow anyone to send magic through it but the Icaral."

Yyzz'ra's fiery glare knifes into him. "Then we use the Icaral and the Roaches to get to Oo'na's Great Tree, where our power will be amplified and we're *sure* to be able to wield Oo'na's Shard. Once there, we kill Vogel and his Black Witch and wall *everyone* out of the Sublands but us, including Wynter Eirllyn, her brothers, and the Roaches."

"Yyzz'ra," the soldier gently refutes, "Wynter Eirllyn just liberated most of the Sublands."

"*Oo'na's Shard* liberated the Sublands," Yyzz'ra fires back. "Not the Icaral. The Shard has brought itself right to *us*, its rightful owners. We can't trust an Alfsigr Elf with it. Just as we can no longer trust Mynx'lia'luure, who is quite literally *in bed* with an Alfsigr Elf."

"You're too hard on Mynx," another soldier puts in as Gwynn's concern mounts. "She and Cael Eirllyn, they're just friends."

Yyzz'ra coughs out a biting laugh. "She let the Maggot into her pants! Ghuy'lon overheard them rutting. And Wynter Eirllyn *cannot* be trusted—at Verpax University, she was *friends* with the Black Witch! They even shared lodging. The same Black Witch who waged war on Voloi. Have you noticed that Wynter Eirllyn has stayed silent on the point of killing Elloren Gardner Grey?" Yyzz'ra slashes the air with her hand. "You cannot trust the Maggots or the Roaches," she growls, casting a sidelong glare at Gwynn.

Swallowing against the knot in her throat, Gwynn retreats inward, her mind whirling from all this information. She looks down at the food, her stomach tightening as the steam's fragrant spices waft up. Everything about it is unfamiliar—some type of blue-glowing mushrooms floating along with the wormlike shapes in the murky broth.

She's landed in another universe here in the Sublands, she realizes, swallowing back a surge of choking anguish, unable to fight back the image of both the armory and her childhood home exploding with runic fire. Unable to bear the thought of her mother's face when she takes in what her formerly beloved daughter has wrought. And unable to bear the thought of both her mother and father taking in the Wanted postings that will soon appear with Gwynn's evilly rendered face on them beside Wanted postings for Mavrik Glass and Wynter Eirllyn.

That night, Gwynnifer lies in a small side cavern on a thin bedroll, a silent sob shuddering through her chest as she clutches her hair. A sudden scud of boots on stone has her swallowing back her raging emotions. Roughly wiping the tears from her eyes, she turns to find Mavrik standing in the rune-lantern-lit tunnel just outside of her cavern's arching entryway.

"May I come in?" he asks, and Gwynn nods, unable to speak, her throat too thick with turmoil.

Mavrik enters and sits down near her. She studies him, feeling like a shell of herself, stripped raw. She distantly notes that his hand has returned to its normal Mage-green shimmer. He leans back against the crimson stone, his intense gaze fixed on the small alcove's opposite wall, his expression unsettled.

"The first few nights are the hardest," he states, the green lantern light just outside the shadowy space flickering over him.

Gwynn lifts her hand and stares at her black, looping fastmarks. A fasting that was *everything* to her. A fastmate who was *everything* to her. And her family . . .

The knot of grief in her throat tightens as she struggles to swallow the soul-shredding despair.

Her thoughts swing to Bloom'ilya and Ee'vee being held down and brutally mutilated. And the Smaragdalfar children fleeing East, Watchers perched on their shoulders. And suddenly, Gwynn is having trouble catching her breath for an entirely different reason, desperate to do penance for everything she was ignorant of for so long. Flooded by remorse she shuts her eyes so tight that they hurt.

A warm touch finds her cloth-covered wrist and she slides her hand up to grip Mavrik's. A sparking rush of magic passes between them as her affinity lines open and weave into his, the sensation making them both shiver.

She opens her tear-soaked eyes to meet his intense green gaze, sparks of the same verdant color flashing in her eyes as she's flooded by a sense of his *power*. She glances at their outrageously entwined hands, threads of prismatic lightning shivering over both his skin and hers, both of them seeming so frozen in awe over this sensation, this *linkage*, as they remain silent for a stretched-out moment.

"We need to find out exactly what's happening to our magic," Gwynn finally says in a hoarse whisper. She knows she should let go of him but can't bring herself to pull away.

"We do," he agrees, swallowing. "I'm trying to . . . get a handle on it."

A breath shudders through Gwynn as she finds herself unable to control the tempest she's set into motion.

What she's followed the Watchers and the Verdyllion into.

"Yyzz'ra is planning to take the Wand from Wynter," she reveals. "When we get to the Northern Forest."

His eyes widen. "You speak Smaragdalfarin?" he asks as they hold on to each other, their power caught up in a magical embrace they both seem loath to break.

"My light magery," she explains. "Trapped as it is, it still gives me the power to visually imprint. I have every dictionary I've ever flipped through in my head. Every grimoire. Every military text." She gives him a searching look. "What did the Vu Trin tell you when you were gone?"

Mavrik hesitates, his jaw ticking. "Vogel's story is true. Elloren Gardner Grey attacked Voloi, along with an army Vogel had hidden in the Vo Mountain Range. They destroyed the Wyvernguard and leveled Voloi. Thousands are dead. The Black Witch was struck down by the Icaral Yvan Guryev at the same time that some unknown force exploded the Vo Mountain Range housing the bulk of Vogel's forces before they could emerge and destroy the entire East."

Gwynn huffs out a hard breath. "And now, the Black Witch is being portaled to the Northern Forest?"

Mavrik nods. "We just got word that Lasair Fae working with the Vu Trin have detected Yvan's fire power caught up in the lag of a Dryad portal and moving toward the Northern Forest, along with Elloren Gardner Grey's Shadowfire. Both the Black Witch and the Great Icaral will soon be under Vogel's control, if he gets hold of them before we do."

"The entire Prophecy in Vogel's hands . . ." Gwynn murmurs, horrified by the ramifications.

Mavrik launches into his history with Yvan Guryev and a description of his work, for years, as a double agent for the Vu Trin. How Vogel sent him to assassinate Yvan, and how Mavrik worked with the Vu Trin to fake the Great Icaral's death, inflicting substantial enough wounds on Yvan to fool Vogel's multi-eyed raven spy—wounds that Yvan later healed with his Lasair powers.

Mavrik grows silent, but that fierce edge to his gaze is undimmed. It's heightened, in fact. "I need your help, Gwynn," he says with unvarnished force. "And not just to break through the Northern Forest's Dryad wards so we can free Yvan and strike down the Black Witch. We're concerned that Vogel's Shadow magic will soon be powerful enough for him to take control of every fasted Mage and Zalyn'or-imprinted Alfsigr Elf via their fastlines and Zalyn'or necklaces. He's already done it on a small scale. Wynter read his intent briefly, while she was imprisoned by a Zalyn'or necklace. Vogel tried to overtake her through the necklace but fled when he sensed her empathic ability to read him."

Gwynn tenses, needing to force calm in the face of this mounting nightmare, suddenly hyperaware of her own fastmarked hands and wrists as well as Mavrik's. "How can I help?" she inquires.

Mavrik gives her a level look. "For *years* I've been working on trying to break down the spells embedded in both the fasting spell and the Zalyn'or necklaces to no avail. *You* have a library of grimoires in your mind. Perhaps if we work together—"

"The fasting and Zalyn'or spells," Gwynn cuts in, "they're *unbreakable*. The magic too solid. Too brilliantly fused when set."

"They have a similar magical base, yes," Mavrik admits, holding up his fast-marked hand, "but Gwynnifer, we *have* to find a way to fight this."

Even though the odds are insurmountable, he means. Gwynn's heart thuds against her chest as she thinks, once more, of all the Urisk and Smaragdalfar children. Of the nightmare bearing down on all of them. And, once more, of her and Mavrik's fastmarked hands and wrists.

"I'll help you," she vows, lips trembling.

Her stubborn rebellion abruptly implodes, cracked apart by the sheer force of trauma and exhaustion, and she finds herself blinking back tears.

Mavrik's grip on her hand tightens, his magic winding around hers in an enthralling rush, the intensity of its flow mirrored in his eyes. "Gwynn," he says, "I know what it is to lose *everything*."

Gwynn nods, his presence and the feel of their combined magic the most tenuous of anchors. But then, he gives her a conflicted look, his grip on her loosening, and she can sense him readying himself to leave.

"Please . . . stay?" she asks as she tightens her grip on him, knowing this request is unspeakably outrageous. Knowing she's just crossed a million lines, asking this male Mage she's only just met . . . whose power her magic wants to merge with . . .

to stay by her side tonight. But in this moment, the chasm inside her feels too great. Too terrifying to handle. No solid ground anywhere.

"All right," he concedes, his voice barely a whisper as he lets go of her hand.

Their magical connection snaps away, and she immediately feels bereft, her retrapped lightlines *straining* toward him once more. Mavrik lies down beside her and silently offers her his wand hand, palm up.

Tension ignites.

Her pulse quickening, Gwynn slides her fingers through his once more, and multicolored sparks streak through her vision as her magic releases into him and they both stiffen against the rush of energy coursing through their entwining lines. Her emotions laid bare, Gwynn's lips start to tremble, and hot tears brim in her eyes.

"I won't leave you," Mavrik assures her, his tone holding the force of a vow, their fingers and magic tightly linked. "I won't leave you, Gwynnifer."

She nods, weeping silently, as she once again pictures her parents finding their home destroyed. The armory destroyed. Choking back the agony of what she's done, of what she knows she'd do again, she soon finds herself drifting off to sleep, Mavrick's intense green gaze the last thing she sees before she's lost to the dark.

Gwynnifer wakes up in Valgard, sunlight streaming through her bedroom's circular window. Disoriented, she turns to find her fastmate, Geoffrey, in bed beside her, his drowsy green eyes set on hers with loving affection, a gentle smile tugging at his lips.

No Shadow-gray glow around his irises.

A sob of relief bursts from her chest. It was all a nightmare. *All* of it. A monstrous dream in which all of Gardneria embraced the Shadow and devolved into a nightmare of cruelty. But *none* of it was real. And now she's back in her safe home, her safe life.

Swept up in elation, she slides her arms around Geoffrey and draws him close, kissing the nape of his neck, nuzzling him, before bringing her lips to his.

Geoffrey seems surprised by the kiss for a moment before he begins to return it, lazily at first, as if he's half-awake . . .

Then intently seeking.

Then hard and deep.

Heat shoots down Gwynn's spine, sparks igniting on her lips in response to the surprising level of passion running through that kiss, sparks bursting through her every line.

Geoffrey's never kissed her like *this* before.

She lets out a moan and surrenders to the kiss, thrills to this new, wantonly insistent Geoffrey, his usual hesitancy gone. An excited shock sizzles over her skin as he rolls his body onto hers and coaxes her thighs apart, his body rapidly firing up, responding to her so quickly when she's used to Geoffrey's usual slow workup.

And his effect on her *lines* . . .

She arches against this new, assertive Geoffrey, wraps her legs around him, his desire pressing against her with startling pressure that sends flares of pleasure raying out from the contact, his arousal so quick, so intensely hard . . .

Abruptly, Geoffrey rolls off her.

"Gwynn," a rough voice says, thickened by what sounds like mingled desire and conflict. A lower-pitched voice than Geoffrey's.

A voice that is *not* Geoffrey's.

Alarm shocks through Gwynn's system, and her eyes bolt open as she's jerked violently out of the half dream to see Mavrik beside her. A glowing prism of hues pulses all over his lips and the base of his neck, the streaks of color practically incandescent in their intensity. He's sitting up and has put some distance between them as they stare at each other with mutually stunned expressions.

Mortification explodes through Gwynn as her sleep-fogged mind assembles what just happened.

"We . . ." Mavrik swallows, his face flushed, lust still swimming in his eyes along with a look of discomfort. "We must have been dreaming."

Gwynn sits up, her head spinning, her thoughts cast into turmoil.

What just happened? Those things she dreamed . . . did she do them with Mavrik? That *kiss* . . .

She can't speak, the shame too tremendous.

She reaches up to massage her swollen lips and sees rainbow light reflecting from her mouth onto her hand.

"I woke fully when you . . . threw your legs around me," Mavrik rasps. He bites at his light magic–infused lips. "Gwynn, I thought it was a *dream* . . ."

"I . . . I thought you were my *fastmate*," Gwynn stutters, her flush heating to a scald, the shame intensifying.

"I'll sleep somewhere else," Mavrik offers hastily, rising to his feet, and Gwynn notices, with heightening embarrassment, the lingering evidence of his arousal.

Because I threw myself at him so unforgivably.

Wildly distressed, she imagines what her family's priest would say as if he were here. She can imagine those judgmental, condemning eyes. And she's certain Mavrik must feel the same way about her.

He hesitates, raking a hand through his tousled hair.

Hair I tousled, Gwynn thinks, her flush growing so hot it feels like a sickness.

"I'll . . . I'll keep my distance from you," Mavrik offers, the multicolored glow on his mouth constricting to forking threads of color. "I'll *never* let that happen again. I promise you. I've never pushed myself on a woman . . ."

At first, Gwynn is thrust into confusion by his words before she realizes, with stunned comprehension, that he's not angry at her. He's angry with *himself*.

The radical idea calms an edge of her distress.

"Mavrik," she ventures, seeming to startle him by her use of his name, "I believe you."

He shakes his head. "I did *not* mean to attack you. I'm *so* sorry, Gwynnifer."

Heat spreads down her neck as she remembers the thrilling feel of him. His unfamiliar, excitingly aggressive kiss. How she wrapped her body around him, her magic straining toward his, unforgivably wanting *more*.

"I didn't mean to attack you either. I'm sorry," she apologizes.

"I don't feel attacked," he insists with a look of wild contrition. "Gwynnifer, the *moment* I realized what was happening—"

"I know. I stopped, too, the second I realized," she agrees hastily as he hovers near the cavern's entrance, color still flashing over his lips. Her own mouth tingles, and she realizes they probably look the same.

"What I just did," he says, sounding tortured, "it was *dangerous* . . . your fast-lines . . . we could have . . ."

Gwynn glances down at the dark, looping lines, the claustrophobic feel of a cage descending. More and more these past months, she's felt this way about her fastlines, but never as strongly as she does now. Now that she knows Vogel might break into their fasting spells . . . *control* them both through them . . .

It only adds to how disoriented she feels in this moment.

Lost and beyond redemption.

"I'm homeless," she manages hoarsely, lips quivering. "In every way."

The energy between them shifts, Mavrik's eyes taking on a pained, commiserating look. "You are," he says with firm compassion. "But, Gwynn, you're not alone. You'll go north with us. In a way that involves absolutely *no one* throwing themselves at you." He gives her a pointed, contrite look before letting out a hard sigh, then lifts his wand hand and considers it. "It seems like Wynter's Wand of Power . . . it bound us more intensely than we realized. I had a clearer sense of the strength of that binding . . . in your kiss."

Gwynn swallows and nods, surrendering to their full honesty with each other. "I stole the Wand from the Valgard armory when I was quite young," she confides. "I could feel it *calling* to me. Looking back, I thought I was simply being dramatic, imagining myself part of some great Mage story where I rescued the Wand from demonic forces. It turns out, I was *right*. I was truly in possession of the Great Wand of Myth. But in the end . . ." Her throat constricts, caustic remorse rising. "I betrayed my closest friend, Sage Gaffney. A fellow Bearer of the Wand. Because I believed in the Mage faith."

Mavrik studies her, his expression turning hard and stark. "I enlisted in the military as soon as I came of age and went to war, then watched a group of Fae get cut down. By soldiers I had aided by transporting supplies and weapons to them. Because I believed in the Mage faith. During the same deployment, I witnessed Urisk being herded into wagons so they could be shipped to the Pyrran Islands. I was told they were all criminals. But I could tell they were just families. How can a child be a criminal against the Magedom? And their cries and screams . . ." His face constricts and he looks away, his jaw hard as stone, his whole body brimming with pent-up tension.

"How old were you?" Gwynn asks in a near whisper.

"Eighteen," Mavrik says, grimacing.

"How old were you when you turned against the Mages?" she presses.

He swallows and fixes his eyes on her, a lethal light entering his gaze that sends a chill down Gwynn's spine. "Eighteen."

They're quiet for a moment, tension tight in the air.

"How old were you when the Wand first came to you?" he finally asks.

"Twelve," she says before pulling in a deep breath and launching into the story of her time with the Wand. Conveying the whole of it as faithfully as she can. Mavrik listens patiently as she relays the story of her time with Sage, the Light Mage. And how, in the end, she unwittingly and unforgivably betrayed her.

He's quiet for another long moment as she grows silent, adrift in turmoil.

"You're equal to this," he finally states, emphatic. "You managed to keep the Wand from two of Vogel's Shadow-bound pyrr-demons. They're incredibly powerful,

Gwynn. But you managed to elude them and send the Wand to safety in Halfix with Sagellyn Za'Nor when you were just a girl of thirteen. You saved a Wand of Power from falling into Vogel's hands. The same Wand that just freed the bulk of the Western Sublands. The Wand Vogel very much wants to get his hands on. And you helped us take down the Gardnerians' largest wand armory and military library, even though you knew it would result in the destruction of your family's home. Even though you knew you'd become a hunted outcast. Believe me, you're equal to this."

Gwynn holds his stare as a strangled sob lodges in her throat. "I don't know what my family will do. What they'll think of me."

"They'll Banish you," he states, his expression blade hard.

Protest rears up in Gwynn, quashing her tears. "They would *never—*"

"They'll Banish you, Gwynn," he insists, an impassioned ferocity entering his eyes. "Harden your heart. Don't wait to do it. I made that mistake."

The choking feeling grabbing at her throat intensifies. Gwynn can barely breathe around the thought of her mother and father performing a ceremony marking her dead to them.

"I . . . I'm not sure I can," she admits.

"You *have* to," Mavrik counters, his gaze filled with sympathy. "You *can.*"

She nods, blinking back tears as she holds his kindred stare, this Mage who walked away from Gardneria for an unknown future, as well. She glances at his fast-marked hands and wrists, barely able to get the question out, but she has to know. "Are you truly fasted?"

She knows, from his small wince, that he catches her subtext.

Are you still with her in any true way?

"No," he says, his lips twisting with derision. "Not for years. She *believes.* In everything the Mages are doing. Helps them, even."

The information strikes deep. And overcomes Gwynn's storming hesitation.

"Mavrik," she says. "Please, stay."

Mavrik looks probingly at her, then concedes with a tight nod before lying down against the wall, too far away to touch.

They lie there for a while, his eyes locked with hers, intensity crackling through the air between them, *magic* crackling between them as turmoil churns through Gwynn. The last thing she hears before sleep claims her is Mavrik's low, drowsy voice, murmuring, "Gwynn . . . I should wandtest you. Our magic . . . it's been upended by each other."

"I've never had access to my own power," she murmurs back.

"But that was before the Wand linked us. I should test you while touching you. And without touching you, as well."

"All right," she says. Lost to the magical tension flashing between them, she dares to voice the forbidden. "I want to hold your hand."

Mavrik lets out a harsh breath and looks at the ceiling. "It's best that we don't," he says in a constrained voice before giving her an intense look. Gwynn reluctantly nods, all too aware of the fastmarks all over their hands.

As well as the prismatic color still sparkling over both their lips.

Did you ever love your fastmate? she wonders, her grief for Geoffrey slicing through her. *Is your heart broken like mine?*

The devastating emotions churn, and Gwynn's heart fractures against them, so painfully that it's a blessing when her eyes finally flutter closed and she falls to sleep, the Verdyllion Wand–Stylus strobing in the back of her mind all through the night.

CHAPTER NINE

QUEEN OF FRACTURE

Queen Freyja Zyrr

Western bank of the Vo River, north of Voloi
Fifteen days after Xishlon

The Eastern Realm is in chaos, Freyja Zyrr considers as she stands on the Vo River's broad bank. Her gaze slides along Noilaan's runic border wall, the Vo River just beyond. She narrows her gaze at the Vu Trin forces positioned along the sapphire-glowing border's base and takes stock of the situation, the overcast day as grim as her thoughts. Four of her Queen's Guard soldiers surround her, her people having emerged from a portal lag into this stretch of wilderness north of Voloi one day prior.

A chill wind whipping at her black hair, Freyja battles back a surge of grief for her beloved Queen Alkaia, brutally slain by the cursed Mages. She pulls in a measured breath, struggling to adjust to the mantle their slain monarch placed upon her too-young shoulders—queen of the Amaz. Leader of a people who are suddenly refugees in a land where it's *clear* they are thoroughly and completely unwanted. And leader of a people who would hate her if they knew how much she yearns to find out if her secret love, Clive Soren, made it to the East.

Is Clive even alive?

Freyja stiffens her shoulders against the rush of emotion, the pull of the straps attaching her runic axe to her back a steadying thing. Her people need to come *first,* above all things.

Even her own heart.

Willing fortitude, she glances over her shoulder at the half-decimated Vo Mountain Range, the upper half of the peaks now a dark, melted apex of Shadow-smoking stone. She turns back toward the runic border, which grows higher and moves farther north each day.

THE DRYAD STORM

To wall Westerners out of Noilaan, including us.

Ire flares, burning hot in Freyja's chest as she remembers the military support her people gave to Noilaan during the last Realm War. How courageous Amaz battalions took down legions of Mage forces after the last Black Witch was killed, countless women struck down, their sacrifices key to halting the Mages' incursion into the East.

Now that the Amaz have landed on Noilaan's doorstep, it seems the East has a very short memory indeed.

Go ahead and wall us out, Freyja seethes at the entirety of Noilaan as the wind grows stronger. *We'll claim the Northern Vo Forest as our own and wall you out in turn.*

A hard crack of thunder sounds, and Freyja glances north toward the storm that's moving in, the clouds ominous masses of gray. Galvanized by the incoming storm, her people call out to each other from both the riverbank and the wilderness to their west as they hastily fortify the small city of rune-marked shelters they've erected inside the Vo Forest's tree line, an army of Amaz soldiers ringing their new-found territory's hastily established periphery, guarding it with warrior focus from intruders.

Freyja surveys her soldiers' weapons, a growing number of the axes and blades, arrows and battle-staffs glowing Varg emerald against the day's stormy gray, the Varg runes swiftly crafted by their Smaragdalfar runic sorceress, Vestylle Oona'rin. There's a martial light in her soldiers' eyes as they study the Vu Trin forces stationed along the border wall.

Ready to war with them if need be.

Freyja's response to the Noi Conclave's firm "request" to "portal back West" was an immediate call to arms that seemed to catch the Conclave off guard. The sight of a few thousand Amaz, both soldier and civilian, leveling their weapons in unison at the three Conclave members and accompanying Vu Trin tasked with relaying the "request" was a formidable sight to behold.

Force us into a corner, Freya fumes, *and we'll simply annex a piece of Noilaan for the Goddess's Own.*

Defiance on behalf of her people surging, Freyja makes the Goddess's symbol on her chest, kisses her fist, and thrusts it toward the heavens, ready to face down every force on Erthia as she booms out the Goddess's Warrior Prayer for the Defense of Her Free Daughters—

"We will fight with the Goddess's Own Fury!"

"We will fight to avenge every Blessed First Daughter!

"We are the Ever-Unbroken *Free People of Amazakaraan!"*

A roar of alliance rises, women's voices vehemently echoing Freyja's Goddess blessing all around her. A knot of emotion tightens Freyja's heart as she turns and scans the countless tattooed faces turned to her, young girls and adults alike, their fists raised to the heavens, expressions of alliance on every face, including little Pyrgomanche, the adopted Icaral daughter of the warrior Alcippe Feyir, the young, winged child held in the arms of Alcippe's longtime love, Skyleia.

Fierce tears stinging at Freyja's eyes, she nods stiffly in response to her people's show of support, determination to be worthy of them, no matter the odds, burning in her core.

Even if it means giving up Clive forever.

"My queen."

Freyja turns at the sound of Alcippe's rough voice, the imposing warrior striding toward her through the throngs of Amaz, her newly Varg-rune-marked axe sheathed across her broad back. Alcippe is flanked by two Amaz soldiers—the silver-eyed, gray-hued Elfhollen-Amaz archer Teel and the sky blue–hued Sorcha Xanthippe, former lover of Andras Volya.

Freyja's shoulders stiffen as she takes in the simmering hostility in Alcippe's rose-hued gaze and Sorcha Xanthippe's penetrating golden eyes. Freyja is quite clear that she's the absolute *last* woman Alcippe and Sorcha would have chosen to replace their beloved queen, Freyja's hidden relationship with Clive Soren an ill-kept secret—one that Freyja knows dredges up Sorcha's own suppressed conflict over giving up both Andras and the male child they created together. Freyja also knows both Alcippe and Sorcha are guardedly willing to countenance her, but only because Queen Alkaia named Freyja monarch.

Confusion knots Freyja's brow as she stares Alcippe down. "Where is Alder Xanthos?" she asks. "I have assured the Vu Trin that we will bring her to them for questioning."

"She's disappeared without a trace," comes Alcippe's harsh reply. "And so has a surviving flock of giant Issani eagles."

Freyja's jaw tightens, this development potentially alarming. The Noi have temporarily backed down on a multitude of demands as Freyja tensely negotiates with them for a new Amaz homeland in the East, but this is one demand she knows there will be no negotiating over—the possible past and present allies of the Black Witch are being hunted down.

Freyja is well aware that Alder and the former head of the Queen's Guard, Valasca Xanthrir, bonded with Elloren Gardner when they all worked together to rescue the Selkies. Now, all of Elloren Gardner's allies—including Alder—have up and disappeared. And through Freyja's own negligence in not thinking to post a guard around Alder, the Black Witch's allies potentially have access to flight.

Freyja catches the accusatory glint in Alcippe's eyes, the unspoken thunderously loud between them. *You're already failing at being our queen.*

Freyja closes her eyes and prays to the Goddess for clarity and strength. She curses herself for ever entertaining the idea that the last Black Witch's granddaughter, Elloren Gardner Grey, should be allowed to live when Elloren journeyed to Amazakaraan, all because Elloren seemed powerless and was heroically bent on freeing Selkies, the Goddess's own Sacred Wand-Stylus having inexplicably chosen her as its Bearer. In reality, the Mage was hiding her vast power the whole time and holding the Wand-Stylus hostage to eventually wield it as the Great Prophecy's Black Witch.

Remorse strikes through Freyja as she wonders how much more she can fail her people before they see her for what she is—too young and morally compromised to succeed at being queen.

Tension taut in the air, she meets the gaze of Alcippe and then the soldiers bracketing her, unable to battle back her sinking feeling in response to the wavering faith in their eyes.

How much worse can the chaos get?

"Freyja!"

Her heart seizes at the sound of the deep and familiar masculine voice.

Her pulse kicking into a hard rhythm, she looks south toward the voice's source and sees a tall, brown-haired Kelt striding briskly toward her, a line of Vu Trin behind him. He's dressed in a crimson Keltish military tunic and black pants, a Varg-marked axe and assorted blades affixed to his body. His dark-brown gaze meets hers, and it's like a firebolt of emotion straight through Freyja's heart, a wave of incandescent love barreling through her.

"Clive," she breathes in a harsh whisper as the line of Amaz soldiers before her draw their weapons as one.

"You will address our queen with respect, roikuul," Teel snarls, aiming her nocked runic-arrow straight at Clive's chest.

Freyja tenses over the aimed weapon and the slur Teel has just hurled at Clive, as well as the scowl she catches Alcippe leveling at her. She knows Clive is well aware that the Amaz slur *roikuul* is a direct reference to his male member, a part of his body Freyja is well acquainted with. Which would be acceptable if she only wanted daughters from him and hadn't been seeking him out again and again because of true love and genuine desire.

Clive ignores the slur, his blazing eyes locked with Freyja's, his whole body coiled as if he wants to leap through the line of soldiers and sweep her into his arms.

You're alive. You're alive, pounds out with every thundering beat of Freyja's heart, the desire to leap toward *him* almost impossible to suppress. But she forcibly restrains herself, even as her heart catapults over itself. Because she has the full weight of the queendom on her shoulders. Which comes before *everything.*

"Halt where you are," she orders him, tone firm, struggling to harden her traitorous heart. "What is it you seek, Clive Soren?"

Clive straightens. "As leader of the Western Realm Resistance, I come to petition you on behalf of the Keltish and Vu Trin forces," he informs her, even as the edges of his eyes blaze with barely contained feeling. "We seek to broker an alliance."

Angry gasps erupt all around, and Freyja inwardly curses. Clive must have been pressured to relay this controversial message himself by someone who understood the blow having her secret lover convey it would level. Straight at her.

She pulls in a slow breath, willing glassy calm. She's already met once with Vang Troi—the high commander of the Vu Trin—to broach the possibility of a military alliance with Noilaan's mostly female forces. But the *Kelts*, with their male-only forces and their male-dominated culture and religion . . .

Great care must be taken here if she's going to move her people forward in this new land, unified, instead of coming apart at the seams. All this division playing *completely* into Vogel's hands.

"Stand aside, Blessed Daughters," Freyja orders her guards.

The women swiftly step to the side of her, but keep their weapons aimed at the "evil" man in their midst as Freyja strides through the gap toward Clive and the Vu Trin.

"Walk with me," she orders Clive, beckoning him with regal coldness and a flick of her hand, ignoring both the effect his proximity has on her as well as her guards' hostile silence at her back.

The Noi soldiers before them convey permission to pass through their ranks, and

Freyja strides briskly through the black-clad and equally silent Vu Trin and away from the Amaz's tenuously claimed territory, not daring to turn and glance at Clive behind her.

Her heart thuds along with every one of his heavy booted steps as Clive follows her away from both the Amaz and the Vu Trin, then around a long curve in the Vo River's bank, his fierce love for her seeming to thrum through the very air.

Like a firestorm at her back.

Freyja veers into the purple wilderness, and he follows, thunder rumbling overhead, the storm closer now. Still not looking at him, Freyja presses deeper into the forest, the voices sounding from the riverbank behind them growing fainter as she steps over a tangled mass of dark purple roots and weaves around trees, eventually striding toward a large, rocky hillock, then around it.

She ducks into a stone alcove, a robust wind beginning to lash against the violet canopy above as tension mounts between herself and Clive, strong enough to rival the brewing storm.

Freyja stops and turns to him, Clive's searing gaze like a thunderclap.

Their storm breaks, his lips crushing down onto hers. She lets out an impassioned cry against his mouth, her back meeting stone as she grabs fierce hold of his military tunic's sides, pulling him toward her, their mouths and tongues desperate and devouring, a sob of joy tearing through her to find him suddenly here, *alive*.

"My love," Clive rasps as he finally breaks the kiss, bringing his forehead to hers, tears escaping both their eyes. He reaches up to cup her cheek, his mouth tilting into a bittersweet smile. "Queen Alkaia chose you, then."

Freyja nods tightly. "She did," she chokes out, her bottomless, soul-crushing grief for her queen breaking free, her chest pummeled by it as the grief sparks a vengeful fury that could level mountains. She yearns to portal back to the Western Realm this instant. To wield her axe and cut down as many Mages as she can before they strike her from this life.

Seething with rage, she holds Clive's fervid stare as he keeps hold of her in turn. And she knows, from the compassion in his eyes, that he understands the full force of her fury.

"I'm not worthy of this," she grits out as lightning cracks above, her mouth twisting into a grimace. "I'm not worthy of *her*—"

"You *are*," Clive insists, emphatic as the thunder rolling in.

"I'm not," she bites back, motioning between them. "Look at where I am *right now.* I'm at full odds with my people surrounding this most *central part of my life.* This secret I dare not speak of."

Clive's jaw tenses, a wild defiance in his mahogany eyes. "She *knew,*" he growls out. "Queen Alkaia *knew* what was coming. She also knew that there is *no hope, no path forward* with all of us divided. *That's* why she chose you. What did she say to you when she made you queen?"

Freyja swallows against a painful knot of unbearable sorrow. "She said . . ." She blinks hard against the tears. "She said 'lead my people into the future.'"

"She *knew,* Freyja," Clive insists, his voice rife with passion. "She knew about the alliances that will be needed to bring down the Mages."

"Clive," Freyja cautions, her jaw tightening, "I am not completely against Amaz separation from men. To coexist with the bulk of malekind requires a firm hand. And a ready axe."

She glowers at him, almost daring him to refute her, knowing, in this moment, that her reflexive flare of anger toward him as a male is misplaced even as it rises. But she also knows that, on some level, Clive understands. That he's cognizant of the evil done to femalekind in every land. Evil that Freyja *cannot* invite into Amazakaraan's new territory.

But she also knows her people can't stand on their own against the Magedom.

"What's the state of Noilaan's governance?" she presses, wanting the unvarnished truth. *Demanding* it. Trusting him more than the Vu Trin to tell her.

Clive's hands come to his hips, and he spits out a breath as if it's an epithet. "The Noi government is in shambles. Most of the former Conclave members are dead. Noilaan is under emergency military rule while they cobble together a full Conclave. Noilaan's reactionary Vo'nyl political movement is poised to take control of it, and they're bent on quickly rebuilding and enlarging their runic border and forcing all Westerners out of the East. No exceptions."

Freyja curses, her mouth tensing with frustration. "Who's in charge right now?"

"As high commander of Noilaan's military, Vang Troi is, effectively, the de facto leader for the moment," Clive answers flatly. "But Vang Troi is dealing with more than a decimated capital city. Vogel's Shadow tide is clinging to the land around Voloi, graying the sun and moon, poisoning crops and fisheries. It's a real threat to Noilaan's food supply. And now, Vogel's forces are deploying east of the Verpacian Spines. The only thing that seems to be keeping the Mages from deploying farther east are the Wyvern-crafted storm bands crisscrossing the Central Desert. And, in a completely unexpected turn of events, a Selkie-led army has invaded Southern Noilaan and managed to drive back a massive Shadow attack Vogel sent in from the south sea. But now, the Ocean Peoples have imprisoned Southern Noilaan under a runic dome the Vu Trin can't get through, and the Magedom has sent a net of Shadow over that dome."

"So, the Vu Trin are fighting a war on two fronts?" Freyja asks, stunned.

Clive nods. "Asrai Vu Trin just deployed south, along with a large number of Weather Wyvern Vu Trin, to break through both Vogel's and the Ocean People's shielding to retake Southern Noilaan for the Noi."

"Avenging Goddess," Freyja huffs out, mind spinning. "What of Voloi? What's going on beyond the Noi's cursed wall?"

He shoots Freyja a jaded look. "Most of Voloi's survivors of the Mage attack, including the refugees trapped outside the runic border, fled to Voloi's Sublands. The ironic crux of this is that many of Voloi's civilians are now Subland refugees, dependent on the largesse of the Smaragdalfar, who have the skills and magic to live underground."

"An ironic turn of events, indeed," Freyja cuts back, just as jaded. She knows, as well as he does, that much of Noilaan's rune-stone-based power is dependent on Alfsigr-mined lumenstone. Mined by imprisoned Smaragdalfar in the West.

A fact not lost on the Smaragdalfar refugees here in the East.

"The turmoil is just beginning," Clive continues. "The Smaragdalfar are deeply divided about having non-Smaragdalfar in the Sublands."

"Well, that's justifiable," Freyja says. "The East never once prioritized freeing the Smaragdalfar in the West, or providing them asylum."

Clive nods, acknowledging the point. "And there's the thorny issue of Ra'Ven Za'Nor and his Light Mage partner, Sagellyn, having disappeared. Along with a number of the Black Witch's other allies."

Freyja holds his grave look. "I should have killed Elloren Gardner Grey when I had the chance, when you sent her to find me. It was a mistake to let her live."

A pained look slashes across Clive's visage, and he nods tightly, holding Freyja's troubled stare. "Yvan Guryev brought her to meet with me in Keltania. He's in love with her." He shakes his head, conflict knifing through his gaze. "I've known Yvan for most of his life, but I never knew what he was." He grows silent, jaw flexing, before he lets out a frustrated huff of a breath. "And now, Vogel's fully turned the Gardner girl into his hellish Black Witch, and Yvan's foolishly gone after her. Or maybe she's imprisoned both Yvan and the Dryad Fae who portaled them out of Noilaan. In any case, both Yvan and the Black Witch are headed for the Northern Forest, caught up in a *long* Dryad portal lag. She'll likely kill Yvan when they get there and bring about the damned Prophecy."

"Or worse," Freyja responds, harsh and unsparing as she thinks of Vogel's gray-eyed soldiers.

Clive winces, a tortured look entering his gaze. "When I met the Gardner girl in Lyndon, gods help me, *I* should have killed her."

"Yvan Guryev might have burned you down."

"He might have," Clive soberly agrees. "But he wasn't the warrior then that I hear he is now. A student more than anything. Ignorant of the extent of his power. He's been training with Wyverns. With Lasair." A guarded hope lights Clive's eyes. "He might survive her yet."

"Clive," Freyja cautions, a trace of sympathy edging her tone, "he's not strong enough to stand against both the Black Witch and the entire Magedom."

Clive's mouth forms a tight line, his expression darkening. "I know it, Freyja."

She straightens against the impossible situation bearing down, suddenly all business.

Queen's business.

"Why did you come as messenger," she challenges, "knowing it would undermine me?"

"They gave me no recourse," he answers, his tone edged with anger. "Yes, Noilaan's reactionary, sorry excuse for a Conclave wants to undermine you. Their rising Vo'nyl majority *wants* conflict *between and against* all Westerners. To give them an excuse to drive every Westerner out of the Eastern Realm."

Outrage burns hot at the base of Freyja's throat. "So, they want me to fail as a leader."

"Yes," Clive bites back. "So, *don't indulge them.*"

They exchange a loaded look. "What do Vang Troi and your army seek?" Freyja finally asks, fighting back the urge to draw him nearer.

"Well," he says, his gaze flicking over the Varg-rune-marked weapons strapped all over her form. "For starters, we'd love the help of your Smaragdalfar runic sorceress." He takes her hand, and Freya's breath hitches as that familiar heat rises between them. Turning her hand gently over, he studies the Varg weapon-retrieval rune marked on her palm, its emerald color flashing and fully charged,

Freyja's hazel skin tough and calloused beneath it.

His brown eyes flit to hers. "The Vu Trin also wouldn't mind a few more Varg-charged weapons in their own hands either." Rebellious heat smolders in his eyes as he lifts her hand, holding her gaze, and presses his lips to the rune. Freyja's heart trips into a pounding rhythm.

"Freyja," he says as he lowers her hand, a martial glint edging into the adoration in his molten-brown eyes. "We all need to align, and quickly. Vang Troi wants the Amaz to lead a new division of the Vu Trin."

Surprise strikes through Freyja. This would be more than just an alliance.

This would be a merging of armies.

"Their Conclave will *never* approve that," she says.

"The Noi Conclave can go straight to the deepest of hells," Clive shoots back, keeping firm hold of her hand.

For a moment Freyja is caught up in tumultuous conflict, the East's sheer political chaos a monstrous obstacle to overcome. Yet Vang Troi wants to pursue unity. The underlying ramifications crackle through the air between them.

"Is Vang Troi about to go rogue?" Freyja presses.

Clive simply gives her a knowing smirk. "Lead your people into the future," he challenges, as gooseflesh ripples down Freyja's back, a sense of the momentous cycling down.

"What future would that be, Clive," she challenges back, her head spinning from the impossible idea of merging three militaries, three peoples—one of them zealously set on isolation from men.

"Not fracture," Clive shoots back. "Not if we're going to have any future at all."

CHAPTER TEN

RUNIC TWINNING

Gwynnifer Croft Sykes

Agolith Desert
Twelve days after Xishlon

Gwynn ascends the spiraling red-stone staircase to the Sunlands, the exit bracketed by two grim-faced Smaragdalfar soldiers. Predawn's indigo light filters in from above, and breathless anticipation wells inside her.

Gwynn was surprised by the ache in her heart and the pull on her lines that took hold when she woke up to find Mavrik gone, her magical draw to him stronger than it was the night before, leading her to rise and follow it through one Subland tunnel and up one spiral staircase after another, past throngs of heavily armed soldiers to where she's *certain* she'll find him.

Gwynn pauses at the cavern's mouth before an elevated, scarlet-stone ledge, awe expanding her lungs as she takes in the sight in the distance.

Lightning-spitting storm bands high as mountain ranges line every horizon.

She's read about these vast streaks of Wyvern-crafted storms that crisscross the continent's center, the storm bands' deadly, Wyvernfire-infused lightning magicked to deploy killing strikes at anything unwarded attempting to fly over them. But it's one thing to read about the storm bands and another to come face-to-face with them.

Gwynn watches the bands, transfixed, as white lightning flashes through their long, roiling expanses. A deep-rose sunrise is forming over the eastern storm band, the Agolith Desert's startlingly red stars still asserting themselves against a brightening cobalt sky.

A pleasurable tingle rushes through Gwynn's lightlines, and Agolith-red sparks flicker through the corners of her Light Mage vision as she takes in the great swaths of ruddy stone arcing over the crimson landscape. And the scattered groves of *trees*.

Some dark and bulbous, some a luminous, buttery yellow that seem to glow from within.

A vision of the Verdyllion pulses through Gwynn's mind, as if it, too, is caught up in the shimmering pull of forbidden Fae color. The Wand gives a directional tug on Gwynn's attention, and she slides her gaze that way, searching across the crimson sands and then freezing as she spots a pale, winged figure in the distance.

Wynter Eirllyn is sitting under one of the yellow-glowing yucca trees, her slender form luminescent against the predawn blue, her dark wings fanned out. A ring of suspended silver Alfsigr runes Gwynn is unfamiliar with surround her, as well as countless birds, some of them on the red sands, some perched on the yellow branches above. The Verdyllion a slim, iridescent speck of green held loosely in Wynter's hand.

Gwynn's gut clenches over how small and vulnerable the Wand seems. Just a trace of green in a huge, lethal world, Vogel's Shadow behemoth rapidly closing in around them all.

Fighting the urge to cower in the face of the dangerous unknown, Gwynn forces herself to stride onto the elevated ledge before her. Pausing there, she sweeps her gaze down toward a knot of soldiers gathered around a runic green bonfire in the center of another flat ledge beneath hers, the winding path of red rock at Gwynn's feet leading down toward that broad, lower ledge.

Her gaze snags on Mavrik, her pulse quickening, a flush heating her face as she remembers his *kiss*.

He's seated amidst the circle of soldiers and talking to them in low tones, the soldiers mostly Subland Elves save for Wynter Eirllyn's intense brother, Cael, and Cael's quiet Second, Rhys. Mynx'lia'luure is pressed against Cael's side in an overly familiar way and sipping from a mug while the commanding Subland soldier with the half-shaved head, Yyzz'ra, glowers at them both. The Amaz, Valasca, sits to one side beside the lavender Urisk woman, Sparrow, both women now garbed in Subland-green tunics and pants, their throats curiously ringed by emerald-glowing Varg runes.

Gwynn's gaze swings back to Mavrik like a compass finding true north, and she begins to pick her way down the stone path. An almost hypnotic rush of magic sizzles through her in response to the way Mavrik's green Mage shimmer is so dazzlingly enhanced by his shockingly emerald Smaragdalfar garb, her lines giving a hard, covetous lurch toward his.

As if sensing her magic's yearning, Mavrik looks up, and their eyes meet.

Gwynn's pulse jumps as sparks of luminous color flash to life on Mavrik's lips, mortification dizzying her as her own mouth tingles, likely with matching threads of shimmering color.

Gwynn freezes, one hand covering her lips as everyone in the circle turns their eyes on her and quiets. Yyzz'ra's belligerent gaze flicks toward Mavrik and then back to Gwynn, the Subland commander clearly having noticed the luminous color stinging both their mouths, an unkind smile forming on her own lips.

An almost unbearable shame swims through Gwynn.

You're fasted, she chastises herself, a tight anguish clutching at her throat. *You threw yourself at Mavrik so shamelessly, and you're both fasted.*

Fasted and Sealed.

"Gwynnifer," Mavrik says, his voice constrained but warm as he beckons her near, "come, have some tea and food."

Gwynn's shame is only marginally softened by Mavrik's air of genuine welcome. Painfully self-conscious over the way her lips are still tingling with light energy, she goes to him and takes a seat between him and Mynx, careful not to touch Mavrik as Rhys quietly pours her a cup of tea from a copper kettle hanging on a tripod over the fire.

"I hope you were able to get a bit of sleep," Mynx says, pointedly ignoring Gwynn's and Mavrik's color-infused lips as she hands Gwynn a plate of steaming, nut-scented cakes, flashing her a sympathetic smile before formally introducing her to Valasca and Sparrow, Cael and Rhys, and some of the others. Gwynn mumbles greetings in return, her gaze drawn repeatedly to the sparkling violet crystal Sparrow is worrying under her fingers like a talisman.

It's a rebellious act, Gwynn knows—Urisk females are forbidden by their religion from handling their class's kindred stones, because Urisk women do not possess the "divine gift" of geomancy. Gwynn meets Sparrow's level gaze, a glint of defiance simmering in the Urisk woman's amethyst eyes.

"Ready for your wandtesting after you've eaten?" Mavrik asks.

Gwynn's pulse kicks up and she turns to him, the glow of forbidden color still dancing over his lips drawing her eyes like a thrall. They exchange a loaded glance.

"Ready," she staunchly returns, even though she feels like a fish cast clear out of a familiar pond and flung leagues away. Famished, she wolfs down the food, her gaze snagging on the Varg runes necklacing Valasca's and Sparrow's throats once more, her confusion gaining ground as she identifies the spell work at play. This combination of Varg runes gives anyone possessing the rune stone used to mark them the power to cut off the air to Valasca's and Sparrow's lungs at any moment.

"Why are you marked with imprisonment runes?" she asks them.

Yy'zzra gives Gwynn a confrontational look. "I marked them. They're both wanted by the Vu Trin for being allied with the Black Witch. They helped Elloren Gardner Grey escape Valgard so she could go on to raze Voloi."

Valasca's dark eyes flash at Yyzz'ra. "We were allied with Elloren *before* Vogel took control of her."

"She was *always* Vogel's Black Witch," Yyzz'ra bites back.

"No, she really wasn't," Valasca emphatically counters. She shakes her head, looks to the heavens as if praying to the Amaz Goddess for strength, then spits out what sounds like a curse before setting her grim gaze back on Gwynn. "We underestimated Vogel. And it's best if none of us ever do that again."

"We might yet give him a run for his money," Mavrik says, a lethal edge to his tone.

Valasca raises a brow at this. "That you may, Glass. Appreciate your deft rune work with the spiders." She raises her teacup, toasting both him and Gwynn with it before narrowing her gaze on Gwynnifer. "And kudos to you for keeping the Verdyllion Wand-Stylus away from the Magedom." Valasca looks toward Wynter's distant, still figure, and Gwynn follows the Amaz warrior's line of sight.

Surprise shocks through Gwynn.

A dome of silvery runes now encases both Wynter and the bright yellow yucca tree she's meditating under. Multiple thin lines of silver power flow from the Verdyllion toward the dome's undersurface, giving the dome's interior magic a dandelion-puff appearance with Wynter at its epicenter.

"How did you know I had the Wand?" Gwynn asks Valasca, thrown by the shrewd look the Amaz is giving her.

"I'm well acquainted with Sagellyn Za'Nor," Valasca answers.

Gwynn stiffens, guilt rising. "Then you know I wasn't a very good friend to her."

Valasca's piercing stare doesn't waver. "Well, you seem set on a decent path now, Gardnerian, which is what's important in this life."

Yyzz'ra snorts, leveling an unkind smirk at Gwynn. "I don't know about decent," she says, exaggeratedly eyeing the chromatic energy still stinging over Gwynn's and Mavrik's lips. "You fasted Mages get on with it rather quickly, don't you?"

Another stab of remorse spears through Gwynn, and Mavrik lowers his mug to his knee, his piercing gaze homing in on Yyzz'ra, his lips curling into a cutting smile. "Jealous, Yyzz? Secretly pining for me?"

Yyzz'ra laughs, jabbing her thumb toward Gwynnifer. "Well, at least I could do more than kiss you, unlike this one here. Such a pity she's fasted, isn't it? Sealed too."

Mavrik's eyes turn cold as Gwynn's remorse turns suffocating.

"You couldn't take each other if you tried, could you?" Yyzz'ra continues. She flicks her finger at Mavrik. "Well, I suppose *you* could without consequence, being a man."

"Silence yourself, Yyzz," Mynx cuts in, silver eyes incensed.

"Why?" Yyzz'ra protests as she sweeps a hand at Gwynn. "I'm just pointing out the barbarity of their wandfasting traditions."

Outrage lights in Gwynn, every nerve bristling to hear Yyzz'ra commenting so assuredly on something she doesn't *live*, wandfasting so trussed up with conflict and joy and pain and confusion, it's like a choking force lodged in the center of Gwynn's chest. And increasingly like a prison cage around her heart as well as a potential route for Shadow horror. *You don't understand*, Gwynn wants to lash out at Yyzz'ra. *You're only right in a shallow, skirting-the-surface sort of way.*

Mavrik has gone very still, his gaze pinned on Yyzz'ra.

Gwynn's guilt rears its head once more, over having approached another man as if he were her fastmate. The nightmare of Geoffrey's gray eyes shudders through Gwynn's mind. His unyielding *belief*. His heart-shattering descent into Shadow . . .

"When did they fast you?" Yyzz'ra challenges Mavrik, as if he's somehow to blame for the invention of this tradition that was foisted on them both. "You're both Styvian," she presses, leaning forward. "Was it at thirteen?"

Gwynn winces, hyperaware of her own fastlines.

Placed when she was thirteen.

"I know what it is to have a binding forced upon me," Cael cuts in.

Gwynn's eyes snap toward Cael's intense silver gaze.

"The Zalyn'or necklace I used to be marked with was forced upon me at only ten years of age," Cael comments. "I tried to fight my people, but they held me down and placed the binding on me in an effort to subdue my will and make me hate my sister."

Emotion balls in Gwynn's throat in response to the pain in Cael's eyes.

Yyzz'ra's biting voice cuts through the moment. "See," she crows at Mynx, "even your Alfsigr agrees that these bindings are barbaric." Yyzz'ra loses her jeering smile as her gaze swings to Mavrik. "And now, there's a growing risk that Vogel might take control of every Zalyn'or-marked Alfsigr and every fasted Mage via your fastmarks, isn't there?"

"The Mages are poised to take over *everything*, Yyzz," Mynx angrily counters.

Yyzz'ra rounds on her. "No, Mynx. These two Mages are a *particular* danger, and you know it. They need runic imprisonment collars around their necks. As do the Alfsigr, Zalyn'or marked or not."

"All my wands are rune marked to self-destruct if I try to cast spells corrupted with Shadow magic through them," Mavrik flings back at her. "Satisfied?"

Yyzz'ra's glower turns white-hot. "No. I am *not* satisfied. And I won't be until your kind are thrown out of the Sublands and wiped clear off the face of Erthia! The Alfsigr too!"

Mavrik slams down his mug and gets up, lightly touching Gwynn's shoulder. "Come with me, Gwynn," he stiffly offers. "Let's get to work."

Gwynn swallows thickly as she rises, so troubled and flustered she's barely able to meet Mavrik's gaze. When she finally dares to, she finds a blazing understanding there, but it does little to temper her lashing turmoil.

"Mavrik, we know you're on our side," Mynx starts, seeming concerned.

Mavrik gives Mynx a harsh, cautionary look that silences her as Gwynn follows him down a rocky path toward the desert sands, an argument breaking out behind them in Smaragdalfarin.

An argument about *them*.

Gwynn does her best to blot it out, feeling as if the whole world is battering her like the winds roiling inside the storm bands in the distance, even though the sheltered predawn space surrounding her is cool and still and dry.

Arms splayed out for balance, Gwynn follows Mavrik down from the ledge and over the Agolith's crimson sand. Rose sparks suffuse the edges of her vision in response to the deep-rose light of predawn brightening as the sun moves closer to the storm bands' apex.

They pass Wynter's distant form, the Icaral's eyes closed in concentration. The Verdyllion in Wynter's hand is raised as she murmurs spell after spell, small runes forming around her like suspended silver rain.

Gwynn's shrewd eyes scan the designs of these newly conjured runes.

Storm-amplifying runes, all of them.

"Why is she crafting storm runes?" Gwynn asks Mavrik as she follows him under one of the Agolith's towering scarlet-stone arches, decadent red sparks flashing through her Light Mage vision and over her wand hand.

"She's getting ready to feed more power into the storm bands so we can overtake them and deploy them against Vogel's forces," Mavrik answers as they stride into a sheltered semicircle of stone, the stone's rose striations alternating with lines of vivid purple, the streaks of forbidden color dizzyingly alluring.

Gwynn lifts her gaze toward the dark storm bands. They're flashing with bright energy, a wall against Vogel's forces, about to be strengthened and controlled by the Verdyllion. A slim bit of relief edges into her, but it's doused by her memory of Yyzz'ra's angrily voiced concerns.

"Yyzz'ra is right about us being a potential danger," Gwynn admits.

Mavrik turns to face her. "She is," he concedes, the color still crackling over his lips with provocative force. "So, we exhaust every magical course of action to fight Vogel and our fastings. Pool our knowledge. Pool our power. See what you're capable of. And, what we're capable of *together*."

He pauses as their magic gives a palpable, insistent pull toward each other, the tingle of magic dancing over Gwynn's lips intensifying along with the color flashing over Mavrik's mouth.

"This is a good, open site to wandtest you," Mavrik comments matter-of-factly, all business as he draws one of the four wands sheathed at his hip—the golden, Issani-rune-marked one—but Gwynn can detect pent-up emotion in his tone.

She glances at his fastmarked hands and wrists, her own pent-up reaction to what transpired between them last night lapping against her in a damning tide. She tenses her hands against her looping fastlines—a fasting that was once the most precious thing in all the world to her. When tears threaten to make a play for her eyes, she blinks hard to press them back.

None of this matters, she chastises herself. *The only thing that matters is fighting Vogel's Shadow.*

But still, the question clamors for release, and she's unable to stop it from bursting forth. "Did you love your fastmate?"

Mavrik freezes, his expression turning as impenetrable as the Agolith's crimson stone. He lets out a harsh sigh, his lips compressing into a tight line. "I was thirteen when I was fasted, same as you, I'd imagine." His jaw ticks as he glances toward the storm band lining the horizon, before turning his blazing green eyes back on her. "It was forced on me."

"But . . . you're also Sealed," Gwynn blurts out. Both of them, bound not just in a fasting but also in a Sealing at or past eighteen years of age, the consummation of the fasting nonnegotiable.

Mavrik narrows his eyes at her, a flash of intensity heating them. "I went on my first deployment the day after our Sealing. By the time I returned, I was hells-bent on resistance. And quickly found out I had been paired with a woman who's like your Geoffrey. Who fully supports slashing the tips off the ears of children like Bloom'ilya and Ee'vee, then deporting them to 'purify the Magedom's Holy Soil.'" He grimaces and glances away before casting her a troubled look, jagged pain in it. "It was an *impossible* situation. I quickly found myself very much alone." He looks away again, mouth tensing before he turns back to her. "I was soon undercover to the Vu Trin, lying to every Mage around me." His eyes take on a haunted look. "Gwynn . . . if you'd seen the Fae slaughter going on in the north . . ."

He stops, appearing momentarily stricken with both devastating remorse and remembered horror.

Contrition tightens Gwynn's gut. "I'm sorry," she says, understanding, all too well, a piece of his remorse and horror. And what it is to find your life suddenly spinning out of control, the image of the armory and her family's home exploding surfacing again and again. Leaving her fastmate and throwing her lot in with the Resistance went against every last thing she was taught her whole life.

As did falling into alliance with a rebel like Mavrik.

But she also can't shake a series of even stronger images—the frightened Smaragdalfar children fleeing through the Sublands. Bloom'ilya's and Ee'vee's terrified faces as their ears were cropped. And from what she's learned since then, that's only a *trace* of the barbarity the Gardnerians have rained down on the world.

"I know how hard it is," Mavrik says, cutting into her thoughts, his tone and gaze softened with compassion, "to go against everything you were ever taught. And I know what it is to have your heart broken by reality."

Gwynn pulls in a harsh breath, blinking back the sting of tears as she holds his gaze, the memory of how kind he was to Bloom'ilya and Ee'vee only escalating her draw to him. "I fell into your magic last night," she admits, struggling not to feel like a criminal. She can tell, from his knowing expression, that he can read the forbidden subtext she can't bring herself to voice.

I fell into you.

"I fell into your magic, as well," he admits before he coughs out a self-deprecating laugh, biting at the color still forking over his lips. He gestures toward his mouth, an ardent intensity overtaking his expression. "I loved kissing you, Gwynn, I won't deny it. Our thrall is making that a bit too obvious. The Verdyllion seems to have enhanced the magical attraction between us when it linked our lines. It's quite adept at creating strong linkages, among other things."

"Have you tried wielding the Verdyllion on your own?" Gwynn asks, cognizant that he was Gardneria's premier wandmaster before the Magedom marked him as its enemy.

He nods. "It won't let me send magic through it. The Wand seems to have a mind of its own. For the moment, only Wynter seems able to wield it as a runic stylus."

"I feel like . . ." Gwynn hesitates, biting at her own tingling lips. "My magic wants to leap into yours."

His eyes sharpen with a knowing light, and she struggles to not fall into the gorgeous *green* of them. "Your magic perfectly complements mine," he says, his tone low and confidential. "I think that's why the Wand was able to forge such a strong link between us. I'm a Level Five Air, Wind, Earth, and Fire Mage. I'm only lacking in light magery. And you have a *very* strong line of light power. Last night, when we . . . *connected* . . . I felt like that link was reforged. Amplified, even."

He rubs at his lips as Gwynn turns this over in her thoughts, the space between them suddenly crackling with forbidden possibility.

"When we kissed . . ." Gwynn forces out, an ocean of conflict rising ". . . I *did* think you were Geoffrey."

"I'm clear on that," Mavrik says, his voice and stance hardening. "Gwynn, I'm *not him*."

So much is conveyed in those two words. A tingle races down Gwynn's spine as she holds his blazingly intent gaze.

No, she considers, *you are definitely not Geoffrey.*

Caustic misery and guilt and anger dig their claws in.

Did Geoffrey witness slaughter? What atrocities was he party to after he deployed?

Yet, unlike Mavrik, he *stayed.*

"Geoffrey's eyes . . ." she tells Mavrik in a strangled voice. "A few months back, they took on a gray glow. He's ensorcelled in some way . . . probably by that Wand of Vogel's. Perhaps not of his own volition—"

"No, Gwynn," Mavrik cuts in. "It's a choice for Mage soldiers to take on Shadow magic. I was offered it, as well. Geoffrey saw what they're doing. He saw it, Gwynn. But he wanted *power*."

His words are a strike to the heart. A part of her guessed this already. Sensed the change in Geoffrey before his eyes started to turn gray. She remembers him railing against his Level Two earth magery, increasingly bitter over how his low level of power robbed him of rank and prestige.

And as much as she had once loved him, she can see the brutal truth so clearly now—Geoffrey would have *absolutely* traded in his humanity for power and acceptance. As it was, his humanity was already slipping away, to the point that the torture of children was acceptable to him. And to her parents, as well.

Her misery slides into blistering outrage then reckless defiance, the will to fight resurfacing. She gives Mavrik a hard stare. "Let's see what I can do with a wand."

Mavrik's eyes glint, as if he's seeing something new in her that he adores. He flips the wand in his hand and holds its hilt out to her. "Try it," he prods. "Send out a spell."

Gwynn nods and takes it, a thrill coursing through her as she considers the wand in her hand, noticing its wood is the exact same hue as the tree Wynter is sitting under. There's a small grove of the same Golden Yucca trees huddled together in the near distance, their bright color gaining ground as the rising sun inches closer to the storm bands' top edges.

Drawing in a shivering breath, Gwynn lifts the golden wand and murmurs a simple Mage light-orb spell, her light magery flashing to life through her lines and sparking toward her wand hand.

Her magic flashes against her palm's underside, triggering an explosive ache as it shimmers fitfully there, unable to break through to the wand in her hand. Caught up in the wildly frustrating yearning for magical *release*, Gwynn grits her teeth, her voice rough when it comes. "My magic is still blocked."

"Then let's try the spell with us touching," Mavrik offers, his tone full of a patient warmth that skims the edge off Gwynn's frustration.

Beating back her turbulent emotions, Gwynn nods, stiffening against the way her magic leaps toward Mavrik's as he slides in behind her, reaches out, and closes his wand hand around hers.

The flashing exchange of their power shocks through Gwynn as their lines connect.

She inhales at the same time that Mavrik does, his hand tightening around hers.

"What magic should I try?" she murmurs, flustered by the surge of her light magery and Mavrik's proximity.

"Fashion Mageline-connection runes," he slyly suggests.

She glances at him over her shoulder as comprehension of his intention triggers a more complicated idea.

"I should try *Issani* power-connection runes," she counters. "I can imprint one on each of us and set down a Noi flow rune between them to amplify the connection. It might set up a transient linkage that's *much* stronger than a Mage ward."

Mavrik's brow lifts with obvious surprise before he grins wolfishly at her. Gwynn's thoughts scatter a bit, the feral masculinity of that grin combined with the feel of his hand wrapped around hers bringing her *right back* to his exciting kiss.

"That's wickedly clever," he purrs, looking her over as if seeing her, once more, in an expanded light. "Try it," he prods with a devilish grin. "Access your magic, Light Mage."

Giddy from his encouragement—encouragement to own her power that no one has ever given her before—Gwynn pulls in a deep breath and murmurs the spell.

Small sparks of bright yellow light spurt from the wand's tip, and a startled sound escapes Gwynn, her pulse accelerating. As her wand hand trembles in Mavrik's grip, the yellow sparks fizzle out before they can even begin to form a rune, but still.

Still.

She coaxed actual light magic into existence.

Her magic.

From a *wand*.

For a moment Gwynn can barely summon a breath. She chances a look at Mavrik to find him grinning dangerously at her, the threads of color shimmering over his lips brightened along with the energy tingling over hers at the remembrance of how his thrilling kiss blasted their magic to more potent life.

The thought slips out before she can fully process it—

"We should kiss to amplify my power."

Mavrik's eyes widen slightly, and she stiffens, nearly overcome by the strength of the ingrained, cultural pushback ricocheting through her over so brazenly wanting things a Styvian Gardnerian woman is *never supposed to ever want* unless it's sanctioned and controlled by the Magedom itself.

Power over her own magic.

And Mavrik's lips on hers.

Religious conflict storms through her, fiercer than the inside of any storm band, and she looks at the red sand at her feet, readying herself for the Ancient One Himself to strike her down.

Mavrik's hand comes to her shoulder. "Gwynn, look at me."

Raging against the rise of mortal fear, she does.

"I think you might be on to something," he offers. "But we need to be honest about how overwhelming this thrall between us feels. Which makes it dangerous. We can kiss to try and free up your magic, and not go any further with it. Gwynn, we *can't* go any further with it, *ever*. It has to be said."

The full cruelty of her fasting is suddenly bearing down on Gwynn, her fast-marks an unbreakable prison. She can sense, in the mutual desire flickering in Mavrik's look, that the subtext blazing between them doesn't need to be voiced. They're both clear that what transpired between them last night wasn't just about a magical bond. His kiss was an explosively thrilling pleasure and a comfort, lighting her up in a way Geoffrey *never* lit her up. Leaving her both frustrated and ashamed to be suddenly considering that type of connection with someone she's not fasted to.

"I loved my fastmate," Gwynn admits, feeling poised on yet another life-altering, unforgivable precipice.

"I'm sorry, Gwynnifer," Mavrik says with a look of pained commiseration.

She holds his gaze, impassioned conflict rising. "I never thought I'd ever want anyone else . . ."

Mavrik takes a step back, shaking his head as if warding off their magical pull. "We can't dare to think that way. Not bound up in fasting spells." He gives her a stricken, searching look, gesturing toward the wand in her hand. "Gwynn, what do you want to do?"

Gwynn looks to the storm bands and thinks, yet again, of the Urisk she witnessed being herded into wagons, the Smaragdalfar children fleeing for their lives. The monster of the whole Magedom bearing down. And then, the memory of how kind Mavrik was to Ee'vee and Bloom'ilya, to the point that Ee'vee was reluctant to leave him.

She meets Mavrik's piercing gaze. "Geoffrey is *gone*. But our power—it's *right here*. This fight is *right here*. I want you to kiss me. Help me access my power. For the good of Erthia."

Mavrik stills, then nods, his breathing tripping into a faster cadence as he steps close, brings his hand up to caress her arm, then leans down and brings his lips to hers.

A shock of multicolored light cracks through Gwynn, an explosion of wanton pleasure flashing through her as they both gasp against each other's mouths and their magic breaks free to surge through each other's lines. Swept up in their powers' prismatic undertow, they draw each other closer, and Gwynn can feel, in the twining of their power, their instantaneous mutual desire to *fuse*.

Something shocks through Gwynn, the sense of trapped magic in her center breaking open in a burst of light as she grips his tunic's side.

Breaking the kiss, Gwynn looks around, dazed, to find that every color in the crimson desert around her is brightened, Mavrik's face and form limned in an aura of shimmering multihued light.

"Try the spell again," Mavrik huskily prods as he slides around her once more and clasps his wand hand around hers.

Forcing focus, Gwynn lifts the wand, Mavrik following her motion as she murmurs the runic spell.

A clean, luminous yellow line sweeps from her wand's tip, and Gwynn's heartbeat leaps, utter disbelief surging. "Holy Ancient One," she rasps out.

"Go on," Mavrik prods, "finish the rune."

Getting hold of herself, Gwynn finishes crafting two small suspended golden amplification runes then drags and fuses one to her wand arm and the other to Mavrik's. Deciding to experiment, Gwynn hands Mavrik's gold wand back to him and places her hand around *his* this time.

Murmuring the Noi flow-rune spell, Mavrik fashions a suspended sapphire rune, seeming stunned by his new Light Mage ability to create runes. Visibly gathering himself, he connects the Noi rune's power to the golden runes on their arms via two luminous rays of sapphire, Gwynn's light power running bright through his lines.

"This changes *everything*," Mavrik says, seeming awestruck by the Noi rune suspended before them, raying out light. He turns to her. "Do you have any idea of the magic we can do *together*? We have access to *all five* elemental lines." He hands her back the wand. "Try to cast a spell without me touching you."

Drawing in a bolstering breath, Gwynn raises the wand and murmurs the Mage light-orb spell once again.

Her magic surges toward the wand and flashes against her palm's underside once more, triggering an even stronger ache as it remains blocked. Frustration swamps her, but before she can give voice to it, dawn breaks over the distant storm bands' towering apexes. Gilded sunlight washes over the desert's breathtakingly vermillion expanse, and Gwynn's heart lifts as her lines fill with a euphoric energy. A bright orange hawk soars into view overhead, then another, the raptors circling each other like two spots of saffron flame.

A small gasp escapes Gwynnifer. "Those are Agolith Flame Hawks," she tells Mavrik. "They pair for life." Her voice hitches around the words as she watches the hawks wheeling through the sky. She turns and meets Mavrik's intense stare as an idea lights, bright as the hawks' feathers and sudden flood of sunlight. "We could join ourselves with Issani twinning runes," she ventures. "The Issani twin their high-level sorcerers. That way, they have full, permanent access to each other's magic. Without needing to touch each other."

She can sense the wheels of Mavrik's wandmaster mind turning as he peers more closely at her. "That's Issaan's most powerful military magic, Gwynn," he says, a strong note of caution in his tone. "A complete fusing. As permanent as fasting. *More* so. And the amplification of power it triggers . . . it can be *lethal*. Which is why it's rarely cast." He shakes his head. "If you were to set down that twinning spell and we survived its fusing, we'd *never* be able to remove it. We'd *never* function as separate Mages again. We'd have to stay in the same location. Always. And if one of us died, the other would die too."

Gwynn pulls in a deep breath, peering up at the hawks as her lines strain toward Mavrik's. Undaunted, she lowers her gaze to his, tension igniting between them.

"It's too dangerous, Gwynn . . ." he insists, slicing his hand emphatically through the air. "We *can't*—"

An explosive *CRACK* booms out from every horizon, knifing through Gwynn's ears and breaking off Mavrik's words as the image of the Verdyllion pulses *hard* against Gwynn's mind.

Startled, they turn toward the sound, and shock lances through Gwynn at the sight they're met with.

The tall black storm bands in the distance have morphed to dark gray and are rising higher into the sky, rapidly gaining height as they flash and boom with a strange, curving black lightning, their bright white lightning *gone*.

"Bloody hells . . ." Mavrik exclaims as the morning's golden light dims and Gwynn realizes that the storm bands are not only enlarging but moving toward them. The Verdyllion pulses against her mind once more with dire urgency.

Her eyes meet Mavrik's as the horrific understanding crystallizes. "Vogel's taking over the storm bands!" she cries. "And he's coming for the Verdyllion. We've got to get everyone below ground and shielded!"

Mavrik draws his Varg-marked wand and grasps hold of Gwynn's wrist, their magic bolting through each other's lines as they launch into a run toward Wynter, skidding over the sand, the wind picking up as the sky rapidly grays. A series of earsplitting rumbles of thunder crackle, and Gwynn winces, the surrounding storm bands barreling closer.

They speed under a crimson stone arch, birds and wildlife scampering and darting away from the advancing storm bands. Gwynn glances over her shoulder just as a dark swarm of flying creatures bursts from the incoming wall of roiling gray chaos and soars rapidly toward them.

"Wraith bats!" Mavrik cries out.

A rush of pure terror courses through Gwynn as the bats fly nearer, wind and sand scouring her back as her mind runs through everything she's read about the beasts, almost immediately realizing her fatal mistake.

"Control your fear!" Mavrik yells over the wind. "They feed on it!"

Gwynn forcefully stamps down her panic as she's filled with a sense of the bats' vicious energy pressing into her mind, drawn to her terror.

"*Wynter!*" Mavrik booms out as they run.

Wynter is sprinting toward them, the Icaral's pale form pummeled by gray gusts, her eyes alight with silver fire, wings drawn in tight. The Verdyllion is clasped protectively against her chest, her bird-kindreds winging around her in panicked, wind-battered flight.

Mavrik releases Gwynn's wrist, and her magic slingshots painfully back into her center as Mavrik throws himself between Gwynn, Wynter, and the incoming wraith bats. He drops down on one knee, thrusts his wand forward and grinds out a spell.

Emerald energy blasts from his wand's tip. A translucent green half dome-shield shimmers into existence, high as a barn's rooftop, and multiple wraith bats crash against it, their shrieks knifing through Gwynn's ears as they burst into green flame. Wind roars against the shield as Mavrik springs back up, and the three of them race toward the Subland cavern's entrance.

Cael, Mynx, and Yyzz'ra are running down the rocky path toward them, along with Valasca and Rhys. Mynx waves Gwynn, Mavrik, and Wynter forward as she skids to a halt along with Cael and Rhys, all three of them swinging Varg bows off their shoulders before nocking emerald-glowing runic arrows.

"Fight back your fear!" Mavrik yells at the incoming soldiers. "They can paralyze you with it!"

Gwynn glances over her shoulder as a huge incoming wraith bat opens its fanged mouth. Dark lightning bolts from its maw and explodes against Mavrik's storm shield, blasting it into Shadow mist.

Panic rises inside Gwynn once more, and before she can tamp it down, she feels the huge bat hooking into her fear, its vicious energy shouldering straight into her mind. She stumbles and halts as the bat amplifies her panic, mushrooming it into paralyzing terror.

"Gwynnifer!" Mavrik shouts, grabbing tight hold of her arm as Cael and Rhys and Mynx release arrows at the screeching bats while Valasca and Yyzz'ra hurl Varg-marked blades.

The bats shriek as they fall, but Gwynn can hear scores more soaring toward them as Mavrik drags her rigid body toward the Subland entrance. Wynter throws herself between Gwynn and Mavrik and the bats as a much larger swarm soars straight toward them.

"Get back, Wynter!" Mavrik cries, and Gwynn manages a glance behind her.

Wynter remains fixedly in place, snapping her wings out to their full breadth.

It's over. It's all over, Gwynn's heart pounds out as Wynter throws her wings down, rises into the sky and raises the Verdyllion in her hand.

Gwynn's breath stutters in her chest as raying lines of silver energy blast from the Verdyllion in all directions, each line of power rapidly coalescing into the translucent form of a rune-marked bird made of spiraling silver lines.

With a warrior cry, Wynter thrusts her free palm forward, and her runic birds wing toward the wraith bats and collide with them in sprays of silver light.

The bats shriek as the aura of Wynter's magical energy hits Gwynn, flashing silver light through every line.

The light filled with pure, undistilled courage.

The fearlessness of a true artist.

Wynter's power rushes through Gwynn, dissolving her fear and galvanizing her to *move* as bats *explode into silver flame and Mavrik pulls Gwynn into a sprint.*

"*Get inside!*" Mavrik growls at everyone as they race up the rocky path to the Subland entrance and Wynter soars in above them then touches down on the entrance's ledge.

They all burst into the cavern, Wynter's panicked birds swarming around them along with the paired Agolith Flame Hawks.

Wynter leaps through the entrance, and they all turn toward it just as the Shadow storm band blasts against the cavern, a violent gust slamming through its opening and into them all.

Gwynn's breath is punched from her lungs as she's tossed clear across the cavern with the others, their backs colliding with the stone wall as they're pinned there, the ferocious power of the wind rattling Gwynn's very bones.

Cursing under his breath, Mavrik grits out a spell and thrusts his Varg-marked wand forward, blasting out another green half dome-shield that punches the Shadow storm back a fraction.

The wind releases, and they all drop to the ground in a heap.

Seizing the window of opportunity, Gwynn lurches toward Mavrik and throws her wand hand around his, their magic intertwining, Gwynn's light magery releasing into his lines.

They thrust out the wand together, and Gwynn hastily conjures interconnected Varg, Mage, Noi, and Issani storm-repel runes shot through with multicolored lightning.

Huffing out another snarling spell, Gwynn blasts the runes forward.

Rays of color flash from the linked runes and flow through Mavrik's shield, then crash into the Shadow storm with a resonant *BOOM*, driving the gray chaos clear out of the cave.

Mynx and Yyzz'ra hastily leap forward and press their palms to the Varg runes marked along the cavern's entrance. A crystalline-green wall closes over the opening, sealing it shut.

Shadow power slams against the conjured barrier in a concussive *BOOM*, and Mynx and Yyzz'ra leap back as the very ground shakes beneath them all, sprays of stone raining down from the cavern's ceiling.

"It's Vogel," Wynter states, silver fire guttering in her eyes as she clutches the Verdyllion to her chest, her birds flapping around the cavern in panicked, aimless trajectories. "That entire storm . . . it's shot through with his Shadow power."

"We need to get farther underground and strengthen the Sublands' Varg shielding," Mavrik urges them all.

Another explosion hits the cavern's barrier, and they set off in a sprint down the spiraling stone stairs until they reach the cavern's base. Following Mynx and

THE DRYAD STORM

Yyzz'ra, they race through a narrow tunnel, then into the expansive crimson cavern at its terminus, its huge ceiling covered in a net of interlocking Varg runes, part of the huge web of runes shielding the entire Central Desert's Sublands.

Two young Smaragdalfar soldiers are there—Yyzz'ra's comrades, the perpetually angry Gavryyl and quietly dangerous Valkyr—along with Sparrow, who rushes over to greet Valasca. The two Subland soldiers are casting Varg rune after Varg rune into the air from precharged runic stones, swiftly spelling each rune upward to strengthen the rune net as fast as they can.

"All the tunnels to the south, west, and east of us have collapsed," Valkyr calls to Yyzz'ra as he fashions runes. "We're trapped. Cut off from the rest of our forces—"

Another seismic blow rattles the earth, and the Varg rune net gives a worrisome flicker to gray.

"Holy gods," Valasca snarls. "Vogel's storm bands can overtake Varg magic!"

Wynter's artistic courage still reverberating through her, Gwynn calmly narrows her eyes at the rune-netted ceiling and can tell, by reading which details of the runic design are flickering out, that the Smaragdalfar's Subland barrier is a few minutes away from falling.

"It won't hold," she says to Mavrik, harsh and emphatic. "We need to fuse our magic with the Issani twinning spell, then link it to the shield." She meets Wynter's silver-fire-rimmed eyes. "Using the Verdyllion." Gwynn's eyes snap pointedly back to Mavrik's, a fervid look passing between them before he nods.

Without a beat of hesitation, Wynter tosses Gwynn the Verdyllion, and she catches it. A tremor passes through her as the Wand's prismatic energy shoots through her every line. Her trapped power expands, a sense of pure *rightness* filling her core as the Verdyllion's green glow spreads over her wand hand and straight up her wrist.

Mavrik's arms come around her from behind, his wand hand closing around hers.

Their combined power floods Gwynn's lines, her light magery streaking toward the Verdyllion. She sets about fashioning two large, bright gold Issani twinning runes to hover in the air before them, the potential consequences of the twinning magic be fully damned.

Another violent BOOM sounds, like a monster battering against the earth, its intensifying roar against the Subland ceiling a nightmare of fury. The Varg rune net above them shivers to a grayer green, a few pieces of the ceiling cracking off and crashing to the floor, a small preview of the devastation to come.

"Pull up your tunic," Gwynn orders Mavrik. He releases her hand, her light magic snapping into its trapped state as he wrests off the garb.

Ignoring her neck-prickling rush of heat from staring at his naked upper body, she grabs the side of his belt and drags him close. He takes hold of her wand hand once more and follows her movements as she touches the Verdyllions's tip to one of the runes then drags the rune onto his body, murmuring an Issani spell to fuse it there.

Mavrik shivers as the rune brightens in a rush of golden sparks then settles into a luminous golden design against his taut abdomen.

Another devastating *BOOM* sounds, spiking through Gwynn's ears. A hail of rocks rains down as the Subland Elves furiously cast Varg runes, the runes fragmenting to gray as quickly as they're cast.

Hurling modesty aside, Gwynn pulls up her own tunic and drags the second rune onto her skin, fusing it there in a prickling profusion of sparks, Mavrik's grip firm around her hand.

Wasting no time, she fashions a third golden rune in the air before them. Bolstered by Mavrik's steady grasp, Gwynn clamps her teeth together to dampen the dizzying clamor of nerves, and crafts golden lines connecting the suspended rune hanging before them to the runes marked on both of their abdomens. Feeling like she's about to jump off a cliff leading straight off Erthia, she draws in a deep breath, exchanges one, last fraught look with Mavrik . . . and murmurs the Issani twinning spell.

Searing gold cuts through her vision. A startling pain strikes through her every line, her affinity lines tearing toward Mavrik's with eviscerating force.

She cries out, Mavrik grunting out a sound of agony as they collide against each other, desperate to relieve the terrible pull, Gwynn's lungs feeling on the verge of collapse as the agonizing tension nears breakage.

Fumbling for a way to connect and survive, she crashes her lips onto his.

The pain exploding through Gwynn's lines abruptly morphs into a stunningly intimate sense of Mavrik's every line of power fusing to hers, a startled energy blazing through his magic as a bright Issani gold overtakes Gwynn's sight. They break the kiss, both of them pulling in great gulps of air, the gold in Gwynn's vision rapidly clearing . . . to reveal Mavrik before her, his irises now an incandescent gold that Gwynn can sense shimmering through her own irises. Her eyes flit to Wynter

THE DRYAD STORM

Eirllyn's silver-burning gaze. The two Agolith Flame Hawks are perched on Wynter's shoulders, their feathers illuminating her slender form in vivid orange light.

Another cave-rattling *BOOM* sounds.

Flooded with a resolve she can feel blazing through Mavrik's power as well, Gwynn releases her hold on Mavrik and aims the Verdyllion at the Varg shielding while gritting out an Issani rune-connection spell, intimately aware that her and Mavrik's connection no longer involves touch.

An iridescent bolt of their twinned power rays out from the Verdyllion and spears toward the cavern's ceiling, the golden light startling Gwynn with its beauty. The rays furcate as they streak through the ceiling's grayed Varg runes, blasting away the Shadow and recharging them all, each rune flashing into multihued light until the entire cavern's ceiling pulses with Gwynn's full spectrum of color power. The rain of stone lessens then abruptly stops, the Shadow storm's onslaught muting to a faint, distant roar.

Gwynn pulls in a hard breath, filled by the heady, intrinsic sense of every Varg rune cast throughout the Central Desert's Sublands now merged to her and Mavrik's twinned power to create an impenetrable net of protection, the Sublands now a fortress.

Walled off from the Magedom.

Gwynn's legs buckle. She's caught by Mavrik, the two of them sinking to the ground, their twinned power momentarily spent, everything in them sent into the Subland shielding.

"You did it," he murmurs, kissing her forehead, seeming overwhelmed. "Well played, Gwynnifer."

Gwynn clings to him as Mynx, Cael, Valasca, and others race over to them. She shivers, the full interconnection of her and Mavrik's lines disorienting, the two of them like one fused entity. Gwynn can sense his emotions through their merged lines, almost as clearly as she feels her own, Mavrik's potent determination to protect her rushing through her while her equally potent desire to protect *him* shimmers through them both in a sizzling aura of light.

"Don't move!" Valasca orders, raising the Varg-marked blade in her hand, her eyes pinned on something above and behind Gwynn and Mavrik.

Gwynn turns just as a raven soars from a stony alcove and Valasca hurls her weapon. The blade impales the raven. A chillingly multitone, too-low *caw* sounds from the raven as it falls, the pair of Agolith Flame Hawks screeching out sounds of distress as they wing away to perch on an outcropping of stone.

Valasca runs to the flapping, fallen raven, and Gwynn notes, with a sharp recoil of fear, that the bird has eyes of swirling Shadow massed all over its upper head, with a single pale green eye set in their center.

And there's a Shadow rune on the raven's side.

Valasca grabs the raven and hoists it by its feet, the pale green eye fixing on her with a look of palpable hate that sends a dart of fright down Gwynn's spine.

"I've encountered this type of beast before," Valasca growls. "Vogel's in it. He's watching us through this runic spy. It's likely he's been watching us for a while now."

With a sweep of her blade, Valasca decapitates the raven spy, and its head thumps to the ground, its Shadow eyes deadening to black, but the pale green eye—the *Vogel* eye—remaining brutally fixed on Valasca.

Growling, Valasca thrusts the thing's body to the side, grabs hold of the raven's decapitated head and stabs her blade straight into the Vogel eye, scouring it out.

Everyone stills while Wynter lowers herself beside the raven's body and places her hand on its rapidly disappearing Shadow rune. A slight shiver ripples through her.

Valasca is breathing hard, her blade's hilt gripped tight in her fist, as they all take in the horror before them. "So, he knows we're here and that we have the Verdyllion," Valasca states. She looks to Yyzz'ra and the two young Subland soldiers bracketing her. "Which means he knows quite a bit about your Subland army." Her dark gaze swings to Wynter. "And there's a chance he knows what Wynter can do with the Verdyllion." Valasca turns to Mavrik and Gwynn, her eyes flicking toward the prismatic Subland shielding they just conjured. "And he knows that you've twinned your magic to wall the Magedom out of here."

"So he has his little spy," Mavrik snarls back. "He can't get through our shielding."

"He can," Wynter murmurs.

Everyone's gaze swings toward Wynter.

She draws her hand back to cradle it against her chest as the Shadow rune marked on the raven's side vanishes, her wings drawing in protectively around herself. "Vogel is going after the wilds," she warns. "I read his intent through that Shadow rune's tether to his power. He's not just targeting Elloren and Yvan, but the entire Northern Forest."

"To get hold of the Black Witch," Yyzz'ra impatiently snaps.

"Not just that," Wynter counters, looking to Yyzz'ra. "To destroy the forest itself."

"Well, we best hope the Dryad wards surrounding that forest hold," Mavrik says. He narrows his gaze at the prismatic shield above them, the chromatic runes pulsing every color over the cavernous space before he lowers his gaze back to Wynter's. Gwynn stiffens as his worry sizzles through their twinned power. "If Vogel destroys enough forest," Mavrik says, "he might be able to break through our shielding."

Gwynn furrows her brow. "I don't understand," she says. "How could destroying forests break through our shielding?"

Mavrik gives her a grim, searching look. "Gwynn," he says. "We're *Dryads*."

A reflexive protest rears over this outrageous claim. "We're *Mages* . . ."

"Yes, Gwynn," he agrees, a hard edge entering his tone, "we are. And all Mages are part *Dryad*. Trees are the source of *all* our magic. Magery flows from the rooted forest, through our lines, then out through our wands. If you kill enough trees, you destroy our magic." His gaze darkens. "Unless you replace the elemental power in our lines with Shadow power."

Gwynn blinks at him, pinned by the intensity of his stare, her thoughts at war. Just uttering that thought is the highest sacrilege in Gardneria.

"Did you ever think about the dead trees that decorate practically every Gardnerian home?" Mavrik presses, unrelenting. "The dead trees set into the Valgard Cathedral itself? The forest decor *everywhere*, in every Mage home? The wands of layered wood? The religious obsession with Ironflowers, which are the beginnings of *trees*? The Sealing ceremony full of dominion over the elements of nature culminating with control over the trees themselves?"

Gwynn's disorientation intensifies, and she can feel the blood draining from her face.

"We're part Kelt, part Dryad," Mavrik vehemently continues. "We're not 'First Children,' sprung from the Great Ironwood Tree. Gwynn, we're part *Tree Fae*."

The undeniable truth cycles down, slamming through Gwynn with the force of a thousand runic storm bands. *Part Tree Fae. We're part Fae.*

She gapes at him, stunned, as Vogel's muted power thunders against the world above. "How have I never pieced that together?"

Mavrik's lips give a bitter twist. "The power of religion. Able to make us deny even the most glaringly obvious of truths." He glances up at their color-pulsing shielding. "Wynter's right," he says, warning in his eyes. "We're not just walled off from the surface of Erthia by Vogel's Shadow storm bands—"

"We're walled off from the *trees*," Gwynn finishes for him, holding his piercing gaze with burgeoning alarm.

"Vogel is going to keep us trapped underground," Wynter states with terrible certainty. Her eyes flick toward the Verdyllion in Gwynn's hand before she meets her gaze. "And while we're trapped, he's going to destroy Dryad magic, bring down your Subland shielding, and take hold of the Verdyllion."

CHAPTER ELEVEN

SHADOW STORM

Marcus Vogel

Agolith Desert
Twelve days after Xishlon

Marcus Vogel holds his Shadow Wand aloft, grayed wind power rotating outward from its tip like a dark hurricane. Hawk-focused, Vogel watches as the roiling spirals radiate over the Agolith Desert's huge expanse of graying land and sky.

The view is sweepingly panoramic from the apex of this highest of stone arcs he's flown onto, one of the multitudes of giant, graying stone formations adorning the Agolith. Vogel's elevated position allows him an unimpeded view of his black-lightning-lit Shadow storm bands moving toward him from every horizon.

Storm bands newly overtaken by the Magedom's sanctified Shadow power.

Vengeful excitement swells against Vogel's chest and sears fire through his lines as he murmurs spell after spell, pulsing radiating bands of Shadow magery toward the Wyverncrafted storm bands. *Linking* them to his power.

And drawing them in like Shadow-tethered wraith bats.

His storm bands now.

Storm bands that will soon hold enough power to smash through the Northern Forest's Dryad warding, so he can take back his Black Witch fastmate—who belongs to *him*.

Vogel glances at his fastmarked hand. He's linked a Shadow tracking rune to his fastlines, and he can *feel* the trajectory of his fastmate through the stretch on his lines. The desire for domination over Elloren lashes hot through his power, the Black Witch caught up in a days-long lag as she streams toward the Dryads' Northern Forest.

Giving him time to close in.

Oh, he'll be ready to regain hold of Elloren as soon as she touches down in that forest. And then he'll use her to bind the Icaral demon and strike down the Dryad Fae surrounding her, along with the Subland filth converging on her with their Heathen Wand.

Wind lashing through his dark hair, Vogel continues to hold the Wand aloft. His multi-eyed Shadow dragon is preternaturally still beneath him as the Shadow Wand's power courses outward and the storm bands rumble in from all directions, enveloping every crimson stone arc in their path, instantly graying them, the arcs' highest curves jutting up from the storm-sea like forlorn, color-stripped islands lost to the churning chaos.

A simmer of holy purpose burns through Vogel as he surveys the huge swarm of Mage soldiers on dragonback flying in from the West. Ready to join those already massing on the pinnacles of the giant, rocky arches—an unstoppable Mage force about to annex the entirety of the Central Continent to the Blessed Magedom.

A verse from *The Book of the Ancients* reverberates through Vogel's mind. *Nothing is beyond the Ancient One's reach. Not the lashing storm nor the moon nor the tides.*

Gnashing his teeth, Vogel sends another pulse of magic out toward the storms.

A returning wave of storming energy floods his body, his back arching in pained ecstasy. The silver gray fire he can sense blazing through his lines heats to darker flame as his Shadow power feeds on the elemental power in the desert trees and plants and wildlife being consumed then morphed into Shadow might.

The land increasingly purified of its vile Fae stain.

A Mage soldier on dragonback soaring over the consolidating storms catches Vogel's eye, the Mage's Shadowed water-and-wind aura breaking into hot steam against Vogel's fiery lines. The Mage angles down toward the pinnacle of Vogel's towering arch, his multi-eyed broken dragon touching down beside Vogel's in a *whoosh* of powerful wingbeats.

"Excellency," Damion Bane greets Vogel, his green eyes glinting with a flash of awe as they sweep over the slowly rotating sea of storm surrounding them, dark lightning and thunder forking and crashing through it. Like a steely hurricane pulled down to hug the land.

Brought to *heel*.

A slash of vicious ire breaches the awe in Damion's expression. "We're unable to break through the shield of magery that's been sent out over the desert Sublands," he admits. "Fallon and a squadron of our finest Level Five Mages are throwing everything they have at the shield-net, but she can't blast through even a small section of it. The Level Five power at play is impervious to elemental attack as it contains all five affinities wrapped in an Issani twinning spell. The source of the twinned spell is just under us. Their Smaragdalfar army is under us, too, trapped to the south. The army was moving north before we blocked their route."

Toward my Black Witch, Vogel seethes, lightning crackling through his lines.

"My runic crow spy sighted all this before it was cut down," Vogel murmurs as he peers north along with Damion, keeping his Wand aloft. "The Subland shielding is the work of Mavrik Glass and his whore, Gwynnifer Croft Sykes. It was cast using the corrupted Wand of Myth. They've escaped our attempt to cut them off from the Subland route to the north, as have the runic sorceress, Valasca Xanthrir, and the Icaral demon, Wynter Eirllyn."

Damion's mouth tightens, the unspoken filling the silence between them: the Heathen Wand headed straight toward Elloren Gardner.

Hatred spits through Vogel's internal fire as he contemplates how he underestimated the winged Elf-bitch, Wynter Eirllyn. How she fooled not only him, but the entirety of Alfsigroth, all of them mistaking her for a weak little slip of a woman. Easily broken. Easily destroyed. And now, she's wrested control of a Wand of Power and unleashed a Smaragdalfar army.

But their Resistance force has been fractured, as has the continent-wide Resistance, Vogel muses, the Icaral and her allies successfully cut off from their Subland army.

"Mavrik Glass and his whore's twinned magic poses a serious threat," Damion warns.

"For the moment," Vogel responds as he lowers his Wand, a more controlled lash of fire burning through his lines now. Because he knows how he'll eventually break through the Subland barrier. Knows how he can get through every defense Glass and his little whore and the Icaral demon can spell into being, even one cast by an evil Wand of Power.

And he knows how to keep them trapped underground until he's ready to overtake them.

Vogel angles his Shadow Wand down and murmurs a spell.

Gray fog jets from the Wand's tip and pierces through the mass of storms surrounding them. Vogel can sense his Shadow net fanning out over the Central Desert

Sublands—a net that will trap the twinned Mages as well as Wynter Eirllyn and her allies underground.

Two can play at the shielding game.

Satisfied, Vogel lifts his Wand. "Prepare for our invasion of the Northern Forest," he orders Damion before pulsing out a hard flare of Shadow power toward his Shadow-tethered Mage forces.

Damion gives a stiff nod, his green eyes flashing with brutal excitement before he growls out a command to his dragon and the multi-eyed beast takes flight.

Vogel's grip on his Wand firms, anticipation sizzling through his power, his path back to controlling the Black Witch imminent.

Elloren Vogel.

A remembrance of Elloren's Black Witch majesty suffuses his mind, his beautiful, green-glimmering witch atop that immense Shadow tree of her own conjuring, ready to smite the entire Eastern Realm.

"My destiny," Vogel murmurs as he peers north. He can still feel the heated echo of the charge that detonated through both his fire and Elloren's when his mouth pressed onto hers, *binding* them.

A flare of desire ignites, a firestorm searing through his lines.

Oh, yes, he'll have her again, that one kiss triggering a ferocious, bottomless *hunger*. He wants her underneath him, under his complete control. Wants to furiously thrust his fire into her until he burns all resistance out of her, their joined inferno powerful enough to scorch the corruption from his own body and soul, as well.

Purifying and transforming them both into an unstoppable weapon for the Holy Magedom.

Elloren can't win against his hold on her fastlines. He'll subdue her once more and transform her into a pure and righteously submissive vessel. He's rolled it over in his mind night after night, day after day—how she'll get on her hands and knees and kiss the ground before him. Thank him for making her whole and pure again.

A hot shiver runs down Vogel's spine at the thought of all that power bowing to him.

She was *almost his.*

His lips lift into a snarl as he inwardly curses that staen'en traitor Lukas Grey and the Icaral demon Yvan Guryev. It's their fault that Elloren is hurtling toward the Dryad's Northern Forest instead of standing here, by his side, under his complete control.

THE DRYAD STORM

Tensing his shoulders, he draws in the storm bands' power through his Wand, the desert's sanctified gray magic filling his lines.

The imperfect vessel can be purified, Vogel silently recites before he mounts the dragon beside him and sends out a mental command to the tethered beast. As if hit by a shock of pain, the dragon tenses its neck then fans out its wings, beats them down against the air and rises along with Vogel's army, all of them soaring above the spiraling sea of Shadow storm.

Vogel angles the Shadow Wand down and tugs on the storming mass beneath them.

Dragging it forward.

The sea of Shadow storm advances, moving toward the Northern Caledonian Mountains along with Vogel's airborne forces. Vogel smiles, his spite igniting to battle lust.

I'm coming for you, Elloren.

He narrows his gaze on the Dryad-green mountain range lining the horizon, the Northern Forest just beyond.

And lo, the Holy Ones shall smash through the corruption of the wilds and redeem them.

Emboldened by the sacred verse, Vogel draws in Shadow power, his path forward clear—to wrest the Black Witch and the corrupted Wand of Myth from the grip of the heathen Northern Forest. As he razes it and siphons up its elemental power while he consumes the Fae wilds of the Eastern Realm via his Shadow attack on the East's water.

The Central and Eastern Continent's Natural World about to fall to the Magedom's Shadow.

And the entirety of Dryad and Fae power about to fall with it.

CHAPTER
TWELVE

VU TRIN HUNT

Vang Troi, high commander
of the Vu Trin Forces

Wyvernguard, North Island command tower
Sixteen days after Xishlon

"The Black Witch's allies have all fled," the young Vu Trin soldier Heelyn stonily reports. "And the Resistance to Gardnerian Rule in the West has been smashed to pieces."

High Commander Vang Troi bites back a groan of frustration over Heelyn's unwelcome news as she stares the woman down from where they stand amidst a gathering of Vu Trin and potential allies in the Wyvernguard's circular command tower. A ring of large, arching windows surrounds them, offering a panoramic view of the rune-shielded Vo River, the devastated city of Voloi, and the gray skies above.

As her mind processes this information, Vang Troi coolly takes in Heelyn's straight-backed form, the young sorceress's weapons and uniform a mirror of Vang Troi's own, save for the metal high-commander headpiece gracing Vang Troi's brow, two curving, steel dragon horns rising from it.

Like the other Vu Trin in the room, both Vang Troi and Heelyn are garbed in a black military tunic and pants with a line of silver runic star weapons affixed diagonally across their chests, curved runic swords at their sides, the weapons' Noi runes glowing bright sapphire with a touch of emerald coursing over them from their anchoring Shadow-resistant Varg runes.

The Wyvernguard's commander, Ung Li, and three of the Vu Trin's surviving legion commanders wait silently for Vang Troi's response to Heelyn's report. Along with Queen Freyja Zyrr, the newly named and shockingly young monarch of the Amaz, and Clive Soren, head of the Keltish forces and former Western Realm Resistance leader.

Vang Troi notes that Queen Freyja is standing clear across the room from Clive. Two of Queen Freyja's stony-faced Queens Guard soldiers, Teel and Sorcha, bracket her, both of them glaring at Clive, looking hells-bent on wielding the huge runic axes strapped across their muscular backs against the sole man in the room.

Vo preserve us, Vang Troi inwardly grinds out, clear she's navigating the equivalent of a runic minefield trying to bring these varied groups together.

The East is devolving into chaos, with Southern Noilaan and the entirety of the Vu Trin navy embroiled in a war with the Selkies and other Ocean Peoples that her army can't get to because the entire area was runically domed off by two shields they can't break through, one cast by the Black Witch's ally Gareth Keeler, the other a dense Shadow net cast by Vogel over Gareth Keeler's shielding that blocked out their view into Southern Noilaan.

When Vang Troi ordered the Vu Trin's Asrai Water Fae Division south to attempt to break through the dual shielding and to fight against the Shadow sea weapon positioned to its south, she was shocked to learn that Fyordin Lir, one of the Vu Trin's most powerful Water Fae military advisers, had disappeared, all attempts at magically tracking him proving futile.

Powerful magic is clearly at play in his disappearance, and in the disappearance of all three Vu Trin Death Fae, including the spider-shifter Sylla Vuul, whose Deathkin webbing saved the Wyvernguard's North Tower.

Vang Troi's hands tighten on the hilts of the curved runic swords sheathed at her sides, her gaze flickering out of the tower's ring of windows toward the Shadow-smoking rubble of the Wyvernguard's leveled South Island. A gray dawn is breaking over the decimated Vo Mountain Range, their runic border wall being *slowly* rebuilt, Noilaan's shielding *gone*. The beautiful purple hue of Voloi's forests has been stripped away, only the moody blue coloration of the Asrai and Deathkin warded Vo River remaining. The cropland surrounding Voloi is now tinted as gray as the skies above, the whole world seeming polluted by Vogel's Shadow filth, the East's food supply in serious danger.

"Both the Lupine alphas are gone?" Vang Troi inquires, setting her penetrating gaze back on Heelyn, tension rife in the tower chamber's air.

Heelyn gives a grim nod. "Trystan Gardner is gone, as well. Along with Sagellyn

Za'Nor, Ra'Ven Za'Nor and others . . . every ally of the Black Witch has disappeared and been rendered untraceable by runic magery."

Vang Troi pivots her attention to Queen Freyja. "And your Dryad, Alder Xanthos?"

Freyja returns her hard look. "Gone and untraceable," she replies. "Along with a flock of giant Issani Saffron Eagles."

Vang Troi inwardly curses.

Oh, how we underestimated you, Elloren Gardner Grey. A shard of pain lances through Vang Troi's war-hardened heart over the brutal murder of so many Noi'khin and the destruction of the tiered city of Voloi, the dangerous Shadow pollution seeping into a wide swath of Noilaan's beautiful lands.

Never again will she so egregiously underestimate Vogel and the Black Witch.

A battle-ready simmer fills Vang Troi's center, her aura of runic sorcery sapphire bright, grounding her as she turns back to Heelyn. "Any word on the Icaral of Prophecy, Yvan Guryev?"

Heelyn nods in affirmation. "His fire is being tracked as we speak." The young sorceress glances toward the tower's ebony, dragon-embossed door.

"Show them in," Vang Troi directs.

Heelyn strides to the door, pulls it open, and steps back in silent invitation.

A woman of about Vang Troi's age sweeps into the room like a firestorm. Her green eyes are shot through with incandescently lethal golden flame, her long hair a blazing Lasair Fae red. She bears a striking resemblance to the Icaral of Prophecy, her angular features as stunning as they are formidable.

Yvan Guryev's part Fire Fae mother, Soleiya Guryev.

Every Vu Trin in the room, including Vang Troi, brings their fist to their chest in heartfelt military salute, Soleiya a highly revered figure in the East. Everyone in the country is cognizant of Soleiya's decades-long Resistance work and the sacrifices she made during the last Realm War, her Icaral husband, Valentin, cut down by the last Black Witch as he struck Carnissa Gardner down in turn.

Saving the East.

Six other crimson-haired, point-eared Lasair Fae stride into the room behind Soleiya, all of their eyes burning the same furious gold. Vang Troi can practically feel the scorching fire from across the room as she meets the gaze of one of them, an arrestingly attractive young Lasair woman.

Vang Troi places her immediately. *Iris Morgaine.*

Iris has been a major thorn in Vang Troi's side. Granted refuge in the East, she arrived only to rapidly fall in with a renegade contingent of Fire Fae set on annexing a section of Noilaan's northeastern territory for Lasair rule, successfully laying claim to a section of it. They're stunningly powerful, these Lasair, able to stave off every Vu Trin attempt to take them into custody.

"We welcome your alliance, Lasair'kin," Vang Troi carefully greets these most volatile of Fae'kin before meeting the fiery gaze of Soleiya Guryev. "I've been informed you are tracking your son, Yvan, through a link to his fire."

"I am," Soleiya affirms, her tone full of emotion. "My son is *alive*. The Crow Witch has abducted him." Vengeful tears glaze her eyes. "I can *sense* where he is through our matriarchal Lasair fire link." She levels her index finger toward the northeast, her gaze spitting a furious light. "After the Black Witch attempted to rip the wings from my son's body, she managed to get hold of him and pull him through a portal containing every strand of elemental power. I could sense the portal's magic swirling around his fire. He was caught in the portal's lag for *days*, but he's arrived in the Northern Forest."

Iris Morgaine steps forward, her eyes burning almost as bright as Soleiya's. "We're ready to rescue Yvan and slay the Black Witch," she snarls. "Mark us with Varg iron-protection runes. Grant us portal passage and dragon flight. And we'll take the witch down."

"I should have killed her long ago," Soleiya rages as a tear streaks down her cheek, her body trembling with a mother's undistilled fury. "I met her months ago in Keltania. She'd enthralled my son by then. I *knew* it, even as he was ignorant of it. I *knew* her for the fiend she was." Her gaze sweeps condemningly over the Vu Trin soldiers in the room. "I *never* wanted my son to be a weapon in this war. But now that Yvan has been thrust into it, be very clear. *I will war to save him.*" Soleiya thrusts up her palm, and a sphere of fire explodes to life and hovers over it, violently licking the air, the temperature in the tower room growing instantly, oppressively hot.

Battle-fire hot.

Iris Morgaine's mouth twists with rage. "The Black Witch helped a number of us get East, but I always held her suspect. And now we know what her true intention was all along—to gather us all here so that her Mage army could strike from the Vo Mountain Range and kill us *all*."

"So now we must strike *her* down," Vang Troi rejoins, scanning everyone assembled. "Along with everyone foolish enough to remain allied with her. But to achieve this, we *must* unite."

Commander Ung Li gestures her desire to speak, and Vang Troi nods her permission.

"A Western Wyvern horde attempted to slay the Black Witch," Ung Li states, "during the Battle for Voloi."

Vang Troi nods at the tall, spiky-haired commander. "Led by Naga the Unbroken's horde," she affirms. "We stand in alliance with them."

"And what of the Amaz?" Iris demands, her fiery gaze swinging toward Queen Freyja Zyrr with a heat that's so confrontationally charged, it could melt iron.

Queen Freyja meets Iris's domineering gaze with formidable calm, her eyes like twin blades, the dark runic tattoos on her hazel face only enhancing Freyja's aura of queenly might. *You're going to grow into this position quickly,* Vang Troi notes with guarded approval.

"The Mages have laid waste to our homeland," Queen Freyja levels at Iris in a low, implacable tone. "Murdered our women and daughters." She fixes her formidable gaze back on Vang Troi. "We will ally with you to kill the Black Witch. But in a female-only legion. My soldiers will not be sullied by proximity to men."

"You'd put that *first?*" Iris lashes back in a fury. "Over slaying the Black Witch and rescuing the *Icaral of Prophecy* from Vogel's grip?"

Freyja's guards stiffen, battle ready as they stare Iris and her Lasair allies down.

Inwardly cursing, Vang Troi takes in the fractured situation, the words of her deceased mentor, Chi Nam, edging into her mind: *Politics is the art of the possible.*

Vang Troi's gut tenses with grief over the loss of Chi Nam and regret over her mentor's disastrous final decision to help the Black Witch survive, as she curses *herself* over how she allowed so many of the Black Witch's allies into Noilaan and its Wyvernguard, as well as the Death Fae who refused to fully align with any army or land.

Still, the wisdom of Chi Nam's words remains relevant in this fraught moment. What's possible here might be messy, but coalition building is messy. And Vang Troi knows there might be room to negotiate.

She's well aware of Freyja Zyrr's hidden relationship with Clive Soren. Which means further compromise might well be on the table, unlike with the late Queen Alkaia, who Vang Troi greatly respected save for Alkaia's zealot-like inflexibility regarding men. But from her shocking choice of young Freyja as her successor, it's clear that Queen Alkaia saw the necessary direction of the future.

"We will deploy with a female-only combined force," Vang Troi declares, looking to Clive Soren. "Our coalition's male forces will remain stationed in the Eastern Realm, guarding the East with the bulk of our Vu Trin forces."

Clive stiffens then nods, and Vang Troi catches the intense, covert look that passes between him and Freyja.

"And what of Vo's Sacred Zhilin Stylus?" presses Commander Hung Xho, the bald portal sorceress's brown brow deeply furrowed. "Is it still in the Crow Witch's possession? She was the Zhilin's Bearer when I was with her in the Agolith."

"During the Battle for Voloi," Vang Troi replies, "the Black Witch was seen holding a gray wand. The glimpse was fleeting, but our forces did not spot Vo's Sacred Stylus on her." She peers at everyone assembled. "We *must* locate it. I've received intelligence that Vogel is intent on finding it, which means it is either dangerous or empowering to him." She inhales, jaw tensing. "It is clear now that Elloren Grey was never a true Bearer of the Zhilin—" her eyes flit to the Lasair "—or the Wand of Myth, as some in the West call it."

Iris spits out an irate sound, eyes burning. "*We* call it no such thing. It is the fabled Myyr'vhhyo Shard! Rightful amplifying tool of the *Lasair*!" Angry sounds of agreement rise up from the Lasair surrounding Iris.

Sweet Holy Vo, preserve us, Vang Troi grinds out in the back of her mind, but she beats back her resurgence of frustration.

"Regardless of the Shard-Stylus's true name," Vang Troi says, "the Black Witch was clearly not its Bearer, but its *kidnapper*. And now, we must *reclaim* it." Her stance tightens, military formal. "My allies, we are in a race against time to slay the Black Witch, rescue the Icaral of Prophecy, and take hold of both the Wand-Stylus of Myth and Vogel's Shadow Wand. If we fail in these tasks, not only the Eastern Realm, but the entirety of Erthia will fall to the Magedom's Shadow."

A potent silence descends. Most everyone in this room is old enough to remember the last Black Witch's sweep into the East and her cruel reign of fire. And Elloren Gardner Grey's attack on Voloi hammered home the horrific, inescapable point—Elloren's power dwarfs her grandmother's.

"The Prophecy's time is *here*," Hung Xho proclaims, and Vang Troi is hard-pressed to disagree. Yvan Guryev's prophesied triumph over the Black Witch is essential, not just for the survival of the East, but for all that is good on Erthia.

Vang Troi's gaze sweeps over those in the room, the path forward solidifying.

"Send a larger contingent of our most elite trackers after the Black Witch's allies. And prepare to portal northwest." She hardens her expression, growing predatorially focused. "We will meet Vogel's forces with storm and fury," she vows. "*Together*, we will fight them and hunt down the Black Witch. *Together*, we will slay Elloren Gardner Gray and rescue Yvan Guryev." Ferocity burns hot through her core of sapphire power. "And *together*, we will strike down Vogel and his 'Most Holy Magedom.'"

CHAPTER THIRTEEN

FOREST DIVINATION

Alder Xanthos

Warded cenote cavern, Vo Forest, north of Voloi
Sixteen days after Xishlon

"Elloren is no longer under Vogel's control," Alder Xanthos states before growing quiet, letting her words sink in.

Elloren's allies surround her in the cenote sinkhole's sheltered, belowground depths. Overcast light shines down through the circular, warded opening above. The cenote's underground lake is mirror-still beside them, reflecting the water-falling violet roots of the Noi Oak that rises like a sentinel from the cenote's upper edge.

Alder slides her hand over one of the oak's cascading roots, lifting her gaze toward the interconnected Alfsigr and Varg glamouring runes hovering over the cenote's entrance—runes to glamour the hole to appear, to those above, like a mass of stone and repel tracking spells. To defend against Vu Trin attack.

A military hunt is underway for every possible ally of the Black Witch. Alder's ability to summon and speak with eagles, including the small eagles of Eastern Realm, is the only thing that enabled her to evade Vu Trin and Amaz capture and quickly locate this hiding place of Elloren Gardner Grey's supporters.

The eagles of Noilaan have proved to be far better trackers than even the most elite Vu Trin.

Alder's Dryad rootlines abruptly seize, pulled taut, a vision from the tree root flowing in and overtaking her empathic mind, tree after tree being blasted to bits in explosions of Shadowfire as Vogel's forces attack the last remaining league of her Caledonian Forest in the Western Realm.

"*No . . .*" Alder rasps, devastation gripping hold of her lines. She shuts her eyes tight against the nightmare consuming her Forest, the Natural World being torn to shreds . . .

"Alder."

The kindness in Trystan Gardner's voice cuts through the agony, his gentle hand now on her shoulder. Trembling, Alder opens her eyes, the vision fading to reveal the angular green face of Elloren's younger brother, who is down on one knee beside her.

"My *Forest!*" Alder sputters to him as another vision blasts through her mind— images of terrified, burning animals, trees burning and *screaming* for her . . .

An aura of comfort flows in around her as the second vision fades, the energy warm and embracing. She looks up at the canopy of the cenote cavern's Noi Oak sentinel as the tree sends an aura of invisible branches to gently brush Alder's back and arms, the loving oak like a child caught up in a war, desperate to give comfort to a loved one. Which both shatters Alder's heart anew and stokes her courage.

Vogel will be coming for this new kindred Forest of mine too, she knows. *He'll be coming for this very tree . . .*

"Dryad." Diana Ulrich's low, commanding voice sounds, the Lupine coming down to one knee by her other side.

Alder pulls in a shuddering breath and meets the alpha's amber stare.

"Tell us what you know of Elloren," Diana bids, the fierce compassion in her tone a lifeline as the last screams of Alder's Caledonian Forest rip through her. Determined to fight back, Alder holds Diana's ferocious gaze, remembering what she overheard a Vu Trin soldier telling Vestylle and Alcippe soon after their arrival in the East—

The Lupine Diana Ulrich was a force of nature during the Battle for Voloi, ripping the heads off Mages and their broken dragons with unmatched fury. Slayed over a hundred of them. Nothing left but scattered pieces of their corpses . . .

Another Lupine kneels behind Diana—her mate, Rafe Ulrich—and Alder's tracery of Wyvern blood stirs.

It's *strong,* she scents, the mating bond that exists between these two alphas, as it always is with Lupines, like a shaft of molten-amber steel running between them, love burning bright in it. The power of that love is so compelling that when Diana places her hand on Alder's shoulder, Alder finds she's able to swallow back the edge of her wild grief and regain her voice.

"The Great Source Tree, III," she falteringly tells them, "it's broken Elloren

Gardner Grey's Shadow fasting." Her eyes slide to the amber gaze of another tower-ing Lupine, Andras Volya, his Amaz runic facial tattoos incongruous on a male face but comforting in their familiarity, being so similar to Alder's own. "Elloren is now both Dryad Witch and Forest Guardian," she tells them.

Elloren's allies trade looks of surprise.

"What is it you see?" Diana presses. A command to answer, but kindly leveled.

Alder grips a purple root spilling down from above, the entire Forest's mosaic of thought filling her mind. "The Forest has absorbed Elloren," she answers. She grows quiet once more, flooded by the sensation of a cataclysmic shifting of energy throughout the entire Forest Matrix of Erthia, all of it contracting toward a single point.

Elloren.

"What do you mean by 'absorbed'?" Trystan asks.

Alder closes her eyes and lets herself slip back into the Forest's mind's eye. "I see an image of Elloren the Forest Witch," she says. "Surrounded by branches. Roots flowing down from her feet. Green light sparking through her rootlines—"

"Rootlines?" Rafe cuts in. "Has the Forest imprisoned her?"

Alder opens her eyes to find Rafe's amber eyes glowing with intensity, his fists flexed, every muscle coiled, as if he's ready to rip through the entire Forest to find his sister.

"No," Alder clarifies as she struggles to maintain her link to the Forest's full aura, the Lupine alphas' air of command a difficult thing to think past. She closes her eyes once more and concentrates. "I'm piecing out more. The Great Proph-ecy . . . it's still written in the trees, but . . ." Her eyes bolt open, and she looks to Elloren's allies in great confusion. "The Forest has flipped its allegiance."

The black-haired, green-glimmering Lupine, Aislinn Ulrich, gasps, her amber eyes widening. "But that would set the Forest against Yvan—"

"The Prophecy is *rubbish*," Trystan cuts in. "We shouldn't be giving it any cre-dence, whatsoever."

"Can you read where Elloren is?" Sagellyn Za'Nor presses, her purple-hued expression tight with urgency as she clenches her wounded hands, chains of pain-dampening runes wound around them to assuage the bloodied gashes from her broken fasting. Sage's heavily armed mate, the Smaragdalfar monarch, Ra'Ven Za'Nor, stands beside her, his silver eyes intent.

"Elloren is in the Northern Forest," Alder states.

They're all silent, trading sober looks.

The Northern Forest.

Leagues and leagues away.

Another series of images flashes through Alder's mind, and she holds up a hand. "There is a man of fire in the Northern Forest . . . waiting for Elloren to emerge from the Great Tree . . . the prophesied Icaral the trees are aligning against—Yvan Guryev. And there's a flock of giant ravens and two Fae'kin traveling through a Dryad portal toward the Forest Witch's location . . . an Asrai Fae woman I know . . . Tierney Calix . . . and a Man of Death and Serpents."

A human-size spider emerges from the cavern's shadows, and Alder startles, recoiling as the spider swiftly scuttles toward them. Her breath caught in her chest, Alder watches as the great spider morphs into a petite, dark-hued woman with tight black curls, her posture almost demure, save for the extra six dark eyes set around her two main ones. *Sylla Vuul*, Alder registers, awe mingling with her fear—one of the three Wyvernguard Deathkin she overheard the Amaz speaking of.

"Viger is the Man of Death and Serpents you speak of," Sylla Vuul tells Alder, her voice's subterranean thrum sending a cool shiver down Alder's spine. "The giant crows," Sylla continues, "are Errilor Death Ravens. They have returned to align with the Forest Witch. I have read the reverberations of this bond-intension in the web matrix of my spider kindreds."

"Vogel will come for Elloren," Alder warns. "With an army the likes of which Erthia has never seen."

"Well, we'll be coming for the Magedom with our own army," Diana Ulrich snarls, exposing sharp, gleaming canines.

The fine hairs on the back of Alder's neck bristle.

Gray smoke abruptly tendrils across Alder's tree-vision, Elloren's allies whisked from sight as a more potent Forest-vision invades her mind.

Marcus Vogel—staring straight at her through her withering root connection to the destroyed Wilds of Amazakaraan. As he siphons their elemental power up into his Wand. His cruel mind touches Alder's, his slithering Shadow winding tight around her rootlines. The images of Elloren then Yvan then Shadow wrapped around a spiraling green-glowing wand blast through Alder's mind with agonizing force.

Alder cries out and wrests her hands from the purple root, falling back onto the cavern's stone. The terrifying connection snaps loose, her body trembling from it.

"I briefly linked to Vogel," she rasps. "He's not just going after Elloren and the Wilds."

"What else does he seek?" Wrenfir Harrow demands, the Mage's kohl-rimmed, spider-tattoo-bracketed green eyes hard as granite.

Alder meets Wrenfir's furious gaze. "Vogel seeks a Wand of Power," she answers. "The green Wand-Stylus crafted from a branch of the Great Source Tree, III. The Verdyllion."

"The Sacred Wand-Stylus of Myth," the bespectacled Kelt, Jules Kristian, comments. "Known to every culture on Erthia by a unique name." He exchanges a pointed look with Mage Lucretia Quillen beside him, and Alder's empathy is momentarily distracted by the sensation of Lucretia's invisible water aura ardently encircling Jules.

"Elloren had possession of the Zhilin Wand-Stylus," Kam Vin notes from where she stands beside her silent sister, Ni Vin, lines of Vu Trin silver stars strapped across the sisters' black uniformed chests.

"It's unlikely Elloren has it still," Andras postulates, "or Vogel would have taken hold of it when he had control of her."

"Wherever its location," Alder says, "Vogel is coming for this Wand-Stylus. And he's coming for both Elloren and Yvan. He wants to force the Prophecy."

"We need to get to Elloren and Yvan and the Wand-Stylus before Vogel does," Jarod Ulrich insists, his tone decided, his hand tight around Aislinn's, unbreakable love swirling around them both.

The young Mage, Thierren Stone, steps toward her. "Vogel will go after the Dryads with Elloren and Yvan," he warns, his severe features drawn with an ever-present tortured look. "I'm ready to go West and fight with the surviving Tree Fae."

Compassion rises in Alder—one touch of Thierren's hand was all it took for her to read the unassuageable grief inside him over the capture and certain death of his beloved, the Urisk woman Sparrow Trillium, lost to him when the Vo Mountain Range exploded around her. But Alder can also read Thierren's single-minded willingness to give his life for any Dryads that might remain in the Northern Forest, due to having witnessed a massacre of the Tree Fae during his brief time as a Mage soldier.

"Vogel's army will be on dragonback," Fain Quillen, Lucretia's brother, cautions. The powerful Water Mage exchanges a somber look with his horned life partner, the Zhilon'ile Wyvern-shifter Sholindrile Xanthile.

"That gives them a huge logistical advantage," Sholindrile agrees.

"You've dragon flight," Sholindrile's nephew, Vothendrile Xanthile, offers Trystan. Vothe flexes his onyx wings, threads of lightning forking through them, the silver tips of his dark, spiked hair catching the light.

He wants to claim Trystan Gardner as his mate, Alder can't help but scent, Vothendrile and Trystan's mutual attraction one of the strongest she's ever encountered.

"We'll need access to more flight than just Sho and Vothe," Rivyr'el Talonir challenges, the pale Elf's rainbow-glitter decorated eyes sparkling in the silvery light.

Alder tips her head toward the cenote's rune-warded opening and sends out a call with her mind. Powerful wings beat down on the air above, and her kindred flock of Giant Saffron Eagles soars down through the cenote's oval opening, Fireling in the lead, the mammoth wingeds alighting all around.

Fireling, the Great Eagle of the Agolith, steps forward and touches her forehead to Alder's, flooding her with the entire flock's love and willingness to *fight*.

Alder reaches up to stroke Fireling's huge head, feeling the arc of destiny sweeping down to gather them all up in its arms. She turns to Elloren's allies, readiness to do battle for the Forest sizzling through her. "We'll give you flight," she offers.

Rivyr'el shoots her a wide, dazzling smile as he reaches into his alabaster tunic's pocket and draws something out. He unfurls his pale fingers to display two sapphire-rune-marked, fully charged portal stones. "These can speed us there," he offers. "They're linked into the magic of a powerful Vu Trin sky portal."

"How in the name of Vo on High did you manage to get hold of *those*?" Kam Vin marvels.

Rivyr'el jabs his alabaster thumb at Bleddyn Arterra, the tall, broad green-hued Urisk woman grinning conspiratorially at him.

"Turns out," Bleddyn crows, "Rivyr'el, Or'myr Syll'vir, and I have a talent for pilfering from the Vu Trin military."

"Well, all right, then," Rafe Gardner says, giving them both a dangerous, teeth-baring smile. "Let's go find Yvan and my sister."

CHAPTER FOURTEEN

HORDE

Raz'zor the Unbroken

Top of the Northern Voloi Mountain Range, north of Voloi
Sixteen days after Xishlon

Raz'zor is bowed down, his head lowered to the purple-veined, isolated cavern at the top of the Voloi Mountain Range, Ariel Haven beside him. His battle-scarred wings are fanned out in supplication, as he and Ariel wait for Naga the Unbroken's answer to their Erthia-shattering request. Only the chill wind breaks the silence as Raz'zor holds his position, stridently ignoring the wounds the Mages lashed across his scaled hide when they briefly captured him along with Or'myr and his horde mate, Elloren.

Before Lukas Grey blew the top off the Vo Mountain Range.

Now, Naga the Glorious Unbroken One, Liberator of Dragon'kin, stands before him and Ariel in all her gleaming, onyx glory. Naga's horde of sixteen unbroken Western Wyverns encircle them, the Wyverns' black scales gleaming like opals even in the East's Shadowed light, their eyes a uniform, golden blaze.

"You ask much, unbroken ones," Naga hisses in the Wyvern tongue before drawing her head back, two tendrils of smoke rising from her nostrils.

The horde's combined heat sizzles through the air, and Raz'zor's vermillion fire leaps with yearning to be bonded to it. But still, a hot tension remains. Because as much as he yearns to be part of Naga's horde, he can't abandon his chosen horde mates. His bonded ones.

Elloren and Yvan.

Raz'zor remembers how hastily he had to horde-bond to Yvan to give the Icaral the power to track Elloren through that bond. Raz'zor remained behind, to surrender himself to Naga, heal from his wounds, and, in a leap of ferocious faith, work to gain the trust of this powerful horde in the hope of bringing them to his small horde's side.

That quest has proven to be prescient.

Raz'zor was hit by the change in Elloren just after dawn—hit by the sudden greening of her fire, a line of verdant flame shooting straight through their vermillion fire connection as she was blasted free of Vogel's corruption by a Tree of Power, a vision of the Great Tree flashing through his fire.

"You ask us to horde to the *entire Prophecy*?" Naga hisses, her eyes like two suns. "Elloren Gardner has been overtaken. She is Vogel's Black Witch . . ."

"She does not *belong* to him!" Ariel snarls, the golden fire in her eyes sparking with a force to match Raz'zor's own flame, the raven kindred on her shoulder ruffling its feathers.

"My horde sistren is no longer the Black Witch of her vile people," Raz'zor growls with blistering vehemence. "She has risen from the rooted ground as the Dryad Witch!"

The fire in Naga's eyes intensifies, and Raz'zor's internal fire gutters, his whole world suspended in the radiating heat of Naga's volcanic internal flame.

"Then come forward, unbroken one," Naga hisses to Raz'zor, her eyes narrowing to molten slits. "Come forward, and I will read your fire."

Raz'zor's internal fire rears, vermillion-hot. His pulse a powerful hammer, he approaches the Great Unbroken One. Stilling before her, he tilts his horned head, exposing the side of his long neck to Naga the Unbroken.

Naga closes in on Raz'zor, opens her jaws and clamps them down around the base of Raz'zor's neck.

Raz'zor stiffens as the tips of her sharp teeth press in, then *puncture*.

An oceanic roar of golden fire races through Raz'zor. He shudders from the force of it, Naga's glorious heat singeing through his every vein. Both of them still as Naga's fire whips around Raz'zor's power and she reads his vermillion, green, gold, and purple fire—reads the essence of Yvan the Unbroken and the Dryad Witch in it. Then ripples her fire along Raz'zor's slender line of purple flame, gifted to him by his runic liberator, Or'myr Syll'vir—the Sorcerer of Stones.

Raz'zor waits, breath suspended, as Naga's fire whips outward toward her entire horde, her teeth still lightly piercing his hide. He can feel the heated conversation happening through their horded fire, the flaring of flame from different horde-points leaping toward her, including Ariel's sparking-hot advocacy for Elloren, followed by the darting connection of Naga's answering flame.

Stillness descends once more, tension high as Raz'zor waits. And waits.

Naga's jaw suddenly clamps down harder, her teeth fully impaling.

Raz'zor inhales as Naga's golden fire bolts into him, his vision flashing to molten gold as the fire of the entire horde blazes through his core. Flame breaks out all over his ivory scales—world-melting, glorious flame, his heart expanding to the point that he fears he may be undone by joy as Naga and the horde not only accept him, but send their horde link out toward his bite-bonded Witch and Icaral. All of them soon to be bonded as *horde. Naga's* horde.

Naga's mouth unclenches, and Raz'zor shivers as the flame on his scales is drawn into his core of fire. He can feel Naga's horde mark burning at the base of his neck, a twin to the bright, glowing gold mark on Ariel, the raying fire mark like a glorious, longed-for star. He can sense the invisible, reverberating line of hot aura fire pulsing out to Elloren and Yvan, ready to fuse them to Naga's powerful horde once it spans the great distance to reach them.

Overcome by a mingling of hot emotion and pride, Raz'zor drops to the stony ground, wings splayed out before the entire horde, as he sends out his powerful vow. *Fealty.*

The strength of the entire horde flares, their combined fiery alliance rolling through him, a euphoric burn tightening the long column of Raz'zor's throat.

Rise, free dragon, Naga sends into his mind, her eyes ablaze with golden Wyvern-fire. *Rise like the strong Wyvern'kin shifter you are. Unfettered.*

Confusion over the word *shifter* darts through Raz'zor's joy as he remains prostrate before Naga the Unbroken. *I cannot shift to human*, he sends out to her and his entire horde, thrilling to their newly minted mind connection even as his confusion churns. *We are, all of us, locked in dragon form through cruel magicks set down on Western Wyvern'kin during the last Realm War. None of us full Wyvern'kin. None of us true shifters.*

Naga smiles, affectionate amusement shivering through her flame. *Look to me, brave one*, she charges, and Raz'zor does, catching the sly gleam in her searing eyes. She lifts her chin, her heat rising, all amusement whisking away. *The Wyverns of the East have broken our bonds. Behold our reclaimed power.*

Naga the Unbroken's whole form contracts, and Raz'zor's eyes widen as the midnight scales of her head morph into onyx skin, her large dragon form constricting into a tall, muscular human frame. Her lips full and gilded. Her vertically slit pupils set in fiery irises, and her short hair tightly curled and edged with fiery gold. Her scaled hide has turned to scaled armor, their horde's golden starmark fire-branded on her side where the Mage *M* used to be. One of her onyx ears is sharply pointed, her other ear ripped off by the vile Mage Damion Bane. Her horns a glorious, gleaming obsidian.

Naga the Unbroken fans out her wings then blasts a shock wave mind-charge to their unified horde that sends heat scorching through Raz'zor's spine. The horde mates surrounding them suddenly shift to onyx-hued human form as well, the fire-star horde mark emblazoned at the base of their necks. Raz'zor's multihued fire sings through his veins with ravening elation, as he's overcome by the sense of his full power unfurling.

"Shift, Raz'zor the Unbroken," Naga the Unbroken hisses, her voice serpentine and triumphant. "Claim power over both your dragon form and your human Laz-ra'xor state."

Raz'zor grits his sharp teeth and draws in the static, shifter energy coursing through his spine. His limbs tighten, and his pale body contracts with bone-aching force, his wings splaying stiffly out . . . and he finds himself suddenly on his hands and knees.

In the form of a man.

Stunned, Raz'zor rises with serpentine smoothness, thrilling to this new way of consolidating his vermillion flame in such a compact form. He can feel the heightened fire burning in his eyes, the tight sting of his horns against an unfamiliar scalp, strands of short, silken hair tousled around his temples, the nape of his neck.

Raz'zor focuses in on Yvan's and Elloren's green and golden flame connections to him, their fire intermingled with his, spitting through his core. His pull to them directional.

Our horde'kin are northwest, Raz'zor thinks out to his new beloved sistren and brethren.

Naga, Ariel, and the entire horde nod in affirmation, horded Wyvern'kin able to track the location of every horde'kin. All of them separate, yet part of a unified whole.

Naga sweeps her golden eyes over her unbroken ones before swiftly shifting back to full dragon form. She breathes a line of fire through her nostrils, her expression turning raptorial.

We fly, free Wyverns, she sends out to them. *We will journey to the Northern Forest.*

THE DRYAD STORM

To find Elloren the Unbroken and Yvan Guryev, our Icaral'khin. And to battle Vogel and his Shadow horde alongside them.

A collective ferocity rises in the air, the horde's linked fire mounting in potency, and Raz'zor thrills to it as they all move to the cavern's large mouth and shift to dragon form once more, save for his Icaral horde mate, Ariel the Unbroken.

A slice of emotional pain singes through Ariel's fire and Raz'zor's gaze snaps to hers, catching her feral look of frustration to be so firmly anchored in human form. An unbearable yearning is spearing through her fire that Raz'zor understands on an intimate level. The yearning to be fully dragon.

His heart aching for her, Raz'zor joins Naga and their entire, gathered horde as they send out a hot rush of bolstering fire to Ariel. Sparks light all over Ariel's wings, and she shudders as the yearning in her fire whips through them all with tortuous force.

Someday, unbroken one, Naga sends out to Ariel. *Someday, you will rise in full dragon form. Your true form. Have faith, fierce one.*

Ariel holds Naga's flaming stare for one tortured moment, but then her fire surges, whipping through the horde's. She flicks her sparking wings defiantly out to their full span and lets loose a teeth-baring growl. Raz'zor's own growl bursts forth as the entire horde roars out their approval through the horde bond in sound and in flame. A unified army of fangs and claws, muscle and fire. *Shadow-burning* fire.

Naga roars out a battle cry and throws down her wings, and they take to the sky as one, Ariel's raven soaring beside her, the mountaintop air deliciously cold against Raz'zor's fire-hot wings. They soar over the huge Vo River, then north over grayed Vo Forest, their horde taking on a V formation, Naga the Unbroken in the lead. Ariel and Raz'zor exchange a fiery look of alliance, and they all blast through the unnaturally bunched gray clouds and spear forward like huge arrows toward the Vo Forest hiding place of Elloren's allies, a location Raz'zor is aware of through his connection to Or'myr's line of purple fire.

We're coming, Dryad Witch, Raz'zor vows as their horde fans their wings out as one, their combined fire rapidly heating to a churning inferno filled with one unified will.

To save the Dryad Witch and the Icaral of Prophecy before Vogel can take hold of them.

And to burn the Magedom to *ash*.

CHAPTER FIFTEEN

VO GUARDIANS

Tierney Calix

Northern Forest
Eighteen days after Xishlon

Tierney watches, transfixed, as Yvan and Elloren draw each other into a passionate kiss beneath the Great Ironwood Tree, III. The giant raven beside her shivers, Tierney's palm pressed to the great bird's onyx feathers, as Elloren and Yvan *ignite*.

The conflagration enveloping Yvan and Elloren blazes gold, then . . . *green*.

The backflow of their magic's green aura blasts through Tierney's rising water power, the surrounding world briefly tinting with the color. The Great Tree's planet-strong magic pulses through it all, its verdant mist flowing outward to enfold the surrounding Dryads and giant ravens and kindred animals as well as both Tierney and Viger, who's standing behind her. A buzzy static still tingles over Tierney's skin from her Dryad-portal journey here with Viger and the giant ravens.

The Great Tree's mist flows into Tierney, a sudden craving for the Natural Balance overtaking her, filling her with vertigo as she's swept up in the unmooring sensation of the whole of Erthia tipping off-kilter, desperately needing to be righted, her water magic taking a swirling turn for deep-water *dark*.

Abruptly hyperaware of Viger's primordial magic pulsing against her back, Tierney stiffens against the urge to let her magic fall into his, the memory of his all-consuming Death Fae kiss quickening her breath.

The green-tinted world shudders into a darker hue, and she turns to find Viger *right there*, his horns up, his midnight eyes intent on hers, as if he's caught up in the same memory, the palpable flare of his low-resonating, primal energy deepening her pulse.

She swallows as a phantom-caress of Viger's living Darkness traces her lips, the

Great Tree's powerful aura swirling through both his thrall and her water aura, intensifying the potency of their attraction.

As if the whole of Erthia *wants* them to fall into each other and fully join their magic.

Asrai . . . Viger's rattled voice shivers through her, achingly resonant.

"What magic is this?" Tierney wonders aloud as she holds Viger's stare, the feral current rising between them like blackened water crashing against a dam that Tierney yearns to *break*.

On instinct, she grasps hold of Viger and pulls him close at the same time that his strong hands take hold of her and he fully wraps his thrall around her, her heart tripping over itself as he draws her into a kiss and she's enveloped in a swirl of his intoxicating Darkness.

A moan escapes Tierney, the darkening scene wavering and growing blurred as the Forest and the Great Tree and everyone surrounding them is overtaken by Viger's deep-night thrall.

Tierney arches against him, all rational thought swept away as they go skidding, rapids-fast, into a whirlpool of pure, magical *want*.

Give me all your fears, Viger shivers through her mind as he deepens the kiss, gravity giving way as Tierney surrenders to the swooping sensation of dropping down with him into Erthia's center. Trembling with want, she opens her mouth to him, opens herself up to his flickering, purple tongue as it twines around hers in an entrancingly serpentine way that has heat curling through her body, the intoxicating motion of his tongue hinting at the things he might be capable of if she joined with him fully.

Sweet holy gods.

A ravenous energy enters his kiss, and an undertow of her darkening water power breaks loose to capture them both.

Viger shudders against her as they lapse into a frenzy, as if desperate to meld power, their kiss turning devouring as gravity gives way, the two of them now prone and submerged in Tierney's dark waters, waves whooshing around them.

A sense of Tierney's Vo River bond abruptly rises, deep in her core, then gives a magic-upending *pull*.

Shock flashes through both her aura and Viger's as they liquefy, the two of them suddenly flowing through the aquifers under the Northern Forest, racing southeast through nature's watery Matrix, pulled by Tierney's tether to her kindred Vo River, the tether now startlingly and fully bound to another power . . .

Viger's thrall.

Tierney's natural sense of Erthia's waterways blurs as their speed increases, their fused auras funneling, flowing, and switchbacking through underground waterways, then up through countless aboveground tributaries, rivers, and streams.

Before sloshing to a sudden halt.

Abruptly, they shift to solid form, still caught up in Viger's Darkness, their bodies wrapped around each other, the two of them lying on what Tierney immediately senses is the Vo River's damp, sandy riverbank, at least a league upstream from Voloi . . .

Dizzy with vertigo, Tierney blinks, Viger's Darkness receding to reveal an unnaturally gray twilight. Viger is on top of her, their limbs entangled, his tongue flickering against her neck as they lie there entwined.

At Fyordin Lir and Or'myr Syll'vir's feet.

With a stinging bolt of alarm, Tierney takes in Fyordin's expression of burgeoning fury and the explosion of purple lightning in Or'myr's green eyes.

Before she can voice her protest, Or'myr and Fyordin launch themselves at Viger and haul him off her, Fyordin's water aura rushing out to lash around Tierney with protective force. Viger wrests himself from their grip in a blur, horns up, dark claws snapping out as he thrusts his palms forward.

A sonic *boom* splices through Tierney's ears as an arc of Viger's power blasts from his palms and punches both Or'myr and Fyordin backward through the air.

They hit the riverbank, and Tierney flinches, but they're back on their feet in a flash, Or'myr pulling a wand and Fyordin conjuring a roiling ball of water above his palm.

"Stop!" Tierney cries as she hurls herself between Or'myr, Fyordin, and Viger.

"Release her from your thrall!" Or'myr growls at Viger, his eyes spitting purple lightning as he levels his wand at the Death Fae.

"I'm not under his thrall!" Tierney counters in an unfortunate shriek. "If anything, he might be a bit under mine!"

"You dare summon *Death*?" Viger booms at Or'myr and Fyordin, his disturbingly low-pitched voice pulsing in from all sides, every hair on Tierney's body rising, the twilight world strobing Dark with his primordial power.

Ridiculously unintimidated, Fyordin and Or'myr take a confrontational step *toward* him.

"Why are you linked to her, *Deathkin?*" Fyordin demands as he readies a hurricane level of power in his suspended ball of water. "I can feel your incursion into our Vo bond! We summoned *Tierney* here. *Not* you." His storming eyes flick up and down Viger. "What have you *done* to her?"

"He didn't do *anything* to me," Tierney snaps, swiping her hand at Viger. "And I can handle his thrall!"

Viger swivels his gaze to hers, eyes gone fully Dark.

A single pulse of his power sends Tierney's thoughts careening, the world flashing to black, a chill, claw-sharp warning racing down her spine, his unspoken message clear—*No, in fact, you really can't handle my thrall.*

He's holding back, Tierney realizes. *He's been holding his power back all along.*

Viger turns and squints at Fyordin, twin black snakes now looped around his shoulders. The serpents let out a hiss that seems to come from everywhere at once, and Tierney is momentarily lost to the siphoning sensation of Viger reading the full extent of Fyordin's and Or'myr's protective fear pertaining to her, his power strengthening against it.

"Tierney and I are now linked," Viger states in a bone-resonating tone, his Darkness consolidating into ropy lines of black smoke, suspended around them both. "Bound by our Xishlon kiss."

Shock explodes through Tierney, every last trace of intimidation falling away. *"Bound?"* she sputters.

"Wait," Fyordin exclaims, outrage gleaming in the Vo-hued eyes he's locked with hers, "you took the *Death Fae* as your *Xishlon'vir?*"

Tierney gapes at Fyordin, bristling at the ire in his tone. But the angry response clamoring in her throat lodges tight as she takes in the betrayal flashing through Fyordin's gaze.

"Tierney," Or'myr says with lethal calm, his eyes narrowed on Viger, the threat of violence flashing in them, his wand still leveled, "are you certain you're acting under your own free will?"

Tierney inwardly curses. "I am," she admits, a fitful storm cloud forming above her head.

Or'myr eyes Viger warily, seeming wholly unconvinced as Tierney's rain starts to fall. Or'myr's eyes flick toward hers, his voice tight when it comes. "May I ask, approximately, *when* on Xishlon that this kiss took place?"

Chagrin slams down, Tierney's chest stiffening against it as she remembers how she slid that Xishlon'lure necklace around Or'myr's neck. And how much she wanted to kiss *him*. To be with *him*. And how crushed she felt when they did kiss and his lightning aura sent that unbearable shock of pain through her lips.

"Before Vogel's invasion," she rasps. "I kissed Viger soon after I kissed you, *all* of it of my own free will."

She can feel the sudden press of Viger's penetrating stare as well as the jealous disturbance sputtering through Fyordin's water aura, a pained slash of violet lightning striking through Or'myr's green eyes.

"Hold up," Fyordin demands, his storming power barely contained now, a scandalized look on his face. "You took them *both* as your Xishlon'virs?"

Tierney's temper snaps its leash. "That's right," she bites out, her rain beginning to sheet down, thunder rippling through her enlarging cloud. "I took them *both* as my Xishlon'virs. And you know what, Fyordin? *None* of this matters right now!"

"Oh, it matters," Or'myr rejoins, his flashing green eyes fixing on Viger like twin blades. "Did you fully inform her what kissing you *means*?"

Viger's snakes hiss at Or'myr as Viger's horns elongate, forming sharper points than Tierney has yet seen on them. Angled threateningly toward Or'myr.

"What does it mean, Viger?" Tierney demands, undaunted by his spiky horns.

"It *means*," Or'myr cuts in, "that he can enter your dreams now. And he can infiltrate your mind through your fears. Isn't that right, Viger?"

Viger hisses, a larger portion of his thrall breaking free to encircle Tierney in a powerful whirl of dark mist just as Fyordin hurls out his invisible water aura to lash around her and batter against Viger's power . . . and then, incredibly, purple lightning forks through all of it.

Tierney's temper turns cyclonic.

Gritting her teeth, she balls her fists and swipes her arms outward, releasing a huge blast of her own power's aura.

Their magic explodes, her magic forcing theirs back as her rain sheets down with pummeling force.

They all gape at her, even Viger's snakes seeming a bit stunned by her magical outburst.

"I said, this isn't *important!*" Tierney growls, lips rain-slicked. "I don't care if you can *all* invade my dreams and infiltrate my fears! Maybe I took a hundred Xishlon'virs!" Fyordin draws back, eyes wide. "Maybe I kissed everyone who crossed my path on Xishlon!" she exclaims. "*None* of that matters right now!"

THE DRYAD STORM

"Yes it does, Asrai!" Fyordin booms, a storm spitting to life over his own head as he levels a finger at Viger. "You disappearing with . . . *him*, matters! Because I've needed you for *eighteen straight days* and couldn't find you!"

Eighteen straight days?

Panic rears. Tierney thrusts her hands out then slams her palms down. Her rainstorm falls along with Fyordin's, clouds meeting earth and instantly turning into mist twining up from the riverbed. Her gaze sweeps up toward the unnaturally gray sky, and she zeroes in on the gauzy half-moon in the darkening twilight where a full purple Xishlon moon hung what seems like only the night before.

The world tilts from the force of her disorientation, and Tierney's eyes snap toward the Shadow-free surface of the Vo River, the Shadow-smoking, half-decimated Vo Mountain Range just beyond. The runic ward-net she and Viger placed over the entire Vo River to keep magic out of it is still blessedly in place, their runes rippling against its waters. The invading Mages and their broken dragons and other nightmarish Shadow creatures—she can't spot them anywhere. It's as if the skies have been stripped clear of them.

Eighteen straight days . . .

"My . . . my family . . ." Tierney stammers.

"I checked on them," Or'myr reassures her. "They're fine and sheltering in the Sublands."

Her thoughts spin. "We went through a Dryad portal . . ." she starts, eyes still pinned on the Vo.

"Which are *slow as pine tar*," Or'myr rigidly supplies. "Alder Xanthos surmised as much. She read your location in the trees."

Tierney's rattled gaze swings to Or'myr's drenched form, his flashing eyes. She takes in the emerald Varg color-fixing rune on the side of his glistening purple neck, there to hold his color against Shadow. A type of rune that takes *days* to fabricate . . .

Portal lag, Viger hisses into her mind, and her hackles rise over the potent clarity of his voice right in the center of her head.

She shoots him an acid glare, and Viger gives her an unrepentant look in return that sends a chill through her, whatever ardent emotion there was in him in the Northern Forest now gone. Replaced by that impenetrable Death Fae veneer. But there's no time to think too deeply on any of it as a fuller clarity of exactly what's happened descends—

The Dryad portal she and Viger traveled through with the flock of giant ravens contained a huge lag. And then, not long after they arrived in the Northern Forest on the heels of Elloren and Yvan, Or'myr and Fyordin figured out a way to pull her back to the East through the Vo River bond she shares with Fyordin.

And Viger was drawn back with me, she pieces together, *through some Death-magic binding in his kiss.*

"Why did you pull me back?" Tierney shakily demands of Or'myr and Fyordin, her anger sliding into overwhelming concern in response to the tidal energy running through Fyordin's aura.

"Vogel is going after the East's waterways," Fyordin growls. "He attacked the Salish Ocean with a huge mass of Shadow that's making contact with the Southern Vo River, and the shielding you set down won't hold for long against it." He glances south, eyes storming. "I need to more powerfully shield our River to protect its southern waters. But I can't cast spells into the Vo because you warded it against all magical incursion. Working with *him*." He shoots Viger another furious look, maelstrom intense.

Her alarm exploding, Tierney abandons them all and rushes into her Vo, water sloshing around her legs. She throws out her arms and dives headfirst into the River, her beloved Vo's cool waters closing around her in an impassioned embrace, a school of silvery fish affectionately brushing by.

Tierney glides toward her River's center and arrows down to the Vo's bed, immediately sensing that the River's power is braced defensively against an incoming threat. She splays out her arms, closes her eyes and meets with the riverbed, pressing her body against its soft, wet earth.

Flashes of images accost her mind.

A Void sea.

The dark, raised mass of it looming at the Vo River's southern base. Multi-eyed kraken and other grotesque, Shadow-elongated sea animals and flying Shadow sea demons ready to rush in with the sea to terrorize Noilaan.

But then . . . the rise of a wall of monumental, storming water magic, battling back the Shadow sea to hold it at bay. The water magic linked to a young man who is part Selkie, part Mage . . .

Gareth Keeler.

Shock flashes through Tierney, her focus suddenly whiplashed away from the South and toward the North by some other force, the images not coming from her River this time . . .

. . . but from her *kelpies.*

Tierney's every muscle goes taut, her bond to her kelpies abruptly shot through with vivid alarm as Tierney is filled with the awareness of them bound in the North somehow, sending out flare upon flare of distress to her for *days,* desperately searching for her to no avail.

Her throat tightens as images of what her kelpies are witnessing in the Vo River's northernmost reaches blast through her mind . . .

Gray Shadow curling above the Vo's northern waters. Ready to choke the life out of water and fish and plants and surrounding trees as it siphons up the Vo's elemental power, the Vo-protecting wards she and Viger extended there encased in Shadow and rapidly graying . . .

Terror spikes through Tierney, and she thrusts herself up from the riverbed, breathing in gulp after heaving gulp of water. She's sensed this Shadow power before, when Elfin Marfoir assassins came for Wynter Eirllyn.

But now it's coming for her *River.*

A scream straining to tear from her throat, Tierney darts up toward the Vo's surface and breaks through. Water power surging, she swims rapidly back to shore, another storm cloud bursting from her and expanding overhead, rain spitting over this entire swath of Vo and riverbank.

"Vogel's forces are about to break through our Vo warding!" she cries out as her feet meet land and she looks to Viger's, Or'myr's, and Fyordin's rain-slicked forms. Pausing waist-deep in the Vo, she meets Viger's solid black gaze. "Our wards are decaying. Vogel's forces are getting ready to send a Shadow mass into my River's northernmost reaches. What's happening in the South . . . it's part of a two-pronged attack on the Vo. We need to get *North.* We need to strike this magic down!"

Viger bursts into dark mist and Fyordin morphs into water, and then the two of them are suddenly right there, beside her, waist deep in the Vo as Or'myr launches himself toward her, splashing through the water until he, too, stands by her side.

"*Read my fears!*" Tierney cries to Viger, gripping his pale wrist.

Viger stiffens at the contact, an unsettling shiver of his Darkness passing through her.

Undaunted, she tightens her grip on him. "Read them *all!*"

Viger's brow tenses, his eyes going half-lidded as a shudder passes through his body. His eyes snap fully open, and his otherworldly gaze turns knowing. Tierney almost draws back from the way he's looking at her as he brushes her fear, his purple tongue flickering out, forked, as if tasting it on the very air. He grimaces, stretching black lips over elongating teeth that he snaps once, as if he's seeking to bite the fear out of her.

"You *see*?" Tierney implores, her heart thundering with fear for her Vo.

I see, Asrai, he answers in her mind, dread lacing his words.

Tierney lets go of Viger and rounds on Fyordin, her urgency reaching a fever pitch. "We need to flash through the waters and get to the Northern Vo. *Now!*"

"*Not alone, Asrai*," Viger hisses, grabbing hold of *her* this time, claws digging in.

Furious lightning flashes through Tierney's storm above. "Unhand me, Viger," she growls, ready to throw her full tempest at him.

"You need more power," he growls back. "*Death* power. Vogel's forces will *destroy* you."

"They'll destroy *all of you*," Or'myr tersely interjects, shooting Viger a cutting glare. "You're all Fae. Mark my words, they'll be ready for you. With *iron*. Which I can easily subdue." He unsheathes his purple, gem-encrusted wand. "Geomancer," he throws down in challenge. Like a leveled weapon. "I can subdue all stones and metals."

"You can't travel as fast as us!" Tierney cries at Or'myr. "It would take *days* for you to get that far north! There's no time! The Shadow is about to *tear my River apart*!" She looks to Fyordin, her water aura churning with desperation. "We need a Noi portal to get Or'myr north with us! We need to go to the Vu Trin!"

"We *can't* go to the Vu Trin," Or'myr shoots back. "Why do you think we're here in an isolated area above Voloi, instead of *in* Voloi? The Vu Trin are hunting down *every last one of Elloren's allies*."

Or'myr quickly outlines the cenote cavern hiding spot and portal stones he helped Elloren's allies obtain and how he briefly encountered Alder there before he aided them in portaling to the Northern Forest. Afterward, he returned here to help Fyordin draw Tierney back East.

So they could all find a way to keep Vogel from overtaking Noilaan via the Vo River.

Tierney's mouth drops open as she listens, her heartbeat quickening over this turn of events. She looks to Fyordin to find his eyes a raging storm, his water aura clashing against her own. As she realizes, with a chastening swoop of gratitude, that Fyordin broke ranks with the Vu Trin and the Asrai to find her.

And bring her back to their threatened Vo.

"Do you know what's become of my cousin?" Or'myr asks her and Viger both, an edge of desperation in the question.

Fyordin's glare swings to Or'myr. "You mean the *homicidal Black Witch* who leveled Voloi?"

"I mean *my cousin*," Or'myr counters, his tone dangerously clipped, a few strands of violet lightning forking around him. "Who was overtaken by Marcus Vogel and forced to do his bidding." He levels his green eyes back on Tierney. "Alder sensed a change in her through an empathic reading of the trees."

"Viger and I were briefly with Elloren in the Northern Forest," Tierney supplies. "Elloren has broken free of Vogel." She swiftly recounts what transpired in the Northern Forest when she and Viger went after Yvan and Elloren through the Dryad portal, along with a flock of giant Errilor Death Ravens. "Elloren is united with Yvan Guryev," Tierney staunchly insists, "in the defense of the Natural World."

Fyordin's power turns ballistic, raging against her own so intensely, Tierney takes a step back. "Elloren Gardner Grey nearly destroyed the entire East!" he thunders. "To go after her for any reason but to *strike her down* is madness!"

"Fyordin, *please*, you have to believe me!" Tierney chokes out, desperately needing his full alliance. Overtaken by terror for her Vo. For her kelpies. For the entire Natural World of the East. Strangled into silence by the Shadow horrors once more flashing through her mind, she looks beseechingly to them all and can see it in their eyes and posture—fierce concern for her, even Viger's Death Fae remoteness shattered.

A knot of wild emotions forms in Tierney's throat. It's a complicated mess of a grouping, the four of them. But, nonetheless, they're true allies.

And true allies of her Vo.

Viger's thrall intensifies, like deeper night closing in. "If I link all of you to my bond to Tierney through a blood tether," he hisses, low and even, "I could swiftly draw you North inside my thrall mist."

Fyordin rounds on him, power rearing. "Oh, you'd bind *us* as well, would you? Infiltrate our dreams, too, and control us through our fears?"

Viger's snakes bare their teeth, tongues flickering, a confrontational half smile forming on his mouth that sends a shiver down Tierney's spine. "I'd need to *kiss* you to infiltrate your dreams."

"Tether me, Viger," Or'myr offers, resolution in his eyes as he holds out his wand hand. "Get us all to the Northern Vo so we can drive off the Shadow bastards." He glances pointedly at them all. "If Vogel poisons the Vo River, Noilaan will fall. There will be a severe shortage of drinking water. Noilaan's farms will fail. Most of the fisheries too." He sets his lightning eyes back on Viger. "I suspect you're a danger to us, Deathkin, but you're an even greater danger to Vogel. Which makes you my ally."

Warmth shoots through Tierney's power as she takes in Or'myr's stance, finding him wildly heroic in this moment, chagrin again rising that she was unable to withstand his kiss on Xishlon.

Fyordin lets out a vicious epithet as the Vo's waters swirl around them all. Shooting a murderous look at Viger, he thrusts his hand out, as well.

Viger grabs hold of Or'myr's and Fyordin's wrists, a disconcertingly wicked grin forming on his mouth as he sinks his dark claws into their skin.

Tierney flinches as a sudden flash of his Darkness bolts through her power, blood trickling down both Or'myr's and Fyordin's wrists as black mist bursts into being to encircle their forms. She shivers as a connection to *all* of them ripples through her magic, threads of Or'myr's lightning now crackling through her power alongside her rippling water bond to Fyordin, all of it spiraling through Viger's tether of Darkness.

Bound.

A hot impulse races through Tierney as their binding consolidates, the unsettling urge rising to take hold of each one of them, draw them into a deep kiss and more tightly meld their magic to hers. The desire overtakes her so intensely that she has to tense every muscle against it. And worse, she can feel their return rush of yearning in Viger's swirling Darkness, Or'myr's spitting lightning and Fyordin's water aura, all of which are now desperately encircling *her.*

"Asrai," Viger says to her, a hardened glint in his pitch eyes. "This bond is centered in you and me. If we draw each other close, it will enhance our speed north." His aura closes in around her in a dark mass, edging away Or'myr's and Fyordin's auras of power, and Tierney can read in its covetous thrum how much Viger wants her to prefer him to the other men here. But also, how he's struggling to restrain that want and put the Vo first. Which, despite everything, feels extraordinarily valiant.

"All right, Viger," she concedes, emotion knotting in her throat as she steps closer to him, surrendering to the pull of his Darkness. "Bring us north."

Viger nods before sliding his arms and thrall around her. The shivering sensation winds a breathless want through her as the world darkens. A ravenous, unyielding look of hunger passes over Viger's face, and he draws her close and into a kiss with sudden, breathless force.

Tierney gasps, careening into his kiss, Viger's thrall intensifying as he spins Tierney, Or'myr, and Fyordin into his Darkness.

A vision of the Great Tree, III, flashes in Tierney's mind, gravity giving way as they all turn to mist and spear north, as one, through the midnight black.

✦

PART ONE

✦

Shadow Wand Rising

WYVERNBONDED MATE

Elloren

*Northern Forest
Eighteen days after Xishlon*

I shudder against Yvan, his lips on mine, my heart fracturing open as our Wyvernbond reignites under the Great Tree, III.

Our bond's churning flame visibly lights up the world, and I'm barely able to hold back sobs as Yvan holds me to his muscular form and the Forest sizzles out of sight, my vision overtaken by our joint blaze's golden-green glow.

Yvan deepens his firestorm kiss, fire to fire, the feel of our bond enveloping me, sending a volcanic charge through my rootlines. I surrender to it fully. Overcome by the *power* in it.

Overcome by the power in *him*.

As Yvan's heartbeat pulses strong against mine, I'm hit by a rushing wave of Tierney's magic at the same moment the Northern Forest's aura flows around my restored Wyvernbond to Yvan, the trees and III *linking* into Yvan's Icaral of Prophecy fire through my rootline connection to the surrounding Forest.

Tierney's magic fades, but before I can wonder at it, revulsion explodes through III and the trees, lashing through the very air. Alarm tightens my gut as leaves rustle and trunks bend and creak all around us, the image of leagues upon leagues of trees consumed in flame slicing through my mind.

The Forest gives a painful, wrenching *yank* on my rootlines, violently intent on severing their connection to Yvan's Wyvernbond, the caws of my huge kindred ravens sounding, the scene around us snapping back into sight.

Shocked, Yvan and I break our kiss, and I cry out, tensing my rootlines against the strangling attack of Forest power and the planetary force of III's *pull*.

Yvan hisses, tightening his protective hold on me as he hurls fire into our Wyvernbond, and I'm caught up in the feel of his power thrashing against my Forest's yanking assault.

"An Icaral cannot link to our Forest!" the Dryad Oaklyyn's rage-filled voice spears out. "He's all *killing fire!*"

My gaze flits to the Dryads, who all stand against us.

Oaklyyn's fern-hued face is twisted in a scowl, her oak staff gripped tight in her hands, its luminous forest green runes charged for battle, her brown wolverine kindred snarling at us. The stance of the mushroom-tressed Dryad Lyptus is just as combative, her mint-green, lightning bolt–marked face livid, her silver panther kindred emitting a low, threatening growl. The Dryads' branch-horned and pine-haired leader, Sylvan, as well as graceful, flower-tressed Yulan, the Deathkin-Dryad Hazel, and the huge branch-horned Dryad whose name I don't yet know, are all glaring at us with equal parts horror and outrage, the huge Dryad's black bear kindred dropping into a threatening crouch.

Alarm spiking, I realize that Tierney and her Death Fae companion have disappeared, along with that great *whoosh* of water power I sensed, and only the semicircle of six Dryads, their kindreds and my flock of giant Errilor Ravens remain in the clearing around III, Errilith and the other ravens moving in to encircle Yvan and me.

"Where's Tierney?" Yvan demands of the Dryads as he keeps tenacious hold of our bond.

My same urgent question is torn away as the surrounding Forest intensifies its assault on our Wyvernbond with furious, wrenching force. My whole body constricts with pain, a gasp ripping from my throat, the full might of the Northern Forest's Natural Matrix slashing against Yvan's bond to my rootlines. Yvan's invisible aura rears, half of it burning protectively around me, the other half whipping against the Forest's attack in a potent firestorm.

Errilith lets out another thunderously loud *CAW*, as if threatening the Forest in return, my kindred raven's ground-shaking cry quickly taken up by the rest of the Errilor flock, the world pulsing with their strange Dark aura mist, even as III's immense power whirls around Yvan and me in ever-tightening spirals.

"Tell the Forest to *stand down!*" Yvan snarls at Sylvan, Hazel, and Yulan.

Hazel's otherworldly night-dark eyes scan my ravens, his lime-green face tensing with a conflicted look as the world strobes with the ravens' world-dimming aura.

THE DRYAD STORM

Hazel's gaze snaps to Sylvan's and Yulan's equally tumultuous gazes, and a conflicted look passes between the three of them.

As one, Sylvan, Hazel, and Yulan thrust their III-marked palms out toward the surrounding wilds.

I gasp, hit by a radiating blast of Hazel's dark mist and Sylvan's and Yulan's powerful elemental auras, their combined magic flashing against the Forest's relentless assault to no avail.

Oaklyyn cuts Sylvan, Hazel, and Yulan a murderous glare and jabs a finger at Yvan. "Our Forest sees him as an *enemy!*"

"He's my *ally!*" I snarl back, as the Forest sends a series of images screaming through my mind . . .

Dark wings erupting into Shadowfire.

The wings enlarging, overtaking a distant Forest canopy before beating silver gray fire down on the trees.

Leagues and leagues of trees burning . . .

Clarity descends as I realize the source of the Forest's confusion—the Wyvernfire Vogel stole from Yvan when he wrested hold of our Wyvernbond during the battle at Voloi . . . a trace of it must still be present in Vogel's Shadow-corrupted firelines. And now the trees are sensing that same fire in Yvan through our Wyvernbond.

My gaze locks onto Yvan's. "The trees think it's *you* destroying the Western Forest," I force out through the line-stretching pain, while Yvan fights the Forest off with an encircling wall of invisible fire, his body beginning to tremble from the effort. I swing my gaze toward III. "Yvan's fire isn't burning you down! The *Magedom's* is!"

III responds with a more urgent pull on our bond, desperation overtaking me as the Forest's visions gain potency, the Prophecy *flipping* in the Northern Forest and III's mind.

Setting itself fully against Yvan.

"*No!*" The word erupts from my throat in a growl, Erthia-tilting in its intensity as Yvan keeps hold of our bond and I face down III, the Dryads, the entire Northern Forest—the entirety of *Erthia*. "He's not your enemy! He's my *Wyvernbonded MATE!*"

My heart seems to burst open around the word, while Yvan's fire *explodes*, our energy shot through with my intention to be with him *always*.

Yvan's incandescent gaze collides with mine, a look of pure passion blazing in it.

An emotional snarl escapes him, defiance bolting through us with the strength of worlds cleaving, our bonded fire power rising to blistering heights.

Yvan's shoulders stiffen, and his expression turns feral as his power sears through my lines in a scorching blast of heat. I draw the living branch III gave to me, life flooding through it via my Forest connection, both of us ready to go to elemental war over this huge, flaming line in the sand, even though I know nothing about wielding magic as a Dryad.

Because we're *done*.

Done with being forced away from anyone we love. Done with being coerced into a prophesied fight that only brings division and destruction to Erthia.

The Prophecy ends *here*.

Without warning, Oaklyyn thrusts her runic staff toward Yvan.

I thrust out my branch and murmur the words to the Mage fire-blast spell to no effect, while Yvan bolts out a line of golden fire from his palm. At the same moment, Sylvan levels a pine branch at Oaklyyn and sends a line of deep-green flame toward her staff and Hazel lashes out blurred tendrils of black mist at the staff from his clawed fingertips.

Hazel's magic whips around the staff and wrests it from Oaklyyn's grip just before Yvan's and Sylvan's bolts of fire slam into the weapon.

It bursts into gold and green flame.

Oaklyyn's expression turns murderous as she glares at Hazel and Sylvan and spears her finger at Yvan. "Our Forest has named him *enemy!*" she cries. "But beyond that, he's *Lasair Wyvern!* He's *all fire* with no other elements to temper it! *Tree-killing* fire! His bond to the Black Witch *must* be broken before his power fully connects to our Forest and burns it to *ash!*"

A maelstrom of conflict shudders through Yvan's fire, while my ravens' caws and pulsing auras gain more urgent force.

Yvan hisses out what sounds like a Wyvern curse, his fervid gaze swinging to meet mine. "She's right," he grits out. "I can't war with the trees to keep hold of our bond and risk the Forest's destruction. The Forest is the source of all your *power* . . ."

"The Forest needs to find a way to ally with you," I counter. "It *can't* be aligned with me while warring with you. We can't fight Vogel divided like that. The Prophecy *cannot* stand!"

My words are cut off as III's potent aura descends through the storming chaos, a sense of vast, invisible weight bearing down on the entire Northern Forest, on Yvan and me and my rootlines. We all flinch, including the Dryads, my ravens' caws ceasing and their pulsing power dissipating as all of us look to the Great Ironwood Tree.

"Let III decide!" Yulan's impassioned voice chimes out.

I meet the lichen-lashed gaze of the petite Dryad, struck by the dead certainty I find in it that this is Yvan's and my only chance to convince the Forest to see past the Prophecy.

To convince *III* to see who Yvan truly is, as it did with me.

"Put your palms on III's bark," I urge Yvan while fighting against the surrounding Forest's rootline-stretching pull *away* from him. "Let III read you."

"*No!*" Oaklyyn cries, her tone one of pure desperation. "Icaral, *no . . .*"

"I'm all killing fire, Elloren," Yvan rasps. He glances at III, conflict whipping through his power even as he rages to hold on to our bond. Eyes bright with pain, he grips my shoulders. "Our Wyvernbond is directly connected to my core of fire. I'm set apart from this. I'm set apart from *you*—"

"No, you're *not*," I protest as the surrounding Forest flings another fiery warning full of dark wings through my mind. But there's another image blooming inside me once more. *Rooting* itself deep in my beleaguered center—III's vision of *everyone* encircling the Great Tree's broad trunk, all of us joined to III and intimately linked to the Natural Matrix. Intimately joined to the power of Life.

Everyone.

No exceptions.

Defiance rears through my chest, scathingly hot. "Yvan, I'm asking you to trust me in this. As your fire-bonded *mate*."

The word *mate* triggers another palpable surge of Yvan's fire, a ravenous look passing over his face, every nerve inside me heating and contracting toward that lightning-bolt look. His power streaming hot around me through our bond, he nods then turns and brings his palms definitively to III's trunk.

I gasp as golden light rays out from where Yvan's hands meet bark, at the same moment that Oaklyyn, Lyptus, and the huge Dryad with the bear kindred cry out and lunge forward, leveling branches and staffs at Yvan while Errlith's *caw* splits the air, a misty shield of Darkness flowing out of my flock's midnight feathers and Hazel's raised palms to enclose Yvan and me.

Yvan shivers, and a *CRACK* sounds on the air as the attacking Dryads blast bolts of deep-green power at our Deathkin shield.

The shield explodes into black mist while bark forms all over Yvan's body, and Oaklyyn, Lyptus, and the huge Dryad ready another magic attack just as Yvan's whole form is drawn into the Great Tree.

"NO!" Oaklyyn cries.

I blink once then stagger back, my pulse roaring through my ears, barely registering her alarmed cry and the Forest's sharp spike of terror as my newly reformed Wyvernbond to Yvan gives a sudden, brutal stretch . . .

. . . and *breaks*.

A shock of pain blasts through my rootlines, and I cry out and drop to my knees, Yvan's volcanic, all-encompassing heat wrenched away, only his hands' glowing imprints shimmering bright gold on the Great Tree's night-dark bark. Until those, too, are consumed by III.

SHADOW STRIKE

Gwynnifer Croft Sykes

Agolith Desert Sublands
Fourteen days after Xishlon

"We have to get to the Northern Forest before Vogel invades it!" Yyzz'ra snarls, her livid silver gaze boring into Gwynn and Mavrik. "How long until this damned portal is charged?"

Gwynn's hackles go up, sweat lining her brow. Down on her knees, she murmurs spell after spell, holding the Verdyllion to the Vu Trin portal's runic frame, one of a multitude of hidden underground Noi military portals, their runic charges long since spent. Mavrik is on his knees beside Gwynn, every nerve in her body hyperaware of his palm lightly cupping the back of her neck, his direct touch amplifying their merged power.

"I asked you a question," Yyzz'ra snaps as a rainbow of sparks sprays across Gwynn's vision. She shivers, her and Mavrik's twinned power coursing through her arm and wand and then into the Noi portal runes, flashes of sapphire magic igniting in them.

"Will you do your level best to be *quiet*?" Valasca aims at Yyzz'ra, the Amaz warrior's tone crisp. Valasca's grayed arms are crossed in front of her chest, the runes of her imprisonment collar glowing emerald against her neck.

Yyzz'ra rounds on Valasca, quietly lethal Valkyr and intense Gavryyl bracketing her, the two young Smaragdalfar soldiers mirroring Yyzz'ra's scowl. "Aren't you my *prisoner*?" Yyzz'ra snaps.

"Stupidly, yes," Valasca drawls as she splays her hand out toward Mavrik and Gwynn. "But that doesn't change the fact that they're *clearly* trying to charge that portal as fast as they can."

"Well, they need to work *faster!*" Yyzz'ra seethes. "Or by the time we get to the Northern Forest, Vogel will have already found a way to crash his storm bands *clear through* the Forest's warding!"

Distracted by Yyzz'ra's and Valasca's constant sniping, Gwynn struggles to hold her focus. Wynter stands behind Mavrik, preternaturally still, even the Icaral's smattering of kindred birds unnaturally motionless from where they watch, perched on stony outcroppings all around them, including the two Agolith Flame Hawks who, Gwynn notes, almost always have their flame-hued eyes set on her and Mavrik.

Willing calm, Gwynn murmurs the Noi interlocking spell, and a harder swoosh of light magery courses from her to her wand, the emptying sensation stealing her breath. Their woven spells snap through the portal's runic frame with a sharp *ping*.

A burst of chromatic light rays out from every rune, and anticipation grips hold of Gwynn, the suspended Varg, Issani, Gardnerian, and Alfsigr charge-acceleration runes she and Mavrik have painstakingly crafted and connected to the portal all pulsing with her multihued light magery.

The normally sapphire Noi portal runes shift into a full rainbow of light as they begin to rotate and charge, and a swell of elation suffuses Gwynn's every line.

Beautiful.

Sensing emotion searing through Mavrik's power, she turns and meets his glowing golden gaze. That familiar flash of multicolored sparks ignites along the edges of Gwynn's vision, a triumphant smirk pulling at Mavrik's lips, words wholly unneeded in this moment. They can both sense that their spellwork has fully taken hold. And to have the power to charge and magically recalibrate a portal in a way that sets its course, speeds its charge and removes its lag . . .

Gwynn pulls in a hard, shaky breath.

It's a formidable advantage.

"It shouldn't be long now," Mavrik assures Yyzz'ra, pulling his gaze from Gwynn's with what seems like great effort to focus back on the portal. He touches the tip of his golden wand to the portal's frame, tracing one of the runes in a way Gwynn knows will measure the portal's charge and lag. "We've amplified the charging process with quickening runes from multiple runic systems," he adds, "which should speed both the portal's charging time and our journey through it."

Gwynn glances at Yyzz'ra and her cohorts, still glowering beside her. Cael and Mynx are leaning against one of the narrow cavern's rough walls, and Gwynn's focus briefly snags on how the portal's color dances over Cael's snow-hued features and Mynx's billiantly emerald visage, the two lovers boldly holding hands in blaring defiance of the near constant censure Yyzz'ra, Valkyr, and Gavryyl hurl their way.

Cael's Second, Rhys, is hanging back to their left, one pale hand resting on an outcropping of crimson stone. Serious, watchful Sparrow stands by his side, the two having struck up a quiet friendship over the past days.

Gwynn considers how sympathetic Yyzz'ra, Valkyr, and Gavryyl initially were toward Sparrow, the three Smaragdalfar soldiers vocally outraged over the oppression Sparrow's Urisk people suffered at the hands of both the Magedom and Alfsigr. But every trace of their sympathy was whisked away the previous night, when Sparrow grew incensed over the verbal abuse they were yet again aiming at Mynx'lia'luure and Cael.

I'm not so good at purity myself, Sparrow announced, rising to her feet, her violet eyes fair burning with confrontational light. *I'm in love with a Mage.*

It was like a runic explosive had detonated, Yyzz'ra, Gavryyl, and Valkyr glaring daggers at her. Sparrow promptly went to sit beside the blaringly Alfsigr Rhys, and now Sparrow and Rhys are near inseparable.

A small firework of prismatic sparks bursts from the tip of Mavrik's wand, yanking Gwynn from her fitful thoughts as the portal frame's runes whir into a faster rotation.

"This portal will be charged in about six hours," Mavrik postulates. "Give or take. In any case, we should arrive at the Northern Forest's southernmost Subland edge before tomorrow eve." He glances at Wynter. "That's close to when you sensed Elloren Gardner Grey and Yvan will arrive there."

"And well before Vogel arrives with his Shadow storm bands," Wynter adds with a look of genuine gratitude, a Crimson Cactus Wren landing on her shoulder. Wynter's silver eyes flash worriedly toward the bird, and Gwynn guesses she's getting another reading on the Shadow storm bands' locations through the vibrations the birds can detect in the overhead root system.

Gwynn glances up at the root network interspersed amongst the ceiling of crimson Subland stone, the glowing, prismatic runes of the net-barrier she and Mavrik twinned their power to hugging the ceiling, the dark runes of Vogel's Shadow net fused to its back, the Magedom angling to outpace them to the Forest . . .

"We'll have a strong lead," Wynter assures them all, seeming to read Gwynn's worries, "thanks to the Verdyllion's twinned Light Mages."

Mavrik turns his head slightly and casts an almost-glance toward Gwynn, a spark of emotion flashing through their fused firelines once more, an echoing line of feeling shivering through Gwynn, her heartbeat quickening.

"Our weapons are charged," Mynx states, and Gwynn glances around at the rune-marked blades, swords, and bows and arrows strapped on the Smaragdalfar soldiers.

"Well, that's a good thing," Mavrik says. "Because in a few hours we'll portal to the Sublands just outside the Northern Forest, break down its Dryad warding and surface inside the Forest. Hopefully amidst an army of Dryad Fae."

Valasca coughs out a laugh. "Who might try to kill your Crow ass on sight."

Mavrik's lip twitches as he shoots her a sardonic look. "I'd appreciate it if you intervened, if it comes to that."

Valasca shrugs. "They might try to slay my ass, as well. Folklore has it the Tree Fae are about as charitable toward intruders as, well, we Amaz are toward men . . ." Her grayed, angular face tenses, a tremble suddenly kicking up along her lips. Gwynn's heart tightens, certain Valasca is being swept up in the horrible remembrance of her destroyed country . . . and the Magedom's murder of thousands of Amaz.

Mavrik's eyes narrow on Valasca, and his jawline firms as he stands. "Amazakaraan will rise again," he insists, adamant, his eyes blazing with a defiant compassion.

Valasca draws in a sharp breath and nods. Straightening, she makes the Amaz Goddess symbol on her chest, kisses her fist, and thrusts it toward the heavens, meeting Mavrik's unwavering gaze once more in a flash of alliance.

"When we get to the Northern Forest's Sublands," Mavrik says to everyone, "Gwynnifer and I might be able to draw on the elemental power of the roots of a primordial Ironwood tree that Wynter's kindreds spotted near the Forest's southern border."

"The Great Tree of all Erthia's myths," Wynter murmurs, the image of the Sacred Ironwood Tree shivering through Gwynn's mind.

Mavrik nods. "If some of the myths are true, we might be able to further amplify our power via the Great Tree's fabled light magic—"

"Not fabled," Yyzz'ra snaps, grimacing at Mavrik. "That magic is the Goddess Oo'na's own, emanating from her Sacred Roots. Her Holy Tree has been unjustly cut off from my people for *generations*." Yyzz'ra spits out a disdainful sound. "Because the Dryad Fae know we will wield the Subland magic of Oo'na's Roots to return the entire Sublands to its rightful dominion—*ours*." She scowls at Mynx and Cael, her thoughts about their linked hands blisteringly clear.

Valasca lets out a beleaguered sigh and stares at the Subland ceiling for a moment, her lips moving, as if she's either cursing or praying for her Goddess's strength, before she levels her gaze at Gwynn and Mavrik both. "You two should get some rest," she prods before glancing at everyone else. "Everyone should. We've done what we can for the moment, and we'll need everyone in fighting form when we get north. Let the portal charge. I'll stand guard."

"I'll join you," Cael offers.

"I will, as well," Mynx chimes in, prompting a chilly look from Yyzz'ra.

"No," Wynter states with calm authority. "Everyone go, rest. My wingeds will patrol the surrounding caverns and routes, and I'll read what they see. I'll sound an alarm if danger comes."

A beat of hesitation ensues before everyone concedes. The Verdyllion, still glowing in Gwynnifer's hand, gives a sudden, tingling pull toward Wynter, and Gwynn hands the Wand-Stylus off to the Icaral while most everyone departs into the small side caverns surrounding this larger area.

Gwynn sets off for the circular cavern where she and Mavrik have grabbed a few fitful hours of sleep in the past two nights, hyperaware of Mavrik following her, the rich crimson of the stone surrounding them triggering a sizzle of ruddy sparks through their fused lightlines.

Amplifying her pull toward him.

Their twinned magic has made it difficult to be separated from each other, the two of them careful to sleep just out of reach.

Which is increasingly an exercise in magic-provoking torment.

Which means, Gwynn realizes, that it's been over three days since she's had any real semblance of sleep, exhaustion bearing down like a leaden weight.

Gwynn steps into the cavern and stills, engulfed by the sudden, potent sense of Mavrik pausing on the cavern's threshhold, their prismatic draw intensifying. Flustered, she turns and meets his eyes.

Their twinned bond bursts into color, and a rush of magic sizzles straight through Gwynn's entire form, the unbidden sensation prompting a rise of illicit heat.

Mavrik quickly looks away, biting at the tracery of prismatic color now forking over his mouth.

He wants to kiss me, Gwynn realizes, breath catching.

Light power crackles mortifyingly to life over her own lips, and she stiffens, the gold color of Mavrik's eyes spangling over her wand hand.

Mavrik's hands come to his hips, his jaw tensing. "It's getting stronger," he says.

"It is," Gwynn admits, giving him a sheepish look. "We need to stay focused on spellwork. It's an awkward time for this to kick up."

"Or a good time," Mavrik suggests. "We're going to need the full might of our twinned power when we get north." He sighs, shooting Gwynn a heated look. "This draw, frustrating and dangerous as it is, seems to be part of it."

Gwynn bites at her tingling lip and nods, railing against her physical pull to him. "I know we need sleep," she says, "but we should take a moment to pool our knowledge of ward-breaking spells."

Mavrik nods, seeming as if he's struggling to assemble his scattered thoughts. "There's a cavern farther down this tunnel," he says, angling his head toward it. "It's shot through with obsidian. The black in it is absorbing much of the charged color so the cavern . . . it's less likely to amplify our . . . light draw." He casts her a meaningful look as another tingling rush sweeps through their twinned magic.

Gwynn's thoughts fragment, muddled by both their dangerous attraction and the way their magic is increasingly intertwined. She remembers Mavrik's words. *A complete fusing . . . as permanent as fasting . . . we'll have to stay in the same location, always . . . and if one of us dies, the other dies too.*

Holding his gaze, she nods and follows him toward the obsidian cavern.

"Vogel is going to strike at those wards with everything he's got," Mavrik notes.

Gwynn nods, down on her knees beside Mavrik, his golden wand clasped in her hand, all of their rune-marked blades and wands, save the ones in their hands, strewn around them to experiment with.

The complicated runic diagram they've drawn on the floor of the black cavern is splayed out before them, ward designs fabricated with streaks of golden wand light that illuminate the room in a buttery glow that's so gorgeous it quickens Gwynn's pulse.

Mavrik taps a section of one of the ward designs with his midnight-black wand's tip, the rune drawn from Gwynn's memory of a diagram of the Northern Forest's warding that she uncovered in the Valgard armory. "I suspect Vogel will siphon energy from his storm bands and attempt to link that energy to the Forest's warding *here*," Mavrik postulates, "to blast the Dryad barrier apart."

"Hmm . . . most likely," Gwynn agrees, glancing at him. "We'll need to mark everyone's weapons with runes that can counter every known angle of Shadow attack. In case Vogel gets through the wards before we do."

Mavrik nods in affirmation, his eyes fixed on the sprawling diagram. "I'm going to stay up a bit and mark our weapons with a linked combination of Noi mirror-strike runes and Varg spell-dismantling wards."

Comprehension clicks. "Ah," Gwynn breathes out, her mind thrilling to his cleverness. "To neutralize Mage deflection runes."

He shoots her a mischievous glance. "That might cause a time lag in the deflection spell's rebound."

Gwynn smiles. "And give us an unexpected edge." She taps her light-infused lip, deep in thought as they both mentally tussle with the likely avenues of attack. "You could cast an Amaz shield spell over those two spells," she ventures. "You'll get a longer lag."

Mavrik's embracing magic stills around hers. "Gods, you're brilliant," he breathes.

Surprised by the emotion in his tone, she meets his eyes, the openly enraptured look he's giving her catching her off guard. The flush that rises on his face matches the heat she feels in hers, prismatic color pulsing to more intense life on their lips.

"Gwynn," Mavrik says, swallowing, a pained look tensing his face as he rubs his mouth. "This draw is insanely difficult to manage." A more potent heat sears through their merged lines, and Gwynn's emotions burst into a turbulent storm of conflict as she struggles to formulate a response . . .

. . . just as a stinging pain takes hold of her fastlines.

Gwynn flinches at the same time Mavrik does, a strangled cry escaping her lips. They both drop their wands and jerk their hands protectively inward. Dread sluicing through Gwynn's veins, she glances down, her gaze zeroing in on the tendrils of Shadow smoke coiling up from her rapidly graying fastlines.

And Mavrik's.

Terror constricts her chest and she meets Mavrik's equally horrified gaze. "Ancient One," she rasps, "Vogel's coming after our fasting spells *right now.*"

"Then we need to wrest hold of the spell," he snarls. *"Right now."*

"How?" Gwynn challenges, trembling now as she forces herself to mentally flip through every remembered runic grimoire, spells flying through her mind.

"I'm working on a hunch . . ." Mavrik says, grabbing his midnight-black Noi rune–marked wand from the floor before taking her free hand and bringing his wand's tip to her palm. "The runes of our Issani twinning spell and the wand motions needed to craft the fasting spell . . . they're based on a similar sequence of primordial linking glyphs. We could use a Noi weaving spell—"

"—to pull our twinning linkage straight through our fastings," Gwynn murmurs, her mind rapidly assembling his plan as gray pulses alarmingly through her vision.

Mavrik nods. "The fasting spell can't be broken . . . but we might be able to *overtake it.*"

"We'll need to cast the magic at the same time," Gwynn cautions. Mavrik nods once more as Gwynn grabs up her wand and they point their wands at each other's Shadow-smoking fastlines just as the scene around them abruptly cuts out.

Gwynn pulls in a hard gasp, the two of them thrust into a vision of an aboveground, Shadowed world. Huge arches of stone tinted a steely hue surround them, Shadow mist smoking up from grayed sands, the images wavering and dreamlike at the edges.

The Agolith Desert above us, Gwynn realizes, *but completely stripped of its ruddy coloration by Vogel's Shadow.*

Her pulse pounds out a panicked rhythm, and she turns to find Mavrik crouched beside her on the Shadow-smoking sand, a combative look in his eyes.

Vogel appears in the mist before them, swiftly closing in, his dark cloak flowing out behind him and a multi-eyed raven perched on his shoulder.

Gwynn recoils, fear striking through her. Vogel's upper face is a grotesque mass of glowing gray eyes, his darkened teeth bizarrely elongated, the Shadow Wand gripped in his glimmering gray hand.

He's here with us, she realizes, staring at the true nature of what Vogel has become, all of them drawn inside his Shadow Wand's link to their fastlines.

"Cast the spell!" Mavrik cries as he grabs hold of her free hand and presses his wand's tip to her fastlines. Battling back her fear, Gwynn brings her wand's tip to Mavrik's fastlines at the same moment Vogel levels his Shadow Wand and blasts a bolt of wind at them.

Before either of them can get a spell out, the wind slams into Gwynn and the breath is crushed from her lungs as both she and Mavrik are hurled apart and through the air, their wands blown from their hands.

Gwynn slams down onto the vision's smoking sand, crying out as her shoulder and hip painfully absorb the blow. Nightmare-swift, Vogel lunges forward and grabs hold of her arm with a clawed hand, gnashing his too-long teeth close to her face. "You little staen'en *whore*," he snarls, every glowing eye boring into her as he bares sharp, gray teeth. "I will *bite* my Shadow into you!"

Out of the corner of her eye, Gwynn catches Mavrik leaping toward his wand, and the primal will to live sparks. Yanking herself from Vogel's grip, she lunges for her own wand, just as Vogel springs for it, bizarrely fast, his bootheel slamming down on the golden weapon as he angles the Shadow Wand toward Mavrik and bolts more wind at him, blasting his wand from his grip again and punching Mavrik back to the ground.

Smiling, Vogel thrusts his Wand skyward.

A giant tree of Shadow blasts up from the ground behind him, and Gwynn's eyes widen with fear. It's taller than the tallest desert arch, its smoking canopy rising higher than the clouds and rapidly branching out to cover the whole desert scene. A grotesquerie of Shadow roots emerges in arcs beneath it, giving the gigantic tree a spiderlike appearance, a small root cage at the end of each appendage.

Thousands upon thousands of cages.

Most cages hold dazed-looking Mage soldiers, with ropey lines of Shadow extending from the root bars to their fastlines, with a few scattered cages enclosing shirtless Alfsigr soldiers, connected to them via their Zalyn'or imprints.

Prickles of fear shoot down Gwynn's spine as she realizes she's looking directly into Vogel's growing network of Shadow power.

Desperate to fight back, Gwynn lunges for her wand under Vogel's heel at the same time Mavrik races toward his wand. Two of the Shadow tree's roots whip up and slam root cages down around each of them and Gwynn cries out and falls, both she and Mavrik now pinned, backs to sand, several paces apart.

"You cannot defeat the Ancient One's Holy Will," Vogel intones, his grotesque, multi-eyed appearance giving way to that of a normal-looking Mage as Gwynn senses his anger abating, something akin to twisted compassion gleaming in his green eyes. "My control over you both will be your salvation."

Gwynn meets Mavrik's gaze through the root bars, a blazingly poignant look in it, as if he's desperately trying to convey something. His covert intention flashes through their twinning spell as he curls their internal light magery into a golden shape—an Issani power-blast rune.

An obscure memory lights in Gwynn's mind, a footnote in the back of one of the armory volumes on Issani military-grade sorcery detailing how twinned sorcerers can manifest runes on their palms without styluses.

Gwynn draws in a harsh breath, a look of understanding passing between her and Mavrik. Drawing power from their twinned lines at the same time Mavrik does, Gwynn mentally draws the rune on the palm of her wand hand, the lines of magic sizzling over her skin.

With a quick nod to Mavrik, she thrusts her rune-marked palm toward Vogel at the same time he does. Their twinned power surges as, in unison, they slide their thumbs over the runes' central triggers.

A pulse of golden energy detonates from their palms and collides with their cages. The bars light up gold then explode in earsplitting *cracks* before the power rushes forward to slam into Vogel, hurling him backward.

Seizing their chance, Gwynn and Mavrik leap toward their wands, grab them, and race toward each other as Vogel rights himself with a hissing growl and thrusts his Wand up toward the Shadow tree.

Another colossal root cage barrels down toward Gwynn and Mavrik as they reach each other and touch their wands' tips to each other's smoking fastlines, murmuring the Noi weaving spell in unison.

The root cage slams down with killing force just as gold light rays out of their fastlines and their twinned power blasts through their fastmarks.

The scene around them shatters, Vogel's snarling cry reverberating straight through Gwynn as the obsidian Subland cave reappears around them. Mavrik is crouched beside her, both of them breathing hard and clutching each other's wrists.

Dizzy with vertigo, Gwynn lifts her hand and gasps as she takes in her newly gold-glowing fastlines. Looking rattled, Mavrik holds up his hand beside hers, the tendriling Shadow *gone*, their designs completely altered. No longer do they have different looping black designs—their fastings are now identical golden lightning-bolt patterns limned with iridescent *color*.

Astounded, Gwynn meets Mavrik's intent gaze. "Do you think it worked?" she asks, barely able to get the words out.

"I think it just might have." He huffs out a stunned breath and shakes his head as they both rise to their feet on unsteady legs. "To my knowledge," he says, "no one's ever tried to flow Issani twinning magic through a wandfasting spell . . . I didn't fully expect it to be able to infiltrate it."

"Do you suppose that's how Vogel took over Elloren Gardner Grey's fastlines?" Gwynn presses, heart pattering hummingbird-fast. "Using Shadow-corrupted twinning magic?"

Mavrik's eyes narrow, riveted on hers. "It's a distinct possibility. It's the strongest sorcerer-linking spell there is."

"He might have used this route to link Shadow power to the Alfsigr Zalyn'or necklaces, as well," Gwynn postulates, the words coming out in a breathless rush.

Mavrik grows very still and Gwynn can feel the contained, prismatic tempest forming in his magic. "Do you realize, Gwynnifer," he says, his words low and measured, "that if what you say is true, we might have just found a way to break into not only Vogel's fasting tether to his bound Mage soldiers . . . but into the magic that could bind all of Alfsigroth through their Zalyn'or necklaces?"

Tension sparks in the air between them as Gwynn slowly nods. She swallows, considering their hands again, studying the identical lightning marks now emblazoned on them both.

"Mavrik . . ." she says, her awareness of what this means, not just on an Erthia level, but on a personal level, consolidating. "Do you think . . . that we're truly fasted to each other?"

He blinks at her before taking hold of her hand and placing his wand's tip to the luminous fasting designs marked there, then murmurs spells.

Ah . . . clever, Gwynn thinks as her light magery stirs, a shiver of intellectual appreciation coursing through her over how *smart* he is, as he draws on her light power to cast a suspended Noi linkage-detection rune combined with an Alfsigr linkage-breaking rune just over their hands, then connects both runes to their fastlines via slim sapphire and silver lines.

Their fastlines flash sapphire, then a stinging silver, before settling back into luminous gold, the Noi and Alfsigr runes disappearing.

Mavrik's eyes widen as he stares at their fastlines, seeming stunned anew. "I think we've taken true hold of the fasting spell," he rasps. He meets her astonished gaze. "Gwynn, I think we might be truly fasted."

"Moving that spell . . . manipulating it . . ." Gwynn stutters.

". . . is the first step in figuring out how to destroy it," he finishes for her.

"Do you know how many 'unbreakable' spells are based on the same spell segments as the fasting spell?" she asks, her tone awed over what they've wrought.

He nods tightly, swallowing as the ramifications bear down more intensely. "*All,*" he responds. "All the higher-level Mage spells. And all the higher-level Alfsigr spells, as well . . . and so many of Erthia's other magical systems . . . their strongest spells are all based in similar primordial magic . . ."

Gwynn ceases to hear him as her eyes fixate on her wrist then his, and she realizes, in a sudden, throat-tightening wave of dread, that their fastlines might be transformed to golden streaks of lightning . . .

. . . but the Sealing lines around their wrists are still black.

A frisson of urgency breaks through.

"We need to own the entire spell," she breathes, lifting her gaze to Mavrik's. "Mavrik . . . our *wrists*."

He pales. "Ancient One . . ."

Gwynn freezes as the forbidden idea grips hold.

"There's only one way to fully overtake a fasting spell," she forces out, an uncomfortable flush heating her face. "Only one way to completely lay claim to it."

She watches him furtively as he stills, a flush pinking his skin as well, the pieces falling into place in his mind.

"Seal it, you mean," Mavrik says, and they regard each other soberly.

She gives him a slow nod, a momentous tension burgeoning in the air between them.

Mavrik gives her a deeply searching look. "Gwynn, if we're wrong and we . . . consummate this fasting—" He shakes his head, glancing down at his fastlines before bringing his gaze back to hers, his expression fraught with concern. "Your hands and wrists could be painfully scarred. *For life.*"

"And I'm safe now?" she challenges, defiance flaring. "Are either of us 'safe' if Vogel takes hold of our Sealing? You know as well as I do that the Sealing spell is a stronger spell. It can overtake the fasting spell in a *heartbeat*."

Mavrik tilts his head in grim acknowledgment, his gaze riveted to hers.

"We need to Seal this fasting," she insists as her heart thuds and her emotions storm. "We need to Seal it *now*, before Vogel draws up enough power to overtake us again."

"Gwynn . . ." Mavrik starts, his tone troubled as his magic churns fitfully against hers.

She rises and draws off her cloak, fingers trembling, then hangs it over the cavern's narrow, arcing entrance and raises her wand to affix it there with three small bolts of earth magery drawn from Mavrik's lines. Then she lifts the edge of her tunic and marks a small Issani contraceptive rune just above her hip, conflict twisting her heart as she beats back a memory of Geoffrey *before* he fully joined with Vogel's forces. Caught up in a wilderness of feeling, she turns to Mavrik, hoping he'll make the first move, because she finds herself unable.

"We need to do this," she says in a tight whisper, unable to reconcile how much she wants him. Warring against how much she wants him. "Please, Mavrik."

For a moment Mavrik doesn't move. But then he gets up and draws near, his hand gently finding hers, prompting a welling of tears in Gwynn's eyes.

"You know," Mavrik says as he lifts her hand and gently traces his thumb over one of her golden, color-limned fastlines, "in Noilaan, instead of fasting at thirteen, when Noi'khin reach eighteen or older, they decide how they're going to 'dwell in the garden.'"

Gwynn stares at him in bafflement, thrown by the direction of this conversation. "The 'garden'?" she asks, swiping away a tear streaking down her cheek.

"It's a euphemism," he clarifies with a slight smile, compassionate warmth sparking in his golden eyes. "Meaning, 'ways to be romantically intimate.'"

Her flush deepens. "What are the 'ways'?" she asks, grateful for his momentary foray into unexpected terrain.

He shrugs. "There are quite a few of them. Some choose 'one flower, and to dwell in a single aspect of the garden.' Some opt to 'create their own garden.' Some decide to 'gather many flowers.'"

"Many flowers?" Gwynn repeats, thrown.

His lip twitches up. "More than one partner," he clarifies.

"Ancient One . . ." Gwynn huffs, unable to get her mind around such an idea.

"They accept men with men, as well," he says as he continues to caress her hand with a gentleness that stays some of Gwynn's emotional upheaval. "Women with women. They have these concepts of some who are fluid in their gender. It's complex and *very* different."

"Quite a bit different from our upbringing," Gwynn notes as they share a small smile, the Noi traditions sounding truly astounding. But then a shard of pain intrudes. She can sense it cutting through the small flare of humor for both of them. She holds up her hand. "No fasting at thirteen for them, then?" She immediately feels an even deeper jab of pain, along with another rush of longing for Geoffrey. For what he was, *before*.

He's gone, she reminds herself, the ache cutting deep, her throat closing around it. *Forever gone. And he chose the Shadow of his own free will.* Tears well in her eyes as she looks at Mavrik, finding the same unsettled conflict in his gaze.

And understanding.

"If you were Noi," she asks, voice rough, "what part of their garden do you think you'd choose?"

Their magical draw shimmers in the air between them as Mavrik holds her challenging stare, the intensity in his eyes remaining unbroken. "*One* flower," he states with unsparing emphasis. "*One* garden."

Her heart trips into a faster rhythm. "That's what I want, too," she says, tears coming to her eyes as they consider each other. "My pull to you keeps intensifying," she shakily admits.

"It's not just the magic, Gwynn," he states, eyes burning with certainty. "If we were magic-free, I think I'd be drawn to you just the same."

Gwynn instantly grasps what he means, the two of them a perfect intellectual and emotional match. So easily getting lost in each other, despite having known each other for only a few days. Complete harmony on every level.

Still . . . the thought of being intimate so soon . . .

But if they're going to truly wall Vogel off from their lines, it has to be done. And *quickly.*

Mavrik reaches up to gently caress her cheek, and a pleasurable frisson courses over Gwynn's skin that only intensifies her searing guilt. "Gwynn," he says, voice low and serious. "We've both done this before."

She meets his gaze to find him giving her a knowing look as her thoughts lace with pain.

With someone I loved, she rages, not able to choke out the words to him. *With someone I was fasted to. Someone I'm betraying.* But then her thoughts tilt once more toward the Magedom's horror, and a harsh tremor runs down her spine.

Someone who chose to be part of the monster.

She averts her eyes once more from Mavrik's compelling golden gaze. Fights the sense of *rightness* in her pull to him. Because if this is right, why didn't the Ancient One lead her to Mavrik instead?

"Let's Seal this fasting," she insists, battling against the fact that she's falling in love with him. And battling against how much she wants this. How much she wants *him.*

"Gwynn . . ." Mavrik says, concern in his eyes. "This is a pressured situation for us both . . ." He pauses, swallowing thickly, clearly thrown, as well. "But it doesn't have to be bad." His voice lowers to a more intimate register. "I can feel your magic *constantly* reaching for mine. I feel it now."

His hand comes to her arm, and gooseflesh rises as the contact intensifies the breathless urge to *fuse*, her magic clamoring for his in a prismatic conflagration. "What would make this easier for you?"

Heart throbbing, Gwynn shakes her head, pulses of wanton color flashing in her vision and through their lines, her body growing warm from it.

"Nothing will make this easier," she forces out. *Because it's wrong to love you and want you.*

Mavrik stiffens, his expression gaining a stubborn edge even as his magic twines through hers with more wanton energy. "Gwynn, I cannot do this against your full will."

Her own stubborn rebellion flares, scarlet sparks exploding as her magic ignites against his with bright force. She grabs hold of his tunic, pulls him close, and kisses him with sudden fervor, sending a shock of flaming red straight through him.

Mavrik grips her upper arms and firmly pushes her back, breaking the kiss, the gold of his eyes intensifying as his power heats around hers, growing crimson with desire as he looks deeply, relentlessly into her eyes, and Gwynn can feel him reading everything she can't voice . . .

Ancient One help her, she knows he's reading the truth of it.

She wants him.

She wants him in every way.

"Are you *sure*?" he demands as his power gains bright ground against hers, his breathing growing uneven, his face flushed with want.

Their chromatic draw surging to unbearable heights, Gwynn holds his gaze and gives a tight nod.

His mouth comes down on hers, every hue exploding through her vision as their power merges more intensely, her back arching against the sensation of falling into his magic.

She tries to hold back her hungry response to his open passion. Tries to tell herself she doesn't truly desire it when he draws her down onto a bedroll and frantically undresses her, the two of them kissing each other brazenly, lost to the magic as he yanks off his weapons and clothing with an intensity bordering on desperation, his hands caressing her *everywhere*.

And then, caressing her in a way that makes her feel as if she's going to dissolve into a marbled puddle of color before they powerfully join.

Gwynn gasps, her eyes widening at the sensations of fullness and their magic amplifying through their merged lines, an exquisite pleasure coursing through her as every resplendant hue flashes through her body and vision. Giving in to the thrall, she wraps her legs tightly around his, driving his magic—driving *him*—deeper into her.

Mavrik groans, low and gutteral, their connection to each other strengthening in a flood of color and wild pleasure as he and his magic move within her, and Gwynn moans against his mouth, their bodies and fused magic burning as hot as a prismatic star.

She tries to hold back her cry of ecstasy as the chromatic pleasure builds with astonishing intensity, a gilded heat rising through her every line even as conflict rears and she resists her out-of-control desire.

Fights the building tide.

But then Mavrik growls into her shoulder and his magic and want detonate, the force of his release tipping her over into her own starbright explosion, pleasure and light flashing through her in a radiant blur.

And then his eyes meet hers through the bright haze of light . . . and Gwynn comes undone.

That *look* . . . it steals her breath, the prismatic color suffusing his eyes like a molten rainbow that she wants to fall into *forever*.

She's unprepared. Unprepared for this much emotion toward him igniting inside her.

"Gwynnifer," he says, his voice and magic full of such raw feeling that Gwynn's heart clenches. He runs a hand down her arm, trailing shimmering sparks as he glances toward her fastlines. "Your hands . . . are you all right?"

"I . . . I think so," she murmurs as she flexes her hands and looks at them, noting, with a jolt, that both her hands and wrists—and his—are marked *only* in glowing gold lines, the patterns on their wrists now identical to the fastline designs marking their hands.

Her magic and feelings suddenly upending, Gwynn tenses and gives him a slight push away, even as everything in her yearns to keep him close.

Mavrik responds immediately, unlinking their bodies, but his magic keeps hold of her in a fervid embrace of color, their bodies lit up with it

Gwynn moves away, her heart constricting. She catches his quick look of concern and confusion as she draws on her clothing. Mavrik tugs on his pants, his magic a tempest of emotion, eyes blazing as he lifts his hands to study his wrists' new golden Sealing lines.

"I think we did it," Gwynn manages, conflict brewing inside her like a storm.

Because she loved it. Even though she fought the feeling, she *loved* being with Mavrik.

Much more than she ever loved being with Geoffrey.

"I think we're fully Sealed," she roughly states, her out-of-control emotions surging as she takes in his body once more.

His handsome form glimmers with incandescent streaks of rainbow *everywhere* they touched. For a moment her gaze is riveted on him, her pulse thudding as her eyes flick over the lingering effects of their impassioned coupling.

Mortification rises in a relentless tide because she knows, from the tingling energy coursing over her own skin, that her body shines in a similar way.

Mavrik moves toward her, his power shimmering around her in loving embrace, as if he can read her conflict, read her drawing away from him. "Gwynn," he says, taking gentle hold of her shoulder. "There's something deeper here than just over-taking a Sealing—"

"Stop." Gwynn cuts him off, the fault lines of religion and culture threatening to pull her into their gaping chasm. "Please. I can't."

"Hey," he says, holding his ground even as she flexes her shoulder, attempting to shrug him off, even as every speck of her magic strains toward him. "This isn't evil," he sets down in firm refute of the internal war Gwynn knows he can feel sparking through their magic. "No matter what you're thinking," he insists, "what just happened between us . . . it wasn't wrong. I genuinely want you, regardless of this situation."

His hand slides down to caress her upper arm, his touch tentative, and she shudders against it. Fights her magic's bucking pull toward him.

And then Mavrik releases her arm and holds out his gold-fastline-marked hand, palm up.

Gwynn stares at it, tears stinging her eyes, his power caressing hers with loving strength.

She slides her hand into his, and the two of them study each other for a protracted moment, the fierce alliance in their shared gaze sending a flush of heat through Gwynn's lines.

His lips ticking up, Mavrik lifts her hand and gently kisses her palm, a potent rush of his magic flowing into her, as if his floodgates have been fully breached.

Hers blown wide open.

"Allies," Gwynn forces out. "It's all I can be to you right now. Allies fighting against the cursed Shadow."

His jaw tightens, and Gwynn's heart clenches over the hurt that flashes through their intimately linked magic—a connection that's stronger than anything she *ever* had with Geoffrey.

Remorse surges, turning her magic into a rioting tempest of dark blues.

"All right, then, my *ally*," Mavrik drawls, challenge in the word. She can sense him holding back the hurt. Holding back a thousand protests to the contrary.

A more intense warmth for him sparks in her.

Because she can also sense him giving her space to work this out, as he puts the bigger picture ahead of this thing building between them . . . and ahead of his turmoil over her response to it.

"This Sealing," Gwynn forces out. "It's strengthened our connection." Her throat goes dry as she meets his gaze once more, color raying through them both.

He nods, and Gwynn can sense it's taking everything in him to mirror her formal distance, his eyes piercingly serious as he traces his thumb over the back of her hand, the enticing motion making her shiver.

"We should get some sleep, my beautiful . . . *ally*," he offers, lifting her hand once more and gently kissing the back of it, the mischief lighting his eyes cutting through the confusion of the moment. "And tomorrow," he croons, "we'll portal to the Northern Forest, break into it, and intercept the Prophecy." A harsh look enters his golden gaze. "And then we'll find the Forest's Great Tree, bind its magic to ours, and run every forbidden color straight through Vogel's Shadow power."

FOREST FIRE

Elloren

Northern Forest
Eighteen days after Xishlon

"Ancient One . . . *no* . . ."

I throw my palms to III's bark, desperation burning through my core. Because my Wyvernbond to Yvan has been *severed* by III, Yvan completely absorbed into III's huge expanse.

Every nerve lit with concern, I claw the wall of bark before me with newly sharp, deep-green nails, fearful that III will douse Yvan's Icaral of Prophecy fire and slay him, mistaking his power for Vogel's. The sudden absence of my bond to Yvan is an excruciating thing, like a crucial piece of me has been torn away.

"*Release him!*" I cry, pressing my palms to III's trunk, wanting to dive in after Yvan, even if it means the obliteration of us both.

My surrounding bonded Forest is disturbingly still, its elemental aura like a trapped breath. And more intimidating yet, III's energy and encircling green mist are gone, only a residual tang of monumental power reverberating in the air, as if the Great Tree has drawn every last trace of its elemental might and focus inward.

Toward Yvan.

A gentle hand comes to my shoulder. I turn to find Yulan beside me, a deeply concerned light in her lichen-lashed eyes, her heron kindred hugging her side.

The dam holding back my flood of heartache shatters.

"I *can't* lose him," I tell her as the tears break free. "I've already lost my fastmate, Lukas. I *can't* lose Yvan too." I draw my wand hand toward my chest, as if searching for a cinder of Yvan's Wyvernbond there. But find *nothing*.

I slump, begging III through tear-soaked lips, begging the entire Forest, to spare Yvan, to no response.

Only silent, immovable bark.

Errilith lowers his giant raven head to my arm and nudges me with his midnight beak, his power coursing around me in protective ropes of pitch-hued mist, an otherworldly stillness flowing into my lines via our kindred link. But Errilith's eerie Deathkin reassurance does nothing to assuage my wild fear. Two obsidian snakes slither onto my lap, then another, dawn's light momentarily dimming.

I turn and meet Hazel's black stare. The slender Death Fae-Dryad has lowered himself to one knee beside me, branch-horned Sylvan just behind him. Hazel's coal-black eyes are focused on mine, horns rising from his short, midnight hair. He holds up his III-marked palm. "The Forest aligns with unlikely ones," he reassures me, his subterranean voice vibrating over my skin as more dark snakes slither up from the ground and curl around his lower body.

A sudden thought strikes. "How much of a lag did your portal have?" Fear spiking, I look to Sylvan and meet his penetrating, pine green stare. "And how long was I in III?"

"Our portal held a fifteen-day lag," Sylvan answers. "You merged with III for three."

My mind whirls, my time in the Dryad portal having seemed to span a matter of seconds, not *fifteen days*. An unmooring sensation grips hold. Because I've just made a horrible mistake. Even if Yvan survives, time has been on Vogel's side. Vogel's forces are likely almost *here*, poised just outside this Forest. And if Vogel strikes while Yvan is still caught in III . . .

"Are there other Dryads in this Forest?" I question Sylvan, Yulan, and Hazel, my alarm burgeoning.

"Our Dryad'kin live in the Forest canopy to the north," Sylvan says, giving me a severe look. "We are soldiers who protect the Heart of the Forest."

"Vogel is *coming*," I warn them. "He warred with III to keep hold of me. He knows where I am. And he's coming for Yvan and for me . . ."

"Well, he won't get through our warding!" Oaklyyn spits out, her fists tight around her branch weapon, her wolverine growling as she glares daggers at me along with mushroom-tressed Lyptus and the huge Dryad with the bear kindred, who they call Larch. "Our wards have stood for generations," Oaklyyn cries, "keeping all non-Dryad'kin *out*. Especially those who would *burn down our Forest*."

A flash of defiance blazes through me. "The Forest is *wrong* about Yvan," I snarl back. "The trees think Yvan's and Vogel's fires are one and the same, but they're *not*." I swiftly explain Vogel's brief theft of our Wyvernbond.

I give Sylvan, Yulan, and Hazel an imploring look. "You have to convince III to spare Yvan. *Please*."

Feeling as if the world is spinning off its axis, I turn and press both palms against III's dark trunk once more, desperate to sense even a *trace* of Yvan's fire.

"The Forest aligned with you despite your fiery lineage," Yulan says, her melodic Dryadin shot through with vast compassion. My tear-blurred eyes swing to hers as I grasp the trace of hope in her tone like a lifeline. "Over the past few days," Yulan softly continues, "I gained a sense of your Icaral's valor. III will get to the root of who he really is. And III will accept him."

"III will *not*," Lyptus snaps, like the lash of a whip. The expression on her face is unforgiving, her words a blow, devastating in their finality. "Forest binding magic requires *connection*," she stresses and glances pointedly at her silver panther, who lets out a low, resonant growl at me. "The kindred bond is a *conduit* for that connection." Lyptus nods brusquely toward my flock of giant ravens, a merciless light filling her green eyes. "There is *no Forest creature* that can withstand an Icaral of Prophecy's fire."

"Then what will happen to him?" I demand, feeling like the ground is giving way.

"Dryad'kin, listen to me," Yulan prods, the sympathy in her gaze willing my attention. "To dwell inside the Natural Matrix is a journey of faith."

This does *nothing* to assuage my fear.

I look to III's canopy, to the sky above. *Please*, I implore the heavens, sending my words out to any deity that will hear me. *Please bring Yvan back to me* . . .

A burst of shimmering green light blasts from III, and I flinch back, along with the others, III's aura of elemental might and green mist suddenly whirling around me, blazing from the Great Tree's core, my kindred flock of ravens cawing.

III's bark bulges outward and morphs rapidly into the shape of a man before the bark gives way and Yvan is crouched before me, my palms pressed to III's bark just above his shoulders, his chest heaving with ragged breaths, his wings extending.

He raises his head, and his shocking newly violet-fire eyes don't so much meet as collide with mine, his gaze burning through the space between us.

A strangled cry escapes my throat as I hurl myself at him at the same time he surges toward me, my rise of emotion so strong I fear I'll blaze apart. Yvan grabs tight hold of me, toppling us both to the ground, the two of us hurtling into a kiss.

Violet-tinted fire blasts through me, and I arch against Yvan as he sears our Wyvernbond back into being with potent force, III's enveloping aura flowing through the connection.

The love in his kiss sends a volcanic line of emotion through me, his fervid mouth feeding the whole, heightened force of his fire into mine as I send my Dryad-fire into him, hot tears giving way.

Yvan breaks the kiss and draws back, his eyes glowing such an incandescent *violet* it steals my breath. Our bond pulses hotter than ever before, in an unbreakable pillar of intermingling violet and green flame.

"Elloren . . ." Yvan says, my name torn from the base of his throat. He lifts his hand to show me his palm.

My heart stutters.

There, marked on his palm, just as it is on mine and on the palm of every Dryad in this circle, is an imprint of III.

"This *cannot be*," Oaklyyn rages as Yvan and I both rise. Her elemental aura lashes at us with such vehemence that I startle, her wolverine bristling as her hand lashes out toward Yvan. "He has no kindred and never can have one!"

Yvan meets Oaklyyn's blistering stare without flinching as III's embracing green mist twines around us both. "I have been linked to a kindred," he tells her in fluent Dryadin. He stops, his eyes widening as shock ripples not only through his fire, but through everyone's elemental power in response to his sudden fluency in the Forest'kin language.

Yvan closes his III-marked palm into a fist, then unfurls it once more, revealing a compact, deep-purple pinecone.

Sylvan, Yulan, and Hazel step forward to scrutinize it, an astonished expression overcoming Sylvan's raptor-sharp, pine green features as he lifts his gaze to Yvan's. "III has given you a kindred Forest in the East."

Yulan's shocked expression is a mirror of Sylvan's. "This is rare," she marvels, her heron's wings fluttering, "to be kin-bonded to an *entire Forest* . . ."

"Which he'll *promptly burn to the ground*!" Oaklyyn snarls, her stance a tight coil of fury. "Sylvan, don't let this happen! He'll be the *death* of it!"

"How can this be?" Yulan presses Yvan, her lovely features tensed with concern.

Yvan silently, almost ceremoniously, steps back from us all, lowers himself to the ground and pushes the cone's lower half into the mossy soil. Then he raises his hand, palm down, just above the cone. The violet flame in Yvan's eyes takes on a hotter glow, his fire aura suddenly burning with such potency it sends a current of heat through my rootlines. I shiver against the sensation as Yvan's III-imprinted hand begins to glow violet.

He splays his fingers with emphatic force, and a stream of purple fire blasts down from his palm. I flinch as the fire meets the cone and it bursts into flame, its coating of shiny violet resin beginning to melt. I wait anxiously, confused by his actions, the entire surrounding Forest seeming to hold its breath alongside me.

But then, the unexpected happens.

Yvan's flame dies down, and the cone unfurls and sprouts thin, violet pine needles and soil piercing roots. The needles rapidly fan out and multiply, new branches forking and needling until a small purple pine seedling stands below us.

Surprise echoes through the Northern Forest's aura as the Dryads trade astonished looks.

All except one.

"I know this tree of the East," the huge, branch-horned Dryad—Larch—rumbles, his enormous black bear kindred lumbering behind him as he approaches. He points a thick, green-glimmering index finger at the seedling. "This is a Nightwood Pine. From the Eastern Realm's Zhilaan Forest. It needs fire to germinate. Fire *regenerates* this Forest."

Oaklyyn is blinking at the pine seedling, a look of internal war ravaging her face. Hazel smirks at her, his expression one of triumph as snakes twine around his black-clad form.

Yvan meets my eyes in a blaze of heat that sends a shiver of warmth down my spine. "III bonded me to the Zhilaan's Nightwood Forest," he explains as powerful energy wraps around both our bond and his core of fire, tugging him toward the northeast and channeling our bond's violet-green flame toward this Forest that loves fire. "Bonding to the Zhilaan was like being welcomed *home*," he enthuses, his voice hitching around the Dryadin word for *home* before his words break off, his fire charged with emotion. His gaze swings to the Dryads. "I never wanted to be a force of destruction," he tells them. "This *weapon* of the Prophecy. It always went against my Lasair pull to *heal*."

"I believe this of you, Lasair'kin," Yulan assures him as she affectionately strokes the head of her heron kindred.

"But when III showed me the Zhilaan Forest," Yvan says to her, "I learned that my fire is able to spark new life and protect it." He gives me an emotion-saturated look. "I felt like, for the first time in my life, I was being shown a place where I truly belong."

"I imagine we have much in common, Winged One," Hazel quietly interjects. "Both of us widely reviled, you as Icaral and I as Deathkin. Our 'vast evil' condemned by the pious while they mutter prayers of protection against us both." Hazel's expression darkens, bitterness in the depths of his midnight eyes as he casts a chilling look at Oaklyyn. "But the Forest cares not for the boundaries of human-kind. The Forest is creating its *own* circle of Dryad'khin, and *no one* can keep you out once the Forest has welcomed you home."

The word *Dryad'khin* strikes me as revolutionary in its implications—a term that embraces not only the Dryad'*kin*, like me, who possess actual Tree Fae lineage, but also the *khin* of the Dryads, including those who are simply aligned with both them and the Natural World.

My thoughts careen toward Lukas and his insistence to me on the night of the Yule Dance that Mages had Dryad lineage. An achingly vivid memory surfaces, of Lukas's subversive smile and the flecks of snow catching on his black hair. My throat tightens, sorrow piercing my heart as tears sheen my eyes, the sudden desire to have him here with us so intense I feel gutted.

"Lukas should have had this," I rasp out to Yvan in a ragged voice as I rage against Lukas's selfless end. "He would have been transformed by III too."

Yvan's invisible fire flows around me, and he nods and draws me into an embrace, my forehead pressed to his hot skin as he holds me tight and I rail against both the loss of Lukas and what was lost to *him* his whole life—his connection to Forest power.

And to the Dryad he always was.

"He lost *everything*," I whisper as the tears come, Yvan's hot hands splayed against my back, keeping me close. "He gave up everything, for all of us."

"I know it, Elloren," Yvan says, voice raw, empathy blazing through our bond. "I know he did."

I tense against the undertow of pain, devastatingly clear on what Lukas would say if he were with me at this moment.

Have your moment of grief, Elloren. One *moment.*

Then pull yourself together and fight back.

I meet Yvan's searching look as he raises his palm to cup my cheek then leans in to kiss my forehead, his warmth suffusing every inch of me, the love he's flooding through our bond an anchoring force, enabling me to quickly pull myself together.

"I was offered a binding to the Zhilaan Forest," Yvan confides, his violet-fire gaze locked on mine. "I accepted. And vowed to use my power to protect it." Sparks flash at the edges of his eyes. "I'm being called there, Elloren. It's like a migratory pull. We need to gather everyone together—my mother, your family, and all our allies—and join them *all* to the Natural Matrix. I understand now, what you felt and saw inside of III. This fight . . . it isn't what we thought. We're standing at the precipice of a complete unraveling of the Natural World."

Yvan's mention of our families and allies sparks a renewed awareness of Tierney's disappearance, and worry for her rises. I turn to the Dryads. "Where is Tierney?" I ask. "And the Death Fae she was with?"

"After they led the Errilor Ravens here," Sylvan answers, "they were drawn east through an Asrai water bond. I sensed it empathically as they disappeared."

My mind whirls.

East. Perhaps drawn back to the Vo River by Tierney's Asrai'kin to fight the Shadow in a land decimated by Vogel's forces. And Vogel has had eighteen days to regroup and plan attacks, not just against Yvan and me, but against the entire East.

Yvan turns to Oaklyyn, a conciliatory light in his eyes. "I have more of an understanding now," he ventures, "of why you were willing to battle me if it meant saving the Forest from being destroyed—"

"You understand *nothing*, Icaral," she spits out at him, her eyes bright with hate.

"Then *teach me*," he rejoins, meeting her ire with impressive steadiness as he wraps his hand around mine. "It's true. I have Icaral of Prophecy power. So *use it.* Use it for the Forest."

Hazel tosses a sly look at Oaklyyn. "So many unlikely ones being called into the Forest's circle," he croons. "Having trouble keeping them out, Oaklyyn?"

Oaklyyn's livid gaze swings toward him. "Just like I had trouble keeping you out, *halfling.*"

The world pulses aggressively with Hazel's power as he gives Oaklyyn a chilling look.

Oaklyyn takes a confrontational step toward him, slashing her hand toward Yvan and me, her lips trembling, "Just like them, you'll bring nothing but death to the Forest. And then you'll *feast* on it."

Hazel's black lips pull back into an otherworldly snarl, his teeth blackening and elongating. "You know *nothing* of what I am," he bites out, gnashing his jaws at her.

"We need to *align*," Yvan says to both Hazel and Oaklyyn. Their combative gazes snap toward him. "III's message to me was clear. We're *all* needed in this fight."

Yulan's gaze lights on Oaklyyn, a beseeching look on her delicate features. "Things are changing, Dryad'kin," she murmurs.

"Things are *always* changing," Hazel agrees, his deepened voice seeming to rumble up from under the ground. "But even more so now." His midnight gaze slides back to Oaklyyn. "Hold on to the rigid lines of the past at your own peril, Dryad'kin. It will bring *Void Death* down on us all. I stand with *Natural Death*." He swipes a black-taloned hand toward the giant ravens surrounding us. "As do they. The Errilor are here because there is a Reckoning at hand, and we *must* subvert it. *Together.*"

Answering strands of black, misty power flash into being around my ravens, the suspended mist flowing out to encircle us all as confusion blazes through both my fire and Yvan's.

"What's a Reckoning?" I ask Hazel.

Hazel levels his enthralling gaze on me, the world pulsing darker as Errilith pulls our thread of connection toward the ground, images of mass extinctions of animals and plants and humans flashing through my mind, gooseflesh rising on my skin.

"A Reckoning," Hazel warns, "is when Natural Death is forced to wash over Erthia. It descends in response to a severe Unbalancing of the Natural World."

I briefly meet Errilith's mournful stare before Yvan and I exchange looks of alarm, and I remember III's vision of Shadow power advancing on Erthia's last stand of the living Forest.

Yvan meets Hazel's otherworldly stare head-on. "We need to pool our power and get our defenses ready to protect this Forest. Vogel *will* attack—"

Black Witch!

A flash of vermillion and gold fire blazes through my vision, and I startle, an urgent hiss invading my mind, everything around me searing from sight.

Raz'zor? I send out through the fire, grasping for a connection, but Raz'zor's fire disappears as quickly as it ignited in a spangle of red and gold flame, a trace of purple sparks trailing in its wake. I whip my stunned gaze toward Yvan and catch a trace of gold, red, and purple fire streaking through his eyes as well, a mirror of my own surprise evident on his angular features.

"What just happened?" Sylvan demands. "I sensed incoming Wyvernfire."

"It's . . . a dragon we're horded to," I answer as my thoughts spin. "Raz'zor . . ."

Yvan's nostrils flare, as if he's scenting the flame. "I sensed Naga's fire merging with Raz'zor's, along with a host of other Wyverns."

Another flash of Raz'zor's fire hits me, my vision searing to flames once more, my heart launching into a hammering beat. Because I can read danger in the urgent way Raz'zor is sending his power out to me. Rough images form in his fire: *a winged horde of broken dragons, taking flight; a line of portals, arches flickering; a curved Noi sword; an Amaz axe.*

"Multiple armies," I gasp, looking to the Dryads as my vision clears. "Multiple forces are setting out. And they're all converging." My gaze collides with Yvan's, alarm surging through our joint fire. "Yvan . . . they're all coming *here*."

CHAPTER FOUR

STORMING RAINBOW

Gwynnifer Croft

Northern Forest Sublands
Sixteen days after Xishlon

Gwynn sweeps through the portal in a color-flashing blur, hurled at the speed of light from the Agolith Desert Sublands toward the southern underground edge of the Northern Forest.

She stumbles from the portal, knees hitting stone. Wynter, Sparrow, Valasca, and most of the others stagger to their feet before her. Gwynn blinks, and the multihued crystalline cavern surrounding her triggers a hail of chromatic sparks through her vision at the same time that she's assailed by a stretching agony in her Magelines, her body jerked painfully toward the portal at her back.

"Mavrik!" she cries, multicolored light strobing across her vision as she skids backward over rough stone toward the portal, her twinned lines desperate to get closer to Mavrik before they stretch to the breaking point. In a flash of dread, Gwynn realizes that if Mavrik doesn't exit the portal soon, their lines will snap and they'll both die.

"Gwynn, what's happening?" Mynx cries, the willowy Elf rushing toward her along with Cael, Valasca, and Wynter, just as Mavrik bursts through the portal's golden mist.

He falls to his hands and knees, and their eyes lock in an explosion of color. A strangled cry escapes Gwynn as they lunge toward each other and grab desperate hold, the agonizing stretch of their twinned lines releasing with a swoop of vertigo. Hugging each other close, they breathe in staggered gasps as their magic re-fuses, the pain strafing through Gwynn's lines replaced by a rippling surge of relief.

"Let's not try that again," Mavrik rasps against the base of her neck, his magic twining around her with such covetous fervor that it sends a shock wave of emotion through her. Because everything in her is surging toward him just as intensely.

Including her heart.

Swept into upheaval over the power of their connection, Gwynn draws away from him and glances around. She pulls in a deep breath, color strobing through their twinned power in raying blasts as they take in the surrounding scene along with their traveling companions.

They're on a large, flat bridge of stone spanning the center of a huge, crystalline geode-cavern, an expansive river rushing by far below. The geode's luminous crystals are a mosaic of every color in the rainbow, the river's reflection of the iridescent hues brilliantly marbling the swirling waters streaming beneath them. Huge dark roots undulate through the cavern's ceiling, and a vision of the Great Ironwood Tree pulses through Gwynn's mind.

A reflexive ecstasy takes hold of Gwynn as the translucent images of hundreds of Watchers, perched on the largest roots, appear and then vanish just as quickly.

Gwynn looks to Wynter, shocked into continued silence as they both take in how the Verdyllion Wand in Wynter's hand has turned fully prismatic, as if drawing on the explosion of color surrounding them. The Agolith Flame Hawks are perched on Wynter's shoulders, their eyes intent on Gwynn and Mavrik, a number of Wynter's other bird kindreds winging around the mammoth geode's interior in joyful arcs.

"Mavrik . . . the *color*," Gwynn barely manages. She meets his golden eyes to find them fired up with almost as much emotion as they were after they . . .

A flush sears Gwynn's skin, and she averts her eyes only to be swept up anew in the gorgeous barrage of forbidden Fae hues. Awe tumbles to life inside her as she remembers what she's read and overheard about the Smaragdalfar religious myths that speak of the Goddess Oo'na's Sacred Roots—roots anchored in all the Light of the world and suffusing the root systems and Sublands around them with their light power for leagues and leagues.

Roots that feed and anchor all of life.

"The Smaragdalfar myths," Gwynn marvels, looking to Mynx'lia'luure as she and Mavrik rise to their feet, "they're true in this."

Yyzz'ra, Gavryyl, and Valkyr all scowl at Gwynn.

"Our 'myths' are true in *all things*, Crow," Yyzz'ra snipes. "Did you really think your pious Mage delusions defined Erthia?" She draws back, a mocking look overtaking her expression. "You *did*," she spits out with a disgusted laugh. "You actually thought your *Book of the Ancients* ruled above all else."

Yyzz'ra's words are an unmooring blow, and Gwynn feels the chastising sting of them, so much so that she barely hears Valasca and Mynx'lia'luure as they, pointing upward, comment on the broad reach of Mavrik and Gwynn's Subland shielding.

Gwynn looks up and can just make out their shimmering net-shield beyond the network of roots as she's overtaken by the implosion of her lifelong religious beliefs. No solid ground to land on anywhere. Nothing but a storming swirl of forbidden color and a forbidden heart-pull to Mavrik Glass.

"Do the Alfsigr myths speak of a Great Tree filled with light power?" Gwynn asks Wynter, meeting the Icaral's serene, silver gaze.

"They do," Wynter says.

"The Amaz, Noi, and Urisk myths do, as well," Valasca offers.

Gwynn nods in dazed agreement even as she struggles against the damning sense of being hopelessly, irredeemably lost to sacrilege.

Wynter peers closely at Gwynn. "All of Erthia's myths speak of the Watchers as well, in some form or other." She glances meaningfully around the cavern, where the multitudes of Watchers were just perched, before lifting the Wand-Stylus in her hand. "And they all speak of the Verdyllion."

"How will we find Oo'na's Tree once we get past the Dryad wards?" Mynx wonders.

As if in answer, the Verdyllion pulses out a flash of color.

Everyone's gaze flies toward it, Rhys's, Wynter's, and Cael's bone-white features briefly suffused with the Verdyllion's chromatic light.

Wynter lifts the Verdyllion, and a stronger burst of multihued light fans out from it, rapidly coalescing into a gigantic, translucent compass that fills the huge geode's center, the lines of its chromatic design passing harmlessly through anything it touches, including Gwynnifer and her companions. The compass's suspended circular form is divided into seven sections, each colored with one of the seven colors of prism-diffracted light.

Gwynn passes her hand through the golden section of the compass, awestruck as she takes in how its huge, silvery needle is not pointed toward any of a compass's usual directional points, but toward the image of a color-flashing Ironwood tree.

"How did you conjure this compass?" Yyzz'ra demands of Wynter, seeming shaken as the compass contracts inward until it's the size of a small plate, hovering around the Verdyllion's tip.

"I'm finding that this Wand-Stylus is many things," Wynter answers. "Things dangerous to the Shadow. It breaks cruel bonds—" Wynter's silver-fire eyes pass over everyone gathered, a small smile lifting her pale lips "—and brings unlikely people together."

"And it's a compass," Gwynn breathes out.

Wynter's serene smile widens. "It's a compass," she agrees. "So, let's follow it." Compassion lights the Icaral's gaze. "Have faith, Light Mage."

Faith in what? Gwynn agonizes, her religious bulwark a swirl of broken beliefs. Shattered in a matter of months.

As if sensing her disquiet, Mavrik's hand comes to her shoulder, his magic a warm caress. Color stings to life on Gwynn's lips as she fights the urge to embrace him. Flustered, she gently shrugs off his hand and steps away from him, cursing the revealing riot of color flashing over her mouth. And now his. She's barely able to meet his impassioned, questioning gaze.

"Let's keep a fast pace," Valasca commands, cutting through Gwynn's color thrall. Valasca's eyes flick probingly from Gwynn to Mavrik, clearly noting the color flashing over their mouths. "Now that we know the way forward," she says, "we've got a Prophecy to intercept." She levels her runic blade at Gwynn and Mavrik, grinning rakishly. "And *you two* have some Dryad wards to get us past with all that fully twinned power."

Guided by the Verdyllion, they journey through the day and into the night, the Varg time-keeping runes marked on the Subland Elves' wrists tracking the passage of hours.

Gwynn follows Mavrik and the others through a narrow black opal tunnel, the stone veined with every color of Erthia, the color's iridescence so vivid it sends dizzying flash after flash of forbidden color through Gwynn and Mavrik's connected lines, her physical draw to him difficult to think around.

"The Great Tree's Subland light magic," she murmurs to him, "it's intensifying our twinning."

Mavrik casts her a glance over his shoulder, and just that brief eye contact sends another spangled rush of color through Gwynn's lines, along with that unforgivable sting of heated color over her lips and everywhere they touched last night.

"I feel it too," Mavrik states tersely, his gaze snapping away from hers as their magic clamors to *fuse.*

From the slight tightening of his shoulders and the tensing of his neck, she can tell he's struggling with this just as intensely. Heat blooms on Gwynn's face as she's overtaken by the memory of Mavrik's multihued explosion of passion when they took hold of the Sealing spell, and how much she loved being with him in that way, the surrounding riot of color making her crave it now.

Mavrik turns again and gives her a heated look, his lips so intensely suffused with color that she averts her gaze, upended by having such strong feelings for him in so short a time.

It's just your twinned magic, she chastises herself, her throat tight with longing. *You can't be falling in love with him . . .*

As conflict knifes through her, they all soldier on, rounding bend after bend of opal-veined tunnel while Gwynn is increasingly swept up in the sense that she's forever cast out of the Ancient One's favor, not only for so egregiously betraying her fasting, but for wresting hold of the Magedom's most sacred of spells and wrestling them into submission.

Going up against the Ancient One Himself.

And now . . . she's following an Alfsigr Icaral wielding the Ancient One's Wand toward the Subland roots of Oo'na's Tree to tap into the Great Tree's vast elemental power. It's such a roiling ball of blasphemy upon blasphemy, Gwynn can feel herself skidding straight toward every last one of the Ancient One's punishing hells.

Her tortuous thoughts break off as they round another bend, spill into a larger opal cavern and come to an abrupt halt.

The underground river slowly streams in front of them, a dark opal bridge spanning it. Beyond the bridge, there's a broad area of flat stone with a line of huge, forest green Dryad runes suspended above it. A translucent, shimmering green wall emanates from the runes, flowing upward through their multihued Subland barrier above and downward through the cavern's stone floor below, a larger, vividly emerald Varg rune hovering before the Dryad barrier.

They cross the bridge, and Mynx and Cael step toward the Varg rune. Mynx touches the air around it, her nails clinking against an invisible, glass-like barrier.

"This is a primordial Varg'plith'nile rune," Mynx says, her tone awestruck as she reaches up to press her index finger's tip to the center of the rune. Green light rays out from her touch, illuminating both her and Cael beside her, their hands interlaced, and Gwynn is struck once more by how the two of them have stubbornly decided to display their feelings for each other despite the fierce censure Yyzz'ra,

Valkyr, and Gavryyl continue to throw their way.

"It is a Varg'*uuth*'nile," Yyzz'ra sharply affirms, with a cutting look toward Cael. "To protect Oo'na's Sacred Subland Rooting from *Varg'plith*."

Sunland heathen filth. Gwynn inwardly flinches in response to the Smaragdalfar slur, and Mynx'lia'luure's silver eyes fill with outrage.

Gwynn recalls how the term *Varg'plith* is spoken about in the Smaragdalfar's Holy Texts. Heathen filth that, in primordial times, let loose a Shadow pollution to crawl all over Erthia's surface, throwing the world off-balance, the Righteous Children of Oo'na called to rise up against the Evil Shadowed Ones. To cleanse the Blessed Sublands of their unholy taint.

Gwynn is clear, from Yyzz'ra's condemning glare, that Varg'plith includes not only Mynx and Cael, but herself, Mavrik, Wynter, Valasca, Rhys, and Sparrow. Gwynn tenses, finding it jarring to be cast as an Evil One in someone else's religious story, the uncomforable questions ringing out, refusing to be silenced—

Who are the true Evil Ones?

Which religious story is true?

Mavrik draws close to the Varg'uuth'nile rune and studies it along with Mynx as Gwynn wonders, uneasily, what will happen when they reach the Great Tree's roots with such clashing religious beliefs at play amongst their small group. She glances at Yyzz'ra, remembering the conversation she overheard when Yyzz'ra outlined her desire to wrest the Verdyllion from Wynter once they arrived at "Oo'na's Roots."

Are they about to go to war with each other?

"Are you able to cut a path through this Varg wardage?" Mavrik asks Yyzz'ra.

Yyzz'ra shoots him another glare and shakes her head. "The magic is densely layered and impenetrable."

"Gwynnifer," Wynter murmurs, and Gwynn turns to find Wynter holding the Verdyllion out to her.

Gwynn's disquiet intensifies. Swallowing, she reaches out and takes hold of the Verdyllion.

A shockingly potent sizzle of color flashes from the Verdyllion and courses through her and Mavrik's twinned power. Gwynn stiffens, their magic giving a taut pull toward each other.

"Shall we have a go at it?" Mavrik gently prods as she meets his intent gaze.

Gwynn nods stiffly and forcibly presses back her rising pull toward him. She and Mavrik draw nearer to the primordial rune. There's a metallic tang of sorcery emanating from it—sorcery she can taste on the back of her tongue. Tracing the tip of the Verdyllion over the rune, Gwynn murmurs the Varg structure spell.

A translucent echo of the rune's imprint telescopes toward her, an astonished breath escaping quiet Sparrow. Gwynn's eyes remain pinned on the rune as she takes in each component, her mind separating them into their interlocking elemental building blocks.

"It's an ancient version of a barrier rune woven into three different magic-repelling runes," she states, tracing the Verdyllion's tip over the emerald lines. "We need to locate the place they're locked together."

"Right here," Mavrik says, pointing toward one of the rune's sections, his hand brushing against hers.

Gwynn's pulse leaps, and sparks race over her skin as power sizzles through her lines. Rattled, she jerks her hand away from his touch. Mavrik shoots her an intense look, and a flash of unsettled indigo shudders through their twinned power.

Gwynn confers stiltedly with Mavrik, careful not to touch him again as they plot out their magical approach. Struggling to keep her bucking magic from breaking loose to embrace his, she raises the Verdyllion at the same time that he raises his Varg-marked wand, the two of them murmuring a Varg spell in unison.

Streams of emerald light bolt from their wands, the bolts colliding with two different runic sections in an explosion of gem-green sparks, the locked sections bulging out almost to the point of breaking.

But it's not enough power, and the locked sections spring back into place, refusing to give.

Gwynn and Mavrik work straight through the night and the next day, the two of them soon encircled by a suspended rainstorm of amplification runes from every runic system on Erthia. But still, the primordial Varg barrier rune refuses to give way, their every combined magical effort repelled.

Evening descends, the others eventually moving off into side caverns to grab some sleep. Gwynn steps back, sweat beading her brow, her chest tight with frustration bordering on desperation.

Mavrik sheathes his wand and rounds on her, intensity firing in his eyes. "I've finally parsed out what's going on. You're fighting our connection. Gwynnifer. We're *twinned*. If you fight it, neither of us can fully utilize our magic."

Gwynn's heart twists, every suppressed emotion rearing, her magic straining to pull the emotion through it. And thrust it out toward him. "I don't know how to stop fighting it," she admits, her voice breaking, her eyes burning. "I . . . I've developed strong feelings for you in such a short time and . . . I don't know how to handle that."

Mavrik narrows his eyes at her, his magic suddenly sweeping around her in an ardent embrace. "Come with me," he says, offering her his hand.

Gwynn follows him toward a small side cavern, her lightlines storming with every hue of distress—ashen dark blues, bruise blacks, turmoil-laden maroons. She falls back against a wall and tightly closes her eyes, wrestling with her uncontainable longing for him.

"Gwynnifer."

She opens her eyes to meet his, the static in their fused lightlines like a storming rainbow, Mavrik's golden irises flashing with impassioned brightness. But his magic . . . it's held back, only a trace of its turbulent flow palpable against hers.

"What are we going to do about this?" he asks, the storming color firing even more intensely through their twinned magic as he motions between them.

Gwynn can barely pull in a breath, her heartbeat thudding against her ribs. "It's wrong for me to feel this way about you," she manages. "We've known each other for a matter of days—"

"During which we've permanetly fused our magic and have become intimate with each other," Mavrik emphatically interjects. "Gwynn, I can sense your *every emotion*. Even though you're trying to keep us separate."

"I can sense yours, as well," she admits, lips trembling.

"We complement each other," Mavrik says. "And not just because you gave me a line of light power I lacked. Gwynn, it's increasingly clear that we're perfectly compatible in *every single way*. Do you sense it, as well?"

She blinks back the tears stinging her eyes as she clings to the understanding in his gaze and the affection he's flowing around her magic—understanding the likes of which she's never experienced with anyone else.

"I sense it too," Gwynn whispers. "And, Ancient One help me, I want to give in to this."

"Then we should," Mavrik offers. "Gwynn, for so many reasons." He holds out his golden-fastline-marked hand to her, a look of resolve in his eyes. "I can't fight it. I want you. In *every* way."

The deep-hued storm of conflict knifing through Gwynn's lines intensifies, her heart knotting, painfully tight, and she knows he can feel *all of it*.

"I've fallen in love with you," Mavrik admits, voice rough, his magic holding steady against hers, tears sheening his eyes. "For the first time in my life, I'm truly in love. And it's not just our magical or physical draw. I have *never* met someone I can be so honest with. You understand me in a way no one else can. Like I understand you. And I love every last thing I feel about you through our linked magic."

Gwynn can barely hold his gaze, the intensity of the feelings running through his magic shearing straight through her heart, mirroring exactly the emotions igniting in her own lines.

"Ancient One, Mavrik," she manages, her eyes glassing over as invisible sparks of color crackle through the space between them. "I broke a *sacred fasting*. With someone I've known for an incredibly short amount of time." She holds up her fastmarked hand. "I don't want to feel this guilt, but it's ripping my heart in *two*."

"Yes," he fires back. "And in that short time, we've forged a stronger connection than I have with people I've known my *whole life*."

A sob almost breaks free from Gwynn's throat because it's true for her, as well. She knows it's devastatingly true.

"If you had never fasted to anyone," he presses, his whole body coiled with tension, "what would you do? What would you want?"

Pain shears through her heart. "But I *did* fast to someone . . ."

"But if you *hadn't*."

"I'd want *this*," she admits, trembling. "I'd want to embrace this fasting. But it's impossible to get past everything I've ever been taught my *whole life* about virtually *everything*."

"We didn't get to *choose*," Mavrik insists, his acid bitterness jolting through their power. "We didn't get to choose our fastings at *thirteen*—"

"I *chose*—"

"No, Gwynn, you *didn't*," he harshly counters. "You were friends with Geoffrey, and that's a damned sight better than being dragged into a fasting with someone you didn't care for, I'll give you that. But it was still coercion into a magically powerful binding at *too young an age*."

Gwynn grows quiet, biting the inside of her cheek as she wrestles with an onslaught of guilt and grief and flashing magic.

"I loved him," she finally manages in a strangled voice.

Mavrik pulls in a shaky breath. "I know you did. I can feel your grief over it. And I wish I could take it away from you. But, Gwynn, when Geoffrey was tested, he chose the Shadow of his own free will. He saw the full horror the Mages are raining down on the world, and he *stayed*. But you . . . the moment you saw—" he gives her a pained, loving smile "—you sought out the Resistance and went *all in*."

An ache slices through her. Because his words are true. She's seen too much, and it's over. She can never go back to Geoffrey. She wouldn't want to. But there's no solid ground in this confusing, tumultuous new world she's found herself in.

"I'm lost," she admits in a shredded voice, tears blurring her eyes. "Following an Alfsigr Icaral toward a Smaragdalfar goddess tree, the whole thing mixed up with a Gardnerian wand myth . . . everything in our religion, absolutely *everything*, forbidding this type of mixing and confusion. And now I'm falling in love with you, which is *unforgivable*. Mavrik, I'm *lost*."

He moves closer and reaches down to gently take her hands in his. "Sometimes you *have* to get lost," he insists, his voice hitching with emotion. "Sometimes you have to get *thoroughly, horribly, horrifically* lost. Or you can *never, ever* find your true way. Don't you think I felt lost when I was confronted by what our people are doing to the Fae? The Fae, who aren't the monsters of our myths, but just *people*? People we're *abusing* and *slaughtering*? I grew up Styvian, just like you. With that inflexible religion of ours shoved down my throat." His magic's a firestorm as he tenses his jaw, his breathing uneven. "But I've finally found my true way, Gwynn. And it's led me *to you*. And to the Great Tree of all the myths, which most of the Smaragdalfar here don't want us anywhere near." He shakes his head. "I don't know what I believe about the Ancient One or Oo'na or the Shining Ones or any religion anymore. But I think there's a hell of a good chance that maybe, just maybe, the Ancient One is leading us together, not apart. *All* of us."

"*None* of the holy books say that—"

"Then the holy books be *thoroughly damned*! *This* is my holy book." He motions emphatically between them. "*This*, right here. This thing growing between us. And freed Smaragdalfar and Urisk and Fae children. And smiting Vogel's Shadow. The fight for *all of us*, Gwynn. *All of us*, no exceptions. Not Yyzz'ra's way. *Wynter's* way. *Mynx and Cael's* way. *That's* my holy book. The rigid lines be *fully* damned."

"I am falling in love with you," she blurts out, her voice thick with both passion and pain and mind-bending confusion as she holds his equally impassioned stare. "Ancient One help me, Mavrik, but I am."

"Then *choose*," he raggedly states. "*Choose* your mate of your own free will. As a tested *adult*. As your true, strong self who goes all in. Because I want to go all in. Say the word, Gwynn. Say it, and I'm *yours*."

Her pulse thuds hot and hard as she holds his incediary stare. A tear escapes, and her magic and feelings break loose and stream toward him, her voice fracturing. "Mavrik, I'm already *all in*."

He's there in an instant, embracing her, choking out an emotional sound as they pull each other close. She can feel his silent tears on her neck as he kisses its nape, murmuring "I love you" over and over, her own tears fully giving way.

And then his lips are on hers, salt-coated and warm.

Then hotly insistent.

She kisses him back eagerly, and their magic fully releases, surging toward and through each other. She groans against his mouth as he deepens the kiss, an explosion of color detonating, the motion of his tongue swirling a luxurious scarlet craving through her every lightline. Then he's yanking off his cloak, throwing it to the ground, and pulling her down onto it, the two of them hastily drawing off clothing and weapons. She pulls his body onto hers, the surging flow of their magic desperate for connection, desperate for this fully and freely chosen Sealing to each other.

"Is the contraception rune still charged?" Mavrik raggedly asks.

"It is," she answers, aware of the slight sting of the rune on her hip, caught up in the pleasure of his body pressed against hers.

Mavrik brings his lips back to hers, and Gwynn gasps as he pushes forward, joining their bodies. She tightens her thighs around his, and can feel his magic reading her consent in a rippling rush before they take each other more intensely. Thrilling to his passion, his hard *maleness*, and stunned by the whirling rise of pleasure where they're joined, she hugs him close to get *more* of him, splaying her fingers over his muscular back.

Pleasure floods their entwined power in an almost unbearable rush. She arches her head back just before Mavrik lets out a groan against her shoulder and their magic shatters against each other in a raying explosion of light power, a shock wave of ecstasy flashing through their joined bodies and merged lines.

They still, hearts pounding, both of them breathing hard.

Mavrik presses his lips to her shoulder, and Gwynn shivers, their twinned magic looping around their joined forms in a swirling, delirious embrace, their bodies lit up with every color on Erthia.

"I love you, Gwynnifer," Mavrik says against her shoulder, the words rough and impassioned.

She reaches up to sift her fingers through his hair as tears pool in her eyes, her old life fully gone, but a new one just beginning. He raises his head, a profound look of love in his golden gaze as his eyes meet hers, light magery crackling over his lips.

"I love you too," she murmurs as she opens her heart to both him and all of life's confusion and gives in to their binding fully. Gives in to it *all*.

Mavrik slides his warm palm over her cheek, and Gwynn's breath shudders as he threads his fingers deftly through her hair, then leans in to kiss her color-singed lips, his kiss intoxicatingly slow and deep, a kaleidoscope of affection flooding their twinned magic.

"My beautiful Light Mage," he murmurs against her lips before drawing back a fraction, the edge of his light-sparking mouth lifting into a seditious smile. "Now that we have all that established, let's go strike down that Varg rune and open a path through the Dryad barrier behind it."

CHAPTER FIVE

GOLDEN STAR

Elloren

Northern Forest
Eighteen days after Xishlon

Raz'zor's blaze of warning sears across my eyes, his red, gold, and purple flame briefly cutting Yvan, the Dryads, and the giant ravens surrounding me from my vision once more.

"Can your warding of the Northern Forest stand against a military attack?" I demand of the Dryads.

"Our Forest is encircled by both Dryadin and primordial Varg'uuth'nile shielding," Sylvan details, his gaze boring into me. "Shielded aboveground and below. The warding emits two invisible dome-shields that protect both root and canopy of our entire Northern Forest."

Yvan gives him a piercing look, the alarm blazing through our bond unassuaged. "Can your wards hold back a combined attack from *multiple* Eastern Realm armies," he presses, "including Vogel's Shadow forces?"

"Yes, Dryad'khin," Sylvan answers, adamant. "Our Forest's warding held fast during *all* of Erthia's wars and every last attempt to break through it."

"How fast is what you sense approaching?" Yulan asks Yvan and me, her lichen-lashed gaze fraught with tension, her heron kindred agitatedly flexing its fog-hued wings.

"I'm not sure," Yvan answers. His violet eyes meet mine, a stronger line of heat firing through our bond. "I'm going to try to source Raz'zor's fire from a higher vantage point. I might be able to gauge how far away he is."

I nod, and he launches himself at III's wall of black trunk and effortlessly scales the majestic Tree. A shiver courses through me as I take in his powerful grace, the dark Wyvern claws that have formed on his fingertips. I'm suddenly filled with the urge to leap onto III and *follow*. III's encircling power tugs on my rootlines, and my need to ascend with Yvan doubles in potency, every one of III's deep-green leaves emitting an almost magnetic pull.

Urging me *up*.

A sense of my entire Forest taking up III's call and tugging on my rootlines overtakes me. Even the mosses at my feet unfurl, as if seeking to spring me upward.

I leap toward III on faith and throw my hands onto the Great Tree's wall of trunk only to be swamped by a flood of stunned elation when my nails sharpen and lock into III's richly crenelated bark. A wave of strength courses through my body, and I find myself gracefully hauling myself up into an assured climb, my Dryad limbs stronger than they've ever been before.

Built for climbing trees.

Joy expands in my chest, and I rapidly scale branch after branch, my dark purple, moon-decorated Xishlon tunic and pants allowing freedom of movement. Yvan turns, his eyes widening as he finds me rapidly closing the distance between us. An impassioned tension fires through our bond before he resumes climbing, his wings pulled in tight.

I match his pace, emboldened by a sense of the entire Forest's magic flowing through my lines, my Northern Forest's power merging so intimately with my rootlines, it's hard to tell where my power stops and my Forest's begins.

Climbing at breakneck speed, Yvan and I soon reach III's uppermost canopy of branches and hoist ourselves through it.

Sunlight hits my skin full on, my heart warming with euphoria, Yvan and I poised side by side within the spearing bifurcation of III's highest, canopy-lancing branch.

Awestruck, I survey the enormity of the Northern Forest, leagues and leagues of green spread out all around us, a verdant living and breathing miracle with vivid touches of early autumn's coloration painted throughout its breathtakingly beautiful expanse.

My kindred raven, Errilith, bursts from the Forest's canopy along with the rest of my Errilor flock and Yulan's heron. A wave of Errilith's affection ripples through my lines as my Errilor Ravens briefly pulse their powerful Dark aura over the world and they soar through a perfect blue sky, a stiff crosscurrent buffeting Yvan and me. As III's branches sway, Yvan extends his wings for balance while I move in sync with III, as if caught up in a loving dance.

A falcon darts past, and I follow its southern trajectory, my giant ravens and Yulan's heron fanning out over the Forest, the green rise of the Caledonian Mountains edging the southern horizon.

"Can you sense Raz'zor?" I ask Yvan.

"I've lost the connection," he replies, his face tensed in concentration, his gaze turned eastward.

A rose-and-brown-speckled butterfly lights on my arm, a prickle of the small creature's love tingling through my lines that prompts a returning rush of affection from me. The small creature's delicate antennae twitch, and I'm overtaken by awareness of the butterfly scenting the air and gauging the wind through them.

The wind shifts northward, and a sense of wrongness grips hold, a strange, foul scent wafting up from the south.

"Yvan . . ." I start, but my voice cuts off as the butterfly takes to the air and I spot the night-black forms of Errilith and my flock speeding back toward us at a fast pace. Their Deathkin aura pulses through the world, urgent this time, and my sense of gravity wavers as Errilith's black eyes overtake my mind, everything before me telescoping southward, as if Errilith is *willing* my attention in that direction.

"What are you sensing?" Yvan asks, his hand coming to my arm. The image III revealed when I was inside the Great Tree flashes through my mind—leagues of Shadow closing in on the Forest from all sides, ready to destroy *everything*.

"Something's approaching," I say as Errilith's low-pitched *caw* echoes through the sky, the rest of my flock joining in. "It's coming in from the south—"

A bolt of fire power hits me, punching through my words, but this magic is coming from the *east*. My breath sears hot, a gasp torn from my throat as everything around me vanishes from sight. The firestorm streaks through my body and vision, burning straight through my rootlines, a cataclysm of golden flame with a line of purple-sparking vermillion flame in it. A surface-of-the-sun level of fire that has my teeth chattering and my body vibrating against its crackling flow. *Too much fire . . .*

"*Yvan,*" I force out in a strangled cry.

Yvan grabs tight hold of me, his mouth crashing down onto mine. My back collides with the branch behind me as I take desperate hold of him in turn, letting out a cry of distress against his mouth, the burning assault through my lines *excruciating . . .*

THE DRYAD STORM

Yvan draws in a harsh breath, the fire assault pulling toward his mouth as he wrests hold of it, the potency of the incoming flame almost as strong as Yvan's full expanse of power.

He draws in another breath, his claws' tips biting into my upper arms, the sudden elongation of his Wyvern canines pressing against my lips as he consumes the fire, pulling it through me and into him until I can sense the bulk of it churning hot in his core, both of us now firmly connected to it via our Wyvernbond.

The excruciating burn through my rootlines swiftly reduces to a tingling scald, and my thoughts clear. Yvan draws his lips from mine, his eyes brighter than I've ever seen them, gold and red flames leaping through the violet, a small, glowing star newly emblazoned at the base of his neck.

"What just happened?" I barely manage to say, throat parched, mind whirling. "What's on your neck?"

He hisses out a series of Wyvern words then catches himself, his face tensing as his teeth return to their regular shape, my heart racing in my chest.

"It's a Western Wyvern horde mark," he says in Dryadin, reaching up to brush his fingertip along the base of my neck, his touch trailing sparks. I glance down, catching the glow of the flaming star emblazoned on my skin, as well. "We've been connected to a large horde," he explains. "Naga's horde. Which means they can track us both. They're winging in *fast*."

Panicked birdsong rises in the air, a whole sea of birds crashing through the Northern Forest canopy in agitated flight, their wings a beating storm as they flee northeast.

A vision of Vogel's Void tree punches into my mind and I flinch, just as a band of dark gray appears on the southern horizon, rising over the Caledonian Mountains. It rapidly enlarges, dark lightning pulsing through its expanse, a wave of unnatural storm power emanating from it.

My alarm skyrockets. "It's a Shadowed storm band," I warn as a punishing breeze kicks up, my ravens and Yulan's heron darting down through the branches beside us, my line of connection to Errilith suddenly urging me *down*.

"The fire in that lightning . . ." Yvan says, nostrils flaring. "It's all *wrong*."

The storm band begins to barrel down the mountains in a gray tide.

Alarm blasts through III's elemental aura and radiates out toward the entire surrounding Forest, a wave of Dryad power flashing through me from below.

Yvan's gaze swings to mine, our joint flame surging into a chaotic blaze.

"We need to get to the Dryads, *now*," I urge as I take hold of the living branch sheathed at my side, a sense of its connection to my entire Forest surging through my rootlines and washing over me the moment I take it in hand.

Ferocity sweeping across his features, Yvan throws his arms around my waist and launches us both into the air. I cling to him as he angles down toward the canopy, my pulse tripping over itself.

Before we soar through the canopy's upper reaches, two huge translucent green dome-shields burst to life above and around the entire Northern Forest, one inside the other, the inner shield marked with Dryad runes, the outer marked with Varg wards.

The image of Vogel's Void tree punches into my mind once more, and I cry out as Shadow thunder *booms* through the air and Vogel's storm band races toward the domes' southern edge in a roaring tidal wave of Forest-decimating power.

OO'NA'S ROOTS

Gwynnifer Glass

Northern Forest Sublands
Eighteen days after Xishlon

"You two look like you ate a bunch of rainbows," Valasca archly comments.

A flush warms Gwynn's cheeks as she and Mavrik stare down the line of Dryad dome-shielding runes, the Verdyllion in Gwynn's hands. The primordial Varg barrier rune hangs suspended, emerald bright, before the row of Dryad runes.

Mavrik's muscular body is pressed to Gwynn's back, his hands clasped around hers, her flush stoked hotter as she thrills to his power-amplifying proximity. Gwynn knows Valasca's humor is kindly meant, the Amaz warrior prone to outrageous commentary to diffuse the near-constant tension. But still, she finds herself hyperaware of the color shimmering over her lips and body as well as Mavrik's, the two of them lit up with a riot of glowing, swirling hues everywhere they touched when they so recently joined.

Even their hair is streaked with lingering color.

"We *devoured* all the rainbows," Mavrik tosses back at Valasca, his hands tightening slightly around Gwynn's in a private, affectionate squeeze. "And they were *delicious.*"

Shocked amusement bubbles up in Gwynn as Valasca barks out a laugh. Gwynn returns Valasca's smile, even quiet Sparrow's and Rhys's lips lifting as Yyzz'ra, Gavryyl, and Valkyr maintain their ever-present scowls. Cael and Mynx look on silently, their arms encircling each other, and Wynter a quiet presence beside them, the two Agolith Flame Hawks perched on her shoulders.

Gwynn chances a glance at Mavrik, and he winks at her. "Ready?" he asks.

Gwynn nods, her memory of the past few hours expanding. She and Mavrik practiced the unlocking sequence of spells several times before returning here, the two of them near drunk with amplified light power after their coupling.

"Everyone will know what we've done," Gwynn worried when they'd readied themselves to rejoin the others, feeling a bit like a criminal as the pleasurable tingle of light magic danced over her lips and body, their love bond a bright, unmistakable beacon.

Mavrik simply reached up to caress her cheek with exquisite gentleness before pulling her in for a deep kiss that set off another explosion of multihued light through Gwynn's every line.

"Let them know," he challenged. "Gwynn, this is your *life*. Be *bold*."

Gwynn sharply inhaled as his words lit her up, striking deep.

Striking *true*.

Thrilling to the memory, her focus swings to the present. She pauses for a moment, turning to study the dark river snaking through the black-opal cave surrounding them, everything in her suddenly galvanized by the desire to test her light power's unbridled flow, love-fueled rebellion rising.

She gently draws away from Mavrik, and a questioning energy flashes through his power as she levels the Verdyllion at the river and murmurs a spell.

Their twinned power courses through her and into the river, and the entire body of water bursts into glowing, marbled color, gasps rising from their surrounding companions. Delighted surprise lights up Mavrik's lines, the shimmering water filled with undulating, glowing ripples of every hue that throw chromatic light over the entire cave.

Gwynn's eyes widen, her lines filling with explosive joy over what she's wrought, feeling herself suddenly unleashed.

Empowered.

Her heart thundering in her chest, she catches Mavrik's enamored grin as she sweeps the Verdyllion in an arc and murmurs a light spell, the cave's every expanse of dark opal bursting into a mosaic of iridescent rainbow hues.

Pulling in an ecstatic breath, Gwynn catches Wynter's satisfied smile before she shoots Yyzz'ra a narrow look of triumph before turning back to Mavrik, feeling drunk on color.

"There," she says, breathless, "now we match *everything*." Then she reaches up, slides her hand through Mavrik's hair, and draws him into a deep, light-magic-detonating kiss.

She can feel Mavrik's smile against her mouth, feel the jubilant color leaping through their joined power as he eagerly responds with his own surge of forceful passion through their twinned lines.

They break the kiss, the two of them filled with more color than ever before, every single blasphemous shade of it, a wicked smirk on Mavrik's color-infused lips.

My freely chosen fastmate, Gwynn thinks, her heart beating out a strong new rhythm.

The pang of guilt still cuts deep, along with the deeply ingrained fear that she's forever cursed and cast out.

But her defiance and power burn brighter.

Fully ready, Gwynn turns to the runic wall and levels the Verdyllion Wand at the Dryad and Varg warded barrier. Mavrik's hands slide around her from behind once more, and together, they sound out the series of unlocking spells.

A bolt of multicolored light blasts from the Verdyllion and collides with the Varg rune before them, piercing a small gap in the rune's design and spearing into the Dryad ward behind it, both runes overtaken by multihued light.

Both the Varg and Dryad wards split in two, the halves sliding apart and forming a small archway limned with sparking color.

Opening a narrow route into the Northern Forest.

Valasca lets out a *whoop* as Mavrik pulls Gwynn into an enthusiastic hug, the Verdyllion in her hand suddenly tingling with a magnetic pull.

Toward Wynter.

Gwynn turns to Wynter and holds out the Verdyllion. "Here, Wynter'lyn," she offers, grinning from inside Mavrik's embrace, her magic sparking brighter than ever before. "Lead the way."

"Oo'na's Roots . . ." Mynx'lia'luur gasps.

Mynx's stunned gasp resonates through Gwynn, and her heart trips into a pounding rhythm. They all step from the narrow series of tunnels they've been journeying through for hours and spill into an impossibly huge crystalline cavern with an arching ceiling, the huge, jutting crystals filled with an explosion of forbidden color, Gwynn and Mavrik's runic net-shield hugging its ceiling.

Unsteady on her legs from the onslaught of so much concentrated light power, Gwynn cranes her neck, gaping in wonder at the gigantic roots waterfalling from the cavern's ceiling. Thick as a barn, the roots undulate over the cavern's floor, walls and ceiling, their python-size root-hairs entangling with the network of smaller roots flowing in from every direction—a network of thousands upon thousands of interconnected tree roots snaking over the Subland's ceiling that Gwynn has taken note of throughout their entire journey here.

One vast web of Forest.

And now here she and her companions are, in the place all the roots were leading to—the living, breathing heart of Erthia's Natural Matrix, spoken about in all of Erthia's religions and myths.

Erthia's Source Tree.

"Holy Goddess on High," Valasca gasps as the Tree's bone-deep frequency of power shivers through Gwynn and Mavrik's twinned magic, Mavrik's grip on Gwynn's hand tightening.

Watchers blink into existence—hundreds of them—shimmering to life, bright as starlight, and perched all over the enormous roots.

Gwynn's breath seizes, a strangled sound of surprise escaping Mavrik's throat as the Smaragdalfar fall to their knees and perform the complicted Oo'na's Blessing gesture over their chests. Cael and Rhys simply gape at the vision that Gwynn realizes they all can miraculously see. Both Valasca and Sparrow murmur what sound like Amaz and Uriskal blessings, and Wynter's wings fan out to their glorious full expanse, the two Agolith Flame Hawks on her shoulders taking joyous flight to land on the Great Tree's roots amidst the Watchers.

The Verdyllion Wand in Wynter's hand rays out multicolored light.

"You see the birds, don't you?" Gwynn says to Mavrik, relief spasming through her as the starlight hue of the ethereal Watchers shifts to a constellation of every color on Erthia—the full spectrum of light power.

Mavrik nods without taking his eyes off the Watchers. "The Ancient One's birds," he murmurs, emotion crackling through his power.

"Oo'na's birds too," Gwynn offers, tears welling in her eyes, "and the Alfsigr faith's birds . . . the birds of the Amaz and Noi goddesses . . . *everyone's* birds."

Mavrik turns to her, seeming uncharacteristically overcome. "I wanted to believe again." He swallows, looking back to the otherworldly scene before them. "When I first turned away from the Magedom, I figured, well, I'm going to all the hells now." He grows quiet for a moment, his magic crackling with bright feeling. "I missed praying. I missed believing in *something*. But I figured, if I was irretrievably lost, I might as well fight for those who might not be so lost. Who still had something worth believing in."

Gwynn's heart tightens, a luminous tide of love for Mavrik shimmering through their power, tears misting her eyes. "I think we were led here," she says. "By the Wand. And the Watchers. And Oo'na's Roots." An expansive rush tingles through Gwynn. It feels revolutionary to name these roots "Oo'na's"—to embrace the confusing, glorious mingling of Erthia's faiths.

Seeming to understand the seismic shifting of her thoughts, Mavrik raises their linked hands and kisses the back of hers, multihued sparks flashing through them both as the Tree's all-encompassing power tugs on their twinned lines.

"Let's go meet Erthia's Source Tree," Mavrik offers. *"Together."*

Gwynn nods, scared and confused and ready. Gripping tighter hold of Mavrik's hand, she meets Wynter's compassionate silver gaze, and they all set out together toward Erthia's Great Tree.

"Stop!" Yyzz'ra snarls.

They startle to a halt as Yyzz'ra lunges between them and the Tree's roots, Gavryyl and Valkyr closing in beside her. The three Smaragdalfar soldiers swiftly unsheathe Varg hilts and flick them out, the sword blades telescoping from the hilts' emerald runes.

"What's this?" Valasca demands, low and deadly, as she and Sparrow unsheathe their own smaller blades, Mynx, Cael, and Rhys nocking arrows to bows in a blur.

"Lower your weapons, *now*," Cael orders Yyzz'ra, his aim lethally focused.

"Silence, Maggot," Yyzz'ra snarls. "Alfsigr filth have no place here." Her combative gaze swings to Valasca and Sparrow beside her. "Disarm *right now*, or I will activate those runic collars around your necks and choke the breath from your lungs!"

Gavryyl and Valkyr swipe their blades through the air, and a multitude of emerald-glowing Varg daggers blink into existence, suspended before Gwynn and every last one of her allies, the blades' razor-sharp runic points a hair's breadth away from each of their throats.

"Yyzz'ra," Mynx'lia'luure carefully ventures, "what are you doing?"

"What you should be joining us in doing!" Yyzz'ra hurls back at her with a hateful glare at Cael. "This is *Oo'na's Tree*. Not for *Varg'plith!*" Yyzz'ra levels a blistering gaze at Wynter and holds out her hand in emphatic demand. "Give me Oo'na's Shard, *Icaral*."

Gwynn flinches at hearing *Icaral* hurled at Wynter so abusively. Mavrik's magic blazes through hers, a series of runic sequences flashing through their twinned lines—runes that could be deployed to blast Yyzz'ra and the two Subland Elves off their feet.

Gwynn quietly begins murmuring the Issani spells, the sting of the runes she's conjuring beginning to tingle against her palms just as Wynter flicks her wings out to their full breadth with such unexpected, compelling force that everyone turns toward her with evident surprise.

Seeming undaunted by the suspended Varg blade aimed at her pale neck, Wynter serenely holds out the Verdyllion to Yyzz'ra. "Take it," Wynter offers. "And return it to Oo'na's Sacred Tree."

Yyzz'ra glares at Wynter, seeming thrown by her calm response. She springs forward and grabs the Verdyllion from Wynter, then steps backward toward the huge roots and beckons Gavryyl and Valkyr to join her with a quick swipe of her hand.

Backing toward the Great Tree's roots, swords raised, Yyzz'ra, Gavryyl, and Valkyr all reach out their free hands and make contact with the Great Tree.

An explosion of chromatic light rays from their hands, and Gwynn recoils as the suspended Varg blades all blink out of existence and Yyzz'ra, Gavryyl, and Valkyr are absorbed clear into the Great Tree's roots, along with the Verdyllion in Yyzz'ra's hand.

Red shock blazes through Gwynn and Mavrik's power.

Wynter turns and gives them all a beatific smile before she steps toward a colossal root and presses both hands to it in a blasting array of colored light. The Watchers all shimmer out of sight as Wynter, too, is absorbed into the Great Tree.

Wynter is the first to reemerge, close to an hour later—an hour that they all spent in the throes of alarm.

Gwynn's arm rises reflexively to shield her face as prismatic light blasts from the roots, awe spasming through her as Wynter steps from the light and Gwynn takes in the Icaral's dramatically altered appearance.

Wynter's eyes are no longer silver but flashing every prismatic hue, her alabaster complexion tinted to pale green. Her wings ray out silvery light, and two flashing horns that seem made of star-white lightning rise from her head. A Watcher is perched on her shoulder, the translucent bird surrounded by an ethereal green mist.

"My sister," Cael says, his voice splintering.

"The Center of Life is calling us home," Wynter says to them all as she raises her palm. There's an image of an Ironwood tree wrought in dark lines there, Wynter's lightning horns forking out a cavern-brightening light. "There is nothing to fear," she states serenely. "We are being called, all of us, to join with the Natural World's power. To amplify it and save it from Shadow destruction."

Wynter fans out her wings just as Yyzz'ra, Gavryyl, and Valkyr emerge from the gigantic root beside her. The three Smaragdalfar soldiers stumble to their knees, and Gwynn, Mavrik, and their allies immediately fall into defensive positions.

But the three Smaragdalfar make no move to attack. They look dazed, all of them clutching what look like tangles of purple roots in their fists, the Verdyllion grasped tight in Yyzz'ra's alternate hand.

Yyzz'ra looks at Wynter, a shaken expression on her usually fierce visage as she sheathes the prismatically glowing Verdyllion and lifts her palm, turning it outward, Gavryyl and Valkyr displaying their palms, as well.

Gwynn draws in a tight breath.

The same tree image imprinted on Wynter's palm is emblazoned on the palms of the three Subland Elves.

Yyzz'ra's expression shifts to one of intense remorse. "I was *wrong*," she chokes out to Wynter before turning to Gwynn and Mavrik and the others. "I was wrong to shut you all out. Oo'na's Tree, III, bonded us to this kindred." She holds up the tangle of purple roots. "We've been bonded to the Sublands beneath a great Eastern Pine Forest." Yyzz'ra glances in that direction, as if her gaze is being drawn by some internal compass. "The Sublands . . . it's not a cutoff territory like I imagined. It's part of a *whole*. A cradle to Life's root connections. If the Sunlands fall, the Sublands fall, as well."

"The Mages and the Alfsigr," Valkyr roughly manages to say, and Gwynn is startled to hear the brooding Elf speak, "they're killing *too much* of the Forest in the West. If we don't stop them from destroying both this Forest and the Forests of the East, the entire Natural Matrix will *unravel*."

"We saw images of suffering people from every group on the continent," Gavryyl puts in, his silver eyes haunted. "*Children*. From every group on Erthia. Dying of hunger and thirst as the Shadow poisons the land . . . the water . . . *everything*."

"I thought our fight was only for the Smaragdalfar," Yyzz'ra forces out, her silver eyes glassing with tears, "but it has to be for us *all*. Or we're going to lose everything to the Shadow." Yyzz'ra looks to Valasca and Sparrow as she retrieves a runic stone from her tunic's pocket and holds it up, sliding her thumb over the rune and pressing along its edge.

The imprisonment collars around Valasca's and Sparrow's throats vanish in a spray of emerald sparks.

"I should never have imprisoned you both," Yyzz'ra admits. She pockets the rune stone and rises, unsheathing the Verdyllion and holding it out to Wynter. "Here, Wynter'lyn," she offers, her voice tight with feeling. "It wants to return to you."

Gwynn exchanges an astonished look with Mavrik as Wynter smiles, steps toward Yyzz'ra and accepts the Verdyllion, its chromatic glow brightening as soon as the Icaral makes contact with it, a sense of the momentous circling down.

Mythological in its potency.

A shivering sense of rightness blooms in Gwynn's breast, drawing her and Mavrik's lines and power toward the Source Tree's roots with undeniable force.

Gwynn's eyes lock hold with Mavrik's, unspoken agreement spiraling through their lines before they step forward, together, along with Cael and Mynx'lia'luure, Rhys, Valasca, and Sparrow, all of them bringing their palms to the Great Tree's roots.

Gravity gives way beneath Gwynn's feet, her and Mavrik's magic seizing in a shock of multicolored light. They grasp protective hold of each other as they fall straight into the root, suddenly enveloped by darkness and hurled into a shocking free fall. Gwynn's pulse explodes as they plummet through darkness that feels like it has no end.

Then slow to a sudden halt, suspended in the void.

Disoriented, Gwynn clings to Mavrik, his arms clutching her close as they take in the vision shivering to life all around them.

They're standing in a purple forest, its spectacular autumn coloration lit up with dream-vivid intensity. Its brilliant fall hues ray out light at the edges, the leaves' riot of fall color encompassing not just the Western Realm hues of reds, golds, and rusts, but also the fabled autumn coloration of the Eastern Realm—magenta and sapphire, vivid lavender, and bright swaths of turquoise.

Gwynn's lightlines expand, a euphoric shiver rippling over her skin as she drinks in the tapestry of color, the hues so rich they make her Light Mage heart ache.

Watchers shimmer to life, perched throughout the forest's branches, and Gwynn and Mavrik's twinned lines are suddenly flowing down, down, into Erthia and linking into a vast network of tree roots all leading to the Great Tree.

The Great Tree's true name strobes through Gwynn's mind—

III.

THE DRYAD STORM

The Center of Erthia's Natural Matrix.

The scene morphs into a swirl of color, and disorientation overtakes Gwynn again as they're thrust into an aerial vision of an entire continent surrounded by ocean, green and golden trees blanketing its expanse. The image of Vogel's Shadow Wand flashes through Gwynn's sight as a wave of gray closes in over the densely forested continent, the steely mass of corruption filled with black, curling lightning.

And then they're being yanked toward the continent's ground and assaulted by image after image of tree-witnessed horror, the forests burning with steely fire as Shadow armies ravage everything and a toxic gray storm rolls in like a demonic tide and collapses the Living World.

Farms destroyed.

Water poisoned.

The air and surrounding ocean overtaken by gray-swirling corruption.

Families . . . children . . . *dying*.

A scream of protest rises in Gwynn's throat.

The horrific scene disappears in a swirl of malignant grays, and Gwynn and Mavrik find themselves suspended, once more, in the Great Tree's all-encompassing darkness. An eviscerating despair grips hold of them both as they comprehend what Gwynn instinctively knows is coming for their continent.

What's already *here*.

But then, an image of the Verdyllion bursts into being, the Wand-Stylus suspended before them.

Gwynn's eyes widen as a translucent, seven-pointed star, big as a miller's wheel, shivers to life around the Verdyllion, each point glowing one of the seven colors of prism-refracted light. She and Mavrik glance down, the two of them positioned in front of the large star's sole golden point.

Figures shimmer into being in front of the star's other points, and surprise stutters through Gwynn as she takes in the purple-raying, blurred form of Sagellyn Gaffney suspended before the star's violet-glowing arm. Her entire form is tinted with purple hues, a benevolent smile on her deep-violet lips.

"Sage," Gwynn rasps, her heart cracking open with both love and remorse to suddenly find herself in the presence of her long-lost friend.

Another figure gains clarity, and a more potent surprise constricts Gwynn's chest, the female figure's skin shimmering a deep forest green, her ears slightly pointed, a verdant streak in her Mage-black hair. Her face is familiar, so similar to the features carved into the martial statue in front of the Valgard Cathedral depicting the Black Witch doing battle with the Winged Icaral.

Elloren Gardner Grey.

There's a glowing green branch in Elloren's hand and a raven perched on her shoulder, her form poised before the star's luminous green point.

Wynter shivers into being before the star's indigo point, her lightning horns forking out prismatic light. And then, a figure Gwynn does not recognize shimmers to life at the star's blue point, an equally blue woman made of flowing water, the light-raying images of two color-flashing octopi streaming around her, a purple root in the woman's hand, her hair a flash of silver. Another figure, an Alfsigr man surrounded in a rainbow haze, appears at the star's red point.

And then, a final figure, made up entirely of fractals of prismatic light.

The Forest vision from before shimmers to life around them, the forbidden hues of the East's autumn raying out to join with the Verdyllion, the star and everyone gathered around it.

Gwynn looks to Mavrik, swept up in the overpowering sensation that channeling their collective light power through the Verdyllion is somehow key to holding the vast Shadow power at bay.

A palpable sense of invitation ripples through the air. Gwynn can feel its world-shifting energy inside her very soul, a joyful tug on her lines, beckoning her to join with the complex prismatic magic that runs through III and the Forest and every living thing.

III's silent invitation quivers in the air, like a hand, held palm up.

A lifeline for Erthia.

A chance.

Gwynn meets Mavrik's beloved gaze in silent affirmation before, together, they bring their hands to the star's golden point and accept.

An explosion of multicolored light detonates as elemental magic bolts through their fastlines. Gwynn grasps Mavrik close at the same time that he grabs desperate hold of her, and they're hurled through the Great Tree's roots, upward and out into the surface world's light.

The real world solidifies into being, and Gwynn finds herself ensconced inside III's huge, green crown, clinging to a branch, her nails digging into bark, thunder rumbling in the distance, Mavrik beside her.

Gwynn pulls in a shocked breath as she takes in Mavrik's dramatically altered appearance, and his eyes widen with an equal level of shock as he takes her in.

His ears . . . they're pointed . . . and the pale Mage green of his skin has deepened to a rich, late-summer green. His dark, tousled hair is streaked with a rainbow of hues, and his gold irises are rimmed with prismatic light.

Gwynn draws in an expansive breath, overcome by the sensation of herself and Mavrik newly and prismatically rooted to the entire Northern Forest and III via their twinned lines, a rush of the Great Tree's affection suffusing them both.

III's pulsing energy strobes through Gwynn's wand hand, and she turns it palm up. Astonishment sizzles through her as she finds III's image fused there in dark lines that weave into and intimately link to her lightning-patterned, gold-glowing fastlines.

Aware of a stretching sting along her ears, Gwynn reaches up and is stunned to find her own ears coming to the same subtle points as Mavrik's. She grabs at her hair and pulls it forward, finding hers shot through with rainbow color as well, her nails newly deep green and slightly clawed, her skin a deepened forest green hue.

"Holy Ancient One, we're Fae," she gasps to Mavrik, almost choking on the words when they come out not in the Common Tongue but in a whole other language, the sounds dry and leafy, the words feeling intensely true. "Can you understand me?" she asks him, almost light-headed from shock.

"I can," he answers in the same leafy tongue, his equal astonishment sweeping through their twinned power.

In a flash of multicolored light, the two Agolith Flame Hawks that portaled here with them burst out of the Great Tree and perch in a nearby branch, their luminous orange feathers ruffling with what seems like vast surprise over their rapid change in location.

Gwynn's and Mavrik's lines twine into a deeper linkage to the Forest as the hawks take wing to light on her and Mavrik's shoulders, their lines flooding with the birds' affection. An instant, kindred connection flashes into being, love for both birds expanding Gwynn's heart with an emotional ache.

"Our lines . . ." Mavrik marvels as he absently reaches up to stroke the hawk kindred's feathers ". . . they're not what we thought they were."

"They're *roots*," Gwynn breathlessly murmurs as their fully anchored light power flashes through the Forest. "And what you told me when we were in the Agolith . . . it was all true. Magically, we're *Dryads*."

Urgency overtakes Mavrik's deep-green features. "Gwynn . . . where are the others? Where's Wynter? And the *Verdyllion*—"

An Erthia-shattering *BOOM* sounds above them, breaking off his words. Alarm streaks through their lines as their hawks startle.

Gwynn and Mavrik exchange a look of dire concern before they both launch into an upward climb, Gwynn finding herself stunningly agile and strong. A stiff breeze hits her as they burst through the canopy's top, the Northern Forest's panoramic expanse of green spread out around them, the two translucent green dome-shields encasing it.

Gwynn's lungs contract as a roaring tide of Shadow storm crashes against the Forest's nested shields, the storm band's dark, curling lightning breaking into a frenzy, all of it knifing into the Varg and Dryad shields.

"Ancient One," Gwynn gasps, just as muffled shouts rise from the ground far beneath them. Their widened gazes meet.

"The others must be at III's base," Mavrik says, his tone harsh with steel-sharp purpose. "We need to pool our power with theirs and strengthen our Forest's shielding."

Warrior purpose firing through their magic, they climb down the Great Tree's massive trunk with startling rapidity, Gwynn adjusting to her lithe, newly muscular body, her movements strong and assured as her green claws dig into III's black bark.

They careen through the densest portion of the canopy, leaping from branch to branch before they drop down into the clearing surrounding III . . .

. . . and come face-to-face with a band of Dryads, a crimson-haired Icaral man, who can only be the Icaral of Prophecy, amongst them.

A stunned breath shudders through Gwynn as Yvan Guryev's violet-fire eyes meet theirs, his pupils vertically slitted. Dark horns rise from his flame-like hair, and black wings fan out from his back.

Beside him stands the Dryad-Fae Black Witch herself, Elloren Gardner Grey, her ears pointed, her hue deepened to Forest tones, a streak of dark green slashed through her black hair, a flock of giant ravens surrounding her.

Memories of visions sent to Gwynn of Elloren the Dryad dart through her mind as she comes face-to-face with the reality that Elloren Gardner Grey is clearly no longer under Vogel's control.

"Mavrik!" Yvan cries as all the Dryads level Forest-hewn glowing runic weapons at Mavrik and Gwynn, the distant Shadow storm band roaring against the Forest's shielding.

THE DRYAD STORM

"We're on your side!" Mavrik cries, both Gwynn and Mavrik displaying their III-marked palms.

Elloren Gardner Grey's eyes widen as she takes in their III marks before her gaze swings to Yvan's. "This is the wandmaster who pretended to kill you?" she asks in fluent Dryadin. "The traitor to the Magedom?"

Yvan nods, his eyes pinned on Mavrik. "Now our Dryad'kin *ally*," he responds in the same tongue.

"They are no kin of mine!" a female Dryad with coiled hair festooned with oak branches snarls, readying a branch weapon, a growling wolverine hugging her side. She lurches threateningly toward Mavrik and Gwynn just as raptors' cries sound out above them all.

Everyone's eyes snap up as two points of golden light soar down from III's crown, Gwynn's heart and magic surging toward their kindred Agolith Flame Hawks. Both she and Mavrik hold up their forearms, the hawks landing on their arms in a rush of fiery love.

Three of the Dryads, including a fierce-looking man with branch horns, a petite, flower-tressed woman, and a lime-hued Dryad with frighteningly intense black eyes, lower their weapons, but the angry female Dryad with the staff and the two Dryads beside her—a huge branch-horned male Dryad with a bear kindred and a mushroom-haired female with a silver panther kindred—all keep their weapons leveled.

"We were with others in the Sublands," Gwynn calls out to them all, ignoring the hostility aimed their way. "The Icaral Wynter Eirllyn amongst them."

"Wynter?" Elloren exclaims.

"She has the Verdyllion," Gwynn tells her as an image of the Wand of Myth flashes into being in the back of her mind, a directional tug pulling her lines *down*. Gwynn's eyes widen. "I've a sudden sense of the Verdyllion . . . in the Sublands below us."

Mavrik gives her an intense look. "I feel the Verdyllion's tug on our lines, as well." He turns to Yvan. "Wynter's brother Cael and his Second, Rhys Thorim . . . they were with us too," he says. "Along with Valasca Xanthrir and Sparrow Trillium. And three Subland Elf soldiers."

"Where are they now?" Yvan presses, urgency firing in his eyes as Vogel's Shadow storm *booms* louder against the southern edge of the Forest's shielding.

Gwynn meets Yvan Guryev's gaze. "I don't know," she shakily tells him. "I think most of them might still be inside III—"

A huge explosion detonates. Everyone looks up as the nested dome-shields cast over the Forest ray out forest green and emerald light. The ground rumbles beneath their feet, and horror lances through Gwynn as the Northern Forest's shielding blasts clear out of existence.

PURPLE GEOMANCER

Sparrow Trillium

Deep inside III

Sparrow's heart accelerates into a hammering panic as she hurtles through the Great Tree's all-encompassing darkness. Her center fills with aching pressure, as if the Tree is trying to join her very core to its terrifying, endless depths.

Abruptly, she slows to a suspended halt.

Fear and disorientation firing through her in comet-like surges, Sparrow rues how impulsively she went to the Great Tree, mesmerized by what felt like a heart-pull that intensified as she took in the ethereal Geo'din messenger birds of the Urisk pantheon perched all over its roots.

Birds who seemed to be calling to the very center of her being.

Filled with what suddenly felt like glistening, trapped *power*.

Her fear devolving into throat-clenching anguish, Sparrow startles as violet light flashes through her vision and violet crystals emerge from the darkness all around her, big as the Tree's huge roots.

Bigger.

Her eyes widen as she gapes at the crystals, her suspended form but a speck in the face of these colossal, geometric formations, their shimmering purple rapidly overtaking the darkness. She pulls in a shuddering breath as she's swept up in the overpowering feeling that the giant crystals surrounding her are benevolently watching.

And waiting.

As if the Tree is making a startling offering to her, like she's some powerful Urisk geomancer ready to wield these mammoth crystals suffused with her kindred Urisk'viil color, the Great Tree not realizing she's a mere seamstress, lacking the geomancy power only Urisk males are gifted with.

Sorrow grips Sparrow as everything in her strains to connect to the gigantic crystals.

Strains to *merge* with them.

I've no power, she agonizes to the Great Tree as the crystals continue to form all around, some of the smaller formations crystalizing toward her, made up of every variety of the purple-hued stones she's especially drawn to as a member of the violet Urisk'viil class.

A memory of Noilaan's dockside gem market enters Sparrow's mind, how she could afford only a select few purple stones. Her hands were shaking as she purchased then pocketed them, feeling like she was committing a crime, the keeping of kindred-Urisk'viil geomancy stones forbidden to women by the Urisk religion.

I'm in love with a Mage, Sparrow had rebelliously thought in that moment as she brushed her fingers over the taboo stones. *Why not own kindred stones as a man would?*

Thoughts of Thierren constrict Sparrow's throat with a longing so intense, she can barely pull in a breath, her mind swinging to that last, agonizing collision of their gazes as she was flown away on dragonback by demonic Tilor while Vogel's demon tide rippled over Voloi, cutting Thierren from sight as she screamed his name.

Thierren, my beloved, where are you?

Her heart squeezes tighter as the face of her other loved one surfaces in her thoughts—Effrey. Did the child survive Vogel's siege of Voloi?

Thierren's and Effrey's names ring out in Sparrow's mind with heart-shredding force as a formation of iris-hued charoite and deep-violet jasper crystallize toward her. A sizzle of yearning is suddenly tingling against the underside of her skin. Not just to be reunited with Thierren and Effrey, but to wield *geopower.*

Her whole being fills with the certainty that the Great Tree is trying to link this stone world to her in some way. But it's completely misguided.

"I'm *female!*" she cries out to the Great Tree, railing against fate. "Urisk females have no geomancy!"

Sparrow is abruptly flooded with the core-warming sense of the Great Tree *smiling*—a smile of such vast-rooted kindness, tears sheen Sparrow's eyes, blurring the purple-crystalline sparkle of the world surrounding her.

And then the entire purple scene around her contracts, and she's cast into another vision.

THE DRYAD STORM

Head spinning, Sparrow finds herself peering down from the twisted golden branches of a bulbous desert tree, a yellow desert landscape spread out before her. A golden city with gleaming domed structures shines in the distance, great mountains of yellow stone just beyond, everything appearing to waver from the battering-ram heat of a white-hot sun.

Surprise overtakes Sparrow.

Urisk'hiir. A city she's heard about in tales from Uriskan's past. She recognizes it by the three fabled golden stars hanging over the mountains, bright as dragon eyes even in day's full light. The city before her—along with the entire country of Uriskan—destroyed during the last Realm War by Gardneria's Black Witch, Carnissa Gardner.

I'm looking into the past, Sparrow realizes as her gaze lowers to three figures in the small stone plaza beneath the tree she's perched in.

Two of the men are muscular Urisk warriors of the blue-hued Uurok class, lines of blue stones strapped across their chests, blue geo-styluses encrusted with cerulean and indigo gems grasped in their fists. Before them stands a slender bald man with the golden hue of the most-revered priestly class—the Urielle—his form limned in the light-aura that only the most powerful Urisk Strafeling geomancers possess.

The priest's yellow eyes are dramatically lined in sweeping silver, a circlet of tawny diamonds set in gold gracing his brow. A runic stylus of crystalline-gold apatite is grasped in his gem-encrusted hand, chain-linked squares of gleaming gold draped horizontally across his lean chest.

All the men's expressions are stern as they glare at the rose-hued woman on her knees before them.

The woman is bound by glowing cords of golden geopower, her pale pink eyes fierce, the rose-white hue of her skin and hair that of the Urisk's lowest servant class, the Uuril. A stylus made of pink amethyst lies on the ground before her, just out of reach.

"What would you have us do with her, High Priest Vyoor?" one of the soldiers growls, his sapphire-blue eyes aimed hatefully at the woman.

Stunned, Sparrow realizes that the priest she's looking at is the Geo'din religion's most revered prophet—High Priest Geo'duuth Vyoor.

"Speak, witch," the high priest commands as he narrows his merciless golden gaze on the woman. "This is your last chance to repent and beg Geo'din on High for mercy."

The woman gives him an acid glare, then draws back and spits at him.

Growling out their fury, the Uurok soldiers raise their blades and lunge toward her, but the high priest holds up a glittering hand and the Uurok halt.

"The Uuril will rise!" the woman growls at the high priest. "As will the Urol! And *all* the women of Uriskan! Your days are numbered!"

With merciless calm, the high priest angles his golden stylus at the woman.

Yellow light blasts from the stylus's tip. Sparrow flinches as the woman's instantly bound form is knocked to the ground, a golden gag forming over her mouth. She cries out her muffled rage, straining desperately against her bindings.

Ignoring the woman's cries, one of the soldiers turns to the high priest. "A number of Uuril and Urol women have gotten hold of styluses, Your Eminence," he cautions. "They've taken over the Geo'glyph Shrine to protest what they blasphemously call 'the abuse of our lower classes and women.'"

In a flash, Sparrow realizes what she's witnessing.

The "Rebellion of the Demonic Women." When the High Priest Vyoor crushed the "Evil Geo'witchlings" and ushered in the "Gleaming Holy Times."

The High Priest Vyoor brings his hand to the linkage of golden squares draped across his chest and raises his geo-stylus as he begins to murmur spell after spell, his golden Strafeling-aura turning sun bright. Sparrow shudders against the sizzling rise of geopower in the air as she draws back into the shelter of the tree.

"I bind your geopower," Vyoor intones as his golden aura intensifies, everything tinting to gold, the scene suddenly stripped of every other color. "In the name of Geo'din on High, I bind the power of *all* current and potential Geo'witchlings of Uriskan."

A great flash of gold detonates, encompassing the entire city and the leagues around it. The golden blast soon fades, other colors streaming back into the world, the woman's metallic bindings vanishing.

In a blur, the woman lunges for her stylus and levels it at the high priest, furiously reciting a spell, *growling* it out, as the soldiers beside Vyoor combatively raise styluses of their own, only to be halted, once more, by the high priest's upraised hand.

The world stills, save for the slight uptick of the high priest's mouth.

Seeming confused, the woman looks down at the stylus and hastily snarls out the words to the spell once more to no effect, her pale rose hue going even paler, her hand starting to tremble.

"What have you done?" she rasps in a quavering voice, her expression filling with rising horror.

"I have bound all the women of Uriskan," High Priest Vyoor calmly explains. "I have set down matrilineal runic magic to bind you all into a Blessed Submission."

"You monstrous fool!" she lashes out in a shattered voice. "To create this binding, you've ruptured our geomancy's link to the *ground*. Our magic exists to protect *Life*. Not to bring you *power!*"

Quick as an asp, the high priest raises his stylus and murmurs a spell. A slicing line of gold flashes out to impale the woman's chest. Her blood sprays and her eyes bug out, her mouth flying open as she falls to the ground in a crumpled heap.

The scene flashes out of sight as Sparrow is hurtled back into the Tree's purple-crystalline root-world. She swallows, trembling with horror from the desert tree's remembrance. But there's little time to make sense of it all as she's suddenly pulled into another vision, now surrounded by a purple Eastern Realm Forest edged with fall's riot of color.

Sparrow's sensation of trapped geo-energy shimmers back to life, deep in her center, the purple magic possessing an undeniable directional *pull*. But it's not anywhere in the aboveground world that Sparrow is being urged toward. It's not a pull toward trees or the sunlit sky that she feels everything inside her straining to reach.

It's a pull *downward*.

Sparrow lowers her gaze and feels herself abruptly shrinking and plummeting. The world around her telescopes outward, rapidly enlarging as she shrinks smaller and smaller, her microscopic essence drawn down into the *soil*.

Awe consumes her as she takes in the huge, magnified rocks surrounding her and feeding geo-energy into the Forest floor, working in concert with tendriling lines of black twining around the stones to break down rotted debris and feed Life-supporting minerals into the Forest.

To spark the reemergence of Life.

Tendrils of gray Shadow begin to flow into Sparrow's microscopic world from all sides. Dread overtakes her as the gray tendrils siphon up the regenerative black lines, their power leaching away until there is nothing but Shadowed stone and gray filth, all of it devoid of geopower.

Devoid of Balance.

Sparrow's gut clenches, the purple energy ignited within her sputtering as she recoils and finds herself suspended, once more, inside III's root-world of giant crystals, a palpable urgency vibrating through the Great Tree.

Sparrow gives a small start as a constellation of Erthia's most beautiful violet stones blink into being, palm-size, and begin to slowly orbit around her: amethyst, charoite, sugilite, tanzanite, iolite, grape agate.

Grape agate.

Sparrow's heart stretches toward the kindred pull of this stone, which is stronger than all the others. She reaches for it, her fingers hungrily wrapping around the grape agate's bumpy exterior.

Rays of purple light scythe out from Sparrow's clenched hand, all the other stones absorbed into the stone in her hand as Sparrow draws in the deepest breath of her entire life. Geo-bindings of metallic gold are suddenly shivering out of her form like tight twine giving way, twine she never knew she was imprisoned by. Geo'din's Watcher birds spring to life, perched on the huge purple crystals around her, the birds' translucent, multihued forms shimmering.

Sparrow's mind whirls with confusion as she looks at the prismatic Watchers of the Uriskal faith, the vision of High Priest Vyoor's murder of the woman resurging, the story of the murder dressed up in holy language and enshrined in her people's holy text.

Cast into turmoil over this religion she has prayed to all her life, Sparrow looks pleadingly at Geo'din's messenger birds.

What is true and what isn't? she agonizes to them and to the Great Tree.

A warmth pulses in the center of her heart—a warmth she knows is her answer from the birds and the Tree, an energy building in the central Geo'light of her soul.

Waiting to be unleashed.

The grape agate in Sparrow's hand contracts, drawing her gaze toward the newly slender purple rod of fused, spherical stones, energy tingling through it. She pulls in a surprised breath, relaxing her fingers slightly. A *stylus.* There's an image of the Great Tree marked on her palm beneath it, the Tree's true name pulsing through her mind—*III.*

Joy fills Sparrow as the Great Tree's rush of love floods her, invigorating her very soul with the energy of invitation to revolution.

On behalf of Erthia's Life-nourishing soil.

Sparrow's fingers tighten around the stylus . . . and she accepts the call.

Thierren, she thinks as tears mist her eyes, wishing she could send a message to him through the Tree. *Thierren, my love. We're not done breaking boundaries.* A crooked grin is suddenly lifting Sparrow's mouth, her life falling into place all around her like a garment being stitched together. *I'm going to reclaim my geomancy power. And help all the Urisk women of Erthia reclaim it, as well . . .*

A large *BOOM* shakes the world.

A hard sting flashes through the image of III marked on Sparrow's palm, and she's filled with a sense of the entire Tree recoiling. The giant crystals surrounding her begin to tint gray, poisonous tendrils of the gray seeping in from all sides.

Sparrow can tell, from the pulsing sting in her palm, that it's not a vision this time.

It's the true Shadow. Coming for III.

Sparrow grits her teeth and raises her stylus. *"Shield me!"* she snarls out in Uriskal.

Violet light flashes from her stylus, and a translucent violet shield rushes around her in a great orb just as the last of the surrounding purple cuts out and she's hit by the agonizing sense of trees *screaming.* Sparrow stiffens, her terror mounting as Marcus Vogel's image shivers into being in the back of her mind, his pale green eyes lit with silver fire.

"I'm coming for you," he croons, his expression viper calm as he lifts the Shadow Wand and points it at the stylus in her hand. "I see what you've done, and I'm coming for you, Urisk Witch. I will consume every last speck of Erthia's geopower. And you along with it."

I'm trapped, Sparrow realizes as her terror flares higher, an intuitive sense of the Shadow power's every line of attack filling her.

Vogel is attacking the Northern Forest along with its soil, she realizes, her dread surging.

And I'm trapped inside III's power.

CHAPTER EIGHT

DEMON STORM

Elloren

Northern Forest
Eighteen days after Xishlon

"Use my power to reshield our Forest!" I cry out to the Dryads as a wind coming off Vogel's incoming Shadow storm band roars through the unshielded Northern Forest. The unnatural gusts crack off branches as they whip through the terrified trees and begin to siphon up their elemental magic, birds and animals in an uproar.

A rustling cry for help courses through my rootlines as the leaves of the surrounding trees begin to gray at the edges. Flapping dark wings, my kindred ravens quickly fan out around III, their urgent Dark aura strobing through the air. A confusing vision of purple, crystalline imagery flashes through my mind as III's power gives a hard contraction downward, as if the Great Tree is channeling all its elemental might into the soil surrounding its roots.

"Use our power, as well!" the gold-eyed Mage, Mavrik Glass, shouts over the wind, as both he and his equally golden-eyed fastmate unsheathe wands, my empathy detecting how their merged auras orbit around each other in brilliant, golden loops, bright gold fastmarks emblazoned on their hands and wrists, flame-orange hawks on their shoulders. "Gwynn and I possess twinned Level Five power in *every single* elemental line!" Mavrik yells, holding up his wand.

"Get rid of those *wands!*" Lyptus spits out with venomous force, her kindred panther snarling.

"You're not dormant anymore," Sylvan agrees, his gaze lancing into Mavrik. "Forget what you think you know about magic. Dryads do not wield dead *wands.* They wield *living branches* connected to the Forest through their *rootlines.*"

"And your bastardized Mage spells won't work!" Oaklyyn hisses, her wolverine kindred pacing around her as it growls. "The Balance of words is all off! They're built for halflings cut off from the Forest!"

Vogel's Void tree blasts through my mind, reverberating there as the storming roar advancing from the south gains potency.

"That storm band is shot through with Shadowfire," Yvan warns, his wings stiffening. "He's going to burn down this *entire Forest*."

"We need to link everyone's power!" Sylvan calls out to us all as he unsheathes a second living branch and holds it out to me. "Make contact with this, witch. We'll draw on your magic and that of your allies to shield III, then expand the shield over our entire Forest."

I grab hold of the top of Sylvan's living branch, energy from the surrounding Forest streaming into my rootlines as he points the branch in his other hand skyward.

Oaklyyn's elemental power whips into a raging fury. "It's a mistake to link to these halflings!"

Hazel bares suddenly darkened, elongated teeth at her, his eyes going fully black before he swings around and sets his gaze on Gwynn and Mavrik with a look of open rebellion. "Tree'kin," he snarls, drawing two dark branches sheathed at his hips. He thrusts one of them out toward the twinned Dryad'kin, his subterranean Death Fae voice cutting straight through the Shadow storm band's roar of power. "Make contact with this branch!"

"Come, Icaral!" Yulan cries out to Yvan as Mavrik and Gwynn wrap their hands around the top of Hazel's branch and Yulan thrusts one of the two branches she's holding toward Yvan, his surprise flashing through our bond.

"You can't use Wyvernfire to shield our Forest!" Oaklyyn snarls at Yulan.

"I don't seek his fire!" Yulan cries against the wind's roar. "I seek to draw on his Lasair healing energy, which can counter Void Death!"

Comprehension blazing through his fire, Yvan springs forward and grips hold of the top of Yulan's branch, as I catch a whiff of the acrid tang of unnatural smoke drifting in on the poison wind, the screams of trees blasting through me as Vogel's fire blazes through the Forest's southern edge.

Murmuring Dryadin spells in unison, Hazel and Yulan join Sylvan in thrusting one of their two branches toward III's canopy. Oaklyyn, Lyptus, and Larch cast them damning looks before thrusting their branches upward as well, joining their voices to the chant.

A deep-green suspended line of magic bursts into being, crackling out from the Dryads' raised branches and connecting them all in a single line of power.

Sylvan booms out a single word in Dryadin. *"Linkage!"*

A wrenching pull on my power nearly knocks me off my feet as I'm flooded with a harder rush of the Northern Forest's line-expanding magic. The Forest's magic roars up through my rootlines and out through the branch I'm holding, before coursing up through the raised branch in Sylvan's other hand and into the green line of Dryad magic.

A *crack* sounds in the air above as a dense translucent green wall of power blasts up from the line. Its top rapidly fans out to create a dome-shield encasing III and the surrounding clearing, the Shadow wind furiously buffeting it.

I sense the colossal amount of combined elemental magic flowing into our shield, most of it being drawn from my rootlines. It's stronger than any shield I've felt before. Stronger than the shields that used to encase Noilaan and Amazakaraan, rapidly gaining enough charge to spring *outward*.

Branch raised, Sylvan turns to me with a look of shocked incomprehension. "Your power," he gasps, "it's *immense*." His gaze darts toward III's cloud-piercing canopy, his gaze seeming to sharpen with resolve before his gaze bores back into mine. "Dryad'kin," he says with measured force, "I need you to climb to the top of III's canopy to provide an anchor point so we can channel your power and rapidly expand this shield."

He releases his hold on the branch in my hand, a crackling green line of connection springing to life, flowing from my branch's tip to the line of green power connecting the Dryads' upthrust branches as I take hold of the branch's base. "Once you reach III's canopy," Sylvan directs, "we'll send out spells through our linkage and cast our dome-shield outward to reshield the entire Northern Forest with a barrier stronger than *anything* Erthia has *ever seen*."

Yvan and I share an intense look, our unvoiced agreement in it, his fire flaring to embrace me before I sheathe the branch in my tunic's belt and launch myself at III. My dark green nails bite into bark as I scramble up the Great Tree, vaulting myself ever higher. My pulse jumping in my throat, I burst through III's expansive canopy, peer out through our shield's translucent green surface and come face-to-face with Vogel's storming nightmare.

The Magedom's churning storm band is arced around the Forest's eastern, southern, and western edges, rapidly gaining height, its dark lightning raining fire onto the trees in explosion after explosion.

But our fledgling shield's combined power—I can sense that it's stronger than the Shadow storm band. And our linked power is building, our entire Forest standing with us, roaring its power through our rootlines and into our shielding as I draw a deep breath and thrust my branch toward the heavens.

The rumble of my allies' combined power surges into my wand arm, my magic amplifying it to world-bending heights. I can feel the Dryad spells charging into my branch, our shielding around III readying itself to spring outward over the entire Northern Forest . . .

. . . just as Vogel's arcing storm band abruptly triples in height and crashes forward in a nightmarish tidal wave of gray.

Faster than I would have ever imagined possible, the Shadow storm rolls over the Northern Forest's entire southern, eastern, and western expanses, league upon league of trees exploding with silvery-black flame, vast quantities of our Forest-linked power disintegrating with them.

My eyes widen as I'm overtaken by the instant sense of my magic hollowing out, my connection to my Dryad'kin guttering along with my connection to my too-distant dragon horde.

My allies' magical connection wavers, the line of green coursing from my branch's tip sizzling out of sight as the Shadow destruction mows through the Forest with astonishing speed and my rootlines seize.

"Augh!" I cry out, the Forest's scream tearing through my mind.

My lungs contract with choking force. My grip slips from both the slim branch I'm holding and the huge branch I'm clinging to, and I fall, panic exploding as I fight for breath and plummet, Yvan's fire suddenly igniting into a scorching roar through our bond.

He reaches me faster than I would have imagined possible, his strong arms seizing tight hold of me from behind, halting my free fall and soaring us upward into the sky before angling us back down toward III's canopy.

I'm met with one last panoramic look south through our shielding around III. More than half of the Northern Forest has been destroyed, the Shadow storm bands rapidly consuming leagues more, the killing chaos headed straight for III.

"Help us!" I cry out to III, the choked-off scream forced from my throat as my rootlines begin to shrivel, Errilith's caw of alarm sounding out.

An image flashes through my mind via my III connection—Wynter and her brothers along with three Smaragdalfar soldiers assembled underground in front of III's roots, Wynter, Cael, and Rhys now tinted green. The Verdyllion is gripped in Wynter's hand as she blasts a circular shield around the Great Tree's roots, the Verdyllion filled with a huge portion of III's rapidly diminishing power, the rest of the Great Tree's magic focused toward a mysterious purple aura suffusing the soil around its roots.

Dread slams down.

Because as Yvan soars us down through III's canopy, I realize what's happening. III is sacrificing its power to save Wynter and the Sublands and those trapped inside it.

And III is saving the Verdyllion.

Yvan touches down in the clearing surrounding the Great Tree as my rootlines collapse inward and I gasp for air, my vision beginning to black out as what's left of my magic scours out of my body. Everyone, save Hazel and Yvan, is crumpled on the ground and struggling for breath, Yulan's vine tresses stripped of their blossoms. Larch and Lyptus are unconscious, Larch's bear and Lyptus's panther pawing at them, while Yulan's heron frantically rustles its wings. Everyone's green hues are shifting to gray, a sense of our shield's diminishing strength heightening my alarm.

My knees buckle as I struggle for breath, and Yvan tightens his hold on me before I can crumple to the ground. I glance at my quivering wand hand, a cascading sense of doom shuddering through me as I take in how, like my Dryad'kin, my forest green hue is rapidly morphing to gray.

"Our shield is giving way . . ." I force out to Yvan, and he glances up to where the new dome-shield around III is already beginning to gray, its tang of power dissolving.

My ravens let out booming *caws* as Hazel hisses out a string of Dryad spells and lifts his branch. Dark mist explodes from its tip and courses over our decaying shield, lines of power from my Errilor Ravens joining Hazel's Deathkin magic.

"Elloren, what's happening to you?" Yvan exclaims, his violet-fire gaze burning into mine.

"My rootlines are dying with my bonded Forest . . ." I gasp. The scouring sensation inside me turns eviscerating, as if my collapsing lines are about to be ripped clear from my body.

The flow of Yvan's fire through our bond turns searing, a ferocious determination blazing through it. His gaze swings to Hazel. "We need to evacuate everyone to the Forests of the East! *Now!* This magic is too powerful to fight!"

"We will *never evacuate!*" Sylvan growls at Yvan from where he's fighting for breath on the ground, his pine hue morphed to deadened gray and his branch hair stripped of its needles. The ferocity in his ash-tinted eyes remains undimmed. "This is *our Forest!* We are its *Guardians!* Our people . . . if this fire reaches them in the North and consumes that portion of Forest, too, they will all *die*, along with their kindred ones!"

My giant ravens *caw* out a louder warning, Errilith's wings ruffling; a stark urgency lights his coal eyes as the incoming storm band's Shadow winds slam against our decaying shield and all the trees surrounding the shield explode into gray fire.

A strangled scream tears from my chest, and I'm only half-aware of being lowered to the ground before Yvan raises his palm toward the incoming chaos and an inferno of horde-bonded fire ramps up in his core.

"*No fire!*" Hazel snarls, his lime hue stripped away to a haunting alabaster, dark horns raised, eyes fully black. "It will trigger a backblast from my shield that could *destroy III!*"

"It's over!" Yvan hisses. "This Forest and III are doomed! We've got to evacuate everyone *now!*"

"*Never!*" Oaklyyn chokes out, the word cut off as her body seizes and her wolverine snaps at us.

A devastated look crosses Hazel's features as he takes in Oaklyyn and her kindred. He turns back to Yvan, the two of them exchanging one lethally decided look before Hazel's face elongates and he gnashes his extended, blackened teeth, six black insectile legs bursting from his back.

Shock skids through my agony as Hazel drops his branch and lifts both his blackening palms and insectile legs.

Dark mist jets from his hands and insect legs and bolts toward III's shielding, a stronger net of dark mist overtaking the graying shield, the Shadow storm's forking lightning and killing wind battering against it with terrifying force.

"Elloren," Yvan says as he drops to one knee beside me and takes firm hold of my arms. "I'm going to try to send power through you from my kindred Forest. Through our bond."

I strain to voice my assent but am unable and summon a weak nod instead, as large swaths of my vision black out and the rootline-flaying pain intensifies, my surrounding Forest falling and the last traces of my magic falling with it.

Yvan's mouth comes down onto mine and I grab weak hold of him, his violet fire roaring through me in a molten blast. I shudder against his kiss as a vision of his vast kindred Forest scorches through my mind—leagues of gigantic pine trees with midnight-hued trunks and deep-purple needles. I can sense the distant Zhilaan Forest waking up and becoming aware of how my sputtering power has come unmoored, sense it reading the destruction raging all around via my link to III.

The Zhilaan's fury rises like a firestorm and blazes through us, its elemental might suddenly burning purple magic through my lines with lung-opening force. I draw in a desperate breath as Yvan deepens our kiss and his distant kindred Forest forges a tenuous connection to my rootlines via my Wyvernbond to Yvan.

I heave in another ragged breath as Yvan breaks the kiss, gripping my arms, my withered rootlines filling with a slim line of the Zhilaan Forest's distant, fire-fueled energy, a branching tingle racing over my skin.

"Are you all right?" he demands, alarm blazing in his eyes.

I nod, pulling in one great, heaving breath after another. I glance down to find a faint purple branching pattern marked over my grayed skin. Before my astonishment can register over this visual manifestation of my slim Zhilaan Forest connection through our Wyvernbond, the surrounding storms abruptly withdraw and rise in a churning gray mass. Dread overtakes me as a 360-degree view opens up beyond Hazel's shield.

A strangled cry bursts from my throat.

The Northern Forest is no more.

What used to be leagues upon leagues of complex Life has been reduced to charred trees, no color anywhere, the plants and wildlife *murdered*.

Only III left standing.

More horrifying still, I can sense a colossal amount of Shadowed power being drawn up into wands by the huge grounded army positioned to the distant south of us, the consolidating storms above coalescing into a planetary ball of lightning-spitting chaos.

Like a Void moon hovering above III.

Yvan's gaze swings to Hazel, his internal Wyvernfire still burning bright. "We need to get everyone onto Elloren's ravens. Along with whatever kindreds we can."

"I'll *kill* you if you touch me," Oaklyyn rasps, clutching at her throat as she casts Yvan a glare of pure hate. "I . . . won't . . . leave . . . my . . . *Forest!*"

A tortured look twists Hazel's expression as he thrusts his pitch-dark palms and insectile legs toward Oaklyyn. Lashes of dark vine shoot from his palms and the tips of his legs, spearing toward her. She coughs out a vicious protest as Hazel binds her and works to encase her snarling wolverine before giving Yvan a prodding look, his black teeth bared, the wolverine shredding and biting through its bindings as fast as Hazel can create them.

Yvan leaps into action, lifting me onto Errilith's back. Hazel tethers me there, and I sway against the bindings, my power depleted, my withered lines bolstered only by the line of distant Zhilaan Forest power.

"Keep Mavrik and his fastmate together!" I rasp out as Yvan drags a semiconscious Mavrik and his fastmate onto another of the huge ravens. Hazel tethers them to it, their orange hawks agitatedly perching atop them. "Their power," I choke out, "it's intensely linked. I'm not sure they'd survive for long if they were separated."

I hazard a glance toward where I sense Vogel's forces massing, the Shadow magic of his army still ominously motionless, the horrifyingly huge moonstorm above us rapidly gaining strength.

Help me! I silently implore the Zhilaan Forest. *Help me to regain my full power so I can save III!*

A ripple of energy shivers over my palm, a line of III's energy flowing into it, as if the Great Tree is desperately trying to convey something with its last shred of power.

I look at my palm, my heart pounding out a ragged rhythm as a sputtering, prismatic glow flashes through my III imprint. A vision of the Verdyllion pulses against the back of my mind, and I'm filled with the sense of III channeling energy into the Wand-Stylus.

"Go!" Yvan orders, and I'm suddenly lifted into the air on Errilith, my Deathkin flock taking wing alongside Yvan, with Hazel on ravenback, Oaklyyn's semiconscious form bound behind the Deathkin Dryad, Yulan's heron soaring in behind the raven she's bound to. Larch's bear kindred lets out a soul-shredding growl of distress along with Oaklyyn's wolverine and Lyptus's panther as we wing away, the animals' cries splicing straight through my heart.

"We can't leave III and those kindreds to Vogel!" I cry, overtaken by wild despair as Hazel drags his shield away from III and draws it around us, my every nerve filling with the desire to hurl myself back toward III and the abandoned animals, a feral terror overtaking me.

Vogel's Void tree slithers through my mind with what feels like a brutal taunt.

I jerk my gaze south and take in the sea of soldiers massed in the far distance, past where the Northern Forest's southern border used to be.

His forces still disturbingly motionless.

I look toward the Great Tree and take in the slowly turning, massive sphere of dark storm poised above it, curling black lightning and muffled thunder pulsing inside the Void sphere. A seismic dread builds, my weakened rootlines *straining* toward III, along with the energy of the entire purple Zhilaan Forest.

Every Forest on Erthia straining toward III.

As the giant killing moon of storm falls.

A world-shaking explosion of Shadowfire detonates on III and the kindreds, a scream tearing from my throat. A planet-shifting sense of the Natural World ripping apart lances through my every rootline as III burns and Vogel's army launches itself into motion by land and air.

His entire Shadow force coming straight toward us.

SHADOW WORLD

Elloren

Shadowed Northern Forest
Eighteen days after Xishlon

My knuckles whiten as I grip Errilith's dark feathers, despair twisting through my gut with such force, it threatens to undo me. I mentally urge my Deathkin ravens to arrow us toward the living Forests of the East, my semiconscious and unconscious Dryad'kin tied to my ravens' backs.

Vogel's airborne Shadow forces spearing toward us.

I glance down at the Shadow wasteland coursing by beneath us—only leagues of charred trees and stumps with Shadow smoke slithering around them remain where the magnificent Northern Forest once stood, millions of kindred plants and animals slain or fleeing for their lives. And the other Dryads who lived in our bonded Forest—were they all murdered by Vogel's Shadow storm?

Hazel is crouched on ravenback, still morphed into his insectile form, his huge insect legs raised. Misty black shielding emanates from his legs' tips to encircle us all in a translucent, midnight-hued bubble. Yvan flanks my other side, his violet-fire eyes alight, dark wings beating powerfully against air, our bond ablaze.

I teeter, depleted from having the Northern Forest bond cruelly ripped from my rootlines, my tenuous connection to the too-distant Zhilaan Forest through my bond to Yvan not powerful enough to strengthen my lines past sheer survival.

I glance behind me toward where III once stood, majestic and strong, and a vise of panic contracts my chest. Vogel's airborne army is rapidly closing the distance between us.

I look to Yvan in a flash of alarm and am hit by a sense of the inferno of fire power he's drawing from his core, a sizzling flush racing over my skin as his hands take on a violet glow. Yvan and Hazel exchange a quick look before Yvan whips around, midair, lets out a low, vicious snarl, and swipes out his hands in an arc.

Bolts of violet Wyvernfire erupt from Yvan's palms at the same time that Hazel opens the back of our shielding.

Yvan's lashings of flame fly through the sky and collide with the southernmost row of incoming Mages. Screams cut through the air as Yvan sweeps his hands from left to right, his line of fire slashing through the entire frontline of soldiers and their broken dragons.

They explode into violet flame, but bile rises in my throat as I take in the seemingly never-ending dark sea of soldiers flying in behind them to our west and soaring up from the south.

Too many for Yvan to take out.

Yvan hurls out another whipping attack of flame before Hazel swipes an insectile limb, closing the gap in our shielding at the same moment three surviving broken dragons spearing in from the west zoom closer.

I take in three salt-white Marfoir astride the grayed, multi-eyed Shadow dragons, and terror singes through me. The Alfsigr Marfoir assassins are even more grotesquely altered than the Marfoir that came for Wynter in Verpacia. Huge, pale spider limbs splay out from their backs, their gray insectile eyes multiplied to horrifying masses that cover their upper heads.

In chilling unison, they flick their spidery limbs toward me.

"Elloren, look out!" Yvan thunders as gray webbing lances clear through Hazel's Death-mist shielding, sizzling it into black smoke before the webbing collides with me and unfurls to encircle my body.

A cry of protest bursts from my throat, and Errilith lets out an urgent *caw* as the Shadow webbing singes away my tether to the raven and I'm tugged toward the Marfoir assassins, desperately scrabbling to hold tight to Errlith's back feathers.

The Marfoir zoom in closer, everything in me yearning for a living branch, fully replenished Dryad power, and the knowledge to wield it and fight back.

Yvan's rage flashes through our bond as a slim, focused dart of his violet fire sears in from the side and into the Marfoir webbing. The web ignites, the Marfoirs' yanking pull on me releasing just before I can be dragged from Errlith's back.

In a split-second blur, Yvan zooms through the air between me and the Marfoir, his power incandescent with fury as he raises violet-glowing hands. Twin bolts of violet light blast from Yvan's palms and collide with the Marfoir. Two of the Elf assassins and their Shadow dragons burst into purple flames, the Marfoir shrieking as they hurtle toward the ground, but the third Marfoir dodges the blast and flies straight at me.

Before Yvan can attack, the Marfoir reaches me and thrusts the knife-sharp points of its spider legs toward me just as Hazel soars in close, leaps from his raven, and slams into the Marfoir, impaling the pale assassin's body with his black limbs and shoving the Marfoir off its broken dragon, the two of them free-falling through air.

Errilith lets out another booming *caw* and veers us away from their battling forms, the Marfoir's pale spider legs flailing, steely blood spraying. The Marfoir and Hazel fall away from each other, plummeting toward the distant, Shadowed ground, Yvan's concern for both me and Hazel firing through our bond as he incinerates another incoming section of Vogel's advancing army.

"Catch Hazel!" I cry out to my kindred flock.

Their answering aura flare pulses the world black. The raven that was previously carrying Hazel swoops in under him, and he slams onto its back in front of a semi-conscious Oaklyyn.

My heart hammering, I glance back up and take in the next wave of Shadow soldiers swarming toward us from the west. The feel of a Shadow storm rising in legions of wands overtakes my power-empath senses. I open my mouth to call out a warning just as potent roars split the sky to the east—the roars of *unbroken* dragons.

My gaze whips east, and surprise explodes through me.

A horizontal tear in the distant sky has burst into being, its golden interior rimmed with the blue glow of Noi runes—*a sky portal!*—a dragon-borne army streaming through it.

Naga! Raz'zor! I mentally scream, frantically searching for their black and white winged forms, rooting around my diminished fireline connection to them for some sense of their hordefire as the incoming army soars into sharper view—*none* of the incoming dragons moon white, most black, some sapphire . . .

Vu Trin!

My pulse leaps as I remember the warning in Raz'zor's fire of Vu Trin forces coming to kill the Black Witch.

A smaller sky portal blips into being, connected to the side of the larger portal, a compact airborne force soaring in, not astride dragons . . . but riding giant eagles the color of *fire*.

My dread slides into jagged panic, the multitude of forces all converging on us as I sense Vogel's army releasing their power. I whip my head back as a band of churning gray bursts into being before the Shadow army and pummels toward us.

Yvan lashes out a long wall of violet fire, but the Shadow storm roars straight through it, blasting away Yvan's flame before slamming into us. I cry out as Errilith and I are hit by a gust of wind, the two of us hurtled through the air, all sight cut out as we're enveloped in the churning tempest.

I grab hold of Errilith's feathers as the sky spins, my pulse exploding. Errilith lets out a great *CAW*, my kindred's wings flapping wildly against the storm in a desperate attempt to right us as we pinwheel through the storming gray, down toward the tops of the charred trees below.

A bolt of golden fire spears through the tempest and slams into my side, hot pain lancing through me as I'm hurled clear off Errilith and into a terrifying free fall, Errilith sending out another frantic cry before he's swept from my vision. A split-second rush of confusion bolts through my terror as I plummet, because I've an intimate knowledge of the fire that hit me—it's Yvan's flame, only shifted back to its original golden hue.

But . . . why would Yvan attack me?

I hit the ground, pain exploding along my side, stars streaking across my vision as the bones in my left arm and leg snap.

Buffeted by fierce winds, I cast my pain-blurred gaze wildly about, all sight cut off by the churning gray save for the spectral forms of the closest dead trees rising from the Shadowed earth, no sign of Errilith. Gritting my teeth, I force myself up, the booms of magical warfare sounding above, blue and gray explosions cutting through the gray, dragons roaring and shrieking.

"Yvan, I'm here!" I cry, just as another bolt of his inexplicably gilded fire spears through the gray and hits my chest, my breath struck from my lungs as I'm skidded back across the smoking ground.

"Stop!" I shriek, frantic with alarm.

A blurred figure takes shape, advancing purposefully toward me through the whipping storm, a vengeful hatred rippling through their fire aura. A figure that is *not* Yvan.

My eyes widen as I realize who it is—Soleiya Guryev, Yvan's mother, her eyes lit with a murderous golden glow.

"I'm not your enemy!" I cry, raising both palms in protest as Soleiya lets out a teeth-gritted snarl, thrusts her gold-glowing palms toward me and bolts out impressive columns of fire.

Her attack slams into my chest and punches me back against a dead tree, the breath struck from my lungs once more as I burst into flames, my broken arm and leg screaming with pain, but my Xishlon garb that Or'myr magicked to be fireproof holding together. All sight is briefly cut off again by the roaring gold as Soleiya's inferno is quickly and intentionally absorbed into my Wyvernbond to Yvan *by* Yvan, his snarling fury over the attack shuddering through our bond's flame.

Violet light blasts into being above me, and Yvan is suddenly soaring down into the clearing like a vengeful falcon and landing between his mother and me.

"What in all of Erthia's hells are you doing?" Yvan roars at his mother, alight with outrage as a portion of his invisible fire aura encompasses my injuries.

Soleiya gapes at him, wide-eyed, love and relief searing through her power. "My son!" She takes a lurching step toward him. "Yvan, I feared this witch would *kill* you!"

"Elloren is my *bonded mate!*" Yvan lashes back, his wings snapping threateningly out.

Surprise. Shock. Outrage. All of it flashes through his mother's expression and fire power as she levels an incendiary look my way. "You gave this *evil witch* your *Wyvernfire?*"

"I did," Yvan snarls, his fire aura whipping protectively around me with such intensity that an aching love for him streaks through my pain. "If you kill my *mate,*" Yvan hisses, glancing up at the light-flashing explosions of the battle raging above, "I'll be temporarily stripped of all my power. Do you *really* want that happening *right now?*"

"You underestimate her capacity for *evil!*" Soleiya hurls back.

Before Yvan can refute her, a swarm of multi-eyed Shadow scorpios leap through the mist and scuttle toward us from all sides, letting out bloodcurdling shrieks.

Chaos erupts. Yvan and his mother blast back the incoming swarm with repeated explosions of violet and golden fire. I clumsily dodge the swinging forelimb of one scorpio and the lashing poisonous tail of another, cursing my lack of a weapon as Yvan's and Soleiya's forms are repeatedly obscured then swallowed by the churning gray.

The primal will to live spiking, I grit my teeth against the pain, turn toward the tree behind me, reach up and break off a charred Shadow-smoking branch, then level it at an incoming scorpio as I grind out the light-strike spell.

My weakened power doesn't budge.

A remembrance lights—Dryad power requires *Dryadin* spells and *living* branches. Spitting out an epithet, I drop the dead branch and hurl myself to the side.

The scorpio barreling toward me collides with the charred trunk with so much force that its head cracks in two, black ichor spraying everywhere. But my victory is short-lived. My dread surges as a swarm of multi-eyed wraith bats and Mages on dragonback appear through the smoke above me while Yvan's and Soleiya's violet and gold explosions continue to detonate at my sides. The incoming Mages raise wands as they soar near and blast Shadow vines toward me.

I cry out as the vines slam into me and encircle my form. Blinding pain streaks through my broken arm and leg as my limbs are cinched to my body, a strangled scream torn from my throat as the Mages land, brutal triumph in their glowing gray eyes, my fear amplified by the wraith bats touching down all around.

What occurs next happens so fast I can barely process it.

A bolt of vermillion fire streaks in from the churning gloom above and blows up the Mages while streaks of blue and white lightning take out the wraith bats in flashes of bright light, their screams and shrieks overpowered by the roaring, mul-tihued explosions.

A constellation of shock whooshing through me, I look up to find a huge onyx dragon with Vothe's white-lightning eyes and Raz'zor soaring in through the Shadow storm, my brother Trystan carried on Vothe's back, his wand raised.

Dryad Witch! comes Raz'zor's ferocious growl.

My heart leaps into my throat as Ariel, her small raven, and three of the giant eagles fly in, my family members astride the giant saffron-hued birds.

Trystan, Vothe, Raz'zor, and Ariel immediately set about blasting away incoming Mages and Shadow creatures with great bolts of blue-and-white lightning and gold-and-red fire, their forms swallowed by the roiling gray storm as they dart into it to battle back Vogel's forces.

Diana and Rafe leap from one of the eagles' backs, Jarod and Aislinn off another, all of them launching themselves at incoming Mages and Shadow creatures while my spider-tattooed uncle Wrenfir, on eagleback, levels his wand and takes out another incoming Mage and his dragon with impaling bolts of thick, black vine.

Diana lets out a chilling growl, and I turn to her just as she leaps at a Mage in a blur and tears the head clear off his body before ripping the head off the Mage's

Shadow dragon. Rafe punches his fist through another Mage's chest in a spray of blood while Jarod claws the neck of the Mage's Shadow dragon.

And Aislinn . . . I watch, awed, as my previously timid friend leaps at one incoming Mage after another, her dark claws out, shredding through Shadow soldiers while large explosions of Yvan's violet fire blast through the whipping Shadow storm to my left.

A pair of gold-burning eyes appear through the roiling gray, Yvan's mother sprinting toward me, her hand raised.

"*Stop! No!*" I cry as Soleiya bolts fire toward me with enough force to break bone.

A bright white stream of Vothe's wind power jets in from the side and blasts Soleiya's flame away. Pain throbs through my broken leg and arm like rhythmic knife strikes as Trystan knocks down Yvan's mother with vine magic and tethers her, binding her palms to the ground.

Trystan leaps off Vothe's back, and Vothe swiftly morphs to his human form. The two of them rush to me and drop to my level as pain sends stars through my vision.

"We meet again, Black Witch," Vothe says, and I meet his white-lightning gaze, his mouth lifting into a wry smile as he slashes through my bindings with his extended claws.

A dome filled with Yvan's and Raz'zor's combined Wyvernfire blasts into being around us, pushing back both the Shadow storm and the attacking forces and revealing Yvan alongside Raz'zor's huge, white dragon form, the two of them steadily burning fire into their shield, Wrenfir and Ariel, her raven on her shoulder, swiftly adding their own power to the shield's fiery might.

Dropping his hands, Yvan turns and rushes toward me in a blur, passionate urgency burning in his eyes and coursing through our bond. He drops to one knee beside me, his fire aura embracing mine as his hands come to my arm and my leg. "I can sense your injuries through our bond," he says.

"My leg and arm are broken," I rasp, wincing from the pain as Yvan extends his claws and expeditiously slashes away my tunic's sleeve before encircling my arm with his warm hands.

Pain spikes through me as Yvan closes his eyes, his brow knotted with concentration. A rush of his heat flows into my arm and I shiver, the pain instantly halving.

"Let me *go!*" Yvan's bound mother rages at Trystan, giving him a blistering death-stare as repeated explosions ignite against our shield and Raz'zor, Ariel, and others continue to blaze power into it.

"What madness is this?" Diana growls at Soleiya as my Lupine sister drops the multi-eyed dragon head she's effortlessly gripping in her fist and levels a blood-covered finger at Yvan's mother. "Who are you?" Diana demands, her eyes swinging toward Yvan. "I scent her as your kin!"

"She's my *mother*," Yvan bites out, enough angry fire to melt planets searing through him as he rips an opening in the side of my pants and slides his hot hands around my broken leg. My teeth clenching, I hiss against the flare of pain.

"Do not heal that Demon Witch!" Soleiya snarls at Yvan.

A growl erupts from Diana's throat. "Silence, Lasair! You speak of my *sister!*"

Soleiya's fiery gaze darts to Diana with an expression of sheer incredulity. *"What?"*

"Pleased to meet you, Yvan's mother," Trystan calmly states as he levels his wand at Soleiya, his words dangerously clipped, "but maybe, just *maybe*, we could all turn our attention to killing *Vogel's forces* instead of my *sister*."

Ariel tosses me a sharp-toothed grin. "This is unexpectedly entertaining."

"We've got to go, *now*," Rafe urges, and he and Yvan lock gazes. "Our forces are holding back both Western and Eastern Realm forces, *all of them* trying to fight their way toward Elloren."

"This shield won't hold for long," Vothe adds as the gray and sapphire explosions blasting against the fiery barrier gain potency, streaks of gray beginning to appear through it.

"Elloren, can you stand?" Yvan asks, his searing violet gaze triggering another rush of heat through our bond.

"I think so," I shakily affirm.

He throws an arm around me and helps me to my feet, the pain in my arm and leg a fraction of what it was, the bones feeling more solid as I desperately look past the shield for some sight of Errilith or the rest of my flock. I close my eyes and search through my depleted lines for a trace of their aura and find it, all of them above us, encircled by our horde's fire, hopefully with my Dryad'kin still tethered to their backs.

"My ravens and Dryad'kin," I say to everyone, "they're with Naga's horde. Along with two Mages joined with Issani magic, all of them carried on the backs of my flock of giant Deathkin ravens. Our horde is shielding them."

"*Raz'zor*," Yvan calls, "I need you to carry Elloren and my mother out. I'll cover you."

An answering flash of affirming red blazes through our horde bond, and Yvan helps me climb onto Raz'zor's broad back while Raz'zor continues to blast vermillion fire into our shielding.

"Kill the witch while you still can!" Soleiya snarls at Yvan.

Yvan casts his mother an incensed look before turning to Trystan. "You'll need to bind my mother's palms and gag her when you tether her to Raz'zor so she can't attack Elloren with Lasair spells."

Trystan nods once and sets about the task, both he and Yvan dragging Soleiya's bound form toward Raz'zor as she calls for my immediate death and Trystan secures her palms against her sides.

"I'm evacuating you with my *mate*," Yvan sharply informs his mother as he hoists her bound form onto Raz'zor's back in front of me.

"She's ensorcelled you!" Soleiya hurls back at him as Trystan lifts his wand to bind her to Raz'zor. "Look at what the witch has done to the color of your eyes and your fire!" Soleiya cries.

"I brought that about *myself*," Yvan shoots back, livid, as Trystan conjures a gag around Soleiya's mouth. She growls against it, rhythmically slamming against me as best she can, as if striving to knock me clear off Errilith's back.

Vothe fans out his wings. "We'll need to draw in our shielding around us as we ascend!" he calls out to everyone just as a slight motion in the charred tree branch above me catches my eye.

I look up . . . and fear sizzles straight down my spine.

There's a multi-eyed raven perched amidst the burned-up branches, a pale green eye in the center of its head.

Set right on me.

Vogel's dark tree punches into my mind.

"Vogel's found me!" I cry.

Ariel throws a bolt of fire toward the raven, and the multi-eyed creature lets out an unnaturally deep *caw* as it explodes into a ball of golden flame.

"Vogel will be bearing down on us in a matter of seconds," Yvan warns.

Rafe gives him a grim look. "We got here by hijacking some of the magic of the Vu Trin sky portal. A Death Fae ally webbed two portals together and remained in the East to keep them bound. They've got a lag that's only a few hours in length.

We're going to have to fight our way back to the portals, get through them, then destroy them before Vogel can follow us."

"We've got to get my Dryad'kin to living Forest," I stress, "before their rootlines completely wither. Or they'll *die*."

With a determined light in his amber eyes, Rafe turns toward the others. "Let's *go*," he calls out as the explosions slamming against our shield turn seismic.

I lean forward over Soleiya's bound, struggling form and grip Raz'zor's pale shoulder horns as Vothe shifts to dragon form and Trystan leaps astride him, others pulling themselves onto the backs of eagles.

We take to the air, my allies drawing our fiery shield in close as everyone who can flows power into it and it takes on the appearance of a colorful glass bubble, the sound of explosions reverberating above us growing louder and louder as we rise through the Shadow storm.

We break through the storm's uppermost reaches, and alarm skitters through everyone's power as we take in how hemmed in my allies are.

Naga and our horde are positioned around us in a wide circle, blasting flames into an encircling wall of Wyvernfire, their powerful wings beating down on the air. Repeated blasts of Shadow power detonate against our horde's shield from the south and the west while a section of the Vu Trin forces strike sapphire power at their shield from the east. I can just make out a larger section of Vu Trin in the far distance, the Eastern Realm soldiers engaged in fierce aerial battles with Vogel's Shadow legions.

Relief stutters through me to find Hazel on ravenback, still in his terrifying Deathkin form, Oaklyyn before him. He's sending visible lashings of his dark power into the Wyvernfire shield from the tips of the giant insectile limbs still sprouted from his back, my Errilor flock hovering near him, an unconscious-looking Sylvan and Yulan still secured to my ravens' backs along with Mavrik and Gwynn, my Dryad'kin's elemental auras drained to alarmingly wispy traces, Yulan's heron kindred nowhere in sight.

In a split-second glance across the skies, I catch sight of the Amaz Dryad, Alder, and to my surprise, Thierren Stone, the young Mage who aided Lukas and me when we escaped from Valgard. Both Alder and Thierren sit astride giant eagles and feed elemental power into our horde's circular fire-shield with branch and wand. And Fain Quillen is there, carried by what I sense is his Wyvern-shifter partner, Sholin, in dragon form, as well as Andras, a Varg-rune-marked axe gripped in his hands.

THE DRYAD STORM

Sage, Ra'Ven, Kam Vin, and Ni Vin are borne aloft on eagleback, the Vu Trin sisters shooting bolts of sapphire Noi power into the shield from runic swords.

I notice with a flash of dread that two of my Errilor Ravens are missing, along with the Dryads Luptus and Larch. And . . . Jules Kristian . . . he's alarmingly bloodied and unconscious and secured to Errilith's back, with no sign of Lucretia anywhere. Or my cousin Or'myr . . .

A circle of suspended silver Alfsigr and emerald Varg barrier runes shimmer to life just inside my horde's Wyvernfire barrier, and I spot the rainbow-decorated renegade Elf Rivyr'el Talonir astride one of our horde mates, his starbright stylus raised, silver eyes flashing as he casts defensive rune after defensive rune into our horde's barrier.

"Join shields!" Kam Vin commands us, and Yvan joins Trystan and the others in pushing our smaller orb shield's power into our horde's larger, circular shield in a blazing stream.

"Hello, Black Witch!" a jovial voice calls from one side, and I turn just as Bleddyn Arterra soars close on eagleback, a Varg-marked sword gripped in her emerald green hand, an incredulous grin forming on her mouth as her gaze sweeps over my altered features. "Nice ears!" she calls out, motioning toward her own ears' points.

My relief in finding Bleddyn here is overtaken by the sudden, empathic sense of a colossal wall of Shadow storm forming to our west. Vogel's dead tree slams through my mind, a cry forced from my throat.

Yvan pivots midair and our eyes meet, a questioning energy flashing through our bond.

Horde Witch! Raz'zor booms into my mind, red fire swirling around the thought as his pale wings beat down to either side of me and Soleiya. *What do you see?*

"Vogel's coming!" I cry. "I can sense him flying in from the west with more power than we can shield against!"

The smile whisks from Bleddyn's face. "Time to get the hell out of here!" she yells.

"On my mark!" Kam Vin cries, raising her sapphire stylus before swiping it down. *"GO!"*

My allies draw in our shielding around us, and we surge toward the sky portal's huge horizontal maw as one, our shielding forcing back the Vu Trin forces in our way.

A defensive line of Vu Trin, Amaz, and Lasair on Wyvernback hover before the sky portal, the horn-helmeted commander of the Vu Trin forces, Vang Troi, and Freyja Zyrr in the line's center, along with a young Smaragdalfar-Amaz sorceress.

Concern flashes through Vang Troi's visible sapphire aura as her eyes find both me and Yvan's mother. "Hand over Soleiya Guryev and the Black Witch," she booms out, "and we will grant you passage!"

"We need to retreat *together*!" Yvan yells back as we soar in toward their defensive line. "Vogel's about to overtake us *all*!"

My gaze slides to the knot of Fire Fae, surprise slashing through both my fire and Yvan's to find my old nemesis from the Verpacian kitchens there—Iris Morgaine.

"Iris, get East with us, *now*!" Yvan thunders, both anger and concern flashing through his power as we slow before them, my sense of Vogel's incoming power mounting.

"I will *never* let you bring that evil witch back East!" Iris snarls at him, golden fire swirling to life around her upraised, glowing hand.

"This is your last warning!" Vang Troi bellows as she raises her runic sword, its sapphire-glowing Noi runes catching blue fire.

"Don't make us fight our way through you!" Kam Vin roars back.

Vang Troi's aura triples in intensity. *"FIRE!"* she cries.

Her entire line of soldiers attacks as one, hurling bolts of runic power and arrows at us, Vang Troi's lash of might coming at us in a huge column of blue flame, the sky lit up sapphire.

"Draw the bulk of our shield's power *forward*!" Vothe growls as we relaunch our trajectory toward the sky portal.

In one, unified swoop, my allies yank almost all our shielding's magic forward and blast it toward the Vu Trin's magical attack just as a monstrous mass of Shadow power slams into our weakened rear, exploding it out of existence in a spray of chromatic sparks.

I blanch, desperation crawling up my throat as the wall of Shadow power races toward us and the fortified front of our shield slams into the line of Vu Trin and their allied forces, forcing them through the sky portal.

Vogel's wall of Shadow hits our back, speeding us into the sky portal's golden depths.

The world snaps out, my vision cutting to liquid gold as Raz'zor, Soleiya, and I hurtle forward through the seemingly endless gold only to blast out of it what feels like mere seconds later.

THE DRYAD STORM

We streak into an overcast, twilight world, a Shadow-corrupted landscape beneath us, gray smoke ghoulishly rising from the steely ground toward a grayed sky, the Vu Trin forces we pushed through a distance in front of us.

Heart thundering, I whip my head backward, a hot whoosh of relief blazing through our bond as I meet Yvan's gaze, my allies and loved ones streaming from the portal into the sky and rapidly reconjuring a shield around us. But when I look past the sky portal, my relief curdles. Leagues upon leagues of Shadowed wasteland stretch before me, a darker mass of Shadow filth hanging over the distant western horizon, a sickening dread pooling inside me at this visual proof of Vogel's expanding reach.

I slide my gaze to the East as Yvan soars in beside me, recognizing the signature lines of the purple Dyoi Mountain Range through the gray mist ahead. The sight shocks through me, every rootline inside me lurching toward it.

Living Forest. Spread out before and over the mountains like a violet carpet.

Vogel hasn't killed it all, I register with a light-headed swoop of elation.

A *crack* sounds, jerking my gaze backward. Vang Troi's surviving forces stream out of the sky portal and draw up a formidable amount of attacking power as they cast large, sapphire portal-destruction runes around the sky passage, the soldiers we shoved through the portal before us doubling back to join them.

A larger *CRACK* connects with earsplitting force, the portal-destruction runes flashing into gray as Vogel's Void tree knifes through my mind.

Before I can call a warning, Shadow soldiers on broken multi-eyed dragons pour from the sky portal. A battle commences, the Vu Trin attempting to slay the Shadow-shielded forces to no avail before they launch into a hasty retreat eastward, Vogel's forces now hot on the tail of both us and the retreating Vu Trin. I sense Marcus Vogel in his forces' center, his aura a silver gray wildfire blaze.

"*Vogel's there!*" I both cry out and send through my horde bond.

Yvan and my allies throw more power into our shielding as the Eastern forces draw in to flank our left, and I sense the brutal truth as I read our collective power— we're all too depleted to fight off Vogel's Shadow forces *and* battle each other.

Yvan, Raz'zor, and the rest of my allies accelerate, and the instinctual, blazing sense builds through my rootlines that we have to reach that living Forest before Vogel's forces get to it if *any* of us are going to survive.

We will get you a branch, Dryad Witch! Raz'zor blazes out to me through our bond.

It won't be enough! I counter, Raz'zor's powerful alabaster wings beating down on either side of me. *I'm not directly linked to a Forest,* I mentally cry out to him. *And my power is depleted. And I don't know the words to any Dryad spells!*

Raz'zor sears a vision of crimson fire consuming Marcus Vogel through my mind, his rebellion rising to tempestuous levels. *You will regain your power, Elloren the Unbroken!* he mentally hisses. *And rise to strike the Mage fiend down!*

Just get us to the Forest! I send out to Raz'zor in a pleading snarl. *Get us to the living trees!*

Raz'zor growls, speeding us toward the line of living purple, my emotions on fire along with Yvan's as he and Ariel keep pace beside us along with her small raven.

I glance over my shoulder once more just as our shield is hit by a lash of Shadow power. It gutters gray, the image of a branching Shadow network slithering through my mind as my power-empath senses are filled with the impression of Vogel's forces parasitically siphoning energy from both our shield and every newly destroyed tree.

Urgency grips me as I look ahead toward the expanse of living purple Forest. *Vogel's going to kill this Forest, too,* I think to Raz'zor, anger rising.

Then we fight! Raz'zor thinks back in a roar. *We battle to the death for Erthia!*

I can sense Raz'zor's determination doubling down as Thierren Stone's full wind power suddenly swoops in behind us and to our sides in a potent gust, so strong I sense his lines collapsing, the roaring force of his magic exponentially increasing both our speed and the speed of the Eastern forces beside us as we spear forward in a blur, a gap suddenly yawning between us and Vogel's forces.

Thierren slumps forward on his giant eagle as we blast over the edge of the living Forest's purple canopy and soar toward the Dyoi Mountain Range's western-facing ridge. We touch down on an expansively long shelf of stone near the ridge's top, the ledge jutting out from a flat section of Forest, the surviving Vu Trin, Amaz, and Lasair forces landing on the ledge to our north.

"We need to protect this Forest!" I call to everyone as Vogel's swarm wings toward us in the distance. "Vogel is siphoning elemental energy from the destroyed trees and turning it into Shadow power!" I meet my brother Trystan's gaze.

Urgency writ on his face, Trystan turns toward Vang Troi and her Eastern Realm forces. *"We need a combined shield!"* he booms out in Noi as Vogel's forces release power and a wall of Shadow storm blasts into being, churning toward us.

In answer, Vang Troi levels her runic sword not toward Vogel's forces, but toward *me.*

In a blur, a barrage of Vu Trin and Amaz weapons fire, bolts of runic power and arrows releasing, all of it hurtling in my direction.

Yvan leaps in front of me, along with Naga and my entire horde, all of them blasting out a wall of flame before us, every incoming Vu Trin weapon and bolt of power incinerated or deflected as Vogel's Shadow storm reaches the purple edge of the surviving Dyoi wilds.

The Dyoi Forest's westernmost edge explodes into steely flame, the trees' screams slashing through my heart, birds screeching and animals crying out in terror as they flee toward us.

"Stop wasting your power!" Hazel shrieks, his Death Fae voice seeming to come from everywhere at once. He leaps in front of Yvan and my horde mates, striding right up to the edge of our Wyvernfire shield, dark limbs extended from his back, the whole world momentarily strobing with his Dark aura and our shielding rendered translucent as he points an emphatic finger toward the incoming Shadow chaos. *"SHIELD THE FOREST!"*

I can sense the split-second equivocation shivering through Vang Troi's aura, the energy of resolve descending.

"Deploy a combined shield!" Vang Troi thunders.

Her forces fan out across the huge ledge to the north as my allies fan out to the south. Vang Troi's forces thrust their weapons up, swiftly conjuring a translucent emerald-and-sapphire wall of shielding. My allies join our blazing, storming energy to it—one solid wall of power streaking up from the ledge's center to curve over us, along with the mountainous sea of purple trees behind us and the sprawling Eastern Dyoi Forest beyond, lightning repeatedly bolting up from the length of the dome-shield's pinnacle to prevent Vogel's forces from flying over it.

Vogel's storm slams into the western-facing side of our shield with Erthia-shattering force, the mountain's stony shelf shuddering beneath us, my heart in my throat. But our shield holds.

Sweet Holy Ancient One, it holds.

I can sense Vogel's scream of fury, his Void tree image punching through my mind again and again in furious assault as his roiling Shadow rages against our strengthening shield to no avail, the Shadow storm soon dying down to a steady roar.

Hazel shrieks out a multitoned snarl, and the bindings tethering all the semiconscious Dryads to my Errilor Ravens turn to smoke.

My allies pull Sylvan, Yulan, and Oaklyyn, and Mavrik and Gwynn off the ravens and Thierren off a giant eagle and lay them on the ground, all of them gasping for breath and barely conscious. Jarod and Rafe lift an unconscious and bloodied Jules Kristian off Errilith while Yvan rushes toward both Jules and Thierren, our horde forming another defensive line between us and the Vu Trin forces.

Sylvan is grasping his chest over his heart, his pine hair morphed to deadened sticks as he murmurs "My kindred one . . . my *kindred*" over and over, his mysterious, hidden Northern Forest kindred almost certainly murdered. Yulan's flower tresses have turned into ashen, withered vines, all of my Dryad'kin alarmingly grayed.

A heartsick fear for them rises in me as I slide off Raz'zor and stumble toward the Dryads, the pain in my leg and arm now manageable aches thanks to Yvan's ministrations, but my power still disastrously weakened, even as Yvan's Zhilaan Forest thrums its courageous energy through me. I catch sight of a purple branch on the stony ground and lean down to swipe it up. A bolstering shimmer of energy rushes through my lines from the living branch. Grasping it tight, I set my sights back on the Dryads as I approach.

Oaklyyn is splayed out on the ground, pulling in air in great heaving gasps, her hand clasping at her rib cage, as if her heart is seizing. Mavrik and Gwynn are struggling for breath as well, as they keep tight hold of each other, their orange-hued hawks staunchly by their sides and ruffling their feathers with obvious distress.

"These Dryad'kin will die without an immediate linkage to the Forest!" Alder cries as she drops to her knees by Oaklyyn's side, bringing her hands to the combative Dryad's chest. I note that Alder's green hue is undimmed and has a purple branching pattern marked over it, the design bolder and more vivid than my faint Zhilaan branch markings.

Speaking of a full link to an Eastern Forest.

"How can we link these Dryads to the Forest?" Diana demands in an urgent growl.

In answer, Alder raises her hand.

Small eagles burst from the tree line edging the back of the ledge, a purple branch clasped in each eagle's talons.

"Press the branches to my Dryad'kin's hearts!" Alder calls out as the eagles drop the branches on each Dryad and Alder yanks Oaklyyn's leafy tunic open then thrusts a living branch onto her chest.

Bleddyn and I drop down beside Yulan, while Yvan rips Thierren's tunic open, grabs hold of a branch and presses it to his chest while bringing his other hand to Jules's bloodied temple to heal him. Desperate to link Yulan to the Dyoi Forest, I yank her clothing open as well, and Bleddyn presses a living branch to her sickly gray chest. Yulan shivers from the contact, a purple branching design radiating out from where the branch is contacting her skin.

"Where's Or'myr?" I press Bleddyn, fearing her answer.

"Here in the East by the Vo River," she assures me. "He stayed to summon Tierney back—"

"*LUCRETIA!*" Jules Kristian is suddenly crying out as he regains consciousness, breaking off Bleddyn's words. Jules pushes himself up, batting Yvan away as he forces himself to his feet and stumbles toward our shield, looking as if he's bent on leaping straight through it.

"Jules, stop!" Andras cries as he and Rafe lunge toward him and wrestle him away from the barrier.

"What's happened to my sister?" Fain calls out to Jules, dire urgency lighting his green eyes.

"She's trapped in that Shadow *hell!*" Jules growls back as he fights against Andras's and Rafe's holds, eyes wild, spectacles cracked. "We can't leave her there! We can't leave her to *Vogel!*"

As if in cruel mockery of his words, the Shadow storm roars to more intense life in a thickening wall of poisonous gray, a dark Shadow net forming over our entire shield.

"Ancient One," I breathe, sensing the Shadow net's power. "Vogel's trapping us under our own shielding with an impenetrable net."

Sheathing my living branch through my tunic's belt, I rise and take a faltering step toward our shield, transfixed by both the Shadow netting and the parasitical gray might assaulting our barrier. Massive and growing in power while the living wilds diminish.

We've walled Vogel off from the East, I consider, stricken, *but not for long.*

A huge Varg rune blasts into being on our shield, a net of emerald magic coursing out from it. I turn, taking in the young Smaragdalfar-Amaz sorceress standing before it, her glowing stylus raised. From our side of the ledge, Ra'Ven adds his Varg power to hers.

"Vestylle, my friend," Alder calls out to her.

The sorceress's invisible emerald aura flickers with anger as she casts a daggered glare at Alder. "Silence, traitor," she hisses.

I pull in a shuddering breath as the Varg rune rays out emerald light, its net of magic rapidly coursing over the entire shield, my power empathy sensing the amplification of our shield's power, the Shadow roaring against our shield instantly muted.

Slowly, both Ra'Ven and Vestylle lower their styluses, the surviving Forest firmly shielded.

A moment of unbearably tense silence descends, and everyone turns their attention to me.

The Black Witch.

"We've allied with you to wall off Vogel's forces," Vang Troi bites out to my allies in a tone that brooks no argument. "Now *hand over the Black Witch.*"

Yvan rises and faces her down, his hands and wrists taking on a violet glow. "Move against Elloren, and you move against *us all.*"

My pulse quickens as a low growl works its way up Diana's throat and my horde flexes their wings and gathers fire while the Vu Trin and their allies draw up power, all hell about to break loose. Forced into a fight I do not want, I move to take my sheathed branch in hand.

Without warning, several dark vines punch through the base of our huge dome-shield and slash around my ankles. I yelp as my feet are pulled out from under me and the world tilts, my back hitting stone.

"Elloren!" Yvan cries, both his internal fire and Raz'zor's and Ariel's surging with defensive heat as they leap toward me along with Diana, my brothers, kindred ravens, and other allies, Errilith letting out an urgent *CAW* as I'm dragged, in a blur, toward the small opening in our shield where the vines punched through.

An opening, I notice with alarm, that Vestylle's and Ra'Ven's net of emerald Varg magic had failed to reach.

"You need to *freely link*—" Alder cries out to me in Dryadin, her words cutting out as I'm pulled through our shield into the Shadow storm, the hole snapping shut behind me, Vogel's net of Shadow coursing over our entire dome-shield.

Fierce winds buffet me, dark lightning scything above and unnatural thunder booming as I'm dragged away from Yvan and the others. Fighting the pull, I twist onto my belly, my stomach scraping against the huge ledge, my tethered ankles on fire with pain. Yvan's and my allies' magic blasts furiously against Vogel's Shadow net to no avail, even Yvan's violet firestorm unable to break through.

THE DRYAD STORM

"*Yvan!*" I cry out as the living purple world rapidly recedes, Yvan's winged, crimson-haired form obscured by the thickening Shadow net and his repeated attacks on it, Yvan's rage and concern lashing through our bond, his incandescent violet eyes the last thing visible before Vogel's darkening Shadow net blots him out.

I come to an abrupt halt near the edge of the huge stone ledge, the whipping gray storm pulling back to create a roiling dome, a broken dragon's shriek sounding out.

Heart thundering, I yank myself around and look up to find Marcus Vogel flying toward me on a multi-eyed dragon, smiling as he swoops in from his Void storm and lands before me.

CHAPTER TEN

DRYAD WITCH

Elloren

Shadow lands

Vogel dismounts from his multi-eyed dragon and strides toward me across the Shadow half of the huge Dyoi Mountain ledge.

Terror leaps through me, but I hold his gaze, refusing to succumb to my well-founded fright. Vogel's aura of silver gray fire power is stronger than it's ever been, Yvan's stolen Shadow-corrupted Wyvernfire still burning through it. His pale green eyes are ringed with a steely glow and fixed on me, his storm pushed up into a roiling dome above us.

"My Black Witch," Vogel croons in a tone of pained fondness, "stop fighting your destiny. It's time for you to surrender fully to me." He stills and raises his Shadow Wand, the gray storm raging around us dying down to reveal the panoramic view beyond the ledge.

My throat clenches as I peer through the gray mist. The section of his army that came through the sky portal is massed at the base of the mountain range. I take in the destruction they've wrought, that they seek to wreak throughout the entirety of Erthia—leagues upon leagues of grayed land and charred trees.

Vogel's bindings slacken a trace, and I spring up, pulse spiking, and lunge back toward the living Forest, its purple color visible just beyond the Shadow-netted dome-shield.

Vogel's bindings around my ankles reassert themselves with a cruel yank. My belly slams to stone, the breath punched from my lungs as Vogel viciously drags me back.

I claw at the stone and growl out my fury, desperate to get back to Yvan and my other allies and loved ones, their repeated explosions of multicolored power booming against Vogel's Shadow netting.

The branch, I suddenly remember. *I have a living branch.*

Desperation spasming through me, I move to take hold of the branch sheathed at my side before I once more remember Oaklyyn's impassioned words—*Your bastardized Mage spells won't work!* And even if they could, my rootlines are severely weakened, my faint indirect linkage to Yvan's distant Zhilaan Forest stretched too thin.

The frustrated will to fight back pounding through my veins, I slowly turn to face Vogel.

He comes into sharper view as he strides toward me through the Shadow mist. His skin's pale Mage-green glimmer stands out in bright contrast to his color-stripped Shadow world, his irises increasingly overtaken by Yvan's stolen Wyvernfire.

Stolen by this Mage fiend who also murdered my fastmate.

Burning rage ignites, fury for Lukas slashing through it.

Vogel scans my face, my heart like a hammer against my chest as his eyes widen then sharply narrow. A flash of his heat sears through me, his immense fire power almost escaping his tight hold as a look of world-severing hate overtakes his expression.

Viper quick, he lashes out his Wand.

Gray vines bolt from its tip to lash around my wrists. I yank against them to no avail as he stretches my arms out from my sides and magically tethers my wrists' bindings to stone.

He falls to one knee before me, grips tight hold of my face and jerks my chin up. "What have you *done?*" he hisses.

Quivering with rage, I bare my sharpened Dryad teeth at him.

Vogel recoils as he takes in my pointed ears and the branching purple pattern covering my grayed skin, his invisible fire aura spearing out steely, corrupted Wyvern flame at me. Baring his own teeth, he reaches up and takes cruel hold of one of my newly pointed ears, his grip so crushingly hard I have to bite back a yelp of pain. He releases my ear and lowers his hand, his pale green lips sneering as he grips my tunic's collar and gives it a hard, downward yank.

I growl out my outrage as my tunic tears to reveal the faint image of a giant, purple pine tree emblazoned across my chest and abdomen. It catches me off guard, a trace of glimmering violet pulsing through it.

Yvan's fire-loving Zhilaan Forest. The great Eastern Realm Forest of Nightwood Pines . . .

Vogel's gaze slowly meets mine, his eyes filled with flat, chilling hatred. In an arcing blur, he draws his hand back then swipes it toward me.

His blow hits the side of my head with brutal force, a strangled cry ripping out of me. Pain shears through my head, my body thrust sideways, stretching the bindings around my right wrist as Yvan's desperate rage to reach me fires through our bond.

"You Fae *beast*," Vogel snarls, his upper lip quivering with a fury that's so out of control, panic strikes through me. His head draws sharply back, his nostrils flaring. "You let the winged demon *kiss you*. I can sense his fire bond running through you. *Again.*"

Anger takes hold of me in a cresting wave, obliterating all fear as I lunge toward Vogel and bare my teeth, straining against my bonds. "I'll bond to him in every way possible, *Marcus.*"

For a moment, our killing glares war against each other before Vogel's silver aura of stolen Wyvernfire tightens into a molten ball, deep in his core. "I could have saved you, Elloren," he rues, his eyes flicking over me with almost bereaved disappointment before his gaze hardens with a look of terrifying finality. "We could have saved and purified each other along with Erthia."

Vogel rises to his feet, a merciless look on his face as he calmly backs away.

With a jolt of apprehension, I realize that Vogel has made a full mental shift, marking me as irredeemably evil, a lethal target rapidly solidifying on my point-eared form. Pulse spiking, I take advantage of my loosened binding to angle my side away from Vogel so I can grip hold of the branch sheathed at my side without detection, my mind desperately whirling—my rootlines are depleted, and I don't know Dryad spells. I don't know *anything* about my Dryad abilities.

Please, I beg the Ancient One, the Forest, anyone or anything that will hear me. *Help!*

A single word flutters through me, like a breeze sent toward me from the East.

Dryad'kin.

That's not a spell! I want to scream at the Dyoi Forest. *It's just a word in Dryadin!*

An amorphous recognition lights, stilling the breath in my chest as I'm filled with the sudden sense of the entire Dyoi and Zhilaan Forests stilling, as well.

A word in Dryadin.

The words to the candle-lighting spell flow into my mind. Words in the Mage-dom's Ancient Tongue, which, I realize in a flash, is just poorly pronounced Dryadin.

Light-headedness almost brings me to the ground as I realize what Alder and then the Dyoi and Zhilaan Forests have been trying to tell me as Vogel lifts the Shadow Wand and begins murmuring spells, filling the evil tool with killing power.

I already have a route to Dryad spells and magic.

I just need to accept a direct Forest connection to access them.

Remembering how Alder and my Dryad'kin forged a new linkage to the Dyoi Forest, I thrust myself sideways, further stretching the binding around my right wrist, and manage to bring the living branch in contact with my naked chest, right over my heart.

The Dyoi Forest's power instantly floods my rootlines, root linking to root. A tingle prickles over me, the deep-green Dryad hue to my skin reasserting itself while the Dyoi Forest's purple energy races over my faint Zhilaan branching pattern, filling it with more robust coloration as purple leaf garb snaps into being on my body, my torn tunic and my pants falling away.

A spell sounds through my lines as I grip my branch tight.

"Abolish bindings and repel attack!" I cry out in Dryadin as both Vogel and I thrust our weapons forward, his vine bolt spearing toward me.

Energy explodes from my branch in rays of purple light, Vogel's vine bolt exploding as my bindings dissolve into purple mist and wick away.

Vogel's eyes widen, my own surprise swiftly overcome by a fierce rush of warrior energy through my faint link to the Zhilaan Forest. A vision of huge, black-trunked, violet-needled Zhilaan Pines rises in the back of my mind like an incoming army as both the Dyoi Forest's and a trace of the Zhilaan's power floods my rootlines, a Dryadin spell breezing through me.

"Shheer'ith'ruush'hhhiir!" I scream, seizing on my split-second advantage as I thrust my branch toward Vogel once more, suffused by the sense of every tree in the Dyoi and Zhilaan Forests bending their will toward mine.

A spiraling cyclone of violet wind blasts from my branch and hits Vogel, blowing him into the air. Extreme shock sears through his power as he slams to the ground, the fulsome sense of the Forests rising within me surging, my power now not just my own . . .

. . . my power a communal *alliance.*

Our power.

True Dryad power.

"Shield me!" I cry out in Dryadin.

A vision of leagues of huge, purple pine trees lancing the clouds like spears flashes through my mind as a line of fiery purple Dyoi and Zhilaan power blasts from my branch with such force that I skid backward over the stone ledge, the purple flame flying up before me in a translucent, shielding half orb.

Vogel rights himself, hisses, and hurls out lines of forking Shadow lightning from his Wand, the silver gray lightning rapidly branching into the shape of a prone, fire-spitting tree as it lances toward me.

The lightning tree knifes into my orb shield, and pain spikes through my branch arm. Alarm streaks through me as my shield contracts inward from the spearing blow, skidding me farther back, but my orb shield holds. Barely. Its purple glow crackling with gray sparks.

A chilling look of reappraisal overtakes Vogel's expression. He growls out another spell, gray fire overtaking his irises as he snaps out a larger, sharper Shadow tree.

"Tree of fire!" I snarl in Dryadin as I thrust my branch forward, drawing on not only Dyoi and Zhilaan Forest power, but an edge of Yvan's Wyvernfire, as well as a line of my horde's fire. A battle cry erupts from my throat as multihued fire explodes from my branch and passes harmlessly through my shield before swiftly branching out into an attacking tree of flame, my body shuddering from the rush of Dryad and Wyvern power.

Our trees collide. Vogel's Shadow tree bursts into silver sparks as my tree of flame shoots toward his cloaked form only to be fully absorbed by the Shadow Wand, Vogel's eyes taking on a wicked, multihued glow that quickly morphs back to silvery gray.

Confusion rocks through me.

How did he just draw in all that fire? He practically *ate* the fire.

Vogel thrusts his Wand toward the sky, and his army appears, rows of soldiers on multi-eyed dragons rising from just beyond the ledge's precipitous drop. With a jolt, I meet the cruel eyes of Damion Bane, and he smiles, my thoughts immediately skidding to Aislinn.

I blanch and take a step back, the brewing storm of Void magic too powerful for me to best, countless Shadow-corrupted wands rising along with the Shadow Wand . . .

I turn and break into a run toward my allies, heartbeat galloping, pulling my shield with me as I go.

Yvan and my other allies' power is slamming against the dome-shield in bright bursts of color as I sprint toward it, Trystan's blue lightning crackling through Yvan's violet fire along with my Errilor Ravens' streaks of Dark aura.

I glance over my shoulder just as a great *BOOM* of Shadow power slams against the back of my shield, skidding me forward and shattering my shield's molten surface in a raying flash of color that morphs to gray as my shield disappears.

Fear leaping, I hasten my pace as Vogel and his forces close in, broken dragons shrieking and winging toward me, the Mages drawing up another cataclysmic amount of Shadow power.

"Get back!" I cry out to my allies as I reach the Dyoi Forest's dome-shield and pull my rootlines *wide open* to Dyoi, Zhilaan, and Wyvern power while leveling my branch at the shield, bent on elemental strike, the full might of the Dyoi Forest and a potent trace of Zhilaan magic rising within me. *"Break through Vogel's Shadow net!"* I cry out in Dryadin as my allies open a small entrance in our shield.

A sizzling tang of energy hits my back, and animalistic desperation sizzles through me as I'm flooded by the split-second foresight of a Shadow storm about to slam into me just as a column of purple energy bolts from my branch. My power collides with Vogel's Shadow netting, blasting a small hole clear through it.

I throw myself headfirst into the passageway.

Yvan's protective fire aura instantly roars around and through me as his strong hands grip hold of my upper arms and he yanks me fully through the opening with ferocious purpose, my power empathy instantly overtaken by the awareness of Trystan, Vothe, Sage, and my other allies blasting their combined power over the shield's hole to seal it, Ra'Ven and Vestylle's shield-amplifying Varg power flowing over the sealed hole, leaving no gaps this time.

Vogel and his forces' full assault of Shadow slams into our shield, and the shield's entire, cloud-high side contracts inward like a sheet of molasses.

Yvan's fire envelopes me as he pulls me close, my vision spitting stars as I gasp for breath, both of us down on our knees. I feel as if my rootlines are close to collapsing in on themselves, my lines severely depleted from releasing so much magic at once.

Yvan brings his lips to mine at the same moment I grab desperate hold of him, knotting my fingers in his hair and drawing him even closer as emotion surges through our bond, both of us clear that, for me, his kiss is the surest route to both his power and the Zhilaan Forest's. His lips are Wyvern-warm and urgently firm, a hot line of our love for each other searing through us as he blasts not only his power into me, but the elemental strength of his kindred Zhilaan Forest and our entire horde via our Wyvernbond, lighting up my lines like a fiery beacon as both his and the Dyoi Forest's strength floods through them.

My power slowly restoring, I break the kiss and meet Yvan's impassioned gaze before I force myself to my feet, rage surging through me as I lunge back toward the shield, not able to see Vogel through his forces' whipping storm, but able to sense his lurking power.

"*You will not take this Forest!*" I snarl at Vogel. "I will regain my power, and I will come for you!"

"Elloren," Yvan cautions as he moves in behind me.

"He doesn't hold enough power to get to me," I bite out. "Isn't that right, *Marcus*?"

Vogel's figure takes shape through the maelstrom beyond the shield, his black-clad form obscured by the wall of churning magic between us, but his silver, rage-bright eyes shining through. Shadowed magic pounds through his lines as Dryad might fills mine, our powers fully and viciously aimed at each other.

Vogel's eyes flick over me in leering appraisal as he draws his storm's full strength back into his Wand, the terrible truth inescapable.

Our power is an even match. But as more Forest dies, mine will be depleted.

Whereas his will grow stronger.

Vogel's lips lift in a slow, mocking smile as his Void tree shimmers to life in the back of my mind. I stiffen against it. And against the shivering premonition that has always been brewing, from the moment of our first encounter . . .

Vogel and I are destined to battle for Erthia.

But then I look past Vogel and his forces. At the leagues of charred trees and grayed, poisoned sky, the Natural World's vulnerability constricting my heart. Millions of years of complex beauty—beauty that I'm only just starting to meet, to root to—gone in the span of a few hours. The power to destroy Life so much more potent than the power to protect it.

Vogel clearly detects the flicker of fear in my gaze. His eyes narrow to slits, and his slight grin turns malefic as he glances toward the destroyed Forest behind him and then back at me. "Your defeat has already begun, *Fae Witch*."

And then he raises the Wand and releases his Shadow storm, his figure instantly engulfed in the churning gray.

When the storm clears, Vogel and his forces are gone, along with the distant sky portal. Only the leagues of dead Forest and poisoned sky remain, splayed out in front of us in dark warning.

V'YEXWRAITH

Marcus Vogel

Shadowed stump of III

Marcus Vogel speeds west through the overtaken Vu Trin sky portal then emerges to soar over the destroyed Northern Forest, righteous fury running silver-hot through his lines. Damion Bane and his forces fly in just behind him. A forest of charred, Shadowed trees speeds by beneath them all, the trees reaching spectral limbs toward the steely sky.

The Shadow-smoking stump of III comes into sharper view. The heathen tree's stump is wider than the base of the sprawling Valgard Cathedral, a dark abyss now swirling in its center.

The Shadow Wand gripped in Vogel's fist gives a firm pull toward the stump, and Vogel sends a mental order out to the multi-eyed dragon beneath him. The Shadow-tethered creature immediately obeys, angling its trajectory down toward III's corpse, Damion and his forces following.

Vogel takes in the additional Mage forces already encircling the colossal, hollowed-out stump, several of his high-level commanders and Mage priests standing in an arc just before it. Vogel glowers at the huge, destroyed Tree that broke his Shadow fasting to Elloren Gardner Grey, stripping the gray lines from both his hands and hers.

Breaking his control over the Dryad Witch.

But in the end, your might was no match for the Magedom, was it? he sneers at III's stump, struggling to tamp down his rage over both the Tree's countermove and the Dryad Witch's betrayal. And how Elloren *bested* him with her tree and Icaral-linked power.

He huffs out a contemptuous breath, clear that her corrupted magic will be obliterated soon enough.

"Excellency," Damion Bane says as he and Vogel land, side by side, "why did you order us to retreat from the Black Witch and her allies?"

Vogel narrows his eyes at the young commander as he dismounts and Damion does the same. Damion's visage and tone are martially contained, but Vogel can sense the chaotic fury pulsing through Damion's Level Five power. Fury that's been well stoked by the slaying of his brother, Sylus, by the Amaz whore Valasca Xanthrir. And Vogel is well aware Damion has another axe to grind, bested as he was by his staen'en bitch of a fastmate, Aislinn Greer.

"Elloren Gardner Grey is lost to us," Vogel informs Damion, acutely aware of his fastmark-stripped hands. "The Fae Witch was never the Ancient One's intended Black Witch."

"Yet you chose not to smite her?" Damion challenges, the surly edge in his tone eliciting alarmed looks from the priests and commanders surrounding them and sending a surge of heat through Vogel's lines.

Vogel tamps down his fiery anger, choosing to ignore Damion's insubordination. "There will be no smiting the Fae Witch at the moment," he says, voice dangerously clipped. "Her power has been linked to the Fae wilds by the dead Tree before us. She allowed the heathen Tree to turn her into a Fae Dryad. As such, her power, combined with that of her heathen allies, is currently an even match for ours." A faint smile edges Vogel's lips. "But her Tree Fae magic will soon begin to shrivel, along with the elemental magic of her allies."

The insubordination in Damion's eyes shifts to a full-on glare. "How can you be so certain?" he demands.

Vogel's smile takes fuller form as he points the Shadow Wand's tip at one of the charred trees encircling the clearing.

Damion turns and takes in the unconscious Dryad female hanging limply from the tree. The Dryad bitch's grayed face is marked by steely lightning-bolt patterns, the mushrooms growing from her Fae head shriveled, her body pierced by multiple Shadow branches. Dark tendrils of power encircle her, one of the tendrils flowing from the Dryad's unconscious body to the tip of the Shadow Wand.

Vogel breathes deeply, the hidden workings of Dryad power shivering through his mind via his Shadow tether. Vogel lifts the Wand. "The Magedom's Holy Tool can read the secrets of Dryad magic," he explains to Damion. "Through it, I have learned that Tree Fae power is amplified in the autumn by the explosion of light power in fall foliage."

Confusion overtakes Damion's expression. "Then why not strike against the Dryad Witch and her allies now, before autumn grips hold?"

"Because," Vogel slyly answers, "autumn in the Eastern Realm is swift. And when the foliage color withers and winter descends, the Tree Fae go into a state of semidormancy until spring. Their power *plummets*."

"Excellency," tall, bald Priest Alfex ventures, "is it wise to allow the witch's power to increase even for a short span of time?"

"We shall not be idle," Vogel answers. "While the witch and her allies are trapped under the shield of their own making, we will kill off every stretch of wilds we have access to. And we will absorb all that elemental power into our Shadow might as we wait for winter's descent."

A cold breeze gusts in from the northeast, drawing everyone's attention. Vogel looks at the sky, thrilling to the feel of the cold chilling his firelines as Commander Fallon Bane soars in from the Issani front lines on dragonback, a portion of her forces trailing her. Fallon's frigid green gaze meets Vogel's as she lands, dismounts, and strides toward him, briefly tossing a contemptuous gaze toward the impaled Dryad. She sets her gaze back on Vogel, and he suppresses a shiver, sensing an ice storm of rage crackling through her lines.

"You summoned me, Excellency?" Fallon says, her tone a demand as Vogel's fire aura surges toward her, sparked into wildfire by the satisfying lack of mercy in her compelling gaze.

He stiffens his lines, forcing his killing Level Five powers and boundless flame into a contained ball as the Erthia-shifting realization ignites—it was righteous Fallon Bane all this time.

She is the Magedom's true Black Witch.

Destined to slay the Great Icaral Demon, Yvan Guryev.

His fire turning white-hot, Vogel curses himself for being blinded by Elloren Gardner Grey's lineage, her Black Witch *face*, when before him all along was the Ancient One's True, Anointed Witch. A ripple of want sears through Vogel's power, a new target for his fire forming.

"We have annexed Issaan for the Holy Magedom," Fallon announces. "And we have reissued the Magedom's warning to Ishkartaan. But the heathens there are defying us. They have sent word that they refuse to cede their lands to the Holy Magedom."

Vogel nods, having expected this. "Refresh your forces at our Caledonian encampment then deploy south for Northern Ishkartaan," he charges. "Await my order to strike. I will soon join you there."

Fallon nods, her internal ice storm whipping into a violent frenzy. Vogel's power surges toward hers once more, and he fights the draw as she turns and strides back to her multi-eyed dragon, mounts it, and growls out an order. The beast throws out its wings and takes to the skies along with the soldiers who accompanied her, all of them soaring back through the gray toward the Caledonian base.

"There's your winter," Damion carefully suggests.

Vogel smiles at Damion's boldness as they watch Fallon wing away, part of her dragon-borne forces rising and closing in around her. *The Ancient One's winter, indeed*, Vogel considers, a hot hunger licking though his power.

"Have faith, Mages," Vogel commands everyone surrounding him, a zealous warmth overtaking his lines as the Shadow Wand gives a harder pull toward III's smoking stump. Vogel points its tip at it, his gaze narrowing in on the swirling Shadow abyss in the stump's center. "This heathen tree was the central source of Fae power," Vogel says. "Its rootline network is linked to all the continent's wilds. And now, we will siphon that power and transform it into sanctified Shadow might using the Wand's own manifestation—a V'yexwraith weapon."

Vogel points the Wand at the very center of the swirling abyss while sending out a mental order through his branching Shadow tether to his glamoured pyrr-demons. The four demons step forward and surround III's corpse, one at every directional point—north, south, west, and east. They turn as one and set their sulfuric gazes on Vogel, their Shadow horns twining up from their Mage-black hair, horns only Vogel and his Shadow-tethered soldiers can see.

Vogel considers how well they've served him, these foul demons of flame that the Wand drew to him. But it is time to summon a stronger creature to the Ancient One's cause.

"Your Excellency . . ." Priest Alfex ventures, and Vogel turns to him. There's an uncharacteristic glint of concern in the priest's gray-rimmed eyes as they flick toward the Wand in Vogel's hand, then to the four pyrr-demons. "Are you sure of this path?" Priest Alfex cautions. "The V'yexwraith . . . it's the primordial demon, not a weapon, spoken about in texts from the Ancient Elfin Wars. This creature the Shadow Wand can manifest—it has a history of snapping its leash."

Vogel's internal fire surges, straining to burn the doubting priest, but he keeps careful control of it. "The Ancient One on High holds every leash," Vogel states as his gaze sears into Alfex. "Would you deprive the Magedom of *any* weapon?"

The four pyrr-demons and every last soldier in sight turn their attention to Priest Alfex, censure in their gazes. Vogel notes, with a fresh sear of satisfaction, how Priest Alfex's Level Five earth-magic aura instantly withers, deferring to Vogel's dominance.

"I would never deprive the Holy Magedom of anything," Priest Alfex demurs with a chastened dip of his head. "You have my complete and undying allegiance, Excellency."

Vogel's nostrils flare as he empathically roots through the priest's power, sensing the wariness still shivering there.

"Let the Dryad Witch have her moment," Vogel says, his gaze fixing once more on the stump's swirling Void. "And let the Icaral bitch, Wynter Eirllyn, have her shielded Sublands and weakening Heathen Wand." Vogel sharpens his Wand's aim once more toward the abyss and murmurs a series of primordial spells—Shadow spells purified and cleansed by the Ancient One's own hand.

He thrusts the Wand forward.

The swirling center of the abyss darkens, and Vogel smiles, sensing monumental power rising.

Without warning, a huge gray figure claws its way out of the abyss and slowly rises, unfolding itself, its form cathedral tall and ferally slender, like a living Wand.

The primordial demon angles its eyeless head down toward Vogel. Huge steely horns spike up like gray lightning from the Wand-beast's temples, its claw-tipped fingers long and spindly. Its horrifying face is eggshell smooth, except for a dark slash of a mouth. Gray spikes angle back from the sides of its head and body like windswept shards, frozen in time.

Gasps rise all around, Priest Alfex taking a stumbling step back. Even normally unshockable Damion Bane's power is shot through with surprise as Vogel drinks in the swirling, siphoning power of the Shadow Wand's V'yexwraith manifestation.

The V'yexwraith sways before Vogel like a tree in an invisible wind. It lets out a low hiss that quickly morphs into a multitoned, bone-shuddering shriek as it gives a violent yank against the Shadow Wand's tether and sends pain knifing through Vogel's wand arm.

Vogel holds fast and smiles, thrilling to the parasite-beast's vicious testing of its bonds, as well as its magic-siphoning aura. *Ah yes,* Vogel gloats, *here is the tool needed to take down the Dryad Witch and her forces.*

"Elloren and her allies aren't as safe and shielded as they would imagine," Vogel murmurs to Damion and Priest Alfex before closing his eyes and tugging on the Wand's Shadow tethers.

Multi-eyed ravens burst from the surrounding Shadowed trees, their unearthly *caws* resonating through the air. One lands on Vogel's shoulder, the rest darting down the trunk's central, gaping Void and disappearing into its swirling mist.

"My runic eyes are everywhere," Vogel croons as he opens his own eyes and fixes them on the swaying V'yexwraith demon. "And my sanctified Shadow power is strengthening. The V'yexwraith's siphoning power will hasten the Magedom's triumph over all." He holds the demon's terrifying attention. "The Dryad Witch and her allies think they have closed off the East from us with their shielding, but there remains a way to destroy its forests."

"How?" Priest Alfex inquires, his wide eyes focused on the V'yexwraith.

Vogel turns and waits for the priest's rattled gaze to meet his. "The Wand's V'yexwraith can manifest wherever Shadow-tethering runes have been marked. And we have marked those runes at the headwaters of the East's largest river."

An awed look of comprehension washes over Priest's Alfex's face. "The Vo," he murmurs.

"The V'yexwraith will have a fight on its hands," Damion counters. "The Selkie abomination Gareth Keeler has managed to cast an incredibly strong dome-shield over the Vo River's southern spillway. Our Shadow sea hasn't yet penetrated it."

Vogel calmly listens to Damion's warnings as the V'yexwraith hovers over them, a swaying presence.

Vogel flicks his Wand's tip toward the V'yexwraith, and the beast's huge mouth opens wide. In a split second, another fanged jaw accordions from its mouth, then another from inside that one, one after the other, straight toward a now shrieking Priest Alfex, until the terminal long-toothed mouth chomps down around the priest's head.

Shocked sounds rise all around as Alfex convulses then falls to the ground in a heap, a bloodied grotesquerie where the back of his head once was, his green hue rapidly fading to gray as his elemental energy is consumed, a line of gray mist flowing from the traitorous priest's corpse into the maw of the Wand-beast. The V'yexwraith draws in its multiple mouths and bares its teeth, grayed blood streaming down its jaw as it consumes the last of the mist, one bulbous, gray eye bubbling to life on its eggshell head.

A shocked silence reigns.

"My Shadow sea is a diversion," Vogel states before angling his Wand toward the huge, swaying demon and murmuring a primordial spell.

The V'yexwraith lets out an Erthia-shuddering shriek, and its form begins to spin and blur, the Mages surrounding Vogel flinching back as the V'yexwraith is sucked down into III's Void abyss, the swirling mist taking on a paler gray hue before morphing back to steel.

Vogel turns to Damion and gives him a tight smile. "We're going to infiltrate the East from the *North*," he smoothly clarifies. "And bring down the entire East and the Dryad Witch via its largest river—the Vo." Vogel's smile inches wider. "We'll invade the water supply of the forests of Noilaan and strangle the trees at their very roots."

CHAPTER TWELVE

DRYAD WARRIOR

Elloren

Northern Dyoi Mountain Range

"Hand over the Black Witch of Prophecy!" Vang Troi's powerful voice booms out over the Dyoi Mountain ledge as the Vu Trin high commander takes a step toward me.

Yvan's fire rises to a focused inferno, his wings arcing around me. "Vanglira," he warns, "stay back."

Naga and the rest of my horde as well as my Lupine allies have closed in to form a defensive line between me and Vang Troi's surviving Eastern Realm forces, tension mounting in the air, my Errilor Ravens gathering around me.

Fain steps forward, glancing between Yvan and Vang Troi. "Let's all take a deep breath, shall we?"

My breathing labored and my power still depleted by my fight with Vogel, I take in the curved sword gripped in Vang Troi's hand and the runic blades and battle stars strapped all over her body. My concern intensifies as the two formidable Amaz soldiers—Freyja Zyrr and Alcippe Feyir—along with my old kitchen nemesis, Iris Morgaine, close in around Vang Troi.

Our opposing sides are close to equally numbered.

"Move one step closer to my sister, and I will separate you from your head, sorceress," Diana growls at Vang Troi, raising a clawed hand, golden hair coursing over her forearm in lethal warning.

"We're all on the same side," my brother Rafe states calmly but firmly, holding out a conciliatory hand toward Vang Troi.

Vang Troi and her combined Vu Trin, Amaz, and Lasair forces don't budge, their eyes and power focused on me, murderously bright. The rhythmic scald of

THE DRYAD STORM

Yvan's mother's aura knifes into me in pulsing spikes from where she's still bound to Raz'zor, raising the hairs on the back of my neck as a threatening ball of golden fire bursts to life above Iris Morgaine's raised palm.

I can't help but gape at Iris's unglamoured form, her formerly blond hair now a fiery Lasair-crimson like Yvan's and Soleiya's, her ears sharply pointed, her green eyes afire with rage. I tighten my hold on the living branch in my hand, my depleted power recharging too slowly as I draw on the magic of the Dyoi and Zhilaan Forests. Both the Dyoi and Zhilaan are twining their support around my rootlines, the maternal Dyoi filling me with a growing sense of its Life-supporting root network, Yvan's kindred Zhilaan infusing me with pure warrior energy.

Dryad'kin, the Dyoi murmurs through me with embracing affection.

Dryad Warrior, the Zhilaan sizzles through me, its enraged violet fire flashing through my binding to Yvan.

Vang Troi's runic magic rises in the air, a visible penumbra of raying, sapphire power flashing to life around her straight-backed form in an obvious display of power. "Hand yourself over, Elloren Gardner Grey," she orders again, her violet eyes meeting mine. "We watched you fight Vogel with true courage, but you must face the fact that you are too easily compromised by Vogel's power. You're a proven danger to us *all*."

Before I can answer, Yvan blasts out a line of violet flame to wall off me and our allies from the Vu Trin and their forces, our entire horde adding to the flame, multicolored fingers of it blazing up in hot warning from the huge stone ledge, a chilling growl rising from Raz'zor's throat.

"I won't ask twice." Yvan glares at Vang Troi, his fire readied. "Resheathe your weapons and order your forces to do the same. Elloren is my Wyvernbonded *mate*."

A hot charge shoots through our bond that sends a shiver through me, Yvan's arm sliding protectively around mine.

Without warning, Vang Troi lifts her swords and points them toward me.

Hundreds of sapphire spears of runic energy blast into existence and dart toward me, each filled with explosive Noi power.

Before I can react, Yvan yanks me backward and Sage, Trystan, Fain, and Wrenfir lift wands. Alder raises a branch, and Ra'Ven and Rivyr'el level emerald and silver styluses while my ravens send out a hard pulse of Dark aura that momentarily dims the world. A colorful glassy wall of power marked with Varg runes springs to life in front of my horde's barrier of Wyvernfire, foggy lines of my ravens' magic coursing through it.

Vang Troi's surprise attack collides with our runic barrier in an explosion of raying, sapphire light, the spears that manage to pierce it instantly singed away by my horde's wall of fire.

"This is *madness!*" Iris cries out to Yvan, her voice shrill with fury. "Have you forgotten *everything* you stand for?" She levels her finger at Soleiya. "You've bound your own *mother!*"

"Unhand Soleiya Guryev!" a young Vu Trin soldier with a dragon shaved into her close-cropped black hair shouts, her face twisted in an enraged scowl. A chorus of livid voices rise, all demanding Soleiya's release.

Vang Troi arches a black brow at the cacophony of demands before giving Yvan a stern look. My gut tenses as I remember how revered Soleiya is in the East—the heroic Resistance-soldier wife of the slain Icaral who took down the last dreaded Black Witch, my grandmother Carnissa Gardner.

Yvan turns to Trystan, eyes burning. "Unbind my mother," he stiffly directs.

Trystan nods, a cautious light in his eyes as he raises his wand and swipes it at Soleiya.

The vine bindings tethering her to Raz'zor's back disappear, but any hope that Soleiya's hate for me has been tempered is instantly and thoroughly quashed as she swiftly dismounts, steps away from Raz'zor, then rounds on Yvan and levels a damning finger at me. "That witch will forever be your *enemy!*"

Yvan's fire aura explodes, a rush of his heat searing my skin as he gives his mother a look of blazing incredulity. "Did you witness *anything* that just happened?" He thrusts his hand toward the leagues upon leagues of dead Forest just beyond our translucent dome-shield's western-facing side. "*There's* your enemy," he snarls. "This infighting—" he gestures between himself and his mother "—it's playing *right* into Vogel's hands!"

I glance toward our semiconscious Dryad'kin, splayed on the stone ledge, all of them tenuously stabilized through the Dyoi Forest branch connection. Purple branching patterns are forming over the sickly gray skin of Sylvan, Yulan, Oaklyyn, and Mavrik and Gwynn.

"You're being played for a *fool!*" Soleiya snarls back at Yvan, her voice breaking with red-hot emotion. "The Crows are full of deceptions! The witch's show of alliance is a *ploy*. *Think*, my son! This witch and Vogel are *playacting* so that they can infiltrate your power through this ill-fated Wyvernbond you've set down! The only way to save yourself and defeat the Magedom is to *kill* her!"

I draw back from the punishing strength of Soleiya's fire power, anguish spiking through me in response to the level of hate in her aura and in the belligerent look she's giving me, offensive fire gathering in her palms.

Fealty. Raz'zor's vow shimmers through my mind as he readies his own vermillion fire.

Raw panic spears through me over the martial energy rising in Raz'zor. *She's not our enemy!* I insist through our bond.

Raz'zor's fire rears hotter. *FEALTY*, he stresses, baring his teeth at Soleiya.

Alder Xanthos calmly steps forward, staying Raz'zor's rage as she strides up to Soleiya. "Yvan Guryev speaks the truth," she states, her tone as hard as Ironwood. "The Prophecy has been rewritten. I have read it in the Forest. Elloren has become a Dryad Witch truly set against Vogel. She stands with the trees."

"Alder Xanthos," Freyja grits out, her tattooed face tensed with a commanding level of ire, her runic axe gripped in her fists. "As your queen, I *order* you to *stand down.* Elloren Gardner Grey is a murdering Black Witch, just like her grandmother. She *leveled* Voloi."

Surprise lights inside both my and Yvan's fire to find out that young Freyja has succeeded Alkaia as queen of the Amaz.

"Elloren didn't attack Voloi," Vothendrile counters from where he stands beside Trystan, their invisible lightning auras crackling around each other. "Marcus Vogel did. I'm a power empath. Vogel had Elloren under his thrall during the Siege of Voloi through a Shadow link to her fastlines. But she's broken *free* of him, and her fastings, as well."

"What's to prevent him from enthralling her again by some unknown Shadow spell?" Freyja sternly counters.

"What's to prevent Vogel from enthralling *me*?" Yvan challenges. "Or *you*? Or *any* of us?"

"Which he *will do* if we stay divided," I add, unable to remain silent one second longer.

"Silence, witch!" Vang Troi snarls.

"No," I snarl back, stepping out of Yvan's embrace to face her down, "I will *not* be silent." A hot flash of Yvan's support fires through our Wyvernbond, along with a simmering rise of Raz'zor's, Ariel's, and Naga's flame through our horde bond. "If we remain divided," I say, "Vogel will pick us off *one by one* while he kills off the rest of the Natural World. And then it will be truly over. For *all* of us. Erthia's Natural

Matrix was anchored in a Great Tree that Vogel destroyed. And now, that Matrix is close to being irretrievably *broken*. If any more Forest is destroyed, it will *fully break*. We'll have no more clean water. No more food. Nothing but *that*." I level a finger west, at the leagues of Shadow-destroyed land beyond our shielding. "Without the Forest, *everything* unravels."

"And a Death Reckoning will descend," Hazel growls, a wild look in his full-dark eyes, "before the Shadow sweeps in to consume *everything*!"

"These are outrageous lies," Iris growls at Yvan. "Your mother speaks the truth! The witch is still linked to Vogel!"

"I'm *not*," I counter, raising my III-marked palm. "I'm joined to the *Forest*."

"Let us bring you to our trees so you can hear them out," Alder offers Vang Troi, Iris, and their allies, displaying her III-marked palm, as well. "Let us link you *all* to our Forest."

Vang Troi gives Alder a look of pure outrage. "You want us to link to a *dying* forest?"

"No," Alder vehemently counters. "To the remaining *living* Forest. Because if it dies, Erthia is *lost*. We are *all* lost. This needs to be our *unifying fight*."

"It came as a shock to me, too," Yvan offers, impressively paring back the ferocity in his fire's flow. "That there's a bigger fight underneath all the things we've been aligned over. But there truly *is*."

His words don't soften the belligerent flow of Vang Troi's and her allies' power, not one bit. In fact, they only serve to stoke our adversaries' ire higher as Soleiya glares fiery daggers at me.

Hope shrivels in my chest. Because if we can't even convince Yvan's own *mother* to hear us and the Forest out when I know she and Yvan love each other deeply, what hope is there for any type of alliance with the East?

"Do you intend to hold me prisoner?" Soleiya challenges Yvan. She casts a pointed look at the barriers my allies have thrown up to wall us off from Vang Troi's forces.

"Let her pass," Yvan stiffly rejoins, his fiery aura and his mother's battering against each other.

My allies open a portion of our shield-wall, and Soleiya strides through it to Vang Troi's side, anger flickering through Yvan's fire as his mother glares at me, making her alignment clear.

Vang Troi and her forces begin to draw up power once more, and I move to warn Yvan and the others just as Sage lets out a strangled cry and falls to the ground.

Alarm leaps through everyone's magic as Ra'Ven drops down beside her and grabs hold of Sage's arms. "Ti'a, what is it?" he cries, his aura of emerald runic power crackling around Sage with impassioned urgency as he launches into a questioning stream of Smaragdalfar.

Sage raises one shaking, fasting-wound-marked hand, then convulses and lets out a soul-shearing cry, her bloody fastlines flaying open further.

The fasting wounds begin emitting tendrils of Shadow smoke.

Horror singes through me as Sage's terrified purple gaze swings to mine. "Vogel is in me! I can *feel* him . . ."

"Aughh!" Thierren cries out as he, too, drops to his knees, desperately cradling his fastmarked hands as his marks also begin to seep Shadow smoke. "It's happening to my fastlines, as well!" he chokes out. "Vogel is wresting control of me!"

"Get them to the trees!" I cry. "The Northern Forest's Great Tree broke my fasting to Vogel. The East's trees might be able to break their fastings, as well."

Alder, other allies, and I rush to Sage and Thierren, Yvan and I taking hold of Sage's arms.

"This is some trick!" Yvan's mother cries to Vang Troi. "Strike down these Crows!"

Yvan shoots his mother a harsh look and spits out a blistering epithet in Lasair as we hoist Sage to her feet.

"Disarm!" I call out to Sage and Thierren. "Disarm in case Vogel takes you over!"

Sage and Thierren give me panicked looks before hurling all wands, blades, and styluses aside, my allies swiftly requisitioning them before we bring Thierren and Sage to the Forest lining the huge mountain ledge's back edge.

Sage unexpectedly lunges for me, and I stumble back as Yvan and Diana swiftly restrain her. Sage's expression has turned alarmingly wicked, her eyes glowing gray as she bares elongated, steel-hued teeth, Vogel's voice hissing from her mouth. "I will *rip* those pointed ears from your head, Fae Witch. And then I will shove them down your throat, along with the bloody pieces of your Icaral beast's cursed *wings*."

Beating back a pulse-speeding rush of fear, I stare Vogel down. "Push her palms to living bark," I grit out as Sage breaks into chilling laughter before turning feral, attempting to snap at Yvan as both he and Diana drag her to a large Noi Maple, while Rafe and Alder drag Thierren to an adjacent Noi Birch. Diana forces Sage's hands to the bark as Thierren slams his own palms onto the tree trunk and Rafe grabs hold of his wrists from behind, keeping them there.

A slash of fear tears through the Dyoi Forest's aura as Thierren turns and sets his chillingly altered gaze on me, his eyes lit with a gray glow.

"I'm coming for you, staen'en witch," Vogel's voice seethes through Thierren's mouth before he gives me a wide, murderous smile.

The Zhilaan Forest's warrior might shocks through me, my own outrage rising with it. "Oh, I'll be coming for you too, Vogel," I vow. But my bravado evaporates as Sage and Thierren buck wildly against my allies' holds on them.

Please, I beg the Forest, the Ancient One, and any deity or tree that will listen as Thierren and Sage growl and struggle. *Please free them.*

A ripple of the Dyoi Forest's awareness shimmers through my rootlines, a fearful, questioning energy in it that settles into courageous understanding. And then, the Forest's elemental aura swoops around Thierren and Sage . . .

. . . and draws their forms straight into the trees.

Immense relief shudders through me as shocked sounds erupt from Ra'Ven and throughout the ranks of Vang Troi's forces.

Ra'Ven rounds on me and Yvan, an alarmed expression on his emerald-patterned face. "Where has she gone?"

"What have you done to them, Black Witch?" Vang Troi demands.

"The Forest has embraced them," Alder insists. "It will free them from Vogel's hold."

"Just like it freed *me*," I stress.

My adversaries' weapons power up once more, the Forest itself seeming to sense their aggressive intent. A palpable call from the trees reverberates throughout the entire Dyoi Forest.

Birds and animals are suddenly flooding out of the tree line and streaming toward me, many of them color-stripped to gray, some grievously burned by Vogel's Shadowfire, all suffused with urgency and terror. My throat tightens as they gather around me in a stunning show of alliance, a brilliantly purple fox with a singed, grayed ear slinking in against my calf, a moon-white Barred Owl with burned feathers landing heavily on my shoulder, the bird's predatory courage feeding into my own. An almost fully grayed Noi Deer moves in to lean against my other side, both grief and fierce affection for these kindreds firing through me.

The huge congregation of animals seems to stun those set against me, disorientation shivering through their power. Even Iris looks thrown.

I'm about to plead my case once more when there's a sudden, vicious tug on both my rootlines and the roots of the entire Forest. A gasp tears from my throat, and my balance gives way as a cry bursts from Alder and Hazel lets out an otherworldly shriek, his teeth chattering in obvious agony as he falls to his knees.

Yvan catches me, his fiery aura lashing around mine, the owl on my shoulder taking flight and the other animals fleeing back into the Forest's shelter, my ravens letting out loud *caws*. Every semiconscious Dryad'kin, including Mavrik and Gwynn, cries out even in their stupor.

"Elloren, what is it?" Yvan presses, urgency burning through our bond, but I can barely focus on him.

An image overtakes my mind—the Void tree's energy latching on to the smoking stump of III, a gray trunk and branches emerging from the stump's central abyss, growing and burgeoning into a huge tree of Shadow. My rootlines fill with the slithering sensation of Shadow power settling there, the Void stump consuming the elemental power of the destroyed Northern Forest with parasitic fervor while it sends feelers out toward the Eastern Realm.

"III," I roughly force out to Yvan as my rootlines shiver with the Forest's terror. "Vogel and his Shadow Wand have invaded III's rootline connections. And once they gain enough power, they're going to use them as a route to attack the East."

✴

PART TWO

✴

Prismatic Fall

SHADOW WAND DEMON

Tierney Calix

Northern Vo River

Tierney swirls through Viger's Darkness, wrapped in his misty embrace as they tunnel North through the Vo River's waters. She clings to Viger's long form, the two of them whirled into a blur, an echo of his Death Fae kiss brushing her lips. A kiss she can sense him holding himself back from repeating, his mouth firmly pressed to the nape of her neck.

She's stunned by the potent edge of *want* in Viger, shuddering through the tether his Xishlon kiss set down between them, emanating from deep in his center. Their proximity makes it difficult to think around her own bond-fueled desire to merge with Viger's Dark thrall, to fall into another of his tongue-twining, otherworldly kisses, even though she's distantly aware of Or'myr and Fyordin also tethered around the two of them, the collective spiral of their partially dissolved forms accelerating through the Vo River with breathtaking speed.

Viger's Darkness abruptly lifts, his powerful momentum halting.

Vertigo accosts Tierney in an Erthia-tilting swoop, her body jostling to a stop against Viger. She blinks, her eyes stinging from the abrupt switch from Viger's otherworldly Dark to the underwater Northern Vo River's shimmering gray light, she and Viger back in corporeal form, lying on the River's soft bed, Or'myr and Fyordin beside them.

Dizziness swirling through her, Tierney takes in the three males clustered around her at the Vo's base. Viger's lips are still pressed to her neck, his sharp teeth lightly touching down, the flick of his tongue against her skin enticing in the extreme. Or'myr hugs her side, his strong hand grasping her upper arm with covetous force, a shock of purple electricity sizzling through the point of contact in an unnervingly exciting rush that only adds to the bond-fueled thrall of Viger's kiss. And Fyordin . . . he's holding on to her other arm, his kindred water power whooshing through her with emphatic, territorial might, as if seeking to drive Viger and Or'myr clear away from her.

Her own water power churns into turmoil in response to her bond-amplified attraction to all three of them. Tierney huffs out a hard, bubbling breath, struggling to regain her wits. She pushes at Viger, and his enticing closeness immediately breaks away as all three males pull back from her.

Viger's Dark eyes meet hers, his arresting, pale features wavy under the water, and Tierney fights the urge to grab him and pull him back into a world-Darkening kiss.

It's the Deathkin bond you're feeling, Tierney cautions herself. *Force it back! You need to think past it!*

Viger gives her a discomfited look, and she can sense him struggling against the bond's draw, as well. Both ensnared and disconcerted, Tierney averts her eyes from Viger's rattled look only to meet Or'myr's green gaze shot through with purple lightning. A shock of Or'myr's power crackles against hers in a forking array, and Tierney shivers, stunned by her new bond-fueled ability to read Or'myr's emotions in his magic like an empath, the intensity of his feelings for her blasting through his lightning in an ardent line of longing.

A color-streaked Rainbow Trout speeds past them and snares Tierney's attention, her Vo-kindreds pulsing *warning, warning, warning* through her bond to her Waters. Tierney's focus on her River's life sharpens, a school of violet-glittering Noi Minnows as well as a multitude of other aquatic creatures swimming past them in panicked flight.

All of them fleeing south.

Concern eddies through Tierney's water power, cutting through her mind-scattering bond-pull to Viger, Or'myr, and Fyordin, the fishes' collective terrified energy prompting a surge of alarm.

Tierney'lin!

Every one of Tierney's nerves spikes to alert as her kelpies' cries flow in, along with a wavering, watery image of them trapped inside a ring of iron spikes hammered into the Vo's bed.

Tierney glances up, frantically scanning the water above them, a more intense alarm racing through her power as she spots a line of glowing gray runes shivering to life on the Vo's surface to the far north. She squints, her gaze snagging on a slowly advancing tide of gray in the distance, seeping toward them through the Vo's pristine water, gradually overtaking the Deathkin-and-Asrai runes marked on the Vo's surface that she and Viger set down to wall off Shadow power, the runes incrementally morphing to gray.

The sense of a nightmare descending shocks through Tierney's system as she takes in the dead fish and crustaceans floating in the gray tide, the creatures multi-eyed and oddly grayed . . .

Fyordin's flood of shock rushes through Tierney with typhoon force, their eyes meeting in a flash of Asrai horror. Her stunned gaze pivots to Viger, who has gone preternaturally still, his eyes narrowed on the incoming threat, as Or'myr draws his stone-encrusted violet wand, a stark look overtaking his expression. Or'myr's neck tightens, his power bursting into desperate, lightning-flashing chaos.

A dire thought pierces Tierney—*Or'myr can't breathe underwater. And if he surfaces . . . he'll fall into the hands of whatever evil lies above.*

Urgency exploding through their power, Tierney and Fyordin launch themselves at Or'myr at the same moment Viger's ropes of Darkness lash around them all, pulling Tierney, Or'myr, and Fyordin in tight before speeding them south in a blur, away from the killing tide of gray.

Viger tugs them upward, and they surface inside a sheltered rocky inlet, the surrounding black stone shot through with lines of dark purple. The water is waist deep, an overcast twilight above, steely clouds roiling across the heavens.

Or'myr's hand slaps down on the wet stone as he pulls in gasping breaths, brusquely nodding his thanks to Viger, as Tierney finds herself swept up in a sense of the elemental power of the Northern Vo's headwaters being consumed and siphoned *west*.

"The Shadow power . . ." she sputters ". . . it's feeding on my River and killing the river life and my kelpies—"

Her words choke off as Viger raises a silencing hand and opens his mouth slightly, his forked, purple tongue flickering toward the Shadow threat to the north of them, as if he's reading it on the very air.

Slowly, carefully, they rise and peer over the bank's purple-veined, obsidian stones.

Alarm eddies through Tierney as she takes in the swarms of Mage soldiers gathered on the Northern Vo's western and eastern banks, this narrow northernmost section of the Vo splitting into multiple tributaries just beyond.

Most of the Mage soldiers are massed around the bases of a great arc of Shadow runes that spans the River. The rune arc resembles a giant half portal, projecting a rippling pewter flow of Shadow into her Vo's waters to create the poisonous tide that's slowly advancing south toward them—the tide incrementally overtaking her and Viger's warding, a small grove of Vo Cypress trees that grow beside the arc beginning to gray, the other trees edging her River's banks graying, as well . . .

Tierney pivots her hand in the water, fully connecting with her Vo, instantly able to sense her kelpies' weakened, dissolved forms at the base of the rune arc's eastern side. The image of a spiraling Wand made of Shadow ripples through Tierney's water power, the poisonous tide siphoning her River's life into that Wand—the siphoning a full, consuming drain without any replenishing.

Bringing Void Death to her Waters.

A cyclonic whirlpool of rage gathers inside Tierney, a primal scream readying itself in her throat. She moves to launch herself toward the Mages as the Vo's own avenger, Fyordin's power rising beside hers, their combined Asrai might ready to break into a storming mass above them both.

Viger leaps at them, hurling out lashings of Darkness, forcefully binding not only Tierney and Fyordin, but Or'myr as well, his arms clamping around Tierney's upper body.

Tierney opens her mouth to let loose a ferocious snarl of protest, but it gets lost as Viger dissolves them all into his swirling Dark once more, sweeping them down into a tunneling retreat.

Viger swiftly remanifests them all underwater, Tierney hissing and bucking against his iron grip as they surface within another stone-sheltered bank a much farther distance south from the invading Shadow tide.

"Let me *go!*" she snarls at Viger, wrestling against his hold as he keeps both her and Fyordin bound but flicks a hand and releases Or'myr.

BE STILL! Viger's words strike through Tierney's mind with bone-vibrating force.

Both Fyordin's and Tierney's water auras burgeon inside them, Fyordin's expression like a gathering thunderhead. "Release us *right now*, Deathling," Fyordin growls, "or we will send the Vo's power *straight through you!*"

Or'myr levels his wand at Viger, his green eyes afire with purple lightning. "What are you doing, Viger?" he inquires, lethally calm.

"Keeping Tierney's and Fyordin's storms at bay," Viger hisses as Tierney and

Fyordin draw up cyclones of power. "If we are sighted," Viger bites out, "we will be *destroyed*."

Fyordin's cyclonic might stills, prompting Tierney's out-of-control fury to intensify as a swift, dire look passes between the three men.

Tierney snarls, teeth gnashing, thrust into a maelstrom of outrage by their timidity in the face of their River's *murder*. Darkness strobes through her vision, obliterating reason, the sight of the grayed waters and poisoned creatures fueling in her power the rush of a night-dark, cataclysmic force she's never felt before.

She pulls in a harsh breath, readying enough water power to blast through Viger's bonds, just as Viger tightens his hold and Or'myr raises his wand and levels it at her while Fyordin wrests hold of her magic through their Vo bond and yanks its flow toward his center.

"Control yourself, Asrai!" Viger hisses, his claws biting into her arms.

Unable to contain her rage, Tierney wrests her invisible tempest from Fyordin and blasts it at Viger, obliterating his Dark bonds to mist, their powers shuddering against each other with vibrating force, the whole world seeming to tint to midnight.

"It's the Void Death of no beginnings!" she snarls at Viger. "They're bringing Void Death to *my River*!"

"Yes," Viger hisses back, "and they're going to *succeed* if you can't get your power under control. *Look!*"

Viger flicks one clawed finger northward, and Tierney turns and peers through a gap in the stones of the rocky embankment. Her breath stutters as she takes in the huge demonic creature rising from the distant water, just below the arc of Shadow runes.

The beast's horned, pale gray form unfurls and rises higher than the arc, higher than the surrounding tree canopies. Two huge gray insectile eyes bubble out of the creature's eggshell-flat face, smaller eyes bulging into being around the two main ones. The creature sways over the River, its unnaturally long arms extending to embrace the runic arc.

The gray demon shivers, its neck arching back in a grotesque show of ecstasy, and Tierney's outrage crackles through her inner storm as she senses the thing *feeding* on the Vo's power through the killing gray tide.

"What is it?" she demands of Viger, engulfed in pure horror.

"A primordial V'yexwraith demon," he hisses, his solid-black eyes fixed on the thing, a flicker of cold fury running through his Darkness. "Summoned from a runic Striike Void somewhere holding monumental power to the west of here." He turns his Dark gaze on her, a formidable urgency in it. "This demon will be difficult to best."

Tierney fixes her gaze back on the V'yexwraith as her magic continues to surge and darken, whipping stronger and stronger, rapidly drawing on what feels like a line of Viger's Darkness and churning toward reckless violence. A seething tremble kicks up inside her. She can *feel* the tang of the demon's vast power in the air. A sliver of rational thought breaks through as she realizes why her allies are trying to keep her power from visually manifesting—because the only advantage they have is surprise.

Her storm of magic *cannot* break free.

"Help me control it," she rasps to Viger, grabbing hold of his arm. "I think our bond has opened up a pathway from your power to mine . . ."

A faint *click click* taps over the embankment's stone just above them.

Viger lets out an unearthly hiss as a Marfoir's salt-pale head rises above the stone's apex, the Marfoir's huge, bone-white spider legs bursting up. Four more Marfoir-spider Elves explode from the adjacent purple woods and run toward them in a blur of scuttling legs.

Viger releases Tierney and lunges at the beasts in a wild blur of Darkness, ripping off Marfoir heads and limbs with Dark claws and elongated teeth, while Tierney swiftly draws her power into her palms, and Or'myr levels his wand at a Marfoir coming in from the side. Growling out a spell, Or'myr blasts a bolt of purple fire clear through one of the insectile Elves while Fyordin throws out both hands and punches three more incoming Marfoir with a potent blast of water, sending them tumbling back toward the trees.

Frantic for her Vo, Tierney springs out of the sheltered rocky inlet.

The huge V'yexwraith beast's malefic gray head angles toward her.

Tierney's rage fires through every nerve as the V'yexwraith's insectile eyes meet hers, the demon's great slash of a mouth pulling back to reveal row upon row of sharp teeth as she's overtaken by the sense of her Waters *screaming*.

Tierney's Asrai warrior energy turns tidal, her River's distress creating a whirlpool in her rage, spiraling it into a frenzy. With a growl, she leaps over the remaining boulders and makes for the multi-eyed V'yexwraith demon.

She can sense Viger's Dark swoosh of alarmed awareness. He hurls his power into hers through their bond at the same moment Fyordin releases his full Asrai might into her and Or'myr's purple lightning aura flashes urgently to her through the connection.

Latching tight hold of their power through Viger's bond, Tierney races toward the V'yexwraith, an edge of her storm escaping her hold and blasting into existence, dark clouds roiling to life and overtaking the sky, a violent wind whipping up, Or'myr's purple lightning cutting from cloud to cloud as she breaks into a faster sprint toward the huge demon.

The V'yexwraith opens its fanged mouth and releases an otherworldly hiss. It springs toward her, a second mouth appearing inside its maw, then another, more mouths telescoping outward, each holding a cavern of teeth as the throngs of Mage soldiers massed along the bank nock iron-tipped arrows and fall to one knee, all aiming at Tierney.

Gritting her teeth, Tierney runs straight toward the Mages and demon, drawing on the Vo's full power, Fyordin's and Or'myr's might, and Viger's line of *Death*.

Every arrow is loosed and whizzes toward her as the V'yexwraith closes the gap between them, and Tierney realizes, in a flash of Asrai reckoning, that the iron onslaught will hit her before she's drawn enough power to take down the beast.

Or'myr springs past her, surprise jolting through her as he slashes his geo-wand through the air.

A crack of purple lightning scythes from his wand's tip, the bolt bifurcating and crackling sideways to collide with the violet-veined stone edging both of the Vo's banks. The stone's veins blast into purple incandescence, *blazing* with light as every iron-tipped arrow is yanked from its trajectory and pulled toward the stone of the eastern bank, along with the iron spikes encircling Tierney's dissolved kelpies.

A chorus of clangs sounds out, the arrows slamming into the purple-lit stone, quickly followed by every iron sword, axe, spike, and blade.

Magnetism, Tierney realizes in a shock of comprehension as Or'myr wrests every last iron weapon from the Mage forces. Emboldened, she quickens her pace, the Vo River rising within her as the V'yexwraith thrusts its hands forward.

A blast of Void energy scythes from the demon's palms and streaks toward Tierney in dark gray bolts, the screams of destroyed Forest and Waters reverberating through them.

Ready to die as an avenging warrior for her Vo, Tierney screams out an Asrai battle cry and releases her full storm.

Ropes of Viger's Darkness unleash from her palms, surrounded by whooshing streams of both her and Fyordin's Asrai storm shot through with Or'myr's purple geo-energy, the three males' determination ricocheting through her center.

Their attack slams into the V'yexwraith's Void bolts, blasting them into an explosion of purple-lightning-spitting steam before their combined powers spear forward and lash around the towering demon. Tierney draws her palms back, cinching the tethers violently inward and binding the creature tight. The V'yexwraith lets out an earsplitting, multitoned shriek while Tierney swipes her arms in a sideways arc and lets out a guttural cry.

The tethers of Darkness hurl the V'yexwraith clear out of her Waters and crash it onto the western riverbank with an Erthia-shaking *BOOM*.

The battle going on around her shudders into focus, the Mages and the Marfoir racing toward her blasted apart by Or'myr's violet-spitting lightning while Fyordin rushes into the water with raised palms and sends a whirling tide around the Shadow corrupting the Vo. Viger surges toward Fyordin in a blur of Dark, blackened hands thrust forward, the mist emanating from his palms twining through Fyordin's power. Their combined might rapidly corrals the Shadow corruption and halts its spread downstream, then hauls it away from Tierney's kelpies.

Fury and Darkness pounding through her, Tierney stalks toward the prone, hissing V'yexwraith's colossal form where it writhes on the riverbank, pinned there by her bindings.

On instinct, she draws in a deep breath and swipes her hands toward the demon.

River snakes swarm out of the Vo and coil around the V'yexwraith's limbs, a dart of vengeful satisfaction rushing through Tierney as serpentine fangs bite into the demon's gray flesh. The beast hisses out its pain and fury, its long back arching as Tierney's storm of Darkness rages around them both.

The V'yexwraith bares its rows of teeth at her, its multi-eyed expression chilling. "You cannot kill me, Asrai," it chitters, its multitoned voice seeming to come from everywhere at once, vibrating straight through her. "My power is *growing*." A harsh shiver courses through her, and she has to fight the urge to recoil. "I will re-form and come for you, Asrai filth," the V'yexwraith chides, its multiple mouths *smiling*. "I will feed on Forest and Water. And I will feed on *you*."

Images of Shadow consuming the Vo accost Tierney's mind. Her fish and amphibians and plant life . . . all the complex Life of her River corrupted and destroyed, the River's Balance *breaking*. The image sharpens, and Tierney's lungs seize. She's suddenly unable to pull in a breath, the V'yexwraith's vision *choking* her . . .

An explosion of purple light blasts the vision apart, and Tierney finds herself on her hands and knees on the riverbank, gasping for air. Or'myr stands beside her, wand raised, his purple lightning sizzling around the demon in a forking array. The V'yexwraith snarls, its multiple mouths accordioning forward with stretching force, stopped a fraction away from Or'myr's face to viciously snap at him, straining to bite. Its attempt thwarted by Or'myr's lightning, the demon hisses and contracts its mouths back into its large slash of a maw.

"Do you understand what it is to move against a primordial demon," it snarls at Or'myr, giving him a terrifying multimouthed smile. It rears its head back and thrusts out two thick, forked, black tongues. Twin blasts of silver gray lightning shoot from the tongues' tips, scything straight toward Or'myr.

Or'myr drops his wand and thrusts up his arms. He catches the lightning bolts in his fists, then smiles at the demon as the gray spitting bolts rapidly tint to violet, Or'myr's tone chillingly vicious when it comes. "Do you understand what it is to move against the geomancer grandson of the *Black Witch*?"

Or'myr hurls the lightning bolts back at the demon, impaling the V'yexwraith's two largest eyes and pinning its head to the riverbank. The demon screeches as the lightning bolts' purple energy sizzles over it, its huge form catching violet fire.

"I will re-form!" the V'yexwraith shrieks, so loudly that the very earth beneath Tierney quakes.

"Oh, go ahead and re-form, Void-spawn," Or'myr snipes as he splays out his hand toward his dropped wand. The wand flies into his palm, and Or'myr levels it at the V'yexwraith.

Tierney flinches as purple lightning blasts from Or'myr's wand and impales the creature's huge, bony chest, the imprint of a glowing purple Xishlon moon forming around the strike.

"Here's my calling card," Or'myr snarls, low and deadly. "Vogel thinks he destroyed our Xishlon moon. Well, he didn't. And it's *coming for him*."

A chilling grin forms on all the V'yexwraith's mouths. "Your love moon can't defeat us."

"Are you certain?" Or'myr shoots back. He raises his wand to the heavens and sends a bolt of purple light into Tierney's storm.

The lower clouds agitate and roll into bright purple orbs, all of them lit up like Xishlon moons.

Or'myr swipes his arm down, and the moons fall, each one colliding with every surviving and slain Marfoir or Mage soldier, the soldiers bursting into purple fire.

The V'yexwraith's smile vanishes, replaced by a look of teeth-gritted feralness as Or'myr once more levels his wand at the demon.

"Vo's love can turn to vengeance in a heartbeat, syth'vuu'wraith," Or'myr bites out. "And I'm Her Varg-warded Strafeling. Come against me and *feel my wrath*."

An eruption of curling Shadow detonates around the V'yexwraith, and the demon vanishes.

Tierney looks at Or'myr in shock as the whole world quiets, countless dead Mage and Marfoir soldiers burning in violet conflagrations all around. Bolting up, she breaks into a run toward the Vo and into it, while reaching up to grab hold of the vial necklace she always wears around her neck. She unstoppers the vial-pendant and thrusts it into the water while hoarsely murmuring an Asrai command.

An ache constricts Tierney's heart as her kelpies' iron-decimated forms dissolve and stream toward her and into the vial, tears stinging at her eyes over their cruel treatment. Forcibly calming herself, she stoppers the vial and puts the necklace back on, then reaches up to massage her neck, her breathing still labored, her power severely depleted. She looks at Or'myr to find his gaze pinned on the bank where the demon thing just was, his breaths measured, a wild purple light in his eyes.

As her storm dissipates, her gaze catches on the single purple orb left hanging above the Vo—Or'myr's own conjured Xishlon moon.

"I . . . I didn't know that you're religious," Tierney manages, gaping at him. Gaping at what they've all wrought.

"I am," Or'myr says, voice clipped. "A tad."

A huff escapes Tierney. "More than a tad, I'd say." She's still stunned by his outburst. In all the time they spent together in his laboratory at the Wyvernguard, she never once heard him utter so much as a prayer to the Goddess Vo. Or saw him wear Vo's necklace. Or set up a shrine anywhere.

Or'myr's eyes meet hers, purple blazing in their green depths. "You don't know everything about me," he says, sounding sharp.

Tierney inwardly winces. "I realize that, Or'myr," she offers, overcome by the sizzle of intense feeling passing between them through the bond, strong as his purple lightning. A memory pulses through her, of the emotional energy in his Xishlon kiss just before the pain struck, and she averts her eyes, her gaze catching on his conjured purple moon once more.

"You should leave that there," Tierney says, a pang cutting through her heart as she lowers her sight to the corralled swath of Shadow-corrupted Vo. Ferocity rises. "Leave that moon *right there*," she insists, her voice splintering with emotion.

"Oh, I intend to," Or'myr replies, looking at his moon. When his eyes meet hers again, they flash with defiant light. "Vogel doesn't get to take it away from us. And I'm going to hang purple moons all over the skies of the West through spells I sent through Vogel's V'yexwraith."

Tierney's eyes widen. "You're going to torment the Magedom . . . with Xishlon moons?"

Or'myr nods stiffly. "And if I can find a way, I'll color the whole damned Magedom purple before I'm done with them."

A spark flares between them just as the Shadow runes spanning the Vo shiver into Death Fae black, hooking Or'myr's and Tierney's attention. Multiple black Deathkin runes ripple to life over the gray-tinged River, and Tierney realizes Viger must be underwater, casting them.

Fyordin is gliding over the Vo's surface just outside the edge of the Shadow corruption, strengthening his and Viger's compact stormwall of Darkness and sectioning off the gray corruption from the Vo's unpoisoned water. Or'myr lifts his wand and sends lightning through their stormwall, and the unpoisoned waters of the Vo tint purple, the protective wall doubling in height and flashing with violet lightning.

Saving her Vo, the River itself flowing out a sigh of relief.

Fierce affection for Fyordin and Viger and Or'myr surges through Tierney, the unexpected swell of feeling constricting her heart. "Your power has turned my River purple," she marvels to Or'myr, her voice hitching.

She turns to him and is instantly ensnared by Or'myr's heated look of surprise. She flushes, suddenly hyperaware of the possible innuendo. And hyperaware that his invisible lightning aura is pulsing toward her through the bond.

Or'myr swallows and glances away, but their new linkage . . . Tierney can feel in it how much he wants to embrace her. And she's stunned by the strength of that desire.

A flush spreads down her neck. "You're using those Xishlon moons to declare war, aren't you," she says, unable to suppress her own heated rise of feeling for him.

"I am, indeed," Or'myr affirms, keeping his lightning-flashing eyes locked with hers as the bond's pull surges and Or'myr's lightning tingles all over her skin with rampant yearning.

A potent wave of water power crashes into them both, and their thrall breaks. Tierney turns to find Fyordin striding toward her over the Vo's surface then onto its bank, his rapidly replenishing power rushing toward and around Tierney's depleted magic with covetous fervor. An edge of Fyordin's storming might jostles against Or'myr's magic through the bond, to no avail as Or'myr stiffens and keeps his violet aura sizzling around Tierney.

Fyordin shoots Or'myr a narrow look before settling his Vo-blue gaze back on Tierney. "Once your power is recharged," he states, "we need to all work together and ward the Vo using our bonded power." His eyes flick toward Or'myr, the jealous ire in them shifting to a look of unequivocal alliance as the task at hand cycles down.

A task more important than this undercurrent of attraction and competition for her affections their bond is dredging to the surface.

Because Vogel's forces will be back, Tierney considers with grim certainty. And the Shadow Wand's V'yexwraith demon will be, too, likely wielding much more power. A shiver runs down Tierney's spine, a knot tightening her throat as she catches sight of Viger, in mist form, gliding just under the Shadowed Waters, more Death Fae wards shivering to life on the section of grayed water.

Or'myr points at the stony embankments around them, drawing Tierney's attention. There's a calculating look in his eyes, and she can sense the wheels of his Geo-Mage mind turning. "There's purple-veined stone not only along the riverbanks," he says, "but lining the Vo's bed as well, which means I can anchor power to it." He looks to Tierney and Fyordin both. "If I draw on everyone's power, I should be able to cast a shield over most of the Vo. If I link Viger's wards to the shield, that should be sufficient to fend off any new Shadow attacks. For now."

For now. Tierney stiffens her spine against the rise of foreboding.

But still, it's a solid start.

"All right, Strafeling," Fyordin says, giving Or'myr a look of begrudging respect even as his power encircles Tierney along with Or'myr's lightning. Tierney struggles to ignore the churning sizzle and whoosh against her skin as they each attempt to shove the other's power off her, the strength of feeling in their magic making her a bit dizzy.

Tierney turns back to the Vo, and her breath catches, her heart picking up speed.

Viger has surfaced, his tall form standing thigh-deep in the water beside the western-bank base of the Shadow-rune arc, ropes of his Dark power twining around it.

Their eyes meet, and Tierney pulls in a shuddering breath, a shiver racing over her skin as Viger's magic undulates straight through Or'myr's and Fyordin's to twine through hers. There's something off about it—his usual edge of viciousness seems ramped up in a dangerous way.

Abruptly, Viger pushes back the other men's power in a stunning show of force, and the world slants Dark, everything seeming to fade but Viger's eyes on hers, and Tierney realizes how little she knows about the bond he's set up.

How little she knows about the ramifications of his Death Fae kiss.

Viger lifts one clawed hand and flicks his index finger inward.

Tierney gasps as the distance between them contracts, her body leaving the ground, the world a momentary blur as she's pulled toward Viger, Or'myr's and Fyordin's powers surging toward her, filled with resentful, protective energy.

But Viger is too strong, his eyes full Dark, which sets the hairs on the back of Tierney's neck prickling. She slows to a halt, thigh-deep in the water beside him, and Viger motions to the base of the runic arc. Sloughing off her ire at being dragged here by his thrall, Tierney takes in the single Shadow rune he's left amidst the blackened runes, the rune slowly rotating, like something disconnected from a larger set of gearworks.

Touch the Shadow rune and tell me what you sense, Asrai, he shivers through her mind.

Tierney gives him a narrow-eyed searching look then complies, pressing one palm to the vaporous Shadow rune.

The rune's energy slithers over her skin, and Tierney fights the urge to recoil as a vision of the Northern Forest's huge Ironwood Tree, III, exploding into Shadow accosts her mind, the Great Tree's vast root network shot through with a line of gray power as a Void-abyss swirls to life in its corpse-stump.

Shock breaks through her.

"Oh, gods," she breathes out as she wrenches her hand from the rune.

Vogel's taken hold of the Center of Nature, Viger seethes into her mind. *He's consumed the Northern Forest's Great Tree.*

"And linked its root network to his Shadow Wand," she realizes, dread burgeoning.

Viger bares sharp, blackened teeth at her. *And now, that Shadow Wand is going to use this connection to consume all of Nature's power.*

CHAPTER TWO

DRYAD'KHIN CALL

Elloren

Northern Dyoi Mountain Range

"Vogel's overtaking III's rootline network with Shadow!" I cry out to everyone under the Dyoi Forest's dome shielding, allies and adversaries alike. "He wants to siphon up the Natural World's remaining elemental power!"

"Do you have any sense of how we can fight him?" Yvan demands as he firms his hold on me, keeping me from falling to the ground of the mountainside ledge as my surviving Errilor Ravens let out *caw*s in deep tones of warning.

Meeting Yvan's intent gaze, I open my mouth to respond, but all words are scoured away as I'm assaulted, once more, by the image of the Shadow Wand's huge Void tree emerging from III's smoking stump.

"Link me to the Dyoi Forest, *quickly!*" Hazel suddenly shrieks.

Both Yvan's and my attention whips toward the Deathkin Dryad, our bonded fire erupting into crackling tension.

Hazel is on his knees, his huge black insectile legs splayed out around him, larger than they were before. And his mouth . . . it's grotesquely widened, his teeth sharper, his full-black eyes grown terrifyingly huge as they meet mine. A chill snakes down my spine as I realize he's surrounded by my kindred flock, as if under guard. And he's a distance away from all my allies, as if he's keeping himself removed to protect us.

From *him*.

A sizzle of urgent warning from the surrounding Dyoi Forest rushes through my rootlines, the image of purple branches flashing through my mind. With a whoosh of dread, I intuit what the Forest is trying to tell me—that when we connected my Dryad'kins' withering rootlines to the Dyoi Forest with living branches to save their lives, we never did the same for Hazel. And now, Hazel's connection to the Shadowed Northern Forest has opened a pathway from Vogel's great Void tree straight into his rootlines.

Shadow mist bursts to life around Hazel's slender frame. He lets out a multitoned screech, his back bowing, his multiple legs contracting.

"Cut the Death Fae down *right now*," Vang Troi booms out from beyond the shield-wall dividing my allies and adversaries. "Vogel is *taking him over!*"

Before I can protest, Hazel springs up, breaks through the circle of giant ravens, and scuttles toward me in a blur, my ravens surging toward me, Hazel's grayed legs whipping out tendrils of Shadow.

All Death Fae black *gone.*

"*Dryad Witch!*" Hazel hisses in Vogel's voice as Yvan springs toward him, Rafe and Wrenfir joining him, all three men tackling him to the ground. Hazel lets out a bloodcurdling shriek as they pin him to the ledge's stone, his legs violently thrashing.

The Dyoi Forest sends a binding spell rustling through my mind as my lines gain enough power to launch spells. I level my living branch at Hazel, murmur the spell and thrust my branch forward.

Deep-purple vines blast from my branch's tips and spear to Hazel, magically binding him as my ravens lash out ropes of their Death Fae power to reinforce my bindings, and Yvan and I exchange a quick, intense look.

Hissing and screeching, Hazel thrashes against the bindings and those holding him down, his gray eyes fixated on mine. Vogel's snarl erupts from his throat with terrifying force. "*I will impale you, Whore Witch!*"

"Press this branch to his chest!" I cry out to my uncle Wrenfir, tossing my branch to him.

Wrenfir deftly catches it, then rips open the collar of Hazel's leafy black tunic.

Hazel snaps his too-long teeth at my spider-tattooed uncle. "*Mage abomination!*" he hisses, the sound coming from everywhere at once, sending ice down my spine. "*I will turn your lines to Shadow and indenture you as my SLAVE!*"

Teeth gritted, Wrenfir forces my living branch to Hazel's chest.

A purple-branching pattern races over Hazel's grayed skin, and he stops thrashing. His insectile legs vanish into him, and the whites of his eyes snap back into existence as his irises contract to a more human size. His eyes lock with Wrenfir's, midnight black overtaking the gray, a look of astonishment on Hazel's visage.

Wrenfir stiffens, my uncle's fire and earth power suddenly contracting toward Hazel's Deathkin power with a force that seems to stun them both as Yvan and Rafe rise and cautiously step back.

The ropy tendrils of Hazel's aura darken, morphing from gray to black as they whip around him before flowing outward to encircle both him and Wrenfir, as if moving of their own accord.

"Vogel's gone," Hazel rasps to Wrenfir, their eyes still locked, Wrenfir's palms and the living branch beneath them pressed to Hazel's heaving, naked chest, Hazel's skin starting to take on his natural lime coloration.

Wrenfir gives Hazel a terse nod before he rises, and takes hold of the wand sheathed at his hip as my ravens draw their ropes of power back into themselves. Wrenfir angles his wand at Hazel and growls out a spell that bursts my vine bindings to purple mist. Then he hands Hazel the living branch and steps back, my uncle's rattled expression shifting to his usual angry intensity.

Hazel's knife-sharp features return to their otherworldly severity as he and Wrenfir tear their gazes away from each other. But my power empathy can sense the way their invisible magical auras continue to circle each other with stunned, questioning fervor.

"Do you finally see why we need to align?" Rafe is suddenly calling out to Vang Troi as he steps toward the translucent runic shield-wall separating our two factions, his amber gaze boring into the Vu Trin commander. My eldest brother levels his finger at Hazel. "Vogel isn't going to stop finding ways to come at us, even under this dome-shield. We *have* to share every shred of our combined knowledge and every last weapon at our disposal to *fight the Magedom*."

"We will not align with you to be consumed by *trees*," Vang Troi fires back.

"Sage and Thierren will emerge," I insist, catching Ra'Ven's look of worry.

Vang Troi narrows her violet gaze on me, a tense standoff descending just as Mavrik and Gwynn begin to stir.

Blinking dazedly, the twinned Dryad'kin open their eyes, push themselves up to a sitting position and turn toward each other, their golden auras of power springing to life.

"Gwynnifer," Mavrik rasps out as they embrace and trigger an invisible shock of raying, prismatic light. The colors burst against my eyes and spangle through my power-empath senses, the intensity of the feelings flashing through their magic so potent it takes my breath away.

THE DRYAD STORM

The two Agolith Flame Hawk kindreds standing sentinel beside them take on a brighter golden glow, and a sudden vision of the Verdyllion Wand shimmers into my mind as my lightlines give an unexpected, emphatic tug toward theirs.

"Mavrik Glass," Vang Troi huffs out, sounding astonished as she takes in her former double agent's pointed ears, golden eyes, and prism-streaked hair as well as the deepened forest green hue of his skin.

"Nor Vang Troi," Mavrik responds, his voice rough with feeling as he and Gwynn rise, hand in hand, their hawk kindreds flying up to light on their shoulders. "I've much to tell you," he rasps out before filling everyone in on everything that happened in the Sublands and how Wynter Eirllyn and her brother, Cael, and Cael's Second, Rhys, are trapped there along with the Verdyllion Wand, Valasca, Sparrow, and three Smaragdalfar soldiers.

"I can sense the Verdyllion Wand's underground location," Gwynn reveals, golden eyes wide as she swallows, glancing southwest as if her gaze is drawn there by an invisible pull.

"As can I," Mavrik agrees, sharing a fraught glance with Gwynn. "Ever since we were transported to the Sunlands by III."

"Valasca is alive?" Ni Vin exclaims, voice breaking.

We all turn toward her, and my heart twists as I take in how obviously worked up Ni Vin is. She's always been such a grim, silent figure, forever marked by the tragedy of the last Black Witch's reign of fire, Ni Vin's burn-scarred head, melted ear, and singed stump of a hand sustained when she was but a child, permanent marks of my grandmother's atrocities.

But Ni Vin's grim reserve has been blasted clear away, her slim military-uniformed figure and blazing dark eyes conveying the sense that she'd jump right into the middle of Vogel's forces if it meant getting to Valasca.

"I assume you're Ni Vin," Mavrik ventures.

Ni Vin nods once, her throat bobbing, as if she's struggling not to choke on the rise of emotion. Tears escape her eyes and streak down her cheeks, a tremble kicking up in her shoulders, her sister, Kam Vin, placing a bolstering hand on Ni Vin's shoulder.

"She spoke of you often," Mavrik tells Ni Vin. "She spoke of her 'Great Love, Ni Vin.'"

Ni Vin lets out a strangled sound, silently weeping.

Mavrik turns, exchanging a grave look with Jules Kristian, and I recall when

Jules mentioned, long ago in Verpacia, that Mavrik and he were in league with each other in the now-shattered Western Realm Resistance. "Jules," Mavrik ventures, concern writ on his face, "where's Lucretia?"

Jules shakes his head, barely able to get the words out. "We were attacked by Marfoir on dragonback and forced to the ground. They ambushed us, and one of them knocked me unconscious. When I awakened . . . ." Jules grimaces, his lips quavering.

"When he came to," Fain grimly finishes for him, looking heartsick, "my sister was gone."

Ni Vin's tear-soaked face swings to Jules and Fain. "I was the last to see her," she roughly chokes out.

Their eyes widen.

"Where?" Jules demands, desperation clawing through his tone.

"I was fighting Marfoir beside her when they attacked us with their Shadow webbing," Ni Vin tells them. "They used it to wrest the wand from Lucretia's hand. When they closed in on her, she backed away toward a half-dead tree and . . . *disappeared* into its trunk."

Jules and Fain remain frozen for a moment, blinking at Ni Vin.

"She may yet emerge," Alder staunchly interjects.

Jules's gaze swings to her. "How?" he demands.

"The living Forest of Erthia has rootline connections that span the entire continent," Alder answers, her voice and forest green eyes as steady as those of the small purple eagle perched on her shoulder. "If the Dyoi Forest's connection to that half-dead tree remains, Lucretia may yet emerge—"

A flash of purple light rays out from two trees at the ledge's edge, breaking off Alder's words, and Yvan and I turn toward it to find Sage and Thierren suddenly there, kneeling amongst the trees' knotty purple roots.

"Sagellyn!" Ra'Ven cries, his invisible green aura blasting into a passionate sizzle as he rushes toward her.

Breathing hard, Thierren and Sage dazedly take us all in. Both are transformed, their ears pointed, Thierren's skin now a darkened Northern Forest green patterned with purple Dyoi Forest branching, a verdant streak through his short black hair. Sage's bright violet hue is heightened, a deep-purple branching pattern gracing her skin as well, both Sage and Thierren grasping purple living branches.

"Ti'a'lin," Ra'Ven exclaims, falling to his knees before Sage and sweeping her into his arms. My gaze darts to Sage's and Thierren's hands and my breath catches. Their fastmarks are *gone*.

Dyoi Monarch Butterflies flutter out of the Forest, the color beneath their wings' black stained-glass lacings a luminous mosaic of every hue of purple. The monarchs light on Sage in a whorl of kindred affection at the same time that an Eastern Peregrine Falcon swoops in from the Forest and lands on Thierren's forearm. The sleek bird of prey ruffles its night-purple feathers, its lavender eyes shining like two amethysts as they meet Thierren's with a look of fierce, protective alliance. Tears glaze Thierren's eyes, his severe face tight with emotion.

"Ti'a'lin," Ra'Ven rasps, his voice breaking as he reaches down to cradle Sage's fastmark-free hands. "You're *free*."

Sage's eyes glisten as she looks besottedly back at him, butterflies decorating her hair, her shoulders. "I'm free in so many new ways," she says in Smaragdalfarin, lifting her palm to display the image of III marked on it.

Surprise darts through Yvan's and my bonded fire, the Great Tree marking on Sage's palm evidence that something of III's energy still thrums through Erthia's rootline network.

Sage presses her III-marked palm over Ra'Ven's heart. "Tia'lin, I need to bring you to the Forest . . ."

"Sparrow's trapped." Thierren cuts off Sage's words, urgency writ in the severe lines of his face as he pushes himself to his feet, the falcon now perched on his shoulder. "The Forest sent me a vision of her. She was inside III when Vogel struck. She's imprisoned inside the Shadow abyss that overtook the Great Tree."

The blow connects with pummeling force. "Ancient One, Thierren," I gasp.

"We've got to get hold of the Verdyllion," Sage says as she and Ra'Ven rise to their feet. "It holds power that might be able to free Sparrow."

"Explain," Vang Troi demands in a harsh voice from beyond our line of division.

Sage meets Vang Troi's stern gaze. "The Forest showed me that the Verdyllion Wand-Stylus is a counterforce to the Shadow when it's wielded by powerful light sorcerers connected as Dryad'khin." Sage turns to me. "Elloren, there's a reason we were drawn to the Verdyllion as its Bearers. Every one of us holds potent light sorcery." She looks to Ra'Ven. "The Smaragdalfar myths are true in this—multicolored light is a *weapon* that can overtake Shadow, especially when it emanates from seven points, seven Dryad'khin light sorcerers." Her gaze swings to Gwynnifer. "That includes you, Gwynn," she says in the Dryad tongue.

An ocean of feeling rises in Gwynn's and Sage's formidable light auras as Gwynn's mouth trembles into a remorseful frown.

"Sagellyn," Gwynn says in a fractured voice as she releases Mavrik's hand and steps toward her. "You were my good friend, and I *betrayed* you. I betrayed you in Verpacia when I pointed the Mage-hunt toward Ra'Ven, and I'll never forgive myself for that." She gives Ra'Ven a tortured look, tears streaking down her cheeks. "I was *wrong*. I'm so sorry."

Sage and Ra'Ven share a look of intense conflict, a storm of emotion in it before Sage turns back to Gwynn, an expression of resolve on her purple features. She surges toward Gwynn, a cry escaping Gwynn's throat as the two Dryad'kin fall into each other's arms.

"You were like a sister to me," Gwynn sobs into Sage's shoulder.

"You are my sister *still*," Sage insists before drawing slightly back from their embrace, holding on to Gwynn's forearms. "We *both* fell prey to the Magedom's lies." Sage looks to the tree line, brow knotting. "And we were both ignorant of our Dryad rootlines and our true Forest home. But now," she says, smiling through her tears as she holds up her III-marked palm, "we are forever united as Dryad'kin. I forgive you, my sister."

"I forgive you as well, Gwynnifer," Ra'Ven staunchly assures Gwynn, bringing his hand to her shoulder as she weeps.

"We need to follow their example and *stop fighting*," Rafe calls out to Vang Troi.

Thierren levels a finger at the still half-conscious Dryads being tended to by Bleddyn, Aislinn, Jarod, and others. "We need to join with them and their Forest. *All* of us. So we can combine power and get hold of the Verdyllion, then rescue Sparrow and the others and *fight back*."

"He speaks the truth," Alder affirms, the small purple eagle still perched on her shoulder. "As more of us link to the Forest and become Dryad'khin, its power and the power of the Verdyllion Wand-Stylus *grows*." She studies me. "And Elloren, I can sense with my power empathy that you not only have a strong lightline, you're potentially the Wand-Stylus's strongest amplifier."

"I've had enough of these *lies*!" Yvan's mother hisses from beyond our defensive shield-wall, startling me, the vicious look she's giving me like a blow to the gut. She levels a damning look at Alder, pointing at me. "You'd cast this spawn of that *monster witch*, the same witch who killed my *husband*, as some type of *savior*?"

"Her name is *Elloren*," Yvan says, low and adamant, a portion of his internal fire whipping up with angry heat, the rest blazing ardently around me as Raz'zor erupts into a low growl.

"Elloren is not a savior," Alder calmly counters. "She's potentially a *catalyst*. For amplifying the combined, Forest-linked light power of the Verdyllion's Bearers."

Yvan and I share a quick, intense look, the urgency of the situation blazing through our commingled fire.

"The witch needs to *die*," Iris insists from beside Soleiya, her invisible flaming aura whipping out to encircle Yvan.

Diana takes a menacing step toward Iris. "Lay one hand on my sister, Lasair," she growls, "and I'll claw your fire straight out of you."

Rafe places a cautionary hand on Diana's shoulder, his stance pure dominance as he faces both Soleiya and Iris down. "We are *not* your enemies."

"Cast the witch aside!" Iris snarls at Yvan, ignoring Rafe. "You're not even truly mated to her!"

I flinch, her words like the lash of a whip as Yvan sends another reassuring lash of heat around me. "Mav'ya," he says to Soleiya in Lasair. "We need to *align*." His violet-fire gaze swings to Vang Troi. "Nor'hoi'yhir Vang Troi," he formally addresses her in Noi. "All we ask is that you *hear the Forest out*."

It's at that moment that Sylvan, Oaklyyn, and Yulan begin to regain consciousness, Sylvan forcing himself into a sitting position, soon followed by Oaklyyn and Yulan.

Sylvan glances down at the branching purple patterns on his skin and stills, his elemental power rising in the air around him in a gathering storm that has me drawing back.

"Sylvan . . ." I caution, and he slowly looks up, his pine gaze fixing on Hazel.

A vicious growl erupts from Sylvan, and his aura of power explodes as he springs up and rushes at Hazel, fists balled, shock jolting through me.

Yvan, Wrenfir, and Thierren leap toward Sylvan as he slams his fist into Hazel's face.

Hazel falls back, insectile legs bursting from his body once more, his teeth elongating as he snarls, jaw snapping, eyes enlarging and morphing back to full black as Yvan, Thierren, and Wrenfir wrestle Sylvan to the ground.

"*Traitor!*" Sylvan cries at Hazel, struggling to free himself. "You took us from our *Forest!*"

"You would have *died!*" Hazel lashes back, ferocious pain slashing through his Dark aura.

"Where are Lyptus and Larch?" Sylvan growls, eyes wild as he glances searchingly around. "Where are our kindreds?"

"Lost to us," Hazel grits out, the whole world strobing dark.

"I will *kill you!*" Oaklyyn rages as she springs up and hurls herself at Hazel, knocking him back down only to be flipped onto her back and imprisoned in a cage of Hazel's legs.

"Do not *provoke* me!" Hazel seethes, his jaws enlarging and snapping. "Or you will feel the *full wrath* of my Darkness."

"*Stop!*" Vang Troi bellows, slamming her curved runic sword's tip onto the ledge's stone.

A great flash of sapphire energy ignites, my empathic sense of her power streaking through my lines, my very bones, the hairs on my scalp raising. All of us freeze, even the battling Dryads seeming stunned into silence by Vang Troi's powerful display of Noi sorcery.

Hazel withdraws, insect fast, and Oaklyyn lurches to her feet, tears streaking her cheeks as she levels a devastated glare at him, her mouth trembling and her elemental aura shot through with violent rage and grief.

"I will hear you out," Vang Troi levels at us all.

Her words are like a runic explosive, impassioned protest immediately rising amongst her surviving Vu Trin forces and Amaz and Lasair allies.

"This is what my husband's sacrifice has wrought?" Soleiya rages at Vang Troi, angry tears glinting in her fiery eyes. "*Hearing out* the granddaughter of the Black Witch who *murdered* him?"

"Not just her," Vang Troi returns, a serious look in her eyes. She turns back to the Dryads, import flashing through her gaze. "The Tree Fae, as well."

Sylvan wrenches himself from Yvan's and Wrenfir's grips and rises, devastation writ hard on his face as he looks toward the destroyed Shadow lands beyond the dome-shield. "It's too late," he rasps, tears streaking down his greening face. "It's over."

Oaklyyn remains slumped on the ground, violently sobbing.

Sylvan levels his tortured gaze on Vang Troi. "Our people are *dead*. Our kindreds are *dead*. And your infighting will soon destroy what's left of the Natural World. It's *over*."

THE DRYAD STORM

"Your people are alive," Thierren raggedly states.

Sylvan's head jerks toward him.

"The Forest showed me a vision of them," Thierren explains. "The Verdyllion . . . it was able to blast open a small path for your people into the Sublands below the Northern Forest."

Confusion gutters through Gwynn and Mavrik's twinned power. "I sense no break in our Subland shielding," Mavrik says.

"If this is so," Gwynn postulates, "it must have happened when Mavrik and I were semiconscious."

"Our people will *die* without a Forest connection," Oaklyyn lashes out, choking on her tears. Her misery-tight gaze swings to Hazel, blistering hate overtaking it. "Like you should have let *us* die!"

"We need to find them," Yulan cuts in, the petite Dryad's melodic voice frayed, her breathing labored, her lichen-lashed eyes stricken. "We need to find them and tether them to the surviving Forest."

"There can be no true tether!" Oaklyyn snarls at Yulan. "Your kindred is *dead*! As is *mine*!" She breaks into more furious tears, glaring at all of us with a fury so potent, it slices straight through my heart as she glares damningly at us all. "Our wild ones *burned* in the fire of your discord!"

"You are not the only one grieving," Yulan chokes out. "The Shadowed ones blasted my beautiful kindred *apart*. I will *never* recover, but, perhaps, some of our people *might*."

A sting ripples across the III-imprint on my palm as the Forest pulses out what feels like a wordless plea. My heart in my throat, I turn toward the tree line, along with Yvan and all my other III-marked Dryad'khin, as an injured creature emerges from it.

I draw in a tight breath as the Tricolored Heron limps toward us, its normally blue, lavender, and white feathers stripped of color and covered in Shadow ash. The grayed heron drags a limp, broken wing, picking its way toward Yulan before stilling before her.

Yulan lets out a strangled sob as she brings her trembling hand to the bird's slender back, and I have to fight off my own tears, the whole world seeming shattered beyond repair.

But then, the unexpected happens.

Ariel breaks away from our horde's defensive line and strides toward Yulan, eyes set on the crumpled Dryad and the heron before her. Gentler than I ever imagined she could be, Ariel comes down on one knee beside them, her wings fanning out in a protective arc, Yulan and the heron recoiling slightly.

"Don't be afraid," Ariel croons. "I can heal wings."

Yulan raises her trauma-stricken eyes to Ariel's and looks at her deeply. Seeming to gather herself, she nods and gently prods the heron forward.

The bird lets out a frightened squawk as Ariel leans in and sets her hand on the heron's singed feathers with exquisite gentleness. The bird goes stock-still, its grayed eyes now riveted to Ariel's, as if mentally conveying horrors endured. Ariel's expression tenses with a look of outraged understanding before she makes a low shushing sound, and the slender bird takes a stumbling step toward her. Murmuring to the winged, Ariel gently strokes the bird's back, then traces her fingers along its wing, crooning softly the whole time as she carefully assesses it.

And then, as if Ariel's gesture was the spark needed to shift the hopeless tide, a deep-purple vine ripples out from the Forest toward Yulan and flows around her, delicate lavender flowers blooming to life all over it and forming blossoming tresses on Yulan's flower-stripped head to replace the gray, withered vines. I can sense the Dyoi Forest's fragility in the gesture. Its need for Dryad'khin protection.

Its need for us *all*.

Yvan's invisible aura of fire is suddenly blazing toward his mother. "Mav'ya," he says, "*please*, hear us out."

Soleiya simply glares at him, her power rife with outrage and hurt. She turns and walks away from us, along with Iris and almost all the Vu Trin and Amaz, save for Vang Troi, Freyja Zyrr, and the young, muscular Vu Trin runic sorceress with a dragon design shorn into her close-cropped hair.

Vang Troi lets out a Noi curse under her breath and narrows her eyes at all of us before looking straight at me and Yvan. "Well, you have my attention. So . . . *explain*."

Night falls before we finish our story. Vang Troi, Freyja, and the young Vu Trin sorceress have been permitted onto our walled-off side of the ledge, grouped now with my allies and me around a central crackling bonfire. The multicolored runes marking our Dyoi Forest's shielding shimmer against the star-flecked sky, Vogel's Shadow net a faint, ominous presence against the shield's runes. There's another distant bonfire glowing in the center of the ledge's northern edge, Vang Troi's forces grouped around it, all of them encased in a small, emerald-glowing dome-shield.

I lean back against the arm and wing Yvan has wrapped around me. I'm trembling, my grief for Lukas a dredged-up ache after conveying everything that happened, from Yvan's mock death at Mavrik's glamoured hands to Lukas's Realm-saving sacrifice. All the way to my abduction by the Dryads and merging into III.

"We align with the Forest, or we die," I roughly state to Vang Troi. Yvan's fire encircles me in a steady caress as I briefly meet Sylvan's grief-stricken gaze.

"Those are our choices," Yvan agrees. "Our only choices."

"They speak the truth," Yulan affirms, Ariel and Alder beside her, the injured heron hugging Yulan's side, its wing deftly branch-splinted by Ariel, the branches secured by Alder's conjured vines. Yulan sets her compassionate gaze on me. "Tell them what III revealed to you, Dryad'kin," she gently encourages, her words of acceptance stunning me, my heart clenching tight around them. I can sense my giant raven flock converging around me, as well as Raz'zor's bolstering line of invisible red flame.

I glance at Raz'zor, his eyes like two vermillion stars.

Speak, Dryad Witch, he prods in turn.

I look back to Vang Troi, Freyja, and the young Vu Trin soldier with the dragon shaved into her cropped hair who is named Hee Muur, or Heelyn, as some informally call her.

"III showed me that we need the impossible," I say, grief for the Great Tree tightening my throat. "We need a massive paradigm shift if we're going to win this war against the Shadow and have any type of future at all. We *all* need to heal our divisions and bind to the Forest." I gesture toward the East, toward Noilaan. "If, by some miracle, we can come together as Dryad'khin, we need to quickly draw on our combined power and the power of the trees to extend our Dyoi Forest shielding over the entire Eastern Realm. And then, we need to travel southeast with great haste to Voloi to gain the Noi Conclave's aid in bringing *everyone* in this Realm to the Forest."

Hee Muur narrows her dark gaze at me, incredulity twisting her features. "You truly want to bind everyone in the East to an increasingly *fragile* Forest?"

"Yes," I return. "Because if the Forest falls, we all fall." I look to Sylvan for guidance. He's gone very still, his pine green eyes fixed on me.

"Go on, Dryad," he quietly prods, sending a thin line of elemental energy out to my rootlines in a palpable show of support.

A swell of emotion tightens my throat in response to his display of alliance despite his terrible grief. An alliance I desperately want to prove myself worthy of.

"Vogel's Shadow Wand is growing in power," I say to Vang Troi, "but I think we can grow our power too." I briefly meet Yvan's gaze. "When Yvan joined with the Zhilaan Forest, I felt an increase in his power, and gained the ability to draw a line of that Forest's power through my lines. There might be some way for us all to intensify and connect our power in this way."

Yulan nods. "That's how Forest power works," she says. "Through connectivity. Link the trees' roots, and their power amplifies. Cut them off from each other, and their power diminishes."

"As Dryad'khin, I think we're the same as the trees," I say, looking pointedly toward Vang Troi's surviving forces gathered around the distant bonfire. "If we cut ourselves off from each other, our power diminishes." I turn back to Vang Troi. "And the Shadow wins."

"This is unwise," Freyja protests as she motions toward the leagues of Shadowed land. "We can't bind ourselves to something whose magic we don't understand that can be struck down in *one day*."

"I'll do it," Trystan suddenly announces, rising. Love for my brother wells up as I meet his staunch gaze. "I'll join with your Forest, Elloren," he quietly continues. "I feel like it's calling to me . . . its elemental power is tugging on my lines."

I nod shakily, going on instinct now, the safe, sure world gone. But the Living World . . . it's spread out before us.

Calling to us *all*.

Vothe is suddenly rising too. "I'm going with you," he tells Trystan, taking his hand, their invisible lightning auras crackling to life around each other. Vothe casts a glance at the tree line. "I feel a draw as well . . . like the draw I felt to keep coming back to the Zonor." He meets Trystan's eyes, a smile tugging at his onyx lips. "And like the draw I feel to you, my Xishlon'vir."

Trystan's magic surges toward Vothe, and the shifter's power meets it, full-on, in a storming caress. Hand in hand, they step toward the tree line, Sylvan and Yulan along with Alder, Rafe, Yvan, and I following.

Halting in front of the trees, Trystan and Vothe give each other one last, ardent look and place their palms on the same huge Dyoi Oak.

They disappear into the tree as one in a crackle of blue and white lightning and my chest is seized by emotion. I reach out to trace the hand-shaped marks filled with their powers' residual threads of lightning, concerned to be so suddenly parted from my younger brother, even though I've taken this journey myself.

Yvan's hand comes to my shoulder, his touch a warm caress. "They're going on faith," he assures me.

"We all are," Rafe agrees.

"I'll speak to your trees," Vang Troi suddenly announces as she stands.

"As will I," Bleddyn volunteers.

"I'll accompany you," Ra'Ven says to Bleddyn before turning to Sage. "I trust you, tia'lin. This message of alliance rings true."

"I'll join in the tree festivities, as well," Rivyr'el Talonir, the rainbow-decorated Elf, chimes in, tossing us all a dazzling grin as he gives Gwynn and Mavrik a look full of mischief. "I think a streak of color would look *spectacular* in my hair. You lot can keep your lofty reasons." And with that, Rivyr'el strides to the trunk of a huge oak and places his ivory, rainbow-nail-polished hand alongside Vang Troi's, Bleddyn's, and Ra'Ven's.

Before I can blink, they're all whisked into the trees, a spray of silver flashing against the trunk in Rivyr'el's wake.

Our bonfire gutters dark, and a weighty stillness descends. We all turn toward Hazel, his eyes once again morphed to full black.

"You best bring the entire East to the Forest quickly," Hazel urges, the ominous look on his face raising the hairs on my neck. "If Vogel destroys the slim amount of Natural Balance that's left," he warns, "Nature will slide into a Reckoning as merciless as the Shadow to try and regain it." A pained look tightens his features. "It will bring the full might of Death to wide swaths of the Natural World. And the power of *every single Deathkin* will be pulled into it."

CHAPTER THREE

DEATH FAE DREAM

Tierney Calix

Northern Vo River

Something dangerous is happening to Viger.

Jagged unease kindles along every one of Tierney's nerves. She glances up, just above their Vo shielding at the purple moon Or'myr conjured, full night descending. Her fingers wrap around the necklace vial containing her dissolved kelpies as her gaze slides back down toward the warded dome-shield she and her fellow Vo Guardians conjured. It envelopes the Vo River and its bracketing Forest, the shield's translucent surface and its scattered runes shimmering a faint purple from the sheer might of Or'myr's geomancy.

Tierney draws in a long breath, her unease mounting as she recalls how Viger slashed through the Shadow soldiers earlier, merciless as a viper. And then, after it was all over, how strangely agitated his power seemed to grow when they sensed the Great Tree III's destruction, the edges of Viger's Darkness feeling oddly wild and unmoored.

As night began to close in, Viger's magic surged to frighteningly potent heights, culminating in the full-Dark look he gave her—a look so chillingly violent it froze her in her tracks. Overcome by a terrifying sense of his Death thrall roaring toward her in an unfightable onslaught, she stepped back from him, alarmed, just as he managed to wrest hold of his power and yank it back from her before abruptly disappearing in a slash of dark mist, his thrall vanishing with him, his vaporous form darting into the Forest's nighttime hollows.

But Tierney can still sense Viger's Dark bond to her power—a bond linked to Or'myr and Fyordin as well—a thickening, night-deep longing stretching between all four of them, like a Dark tempest brewing.

THE DRYAD STORM

More unsettling still, Tierney is increasingly aware of Viger's bond drawing her power down toward the River's deepest, darkest recesses, mysterious places of cruel endings and fragile beginnings, their Xishlon kiss seeming to have awoken something primal within her.

Tierney's troubled gaze slides back to the violet Xishlon moon replica Or'myr defiantly hung above the Vo. An edge of her stress softens as she basks in the moon's purple glow, feeling, for a moment, like she's being suffused with the calming thrall of the *real* Xishlon moon, the unbidden urge to go to Or'myr and Fyordin and even dangerous Viger and pull each of them into a kiss abruptly surging.

Holy gods. Tierney stiffens against the scandalous bond-fueled urge, a flush blooming on her cheeks. *Get hold of yourself, Asrai!*

She glances sidelong at Or'myr, struggling to keep her thoughts from veering toward the first thrilling moments of the Xishlon kiss she shared with him before his purple lightning struck and everything went to all the hells.

He's standing a few paces away, facing a sizable stone hillock edging the riverbank that they're using as their Vo-shielding's central runic anchor point. Or'myr's arresting expression is tenacious as he casts bright violet runes onto the stone wall.

Tierney mulls over how Or'myr has taken charge of fortifying the Vo River's runic shielding, methodically setting up this area as a base for it, drawing on not only Tierney's, Fyordin's, and Viger's powers through their binding, but on the veins of purple running through the riverbank's stone. A line of Tierney's water power steadily courses toward Or'myr's runes and into the dome-shield, a shield she and Fyordin spent hours helping Or'myr fortify, and now she feels tapped out, exhaustion weighing her down like a leaden anchor. She considers striding into her Vo, curling up at its bottom and falling asleep in its arms, letting the gentle lap of the Waters restore her.

No, she realizes, her Asrai heart tightening. Tonight, she, Or'myr, and Fyordin were the ones doing the restoring. And Viger, too, before he took his frighteningly unhinged turn.

She glances out over the Vo and takes in Viger's Deathkin power, rising in dark, snaking tendrils from the contained section of Shadowed water, the water slowly taking on a purple coloration as it sheds the gray poison. Worry digs its claws into Tierney—if it took such a monumental effort to battle such a small section of Shadow, how can they possibly prevail against Vogel's full might?

As if sensing her tortured churn of emotion, Fyordin meets her gaze from where he's standing waist-deep in the Vo. His palms are resting on the water's surface as he feeds healing Asrai energy toward the Shadowed water from his depleted reserves, joining his magic to Viger's power to hasten the decomposition of the Shadow-killed river life.

Bringing Balance back to their Vo.

A wave of appreciation for her Asrai'kin eddies through her as she notes the way Fyordin's skin, like hers, is such a mirror of the Vo's water, both of them currently night dark and suffused with swirls of Or'myr's dark purple, Fyordin's hair and hers the same night-plum hue.

Fyordin holds her gaze, a flash of mutual fear for their kindred River roiling through their Vo bond. Fyordin's water power streams out to encircle hers in a bolstering caress, and Tierney lets herself melt into it, Fyordin's magical embrace rapidly whirlpooling into a heated longing that Tierney feels she could easily let herself funnel down into . . .

Or'myr's purple lightning shocks through the Deathbond with crackling, covetous energy, and Tierney stiffens at the sensation. Flustered, she glances at Or'myr and catches the unsettled lightning flashing through his gaze just as Viger's Darkness rushes in like a storm making landfall and crashes venomously against both Or'myr's lightning and Fyordin's whirlpooling caress with shockingly potent strength.

Tierney's temper flares, hard and hot—the strength of Viger's attack alarming, like he wants to sink his teeth into their power. Her hackles bristling, Tierney winds up her own storming power, tempest-tight, grits her teeth, and blasts it out against Viger's invading thrall.

A serpentine hiss shudders through her mind, the scene around her pulsing blacker than night. Viger's attack consolidates, a barrier of dark, gnashing fangs forming around the bond, keeping Or'myr's and Fyordin's powers at bay.

"Do you feel what's happening?" Tierney asks Or'myr, both alarmed and incensed.

Or'myr casts a glance at her, his eyes flashing dangerously. "It's a bit hard to miss."

Fyordin curses, glaring at them both before blasting out a powerful rush of his invisible water magic to crash against Viger's hold on their bond, Viger's biting Darkness outrageously entrenched.

"Your Death Fae is getting territorial," Or'myr comments, his tone wry, but the lightning flashing through his eyes spits fire. "He's lucky he has a skill set we currently need."

Or'myr's power surges, crackling through their bond to forcibly shift Viger's biting Darkness to purple. A tingle courses over Tierney's skin, but within the span of a breath, Viger's Darkness bites back down.

"I think he might be stronger than all of us," Tierney warns.

Or'myr's aura gives a hot, purple flare. "You underestimate me."

A shiver runs through Tierney, and it's not unpleasant, their locked gazes generating a disarming heat.

Stop falling into this bond! Tierney chastises herself as she wrenches her gaze away from Or'myr's only to have it snag on his entrancingly violet sorcerer hands. Tierney's thoughts scatter, both Or'myr's violet form and the riverbank's stone lit with a deep-purple runic glow that's so lush, a tendril of sensual heat curls through her, her River shot through with every dark shade of Or'myr's glorious *purple* . . .

A sudden realization floods her.

I've gained some of Or'myr's geo-draw to purple through Viger's bond.

She meets Or'myr's heated gaze once more, a tracery of lightning flashing over his lips, as if he can sense both her newfound color thrall and her flare of longing for him. He shakes his head and spits out what sounds like an Uriskal epithet before casting her a tortured look. "Do you know how hard it is to keep my wits about you now that you're . . . *purple?*"

Tierney's heart skips. Swallowing thickly, she glances toward Fyordin to find him farther into the Vo, his back to them, a jealous tension rippling through his water power.

"I . . . I'm not completely clear on what's happening between all of us," Tierney admits sheepishly.

"Oh, I've a few guesses," Or'myr offers. "I think that bond Viger set down in you during Xishlon is a primordial mating bond, and it's quickening. And now we're *all* caught up in it."

Tierney's power rears, a small storm cloud bursting to life above her. "I suspected as much," she sputters.

"I need to have a talk with him about the meaning of *consent*," Or'myr grits out with dangerous calm. "And by 'talk' I mean 'inflict great bodily harm.'" Tierney cocks a brow at this, as anger forks through Or'myr's eyes. "The only thing keeping me from going after him *right now*," Or'myr adds, "is the fact that the very large Dryad piece of me knows he helped us save a huge swath of Forest along the entire expanse of the Vo. Not to mention the Vo itself. Which is a lot more important than—" he swirls his hand agitatedly between the three of them "—*this* insanity."

Her brow knotting, Tierney glances at the grayed trees edging the Vo, Viger's tendrils of Darkness winding around their bases, their leaves slowly speckling with purple.

Viger's regenerative Death power battling back the gray.

"*I* need to have a talk with him," Tierney firmly states. "Where is he?"

A harder flash of lightning cracks through Or'myr's eyes. "I don't know where your Xishlon'vir is," he rigidly supplies, and Tierney hears him attempt but fail to keep the hurt from his tone. He draws in a deep breath and shakes his head, giving her a pained look. "I'm sorry, Tierney. Being bound to you like this . . . it's incredibly difficult."

Remorse rises inside her, mixed with the trauma of the night, a lump suddenly lodged in her throat over the invisible divide that stands between her and Or'myr. A divide that might not exist if their incompatible magic didn't make kissing, and possibly other types of touching, a lightning-charged agony.

Her pang of remorse tightens.

What must Or'myr think of her, now that he knows she kissed both him and Viger on Xishlon? And what must Fyordin think of her? A flustered aggravation quickly flares, overtaking her rush of cursed Gardnerian *shame*, because none of this matters *one whit*. Not compared to saving the Natural World.

But still, having a primordial Death Fae *mating* bond set down without her consent—that most certainly *does* matter.

Her troubled emotions gathering into a fitful tide, Tierney brings one hand to her hip as she turns and peers into the Forest's darkness. She can *feel* Viger's directional pull through his fang-deep hold on the bond, a subtle tether of his Darkness fastened to her power's core.

Blast this, Tierney curses as she turns and strides toward the purpling woods, a protective flare of Or'myr's and Fyordin's powers encircling her. Fighting the urge to let her power return their embraces, she shoves off their magic with an aggravated burst of water power and strides into the Forest toward Viger at a rapid clip, shoving a hand into her tunic's pocket to retrieve the small purple runic stone that Or'myr magicked for her earlier to light the night.

She's only a few paces into the woods when her sense of Viger's pull vanishes, as if wrested from her grasp. She pauses, frustration burgeoning. The night air is cool, insects chirring, as she casts about for a sense of Viger's aura of Darkness, but . . . nothing.

She curses under her breath. Viger could be *anywhere*.

THE DRYAD STORM

A sudden idea lights.

Stilling, Tierney closes her eyes and draws in a deep breath, her hand coming to the vial around her neck as she focuses inward on her fear for the Vo and her iron-injured kelpies, and for her multitude of kindred river creatures and all the Waters of Erthia.

She can feel Viger's awareness prick up like an antenna's subtle lift as he connects to her fear, but he makes no move to enthrall her or draw her in. She senses his shiver of resentment, but also, the subtle pull toward his location.

Stalking forward, she fumes, resentment welling over everything Viger didn't tell her about their bond but *should have.*

Her sense of his energy strengthening, she finds him in a small clearing, crouching on the ground, his hornless head angled down, eyes closed, claws in, ravens perched all around him.

His palms to the earth.

Her primal attraction to him quickens, and she remembers how he fought off the Shadow forces, all teeth and claws and Dark Deathkin power, warmth rushing to a place she has no wish for it to be.

Why in all the hells would you be drawn in by that, she chastises herself.

Mortified by his effect on her, gnashing her teeth against it, she halts before him.

Viger's gaze slowly rises to meet hers, the ravens and the surrounding trees washed in the purple glow of her runic stone. Keeping his midnight eyes fixed on her, Viger whispers a stream of words to the ravens in a language she doesn't comprehend, his hiss like an insidious wind that she can feel winding around her ribs and everything surrounding them.

Viger quiets, and the ravens take off as one, their multitude of wings beating down on the air, while he remains low to the ground, palms to the soil.

Everything empties from Tierney's head except one, churning thought.

"Is it true you set down a Death Fae mating bond between us?" she demands, condemnation swelling in a fierce tide. She slashes out a hand at him, like an axe leveled. "Be straight with me, Viger. Because I need to trust you completely if I'm going to fight for my River with you. And I will never trust you again if you're not honest with me, *right now.*"

Viger rises, so quickly that Tierney recoils, one second on the Forest floor and the next, standing less than a breath away, the night's darkness seeming to pull in around them both.

"We kissed," he bites out, his pitch-black eyes narrowing. "A Deathbond has been formed."

Tierney's flare of ire crackles hotter. "So . . . that means *what*? That you'll devour my dreams now? That you'll devour *me*?"

His lips curl with obvious disdain. "No."

Tierney glares at him, incensed. "But you *could*?"

Viger narrows his coal-dark stare on her as his horns rise and sharpen. "Yes, Asrai." He flashes his teeth as his thrall pulses Darker, the whole world blackening, including the whites of his center-of-Erthia eyes, but Tierney is undaunted.

"Careful, Viger," she snaps, drawing confrontationally nearer, "I might invade your dreams, as well. And we'll have a little talk. A violent *storm* is likely to be involved!"

She's suddenly swept up in a more intense blur of Dark and she gasps, gravity itself cutting out, Viger's thrall swirling around them as the ground gives way.

"Then invade them, Asrai," he challenges.

A shiver goes through Tierney, but she refuses to cower or give in to the urge to buckle and fall straight into him.

"You should have warned me," she throws down, her voice breaking around the tide of her anger. "You should have told me *exactly* what kissing you meant. Now get your thrall off me and *set me down*."

In an instant, she's back on solid ground, teetering a bit from a rush of vertigo. Viger scowls, his sharpened teeth fully bared, his purple forked tongue flickering out in warning.

Intimidation fires inside Tierney, but she ignores it as an inexplicable hurt rises. "I thought we were *friends*." Her voice seems to split apart at the seams.

Viger gives her a mocking look. "You seek friendship with *Death*?"

The hurt digs in deeper. "No, with *you*," she exclaims, voice breaking.

"You understand *nothing*," he snarls, low and menacing, his elongated teeth snapping. "You do not understand what we Deathkin will be forced to do if Nature's Balance gives way. What I'm already being drawn toward. Nature is *upending*. And we will bring the *Reckoning*. The death of crops. Pestilence. Sickness. A tide of Death the world has *never before seen*."

"Then work to keep it at bay," she cries, "like you're helping us keep the Shadow at bay!"

"If the Balance unravels, it cannot be kept at bay!" he hisses, eyes wild. "Death Fae are beings of *primordial power*. We do not fight for any alliance, no matter what this bond-linkage has wrought. We fight for Natural *Death*. And if the people of Erthia upend the Matrix, *Natural Death will come*. Our Reckoning will rise to fight both the Shadow Death and Nature's Unbalancing, and you will be torn apart by our sickle!"

Tierney takes a stumbling step back, a shiver of intense fear coursing through her hurt and confusion. "But . . . we're *allied*."

Viger leans in, lip lifting in a snarl as multiple snakes appear and slither around his shoulders, all of them hissing at Tierney, fangs bared. "I am *Deathkin*," he snarls, his voice vibrating straight through her. "I am *cruel*. I am every reality you are afraid to face. I am every cherished belief *destroyed*. Do not come to me if you seek comfort or consolation. Do not come to me for kindness or friendship or alliance. You will find *no* solace here."

And with that, he turns into mist and flows into the night, a tendril of his Darkness trailing behind him.

Distraught, Tierney stumbles back to her Vo a distance away from *everyone*. She dives into it, blasting away Fyordin's then Or'myr's incoming flashes of protective, questioning power, making it clear that she wants them to *stay away*.

The Vo enfolds her as she glides toward its bed, her emotions a tempestuous mess, her full fury whirling around Viger Maul's unexpected cruelty.

Have I misjudged him all this time?

Fear rises that Viger is not truly aligned with her beautiful River but with Death above all, ready to send a wave of killing might over everything. Not in the way Vogel would, with demonic power and multi-eyed beasts, but by raining down sickness and famine and cruel natural Death, he and his fellow Deathkin scything through everything she and her allies are trying to salvage and protect.

Everything on Erthia worth fighting for.

Tierney stares up through the water for a long time, her eyes focused on Or'myr's wavering purple moon orb until weariness begins to pull her under. *Does Viger even sleep?* she wonders as she sinks closer to a troubled slumber, her thoughts churning around Viger's cold words. She has no idea where he sleeps, if he does. He's the most solitary being she's ever met.

Solitary as Death.

She closes her eyes and recklessly searches for the bond Viger laid down with his kiss, bristling with offense that even her dreams are no longer her own. But still, she can't get the image of him fighting off Shadow soldiers out of her mind, a terror and a wonder to behold as he drove off Mage and Marfoir power.

Helping her to save her River.

Despite Viger's chilling words, she can't help but remember that glimpse, through his kiss on Xishlon, of how his terrifying magic supports the entirety of the Natural Matrix, the decay and Death giving rise to all new Life, their kiss a mind-bending revelation, leaving her clear about his complexities. But his frightening words . . . she sensed truth there too.

Are you really so cruel, Viger? Tierney frets, remembering the edges of besotted tenderness in his Xishlon kiss. And suddenly, despite her ire, the desire to find him rises once more. Searching for their link to no avail, she starts a slow slide toward sleep . . . then abruptly finds it.

Jolted into wakefulness, she tenses, hyperaware of a thin Dark thread in the Deathbond's center, bound to the deepest recess of her mind.

The dream tether.

It's subtle as the pull of a single strand of spider silk, taut and firmly affixed.

Tierney runs her mind along it as it loosens . . . then slackens.

He's going to sleep, Tierney realizes, astonished to be able to sense this so clearly through the tether. Pulse quickening, she slows her breathing and focuses on the slackening binding, then lets herself fall right into that slender strand, the surrounding world dissolving, Viger's Darkness collapsing in . . .

Abruptly she's on her feet and in another nighttime location, surrounded by green-leafed trees instead of purple.

The Western Realm.

Disoriented, she peers through foliage toward a clearing just beyond. There's a cottage in its center, its windows glowing with amber light.

A tall youth garbed in black disembarks from a carriage and stalks purposefully toward the cottage, his cloak billowing dramatically behind him.

Tierney gives a hard start.

Because it's *Viger*. But . . . a much younger Viger. Perhaps around fourteen. Pale and skinny. But hints of the emerging man are there in the square lines of his jaw, his imposing height. The intensity in his Dark eyes.

A chill pricks at Tierney's skin. *I'm in his dream.*

A fuller realization hits. *The tether he set down in his kiss . . . it goes both ways.*

The eerie Dark of Viger's thrall ripples over her, but it's not controlled and contained. It pulses fitfully, triggering a jolt of fear and despair that tightens her chest. Stunned by the out-of-control potency of teenage Viger's aura, she stands her ground and ignores the instinct to turn and run from him.

His dark form is trailed by a middle-aged Keltish couple—an emaciated brown-haired woman clinging to the arm of a broad bearded man. The bearded man's face is set in a stern-approaching-furious expression, his gaze pinned on Viger's back.

Tendrils of black smoke appear below the hem of Viger's cloak, curling and undulating toward the couple, as if he's trying to scare them into fleeing from him.

Tierney's entire body breaks into gooseflesh as she's hit by side-tendrils of Viger's mist. The scene shudders, the edges of the sky momentarily contracting. Everything stills, no birds, no insects, no trace of a breeze, Viger's ominous wall of quiet pressing down.

The cottage door opens, and a white-haired older Keltish woman appears in the lantern-lit entryway. Her calm, kind voice rings out. "This must be Viger. Come in, come in." Her unflappable composure surprises Tierney. It's as if the woman doesn't notice Viger's eerie black mist or his aura's thrall of frightening doom.

Viger and the couple enter the cottage, Viger's dark fog sucked in behind them as the door snaps shut.

Tierney lets out a breath she didn't realize she was holding as slowly, tentatively, the normal night sounds resume—an owl hoots, followed by a chorus of peepers then the thrum of insects, the chill prickling Tierney's skin receding as the night smooths out.

Tierney creeps toward the cottage and enters it through the back door, walking silently through a dim jarred-goods storeroom, fragrant herbs drying overhead. She nears the amber light spilling from the edges of a slightly open door and peers into a rustic kitchen. She immediately spots young Viger, now seated at the central wooden table, his hands clasped before him, pale face hood-shrouded as he stares fixedly at the oak table before him, his swirling black mist orbiting his straight-backed frame.

The older woman is leaning back against a wooden counter, her hands planted on it. A slender gray-haired Keltish man of about her same age stands beside her, his bespectacled visage intelligent and kindly, the couple's gazes on the angry bearded man as he holds forth.

"You've got to take him back," the bearded man insists with a swipe of his arm toward young Viger. "He's no good. He's got the demonic in him."

"He wasn't always like this," the emaciated woman nervously counters. She's sobbing a little as she speaks, her arms wrapped around her scarily thin frame as if she's desperate for self-comfort. She looks to the white-haired woman, a pleading expression on her sickly face. "He's got good in him. I know he does. When we first took him in, he was such a sweet little boy."

"He was never a *sweet boy*," the man refutes with a vicious sneer. "He was off right from the start." He jabs a thick finger at Viger. "Up all night. Asleep all day. *Peering* out from corners. Like a demon from a nightmare. Eating spoiled food." He crosses his muscular arms in front of himself, eyes set on the bespectacled man, as if only a man will see sense here. "We caught him taking things from the *garbage*." He glances at Viger, his gaze narrowed. "Frightening, is what he is and always was."

"He's quiet and artistic," the woman insists, her voice choked with tears.

The man gapes at her. "He drew multiple pictures of giant gray clouds with horrible eyes devouring villages like a demonic tide, a black tide rising up from the ground to batter against it! Those aren't normal things for a child to be drawing!"

The emaciated woman shakes her head, her mouth a trembling grimace. "He's good. I *know* he's good. You don't see him for what he is. You never did." She looks at Viger, desperation washing over her face. "Viger, why won't you talk to me? I want you *home*."

The man jabs his finger at the youth once more, his expression venomous. "That . . . *thing* can never step foot inside my house again." He rounds on the woman. "Or I will call the Mage Council, Rosalie. I *swear* I will."

The dark thrall winding around motionless Viger ripples out over the floor, thickening. The bearded man lets out a low oath and steps back, but the black mist slithers over his foot.

"You see what he does?" the bearded man cries to the older couple, a slight tremor to his voice. "He's *evil*, I tell you!"

"Please," Rosalie begs the couple, "you need to believe me—he's not what Goryl thinks he is."

"He's *exactly* what I think he is," Goryl hisses at her.

"The Fae have ways that differ from ours," the bespectacled man pipes up diplomatically. But I notice he's regarding Viger warily. The white-haired woman, on the other hand, is fixedly eyeing Goryl, pointedly ignoring the dark mist snaking around her ankles and undulating over the entire kitchen floor.

Rosalie is sobbing harder now, her head falling into her hands. "He's good with animals—kind to them," she murmurs brokenly.

Goryl makes a sound of disgusted incredulity. "Are you going to tell them what *type* of animals, Rosa?"

"No, but—"

"Tell them what *type*, Rosalie."

She looks up and meets his eyes, her face a mask of misery.

"I'll tell you what type," Goryl snarls, turning back to the shocked-looking couple. "Bats. Ravens. Scavengers. Every vile animal you can think of. *Wolves*." He swirls the air with his finger. "Sniffing round the house. We caught him with a *whole pack of them*. More than once. Circled round him, they did. Like he was some *dark lord*. It was *twisted*." He glares at Rosalie. "Should I tell them about the spiders?"

She shoots him a pained, pleading look before glancing imploringly toward the older couple, her cowed voice fading to a whisper. "He's quiet and thoughtful. He's smarter than most—reads everything he can get his hands on—"

"And what does he pick out from it? Hmmm?" Goryl demands. "Marks every page that has to do with death. Or disease. *That's* what he reads." He taps the side of his temple with a finger. "He's sick in the head. Maybe more than sick."

Viger endures it all calmly, black eyes alarmingly feral, his form still and silent. Like Death.

Goryl makes the Ancient One's star sign of holy protection on his chest, murmuring a prayer.

Seeming overcome, Rosalie suddenly rushes through the mist toward Viger. She grasps his arm, but he doesn't look at her. "I know you're good in you," she cries. She looks to Goryl, pleading. "Remember when he nursed the bats?"

"No normal boy has a small sanitarium for ravens and bats!" he booms back. "No normal family has bats flying 'bout the house!"

"He's *not* normal! But he's not *bad*!"

"A mother's love is an all too forgiving thing!"

"As a father's should be!"

Viger rises in one blindingly fast motion. The entire room seems to shudder and contract as his eyes turn solid black and he sets them on Goryl, horns rising from his head.

"YOU. ARE. NOT. MY. FATHER."

Viger's deep voice echoes from every corner of the room, the Dark force of it sending a vicious chill straight through Tierney, and she takes a step back, her heart quickening.

Seeming frightened now, Goryl makes the Ancient One's protection sign on his chest once more before he sets his rattled gaze back on the older couple. "I rue the day I ever let this *thing* in my house."

"Don't speak of him like that!" Rosalie cries, grabbing Viger's arm again as his Dark power whips around the room, sucking Tierney into its thrall, filling her thoughts with death and despair.

Rosalie throws her arms around Viger. "I'm so sorry, my beautiful boy. I'm so sorry. I love you, my sweet one."

"Do you see?" Goryl cries out to the couple. "He has her under his *thrall*."

Viger suddenly grips Rosalie's arms and pushes her back with obvious, otherworldly strength. "Mother, you've got to let me go." His face is devoid of feeling, his eyes a piercing abyss.

"She's not your mother!" Goryl snarls. "She never was, and she never will be! Your mother is *dead*, and it's probably a good thing, too, if she could bring forth the likes of you!"

"Please stop," the older white-haired women shakily states, holding up her palm.

Viger slowly turns back to Goryl. A chilling grin forms on his face, his eyes filling with Dark power, his thrall expanding to fill the cottage's expanse with a suffocating force that Tierney can feel pressing against her lungs.

Viger lunges toward his mother, and Tierney flinches in shock as he grabs Rosalie by the back of her neck and sinks his teeth into the base of her throat, dark mist flowing from the edges of his mouth.

Chaos breaks out.

Goryl and the older couple spring forward to grab Viger, struggling to pull him off Rosalie. She shudders and convulses, her eyes lolling backward, before Viger releases her, all the Dark mist in the room snuffing out.

Goryl punches Viger in the face. Hard. Sending Viger to the floor, blood streaming from his nose.

"Only for *her* did I not slay you," Goryl growls at a crumpled Viger. "Stay away from my family, freak! You *hear me*? The Mage Council is right about you lot!"

Rosalie is staring at Viger, dazed, her hand cradling the base of her throat. "The pain in my hip is gone," she marvels to Viger in a rasp. "What did you do?"

Viger pushes himself up from the ground, his grim gaze fixed on his mother. "When I come into my fullness, I will return for you."

Rosalie seems to barely register his words as she clutches her hip, then her abdomen. "The lumps . . . they're *gone*. What did you do to me, my son?"

"No," Goryl snarls, grabbing her arm. "No more falling into his thrall. This ends *now*."

With that, he drags Rosalie out of the cottage and into the night, slamming the door behind them.

Stunned, Tierney looks at young Viger, two snakes now twining around his shoulders as he stares the older couple down with unnerving, emotionless focus even as blood streams over his lips and chin.

"Here," the woman says, retrieving a cloth and dampening it before offering it to Viger. "For . . . for your face." But she seems scared now, and Viger makes no move to take the cloth.

"Well, Viger," the bespectacled man says stiltedly. He clears his throat, his wariness of the horned teen before him evident on his face. He motions to a room at the end of a narrow hallway. "We've prepared a room for you. You . . . you must be tired."

In a blur, Viger is on his feet and striding down the hall, his dark cloak billowing behind him. He reaches the room, enters, and firmly shuts the door behind him.

The couple stares in his direction for a good, long moment before the man turns to the white-haired woman. "What is he, Emilin?" he asks in a tremulous whisper.

She swallows. "Primordial Death Fae."

The man sucks in a long breath, fear in his gaze. "We can't have a Death Fae living here with us . . ."

"He has nowhere else to go."

The man shakes his head. "Emilin . . . I'm sorry, no. The Asrai and Lasair Fae . . . that was one thing. *This* is entirely different. You can tell him in the morning. He *has* to go."

With that, the man walks out, leaving the woman alone. She stands there for a long moment before she, too, casts one last anguished look toward Viger's room, then turns and follows the man out.

Tierney is frozen, her heart in her throat.

Forcibly getting hold of herself, she creeps through the kitchen and down the dimly lit hall, dark mist seeping out from under the door before her. The closer she gets to it, the more she can feel the troubling vibration of fear and sorrow in Viger's thrall.

Tentatively she takes hold of the cool, metal doorknob and turns it, pulling the door open.

Tierney draws in a quick breath as she finds Viger sprawled out on a bed, facedown, cradling his horned head tightly in his arms as he sobs, chest heaving. A multitude of serpents are slithering over his prone form, more slinking in from the slightly ajar window, as if seeking to offer him solace, but he doesn't acknowledge them, so great is his misery. Tierney's chest tightens with kindred sorrow, a fierce compassion for him cinching her gut. Sympathetic tears fill her eyes as she remembers being ripped away from her Fae parents when she was so small. Remembers how her mother screamed her name as Tierney's painfully glamoured three-year-old self was dragged away.

Forcing back the nightmarish memory, Tierney snaps herself away from the dream tether, the world blurring as she's thrust back under the Vo, breathing in gulp after gulp of water as she opens her eyes, her river-slicked gaze burning with emotion. She sits up, the Vo's cool water streaming around her body as she's filled with the desperate urge to find Viger.

She closes her eyes and concentrates, more easily locating their tether this time and latching hold of it. She burrows deep until she can sense a small, subtle pull toward Viger through the woods. Decided, she swims toward the bank, emerges, and releases her restless kelpies from her necklace's vial into a small, sheltered pool beside the Vo, then whisks the water from her form and follows his dream's pull.

Tierney finds Viger deep in the woods, facedown on the ground, covered in serpents and sobbing in his sleep. Her hand flies to her mouth in anguished surprise. Falling to her knees beside him, she touches his shoulder, his snakes slithering agitatedly over her hand. "Viger . . ."

He swings around and grabs her wrist, instantly awake and hissing along with his serpents, his horns arcing up, his claws digging painfully into her skin, his eyes full Dark and teeth snapping, his face slick with black tears.

A shocked recognition flashes through his eyes and he instantly loosens his grip and retracts his claws and horns, his eyes regaining their whites, his breathing labored.

Tierney gapes at him. She's never seen him look so young and vulnerable. "You healed her, didn't you?" she manages, sliding her wrist out of his grip to take hold of his hand.

He moves to pull away but she tightens her grip, and he allows it, pain slashing through his eyes. "I did," he admits, voice rough and resonant.

"How did you do it, Viger?" she prods, her heart going out to him.

He grimaces and gives her a harsh look before his mouth lifts in a horrible rictus grin. For a moment, Tierney's mind is filled with visions of maggots. Of decaying flesh. A spider piercing its prey with venom. Her own body decaying in the center of Erthia . . .

"*Stop it,*" she firmly grits out, keeping tight hold of him. "Stop trying to push me away. How did you save her, Viger? *Tell* me."

A subtle flinch before his gaze takes on a morbid tension. "Life was killing her," he finally says, his lips quivering into a fierce scowl. "Life *unchecked* . . . growing and eating and consuming and blossoming into its *hideous fullness.*" A furious glint fills his eyes as his gaze knifes into her. "I *killed* it."

Tierney pulls in a long, harsh breath. "And saved her."

Viger gives a subtle nod. "Yes, Asrai."

"What . . . happened?" Tierney asks. "Did you ever see her again?"

Viger's face twists. "I tried to go back. But her wretched husband convinced her that it was my leaving that cured her. The removal of the demonic so the Ancient One could restore her. And then . . . they reported me to the Mages."

"Oh, gods, Viger."

They're quiet as she regards him. No horns, claws, or fangs. No thrall.

Just Viger.

Inky tears glistening on his cheeks. Dark circles weighing down his eyes.

Another black tear courses down his pale face. "I don't want to bring the Reckoning," he rasps, an abyss of misery in his gaze. "I don't want to kill you or your Waters."

Tierney nods, her own tears brimming. "I believe you." An idea lights, deep in Tierney's core. "Come with me," she offers as she cradles his hand.

He nods, seeming too choked up to say more, which both stuns and pains Tierney anew. Decided, she releases his hand, gets up, then holds her hand out to him once more.

Viger hesitates, then takes her outstretched hand and rises, his midnight eyes meeting hers, the bottomless sorrow glistening in them strengthening Tierney's resolve. Silently, she leads him to an isolated bank of the Vo and then into it, heading toward its center.

The Vo's night-dark waters close in around their legs, waists, and abdomens before flowing over their heads. Tierney keeps firm hold of Viger's hand as she leads him down, down, down to the bottom of her River, all the way to the deepest point of the Vo's silty bed.

And then Tierney pulls Viger onto the River's floor and into a close embrace, his arms wrapping tightly around her.

He clings to her in the darkness, and Tierney can feel his powerful, pent-up emotion, leagues deep, pulsing through her and around her as she holds on, a shiver running through his long form.

A sudden vertigo sweeps through her.

The River's bed gives way as Viger pulls her down into it, tunnelling deep into the earth before they both still, their small, cavernous space lit up a dim silver as Tierney draws back a fraction and meets Viger's impassioned gaze, stunned to find she can still breathe so deep inside Erthia's depths.

She draws him into a close embrace once more and can feel the loosening of his breath against her neck as she's filled with the sense of natural Death thrumming through the earth, through her River above, the Magedom's Void Death driven off by it. The River's Balance tenuously restored.

But she can also feel Viger's pain and unguarded fear over being nature's Great Balancer and what that might mean for his immediate future.

"Those pictures you drew as a teen," Tierney whispers. "You were drawing your fear of a Reckoning, weren't you?"

Viger nods against the side of her face.

"The Shadow is throwing off the Balance," she continues, losing herself to their joint upsweep of emotion. And their joint upsweep of *fear*. "It's not *you* throwing it off. I know you fear for my River as much as I do."

He nods again and draws back a fraction, a grim Darkness passing through his gaze. "There's only one way to stave off a full Reckoning," he says in a rough whisper, "if Nature's Balance is destroyed."

Tierney waits, heart in her throat.

"To dissolve myself completely into the Natural Matrix."

Tierney's pulse stutters. "Would it kill you?"

"Only if the Shadow Death wins."

A terrible silence descends.

"And if it doesn't win?" Tierney asks, voice tight as she takes in the stark glint in Viger's eyes.

"I'd reemerge," he says, his voice weighted with a chilling finality. "In a hundred years or more."

Her breath catches. "Are you immortal?"

His gaze on her intensifies. "Yes, Asrai. As are you."

Tierney startles at this, shaking her head in solid refute. "Viger, I'm Asrai."

"You have a much stronger Deathkin line than I realized. I knew there was a sliver of primordial lineage in you, or you would not have bonded to Deathkin kelpies. But it's much more than a sliver. When we kissed on Xishlon, I thought I would be able to stave off a permanent binding between us. But your Deathkin line . . . it overtook the Balance between us when you pulled on your full power battling the V'yexwraith, and I wasn't able to hold back from a full Deathkin mating bond."

Tierney's heart thuds against her chest as she senses, through his line of fear, the truth of his words. That he never meant to create such an intense bond between them.

"You told me that Deathkin don't pair with other Deathkin," she counters, confused.

His eyes ink over, a spark igniting in them. "Not when the Balance is veering toward chaos. The draw becomes too . . . *wild*. If we were to give in to this bond, it could pull us both into Nature's Reckoning."

Longing ripples through their bond, and Tierney senses Viger swiping it back, emotional pain rushing in behind it. And fear. Incredible fear. Tierney follows his line of fear, stunned by what she finds at its base. Three words, buried deep. All his fears swirling around them.

A tear streaks down her cheek, and she can sense it's as inky black as his own. "I think I understand," she says, lifting her palm to his tear-slicked cheek.

Viger lets out a shuddering exhale, his mouth trembling before he nods and draws her close, pressing his tear-damp lips to her neck in an impassioned, tongue-flickering kiss that sets Tierney's heart racing.

And then he stills against her and tugs gently on their dream tether.

The faint, silvery light cuts out, the two of them dissolving into entwined mist before they fall into a deep, Deathkin sleep, both of them soon caught up in nightmares filled with clouds of gray with multiple eyes ready to consume Erthia whole.

CHAPTER FOUR

ICE WITCH

Marcus Vogel

The newly annexed Gardnerian province of Issaan
The Holy Magedom's central continent

Vogel steps toward the center of the dais at the head of Issaan's Sun Hall, its heathen sand-gold hue cleansed by the Magedom's Shadow to gray, the taunting purple moons Or'myr Syll'vir conjured into being above this newly annexed land finally blasted away.

Yes, he's received messages that more purple moons have burst into being over Valgard and other Gardnerian provices. The geomancy Or'myr Syll'vir sent through the Wand's V'yexwraith has been surprisingly difficult to subdue, slyly embedded as it is, through the Shadow Wand's huge network of branching tethers.

Let Edwin Gardner's bastard rockbat of a son have his moment, Vogel seethes. He'll inevitably be ripped to shreds by the Magedom's Shadow.

Gratified by the thought, Vogel stills, lifts his Shadow Wand, and conjures a suspended, steel-hued voice-amplification rune to hover in the air just below his chin.

A sea of Mage soldiers stand straight-backed and silent before him in neat rows, several of his high-level commanders gathered around him in a semicircle, including Fallon and Damion Bane, the power in the room burning with euphoric, violent triumph. The Magedom's huge black flag flaps above them, just beyond the hall's domed glass ceiling, the Ancient One's white bird sewn into its center.

"Most Holy Mages," Vogel booms, his voice shot through with zealous triumph, "our annexation of the continent's entire center will soon be achieved."

A victorious roar erupts, echoing off the curving walls of the domed interior. The sound triggers a silver blaze of excitement through Vogel's power, the muscles of his back straining against it. He glances at the roiling slate clouds gathering above, his Shadow-portal journey from the stump of the Great Heathen Tree to newly conquered Issaan over in the time of a breath. His Shadow Wand's new ability to conjure lag-free portals has been a revelation, new powers emerging as the Wand's power grows, all of it further proof of the Ancient One's blessing of the Magedom's Holy Might.

And the Magedom's unstoppable march east.

A disturbance sounds at the far end of the hall's long, central aisle, drawing everyone's attention. Vogel narrows his gaze at the black-bearded Mage stepping into view at the aisle's distant terminus. Several Level Five Mages have closed in around the man, wands drawn, troubled murmuring kicking up.

"Your Excellency," one of the Mages calls out over the distance via his own hastily conjured amplification rune, "the Magedom's agricultural advisor, Mage Warren Gaffney, seeks an audience. He refuses our order to stay back. Says he brings dire news that cannot wait."

"Lower your weapons, " Vogel benevolently commands as he beckons Warren Gaffney forward. "Approach, Mage," he prods, concealing the spite crackling to life through his power. *This* is the Mage who spawned the light sorcerer Sagellyn Za'Nor, mother to an Icaral demon and ally to the Stae'nen Witch.

Warren Gaffney's gaze darts around as he heads down the aisle, the thud of his boots on the stone echoing through the silent chamber as he strides toward the dais and stills before Vogel.

"Your Excellency," Warren Gaffney starts, forcibly straightening. "I bring news of Gardneria's food supply. The Shadow power cast over Amazakaraan has spread west. A dark cloud of Shadow now covers Gardneria's northernmost reaches, blocking sunlight and raining ash onto Mage fields. And the Magedom's Shadow sea military exercises in the Voltic Sea . . . our fishermen there are bringing in corrupted catches, the fish poisoned and inedible, many with multiple eyes." His eyes focus on the Wand in Vogel's hand. "We're starting to fear that if this contagion spreads, it will bring famine to large sections of Gardneria."

A tense stillness descends, every ounce of elemental Magery in the hall shivering expectantly toward Vogel.

"A sacrifice," Vogel finally states, calm and final.

Warren Gaffney blinks at Vogel. "A sacrifice, Your Excellency?"

"A *sacrifice*," Vogel repeats, enunciating the word. "'The Ancient One's own must walk through the Reaping Times' Shadow before they can emerge into His

Holy Renewal.'" A beatific smile lifts Vogel's lips. "When the Reaping Times are over and the Prophecy has been fulfilled, all will be cleansed and transformed, as the *Book* assures us. The waters will run clean. The air will be purified and your fields, my Blessed Mage, will turn gold with grain."

Warren Gaffney's brow knits tight. "But, Excellency, if there isn't enough *food*—"

"Where is your faith, Mage?" Vogel quietly cuts in.

A dangerous silence overtakes the vast hall, fear flashing across Warren Gaffney's face. "In the Ancient One above," comes his rattled reply. "But, Your Grace, how will the Prophecy be fulfilled with our Black Witch lost to us?"

Vogel smiles. "It will be fulfilled because the Magedom's True, Blessed Black Witch has risen." Vogel turns toward Fallon with bright, predatory interest and is stopped short by her *eyes* . . . they're bright as ice daggers, and they meet his without one speck of intimidation.

Vogel suppresses a shiver, overcome by the heady sense of Fallon drawing up her power, her lines churning with lethal wind and killing cold, her ferocious desire for vengeance *begging* to give way.

Good, Vogel thinks, approval searing through his lines. *I need your thirst for revenge. To annihilate the Whore Witch and her Icaral demon.*

"Show them, my Black Witch," Vogel charges, as his silver-dark fire aura strains toward Fallon. "Show them the power that is bringing the heathens to their *knees*."

Fallon's mouth lifts into a frigid smile before she unsheathes her wand, raises it, and murmurs a spell low in her throat.

A chill wind whips up to encircle her, buffeting her dark garments, her raven hair. A *CRACK* sounds, triggering a collective flinch, a shiver of excitement racing through Vogel, as ice blasts from Fallon's wand to collide with the empty middle of the central aisle.

A huge column of ice bolts up from the point of impact, Mages nearby jolting to their feet to stumble away from it as the column rapidly branches out to form a gigantic ice tree, the air markedly cooling.

Fallon's gorgeous icy-green eyes flash to Vogel's before she murmurs another spell, and the ice tree's branches slam down onto the side aisles in impaling sprays of gravel, shocked sounds erupting as the Mages near the collisions jump back. Smaller ice branches crackle into being at each impaling branch's terminus, spindly soldiers made of ice forming and rising, higher than any human.

The soldiers crack themselves off from the branches, Fallon's ice army encircling the hall now. As one, they look to Fallon with gray-glowing eyes, and the air turns even *colder.*

Vogel's power shivers with excitement as it sizzles against Fallon's frigid magic, his every line *straining* to send fire into perhaps the greatest Ice Witch Erthia has ever known. "My Blessed Black Witch," he intones, "My True Black Witch, the Prophecy rests with you."

Vogel flicks his finger at Warren Gaffney, and Fallon nods once before thrusting her wand toward the Mage.

The ice soldiers leap clear over the crowd, carried on great gusts of wind power, and land around Mage Gaffney.

"No," Mage Gaffney pleads with Vogel. "Excellency, *please . . .*"

The ice soldiers thrust their finger-spears into Warren Gaffney.

"Aughhh!" he screams, then gurgles, then is silent as his bugged-out green eyes shift to frigid gray, his body icing over before shattering into a pile of bloodied shards.

The hall rustles with agitated emotion, a combination of zealous satisfaction and fearful awe stark in the air.

"'Entertain not a disbeliever,'" Vogel intones before he raises his Shadow Wand, bolts out a blast of silver-dark fire at Warren Gaffney's icy remains and quickly renders them to char.

Vogel turns to Fallon once more in unspoken command.

Nodding, Fallon thrusts her wand forward, and her ice soldiers and tree all blast into mist that's absorbed, in a sweep of gray frost, into Fallon's wand.

Vogel scans the now silent sea of Mages. Raising his free hand, he thumps his fist lightly against the white bird marking the chest of his uniform. "Pray with me, Mages."

Vogel launches into the prayer—"Oh Blessed Ancient One. Purify our minds. Purify our hearts. Purify Erthia from the stain of the Evil Ones."

The entire hall joins in reverentially, violence thrumming through the prayer, an ocean of unstoppable Mage power rising.

Vogel senses the ice-cold rush of Fallon's approach before she sweeps into the Sun Hall's command tower, a panoramic view of Issaan's Shadowed expanse visible through the tower's ring of huge floor-to-ceiling oval windows.

Seeking a private audience with his Black Witch, Vogel flicks his finger at the two glamoured pyrr-demon soldiers bracketing the hall's arching entrance. The demons exit, shutting the grayed door behind them.

Vogel surveys his beautiful Ice Witch and breathes in her glorious scent of icy wind as she stills, her power increasingly grayed by the Shadow Wand's linkage to her lines.

"You will deploy back south and annex all of Southern Ishkartaan for the Mage-dom," Vogel commands.

He can sense the glorious surge of anger through Fallon's power as she chafes at this command, a sudden chill overtaking the room.

"I seek to move against the Dryad Whore and her allies," Fallon insists.

Vogel's domineering smile is undimmed. "All in good time, my Black Witch. But we must wait."

The room's temperature dips, hoarfrost needling to life across the oval panes of glass. "Giving their power a chance to *grow*?" she challenges.

Vogel narrows his gaze at her, silver fire flashing along the edges of his vision. "No," he counters, "to *weaken*. Let the Fae Witch and her allies have their shielded moment. Dryad power is seasonal. Linked to Light. And soon, my Ice Witch, the world will darken as your winter descends."

Fallon's eyes widen with evident surprise as Vogel closes his eyes and sends out a mental call. The papery sound of wings fluttering descends, a multi-eyed raven swooping down from the rafter overhead to alight on Vogel's shoulder, talons biting in.

Images from his multitude of Shadow ravens flood Vogel, images the Dryad Witch can't shield.

Vogel opens his eyes and narrows his focus in on Fallon once more. "My runic eyes are in the Dyoi Forest. I am watching the Dryad Witch and those trapped there with her. As the scale of power begins to tip more strongly in our favor, I will draw her to us."

"How?" Fallon demands.

Vogel pulls out a Shadowed stone, the Amaz rune emblazoned on it transformed into a steely clouded gray. Intoning a spell, he closes his eyes and forms a detailed mental picture.

A ripple slithers over his skin, and Vogel shivers then opens his eyes. A dart of glee spikes through him in response to the astonished look on Fallon's face. She takes in the glamour he envisioned and the stone brought into being—a young Mage with vivid blue hair, kohl-lined eyes, a pierced lip, and a blue dragon tattoo running along the side of his neck, a blue lightning design encircling the column of his throat.

"Trystan Gardner," Fallon breathes.

Triumph courses through Vogel as he draws in a deep breath and concentrates on a new glamour, his form shifting to what he knows is that of a tall, purple-hued, young Urisk man with Gardnerian green eyes and violet garb, his features bearing an uncanny resemblance to the Dryad Witch's.

"This must be Or'myr Syll'vir," Fallon murmurs, awe icing through her aura, "the staen'en witch's abomination of a cousin."

Vogel nods, then shifts to one more glamour, viper-focused on Fallon, his stare like a hot brand against her ice power. He can sense the pleasureable rush of goose-flesh breaking out over her skin in response as he morphs into a deep-blue Asrai Fae with a confrontational expression.

Fallon grins wickedly, her eyes narrowing with a sly light. "And this must be the little Water Fae whore, Tierney Calix."

Vogel gives her a venomous smile. "The Magedom's Shadow Wand is close to holding enough power to portal through any shield." His smile sharpens. "Once foliage season subsides and your winter descends, we'll go after the Whore Witch. And I'll draw her to us with bait she least expects."

CHAPTER FIVE

TREE'KHIN

Elloren

Northern Dyoi Mountain Range

I emerge from a few hours of sleep, hazily aware of falling from dreams saturated in swirling color, my senses muzzily awakening. There's a crisp chill to the air that's new, but I'm not cold, my Wyvernbond a constant source of warmth . . . as is Yvan. We fell asleep near each other in an isolated section of the woods, the two of us maintaining a discreet distance. But at some point in the night, we must have reached for each other, because Yvan's lean, muscular form is wrapped around mine, his body like a *furnace*, his heartbeat strong and steady.

A spark of love and desire for him kindles along my every line, more fully rousing me, and my eyes flutter open, dawn's rays of sunlight sparkling against my vision as I take in the Forest canopy above.

A rush of euphoria sweeps through me, a tingle racing through the III mark on my palm, my magic *surging*. There must have been a hard frost last night. Ice glitters at the edges of *everything*. And the cold . . . it's flung the door *wide open* to the Forest's miracle of autumn foliage.

I gape at the dazzling show. The foliage of the East is like nothing I've experienced before. Every hue of the rainbow has exploded into being along the edges of the purple leaves in a kaleidoscope of *color*.

"Yvan . . ." The whisper bursts from my lips, from the center of my very heart as the color connects with my lightlines, every emotion and line of magic amplified by it. I arch more intently against Yvan, everything I feel for him surfacing in a blood-warming rush.

"Elloren," Yvan murmurs, firming his hold on me as he awakens.

His eyes open and meet mine, the whole world stilling on its axis for one power-surging moment. Violet fire ignites in Yvan's gaze and through our bond, a shot of love searing through our linkage that's so intense it obliterates all reserve.

We pull each other into a kiss that instantly deepens, our mutual hunger rising like wildfire, roaring through us. Yvan's fingertips are live flames, his mouth urgent against mine, his seductive heat licking through my lines in a way that makes me want to strip off everything that separates us and merge with him fully.

And the Forest . . . it seems caught up with us, both the surrounding Dyoi and distant Zhilaan feeding heat into our bond, *rooting* us to each other.

"I love you, Elloren," Yvan says as his hands trace heat over my body. "I love you, and I *want* you . . ."

He sweeps me into another feverish kiss, our hands roving over each other with desperate abandon, my pulse racing hot against his. Drunk with light magic and his fire, molten lust kindles in my every nerve. I slide my hands down his hips and wrap one leg around him, urging him closer.

Yvan lets out a small groan, and the low timbre of it triggers a memory that sends conflict surging through my desire.

Lukas. On our Sealing night, and then, again, in the Forest and Agolith Desert.

Yvan pulls back a fraction, his breathing uneven as he gives me a probing look, a hectic red coloring his cheeks as my throat constricts and I'm suddenly swallowing an upswell of tears. I can't think about Lukas. I *can't.* Because this *grief* . . . I'm no match for its undertow.

"Yvan," I rasp out. "I'm sorry."

"It's all right, Elloren," he says, reaching up to caress the side of my face, his voice firm. "I can read you. I understand. And I know what you feel for me."

I nod once, tears escaping my eyes and trickling down my face. Yvan leans in to press his warm lips to my brow, and the cadence of my breath smooths out as his invisible fire embraces me.

He moves to pull me into a reassuring hug but abruptly stiffens and sits up, looking past me into the Forest. My pulse kicks up, and I give him a questioning look, sitting up, as well. He holds up a cautioning finger, an expression of concentration tightening his eyes, his nostrils flaring. "Bleddyn's coming," he says.

Anticipation lights. Bleddyn, as well as a number of our allies, were absorbed into the Forest last night. We've taken turns standing sentry to wait for their reemergence so we could all catch a few hours of vital sleep.

A rustling of brush sounds as Bleddyn emerges from the Forest's breathtaking mosaic of color, my Errilor Ravens flying down from the Forest canopy to alight around us. My eyes widen, astonishment crackling through Yvan's and my bonded fire as we take Bleddyn in.

Her tall, vividly green form is surrounded by a penumbra of verdant light. Her breath misting in the crisp air, she's gripping a striated piece of malachite in her fist that's the same emerald hue as her skin and hair.

"You joined with the Forest," I marvel, sensing a similar line of kindred connection to the stone that connects me to my ravens.

"I just emerged," Bleddyn informs us, a revelatory look in her wide eyes. "I had to find you both. The Forest . . . it gave me back my *geomancy power*."

Shock races through our fire.

Bleddyn lifts the malachite, tears sheening her eyes. "You were right, Elloren. This fight, it's bigger and different than we all thought." She peers in the direction of the broad mountain ledge. "Vang Troi has emerged from the Forest, as well."

My pulse kicks up. Yvan and I exchange a stark look before we rise and follow Bleddyn back to the ledge, along with Errlith and the rest of my flock, my power burgeoning with every step, shot through with fall's power-amplifying explosion of color.

In the morning light, I take in the Shadow wasteland beyond our Dyoi Forest shielding, my grip tightening around Yvan's. The sight is a fresh punch to the gut. To our east lies a fragile Forest caught up in early autumn's glorious, chromatic show of light power. To our west lies a color-stripped, poisoned wasteland, stretching as far as the eye can see.

My lightlines contract just from looking at the Shadowed land, and I recoil from the sensation and exchange a quick look with Errilith beside me, my raven's loops of power tugging my sight back toward the color-rich Forest. I follow the pull of my kindred's magic, turn toward the trees, the tension in my lines slackening as they're flooded with another shimmering surge of chromatic power.

"I see," I whisper to Errilith with a quick caress of his wing, Errilith's returning embrace of Deathkin stillness bolstering me.

A large bonfire still crackles in the huge ledge's center, spitting sparks and cutting through the morning air's chill, most of my allies grouped around it, Freyja Zyrr and the soldier Hee Muur still on our side of the shield-divided ledge. Yvan and I stride hand in hand toward our allies, Bleddyn, Errilith, and the rest of my ravens fanning out around us.

Most of our adversaries are gathered just beyond the translucent shield-wall separating the ledge in half, the rush of Soleiya's aura like a flaming dagger thrown straight at me.

Dryad Witch, Raz'zor growls into my mind, alliance blazing in his crimson-fire eyes. Naga nods to Yvan and me in greeting and we're swept up in an embracing *whoosh* of our horde's fiery support that I return with a blast of power that has Naga, Ariel, Raz'zor, and the others looking at me with widened eyes before giving me fanged smiles.

Those who also hold Dryad lineage seem as caught up in autumn's surge of light power as I am. Mavrik's and Gwynn's golden eyes are ringed a more intense band of glowing color, their twinned magic's looping golden aura shot through with streaks of rainbowed light, a thread of connection to that power tingling through my lines via our common Forest linkage. Even Gwynn and Mavrik's kindred Flame Hawks seeming invigorated, their orange feathers aglow with a prismatic sheen.

Sylvan and Yulan appear renewed as well, their forest green coloration fully restored and shot through with a heightened, branching Dyoi purple, the elemental power running through their rootlines blazing with foliage light. Sylvan's branch horns have shed their gray—they're now a rich brown, his pine hair thick with deep-purple needles. I glance around, wondering who his hidden kindred might be, but find no clue.

Yulan's grayed Noi heron hugs her side, some of the graceful bird's feathers having regained their blue, white and lavender coloration. Ariel and Alder are stationed protectively beside them, Yulan's long vine tresses holding a heartening explosion of delicate multihued flowers.

Hazel and Oaklyyn are conspicuously absent, as are Trystan, Vothe, Ra'Ven, and Rivyr'el, but Vang Troi stands near the ledge's shielding on our side of it, her violet eyes fixed on Yvan and me.

Worry tightens my throat as I take in Vang Troi's stiff stance and her lack of any obvious show of Dryad'khin transformation or kindred creature.

"Did the Forest show itself to you?" I ask, my concern mounting.

"It did," she confirms, determination hardening her sharp features and flashing through her sapphire power. "I held back my assent when it asked for an alliance."

My heartbeat quickens at this news, my fire spiking against Yvan's equally unsettled flame.

Vang Troi unfurls her unmarked palm. "After the Forest revealed the wider fight for the Natural World to me, I wanted to forge an alliance with it. But both the Forest and I are holding back for the moment so that I could stand before my forces as *proof* that what the Forest offers is a true invitation to alliance—freely given and freely accepted or rejected with no compulsion. But what the Forest has shown me—" she gives us a dire look "—it's compelling to the extreme." She turns to our adversaries just beyond the translucent shield-wall, a penumbra of blue power shivering to life around her as she describes visions stressing Dryad'khin unity against the Shadow that the Forest sent to her. "I urge all of you to enter into the Forest as I have done," Vang Troi charges. "To simply listen to what it has to say. And decide, for yourselves, if you will align with it as Forest'khin, as I have decided to."

My heart gives a leap as a troubled murmur goes up amongst our adversaries, Iris, Soleiya, and Alcippe all wearing expressions of outrage. Soleiya's invisible fire aura whips ragefully against me, and Yvan and I both stiffen, but then, the unexpected happens.

"I'll hear the Forest out," the young Vu Trin soldier Hee Muur announces to Vang Troi, her severe expression turning flintier still as she slashes out an emphatic hand toward the tree line. "But that's *it*."

As if galvanized by Hee Muur's shocking declaration, Bleddyn strides away from Yvan and me and straight up to the ledge-dividing shield-wall, her geomancy aura of emerald light gaining intensity. Iris's invisible flame aura burgeons into an out-of-control firestorm as Bleddyn halts a few paces before her, only the shield separating them, Iris's perennially hostile expression turning flat-out belligerent.

Unmoved by Iris's show of ire, Bleddyn holds her III-marked palm up. "Iris Morgaine," she states with impassioned formality, her aura crackling with emotion. "I implore you, as my *friend*. Just hear the Forest out."

Iris doesn't budge, fire spitting through the eyes she has furiously pinned on Bleddyn, her power blazing with enough conflict to level a mountain to charred ash. I know the two of them have a fractured friendship. Divided by cultural lines, like so much of the East.

But something in Iris softens, the angry sear of her fire dampening as she holds Bleddyn's unflinching, forthright stare. And remarkably, Iris's closed-off stance slackens, her defensive look collapsing into one of pained emotion.

"All right, Bleddyn," she snaps, her voice tight and raw, her fire now a discordant flare. "I'll hear your Forest out, as well. But I won't join with it."

THE DRYAD STORM

A gasp shudders through my throat, Yvan's hand tightening around mine as our bond flares with surprise over Iris ceding even one trace of ground.

Alder crafts an opening in our shield for Iris to step through so that Bleddyn, Iris, Vang Troi, and Hee Muur can approach the tree line together, Sylvan and Yulan joining them.

I've a sense of our collective breath, trapped, as Vang Troi, Hee Muur, and Iris all place their palms to the bark of the same Noi Oak . . .

. . . and are abruptly pulled into the tree.

A tense murmur ripples through everyone assembled, just as the Alfsigr Elf Rivyr'el Talonir emerges from a Noi Oak a few paces away in a flash of prismatic color.

A ripple of emotion tingles through me.

Rivyr'el is kneeling on the ground by the trunk's base, a gorgeous, flashing penumbra of color surrounding him. His formerly spiky Alfsigr-white hair is more intensely rainbow-streaked, jeweled dragonflies of every hue zipping around him.

A tear slides down his cheek as Rivyr'el raises his newly multicolored eyes and grins. "It's all so beautiful," he murmurs, before he rises, dragonflies alighting on his shoulders and hair as he turns to Sylvan. "I want to help you save it. Teach us what we need to do."

"Dryad power is seasonal," Sylvan says to everyone gathered around the smoldering bonfire, the strengthening sunlight rapidly overtaking the early morning chill. "Both Forest and Dryad power will peak before long, when the Forest's foliage peaks."

Yvan's mother and a few of our other adversaries linger close to our barrier wall, listening, Soleiya's hostility seeming unmoved.

Iris sits quietly between Sylvan and Bleddyn, more subdued than I've ever seen her. She has been, ever since she stumbled out of the Noi Oak and was caught in Sylvan's strong grip before she could fall, headfirst, to the ground. Seeming dazed and overwhelmed, Iris met Sylvan's green eyes with a shock that I sensed coursing through both their auras before Iris shakily held up her III-marked palm.

Sylvan took firm hold of her hand, III mark to III mark, Iris's fire aura blazing toward his foliage-strengthened magic to whip around and through it.

I watched, surprised, as Sylvan calmly met Iris's grasping heat with a returning blaze of his elemental fire power, the sun's Forest-nourishing heat burning bright at the heart of it.

Common ground.

It was at that moment that a night-black Noi Fire Falcon flew out of the Forest and landed on Iris's shoulder. Iris promptly burst into tears and reached up to caress the bird, its eyes the same flaming gold hue as her own. A bird, Yulan later explained, that uses the flaming branches drawn from naturally occurring and Forest-replenishing wildfires to flush its prey out of hiding.

A bird as fierce and fiery as Iris Morgaine.

My focus sliding back to the present, I take in Iris's invisible aura of fire power circling both the hawk and Sylvan, and I wonder, not for the first time, what Sylvan's kindred might be. I can sense that he has one—a thread of his power flows into the Dyoi Forest in the same way a thread of mine flows out to Errilith beside me. But Sylvan's mysterious kindred remains hidden, a quiet, strong presence deep in the Forest's shade.

"Dryad power is communally amplified magic," Sylvan says, giving us all a pointed look, "which could give us a powerful advantage against the Magedom if we *all* join with the Forest and share our magic as Dryad'khin during peak foliage."

My allies and I listen closely, Ra'Ven now III-marked and reunited with Sage, his fingers interlaced with hers as violet Noi Monarch Butterflies flit around Sage's form. A purple-patterned Noi Subland Gecko kindred clings to Ra'Ven's shoulder, Hee Muur beside them with a sheep-size violet Dyoi Dragon Lizard kindred pressed to her side. Most of my allies show signs of having merged with the Forest—a lavender tailorbird perched on Fain's forearm, a silver dove on Sholin's, a dark-furred, purple-spotted Noi Lynx standing sentry beside Kam Vin and a large black bobcat prowling around my feline-loving uncle Wrenfir.

I catch Rafe's gaze, Aislinn and Jarod beside him. Diana flashes me a toothy grin, their kindred pack of wild wolves silently stationed near the tree line, the Lupines already connected to the Forest via their Change.

And Vang Troi—she went back into the trees and reemerged astride a wild, midnight-black mustang, her sapphire aura shining bright as she rode out to greet us, her horse kindred now grazing near the trees. I can't help but glance at silent Ni Vin, who sits beside Vang Troi on our side of the shield, a III mark now on her palm, her new violet-hued mare kindred nearby beside Andras's purple-speckled black stallion kindred. I remember, with great remorse, how I accidentally killed Ni Vin's beloved black mare with my terrible Black Witch fire so many months ago. I'm deeply gratified by the Forest's gift to her of this horse kindred, my determination rising to use my power to support Life instead of destroying it.

"Everything we are is about natural rhythms and connections," Yulan softly interjects before launching into a deeper explanation of the seasonal and moon cycles and their effect on the elemental power of Tree'kin.

I glance toward where Yulan sits with Ariel, Alder, and Andras. The four of them have been ministering to the Shadow-burned and orphaned animals who fled here from the West along with the rest of us, the terrified, dazed-looking beasts staggering out of the tree line in spurts, their fur and feathers and bodies grayed and mutilated.

My heart constricts with grief, even Yvan's constant caress of fire unable to staunch the sorrow. The loss of habitat cuts horrifyingly deep. But despite all the trauma and Soleiya's intractable aura of hostility, I find a spark of hope in how a generous portion of Sylvan's power is intentionally flowing toward Iris, offering her a sustained mooring as the Forest's magic embraces her.

I glance at Yvan and catch him studying Iris and Sylvan closely, the shimmer of surprise in his fire echoing my own as Iris and Sylvan meet each other's eyes, fire sparking hard through both their auras before they glance away.

Iris stills, a tortured look overtaking her expression. "I wanted Lasair dominance," she blurts out as she abruptly rises to her feet, a slight quaver in her forceful tone. Everyone grows quiet, looking to her. "I wanted a restoration of Lasair rule over the East," she grits out, her eyes sparking with gold fire, a flash of her former condemnation flaring in them. "Which I saw as our right. This land was *ours*."

Everyone is silent for a moment.

"It was," Sylvan agrees, a tremor of unsettled force brewing in his power. Iris turns to him, and their gazes connect, triggering a sharp flare of their elemental attraction. "But the Dryad'kin were here before the Lasair," Sylvan notes.

Iris's gaze locks tighter with his, their auras whipping around each other in a hotter flare. "I know," she finally admits, voice tight. "The Forest . . . it showed me the history of both our peoples. It showed me how my people drove the Dryad'kin from the East with great cruelty. And generations later, what the Kelts did to my people in turn." She pauses, a haunted look overtaking her fiery gaze, her voice rougher when it comes. "So many Lasair massacred with iron . . . almost wiped out . . . my people nomads after that. But we did a similar thing to the Dryads . . ." She reaches up and rakes her fingers through her crimson hair, her face tensing with a look of fierce remorse. "Sylvan . . ."

"And now you'd wipe us out further," Soleiya snipes at Iris from beyond the shield-wall, Yvan's fire aura instantly sparking with frustration.

Iris's expression turns distraught as she turns to Soleiya. "Lasair'kin," she implores her in Asrai, "you have been like a second mother to me all my life. Lasair'lhir'in, *please*, just listen to what the Forest has to say."

Soleiya's eyes catch fire. "Where was this Forest power when we were being *slaughtered* by the last Black Witch, Iris'iyl'ir?" she demands. "Or have you forgotten your true Asrai name?"

Iris winces as if struck, and I stiffen against Soleiya's heated vitriol, an invisible lash of Yvan's angered fire flashing out toward his mother.

"Enough," Yvan levels at her in Lasair, rising to his feet.

"No, Yvan," Soleiya bitingly returns in Lasair, pointing a finger at me as anguish streaks through her power. "This witch has poisoned your mind. These 'alliances' are getting us nowhere but closer to the *complete annihilation* of the Fae'kin—"

"There can be no Fae'kin without the Natural World!" Iris shrilly levels back at Soleiya. "All this division, it simply keeps us too powerless to fight back against the Shadow!"

"No, Iris," Soleiya fires back. "And I will call you that Mage-bastardized version of your name because, apparently, that's what you are now." Soleiya slices another glare at all of us, but most especially at Vang Troi. "You will be the ruination of my people," she snarls. "So, go ahead. *Finish* the work the Mages started."

Vang Troi's expression remains stoic, her gaze fixed on her clasped hands as Soleiya storms off in a tempest of fire power along with most of our adversaries, save for Freyja Zyrr on our side of the shielding, Alcippe Feyir and another member of Freyja's Queen's Guard remaining protectively beyond it, a look of conflict on the Amaz monarch's face.

Yvan's eyes are two points of conflagration as he watches his mother storm off, his aura's churning tension hot in the air, so hot I fear one spark will ignite an explosion.

Iris turns to Yvan. "Yvan'myir," she implores in Lasair, "I'm sorry for the rift I caused between us."

Yvan pulls in a deep breath and shakes his head, a compassionate warmth coursing out to her. "Iris'iyl'ir," he says, heartfelt, "there's no need. All is forgiven."

Iris swallows, tears glistening in her eyes as her gaze slides to me, without rancor for the first time. "Elloren'mysshir," she says in Dryadin, her voice fracturing. "I'm sorry . . . for so many things."

Emotion tightens my throat as the Dyoi Forest's embracing energy flows toward us both, and I painfully recall how I behaved toward Iris and others in the Verpax University kitchen.

"I'm sorry too, Iris'mysshir," I tell her in Dryadin. "For so many things."

"Then let this discord between us end now," she offers, her fire simmering toward me in a passionate stream as she strides to me and holds out her hand, a slight tremble to the gesture. My heart thudding, I rise, a huff of emotion escaping us both as I take her hand then draw her into an embrace, fire to fire, Forest'kin to Forest'khin.

"The Forest needs such a fierce ally," I tell her, tears glassing my eyes.

She nods as we draw away from each other, her cheeks slick with tears. She squeezes my shoulder warmly before returning to Sylvan to take a seat, once more, by his side. "Well, Dryad'kin," she says, turning to him, "it looks like I'm hells-bent on being the worst possible Lasair I can be. So be it. I've pledged my full power to your Forest." She holds up her III-marked palm.

"*Our* Forest," Sylvan gently corrects her as his power encircles her, the Dyoi Forest's embracing energy pulsing out more strongly toward us all.

"*Traitor,*" a female voice snarls from the tree line.

We turn to find Oaklyyn suddenly there, inside the great ledge's forested rear. She looks haggard, her skin still grayed under the Dyoi Forest's purple branching pattern. I can sense that the Forest's attempt to feed elemental power into her lines isn't enough, and there's no kindred in sight. Her elemental energy feels perilously unmoored.

One of the animals Yulan is tending to—a young fisher cat with singed, grayed fur—takes a faltering step toward Oaklyyn and sends out affectionate kindred energy to her, but she refuses to even glance at the injured animal.

"My Dryad sister," Yulan says as she rises to her feet, compassion tightening her lovely face as she takes in Oaklyyn's battered state, "let one of these unbonded ones accept you as kindred—"

"My kindred is *dead!*" Oaklyyn snarls as she levels an incendiary glare at Yulan. Her grayed gaze swings to Sylvan, and she jabs a shaking finger at me. "We should have killed that witch the second we took her prisoner! We should have killed every non-Dryad in existence!" She glances toward the leagues of destroyed land, her eyes wild with grief. "That Shadow was brought down on our Forest by the Black Witch's people, and now you've become an ally to them! I renounce you *all*! I hate you *all*!"

With that, Oaklyyn disappears back into the Forest, her severely depleted aura soon untraceable on the air.

A heavy silence descends in her wake. It's as if a cyclone has departed, devastated looks on Sylvan's and Yulan's faces, Raz'zor's fire giving a troubled flare in the direction Oaklyyn stormed away to.

"We need her," Sylvan comments grimly, meeting Yulan's anguished stare.

"I know we do, Dryad'kin," Yulan agrees.

Sylvan glances up at our dome shielding, Vogel's barely visible trace of Shadow webbing coursing over it. "I'm a power empath," he tells us. "I can gauge the power in our shielding. It may be enough to hold off the Magedom for now, but it's not enough to break through that Shadow net and draw our shielding over the entirety of the East. We need the power of *everyone* under this shield to do that." He glances toward our adversaries, grouped together in the distance. "Or we'll remain trapped here until winter descends, our magic goes dormant, and the Magedom strikes down our dome-shield and levels all the remaining Forests. Which will unleash the complete destruction of the Natural World."

"We cannot afford to lose even one more half league of Forest," Yulan agrees, grave warning in her moss green eyes. She reaches up to caress the grayed sparrow with a splinted wing perched on her shoulder. "Nature's Balance is held by a weakening thread."

"I'll try to convince my allies to simply listen," Iris quietly offers, glancing toward Vang Troi's forces before turning to Yvan with an expression of grim concern. "It's going to be difficult with the widow of 'the Great Icaral Who Saved the East' so set against Elloren."

"I'm quite clear on that point," Yvan responds, voice clipped, an angsty motion to his fire that has me reaching for his hand, a fervent look passing between us as he grips hold of me.

"We need the Verdyllion," Yulan chimes in, looking at Gwynnifer and Mavrik. "Great Balancing energy is said to lie within III's Verdyllion branch. Perhaps enough to make up for what we lack in power. Gwynn and Mavrik possess a trackable link to it that we can follow."

Naga's form abruptly contracts, and my eyes widen as first Naga and then almost our entire horde, including Raz'zor, morph to human form.

Yvan and I gape at Naga, now a tall, black-scale-armored woman, her green eyes overtaken by golden fire. The ear that Damion Bane tore from her head is a slash of a wound, and her skin is the same onyx hue as her scales, her short, tightly curled black hair tipped in gold. Horns rise from her head, dark claws grace her fingers, and the Mage Council **M** cruelly branded on her side stands out in relief. She shoots me a bemused look as I gulp, my shock ratcheting up to roaring heights as my gaze swings to Raz'zor . . . who is now a striking, snow-hued young man with eyes of vermillion flame. Alabaster horns rise from his tousled, chalk-white hair, his body covered in white-scale armor. His head tilts with inhuman, serpentine rapidity as he considers me.

Well, you're full of surprises, I send out to him via our mind-link.

Raz'zor flashes me a toothy smile.

"Get my horde to the Sublands," Naga hisses, her stance full of coiled power, "and we will liberate both the Verdyllion and the Unbroken Alfsigr Icaral who wields it, along with her Subland forces and the surviving Dryads."

Ariel's fiery aura crackles with urgency at the mention of Wynter, the flame in her eyes burning hotter as she looks at Mavrik and Gwynn, our path to the Verdyllion.

"You forget," Mavrik cautions us all, "we don't just lack the power to break out of Vogel's dome-net. He's cast a barrier over our Subland shielding, as well."

"Shielding Vogel will soon break through," Alder cautions. "If we can't best him before winter descends."

"Which will place another Wand of Power in his hands," Vang Troi notes.

"Power Vogel could use to speed his control over every Mage's fastlines and every Alfsigr Elf's Zalyn'or bindings," Mavrik adds. "And keep in mind, he already possesses the ability to glamour and portal."

The whole world shivers into darkness, and we collectively startle as Hazel, in human form, bursts from the woods at a rapid clip, his compact form like a dark star hurtling toward us, the legs of three dead ravens clenched in his fist, the lifeless birds hanging upside down. I inwardly recoil. Swarms of eyes cover the raven's heads, Shadow runes emblazoned on their sides.

Sylvan, Vang Troi, and my uncle Wrenfir bolt to their feet.

"It seems as if Vogel has been with us all the time," Hazel snarls. "I caught four of these abominations."

"You're only holding three," Vang Troi points out. "Where is the fourth?"

Hazel narrows his pitch-black eyes at her. "I *ate* it."

Shock ripples through me as Hazel bares his teeth and I take in the disturbing gray glow sparking to life around his irises. "I'm linking to the energy in Vogel's branching Shadow."

"Take care, Hazel," I caution. "Vogel could consume you through that link."

Hazel shoots me a scornful look, his aura pulsing through the world around us once more. "The blood of the Forest balances the Death in me," he hisses. "As long as my link to the Natural Matrix holds, my power is stronger than Shadow."

"What do you mean, 'blood of the Forest'?" Wrenfir presses, his bobcat bristling.

Hazel tilts his head toward my young uncle, the movement disturbingly quick. "Have you not guessed my kindreds? The source of my shifter self?"

I remember Hazel's huge, eight-legged insectile form, terrifyingly bloodthirsty with slashing teeth. Spiderlike but not completely that, some other, terrible force of Nature within him.

Hazel's thrall loops around Wrenfir. "You cannot guess it, can you, Mageling?" he snarls. Challenge knifes through Hazel's words and power, and oddly, what feels like an attempt to intimidate my uncle as Wrenfir's bobcat begins to growl.

Wrenfir's magic gives a defiant flare, his blackened lips ticking up as he motions to his bobcat for calm and shoots Hazel a narrow-eyed grin. "Why don't you show me, Deathling," he challenges in turn.

Hazel bares his teeth, a foggy rush of his Darkness suddenly flashing straight through Wrenfir.

I flinch, but Wrenfir simply holds Hazel's stare, shooting him a wider, canine-bearing grin.

A twitch of surprise shudders through Hazel's magic before his expression turns to one of viciousness so feral it sends a chill through my lines. Hazel closes his eyes, arches his head back and opens his mouth. It stretches grotesquely wide, tendrils of Darkness emanating from it. A rushing sound erupts from the Forest, and all of us who remained sitting bolt to our feet as an insectile carpet of black flows toward Hazel and Wrenfir.

They're *ticks*, I realize as the stream passes close. So many bloodsucking ticks they could fell us all in a heartbeat. Before we can protest, the ticks flow up Hazel's and Wrenfir's bodies, all the way up to my uncle's raven-tattooed neck, his kindred letting out a distressed snarl.

"Hazel, stop!" I cry out, but am silenced by my uncle's halting, tick-covered palm.

Wrenfir, unflinching, hold's Hazel's full-dark gaze, ticks streaming all over him. And then he smiles.

Hazel tenses, confusion overtaking his sharp features.

Wrenfir flinches as if from the sting of sudden bites, his smile vanishing. *"Enough,"* he levels at Hazel. "I'm your *ally*, Primordial."

Hazel's power shivers, a pained look slicing through his eyes before he murmurs a bone-shivering sound that seems to shudder through the very stone beneath us.

The carpet of ticks flows back into the Forest as quickly as it came.

"You do not fear me," Hazel says to Wrenfir, seeming deeply thrown.

Wrenfir huffs out an incredulous sound. "I embraced Death Fae as my allies from the age of thirteen on," he snaps. "I know you have *bite*. But take care, Primordial. I might bite back. I have magic of my own."

Their eyes remain locked for a protracted moment, and I look away, feeling like I'm intruding on something that just tilted toward the private.

"I will not draw your blood," Hazel promises Wrenfir, his tone holding what feels like formal Death Fae apology in it.

Wrenfir's gaze slides languidly up and down Hazel's slender form, his smile turning wicked. "Oh, I might let you, Deathling. But only if you ask me *very* nicely."

Hazel gapes at him, then barks out a surprised laugh that has Wrenfir's smile broadening, the tension between them bizarrely broken as Wrenfir strokes his bobcat's head.

Hazel abruptly shudders, his body stiffening, the gray glow around his irises intensifying as Wrenfir's power is cast back into fitful flares.

"I'm getting flashes of Vogel," Hazel tells us, and we listen, rapt, as he conveys the rise of a new Black Witch—Fallon Bane—as well as the fall of the continent's center, an invasion of Ishkartaan underway. "Vogel has more raven spies throughout the East," Hazel conveys, "and likely throughout this Forest. Be vigilant. He seeks to unravel any alliance that could form between all of us under this dome."

"Well, we're doing a bang-up job of that all on our own," Bleddyn grouses, before casting Hazel a wary look. "Let's just make sure we keep close tabs on you, Deathkin. This link of yours is risky, whether you think it is or not."

"I'll keep an eye on him," Wrenfir offers, his gaze swinging to Hazel with confrontational force as Hazel's eyes flick toward him and fix hard, all the light surrounding us briefly shuddering Dark once more as their power jolts toward each other.

"Is there any way of knowing when Trystan and Vothe will emerge from the Forest?" I ask Sylvan.

"And what of Lucretia?" Jules Kristian puts in, a haggard desperation roughening his tone. I look at him in concern, Jules having adamantly refused to enter the Forest even though he seems torn over his decision.

Yulan is studying Jules with a look of deep sympathy. "I do not know when or where any of these Forest'khin will emerge," she answers.

An invisible, devastated rush of water and wind power has me turning toward Thierren, and I catch him glancing toward the Shadow wasteland. I can easily guess at the turn of his thoughts, the falcon kindred on his shoulder agitatedly ruffling its night-purple wings in a show of understanding. Because Sparrow is out there, somewhere. Perhaps caught up in the wastelands with Lucretia.

Trapped in Vogel's Shadow.

Yvan turns to me and our eyes meet, fire sizzling through our bond. "I'm going to arrange a meeting with my mother and try and bring her to our side," he says.

"And I'll work on swaying my forces to do the same," Vang Troi announces.

"I'll accompany you," Freyja Zyrr calls out, Hee Muur echoing her offer.

Ra'Ven holds up his stylus. "I'll cast Varg power connection runes on our shielding just in case you're successful," he says to Vang Troi. "They'll speed a linkage of their power to ours if they join with the Forest." He turns to Sylvan. "Can you show us how to strengthen our spellwork with Forest power?"

Sylvan nods. "We can." Sylvan meets my gaze. "We can make use of your foliage amplified magic to aid us."

"My power is yours," I offer, but find myself hesitant to release Yvan's hand as the heat of our bond revs up. I exchange a knowing look with him, the sudden reluctance to part sputtering through our flame as offers of aid sound out around us.

Battling our draw, Yvan and I let go of each other just as Jules Kristian gets up and walks decidedly away from us all, making for the tree line.

"Where are you going?" I call to him, concerned.

Jules swings around, walking backward now, a tortured look on his face. "To scour every inch of this Forest for some sign of Lucretia." And then he turns away without slowing and disappears into the prismatic Forest.

LIVING LIBRARY

Lucretia Quillen

Northern Dyoi Mountain Range

Lucretia is pulled through the Forest's dark embrace for an expanded time, drawn along the thread of a force that runs through the heart of the Natural World, every one of her rootlines lit up bright with it.

Love.

She follows that draw toward the center of her own full-to-bursting heart and careens out of the Forest's darkness. Instantly dazed and disorientated, she finds herself on her hands and knees, palms to moist earth, a dense purple Forest with prism-edged foliage surrounding her.

She pulls in a euphoric breath in response to autumn's power-amplifying surge of light magic, the sound of burbling water hooking her senses. She glances toward the stream rippling beside her, its crystal clear water throwing off sparks of reflected color and sunlight, her water lines straining toward it.

Tears stinging her bespectacled eyes, Lucretia takes in the early morning mist hanging suspended over the Forest's ground like delicate gauze. Her Dryad'kin rootlines thrill to the sense of the water cradled in it. A sense of the watery pathways feeding the Forest's entire root network is suddenly filling her mind and anchoring her rootlines to the ground, every sense alive, alight . . . *connected.*

Her awareness of that thread of love she followed to this place warms as she pushes herself to her feet, then turns and raises her hand to make contact with the pale lavender trunk of the Eastern Birch she emerged from.

Lucretia is flooded by a stronger sense of the tree's connection to *water,* her strengthened water lines rippling to more potent life. Smiling, she closes her eyes, breathes in the water-cradling mist and drinks in her newfound awareness of the aquifer running deep beneath the Forest. She goes deeper, her rootlines linking to the vast network of the East's streams, her lines lit up by the Forest and Water's interwoven nature, the trees not only protecting and replenishing the aquifers by channeling water downward to them, but also stabilizing the very climate around them by drawing water up through their roots and sending it out as water vapor, the whole, swirling dance an intimate partnership.

To support Life and Love.

Joyful tears spill from Lucretia's eyes as her rippling connection solidifies to the Forest aquifer beneath her feet. *My kindred*, she realizes, her newfound bond to the aquifers of the East locking around both her water aura and her heart.

A birch branch drops down before her. Swept up in the tide of the surrounding Forest's affection, Lucretia reaches down to pick up the branch and is shocked anew not only at the feel of the living branch's reestablished connection to the surrounding trees through her rootlines, but also to find her skin has turned a deeper, richer shade of green, its glimmer intensified, a mark of the Great Tree, III, whom the Forest revealed to her, emblazoned on her palm.

The Nature Anchoring Tree murdered by the Shadow.

Grief clenches Lucretia's throat, and she has to swallow it back as she sheathes her living branch, her focus drawn to a lingering stretching sensation along her ears. She reaches up to find subtle points there, a resurgent shock eddying through her.

Home, she realizes. *I've finally come home.*

Yes, she's finding home when it's on the brink of being lost to everyone forever, but still, she's finally found her true place. Not as a Mage at all.

But as a Dryad'kin of the East.

Her tugging sense of that thread of Love tightens, the rustle of approaching footsteps sounding.

Lucretia straightens and peers into the Forest to find Jules in the distance, striding closer, peering into the woods to their left.

Her heart leaps into a tight, impassioned rhythm, every nerve coming alive.

Jules looks as worn-out and fierce willed as she's ever seen him, his clothing mussed, hair a tousled mess, his spectacles a spiderweb of cracks and bent to a slight tilt on his nose.

"Jules, I'm here!" she calls out to him, then gasps, shocked to find herself speaking a whole new language, flowing dry and leafy over her lips, the words seeming like the truer, richer names for things.

Coming to a halt, Jules lifts his gaze to meet hers. His eyes widen.

He breaks into a sprint over the brush, rapidly closing the distance between them, then catches her up in a passionate embrace, an emotional sound bursting from his throat.

A joyful cry escapes Lucretia, love for Jules rushing through her in a euphoric tide so strong that she fears her magic might leap clear through her rootlines and straight into magic-free Jules in a drowning rush of water. Her wave of feeling breaks out into dense, visible mist, swirling around them, as she's inundated with a sense of the surrounding birch grove sending out embracing energy to encircle them both.

"My love," Lucretia cries against Jules's warm cheek, her knees almost buckling at the feel of his perennially tousled brown hair under her fingers, her invisible, Forest-linked water power streaming around him.

He brings both hands up to cradle her face as they draw slightly back from each other, tears streaming down her cheeks, her deep-green face mirrored in his bespectacled eyes, his own tears splotching his glasses, his lovestruck look expanding her heart with an ache that's almost too joyful to bear.

And then his lips are on hers, desperate and devouring, and she kisses him back just as intensely, wanting to flow straight into him and never let go.

Breaking the kiss, Jules huffs a soft sound as he takes hold of her hands and draws back a fraction, his gaze raking over her from head to toe, taking in her transformation. "Lu . . . look at you."

"Join with us," she offers in the Common Tongue, reaching out to grip his arm. She holds her palm up, displaying its mark of III.

Jules's brow knots as he studies the Forest's defiant imprint then tenderly takes hold of her hand. He meets her eyes once more, and heat ripples over her skin, that searching warmth in his gaze able to undo her *every single time*.

"This connection to the Natural World," she tremulously enthuses, "it's like nothing you've ever felt before." It's almost too joyous to bear, the power of the Natural Matrix thrumming through her lines, strong as spring rapids. Fluid with rejuvenation. With *connection*. "Being joined to the Forest," she says, "it's like connecting to the intricate center of *everything*."

Jules lifts her hand and kisses her palm right over III's image, and Lucretia's pulse quickens in response to the level of passion in that kiss. But then Jules's eyes tighten, an expression of intense chagrin in them. "Lucretia, I can't."

"You *can*," she insists, her mouth breaking into a heart-expanding smile. "You don't have to be Dryad'kin to be *Dryad'khin*. The Forest wants you too. It wants *all* of us. I can feel the trees' invitation swirling around you."

Jules glances at the surrounding trees, a grimly serious look entering his eyes as he brings his gaze back to hers. "I'm a historian, Lu. And that has demanded . . . *required* that I not align, to do any justice at all to my calling in this life."

Love eddies through Lucretia, as well as a tight rush of respect for Jules's fierce guarding of his own mind. Along with an appreciation of how it's set him apart, kept him on an often-painful path of intense solitude, reading deep into the night by candlelight, stacks of history books surrounding him, delving into confusion over painful and brutal truths.

Then attempting to use all that conflicting knowledge to work for a more just world.

For *everyone*.

"I know it's your calling, Jules," she concedes as her water aura rushes around him in a potent stream. "But you can't do it justice cut off from all this." She motions toward the prism-edged Forest world around them. "It's *not* an alignment in which you lose your free mind. It's an opening up of the most important library there is on all of Erthia. All the archives. All the libraries. Every page you turn. They're already supported by *trees*."

"Dead trees," Jules reminds her, his expression unsettled as he peers closely at her.

"That's true," she concurs, pointedly glancing at the color-decorated trees, at the glorious, complex, miraculous tangle of Waters and Forest and *Life*. She breaks into a smile once more. "But now it's time to enter the library that's *living*."

Jules's breath shudders through his throat as he blinks at her, his features tensing as he looks up toward the Forest's canopy and then back at her.

"All right, Lu," he concedes, his eyes taking on a fierce, intellectual light. "Bring me to your living library."

Lucretia's breath stills, the charged energy of the momentous shimmering in the mist around them. Pulse thrumming, she takes his hand and raises it, presses her lips gently to his palm and kisses its warm center.

Jules's breath hitches as she takes her time, kissing every part of his hand before she meets his enamored gaze. "Place your palm to the tree, Jules."

With their gazes locked, Jules draws his hand away from hers and brings it to the Noi Birch's smooth, lavender bark.

THE DRYAD STORM

A prismatic glow shivers to life around his hand. He pulls in a harsh breath and suddenly falls to his knees. Lucretia drops to her knees beside him, her magic swirling around him as Jules presses his forehead to the tree, a chromatic glow spreading around his form. Birch bark is suddenly forming around him and then drawing him inward until there's nothing before Lucretia but the trunk.

Heart in her throat, Lucretia waits, her palms on the birch. Erthia seems to still on its axis, and Lucretia stills in turn. One heartbeat. Then another. And another. The pulse of the whole world slows as Lucretia closes her eyes and *breathes*.

And then, after a time, it's Jules's warm shoulders under her palms instead of smooth trunk, and Lucretia opens her eyes and meets his awestruck gaze, an amber-lit late afternoon having descended.

Jules's breath is coming in uneven gasps, a streak of deep green now running through his messy brown hair, his spectacles gone. A Noi Kestrel with silver feathers and bright-violet eyes is perched on his shoulder. Catching his breath, Jules lifts his palm, and the kestrel takes wing and alights on the branch just above them.

Lucretia's heart swells.

There's an image of III marked on Jules's palm, identical to the one marked on her own.

"Where are your glasses?" Lucretia wonders.

Jules glances toward the kestrel. "The Forest merged my sight with my kindred's." He stops, blinking in obvious surprise over the Dryadin language flowing from his lips. "It wanted me to have a more expansive view. Of *everything*." He pauses again, swallowing, seeming overcome, before a fierce determination lights his brown eyes. "A new history needs to be written," he states, voice ragged. "Not centered on just one group of people or another."

Lucretia waits, her heart fair bursting with an outflow of hope.

"The history we need right now," he says, a revolutionary understanding in his eyes, "is a history of the Forest and the rest of the Natural World." He shakes his head and huffs out a frustrated breath. "In all my years as a historian, I . . . I thought I was striving to remain impartial. But I was biased in the worst of ways. I missed the history at the center of *everything*."

He looks to the III mark on his palm, face tense, as if in devastated apology.

"Then stop missing it," Lucretia prods.

He sets his gaze back to hers. "*This* is why confusion was essential. Because none of the other historical points was ever at the true Center of things, although they all tried to be. It was all always . . . off-kilter."

"Except when it was rooted in the Natural World," Lucretia ventures.

He nods, holding her gaze. "And in the force of Love. For all of this. And for each other." He stops for another moment, blinking at her, as if in awe. "Lu, I can sense your water power. This new link to the Forest . . . it's opened up a stronger link to *you*."

On instinct, Lucretia takes his hand and presses their palms together, III mark to III mark. Both their eyes widen as Lucretia is filled with an intimate sense of a trace of her water magic flowing straight into him.

"You can feel all of it, can't you," she marvels, a thrill igniting and rippling through her every rootline.

He nods, his gaze grown a bit liquid. "Lu . . . I *can*. I can feel what your power is like to possess. And your kindred link to the Water Matrix . . . the aquifer beneath us . . ."

"I can sense an edge of your true power, as well," she enthuses, overcome by a glimpse of his mind opening up, the whole history of the Forest clicking into it, straining to merge with her too. A tracery of images flash through the edges of her mind, everything this Forest has witnessed throughout time imprinted in its very wood, shimmering through every internal ring.

A blazing look enters Jules's gaze. Lucretia has witnessed this fire-struck look only a few times over the years, when she caught him reading something truly illuminating—something that vastly increased his understanding, shattering everything he thought he knew.

"I want to read every tree on Erthia," Jules states.

A smile lifts Lucretia's lips, and she places his palm over her own heart. "You can start by reading me, Tree'khin."

The feel of Jules's warm palm has her senses careening back toward his connection to the Forest's library, and she realizes, more fully, how powerful Jules has always been in his own magic-free way.

And then he's pulling her close and kissing her, and she can feel him reading the Waters of Erthia in her as he deepens the kiss and Lucretia connects more strongly with his mind, reading how the Natural World's Waters have figured into all of history.

How they've *driven* history.

And how the world truly needs a *new* history.

THE DRYAD STORM

An *Erthia*-based history.

"You know . . ." Lucretia groans as Jules moves to trail kisses down her neck, her body arching against his with the growing, all-consuming desire to *merge*. "Vo mystics believe that the truth is like a light at the center of a circle," she says. "We all see a piece of it. But we need *all* of us to have a grasp of its full illumination." She draws back, and their eyes lock. "I want you to see my light," she offers, her breath hitching with desire, every swirl of her magic intuitively sensing that joining with him fully will create a stronger link. That *this* is part of Erthia's power too. "Jules, let me *fully* connect you to my waters."

Clearly grasping what she's offering, Jules flicks his tea-hued eyes over her, a molten light seeping into them. His lips quirk, a stronger spark of want lighting his gaze and sending a strong ripple through Lucretia's water power. "You're bold, Dryad'kin," he teases. "It seems you imagine me an easy mark."

Lucretia smiles and runs her hand over his chest, thrilling to how his gaze on her has deepened, growing half-lidded with desire. "All those years of solitude?" she purrs, teasing back. "With that pent-up ability to kiss so well that you buckle my knees? Yes, Jules, I imagine you're an easy mark."

Jules laughs as he embraces her, Lucretia laughing as well as he nuzzles her neck and traces a kiss along its base before glancing at the misty grove surrounding them. "Here?" he asks, voice a bit ragged.

Lucretia answers by lowering herself to pluck some Sanjire root, the Forest floor thick with the small, purple-leafed plants. "Where else?" she purrs. "We're Dryad'khin now."

A huff of a laugh escapes Jules. "So very un-Gardnerian."

Lucretia's smile broadens. "So completely un-Gardnerian. But so completely Dryad'khin."

His expression takes a turn for the ardent as he draws her into a deeper, thought-scattering kiss, Lucretia's chest rising and falling against his, her water power circling tighter and tighter, low in her center and his.

"All right, Lu," he rasps, his lips tracing the edge of her jaw.

She can feel the heat of that contact flowing straight down to her toes. Straight through the low, sensual vibration kicking up through her Forest-bonded lines.

"Root me," he offers in an enticing whisper before kissing her in a way that makes her want to join him to her power's flow. "Root me to your Forest and pull me clear under your Waters."

CHAPTER SEVEN

ZONOR TRANSFORMATION

Vothendrile Xanthile

Northern Zonor River

Light blasts into being around Vothe as he's thrust from the Forest's inner darkness in a rush of elemental power, sure he's been pulled a distance away from where he entered the trees. He looks around, finding himself on the bank of the Zonor River, the leaves of the riverbank trees edged in a mosaic of every color in the rainbow, everything washed in late afternoon's amber light.

The waves of the Zonor shimmer before Vothe, the river's aura of water power flowing out to him in a powerful wave before catching him up in a kindred embrace that has Vothe gasping from a returning upswell of joy. He can sense how much magic it took for the Forest to bring him here, knows deep in his core that the trees must have some compelling reason for marshalling so much might to bring him this distance.

A sense of power crackling into being to his south draws Vothe's gaze just as Trystan emerges from the broad trunk of a Dyoi River Oak a short span away. Vothe is instantly overtaken by a sense of the Zonor River sweeping Trystan into the same kindred embrace. An embrace that's pulling them joyfully toward each other.

Trystan's eyes meet his in a shock of lightning, a jolt of forking energy leaping between the two of them that sizzles over Vothe's skin, his breath catching tight over Trystan's altered appearance and the feel of his foliage-amplified power.

Holding Vothe's gaze, Trystan throws off his tunic, his lean, muscular chest glimmering a deeper, brighter forest green than ever before, a branching purple pattern tracing over it, his Vo'lon faith necklace looped around his neck, the starlight Vo dragon goddess in its center. Trystan's sapphire dragon tattoo seems lit up by the amplified magic racing across his form in forking threads of blue lightning. And Trystan's *eyes and hair*—they're darkened to a deep-river blue, his ears now coming to points like Vothe's.

Trystan strides toward Vothe, an emotional tension mounting between them, Vothe's throat going dry with a sudden river-amplified desire for Trystan, a current of the Zonor's formidable power swirling around them both.

Vothe's pulse pounds hard through his veins as Trystan stills before him and opens his palm. The image of the Great Tree III that Vothe saw inside the Forest is imprinted there, the image the same wavering steel blue hue as Trystan's eyes and hair.

Vothe realizes what this transformed color mirrors as he glances toward the huge river beside them. *Zonor blue.* The river that's marked them both as its kindreds.

Trembling slightly, Vothe unfurls his own palm, the same defiant III image emblazoned there, shot through with an identical rippling Zonor blue, traceries of his white lightning threading over his onyx skin.

"I'm forever changed," Trystan marvels in the Dryadin language . . . a language that Vothe, too, can now understand.

"I'm changed too," Vothe responds in Dryadin, his heart full to bursting with Trystan and the Waters and the Forest and the Air above. "I was always so anchored to the Sky," he roughly states, "but cut off from the Forest and the Waters. Now I'm anchored to it *all*."

Trystan nods, and his expression takes on a pained look, his aura of blue lightning flashing ardently around Vothe. "I feel truly different, Vothe. I don't know if . . ." Trystan pauses, and Vothe can scent the sudden fear storming through him.

Passion rises hot in Vothe's chest, and a wild incredulity rises. "Are you asking me if I still love you?"

A more intense pain slashes through Trystan's power as he stands there, rigid, all the lightning in the world balling up in him, and also balling up inside of Vothe. *All of it* for this man.

"Trystan," Vothe growls, the name ripped from the center of his chest as his lightning aura cuts loose, exploding toward Trystan's power. "Always. *More*."

And then they're closing the distance between them, Trystan's lips crashing down on his, their lightning igniting against each other's in an incandescent firestorm, lighting up the surrounding air with forking white and blue power.

"I love you," Trystan says in a gasp between electric kisses. "I love you, Vothe. I love you *so much*."

"Be my mate," Vothe growls against Trystan's lightning-coated lips. "Be mine with the Zonor. With all of Erthia. But be mine, Trystan Gardner."

"Not on land," Trystan insists, gripping the sides of Vothe's pants, holding Vothe against himself, so tight Vothe feels as if he'll lose his mind if they don't take each other fully. "You can conjure air around me."

Nodding, Vothe pulls Trystan into another kiss, their lips meeting in an explosion of lightning as Vothe flies them into the center of the huge Zonor, Trystan's mouth hot on Vothe's.

Vothe pivots his wings and arrows them down toward the river's rushing surface. They hit the cool water and bolt into it, multihued lightning illuminating their descent as Vothe conjures a bubble of air around Trystan's head.

Trystan pulls Vothe into another kiss as they reach the riverbed, Vothe's hands sliding over Trystan's slick, muscular form, the two of them desperately pulling at and yanking off each other's clothing until there's nothing separating them from each other, nothing separating them from the Life-giving waters of the Zonor.

Nothing separating them from the power of the river merging with the power in their bodies.

Capturing each other's mouths in a deep, tongue-twining kiss that comes close to turning them both into pure lightning, they slide around each other in the churning waters and powerfully join with a crack of lightning, Vothe's mouth clamping down on Trystan's shoulder, Trystan's skin hot against Vothe's lips.

Storming magic sizzles over them both with the power to cleave worlds as Vothe sinks his teeth into Trystan's shoulder and sends his full lightning into him.

The entire Natural Matrix of the river explodes in blue light, merging with them both as they're swept into a wave of Erthia-tilting ecstasy and love and merged Wyvern-Dryad power.

"Are you ready?" Trystan asks from where they later stand, hand in hand, on the riverbank's outcropping of flat, obsidian stone, both of them clothed in pants made of melded deep-purple leaves that Trystan fashioned with a swipe of the branch in his hand.

A steady breeze kisses Vothe's skin, and he can read that Trystan isn't chilled by it, Trystan's physical connection to the world transformed by the Forest and the Zonor and their full Wyvernbonding. More shifter-like than he was before, as a result of their mating bond.

Just like Vothe has become more Dryad Fae.

Vothe pulls in an ecstatic breath, both of them suffused with the warm, shimmering aura of their merged lightning, a bit stunned by their effect on each other, Vothe's emotions and power still swept up in Trystan, his hold on Trystan's hand firm.

Vothe looks to the half-moon Wyvernbond mark on Trystan's shoulder. It glows lightning bright, small threads of silvery lightning crackling from it. A besotted ache constricts Vothe's chest, the Eastern Wyvern mating mark's glow as incandescent as their love for each other and for their kindred river. Their merged power amplified by it *all*.

"I'm ready," Vothe affirms.

Trystan raises the branch in his hand at the same time that Vothe raises his palm to the heavens, and they summon that love-fused power.

Bolts of their fused blue-and-white lightning flash from Trystan's branch and Vothe's palm and merge as they soar upward and fan out to form a domed net of pulsing, forking magic over the entire Zonor River and its bracketing Forest, the Forest's energy joining in to guide the net-barrier's flow in perfect sync with the trajectory of Trystan and Vothe's magic.

Vothe and Trystan continue to feed power into their lightning barrier until they're tapped out, their bonded magic needing time to recharge. But this shield, Vothe considers as they survey it, side by side, it feels strong enough to protect this second largest body of water in the Eastern Realm from *anything* containing Vogel's Shadow.

"My great-aunt Sithendrile told me to go back to the Zonor," Vothe confides in Trystan. They're sitting on the upraised rocky embankment by the Zonor's edge, their fingers interlaced. "Back when you had that first day's leave from the Wyvern-guard, and we went to Voloi," he adds, glancing at Trystan, feeling both lovestruck and dazed as he slides his gaze back toward the river and takes in what they've wrought.

A paintbrush twilight has descended, large swaths of pastel hues brightening the western sky, their net-shield of blue-and-white lightning flashing across the Zonor and its forested banks.

"She told me," Vothe continues, caressing the side of Trystan's thumb with his own, "*that's where you'll find your transformation.*"

Trystan seems to ponder this before he draws Vothe into a close embrace and kisses him long and slow and deep, feeding lightning into Vothe in a way that speeds Vothe's pulse and makes him want to pull Trystan down to the bottom of the Zonor once more.

"Do you feel transformed, Vothendrile?" Trystan asks, giving him a slight, wry smile, his eyes lit with blue-and-white lightning, with the sheer thrill of their combined power.

And their unleashed love.

Vothe bares his teeth in a hungry grin before an upswell of emotion clenches his heart—for this Mage he initially tried to drive away. This Mage who is now his *everything*.

"I do, Trystan," Vothe confides. "Our power . . . it's completely intermingled now. Can you feel it?"

Trystan draws in a deep breath before leaning in to touch his forehead to Vothe's while caressing the side of his face.

"I can feel it," Trystan hisses in Wyvern. He inhales fast, seeming just as shocked as Vothe is to hear the Wyvern tongue sliding through his lips. "I can draw on your power and language now," Trystan marvels, curling his mouth around the sibilant Wyvern words, the motion of his pierced lip so sexy that Vothe wants to eat his words whole. "I feel . . . *merged* to you," Trystan admits.

An ardent spark ignites between them, and Vothe moves to draw him into a closer embrace just as the feel of an incoming storm aura barreling toward them from the East wrests his attention. Alarm crackling through their merged power, they bolt to their feet.

"What is it?" Trystan asks as he takes hold of the branch sheathed at his side, their merged power coiling and readying to strike.

A dark, winged figure soars out of the clouds jutting out over the half-leveled Vo Mountain Range in the distance. Surprise lights through Vothe as he reads the figure's energy, recognizing his great-aunt's power before she soars into closer view above their shielding, alarm forking through her magic.

"It's my great-aunt," Vothe cautions Trystan, his hand coming to Trystan's wrist to halt a defensive attack. "We need to let her through."

They open a gap in their lightning dome, and Sithendrile swoops through it and lands before them. Her dark eyes spit gold lightning, and her horns are up, her claws out, a look of urgency on her crimson-tattooed onyx face.

Her shrewd gaze slides over them, missing no detail, including the lightning-filled mating mark newly emblazoned on Trystan's shoulder, their linked hands, and Trystan's transformed state—his newly pointed ears, deep-green hue and Zonor-blue eyes and river-hued hair—as well as the blue-and-white lightning forking over Vothe's onyx skin.

Sithendrile's eyes meet Vothe's, power zapping between them as her wings snap in. "Zhilaan is sending out a storm force of Zhilaan'whuur to take hold of the power of this river and the Dyoi Forest," she warns.

Vothe gapes at her, rapidly comprehending the full gravity of this.

The Zhilaan'whuur—Elite Weather Forces of the Zhilaan military.

"I felt your energy from a full league away," Sithendrile bites out, her eyes flicking toward Trystan with a conflicted look. "I soared ahead to warn you both to draw down your magic and *get out of the way*. The Zhilaan'whuur are going to send a huge storm band through here at dawn. The largest storm band they've ever created. To wrest hold of the elemental power of the Zonor River and Dyoi Forest and use it to battle back Vogel's Shadow storms in the continent's central lands."

A charged ripple of shock flashes through Trystan and Vothe, the ramifications of this detonating like a runic explosive—to build a storm band that holds enough elemental energy to drive back Vogel's Shadow storms . . . it will require drawing *way too much* power from the Natural World. Both the Zonor River and Dyoi Forest will be destroyed.

"How far away are they?" Trystan demands.

Vothe's great-aunt narrows her eyes at Trystan, and every hackle in Vothe rises. Because he can sense, through the conflict streaking through her power, that she's warring with herself, what she knows of Trystan pitted against what his Black Witch sister almost succeeded in doing to the entire East. But it's what *Vogel* nearly did to the entire East.

"You've half a day at most," Sithendrile bites out, baring her teeth at Trystan. *"So get out of Zhilaan's way."*

The storm churning to life inside both Vothe and Trystan surges. Without warning, Trystan grabs tight hold of Vothe's empathic aunt's wrist. Instantly comprehending Trystan's intention, Vothe lunges forward to grab hold of her, as well.

She hisses, elongating teeth flashing at them both.

"Please! Listen!" Vothe implores, desperate for her to use her empathic powers to read them both.

Sithendrile's brow furrows as her empathic senses connect and read every last thing the Forest showed Vothe and Trystan, as well as everything that's happened to them and their allies since they flew west to find Elloren and Yvan.

Sithendrile's eyes meet Vothe's, a look of pure, unadulterated shock in them. "Holy Vo," she hisses in Wyvern. "Can this all be true?"

Trystan nods emphatically. "If the Dyoi Forest and the Zonor fall, the Natural World falls apart," he hisses back in Wyvern, Sithendrile visibly startling at Trystan's new ability to speak their language fluently. "Destroy the Natural World, and there is no East," Trystan continues to hiss. "No water. No crops. The descent of weather so violent even your Zhilaan'whuur will *not* be able to control it. Then, the complete breakdown of the Living World as the Shadow rolls in."

"Come to the Forest," Vothe begs of her, urgency crackling around them all.

Seeming dazed, Vothe's great-aunt nods and lets them lead her to the riverbank's tree line. Lets them guide her palms to a River Oak's rough, deep-purple trunk.

Sithendrile stiffens and gasps as the golden lightning crackling over her skin flashes to brighter life and she's pulled into the tree.

Vothe whooshes out a shuddering breath, his palm to the bark, turmoil slashing through him. "My brother, Geth," he forces out, "he leads the Zhilaan'whuur." He looks at Trystan, desperate. "We can't let the Zonor and Dyoi Forest fall . . . but how can I fight my own brother?"

"You won't," Trystan rejoins, his hand coming to Vothe's shoulder in an unflinching show of support. "We'll keep the Zhilaan'whuur walled off from both our Waters and our Forest."

Vothe's skin shivers in response to the bolstering feel of Trystan's touch as they stand there for what seems like an eternity, waiting.

Night has descended by the time Vothe's great-aunt emerges, completely encased in dark purple bark, her form softly illuminated by the lightning crackling over the dome-net above.

Vothe and Trystan step back as Sithendrile rapidly morphs back into herself, both gold and Zonor-blue lightning now sizzling over her skin and dark wings as she fans them powerfully out.

"I *see*," Sithendrile raggedly manages, her eyes wide. She raises her III-marked palm, Zonor-blue coursing through the image. "We need all of Zhilaan with us in this fight—"

Her words cut off as a lightning-spitting storm band suddenly appears above what's left of the Vo Mountain Range.

"Holy Vo," Sithendrile hisses. "They're sending a portion of their power out *now*!"

Alarm explodes through all three of them as the storm band begins to avalanche toward the Zonor. Guttural growls escaping them all, they thrust branches and palms forward, lashing their storming power into their shield and tethering it there before sending a wall of energy high up from its apex to prevent flight over their dome-shield's expanse.

The storm band crashes into their shielding with a concussive *BOOM*, then draws back and hits it again, then again, each Zhilaan'whuur blow sending a frisson of potent energy down Vothe's spine. But their shield holds, keeping the powerful storm band at bay.

The sky begins to clear, the dense lightning-spitting clouds parting and then dissipating. Three Zhilaan'whuur fly in, illuminated by the lightning dome, and Vothe immediately senses his brother's energy.

"That's Geth in the lead," he tells Trystan, every hackle rising. "I'm going to let him through."

Trystan nods, and they cast a defensive barrier over themselves and Sithendrile before opening a hole in their shield.

Geth feels like a barely contained storm as he soars in and lands before them, his white-flashing eyes blazing with a violence Vothe has rarely witnessed in his thoughtful, measured brother's expression. Geth's gaze rakes over the mating mark on Trystan's shoulder with a look of combative fury, his face twisting into an expression of open confusion over Trystan's altered appearance before he takes in the blue-and-white lightning coursing over Vothe's skin and the blue-and-gold power forking over Sithendrile's.

He gives them both spearing looks of disgust. "What in *all the hells* have you done?"

"Hear us out, Geth," Vothe implores, grasping for every shred of their history of closeness. "Please, my brother—"

Geth snaps his teeth at Vothe. *"Get. Out. Of. Our. Way,"* he hisses, his eyes flicking damningly toward Trystan.

"No, Geth," Vothe snarls back. "We can't lose any more of the Natural World— Vogel's already destroyed too much of it. If you bring your full power through here, you'll destroy both the Zonor and the Dyoi Forest, and the Natural Matrix will *fall.* Its very tether on the weather will *fall.* It will be weather chaos. And even the Zhilann'whuur will not be able to rein it back in!"

"What are you talking about?" Geth growls back, his eyes flashing with rage. "*We* control the weather! Vogel is at our doorstep! And you speak of protecting *rivers and trees?*"

"I speak of staving off the end of the *entire Balance of Nature,*" Vothe throws back, incensed, desperate. "The old ways of warfare won't work anymore. We might as well wage war on *ourselves!*"

"Gethindrile," Trystan tries, firm and unrelenting, "just hear us out."

Geth shoots Trystan a murderous look. "Silence, *Fae Crow!*"

"Silence *yourself,* Geth," Sithendrile fires back, a circle of gold-and-blue lightning crackling up from the ground to surround her. "They are trying to tell you something *vital.*"

Geth glares at both her and Vothe, rage sheening his eyes. "You're proving yourselves to be traitors to the entire East. Is that what you want? Am I supposed to take down my own family?" His voice splinters, his power infused with an upsurge of tortured conflict. "If you don't relent, I *will* wage war on you both!"

Trystan's power rises, dwarfing even Sithendrile's and Geth's, Vothe's hair prickling from the static spitting from his aura's edges. "This is what Vogel wants," Trystan levels at Geth, his voice low and adamant. "This fracture between us—" he motions between Geth and himself "—and between everyone who needs to stand together with the Natural World. It will be our *undoing.*"

Geth gives Trystan a look of blazing incredulity. "You have *corrupted my brother.* You have brought him and now my great-aunt down a path of *ruin.* I will kill you myself when we sweep through here in storm and *fury.*"

And then Geth takes flight, bolting into the air before pausing to hover just above them as he points a damning finger. "Vothendrile, you are my brother," he grits out, his voice breaking with emotion, "but I will *mow you down* in a heartbeat if you stand in my way of protecting the entire East. You have been *fully warned.*" He glares at their great-aunt. "And *you* . . . you are *dead* to me."

And then he flies off, leaving a trail of lightning in his wake.

They close the gap in their shield and watch him soar away, a tense quiet descending before Vothe's great-aunt breaks it with a hissing stream of Wyvern epithets.

"Well, that went well," Vothe snarls, staring toward the top of the Vo Mountain Range.

"Your brother always was a stubborn fool," she growls.

Vothe levels a glare at her. "You were ready to incinerate my mate or bite his head off when you first landed."

Sithendrile returns Vothe's glare in spades. "Yes, and I'm the *open-minded* one of the family." She lets out a long, teeth-gritted growl. "Please tell me you two have a larger force on your side."

Trystan brings one hand to his hip and rakes the other through his Vo-blue hair before leveling a hard look at her. "All of our potential allies are fighting with each other."

Sithendrile looks to the heavens and curses again before visibly gathering herself, jaw set tight. Her eyes fix on Trystan once more, an edge of apology entering their fierce depths. "Welcome to the family, Dryad'kin."

Pained emotion shivers through Trystan's power before he reins it in, and Vothe is swept up in the almost unfightable urge to kiss away any doubt left in Trystan that his place is by Vothe's side. Then Trystan gives Sithendrile a returning jaded look, coolly collected once more as his eyes flash power.

Sithendrile smirks as she holds Trystan's gaze, her eyes crackling with obvious approval. "Well, then," she hisses in Wyvern as she lifts her hands and gathers gold-and-blue lighting around them, her fingers and wrists flashing bright with it, "we'll just pray to Vo on High for a miracle. And, in the meantime, we'll find out just how much power we can throw into our shielding."

CHAPTER EIGHT

DEATHBONDED

Tierney Calix

Northern Vo River

Tierney swirls her hand through the Vo's night-dark purple water, her vulnerable River's returning ripple of affection squeezing her heart. She can sense Or'myr, Fyordin, and Viger just behind her, the four of them grouped on the rocky riverbank, their joint power so intimately bonded, any boundaries between their intermingling auras have frayed.

"I can sense the Vo's elemental magic gaining importance as more of the Natural World in the West is destroyed," she murmurs. Her eyes widen as a new reading flows in from the Vo's connection to all of Erthia's waterways. "I sense something else, as well. A shield has just been sent up around the Zonor." She looks at Fyordin, who strides knee-deep into the Vo, as well.

"Can you sense its origin?" Fyordin presses, sliding his hands into the water.

Tierney nods. "Trystan's power is in it . . . along with Zhilaan Wyvern magic. Can you feel it? And the aquifers of the East . . . they've just been linked to a Dryad with strong water magic."

Fyordin's Vo-dark stare meets hers. "I've a sense of this, as well."

Astounded by this development, Tierney lets the unexpected magic rush over her for a long moment as she studies her River, her immediate surroundings illuminated by the purple light emanating from the shield-amplifying runes Or'myr has marked on the stone wall beside them. She lifts her gaze toward the Xishlon moon Or'myr crafted in the sky, still hanging just above their dome-shield.

Like a purple battle cry.

Tierney's blood warms, a wave of affection escaping her hold to rush toward

Or'myr. Instantly abashed by this surge of emotion she knows will flow right into him through their bond, she frantically tries to reel it back to no avail.

Her surge of feeling connects with Or'myr like a wave crashing to shore, and she catches him stiffening, their gazes flashing toward each other. Violet lightning flashes through Or'myr's eyes as he gives her a look of such pure *ardor*, a hot flush blooms over Tierney's skin.

They wrench their gazes away, Tierney's pulse cast into a tight, rapid rhythm, as Fyordin's water power lashes around her in an aggravated swirl, her Asrai'kin clearly picking up on what's going on between her and Or'myr.

Viger's line of Dark suddenly courses through it all in a disquieted vibration.

Tierney startles and flicks her gaze toward Viger. He's defying gravity, as he's wont to do, his tall form suspended against the broad trunk of a towering Noi River Elm above their heads like a great spider, his back to the bark, his full-Dark predator eyes set on *her*.

"That's good news, that we have help in protecting the East's waterways," Or'myr states rigidly, drawing Tierney's attention back to his intent, lightning-spitting stare. She can sense him fighting off the bond's pull to her, sense him attempting to keep his emotions from crackling through it. He peers out over the Vo. "I've always known on an intellectual level that this river is one of Erthia's major arteries. But I never *felt* it like I do now . . . connected to you all."

Tierney gulps as Or'myr casts another pained, ardent look her way, prompting a stronger rise of Fyordin's power to roil through them both. Tierney struggles to ignore it. She can feel the way they've all been fighting to see past the bond's pull, wrenching their focus toward the Vo again and again—they're all clear that there are more important things at stake than the tumultuous, impassioned feelings simmering through this binding.

"I feel more fully *Fae* than I ever have before," Tierney confides, keeping her gaze firmly on the Vo, "with so much at stake."

"I also feel more Fae than I ever have," Fyordin admits, his voice gruff, conflict jostling through his power. "When my family arrived here as refugees, they were so desperate to assimilate." He pauses, grimacing as he shakes his head before he glances at them all. "At times, after I pledged allegiance to the Wyvernguard and the Vu Trin, I wrestled with the pull to be Fae *first*. But I realize now, my decision to put the Waters of Erthia above *all else* was the right path all along."

"You aren't alone in feeling that Fae pull," Or'myr admits to Fyordin, his arresting, violet features tightening with a look of frustration as he glances toward the nearby Noi Cypress grove. "I can sense the Dryad Fae in me struggling to come out of dormancy in response to this Vo connection I feel through you and Tierney, especially in response to the trees rooted in the river. And the Urisk in me . . . I can sense that part of me striving to break free in some new way, as well. My Urisk people . . . we were once known as the Fae Guardians of Erthia's Stone. Until my people deemed those ancient ways 'primitive thinking.'" A shot of rebellious energy sizzles through Or'myr's power, making Tierney shiver.

"But those 'primitive Fae ways,'" he continues, "they were intensely connected to the Natural World. I think they were the truer path. I'm increasingly drawn toward that Erthia-connected Fae-ness." His gaze slides to Tierney, a warrior light flashing in his eyes. "And toward being a protector of your Waters' entire bed and its surrounding Forest."

Tierney holds Or'myr's gaze for a protracted moment, another wave of feeling for him sweeping through her in a whirlpool rush. His words have the gravitas of a vow, and she's momentarily overcome with gratitude for his alliance.

Gratitude to them *all*.

Fighting back the sting of tears, Tierney glances up toward Viger's shadowy horned form. "You never lost your connection to your Fae calling, did you, Viger?" she says as she remembers Viger's heartbreaking dream. "Even though you were reviled for it."

A bitter expression crosses Viger's pale face. "Death is reviled by all," he states in a voice so low and chilling it shivers straight through her, the vulnerable friend she felt so close to last night *gone*. "Keep your praise," he hisses, every speck of light around them pulsing Dark. "If this River falls, I will become your greatest nightmare."

Tierney narrows her eyes at him, holding his stare, refusing to be intimidated. Asrai warrior energy surges through her, infused with the strength of churning rapids. "So, we don't let it fall," she shoots back.

A bold idea lights, widening her eyes as her gaze swings to Or'myr's wall of runes. She levels a finger at it. "We should runically connect our Deathkin binding to the Vo's shielding. So we can flow even more of our power through it." She pivots back toward Viger. "Can it be done?"

There's a beat of hesitation, Viger's gaze boring into hers as the ramifications of what she's suggesting shivers through everyone's linked power. "It can be done, Asrai," comes Viger's bone-shuddering reply.

THE DRYAD STORM

They all still, a momentous tension sizzling through their bond.

Or'myr shoots Viger a cautioning look. "Correct me if I'm wrong, but if we runically bind our primordial linkage to the Vo's shielding, and the river falls . . . we're brought down with it. Yes?"

"If this River falls," Tierney cuts in, slicing the air with her hand, "*everything* is lost. There's no 'losing the Vo,' Or'myr."

"I agree," Fyordin says. "We need to do whatever it takes to protect our Waters."

A tidal wave of Tierney's gratitude fair explodes out of her to storm through Fyordin, and he meets her flow of power with an embracing rush, an enamored look liquefying his gaze that has Tierney fighting the urge to throw her arms around him, fully liquefy them both, and merge with the Vo.

Viger lifts a hand and bursts into mist, drawing everyone's attention as a portion of his Darkness takes the shape of a suspended black Deathkin linkage rune. Viger's disembodied hiss sounds out, the rune streaming toward Or'myr until it stills, hovering before him.

"Bind this linkage rune to the Vo's shielding, geomancer," Viger charges as he rematerializes halfway up another tree's trunk, defying gravity once more as he leans against it, his chilling, emotionless tone a wall.

Or'myr casts them all a grim look, then motions toward the suspended rune. "We're all decided, then? We permanently link our binding to these Waters and stand or fall with the Vo and its supporting land and stone?"

Tierney's pulse kicks into a faster rhythm as a palpable assent floods their connected power.

Without another word, Or'myr lifts his wand toward their shielding's largest foundational rune and draws the suspended black rune onto the purple-glowing rune then murmurs a series of spells. Four misty ropes of Dark power flow from Viger's rune to connect with the center of all their chests, just over their hearts.

Or'myr lowers his wand and sets his gaze on Viger.

Viger's lower half shivers to mist, and he pushes himself off the tree and hangs suspended in the air as he murmurs a Deathkin spell, the sound of his voice coming from everywhere at once, sending vibrations through their commingled magic.

A booming *CLAP* knifes through Tierney's ears, and she flinches, the world shuddering to full Dark. A hard pull yanks on their Deathkin bond, a wheezing breath punched from all their lungs as their bond fuses to the shielding's foundational rune then streams through the River's shielding, their connection *amplifying*.

Warmth blasts through Tierney's blood, her attraction to all three of them surging.

All of their eyes snap toward her with raptor-focused intensity, their fused power shot through with a swell of emotion-fueled attraction stronger than the pull of the Xishlon moon.

Or even a hundred Xishlon moons.

Tension crackles in the air, and Tierney can feel all three males striving to beat down the sudden surge of bond-fueled *want*.

"I doubt any trace of Shadow can get through our shielding now," Or'myr mutters, then clears his throat as he looks at the shield, a line of his invisible lightning forking around her and sending gooseflesh breaking out over Tierney's skin. "Everyone should get some sleep," Or'myr suggests, glancing at her. "I'll activate alarm runes to alert us if anyone tries to breach our defenses."

Flustered, Tierney gets up, ready to flee from all of them. She's not even several paces away before steps sound, close on her heels, Fyordin's power eddying through hers, her own steps halting as she turns toward him.

"Tierney'lin," he rasps, his power breaking loose to stream around her in a rippling caress as he takes hold of her arm and leans in close. "Come with me, Tierney'lyn," he huskily offers, his eyes glazed with feeling. "Come rest with me at the bottom of the Vo."

Viger's and Or'myr's powers flash through their bond, the intense jolts startling Tierney, all of them understanding from the flow of Fyordin's power that he's offering more than sleep.

Her pulse thudding, Tierney looks toward the ground, toward the wilds, anywhere but at Fyordin and the Vo, suddenly hyperaware of the Sanjire plants growing everywhere, as common in the East as dandelion weeds are in the West . . .

She dares a glance at Fyordin, swept up in the seductive urge to let him draw her to the bottom of the Vo and feel his Asrai form against hers as they dissolve into each other . . .

"I . . . I need to be alone," she stammers, pulling away from Fyordin's loose grip.

Not daring to stay near any of them for one second longer, Tierney strides away at a fast clip, the caressing stream of Fyordin's power only heightening her wanton draw to give in to this bond-pull.

She can feel the three males' attention fixed on her through the bond, even after she rounds a rocky bend and all three of them are cut from sight.

THE DRYAD STORM

Tierney finds a small, isolated inlet by the water's edge, sits down on an outcropping of stone and remains still for a long time, a small beaver briefly joining her, her lower legs dangling in her Vo's night-dark waters. The River's swirl of love whirlpools through her as she lets her complicated emotions settle.

Eventually, she slumps, unable to fight the pull of sleep any longer. Pushing herself off the stone, Tierney drops into the Vo's waters until she's fully submerged, then swims down into its deep center, fish circling her. Curling up against the silty bed, exhaustion gripping a firmer hold, Tierney melts toward sleep.

She's drifting aimlessly when a misty swirl of Viger's Darkness ripples through her subconscious like a distant caress, triggering a dream. Slipping into her dream like warm honey sliding from a spoon, she finds herself caught up in the seductive sensation of Viger's long form wrapped around hers, his teeth pressing lightly against the base of her neck.

Heat shivers over her dream-form's skin, the cadence of Viger's breathing tighter than it was when they kissed in the Northern Forest, the hungry nature of his embrace prompting an enticing shiver through her. Silvery-black ribbons of Viger's thrall swirl around them, beautifully surreal, as if painted there by an invisible brush. The ribbons still, along with Viger's breathing.

You're here, he shudders through her.

"I am," Tierney responds, heart fluttering, as she reaches up and runs her fingertips over Viger's hard cheekbone, then back through his silky midnight hair, tracing her thumb along the edge of his pointed ear. She leans in and brushes her lips against his, waiting for his dream-kiss. Suddenly *hungry* for it.

Tierney . . . there's danger in this. Viger's thought ripples over her skin.

"Maybe in real life," Tierney whispers against his lips, feeling giddy with desire, "but this is only a dream. Do you want to give in to this draw?"

His thrall stills, his power shivering over her, trailing ardent heat.

Yes, Asrai, comes Viger's low, almost tortured answer.

"Then give in," she urges, a rush of heart-quickening anticipation sizzling through her.

The energy coursing through Viger's thrall takes a turn for the feral, and he leans down and brings his lips to the base of her neck, every one of Tierney's nerves tingling to life as his tongue flickers against it. He slides his mouth toward her shoulder, his teeth touching down once more as he stills, his heart thudding against hers.

"Are you going to bite me?" Tierney throatily teases, every inch of her caught up in pulse-quickening excitement.

She can feel Viger's ripple of amusement. His teeth touch down a fraction more, the pressure dancing on the edge of a sting. *Say the word and I'll consume you, Asrai'ir*, he murmurs, his deep voice vibrating through her power, his lips now tracing a line along the base of her neck, his serpentine tongue flicking against her skin in an enthralling motion.

She presses her body seductively against his, and Viger breathes out a sound somewhere between a wicked laugh and low groan, her desire ramping up, hot and hungry . . . before she stills, a small sliver of her lust-addled mind triggering a pause.

Remembering that he's a primordial Death Fae.

"What do you mean by 'consume'?" she asks. She meets Viger's stare, his pale skin surprisingly flushed. He smiles, giving her a look full of the forbidden edges of midnight. And then, he opens his midnight lips, and his forked, purple tongue flickers out.

A ragged breath shivers through Tierney as she's overtaken by the startlingly pleasurable phantom sensation of Viger's tongue flickering all over her body—all except for the place she's the most lit up for him.

A hot flush suffusing her face, Tierney holds his hypnotic stare. "Since this is just a dream . . ." she suggests, her thoughts scattering as she grows quiet, both fear of the unknown and a brazen lust for it mounting.

Viger's smile gains a sultry edge. *What does your dream-self want, Asrai?*

"What do *you* want?" she hedges, nerves frayed, her desire struggling to break through her nervous trepidation. "Show me," she more firmly insists. "I want to know."

Viger blinks, and her clothing and his tunic disappear.

Tierney is unable to stifle her shocked laugh, amusement bubbling up through her fugue of nerves. "Shy one, aren't you," she teases.

Viger lets out a low laugh, his Dark eyes sharpening on hers. *Are dreams a place to be shy?*

"No," she admits, heatedly aware of his gaze flicking over her form, lighting her every nerve. Her pulse deepens with a stronger want as her gaze wanders over Viger's naked chest, black snake tattoos marking its muscular expanse, their serpentine forms rising from his pants, which only stokes her nervous amusement higher.

She traces a trembling finger over one of the serpents, her breathing growing erratic as the muscles of Viger's stomach tighten against her touch and she continues to trail her finger lower and lower . . .

. . . then slides her fingertip just under the edge of his pants, the desire to consume *him* gaining serious ground.

What do you want, Asrai? Viger asks again, the possibility-fraught words shivering through her.

Reckless hunger rising, Tierney blinks, and the rest of Viger's clothing vanishes.

A hotter rush of desire courses through her widened eyes as she drinks in his entire body, his dark horns rising.

Viger's hands slide to her hips, pulling her insistently closer before he stills, clearly waiting for her to voice her consent.

I want to know what this is, she thinks through their bond in a sudden blaze of emotion, shocked to find her words easily sliding into him via their strengthening linkage. Her breath hitches as she decides to delve deep and bare her whole heart to him. *I want to know what this is before the Shadow War comes. Even if it's just a dream.*

Viger studies her, the whole world stilling, his entire thrall receding. She can sense his desire burning in it like a dark star, yearning to collide with both her power and her heart.

"Sweep me up in your thrall, Viger," she demands. "I want you to."

Viger's question shivers through her. *Are you sure, Asrai?*

In answer, she reaches up to grab hold of one of his horns and pulls him into an intense, tongue-twining kiss, the deepest recesses of her water power coursing out to ripple through him.

Viger groans, his thrall sweeping them into its spiraling power as he breaks the kiss and slides his mouth down to the edge of her shoulder once more, tongue flickering as his sharpened teeth bear down . . .

. . . then lightly pierce her skin.

Tierney cries out as a wild rush of pleasure courses through her. Brazenly pivoting herself toward Viger, their movements dream-blurred, he thrusts forward and they join.

A gasp of pure excitement breaks from Tierney's throat as she grips his strong body, the dream-amplified pleasure more intense than anything she's ever experienced, surging through her, eddying through her magic as she eagerly firms her hold on him, urging him on, and Viger responds with feral vigor.

A groan tears from Viger's throat that vibrates through both their bodies and Nature itself as their joint rhythm takes on a more frenzied pace, a growl working its way out from the base of Viger's throat, his claws biting into her skin.

A spiraling, magic-exploding rush of ecstasy shatters through Tierney, followed by a rapids-strong, cascading shudder of pleasure that widens her eyes and blasts her power into a swirl of molten steam.

Viger snarls her name, pressing himself pulsatingly deep as he floods her with his Darkness, his lips and teeth clamping down on her shoulder. The sting of his bite prompts one last, wild lash of ecstasy that's so strong it catches the Natural Matrix surrounding them in it, and Tierney is overcome by a sudden awareness of a sea of Darkness forming on all sides and rushing toward them as the Balance around them begins to career off-kilter . . .

Viger's silvery thrall flashes to life and blasts outward as their eyes meet, bright with urgency. A look of intense emotional pain tightens Viger's gaze as three words shiver to life in the center of all his fears, bright as beacons. He blinks once, and snaps out of existence, and Tierney is pulled, rapids-fast, into the tunneling Darkness.

The departure of Viger's Deathkin energy dampens the aura whirling around Tierney as her dream-self dissolves into her water form. The Darkness fades, a vivid blue flashing to life all around Tierney as her dream morphs into a completely different scene.

Fyordin's water form wrapped around hers.

"My Asrai'ir love," he murmurs as they both begin to solidify, liquid warmth shifting to strong hands running along her back with fluid finesse, Fyordin's Vo-blue lips catching hers in a kiss shot through with the River's embracing power.

Am I truly daring to dream this too? Tierney questions as she lets her dream-blurred self fall into Fyordin's enticingly fluid kiss, waving away her distant sense of confusion.

Swept up in Fyordin's vortex of desire, they roll through the warming water, the surrounding Vo rippling every glorious shade of dream-heightened blue.

"Tierney'a'lin ruuushh muu Asrai'mir . . ." Fyordin murmurs against her lips, the magic he's swirling around and through her turning tidal as they *merge*.

Caught in the current of their Vo's power, Tierney throws her head back, opens her mouth and draws in a stream of water, arching against Fyordin as his hunger gains ground and she matches his fluid rhythm.

Fyordin's Vo-blue eyes lock with hers, his gaze sharpening into what seems like a more vivid, astonished awareness as a faraway edge of Tierney's mind startles against their outrageous joining.

It's just a dream, she thinks, as Fyordin catches her up in another kiss and Tierney brazenly gives in to the pleasure of it, thrilling to the cresting-wave feel of his body's motion, the Vo's full power coursing through their joining like a tsunami about to break . . .

A hard flash of purple light suddenly overtakes the surrounding blue, casting Tierney into a fuller confusion.

Fyordin grips her harder, his arms flexing around her back with covetous force, hands splayed out in what feels like a desperate attempt to hold on to her as he murmurs to her in a passionate stream of Asrai.

The scene shatters, as if blasted away by an explosion of superior magic, and Tierney is drawn into a new one.

A purple room shimmers into being around her, blurred at the edges. Wavering, deep-purple trees are set in the surrounding walls, everything violet misted.

A purple-hued man pressing her into a bed, kissing her with lightning-rod fervor.

Shock lances through Tierney.

Or'myr.

Tierney gasps as a streak of Or'myr's purple lightning forks through her body and connects with her power, shocking through her inner storm and electrifying it.

Amplifying both his magic and hers.

It's explosive, Or'myr's kiss, but there's no pain in it, the startlingly electric sensation sending her sliding rapids-fast into a sizzling place of pure *want*.

Or'myr breaks the kiss and meets her gaze, lightning pulsing through his eyes with feverish light. "I love you," he says, giving her a look so intense it's almost tortured. "Tierney'lin, I love you so much. I have loved you since our first moments together. And I will love you *forever*."

And then his mouth is on hers once more in a claiming kiss, his magic surging through hers with impassioned force, emotion bolting through Tierney over his ardent declaration as a rush of love for him breaks through her power. She draws him closer, Or'myr's body joining with hers in a surge of purple lightning and her rushing rapids.

Tierney gasps, the explosive energy of their coupling flowing not just through each other, but into the entire riverbed, sending an unexpected wave of re-Balancing energy straight into it.

Tierney cries out as they hold each other, incandescently lit up by the way Or'myr is driving sheer geopower into both her and the Vo's bed, the pleasure Erthia-bendingly intense, every last trace of her power, vivid blue and deepest Dark, shifting into a sensation of ecstatic alignment.

As his power Balances *her*.

And suddenly, Tierney wants this connection more than she's ever desired anything. Wants Or'myr to turn not just the Vo's waters but every last shred of her power blazingly *purple*.

Violet light shudders through Tierney's vision, the whole world igniting as glorious, violet energy detonates more intensely through both their forms, blasting through her straight into the riverbed. A guttural cry escapes Or'myr, his long, muscular form shuddering against her, his heartbeat a hammer.

"Tierney'nuu'fya'lir," he raggedly says in Uriskal as errant threads of his lightning detonate over her skin and his.

Tierney, my beautiful love, she translates through the bond, emotion tightening her throat and blurring her eyes. Overcome, she pushes gently against his chest, and he draws a fraction away, so much lovestruck feeling in his eyes that her heart trips into an erratic rhythm.

Her gaze skims his chest, and surprise lashes through her.

There's an image of the dragon-goddess Vo encircling the Xishlon moon tattooed over its expanse. She meets Or'myr's eyes, stunned anew by the level of passion firing there . . .

. . . and something more.

Something so *right* that Tierney feels the very earth beneath her shift.

Both wildly thrown and wildly drawn in, she struggles to hold herself back from him, rocked by a sudden, ardent longing she's never known the likes of before.

A click of recognition seems to spark in Or'myr's eyes, and he blinks at her, as if seeing her with new blazing clarity. His eyes widen, and pain ripples across his expression before he blinks once more and the entire, purple-tinted dream snaps out of sight.

Tierney shivers awake at the bottom of the Vo. The riverbed is soft beneath her back, and electric energy courses through her like a pre-storm charge.

THE DRYAD STORM

Eyes closed, she pulls a deep, long breath of her River's sweet water into her lungs and stretches her blue limbs, sensually hyperaware of her body, her charged magic flowing seamlessly into the Vo's riverbed, and its surrounding *stone* . . .

Tierney's eyes snap open, a hot flush suffusing her skin as she hurtles into a sudden remembrance of her dreams.

Her pulse skyrockets.

Sweet holy gods.

And . . . Or'myr.

Joining with him, in particular, felt so outrageously *right*, his gloriously grounding energy still pulsing through her, drawing her focus away from the darkest, most forbidding corners of her Waters and more intensely toward the pulsing Life within them.

My sweet love, Tierney sends out to her River and every plant and animal that lives in it. She rolls her head to the side, protectively leaning her cheek against the Vo's bed as she's struck by a fleeting sense of Viger's thrall lashing through their bond like the sting of a whip, there and gone again in a flash of Darkness.

Tierney's pulse amps up because there's something *off* about Viger's power, a brutal edge to its energy that's deeply alarming. Tierney casts about for an explanation, the most obvious triggering a hot rush of chagrin.

Might Viger have sensed her dreams?

No, she assures herself, her flush growing uncomfortably hot. They were all hers, her own private imaginings, played out in her own mind.

Tierney stills, hunting for her central binding to Viger to get a sense of his location, and a brighter spark of concern lights. Her Deathkin bond to him has solidified, tendrils of his Darkness wrapping tight around her power's core.

Covetously tight.

Tierney's disquiet intensifies.

I need to find him, she realizes, beating back the reflexive dart of mortification over the scandalous dream-couplings.

Pushing off the riverbed, she swims to its bank and breaks through the Vo's predawn surface . . . and the scene she's met with whisks her breath away.

The Vo Forest's foliage has transformed into a stunningly vibrant show of colors overnight. The riot of hues edging the leaves are reflected by the Vo's slow-flowing surface, an early autumn chill in the air. The sky has lightened to a deep sapphire, the color glinting off the bond-Darkened runes dotting their dome-shield's entire surface.

Tierney draws in a bolstering breath and steps onto the rocky riverbank, then whisks the water off her body, reassuring herself that, as mortifying as the dream effects of the strengthened bond between herself, Viger, Or'myr, and Fyordin might be, her beloved Vo is more powerfully protected now that it's linked to that bond.

And she can't deny it—a part of her feels decadently lit up by her new dream-knowledge of this thing most everyone at the Wyvernguard seemed to have full knowledge of already, with their Xishlon festival and shockingly open ways. Even though she's never been with anyone outside of dreams, she now owns part of that knowledge, too, and feels powerful in the knowing, both desirable and full of her own potent desire, the feel of her River's power of creation coursing straight through it . . .

"Unbond her, *right now!*" Or'myr's angry voice booms from just past the rocky embankment, and Tierney freezes.

She's stunned by the level of vitriol in Or'myr's tone, a blast of his Geo-Mage aura flashing through their bond in a crackling, purple rush. Alarmed, she rounds the stony bend . . . and emerges into utter chaos.

Viger, Or'myr, and Fyordin are facing off, all of them glaring murderously at each other, fists balled, muscles tensed, seeming ready to tear out each other's throats.

Tierney's concern surges as she takes in Viger's sharpened horns and how his form is shirtless like the others, the snakes tattooed all over his chest writhing to life. His dark claws are out, body coiled for attack as he stares Fyordin and Or'myr down.

Wait, a part of her mind blares, *Viger truly has snake tattoos?*

Viger turns, his solidly black eyes arresting hers.

Before she can react, Viger's snake tattoos elongate and slither toward her, the serpents encircling her and enveloping her in a tight, black spiral. Viger bares his teeth and hisses.

Her feet skid across rocky sand as she's pulled clear to him in a blur, her outrage storming to life.

"What in the name of all the gods are you *doing!*" Tierney snarls.

Viger's hand clenches down around her arm, nails biting. "You're *mine,*" he growls.

Wait . . . what?

Or'myr draws his wand and levels it at Viger. "Get your hands and your bond *off* her."

Tierney's full storm bursts to life inside her as she levels a furious glare at Viger. "I asked you what you're *doing*?"

Viger bares his teeth at her. *Claiming you*, he snarls through the bond.

Tierney's storm surges, rapids-fast, and breaks free. Dark clouds roil into being overhead, a fierce wind picking up around them all as she narrows her gaze at Viger. *"Do. Not. PROVOKE me."*

An aggressive smile rises on Viger's dark lips. *You imagine your power a trace of mine?*

"Unhand her, Deathling," Fyordin growls, his stance confrontational, his invisible water aura bursting forth to rush around her. He raises both palms, roiling spheres of river water blasting into existence to hover above them. "She belongs to me and the Vo."

Tierney's eyes widen over Fyordin's outrageous declaration as well as the staggeringly potent amount of Vo might he's drawing up and readying to unleash straight at Viger.

"Have you given leave of your senses as well, Fyordin?" Or'myr bites out as he aims his wand at the Asrai in emphatic warning, purple lightning forking around it. *"None* of us own her. Stand down. The both of you. Or I swear to Vo on High, I will *make* you both stand down."

A hard punch of realization hits Tierney as she quickly scans the tattoo covering Or'myr's chest—the Goddess Vo's purple dragon manifestation, the purple Xishlon moon held in the dragon goddess's claws . . .

Tierney blanches, feeling as if the bank beneath her feet is giving way, as she's faced with the awful possibility that none of her dreams were solely her own, and Viger was able to read all three of them through their bond.

Her mortification and anger surging to monstrous heights, Tierney yanks her arm from Viger's grip, slashes her hands through the air, and hurls out a powerful wave of storming energy. Viger's serpentine bindings blast apart as she breaks clear of his thrall.

Barely.

"What in *all the hells* is going on?" she cries as her thunder booms and rain begins to sheet down. She levels her furious gaze on Viger's abyss-black eyes, Fyordin's Vo-blue ones, then on Or'myr's lightning-spitting look in belligerent question, hoping against hope that she's wrong.

"Tierney," Or'myr says tightly, "we're all bound more intimately than we realized." He shoots Viger a narrow glare as her winds whip around them all. "When we woke up, we were flooded by an awareness of . . . all of our mutual dreams."

A fiery flush sears through Tierney. "Holy *gods* . . ." she rasps out.

"She is bound to me before *all!*" Viger hisses at Or'myr and Fyordin.

In a blur, Or'myr levels his wand on Viger, his Strafeling geo-aura bursting to purple life and pulsing around his tall frame. "Think carefully, Viger," he warns, his tone low and lethal. "If you want her to hate you, then, by all means, continue down this path."

Viger's lips twist into a vicious smile. "Death is hated by all, Strafeling." He raises his hand and snaps his Dark-clawed fingers, and Tierney is instantly swept into the irresistible pull of his thrall, her feet skidding toward him once more, as if gravity has found a new origin point.

Him.

A shock of hurt pierces Tierney as she digs in her heels and struggles to resist Viger's pull, heart-stricken by his outrageous imagining that he *owns* her. She curses herself. Curses how she truly grew to care for him over these past few months. And suddenly, she can barely pull in a breath, deeply pained and thrown and flat-out *furious* as she holds firm against Viger's mounting draw and the covetous flow of Fyordin's burgeoning tempest.

With a growl, she draws on the Vo's might, pulling it into her palms. A cry tearing from her throat, she thrusts out her hands, and two storming blue bolts stream from them, blasting away Viger's and Fyordin's powers.

Trembling with righteous anger, Tierney meets Viger's ferocious gaze, sensing through their bond that she can't rival his full power as she draws more storming magic into her palms, but she's well past caring.

A shiver of out-of-control conflict slashes through Viger's Darkness as he abruptly draws his thrall down.

But it's too little, *too late.*

Tierney bores her piercing glare into him, wildly upset and breathing hard, furious at *all* of them. Furious at Viger and Fyordin for thinking they own her. Mortified over their collective dreams. And inexplicably furious at Or'myr for the intense, unwanted emotion their dream-coupling triggered to life inside her.

"*None* of you own me," she declares, struggling to hold back a typhoon. "Do you *hear* me? *None* of this matters, and *none* of you ever had a chance with me. I'm *already spoken for!*"

Or'myr blinks at her, seeming thrown. "There's *another* man?"

She glares at him, frustrated beyond all reason as their power strains toward each other's. "That's the *last* thing I need," Tierney cries before turning and storming off toward her River.

"What do you mean 'spoken for'?" Or'myr calls out from behind her, his voice strained.

"She means the Vo," comes Fyordin's harsh reply.

Hands at her hips, her breathing forcefully measured, Tierney's steps halt as her soles meet the Vo's cool water, every terror flooding back, too fast to handle—

The V'yexwraith demon.

The Mages and the Marfoir.

The terrifying Shadow poison sent into the Vo's waters.

So much river life, so quickly *destroyed.*

Tierney reaches up to rake her fingers through her long, tousled hair, the Vo catching her ankles in a swirling embrace as she's flooded with wave upon wave of clarity over how Viger's Death Fae mating bond has caused them all to lose their senses.

She turns to say as much to all of them when a winged, Wyvern-like figure appears in the sky. Her gaze pivots west to find a whole host of winged figures flying in.

Alarm flashes not just through her power, but through Fyordin's, Or'myr's, and Viger's. Viger's low hiss vibrates through their bond, the world around them pulsing Dark as the winged army of black-clad soldiers soar in and hover above their translucent dome-shield, the soldiers horned and night dark in hue.

Zhilon'ile Wyvern-shifters.

Or'myr holds up a cautionary hand as one of the figures swoops lower than the others, flying down to the shield's surface. "I know him," Or'myr says warily. "Vothendrile Xanthile's brother, Gethindrile."

A low growl rises in Viger's throat. "I sense a threat," he hisses.

"By order of the joint Zhilaan and Vu Trin forces," Gethindrile booms, his wings beating on air, "drop your shielding!"

"Can you let only him in?" Tierney asks Or'myr.

"I can," Or'myr answers as Vothe's brother waits. Or'myr glances toward Fyordin and Viger, an unspoken search for confirmation in his eyes.

Both Fyordin and Viger give him quick nods of assent, drawing up their power as Tierney gathers her own. Seeming satisfied, Or'myr calls out, "Only Geth comes through!" before he points his Wand-Stylus toward Gethindrile, murmurs a spell, and blasts out a thin bolt of violet lightning.

A small opening in the shield forms on contact, edged with raying, purple light. Vothe's brother soars through it, the opening snapping shut behind him. Landing gracefully on the bank before them, Gethindrile has a combative look on his chiseled onyx face, bright white threads of lightning forking over his skin.

"Gethindrile," Or'myr greets him, wand leveled.

The Wyvern-shifter's wings snap in tight behind him, Gethindrile's gaze sweeping over them all in a tight glare. "You were all summoned by the Vu Trin to come in for questioning *weeks ago* pertaining to your relationship with the Magedom's Black Witch."

Or'myr lets out an aggravated sigh. "Well, I declined the summons, Geth."

"I flat-out ignored it," Fyordin states, crossing his muscular arms in front of his broad chest as he and Tierney silently continue to draw up a formidable level of water magic, Or'myr quietly gathers his lightning, and Viger stealthily readies his full Darkness.

"You cannot just *ignore* a military summons," Gethindrile counters, lightning practically spitting out of his dark eyes.

A hard pulse of Viger's Darkness strobes through the surrounding world, twin black snakes suddenly draped across his shoulders. The serpents open their mouths, purple tongues flickering as they hiss at Gethindrile.

"You think you can summon Death?" Viger asks, lethally quiet, his lips lifting into a vicious grin. "Death does the summoning, Wyvern'kin." Snakes are suddenly streaming in from the Forest and River to surround Gethindrile, Viger's ire clearly piqued.

Easy, Tierney thinks to him through the bond. *He's not our true enemy.*

Viger glares at her, then glances pointedly toward the Wyvern army hovering high above. *We are depleted.* His voice shivers through her. *The bulk of our power is flowing into the Vo's shielding. And I sense a warring threat coming off of them in waves.*

Unease rises in Tierney. *Point taken,* she concedes.

"You are being ordered," Gethindrile states formally as he eyes the gathering serpents, "by the commanders of Noilaan and Zhilaan's joint Vu Trin forces, to *immediately* unshield the Vo River. Comply, and your ignored summons will go unpunished."

THE DRYAD STORM

Tierney's Asrai power rears alongside Fyordin's. "The Magedom has attacked our River from both ends," Fyordin growls before describing their battle with the V'yexwraith and Vogel's forces. "Why would you want it unshielded?"

"We have need of this river's elemental energy," Gethindrile answers. "To blast through the shielding the Black Witch and her forces have placed over the Dyoi Forest and the Zonor River. We need to draw on all of the elemental power of that land and water to create a storm band strong enough to battle Marcus Vogel's Shadow storm bands to the west of us. The Mage forces have close to total control over not just the Western Realm, but the continent's entire center, including Northern Ishkartaan, and they're about to invade Southern Ishkartaan."

Shock hits Tierney like a hammer blow. She can feel it reverberating through Viger, Fyordin, and Or'myr as well, straight through the bond.

A threat. There's a threat to the Balance here.

Coming from their *own* side.

"If you draw up enough power from the Dyoi and the Zonor for a storm band," Fyordin warns, "you'll consume *too much.* You'll not only throw the East's Natural Balance into utter disarray, you'll completely destabilize the East's weather."

Gethindrile glares at him. "Marcus Vogel has mowed down almost the *whole center* of the continent. If he comes here, he'll destroy the *entire East.* And you're worried about weather that *we* control?"

Fyordin's jaw hardens, a maelstrom in his eyes. "Your arrogance will be your undoing," he snarls. "Zhilaan only 'controls' the weather when working with a Balanced Natural World. But that Balance will be blasted into chaos if you destroy the Zonor and the Dyoi. We're holding our shield."

"The Asrai are right to stand their ground," Viger agrees, serpent calm, but there's nothing calm about his full-Dark stare. "Too much of the Natural World has been lost. Lose more, and you will bring a Full Death Reckoning down on your heads."

Gethindrile's expression turns explosive as he casts a daggered glare at Viger. "Do you even care what's at stake here?"

Viger's teeth elongate as he snaps them at Gethindrile, his snakes flashing fangs. "Do *you* have any idea how close I am to being drawn into a Reckoning, Noi'khin? How close *all* the Deathkin are? Do you have any idea of the cruelty involved in trying to right even *one slice* of a destroyed Balance?"

"I think you have your answer," Or'myr calmly states.

Gethindrile cuts them all an outraged look. "The East *trusted* you. We let you all into our *Wyvernguard*."

"You did," Tierney shoots back. "To protect the East. And we're going to do *just that*. By protecting her largest rivers and adjacent forested land."

Gethindrile's face twists with disgust, lightning leaping through his eyes. "You're no longer Vu Trin," he growls.

"So be it," Fyordin growls back, ignoring the pain Tierney senses strafing through his power. "But we are *Asrai*." He exchanges a look of ferocious alliance with Tierney before pointedly glancing at Or'myr and Viger. "And they are our Asrai'khin."

Fierce emotion strikes through both Viger's and Or'myr's powers, straight through the bond as a surge of love for all three men rises inside Tierney, the power of the Vo swirling around and through them all.

A look of cold reappraisal tightens Gethindrile's features. "You can't fight us off forever."

A laugh escapes Or'myr. "We'll sure as hell try."

Gethindrile hisses at him, baring his teeth. "We should have known better than to let the grandson of the Black Witch into Noilaan."

A dart of anger sparks through Or'myr's power, Gethindrile's cruel words roiling Tierney's internal tempest as Gethindrile thrusts his wings down and takes to the air, soaring toward the shield, angry crackling threads of lightning trailing in his wake.

Or'myr briefly opens an exit for him, and Gethindrile soars through it, then hovers in the air above the shield for a moment to confer with two other Wyvern-shifters, before the entire unit of soldiers fly back west. Throat tight, Tierney watches them wing toward the half-destroyed peaks of the Vo Mountain Range, likely assembling a large military force there to magic their storm band into being.

Holy all the hells.

Tierney turns back to her three Asrai'khin, the strength of their bond pulsing with troubled force. "What now?" she asks, at a loss.

"I will travel to the continent's central lands," Viger states grimly, turning his abyss-like eyes toward the half-decimated Vo Mountain Range. "And get a closer look at these storm bands Vogel has set in motion." Viger's gaze collides with Tierney's, those three words that live at the base of his line of fear suddenly escaping his hold to pulse through her with heart-striking force.

A knot of emotion tightens Tierney's throat, her internal storm rearing, surprise welling to find herself loath to be separated from Viger, despite all her anger and confusion over his actions.

"Viger . . ." she starts, but before she can get out another word, he bursts into multiple crows made of mist and takes to the sky.

Winging west.

Or'myr, Tierney, and Fyordin watch him leave in tense silence.

"He certainly has a flair for the dramatic," Or'myr notes, bringing a hand to his hip before spitting out a few Noi curses under his breath.

"Can we push our shielding west somehow?" she asks him. "To join it to Elloren's and Trystan and Vothendrile's shielding?"

Or'myr glances at her sidelong. "That's what I'm thinking. We'll need two runic focal points of Asrai power to accomplish that, placed north and south."

"Give me a rune-marked stone, and I'll carry the focal point south," Fyordin volunteers, a quiver of fierce reluctance eddying from his power to rush around Tierney. He looks straight at her, a current of love for her streaming through their joined magic and flowing to both her and their River as Tierney struggles to bite back her rise of reciprocal feeling.

"I need to be the one to go," Fyordin insists. "I can more easily evade Vu Trin capture, since I have the most knowledge of how they operate."

Tierney nods, grasping the truth of his words. And as much as she was angered by Fyordin's domineering attitude toward her earlier, she can't help but be impressed by how they're all putting aside their differences and jealousies to save the East.

"Goodbye, Asrai'ir," Fyordin says, holding his forearm out to her.

Tears stinging her eyes, Tierney reaches out to grip him. She can tell from the pained reluctance streaming through his power that he's saying goodbye to more than just their proximity.

Visible lines of their water power flow around each other's forearms, and Tierney blinks back tears, steeling herself as she murmurs the traditional Asrai farewell she's overheard both Fyordin and her other Wyvernguard Asrai'kin use again and again—"Asrai'ir m'yor'ith'illian." *May the full flow of Erthia's Waters go with you, Asrai'ir.*

"Asrai'ir sil'thrier," Fyordin responds. *And with you, Asrai'ir.*

Then Fyordin gives her a bittersweet smile, releases her forearm, takes her hand, and lifts it, tenderly kissing its back, a knot of emotion tightening the base of

Tierney's throat. Fyordin releases her and strides into the Vo, raising a hand to both her and Or'myr in farewell, before diving underwater and dissolving into their Vo, streaming south.

For a moment, Tierney stares in the direction Fyordin is streaming toward. She turns to meet Or'myr's gaze, his body and pants slick with her rain. She finds him studying her, one purple brow cocked, and warmth blooms on her cheeks as an inconvenient spark of attraction rises, an all too knowing look heating Or'myr's gaze.

"Let's just get to work, shall we?" Tierney self-consciously offers.

"Good idea," Or'myr responds kindly. He sighs, a trace of welcome amusement dancing in his eyes as he peers up at their shield, then points his Wand-Stylus toward the stone wall of runes that anchor and feed energy into it. "Let's set up our northern focal point of power, right there." He gives her a quick, loaded glance. "Seems a good place to channel all our pent-up . . . *energy.*"

SHADOW WINTER'S ASCENT

Marcus Vogel

Northern Ishkartaan Mountain Range

Vogel steps through his Shadow portal and out onto a cavernous ledge, the flat surface cut right into the heathen-gold stone of the Northern Ishkartaan Mountain Range's highest peak. Vogel tightens his eyes, brushing away visions his multi-eyed ravens are sending him of the fortified shielding the Dryad Witch's allies have cast over the Zonor and Vo Rivers and Dyoi Forest, all of it an insignificant setback.

Because Commander Fallon Bane stands on the torchlit ledge before him.

Fallon is washed in the overcast light streaming in from the cavern's opening. She's bracketed by ten Level Four and Five Earth Mages, her beautiful face lit up with excitement as her gray-rimmed eyes meet Vogel's, silver gray flame racing through his lines.

Pulling his gaze from hers, Vogel takes in the panoramic view of Southern Ishkartaan in the distance, the peninsula surrounded by the deep-blue waters of the Southern and Salish Oceans.

The last heathen nation of the Central Desert to hold out against the Ancient One's might.

Vogel surveys the Shadow dragons Fallon and her Level Five lieutenants flew in on. The beasts are hunched down near the ledge's long edge, each dragon watching them through multiple gray-glowing eyes. They've sprouted an extra set of legs, many of their dragons becoming more and more insectile as the Magedom's Shadow power grows. Thousands more multilegged dragons and Mage soldiers are perched on countless ledges they've blasted into the surrounding mountain range, Northern Ishkartaan's mountains rapidly being transformed into a huge Mage military base, its creation overseen by Vogel's Black Witch.

Vogel's gaze swings appreciatively back to Fallon. He can sense her excited response to his presence through her quickening heartbeat and the invisible ice crystals crackling to life through her lines as he steps toward her.

Good, Vogel thinks, his gaze sliding over Fallon's curvaceous form. *You've finally let go of your fury over the death of that staen'en bastard, Lukas Grey.*

"Your Excellency," Fallon drawls, her eyes bright and unintimidated, her aura churning into a hungry storm. Hunger so palpable Vogel can taste it on the back of his tongue.

How could I have ever imagined that Elloren Gardner Grey was the Magedom's Black Witch? he wonders as he breathes in Fallon's ruthless aura. *How could I have ever entertained for one second that the Dryad Whore would be the one to bring the Prophecy to fruition and slay the Great Icaral?*

It's been ever-faithful Fallon all along.

And luckily, the Ancient One has finally given him eyes to see it.

"Are you ready, my Black Witch?" Vogel asks as he unsheathes his Shadow Wand and extends its tip toward her, silver fire churning through his lines toward the Wand in his hand, the Mages surrounding them silently looking on.

Fallon's mouth twitches up as she unsheathes her own wand and touches its tip to his.

Tendrils of Shadow flow from Vogel's Wand to twine around hers before winding clear up her arm. A shudder passes through Fallon, and she goes half-lidded, her lips parting.

She tenses, visibly gathering herself before opening her eyes, coolly ferocious once more. "I'm ready, Marcus."

Hot spite sears through Vogel in response to Fallon's daring use of his first name. His fingers twitch, Shadow claws straining to form on their tips, but he holds the power back, excitement chasing his flare of spite. Excitement over her lack of fear of him.

Yes, you always were my Black Witch, he muses, his internal fire simmering.

"Southern Ishkartaan has sent their terms of surrender," Fallon informs Vogel with a sneer.

Vogel can't help but smile at this, bemused. "They imagine there's room for negotiation?" he inquires. They exchange brief lethal smiles before Vogel's expression hardens. "Destroy the country and everyone in it," he orders.

Excitement flashes through Fallon's power, and through the power of every Mage surrounding them, the momentousness shivering through them all.

Fallon gestures toward a dense, dark line edging the Salish coast that extends east from the Ishkartaan peninsula. "Refugees," she informs Vogel. "Huge numbers of them. Shall we mow them down, as well?"

"No," Vogel calmly answers, the Ancient One's Glorious Plan unfolding before them all. "Let them flood the East. It will further destabilize Noilaan and make it all the easier for us to invade."

Fallon's smile widens as she nods and then pulls in a deep breath, tugging on the Shadow tether she's welcomed, drawing the Shadow Wand's gray power into her dominant icelines and windlines.

Vogel shivers in response to her power's connection to his, thrills to the feel of Fallon consuming as much Shadow as she can, the frosty mountaintop air chilling even further.

Raising her wand, Fallon begins to murmur a series of spells.

A compact, icy wind kicks up, whipping around her lower legs before consolidating into thick gray mist. And then, Fallon simply steps up onto the mist and effortlessly glides through the air toward one of the multi-eyed, multilegged dragons.

Fire races through Vogel's lines at the sight of Fallon's magic coming into its own as she and her lieutenants mount dragons, and she sends out a shock wave of mental commands through all the dragons' Shadow tethers.

The Shadow beasts fan out their powerful wings and throw them down, taking flight with Fallon in the lead. Hundreds of Mages on dragonback positioned on the surrounding ledges take to the air as well and converge around her, all of them soaring toward Southern Ishkartaan.

Fallon thrusts her wand forward, and a thick bolt of ice spears toward the ocean-surrounded peninsula, landing in Southern Ishkartaan's distant center in a small explosion of gray.

Vogel's pulse quickens as huge trees made of ice burst upward from the huge peninsula's middle, an icy gray spreading out from the trees' bases and rapidly overtaking the land's every gold or green expanse as Vogel lifts his Shadow Wand and aims it toward the distant Salish Ocean.

His Shadow sea rolls toward the country's eastern coast, the dark mass riding the water's surface like a floating tidal wave. A roaring sound rises from the peninsula, and a deeper thrill shoots through Vogel's fire power. It's a sound he feels the urge to bite his teeth into and devour whole as his Shadow sea crashes over Ishkartaan's coast and Fallon's giant ice trees throw their branches down, detonating explosions of ice that can't completely cut out the thrilling sound.

The soul-expanding sound of thousands upon thousands of heathens . . . *screaming*.

Vogel is there when Fallon returns to the torchlit ledge, a steely twilight descending. She dismounts from her multilegged dragon, strides up to Vogel and stills before him, a wild, victorious look in her Shadow-rimmed eyes.

A cleansed country lies in the distance, even the mountain range's stone stripped of its heathen gold. Vogel's Shadow sea has overtaken the coast, gray-black waters now encompassing the huge peninsula, the coastline submerged. Dark clouds roil in the sky above Southern Ishkartaan, silver-black lightning arcing through them with muffled *boom* after *boom*. Every speck of natural Forest has been frozen to death, Fallon's mountain-high Shadow ice trees spread out over Ishkartaan's expanse. Vogel sets his sights East with burning anticipation, only Noilaan and Zhilaan left to be cleansed to bring the Ancient One's Reaping Times to their fullest fruition.

Fallon strides up to Vogel and holds her Shadowed wand out to him.

Curious, Vogel's hand closes around it. He moves to draw it away from her, but Fallon doesn't let go. Instead, she moves closer, her Shadow-tinged ice power flowing through her wand to coil around Vogel's hand then crackle through his internal fire in icy tendrils that emit steam against his fire, his breath hitching in response to the intimate collision of their powers.

"It was you all along," he breathes, silver sparks igniting in his vision. His fire rears against her ice, the skin of his back twitching, the hot steam breaking out to encircle them.

Fallon draws nearer and tilts her head up, her full lips *so close* . . .

Vogel is swept up in a remembrance of how it felt to devour Elloren Gardner's mouth. How it felt to *burn* that Wyvernbond straight through her body. He heatedly wonders what it would feel like to set down the same type of binding in Fallon Bane. What it would feel like to devour his new Black Witch's mouth instead.

And sink his teeth into her.

"It was always you as well, Marcus," she whispers, waiting, lips tilted, her breath chilly against his heat.

He can sense it, how his fire could so easily dominate her ice. And oh, how he would enjoy that exercise in domination. But he needs to wait. Needs to bring the Reaping Times to their completion before he takes hold of her in that way. Needs the purification of his body and soul that the Reaping Times will bring. His eyes flick toward the cleansed country. Toward the dark line of refugee filth moving slowly and relentlessly east.

"My Black Witch," he croons, meeting her excited gaze, clear that the coming Mage world is *theirs*. "You were always the one destined to kill the Icaral and bring the Prophecy to fruition."

Fallon reaches up and dares to run her fingertips along the edge of his cheek before threading them through his hair.

Vogel's fire rears, Shadow claws threatening to break through, his teeth stinging as his neck arches and silver fire flashes across his vision. He wants to spring at her. To bite into her and bring her to heel. She has no idea what she's toying with.

"Careful, witch," he croons, flashing teeth.

Fallon's lips curve into a sultry smile, the hand she's threaded through his hair tightening to a fist, his scalp stinging. A shock of fiery lust bolts through Vogel, and he lets go of her wand and grabs her wrist, nails digging into her skin. Fallon's breath hitches, her pupils dilating.

"Come with me, Black-Witch," he snarls as he draws his Wand.

Vogel sweeps his Wand's tip out in a wide arc. A thin bolt of Shadow jets from it to form an arc of misty gray portal runes. The air inside the arc turns silvery as it blurs and wavers, like translucent water.

Vogel takes hold of Fallon's arm and guides her through it.

The world flashes silver before they emerge on the apex of one of the Eastern Dyoi Desert's huge stone arches.

Fallon glances over her shoulder at the Magedom's towering Shadow storm band to their rear, spread out over the night-darkened Shadowed lands as far as the eye can see, north to south. She turns her gaze back east and takes in the huge dome-shield cast over the entire Dyoi Mountain Range, multicolored lightning and a cacophony of runes marked all over it, Vogel's imprisoning Shadow net clinging to the dome-shield like a second skin.

Fallon's piercing gaze snaps to Vogel's, a restless tension crackling into being between them. "This waiting is a gamble," she challenges, glancing pointedly toward his Shadow storm band. "We should attack the Dryad and her Icaral *right now*."

"Their shielding is too strong," Vogel responds, meeting her knifing ice aura with simmering patience. "And I don't yet hold enough power to portal through it."

Fallon's expression edges toward the explosive. "So, we simply *wait* while the Dryad Witch and her allies take hold of the *entire East*?"

Vogel gives her a lethal glare, but Fallon meets it fully, her brazen ire undeterred. *Careful, witch*, Vogel thinks, suppressing a snarl.

"This is not a taking hold of," he counters. "The Dryad Witch and her allies have sent one shield up over the Dyoi Mountain Range and Forest, another over the Zonor River and yet another over the Vo, no plan or unity fueling these actions. Because there is no unity in the East."

The temperature dips, ice-pick anger in Fallon's eyes. "So we leave them all be until they can find a way to unite and rise against us?"

"No," Vogel responds. "We leave them be as they tear each other to *shreds*. The Dryad Witch and her allies are drawing on foliage light magic that is nearing its height. When foliage season peaks, the light magic running through the trees reaches its pinnacle." A patient smile forms on Vogel's lips. "But after that, as color is swept from the trees, Dryad power will go dormant. And peak foliage's surge in magic will be blunted by our razing of the Northern Forest and the rest of the Central Continent's wilds."

A calculating glint forms in Fallon's eyes. "So, quite soon, they're about to see a huge drop in their pooled magic. Enough for us to break through their shielding?"

Vogel's expression turns serpentine. "Enough for us to break through their eastern shielding and their Subland shielding, as well. Opening up paths for us to level the East, wrest hold of the Heathen Wand of Power, and bring the Prophecy to fruition."

Excitement overtakes Fallon's expression, her icy magic kicking up steam as it shivers against Vogel's fire power.

He leans in, close, thrilling to the feel of his fire against her ice. "Patience, my Black Witch."

"I'll tear the Icaral demon's wings right from his body," Fallon promises, her breathing uneven, the rise of her desire for him ferally intense, and Vogel knows—he knows in that moment—that possessing her was always the Ancient One's will for them both as she crackles her power against his with more insistent force.

Territorial force.

Which sparks a hard dart of Vogel's anger.

He steps back, angles his Wand at her and murmurs a spell. A look of curiosity flashes through Fallon's eyes as Shadow vines fly out of the Shadow Wand's tip to encircle her arms, her wrist, her body, dragging her onto her knees so fast she barely has time to react.

Rage and alarm shock through Fallon's lines, frost breaking out on the grayed stone surrounding them before Vogel abruptly dissolves her binding. Fallon's expression of fury morphs to a look of rattled reappraisal tinged with an almost reverential awe as she rubs her wrist.

He waits, staring her down, *testing* her. But she remains on her knees.

Good.

"I am naming you commanding witch of the Magedom's entire military forces," he tells her, satisfied by her display of submission. "Rise, Black Witch of the Magedom."

Fallon pushes herself back to her feet, her eyes steady on Vogel's as their power batters and steams against each other's, silver-dark fire against Shadow ice.

"Bring your forces north to our new Issani military base," Vogel orders, "and prepare them for invasion of the East."

"Yes, your Excellency," Fallon demurs, just as a line of glowing purple moons blast into being in front of the Dyoi Mountain Range's shielding, low to the ground, like a line of Xishlon moons walling off the East.

A firebolt of surprise scorches through both Vogel and Fallon.

"More taunting from the Dryad Witch's abomination of a cousin," Vogel hisses, fury searing through his lines that he swiftly reins in.

"Be wary of Or'myr Syll'vir," Fallon warns. "I've been told he has a Strafeling level of geopower mingled with the Mage might of his Black Witch lineage."

"He's a nuisance, to be sure," Vogel returns as he takes in the heretical moons.

"He's sending a message," Fallon bites out. "Perhaps not just to us, but to his whore of a cousin, as well."

Vogel's gaze slides back to Fallon. "Let him send his heathen messages, my beautiful Black Witch," he croons. "We'll soon turn every moon Or'myr Syll'vir can conjure into spheres filled with Shadowfire and send them hurtling down onto the entire East." His focus on her intensifies, silvery hot. "And you can speed that day by sending your power into my Shadow net over the Dyoi, to hasten winter's descent."

CHAPTER TEN

LIGHTNING KISS

Tierney Calix

Northern Vo River

Tierney peers up at the Vo's translucent dome-shield, its purple-limned Dark runes barely visible against the starlit sky. Waist-deep in an isolated stretch of the Vo, she draws in a long, steadying breath as river life affectionately swims and buzzes around her, her storming power steadily channeling into the shield via Viger's bond.

Their protection of Erthia's largest River growing more crucial hour by hour.

The day started on a note of triumph. A potent rush of Fyordin's power flooded their shielding as he placed a second focal-point shield rune on the Southern Vo River to complement Or'myr's northern focal-point shield rune, the linkage of those runes amplifying the strength of their shielding over almost the entire River save for the southernmost portion, walled off by Gareth Keeler. Relief eddies through Tierney over both this proof of Fyordin's success and that the ability to extend their shielding west to link to their allies' shielding of the Dyoi Forest and Zonor River is now a possibility within their reach.

Tierney clings to this victory, desperately needing it.

Because she can also sense, through her River's link to Erthia's tapestry of Waters, that there's been a monumental depletion of Nature's Balance, huge swaths of the Natural Matrix in the continent's southern-central lands consumed by Shadow. Tierney froze in that moment of detection, waist-deep in the Vo as she is now, her fears crashing through her with devastating force. In that moment, fear overtook her, surging with drowning intensity and heightened by her bond-sense of Viger's draw toward a Deathkin Reckoning that grows ever stronger.

Viger is in the West somewhere, she's sure of it. Close to this new locus of

Shadow destruction, his directional pull through their bond like a living cord.

What Shadow horrors have you found out there, Viger? Tierney sends out to him through the bond.

A sense of Viger withdrawing his thrall snaps through her with whiplike force as he mutes their linkage with a silencing snarl.

Their connection going dark.

Viger's violent withdrawal combined with her fear for Nature casts her every emotion into a hollowing implosion.

Disturbed, Tierney's gaze slides toward Or'myr's conjured purple moon, a tremble kicking up as she realizes that what she needs from Or'myr is, perhaps, no longer fully possible.

She needs her *friend*.

Or'myr has been kind but painfully formal with her these past days, both of them focusing their energy into preparing their shielding for Or'myr's enlargement of it once it gains enough power, both Tierney and Or'myr doing their level best to ignore their undeniable draw to each other dredged to the surface by Viger's bond.

A pull that seems to be mysteriously increasing as Nature's Unbalancing gains ground.

Barely aware of the loving swirl of minnows around her, Tierney remembers how she got into the habit of seeking Or'myr out at the Wyvernguard, returning, night after night, to his blaringly purple laboratory high up in the military academy's now-destroyed South Island. The two of them would prattle on about anything and everything while they worked out magical formulations to draw their power into Vu Trin weapons. Tierney's roiling emotions were always put at ease, grounded even, by Or'myr's earthy aura and the intent way he listened as he worked, interjecting a wry comment every now and then and brewing her his signature mushroom tea. Or feeding her, his love of cooking and all things domestic having always charmed the hell out of her. And so, she lingered in his lab with him, night after night, Or'myr never failing to offer her a scientific tome for her to take back to her lodging, a twinkle in his forest green eyes that sent an enticing tingle over her skin as he crooned the same words every evening—*For your reading pleasure.*

Tierney flushes as she remembers a very different kind of pleasure—the lightning-bolt excitement of their shared dream. Her heartbeat quickens even as a pained conflict rears, because she doesn't want her outrageous, perhaps unforgivable dream actions to change what was becoming rock-solid between the two of them.

Tears suddenly stinging at her eyes, she blinks them back and sets out to find him.

Tierney locates Or'myr by the stone wall that holds their shield's northern focal-point rune. He's down on one knee, tracing his Wand-Stylus over it. The sound of his enticingly deep voice murmuring amplification spells sends a disquieting thrum straight through her, and Tierney struggles to suppress her awareness of how his Vu Trin tunic is draped over his muscular physique, the military garb morphed to vivid purple, as is all his garb, by his powerful Strafeling geomancy.

Violet sparks flash from Or'myr's wand's tip and fan out over the rune, its violet light casting a dreamy glow over Or'myr. Tierney's breath catches in her throat, her heartbeat jumping into a faster rhythm.

He doesn't glance at her as he works, but Tierney can sense the static charge of his lightning flaring toward her as she draws nearer, his power crackling against her water magic with unmistakable longing, a memory of their shared dream flustering her once more.

What must he think of me? she agonizes as she stills awkwardly behind him, struggling not to remember the electric feel of his kiss, the balancing energy of his touch . . . and the explosive love in their *joining*.

"I've figured out a way to hasten the enlargement of our shielding," Or'myr comments congenially, still not looking at her.

An edge of Tierney's searing mortification softens in response to his warm, conversational tone. The tone of her friend.

Or'myr glances at Tierney, and a heightened relief sweeps through her in response to the calm, undimmed affection in his gaze. He scans the translucent shield's faintly visible runes. "I'm keeping the bulk of the Vo's shielding porous to all but Shadow power, but I've completely closed off the northern section we're under and the southern section Fyordin is under to protect our runic focal points from both Vogel and the Eastern Realm's forces."

Tierney squints at the glowing purple focal-point rune beside him, as well as the newly crafted series of smaller purple runes orbiting it. She intuitively grasps what he's building, her scientific mind's appreciation of a clever solution further softening her emotional upheaval. But still, an undercurrent of fear remains, prickling under her skin.

"The Natural World's Unbalancing," she warns, "it just accelerated in a monstrous way. Vogel's managed to kill off another huge section of Erthia's wilds."

Or'myr gives her a grim look. "I felt your disquiet through our bond." Letting out a long sigh, he rises, sheathes his geo-wand at his hip, and meets her gaze once more. "Tierney, we're giving this shielding all we've got for the moment. Not much to do but keep it steady and let our power amplify this focal rune as much as possible. Soon enough, we'll shield the entire East and *hold it*."

Leagues-deep emotion is suddenly balling up in Tierney's throat. "Thank you, Or'myr," she says, barely able to get the words out. "Thank you for helping my River and all of Erthia."

Lightning flashes through his eyes as their gazes lock more intensely, and Tierney feels the desire rising to fall straight into his purple-flashing gaze and into *him*. To pour her heart out over the powerful, confusing things that have transpired between them like she's poured her heart out to him about practically everything else in her life.

"You're welcome, Tierney," he says softly, a crackle of his lightning riding out to her, a static tingle rushing over her skin.

Stiffening and averting his eyes, Or'myr moves toward the purple bonfire he's got going on the riverbank, a few stone seats surrounding it that he's carved from the bank's rock. A steel teapot hangs from a tripod over the bonfire, the metal stunningly crafted from the iron spikes that Or'myr pulled from the River, his transformation of iron to steel rendering the metal safe for Tierney to handle. What smells like a root-based stew is simmering in a pot set on the tripod's metal base, sending up a mouthwatering aroma.

Tierney's eyes flick toward the shelter Or'myr is in the process of cutting into the wall of purple-veined onyx riverbank stone just behind them. Stone trees are artfully carved into the walls, along with a variety of shelves, a table, and a bed.

Tierney's lip quirks. "I can't believe you're managing to carve an entire *home* into the bank's stone," she marvels, both charmed and amazed by his ability to do this so rapidly, his thick Urisk strain of domesticity such a bolstering comfort in this moment.

Or'myr glances aslant at her, one brow cocked as he takes hold of the gleaming teapot's wooden handle. "Well, I don't like to be idle. And I can draw only so much amplifying charge into our shielding in a day. Which leaves some gaps of time." He smiles at her as he pours mushroom tea into two cups carved from the bank's stone. "And I can't very well sleep with you at the bottom of the Vo . . ." He stiffens and glances away. Heat blooms on Tierney's face once more because she's *sure* he's remembering their brazen dream, as she, too, careens into a recollection of his astonishing level of passion. And *love*. So much love for her flowing through their bond when they dream-joined.

"It's so . . . *charming*," she comments, as she takes in the small, suspended, purple moon orb magicked into the dwelling's inside corner that illuminates the space with deep violet light, a door crafted from woven purple vines already set into steel hinges and thrown open.

She dares a glance at Or'myr to find him grinning at her. "If you like this," he says, "you'd *love* my Vonor. Oh, wait . . . you saw a bit of that . . ." A flush rises in his purple cheeks and he averts his gaze once more before shooting her a resigned, amused look and holding out a warm cup of tea.

Another rush of affection for him ripples through their bond as she accepts the tea and takes a seat by the bonfire.

"I've never had a safe, permanent home," she confides, her throat suddenly feeling a bit raw. Or'myr stills, listening as she cradles the warm mug and stares fixedly at its rising curlicues of steam. "I was ripped away from my Asrai family at such a young age," she continues, "and my Gardnerian home, loving as it was . . . I was always under the threat of losing my new home, because I had such a hard time hiding my power. And now, my Mage family . . . they're unwanted refugees here in the East . . . their lives torn apart because they took in my younger brother and me."

A wave of turmoil eddies through Tierney's magic and she struggles to contain it. Or'myr sets down the teapot and takes a seat next to her. She can feel the weight of his fervent gaze on her, his quiet like an embracing lifeline as she looks up and meets his eyes. "Your sense of home," she says, "it's so solid and sure, built right into stone. When I'm with you, I feel like I've finally found a place where . . ." Her words trail off as she's overtaken by a gut-deep yearning for this thing in him that she always craved with everything in her but could never pinpoint why until right now, Or'myr's aura of steadiness like a home in and of itself, so solid and true . . . save for the frenzied lightning in his kiss.

Lightning that stands between them.

"Make me a space here," she's suddenly imploring, motioning toward the cavern. "Extend it maybe . . . so my River flows in . . ." The words catch, too much emotion trussed up in them for her to say more.

They hold each other's gaze for a heartbeat. Then another.

"I'll make you a space here," he offers quietly, the lightning flashing through his gaze emphasizing the subtext running through his words. A more heated tension flares, a frustrated energy running through both their auras.

A bitter ache grips Tierney's throat, this sudden yearning for him twisting her heart so hard that she can barely get out a *thank you*. She focuses doggedly on the teacup in her hands, an earthy steam wafting up from the tea inside it, but her yearning for him only intensifies—his conjured moon, the teacup and mushroom tea, the home he's forming even with the Magedom's demonic forces breathing down their necks. It's as much of a defiant battle cry as his readiness to deploy his power against the Magedom with lethal precision.

"Tell me more about your Vonor," she prods, casting about for a distraction. "I've been curious about it for a while."

Or'myr cocks a quizzical brow before his expression lightens. "Well, there are many, many books, as you'd likely expect. As well as a small geomancy lab and quite a few weapons. And I have a mushroom farm in a cavern on one side."

Welcome amusement bubbles up inside Tierney. "You have a mushroom *farm*? You never mentioned that."

"Shhh," he chastises, shooting her a look of mock censure. "Don't tell anyone. You'll ruin my great mystique. Don't mention the teacup collection either."

She lets out a short laugh. "You have a *teacup* collection?"

"I do. And quite a few violins. And drawings that I did." He hesitates. "Mostly of the Vo." He glances at her sidelong. "Quite a few of you."

Tierney's skin prickles as his lightning aura crackles through the warming churn of her water aura.

His expression shifts to one of amusement. "Is this enticing you?"

She gives him a flustered, wry look.

Or'myr breathes out a laugh, mischief in his eyes as he sits back, cradling his tea. "Well, then, you'll *love* hearing about the waterfall."

Tierney gulps, her heartbeat tripping over itself. "There's a *waterfall*?"

His grin widens. "There is," he croons, his voice dropping to a teasingly suggestive octave. "Deep in my Vonor's most cavernous recesses. It flows down from an outcropping of amethyst then out over the Voloi Mountain Range's lower peaks. Its water is suffused with my purple geo-energy and eventually flows down into your Vo."

"I've sensed it," she murmurs in a flash of realization, barely breathing, completely under his spell. "I've sensed your purple energy in the water."

"See, Tierney," he murmurs, his voice like silk, a suggestive thrum in it. "I've been there in your river all along."

Tierney's power shivers. He's so *close* . . . she almost forgets herself as they both draw closer, and she angles her lips toward his . . .

She gives a start and jerks back, remembering the pain of his lightning, their magic dauntingly incompatible, save in that *dream* . . .

Bitter chagrin slices through their thrall and they both stiffen and move farther away, even as Tierney's heart and the rippling energy of the Vo itself seem to urge them to do exactly the *opposite*—a pull she knows Or'myr can also feel through Viger's damned bond.

Or'myr's brow furrows and he gives her a charged look, a sliver of his magic breaking loose to brush against hers in a heated sizzle. The contact only intensifies the ache in Tierney's heart as she forces her water aura into a churning barrier to try and wall off his power, instantly strung up into tighter conflict as she catches the tension around his eyes.

Or'myr forcibly withdraws his magic, then lets out a sigh, peering into the bonfire's leaping purple flames. An uncomfortable silence descends.

"So, you bound yourself to the Death Fae," he comments. "Xishlon night. With a kiss."

Ah, there it is, Tierney thinks, hollowing out. The conversation she knew would rear its head the moment they both had a chance to catch their breath. She meets Or'myr's gaze, a frisson of remorse tightening her gut. His words were idly said, but there's a flash of purple lightning ringing his irises and leaping around the edges of his power. Clearly this has been eating at him, shoved aside as they've dealt with securing the Vo.

And this *bond* . . . it has a way of dredging up matters of the heart and putting them into blaring focus.

"I did," she admits, throat dry and tight. *Go ahead and say it, Or'myr,* she thinks. *"You kissed him right after you kissed me."*

But he doesn't voice the words. Instead Tierney feels them hanging in the air, weighted with tension.

Another uncomfortable silence ensues.

"Was it good?" he finally asks, and Tierney can feel both things in the question—her friend falling into heartfelt conversation with her . . . and the pained bitterness of rejection.

Grasping at their friendship, *needing* their friendship, she decides to level with him as she recalls Viger's astonishing Darkness. And the sensation of being pulled to the very center of Erthia.

"It was otherworldly," she admits.

Jaded amusement flashes in Or'myr's eyes. "Otherworldly?"

She scowls at him. "It's not what you think. It was . . . revelatory."

His eyes widen. "Revelatory?" he echoes, his expression turning a tad too mocking for her taste.

She glowers at him. "You don't understand."

He loses the smile. "Nor will I ever."

Tierney's water power gives a defensive flare. "Bitterness doesn't become you, Or'myr."

He spits out a mirthless laugh. "Says the woman who can kiss anyone but me. Who has a multitude of men mooning over her." He shakes his head and looks away, his unspoken words like a bolt through her emotions. *Including me.*

Ire rises. "Is any of this important right now?" She gesticulates wildly toward their shielding, the Vo, the surrounding land.

"No, Tierney," Or'myr says, leveling his lightning gaze back at her. "But it doesn't change the fact that we're bonded in a way that draws all of this straight to the surface." He shakes his head, cursing under his breath. "This bond feels like someone bottled the Xishlon moon and fed it into our damned veins."

His tattoo flashes into Tierney's mind—the Xishlon moon emblazoned on his chest—as she's cast into another heated memory of the feel of his body pressed against hers. And how good his lightning felt, cracking straight through her . . .

Tierney tenses against the accompanying vortex of emotion, speechless for a moment and feeling frozen. "I don't want to lose you," she finally rasps out. "Even if we can't . . ." She pauses, not able to finish the sentence. Instead, she looks at him full on and bares her heart. "Or'myr, I don't want to lose you." She stops, scared that the tears stinging her eyes might give way in a torrent.

Or'myr loses his guarded look and peers at her, his hand coming to hers in a gentle caress. "You could never lose me," he reassures her, his voice heartbreakingly kind. "We're allies and close friends. *Always.* All right?"

Tierney nods stiffly, blinking back tears. "Everything that's happening in the world right now," she roughly manages, "it's *frightening*."

"It is," he gravely agrees. "But we'll fight the Shadow *together*. And I know that despite the madness of this bond, Viger and Fyordin are with us in this fight too."

Tierney nods again, some of the tension in her shoulders, her body, slackening as she gives him a grateful look.

Or'myr removes his hand, sits back, and regards her squarely. "So," he says, cradling his teacup and taking a sip of his tea, "you had sex with all of us in our dreams."

Tierney's eyes widen. She was used to the unvarnished bluntness of their conversations at the Wyvernguard. But never about a topic like *this*.

Or'myr barks out a laugh and mock-toasts her with his mug. "If I wasn't so busy being jealous, I'd be impressed."

Tierney winces and glances away. When she looks back at him, she finds his eyes narrowed with an all too knowing mischief.

"You know there's a name for women like you," he says before launching into a string of Noi words her translation rune can't make out.

Hurt spears through Tierney, evisceratingly sharp. Because she can just about guess what his words mean, and it's beyond painful to hear coming from him.

Angry tears burn her eyes as she slams down her teacup in a clatter of stone against stone. "I thought you were *different*," she hurls out. "Go ahead, Or'myr. Tell me what that means. What is it? *Slut? Whore?*"

Or'myr gapes at her, seeming wildly taken aback. "Sweet Holy Vo on High, *no*," he exclaims. "That's *barbaric*. Why would you think that about yourself . . . or *me*, for that matter?"

She glares at him.

"It *means*," he emphatically states, "*one who embraces the garden*."

Tierney scrunches her face in confusion. *"What?"*

"The *garden*," Or'myr sputters before repeating the Noi phrase.

"What on Erthia are you talking about?" Tierney cries, throwing up her hands. "I don't speak Bizarre Eastern Realm Euphemism!"

Or'myr blinks at her. "More specifically, it means *one who wants to gather many flowers*."

Tierney blinks at him in turn.

"One of the many ways of approaching romance," he prods.

"There are *many* ways?"

This seems to bring Or'myr up short. He splays out his palms. "Of *course* there are. There are those who 'stand outside of the garden.' Those who 'choose to be their own garden.' Those who 'share the garden and become the flowers' . . ."

This goes on for several minutes as Tierney just stares at him, mired in a confusion that's dancing on the edge of a hilarity over their screamingly huge cultural divide.

"That's a bizarre number of love categories!" Tierney exclaims, frustration making her aura explode in all directions.

"Hold on," Or'myr counters, "are you saying that your limited Western categories . . . *wait*, I mean your *only* allowable *single* category to describe something as complex as love and lust, makes *any sense at all*?"

Tierney is stunned into silence, backhanded by the possibility there could be some truth in his words even though these Eastern Realm ideas about love and lust are bizarre to the point of laughable and smash clear through her rigid cultural framework.

She wrestles with it all, struggling to regain her bearings.

"So," she finally starts, trying to piece together the veiled meanings of each of the multitude of garden metaphors, "do you want to 'gather many flowers' . . . or would you if . . ."

"If not for my terrifying lightning?" Or'myr supplies.

Again, an uncomfortable silence ensues, the two of them staring at each other.

Or'myr lets out a long sigh. "I'm a bit different. There are names for people like me too."

He sets down his mug, gets up, walks over to the tree line, and picks a single, violet-glowing Twining Lily from a vine encircling an Eastern Maple's slender trunk. Then he strides back to Tierney, a pained edge entering his gaze as he holds out the flower to her.

"I'm 'the one who desires the single Xishlon rose,'" he admits, ardent longing crackling through his power.

Forking straight into her.

Warmth spreads over Tierney's skin as she accepts the flower, their eyes meeting. And then, with palpable effort, Or'myr clamps down on his power and whisks it into his core. Sitting back down, he picks up his mug and warms his palms with it, his eyes lit up now with simmering purple heat.

"You're a hopeless romantic," Tierney murmurs.

"It's true," he admits with a rueful smile, even as his tightly controlled power continues to strain toward hers. "But I can never 'partake of the garden' with my true love." His gaze intensifies, both pain and desire in it, the potency of it triggering a surge of Tierney's own power. Her magic jostles against her hold, striving to surge toward him.

Pulling in a harsh breath, Or'myr peers fixedly back at his tea. "I'm cursed to stand on the outside of it all, it would seem." He lets out another long sigh and attempts a smile. "My own personal tragedy to bear. I suppose there's romance in that too." He nods toward the shield above them. "But at least I can make myself useful."

Tierney's throat tightens, thick with longing. "The dream I shared with you," she says, "our connection in it . . . it was the one that brought Balance to my River. But it was more than that. I care for you, Or'myr. As more than a friend." She hesitates, barely able to draw an even breath. "I want you back in my dreams."

A stronger heat fires on the air between them, reflected in Or'myr's eyes.

"If I was able to regain access to your dreams," he says, low and emphatic, "I would *incinerate* them."

Tierney's eyes widen, a forbidden warmth sparking low in her core. "I bet I could handle you," she teases, completely enraptured. "Since I'm such a connoisseur of 'the garden.'"

Or'myr coughs out a surprised laugh, giving her a sly, suggestive look. "You certainly seem to be."

Tierney swallows and looks away, striving to maintain her composure. "If you had been raised by an Easterner," she finally ventures, "do you think you'd be different?"

He cocks a brow. "What do you mean?"

She shrugs. "Do you think you'd want more than . . . just the 'one flower'?"

Or'myr seems to seriously consider this, looking into his tea. "I don't know. I'm private by nature and have a tendency to form strong bonds with those I care for. It's hard to say."

Tierney's ache for him intensifies, and it's not just for his gorgeous tattooed body, or the lightning-rod excitement of their dream coupling. Or even for the Balance their joining brought to her Vo's energy. It's a complex longing for *all* of him. For everything that he is.

"I *really* want you back in my dreams," she admits, surrendering to his draw as their eyes find each other once more, the heat in his gaze shifting to flame as his eyes travel over her more wantonly than they ever have before, a stronger heat sparking through them both as his lightning aura crackles around her form.

He wrenches his gaze away, looking toward the sky as if praying for strength. "This conversation," he rasps, "coupled with the draw of this bond, is making me *so hard.*"

Tierney gapes at him in utter shock.

He lowers his gaze to hers and registers her expression, his lips twisting with incredulity. "You dream-paired with all three of us, and *I'm* scandalizing *you*?"

Tierney huffs out an incredulous sound. "I'm from the West. We don't say those things!"

Smirking, Or'myr gestures toward her with his mug. "You should practice saying scandalous things. I think it would be good for you."

She tosses him an arch look. "Maybe I like being oblique."

"All right, then." Or'myr suppresses a smile as he glances up at their shield. "I, for one, could use an occasional distraction from the end of the world. We can be oblique together. And discuss matters of love and lust in bizarrely metaphorical ways. We'd best work through what's going on between us, though, as it seems you and I are linked in a way that puts our every feeling and desire on full display." He gives her another slow once-over, their powers snagging, his lightning sizzling against her water magic with potent force.

Unable to resist the draw of their bond one second longer, Tierney sets down her tea, rises and holds out her hand for his mug. A questioning look enters Or'myr's eyes before he hands it to her, purple light flashing through his gaze as she sets his mug aside.

Her heart thudding, Tierney brazenly throws a leg over his and lowers herself onto his lap, straddling him. Her heartbeat thudding against his, she presses herself against him, uneven breaths shuddering through both their throats. *Hard, indeed.*

"What are you doing?" Or'myr whispers, his breath warm against her cheek, his hands on her waist, light and tentative.

Tierney swallows, overcome by the wild pleasure of pressing herself against him so intimately, the reality of it so much more intense than their dream. "I'd like to 'dance around the Ironwood tree.'"

Or'myr coughs out a laugh. "Is that a bizarre *Western Realm* euphemism?"

Tierney can't suppress her smile. "It actually is."

"You talk about pairing . . . as *Ironwood trees*?"

"Mm-hmm," she admits.

"That's ridiculous," he breathes against her ear.

"I want to test your lightning," she offers, serious. "To see if it's just in your kiss. I think I'm falling in love with you."

"Tierney . . ."

"Shh, just don't kiss my mouth." She leans in and runs her lips down his warm neck, then kisses him at the base of it.

Or'myr groans low in his throat, his grip on her waist tightening. He draws back and stares into her eyes, his own lit up with incandescent streaks of purple lightning as he carefully searches her gaze, as if affirming that she's sure.

Tierney's heartbeat turns erratic as she leans back and runs one trembling finger down his chest, sliding it lower . . . and lower . . .

The world spins, and the next thing she knows, she's on the ground, Or'myr above her. Her power surges toward his and she gasps, thrilling to the feel of his long, hard form pressing her into the ground, his lips on her neck in a tongue-swirling kiss that shocks radiant, electrified pleasure through her entire body. Her back bows against the sensation and she moans, wanting more of him, as a much stronger shock of lightning flashes from his mouth straight through her neck and a jolt of searing pain knifes through her.

Stars flash against her vision, and Tierney lets out a strangled cry, shoving at Or'myr, barely able to see through the scalding pain lancing through her neck and shoulder.

Or'myr immediately rolls off of her, and she recoils then bolts into a sitting position, wincing from the agonizing pain that feels like a flaming brand pressed into her skin.

"Oh, Tierney," Or'myr says, as tears blur her eyes and he curses himself, the pain swiftly tamping down to a more manageable scald. Teeth gritted, Tierney struggles to catch her breath, her emotions a wild torment as the pain dissipates.

"I'm okay," she insists, feeling wrung out. "It's gone . . . the pain's gone."

Or'myr gives her a stricken look before he gets up and rakes his fingers through his hair, cursing again in Uriskal.

Tierney hugs her knees, shivering as she inwardly curses both her power and his, as well as fate and all the elemental magic of Erthia.

"I can't do this," Or'myr says in a shattered voice, shaking his head, a tortured look in his eyes. "You're right. Compared to what we're facing, this doesn't matter. At all. But it doesn't change the fact that I've been falling for you from the moment I met you and I can never have you. And now I've been thrust into this cursed *garden* with you along with two other men. I cannot do this, Tierney."

Tierney glowers at him through tear-streaked eyes, vulnerability cracking her dangerously open. "So, you're no longer my friend, even?"

"I *am* your friend. *Always*. But I also happen to *love* you. And seeing you with other men, even if it was just a dream . . ." He pauses, lightning flashing in his eyes. "I *want* you. And right now, it's hard not to hate every man who's able to touch and kiss you without causing you terrible agony."

"Or'myr . . ."

"You have to leave me be in this," he sets down, adamant. "Until I can have you, which is *never*, we can't pursue this, even in dreams."

Tierney gets up and tries to go to him, but he steps back, a wild look entering his eyes. "Tierney, you will *shatter my heart.*"

"I'd be with you if I could!" she cries, her voice breaking as a storm cloud bursts to life over her head. "I realized that in the dream . . . I do care for Viger and Fyordin. A great deal. But I want *you.*"

"And I want *you*," he fires back, eyes burning. "*Only* you. But fate won't allow it. Believe me, I've tried to parse out some magical way around our clashing magic, but we're both too powerful." He brings his hands to his hips and forces a deep breath before meeting her eyes once more. "If we survive this, go find your comfort where you can. Embrace the whole cursed garden if it pleases you. But *this*, Tierney—" he motions between them "—we have to find some way to block this attraction. Because I *have to* focus on the possible end of Nature rather than my own yearning for someone I can *never, ever* have. Now, if you'll excuse me, I'm going to take my currently *out-of-control* power and use its force to blast a line of purple moons into being in front of the Eastern Realm."

Tierney nods stiffly, stifling her ocean of tears, and Or'myr giver her one last purple-lightning-spitting look then walks away.

Tierney lies just under the Vo's lapping waters that night, staring up at the sky, watching Or'myr on the distant riverbank as he conjures a line of purple moons in the sky, ready to transport them west through the line of magic he set down inside the V'yexwraith's Shadow power, her emotions a turbulent mess.

Unable to fight off the pull of sleep any longer, she succumbs to its embrace as Or'myr's line of moons flash a deeper purple and blink out of sight.

Viger opens their dream-linkage and comes to Tierney that night.

She startles at his sudden presence beside her, the two of them sitting side by side atop a huge gray stone desert arch, his pulsing draw to her held staunchly back.

Fear ripples through Tierney's power as she takes in the nighttime scene before them—leagues and leagues of Shadowed wasteland spread out around their every side, charred Forest under a poisoned, gray sky, slashes of Shadow storm bands marring every horizon.

"Tell me this is only a dream," she implores as she takes in the Central Continent's devastation. She turns toward Viger. His horns are absent, claws in, his thrall's suspended ropes of Darkness slowly encircling them both.

"It is not only a dream," he says, his multitoned voice low and dread filled, seeming to envelop them from everywhere at once.

Tears sting Tierney's eyes as it hits her anew—what they're up against. What the Natural World is up against. She takes in Viger's contained presence and how he's maintaining complete control over his thrall, even as he allows a slender pulse of what he feels for her to escape his hold, that slim trace of it filled with a mind-bendingly potent rush of sheer *want*.

Realization grips hold.

"You purposefully drove me away," she murmurs, barely able to get the words out.

His dark eyes remain fixed toward the West. "It is not our time, Asrai."

A torrent of emotion churns into being, what Tierney feels for Or'myr warring with what she was starting to feel for Viger too. "Are you saying there will be a time?" she asks, confused.

"Someday, if the Natural World survives," he answers, his power encircling them both. "Soon, I will dissolve myself into Nature to hold off a Reckoning. The dissolution of my power of Natural Death into the living Forest will buy you time and form a bulwark against the Shadow's Void."

Tierney's thoughts whirl, alarm surging. "Viger, *no* . . ."

He sets his full-black gaze on her, the whole world contracting around them as he bares his teeth. "It is the only way to ward off our Unleashing." Pain flickers through his eyes. "There is no Balance between you and me at the moment, Asrai.

You know this. We both felt it when we dream-paired. You hold too much Death-kin lineage. And there is too much Death coming for the Natural World. We can't risk amplifying it."

Tierney's lips tremble as she holds his full-Dark gaze, remembering how he told her, on Xishlon, that two Death Fae never pair because there is no Balance in it. A fuller comprehension stirs. "You used my fears to drive me away, didn't you," she rasps, tears burning her eyes. "You read my fear of someone trying to own me and used it to drive me away."

"I did," he says, still as a Dark star.

She shakes her head and looks back out over the nightmare landscape. The nightmare coming for her Waters. The nightmare Viger is willing to sacrifice him-self to fight.

"I just want you to know," she says, voice shredding, "that I could love you too. I love Or'myr. A great deal. And even Fyordin as a good friend. But, in another place, another time . . . I could love you intensely." She forcibly keeps her eyes on him, holding steady against his hypnotic thrall.

"I know," he says. "I've read your fear of that too."

And I've read your fears, she thinks to herself, her heart twisting. *I've read your greatest fear in those three words you keep buried so deep inside you.*

"It's as I told you," he says, turning his Dark gaze back toward the poisoned land-scape, his two snakes suddenly there, twined around his shoulders, "when we kissed on Xishlon and in the Northern Forest, I thought I could hold back a full mating bond. I didn't expect to unearth such a strong Deathkin lineage in you."

"Viger . . ."

"We can't be together with so much Death power running between us," he states. "Even dream-pairing, we almost drew each other toward the Reckoning that could bring Nature's full fury down on the Living World. If we were to take each other as mates, your Asrai nature would fall away. At a time when your River needs you as Asrai'lir."

Tierney fights back the surge of emotion, those three words that Viger fears most shivering through the bond connecting them. "Can you feel me inside your fears?" she whispers as a tear breaks loose to streak down her cheek.

No answer. They sit there for a long moment, eyes locked, enveloped in his still-ness. And then he lifts a hand to caress her cheek, her breath hitching at the warm contact, his voice a bone-deep thrum when it comes. "You never know someone as well as you do when you know *exactly* what they fear," he croons. "And your fears, Asrai'vhia'lir . . . your fears are *beautiful*."

Tierney gives up trying to contain the tears and lets herself melt into his touch, goodbye shivering in it. "How long will you be absorbed into Nature?" she asks, hoping against hope that the Natural World will survive what's coming.

He tilts his head, as if considering. "A hundred years. Perhaps two hundred. Our power works in those cycles."

"I'll never see you again," she protests, the tears flowing.

Viger's dark mouth slides into a faint smile. "We may yet meet again. It's as I've told you, Asrai. You are immortal because of your Deathkin lineage. Unless pierced through with iron. But the Asrai part of you, after the course of a normal Fae lifespan, it will drop away. You will become, increasingly, one of us."

Tierney stills, shock lancing through her before it settles, so many things about her falling into place. A wavering smile forms on her lips as she holds Viger's hypnotic stare. "The idea should scare me, but it doesn't."

"Until then," he says, low and resonant, his thumb tracing the edge of her mouth, "follow the Waters' Balance."

She can sense Viger's undercurrent of meaning, knows he senses the overwhelming Balance that flowed out of her dream with Or'myr.

A fresh wave of tears pools in Tierney's eyes, and she shakes her head. "I can't be with Or'myr in that way. His kiss, his touch—there's too much fire in it."

Viger's hand slides down to her shoulder, a pained, ardent Darkness in his eyes. "You'll find a way."

"If we do," Tierney shakily offers, "I want your blessing."

Some amusement shines through Viger's pain. "You seek the blessing of a Death Fae?"

She nods.

"His fears are beautiful too," Viger states, his voice shot through with feeling. He takes her hand, their fingers interlacing, ribbons of his Darkness twining around their wrists. "They're noble, like yours." He gives her a wry look. "As are the bulk of Fyordin's."

Tierney coughs out a laugh through her tears. "Your lack of jealousy . . . it's both impressive and confusing."

Viger's expression turns ardent, everything he feels for her simmering Dark in it. "The Strafeling will have you for perhaps sixty years. Seventy. I'll have you *forever*.

If the Natural World survives, I'll be back for you, Asrai'lir."

And then Tierney is being flooded by another of his fears, almost as strong as his fear of those three words.

His fear of her being alone.

Tierney swallows against the pain rising in her throat. "Find me in the future, Viger."

"Bring the Balance, Asrai," he responds, the scene around them wavering. "Restore the Natural Matrix. When the world needs more Death as its Balance, instead of more Life, I'll be back for you with my full Darkness."

And then they're on the Shadowed ground, three huge desert serpents rising from the ashen sand, black as tar. One of them lowers itself before Viger, and he climbs onto its back. He peers down at Tierney, giving her one last, abyss-Dark look, before the serpents coil and turn, then dive into the ground, Viger and the serpents turning into black mist as they go.

Her heart in her throat, Tierney feels a parting brush of Viger's Darkness against her lips and swirling around her in an ardent caress, those three words at the base of Viger's fears simmering through her very soul.

She can feel him sending them out to her through their linkage. Feels them pulsing into the center of her power. A statement and a promise, as strong as eternity.

As powerful as Death.

I love you.

CHAPTER ELEVEN

FOREST'KHIN

Elloren

Northern Dyoi Forest

Vogel's Void tree shivers against the edges of my mind.

My pulse quickening, I dig my sharpened Dryad nails into the canopy-piercing branch I'm clinging to, the Void tree vision blurring my nighttime view of both the Shadow wasteland just beyond our Dyoi Forest shielding and Alder, who's on evening watch beside me.

"Vogel's there," I huff out to Alder, pointing west toward the Shadowed lands, my alarm intensifying as a distant sense of Vogel's stolen and corrupted silver gray Wyvernfire prickles heat over my skin. My surrounding ravens have grown restless, their huge wings ruffling. Errilith lets out a rough *caw* of warning, the ravens' distress spreading to Alder's encircling giant eagles.

"I can sense Vogel, as well," Alder affirms, giving me a stark look as an unnatural frosty power crackles against my lines, the ice magic weaving through the Shadow net Vogel cast over our shielding.

Black Witch strong.

"Holy Ancient One," I gasp, "I'm picking up on Fallon Bane's power."

"I sense her too," Alder confirms, her timber-calm voice low with dread. "It's stealthy, her attack. She's suffusing Vogel's net with enough Shadow ice to speed winter's descent."

The scream of distant Forest abruptly roars in from the southwest through Erthia's rootline network, reaching us after who knows how long. Vertigo swoops through me and my hands flex, my nails digging into bark as both Alder and I shudder, overcome by the sense of the entire Natural Balance of Erthia tilting toward the East. Now *held* by the East.

Flashing images of a cloud-high Shadow forest of ice trees burst into my mind, huge swaths of healthy southwestern land being blasted apart by Fallon's power, the trees' elemental might siphoned into the ice as they die.

"Fallon has killed the Forests of Ishkartaan," Alder rasps, trembling.

"With a Black Witch level of power," I grit out, narrowing my gaze on the West. "Only this time, the Black Witch isn't coming with fire. She's coming with *ice*—"

My words break off as a line of glowing purple moons flash into existence above the western horizon, as if Xishlon itself has joined with us to face Vogel and Fallon down. Stunned, I read the magic at play in those moons, and shock sizzles through my rootlines.

"That's my cousin Or'myr's magic," I gasp, just as my sense of Vogel's and Fallon's presence snaps out of existence.

"They're gone," Alder shakily notes.

"For now," I rejoin, my heart slamming against my ribs as I meet Alder's dire look once more.

"Vogel's Black Witch is about to shorten foliage season," she warns.

Resolve rips through me. "We need everyone under this shield to unite *right now*."

She gives me a concerned look. "Which means we need your Icaral's mother on our side *right now*."

I inwardly curse that impossible task. Soleiya Guryev's campaign against me has only intensified.

"Yvan is meeting with her to plead for an alliance," I say. I focus in on my link to Yvan's fire, engaging fully with his power, and am almost blasted off-balance by the frustration sputtering through it. I cast a fierce look at Alder. "Warn the others that Fallon's magic has been woven into Vogel's Shadow net." I start down the trunk as I send out a mental call to my ravens to remain on watch.

"Where are you going?" she presses.

"I'm going to find Yvan," I return, "and get his damned mother on our side."

I rush through the Forest's upper reaches, leaping from branch to branch, drawing foliage-amplified light power into my vision to allow sight as I follow the furious thread of Yvan's fire. Before long Yvan's burning aura is blazing over my skin . . . along with the scorching Fire Fae aura of his mother, their angry voices audible just ahead.

I drop silently to the ground, my heartbeat quickening as Soleiya's incensed voice rings out clear. "We are open to an alliance, but the Black Witch must be *slain!*"

I halt in response to the level of vitriol in Soleiya's voice, Yvan and his mother now visible through the branches before me, the two of them facing off inside a small clearing. Their figures are illuminated by the blaze of their eyes, their magics' violet and gold auras flaring to wildfire heights.

"Elloren is on our side," comes Yvan's seething reply. "And we've run out of time for anything but alliance with *every single person under this dome!*"

"Even if what you say is true—" Soleiya hisses.

"It *is* true." Yvan cuts her off. "I'm an *Icaral.* I can sense the truth of Elloren's *every* intention."

Soleiya spits out a mocking sound, her mouth twisting with derision. "Oh, such keen powers of perception. You thought you knew her every intention in Voloi. And then she came close to leveling the *entire city!* And don't tell me that it was Vogel controlling her!"

"Even though he was, in fact, controlling her?" Yvan counters.

"I don't believe it!" Soleiya's face takes on a look of sheer desperation. "Her grandmother killed your *father.* Her family is evil to the *core.* My son, how can you *possibly* ally with her?"

"She is my *Wyvernbonded mate,*" Yvan snarls, eyes incandescent.

Yvan's fire roars toward me through our bond, a startled flare momentarily overtaking its heat as he senses me so close. He immediately regains his bearings, catching me up in a blazing aura embrace so full of defiant love it brings the sting of tears to my eyes.

Yvan jabs his finger toward the ground, as if there's a burning line in the sand between himself and his mother, his molten eyes severe. "Stop judging Elloren for her lineage. For her *face.*"

"You ask *too much* of me!" Soleiya cries.

"No, I ask *fairness* of you," he lashes back. "Elloren has the right to be judged based on her *own* actions, *not* her grandmother's. Stop actively undermining her. You're sowing division, and it's playing right into Vogel's hands!"

Emotion surging, I'm about to step out of the shadows to join Yvan in facing Soleiya but am halted by the sudden sense of her invisible, fiery onslaught falling into sparking disarray, my heart twisting in response to the misery crackling through it as she gives Yvan a look of pure devastation.

"You can't be in love with the *Black Witch!*" she practically screams, her voice breaking. "There is nothing but *pain* for you there!"

They abruptly quiet, as if their combined violent storm has been reined in, their twin gazes blazing white-hot, both of them breathing hard, their fiery auras pulsing around them with out-of-control emotion, my own aura swept up in their firestorm of pain.

"Do you wish you'd never been with Father?" Yvan finally asks her, his voice low and harsh.

Soleiya's face tenses with what looks like vast, shattering hurt. "How can you even *ask* that?" she hisses, mouth trembling.

"Yet choosing him brought you great pain."

"Your father didn't bring me pain!" she counters. "The cursed *Mages* did!"

Yvan steps forward, wings fanning out, refusing to back down. "But your relationship, with an Icaral, in the Western Realm. It brought *pain* into your life."

"*Yes,*" Soleiya cries, tears falling as she thumps her chest with her fist. "It ripped my heart right out of my body when that witch *murdered* him."

I wince, a tear escaping my eye.

"Yet, knowing all of that," Yvan says in a strangled voice, eyes burning, "you'd choose him again?"

Soleiya breaks down now, sobbing. "Yes, Yvan . . ." she roughly sputters. She closes her eyes tight, then opens them, tear glassed, her voice a defiant snarl when it comes. "I'd choose your father *again and again and again and again.*"

And then her aura implodes, her shoulders slumping as she weeps, her body quivering.

Yvan's invisible fire blazes out to her, circling her in an embrace as he steps forward and brings a hand gently to her shoulder. "That's what love is, Mav'ya," he says in Lasair, his tone rife with feeling. "A wide-open heart. Wide open to the love *and* the pain."

After a long moment, Soleiya meets Yvan's gaze and brings her hand to his angular cheek, her lips trembling, her fire reaching out tentatively to his. Yvan meets her flame without hesitation, flowing a graceful tendril of fire around his mother's power, his own tears falling.

Soleiya pulls in a shuddering breath, her angular face tightening with emotion. "How did you get to be so wise, my son?"

An incredulous laugh escapes Yvan, his tear-slicked mouth lifting into a wry smile. "Maybe growing up an Icaral in a Realm that hates me?" He loses the jaded look, his expression growing earnest, his form a prism through my own tears as he sends out an invisible, ardent embrace of flame to encircle me. "But then, I met Elloren. And I learned, along with her, that there's another way. Beyond all the rigid lines. And then . . . I joined with the Forest, and found out that I don't have to be this . . . this *force of destruction*. This 'Icaral of Prophecy' weapon. That there's another path for me. Another path for us *all*." The flow of his fire around her flares with insistent, loving might. "Join with us, Mav'ya. This path holds our *only* chance to save Erthia and defeat the Shadow."

There's a prolonged beat of hesitation as Soleiya turns and registers my presence inside the Forest, a startled blaze of conflict igniting through her aura, her power whipping up to tempestuous levels before she sets her sights back on Yvan with a look of outrage.

"Please, Mav'ya,' Yvan urges, holding firm. "Please, just *hear the Forest out*."

Soleiya holds his gaze for an excruciatingly long moment. "All right, my son," she finally concedes. She casts me a look of hatred before turning back to Yvan, her expression tortured. "I'll listen to your Forest."

Yvan pulls in a deep breath, then takes his mother's hand and leads her to a large oak. Gently, he lifts her palm to the bark, and I've a sudden sense of the entire Dyoi Forest pulling in a breath as its power abruptly contracts toward Soleiya.

Soleiya gasps, her hand taking on a prismatic glow. Then, just as it happened for the others, bark swiftly forms over Soleiya's body, and she's pulled straight into the tree.

Yvan lets out a harsh sound, both his palms on the tree now.

My heart in my throat, I step from the tree line and swiftly close the distance between us. I bring my hand to Yvan's hot shoulder, and his fire immediately flares and flashes around and through me in impassioned strokes.

"I'm sorry, Elloren," he grits out. "I'm sorry you have to endure so much hatred."

"Yvan," I warn, "Fallon Bane and Vogel were briefly just outside our shielding."

Yvan's palms drop from the tree as he turns to face me in an urgent blur. "What happened?"

"They seemed to portal out as quickly as they came," I answer. "Alder and I read a message from the Forests of the continent's South, sent out as those wilds were destroyed. Fallon has leveled both Northern and Southern Ishkartaan with her ice. Yvan, she's now capable of a Black Witch level of Shadow ice power. She's thrown a line of her ice into Vogel's Shadow net over our shielding. Which will hasten winter. We need every last person under this dome on our side *tonight*."

Yvan casts me a fervid look before glancing at the trunk Soleiya just entered, a frustrated look sharpening his features. "My mother's as stubborn as me."

"Well, we can only hope the Forest gets through to her."

I tell him about Or'myr's line of purple moons as we wait for what feels like an unbearable stretch of time. Eventually, rays of prismatic light blast from the trunk, and Yvan and I step back, his mother suddenly before us, down on her knees and panting, her palms to the ground.

"Mav'ya?" Yvan says, dropping down to her level and reaching out to take hold of her arm.

Soleiya lifts her head, and I pull in an astonished breath.

Her eyes are filled with purple fire. She unfurls her clenched hand to reveal a dark violet pinecone, the image of III marked on her palm just beneath it, and I can sense it thrumming through her—Soleiya's new bond to Yvan's kindred Zhilaan Forest.

The Forest that needs fire.

"It's . . . it's all more complex and interconnected than I ever realized," Soleiya stammers, her awestruck face slicked with tears as she stares, wide-eyed, at the pinecone and III mark on her palm. She lifts her gaze to me, her brow knotting as more tears pool and streak down her face. "The trees . . . they showed me what you've both been through. And, Elloren . . . they showed me your heart, and what Vogel tried to do to you. They showed me *everything* . . ." Her words trail off as her face tenses with obvious remorse. "I'm *so sorry*."

My throat tenses with emotion as Yvan huffs out a relieved breath and Soleiya rises. I draw her into a close embrace, her lips trembling along with her voice when she draws slightly back. "Perhaps . . . we can start over, you and I?"

I nod with enthusiasm and urgency, Yvan's wings arcing in around us both as his fire lashes around us, the three of us no longer divided as Icaral, Fire Fae, and Mage.

All of us now Forest'khin.

"Vogel's Black Witch, Fallon Bane," I caution Soleiya, my power's flow bright with alarm, "she's woven her ice power through Vogel's Shadow net over our shielding."

Soleiya's fiery eyes widen.

"Which means," Yvan stresses, "we need your help uniting everyone *right now.*"

CHAPTER TWELVE

GERMINATION

Elloren

Northern Dyoi Mountain Range

"I was wrong about Elloren," Yvan's mother calls out to my adversaries beyond the runic wall separating us, the light from Or'myr's moons suffusing the night and Soleiya with a violet tint.

Sylvan, Iris, Yulan, Alder, and Vang Troi bracket Soleiya, a warm shimmer of emotion coursing through me in response to Soleiya's vocal support, my ravens on guard in the sky above us, just below our dome-shield's cloud-high apex.

I lean into Yvan, and he shoots me a quick, fervent look, his arm and fire aura wrapped around me, both the Dyoi Forest and the distant Zhilaan sending out palpable swirls of support around the two of us—Icaral and Dryad Witch united.

Fixed as two fiery stars.

"What of the Prophecy?" one of the Amaz behind our wall of magic snarls—a young, gray-hued, heavily tattooed Elfhollen woman with braids the color of steel. Her silver eyes glint with a battle-hardened ire as she sets her gaze on me.

"*Fallon Bane* is the Black Witch!" my sister Diana growls, her amber eyes aglow. "I warned you of this *many, many* months ago!"

"The Forest is forging a new, more powerful Prophecy," Soleiya insists to the Elfhollen soldier. "It is forging a new Prophecy for us *all*." She holds up her palm, displaying the III mark imprinted there.

An audible gasp rises, and Soleiya turns to me. I meet her incandescent gaze, our magic flaring out to each other in a blaze of alliance that twists my heart with the best kind of ache as she turns back to her allies and launches into a description of what the Forest revealed to her.

"I believe," Soleiya finally states, her voice hitching with emotion, "that if my husband, Valentin, were alive today . . ." She stops, her mouth quavering into a grief-stricken grimace.

Yvan's eyes meet mine before he goes to her. He takes hold of his mother's hand, invisible spirals of his aura winding around their joined hands and arms as tears streak down Soleiya's face. Yvan murmurs something to her in Lasair, and she nods, seeming bolstered by his words as she straightens and peers back out at the crowd of Vu Trin, holding tight to Yvan.

"I believe," Soleiya starts again, her splintered voice stronger now, "that if my husband were here with us *right now*—" she glances at me once more "—that he would not only join with the Forest, but embrace Elloren as an ally and as *family*. As the Wyvernbonded mate of my son."

Yvan's heat shocks through our bond, his gaze flashing to mine with such ardent force that a flush warms my skin.

Hostile murmuring breaks out amongst our adversaries. Their outraged silence descends, everyone's gazes settling on me. Sparks flying between us, Yvan extends his hand to me.

Feeling the press of fate circling down on us all, I go to him and wrap my hand around his, the contact triggering another rush of heat through our bond. An affectionate smile on his lips, Yvan draws me close, the Forest's support flooding my rootlines with shimmering light power. I glance at the purple-lit tree line edging the ledge—the beautiful, complicated, absolutely vital-to-our-survival Living Wilds—my gut tightening against the dire situation we're all faced with.

Reckless courage rises within me like an elemental storm, fueled by autumn's prismatic power. I look first to Yvan, then to my allies and adversaries both, my heartbeat striking against my chest as I briefly meet the gazes of Mavrik and Gwynn, then Sage, Ra'Ven, Rivyr'el, Thierren, and Fain.

Unsheathing the branch at my waist, I drop it to the ground, fully disarming. Recklessly decided, I voice the words that are a leap off a cliff. "Strike down the wall between us."

Shock flashes through Yvan's and Soleiya's power, through *everyone's* power, my airborne ravens pulsing their cautioning Darkness through the scene around me as they land, ready for battle.

"Elloren," Yvan protests, "their hostility has *not* abated."

I meet his blazing stare with my own. "We're out of time," I insist, motioning to Alder, Sylvan, and Yulan. "You heard what my Dryad'kin and I sensed from the trees. The Mages are razing every Forest they can access. And now, Fallon has hastened the descent of a Shadow winter. No matter the risks, we can't remain divided *one second longer.*"

Steeling myself, I meet Errilor's pitch-black eyes and mentally petition both him and the rest of my flock to keep hold of their power before I turn back toward those allies who had a strong hand in crafting the shield-wall.

"Are you sure, Elloren," Trystan presses.

I nod.

They all hesitate for a brief, fraught moment longer, before raising branches and styluses in unison and murmuring spells.

The shield flashes out of existence in a spray of multicolored light.

My adversaries move to take their runic weapons in hand, and Yvan and his mother slide protectively in front of me, but I gently motion them back and step forward, pulse thundering, acutely aware of my vulnerability and my adversaries' battle magic rising.

"Noi'khin'nur, Amazakaraan'veer, and Lasair'shin," I say, addressing my adversaries with the Noi, Amaz, and Lasair terms of highest respect. I gaze pointedly toward the Shadowed wasteland. "We're staring down the possibility of the *true end* to Erthia. My Dryad'khin and I . . . we can't fight this battle alone." I hold up my III-marked palm. "I'm begging you, Noi'khin'nur, Amazakaraan'veer, and Lasair'shin—" I sweep my hand toward the trees "—to simply *hear the Forest out.*"

Silence falls, weighty with portent, my breath suspended in my chest as defensive magic continues to rise, every trace of Yvan's and Soleiya's fire poised to blast around me with weapon-repelling strength.

Queen Freyja Zyrr steps forward, her hazel eyes fixed on me. "Elloren *Guryev,* I will hear your Forest out."

Heat explodes through Yvan's and my bonded fire, Freyja's gutsy move to name me Guryev triggering a shock wave through the magical aura of every adversary.

As well as through my own.

I turn to Yvan and find him giving me a look of such fiery love, I fear I might come undone. The name feels so right, so true, as heart-expandingly right as accepting Lukas's surname finally became. The full withdrawal from the yoke of my Gardnerian surname, grief-marked as it is, tastes like hard-won freedom. And the deepest mark of Yvan's love.

"I'll join you, my queen," a voice calls out, shock further unsettling our collective magic as the Elfhollen Amaz woman steps forward.

Yvan, Soleiya, and I exchange cautious yet hopeful looks as several more Amaz volunteer to connect to the Forest, Yulan and my other Dryad'khin allies accompanying them to the trees.

But one Amaz in particular remains aggressively unmoved—Diana's nemesis, the huge axe-wielding Amaz warrior, Alcippe Feyir. A furious expression smolders on Alcippe's face, her amethyst eyes fixed murderously on Yvan and me, her fists clenched around her axe's rune-marked handle.

A growl erupts from Diana's throat at the same moment that Alder breaks from our ranks and strides toward Alcippe. She comes to a halt before the huge warrior, a grayed Dyoi Eagle with half-singed purple feathers perched on Alder's shoulder.

"Fierce One," Alder greets her in Amazkaraan, an uncharacteristically emotional edge to her perennially timber-calm tone. "You placed my very first runic spear in my hands when I was but eight years of age, an orphan amongst the Amaz. You have been a mentor and a protector to me, and to so many of the Goddess's Own. I ask you, Revered One, not just as a Dryad'kin, but as an *Amaz*, to *hear my Forest out.*"

Alcippe's broad jaw stiffens, her expression flexing with what looks like almost violent conflict. But then something miraculous happens that makes me feel as if the whole world is tilting beneath our feet.

Alcippe nods, quick and tight.

Wasting no time, Alder walks with her into the Forest's tree line, accompanied by Alder's entire flock of giant kindred eagles.

Midnight is closing in, a deep-night chill enveloping the world, when the Amaz, Vu Trin, and Lasair who entered the trees begin to emerge. All transformed.

All imprinted with III's image.

A silver-eyed, purple-furred Noi Grizzly Bear kindred is seated behind Queen Freyja Zyrr, all of us, including a blessedly alive Lucretia, gathered on the huge ledge around one central, runic bonfire when Alcippe finally emerges from the tree line, a gleaming shard of what looks like rose quartz gripped in her fist, a stunned expression on her tattooed face.

Yvan and I rise to our feet, along with Vang Troi, Freyja, and so many others.

Alcippe breaks away from Alder's side and makes a beeline for Yvan, her fierce, pale pink eyes fixed on him. Alarm sears through me—I'm clear that the Amaz are forbidden from polluting their gazes by staring directly at men, unless in the act of using them to create more daughters. Or striking them down.

I grip protective hold of Yvan's arm, but it's his turn to caution calm through the reassuring flow of his hot aura around mine.

Alcippe halts before him, making no move to draw the axe strapped to her back or the blades sheathed all over her body. Yvan's wings draw in tight as he faces her, his fire power a molten ball in his center.

"You saved my Icaral child, Pyrgomanche," Alcippe roughly states, her tone deep and intense. She raises her free hand, and relief shimmers through both Yvan's power and mine as we view the image of III imprinted there.

"The Forest," Alcippe says to Yvan, "it showed me your rescue of Pyrgo from the Mage prison in Valgard. And it showed me how you aided our Selkie'khin, and so many others of womankind. The trees . . ." She falters, an emotional sheen to her eyes as she lifts the quartz gripped in her other hand. "They not only showed me all this . . . they unbound my power. And restored the geomancy stripped from all Urisk womankind by *men*." Disgust tightens Alcippe's features as she holds Yvan's stare with condemning force. "But, perhaps," she allows, the weight of an anvil in her tone, "there is room on Erthia for men such as you."

Shock stills my breath as Yvan snaps his wings out to their full span. "You have my fire, Alcippe Feyir," he vows. "You and your people, and your Icaral child."

"And you have my axe, Icaral," Alcippe vows in turn as my reverberating shock shifts the very ground beneath my feet.

Naga contracts into her human form and leaps onto an elevated ledge of stone, her wings snapping powerfully out as her narrowed gold-fire gaze sweeps over the Vu Trin forces. "Unbroken Ones of Erthia!" she growls. "It is time to create a new kind of force! With a *living* flag and banner! Rise up with us, Dryad'khin, as Defenders of Erthia!"

Vang Troi unsheathes her runic sword and raises it, a flash of her sapphire power illuminating the night. "Who here," she booms, "will unite as a Dryad'khin force so we can combine our power, throw our dome-shield over the entire Eastern Realm, and unite the East to *take back Erthia* from the Magedom's Shadow?"

I suck in a breath as every single one of our former adversaries raises III-marked palms, an emotional sound torn from Yulan.

"Well, then, let's get to work, shall we?" Hazel drawls, a wicked smile forming on his black-lipped mouth where he stands beside Wrenfir, my uncle's large black bobcat kindred hugging his side. Wrenfir's and Hazel's arms are slung over each other's shoulders, their magic looped around each other, a surprisingly intimate energy thrumming through it as the mounting foliage power of the Forest pulses through us all.

"We need Oaklyyn," Sylvan calls out to Hazel from where he stands beside Iris Morgaine. Everyone grows silent as Sylvan levels a finger toward the West, at the Shadow threat bearing down, his pine eyes severe. "Oaklyyn holds a special talent for crafting Dryad runes, including the amplification, linkage, and expansion runes. We need those runes to break through Vogel's Shadow net and throw our shielding over the entire East. We hold great power, but not enough to achieve this before the Magedom's Shadow winter closes in. Not with foliage season shortened. If we're going to outpace Vogel's forces, we need Oaklyyn on our side, but she has estranged herself from us all."

"I have sought her out as well, Dryad'kin," Yulan tells Sylvan, a mournful edge to her tone and in her kindred heron's eyes, "but there is no convincing her to ally with us."

"I went to her, as well," Alder admits, her green brow knotting tight. "But a more powerful enemy than even the Magedom has taken hold of her. She has lost all hope."

"We can't abandon her," Aislinn insists with a vehemence that sends an ache through my heart—I'm certain that my Lupine sister is all too clear on what facing misery without hope or aid can do to a person.

"Aislinn's right," Jarod says from beside her, his arm wrapped around Aislinn.

"She needs us to be her khin," Thierren passionately agrees.

"Raz'zor and I sought her out soon after she retreated into the wilds," Ariel reveals, a troubled look tensing her sharp features, the raven kindred on her shoulder bristling. "She's ready to attack anyone who comes near. Raz'zor asked me for the chance to try and break through to her alone."

Troubled, I send a line of my fire out to Raz'zor. His returning ruddy flame is suddenly streaking through our horde bond with an impassioned red sizzle I've never felt in my horde mate's fire before. Along with a cautioning flare, emphatically fierce, and I struggle to respect the demand for distance I feel in it.

Because we're running out of time.

CHAPTER THIRTEEN

FIRE FOREST

Oaklyyn

Northern Dyoi Mountain Range

The Wyvern Raz'zor and the Icaral Mage Ariel Haven sought me out soon after I broke from their allies' cursed ranks, the two of them ignoring the violently clear message I gave to my Dryad'kin.

Leave me be.

I empathically sensed the Wyvern's and Icaral's approach before I sighted them from where I'd retreated, deep into this doomed Forest. I could sense their cursed *fire*.

Their cursed *non-Dryad'kin* fire.

Rage lashed through me, and I reached for my staff, ready to fight them off here in the dawn-lit wilds. Ready to unleash revenge and scream until the heavens shook. As their wicked fire drew nearer, I sprang to my feet, trembling with grief-stricken fury.

Wanting them *dead.*

Wanting to *be* dead.

The memory of the sound of my bonded Northern Forest and my kindred wolverine screaming echoed through my soul, echoed through my destroyed heart again and again and *again*.

"Leave me *be!*" I snarled at them, spittle flying from my mouth as the Wyvern and the Icaral slunk through the trees with their terrible serpentine fluidity.

Non-Dryad nature killers! I yearned to scream at them.

All of them nature killers.

Hate pummeled though me as the Icaral and the large white dragon slid into fuller view. Their gold- and red-fire eyes took in my murderous stance, unintimidated ferocity blazing in them.

THE DRYAD STORM

I raised my staff and moved to attack as the Wyvern suddenly contracted inward.

I halted, dead in my tracks, as his form snapped into the shape of a serpentine young man, his startlingly abrupt change throwing me off-kilter, his form clothed in hard white scales, the crimson fire burning in his eyes undimmed. His wings fanned out just as two Noi Doves with half-grayed feathers soared down from the Forest's canopy and perched on my shoulders, the birds flooding me with a pleading, gut-wrenching affection that was unbearable to sense, hopelessly doomed as they were.

Undaunted by the hardening of my aggressive stance, the doves flashed images into my mind of the Icaral woman before me placing healing salve on their burns. Cooing them to sleep.

But I wanted *none* of the wingeds' false hope.

I shrugged them off, struggling to harden what was left of my shattered heart against their startled flare of protest as they flew off to the branches above in a flurry of hurt and confusion.

A misery so acute I feared I'd retch swamped me, and I doggedly avoided looking at the winged innocents. Unable to bear the pain of any type of connection forming between us or with the surrounding doomed Forest—a Forest that kept swirling unbearable, embracing love around me.

Because it would soon be dead. Like my Northern Forest was dead. Like *I* wanted to be dead.

It's over, my broken heart beat out.

Nature is over.

"I know what it is to want to die," the Icaral, Ariel, blurted out, her tone blade sharp.

My gaze snapped to her, the Icaral's expression shot through with such a blazing level of sincerity that my misery whipped into even greater turmoil.

And fury.

So potent it could level galaxies.

I took a menacing step toward her, my grip firming on my staff, ready to smash her Icaral head right off her Wyvern'kin shoulders.

I took another warning step, snarling, my rage so intense it singed acid into my lungs. "You know *nothing* of what I feel, Wyvern!" Casting a belligerent look toward Raz'zor, I found his crimson-fire eyes focused on me, unblinking. Everything about him disturbingly *other*. More reptile than human.

But that wasn't the most disturbing thing about him.

The most world-upending thing was the intense understanding simmering in his blazing red eyes, his gaze shot through with such leagues-deep pain it prompted a tidal-wave rise of my own misery, the swell of agony unbearably intense.

"Get away from me!" I screamed at them, drawing on what shreds of Forest power I could without a kindred connection to conjure a cyclonic ball of elemental power above my staff.

NOOOOOO! the Forest shuddered through my every withered rootline as the doves and other wingeds broke into agitated squawks and wing ruffling, every tree and kindred clamoring for me to *stop*.

I was unmoved by their protest, ready to blast these Wyvern'kin straight through their futile dome-shield and into the waiting Shadow.

The Wyvern'kin said nothing. Instead, they remained fixed in place, eyes locked with mine, their stares full of that wildly unsettling understanding. And then, as one, they threw their wings down in an emphatic *whoosh* and launched themselves into the Forest's canopy, where they perched on branches high overhead.

A hissing conversation in their Wyvern tongue ensued before they seemed to come to some agreement, the Icaral flying off after giving me a long, pained look, and the pale Wyvern remaining.

Refusing to leave.

I snarled and hurled out curses at him before turning and stalking deeper into the woods, pointedly ignoring the curious animals that followed, rippling out their vulnerability and love to me. Because it crushed the remaining shreds of my heart to know that their home was about to die.

The Wyvern found me that evening.

He remained there, straight through the night, watching me from up high in winged-human form. He retreated briefly when I shook my fist and screamed at him. But then, as I crumpled into a ball of utter despair, he reappeared in the canopy above, a silent, stubborn presence, refusing to leave.

The next night, I'm balled up on the Forest floor, sobbing for my destroyed Forest and kindreds.

That's when the Wyvern approaches me once more.

I'm too worn down by grief to scream at him. To summon power and attack. To do anything but grieve for my dead Forest. For all the soon-to-be-dead remaining Forests.

He crouches down in human form on one knee, pale wings pulled in, alabaster horns curved above snow-hued hair. "Horde to me, Fierce One," he says.

I blink up at him. *"What?"* I spit out, not believing his sheer audacity.

"Horde to me," he hisses again, emphatic, his crimson eyes lighting up the night. I want to hurl every last shred of my power at him. I want to hurl it at them *all*.

"Why are you doing this," I rasp at him, voice choked.

"Horde to me," he says once more, fierce. "You are *not* alone."

Incredulity leaps through me, tightening my every muscle. I spring up at the same time he does in an otherworldly blur. Balling my fists, I lunge toward him, staring into those burning crimson eyes, not caring about the monumental Wyvern power I sense radiating from him.

Power that can incinerate trees.

That can destroy Forests.

"I am a *Dryad*!" I cry, my voice splintering from the sheer force of my rage. "I am not a *Wyvern*! I wish you were all *DEAD*!"

He doesn't budge. His crimson eyes only burn hotter. "Horde to me, Fierce One," he hisses, infuriatingly stubborn, everything surrounding us lit up by the flickering red glow of those eyes. "We will protect Erthia's surviving Forests together. As *one*."

I spit out a sound of blistering fury. "You want to protect *Forests*? You're all *fire*." I splay my arm out, gesturing around us, tears blurring my eyes. "How can you protect *any* of this?"

He's unmoved, his stare pierced through with ferocity. He leans in, teeth bared. "By protecting *you*."

I bare my own Dryad-sharp teeth at him. "I don't *want* your protection!"

Again, he doesn't budge. "I was alone for a long time," he growls, low and emphatic. "Unhorded. Imprisoned by runes. My fire . . . it couldn't *breathe*. I was like a lone tree without a Forest."

My face twists with feral offense. "You dare to compare your horde to my *Forest*?"

"Yes," he snarls, flashing his canines. "A Forest of *fire*."

And then it's all crashing in—the never-ending barrage of horrific images.

My beloved Forest, caught up in the Magedom's Shadow conflagration, rapidly singed to nothing. The wild innocents who trusted me as their protector all *decimated*, my Dryad grief consuming me in the Shadowfire's cruel wake.

"GET AWAY FROM ME!" I scream, readying every last shred of elemental power I can summon to deploy against him, even at the risk of fatally collapsing my rootlines.

He gives me an incinerating look, the understanding in it holding the power to destroy me. But before I can unleash my full rage against him, against the entire Forest-murdering world, he snaps out his wings, throws them down, and soars away.

I fall to my knees and scream out my despair, wanting to shatter the heavens, as the Forest gently sends multicolored leaves and fluttering kindreds and lovely, tendriling vines out to me, shattering what's left of my heart.

Raz'zor is back again later that night, the Forest washed in violet light emanating from a line of purple moons that sprang up over the Dyoi Forest earlier this eve, an image of the moons sent to me through the trees, as if they should give me cause for hope.

There is no hope in this cruel, Nature-destroying world.

I look up, bleary-eyed, and spot Raz'zor's pale human face in the trees, surreally illuminated red by his crimson-fire eyes. He's perched on a low-lying branch, wings tucked tightly back, his unblinking Wyvern gaze set stolidly on me. *Blazingly* on me.

"Don't you ever give up?" I ask, my throat raw and tight.

"Horde to me, Fierce One," he replies, steadfast and adamant.

I hold his gaze, too worn-out by grief to keep my defenses up.

"Raz'zor," I say, startling myself with the intimate strangeness of his name on my tongue. I shake my head, a mournful sorrow tightening my throat. "You're all fire. I'm *Dryad'kin*. We can never be khin."

In a pale blur he's next to me, crouched down, stubborn fire in his otherworldly slit-pupiled eyes. His pale lip ticks up, defiance sparking in his gaze. "Your trees consume the sun, Fierce One. And that sun is made of *flame*. Your Forest and your power, it pulses with that connection. Pulses with the light power of *fire*. *Horde to me.*"

I choke back a startled sob. Stunned by his idea—the Erthia-upending idea of a Wyvern-Dryad'kin horde bond able to support and defend the Forest rather than singe it to the ground.

THE DRYAD STORM

The Dyoi Forest stills, as if holding its breath, as if it, too, senses the revolutionary power in his idea.

A hot tear rolls down my cheek. "It's lost," I choke out to him as images of leagues and leagues of my Forest burning with Shadowfire ricochet through my mind in eviscerating spasms. Combined with the root-deep awareness of ever-increasing leagues of Western and Southern Forests being murdered, all of it slicing clear through my soul. "The battle you seek," I tell him, "it's already lost."

He draws even closer, bringing his fiery eyes level to mine, and I feel as if I'm staring into a never-ending inferno.

"Horde. To. Me," he says again, baring his teeth. "We will fight for every last remaining tree."

Startlingly, the boundaries between us begin to fall, searing to flame under the relentless force of his stubborn fire.

And the compassion burning in his eyes.

I force myself to sit up, mouth trembling, holding his relentless stare. "All right, Wyvern," I raggedly concede, with absolutely nothing left in this world to lose. "I'll horde to you."

Raz'zor's lips lift in a canine-baring smile. He takes hold of my hand and coaxes me to rise with him, before drawing me into a loose embrace and bringing his lips to the base of my neck.

A shiver of sparks radiates from the contact, the pleasurable sensation startling me.

He tightens his embrace, his teeth piercing my skin, and I gasp, my eyes widening as my rootlines open and I'm flooded by his entire horde's sunbright, revolutionary fire.

CHAPTER FOURTEEN

FOREST MAGIC

Elloren Guryev

Northern Dyoi Mountain Range

I startle awake after only a trace of sleep, the shock of a new, green blaze of fire power roaring through my horde bond, a flare of Yvan's heat lashing out to wrap so hungrily around me, it sparks a rampant warmth through every line.

Yvan lies beside me in a mossy Forest alcove inside the ledge's tree line, both of us catching a few hours of much-needed sleep after the grueling work of connecting everyone's power to the Dyoi Forest's shielding as strongly as we can without Oaklyyn's runic amplification.

Yvan's eyes snap open and meet mine in a rush of green sparks, my pulse quickening over both the feel of this unexpected verdant flame and the powerful hunger in Yvan's fire.

"What just happened?" I ask, fighting off the urge to draw him close, shocked by how much this rush of fire is making me crave his lips and body against mine, a firestorm having flared between us.

A glazed look enters his eyes, his breathing uneven. His brow tenses, and I can feel him forcibly wresting a line of his fire magic away from me to search our horde connection for the source of this new flame while our bond *burns* as if fanned to new heights by this unfamiliar fire, green-and-vermillion fire blazing through it with spitfire energy.

"Someone has joined our horde," Yvan huskily states, focusing his green-flame-streaked gaze back on me. He swallows, a hot flush coloring his angular face. "Raz'zor . . . his fire brought them in. There's an energy of attraction in it. Can you feel it?"

It's my turn to draw inward, to search the horde bond for a deeper reading of Raz'zor's vermillion line of fire, and sure enough, I find his red flame embracing this new green power.

Raz'zor, I send out through our fealty bond.

Dryad Witch, comes Raz'zor's low, simmering reply.

Who have you horded to us?

A triumphant rush of his vermillion flame streaks through my vision.

The Dryad, Oaklyyn.

Red sparks explode through our fealty bond, and it surprises me, the amount of fire Raz'zor has wrapped around Oaklyyn's name.

"It's Oaklyyn, isn't it?" Yvan surmises, giving me a sly look.

"It is," I confirm, astonished. "I've never felt Raz'zor's fire this worked up."

Yvan's expression takes a turn toward the knowing, a molten heat entering his gaze that sends a flare of his warmth straight down my spine. "He wants her for his mate."

He wraps his hand around mine as the unspoken simmers between us, the hot brand of his gaze and the Wyvern warmth of his touch surfacing a memory from what feels like lifetimes ago—that time Yvan and I danced in Verpacia under a starry sky, loved ones gathered around us, Trystan's violin music light on the air. I remember being entranced by Yvan's seductive Lasair grace and assured lead, by the feel of his body moving against mine with unerring rhythm, the two of us perfectly in sync, our faces flushed, the caress of his hot hands on me lighting a fire down low. A fire that's drawing me to him right now.

"Do you remember when we danced?" I whisper, the question escaping before I can swallow it back, my pulse thudding around it.

The sparks crackling through our bond strike into a blaze, fast and hot. Suggestive amusement dances in Yvan's eyes as he lifts his free hand and authoritatively swipes it down, pushing our horde's fire clear away, only the firestorm of want in our bond remaining.

"Do you want to dance with me, Elloren?" he asks, voice sultry, a serious glow entering his eyes as he strokes sparks along my hand.

I swallow, not able to pull in an even breath as I fall into the ravishing heat of his fire, finding him so achingly handsome in this moment I can barely get the words out. "I do."

And I mean it. I'm almost ready to move past the grief that has an aching grip on my heart and embrace him in every way.

Almost.

Yvan's fire gutters, and I know he's sensing the *almost* in my emotions. I can sense it in the fleeting tension in his body and how his hand stills around mine. And in the way he's now drawing back some of his fire and taking a steadying breath.

The energy of understanding ripples through our bond, and he reaches up, his warm hand caressing my face before he leans in to press his heated lips to my temple. "When you're ready," he whispers, and I have to blink against the sudden burn of tears in my eyes.

After a moment, Yvan draws back, lifts his hand, and flicks it open, our horde's fire streaming back through our power, Raz'zor and Oaklyyn's intertwined green-and-vermillion sparks still crackling through it.

"We should find our horde," he throatily offers, his hand caressing my arm, and I nod, distantly wondering if Raz'zor and Oaklyyn wanting to be Wyvernbonded mates could possibly be true.

Oaklyyn blasts onto the predawn mountain ledge like a Dryad storm. Her runic staff is in hand, verdant runes glowing all over it. Three midnight-purple Noi Wolverines trail her, and my heart lifts at the sight of her newfound kindreds. The wolverines are all as growly as Oaklyyn, their purple fur bristling, their combined ferocity at full odds with the delicate beauty of the dew-speckled morning, a mounting, prismatic riot of color close to overtaking the trees, a gauzy fog rising from the ledge's stone.

"Dryad'kin," Sylvan states as he and Yulan step toward her, their magic awhirl with a sudden rise of feeling, powerful relief shuddering through everyone's power, even Hazel's magic briefly eclipsing the world in Darkness.

Because Oaklyyn is transformed, her green hue fully restored, the purple branching pattern shimmering over her skin heightened. The same golden-star horde mark emblazoned on my entire horde shimmers against Oaklyyn's inner shoulder.

Raz'zor stalks in beside Oaklyyn in human form, his crimson eyes lit up as they swing to me. He shoots me a smug, triumphant grin that I raise a brow at, his aura's ruddy power flowing embracingly around Oaklyyn.

Naga and the rest of our horde rise as Ariel sends a welcoming line of her golden flame out to Oaklyyn, the rest of our horde joining her and flowing power into a communal blaze.

Oaklyyn stiffens, her elemental power held tight in her core, emotion churning in it. She glances toward our dome-shield, taking in the multicolored mosaic of runes shimmering against its surface, Vogel's Shadow net slithering over it all like a giant, clawed hand shot through with Fallon's winter-hastening magic.

"We need to flood that shield with amplified power to blast through Vogel's Shadow net," Oaklyyn bites out. "I've a few Dryad amplification and expansion runes that should do the trick, especially when I draw the power of our Dryad Witch through them." Her newly green-burning gaze swings to mine, a rush of her verdant flame blazing through my rootlines, green sparks crackling in my vision. Oaklyyn levels her staff at me, a staff I've felt the blunt end of a few times, before her gaze slides to Sylvan and Yulan. "I'll rune-bind the witch's rootlines not only to the shield but to our rootlines as well, via a linkage rune," she states. "I'll do the same for the other Mage-born Dryad'kin. To give their rootlines full access to our knowledge of Forest magic so they can become true soldiers for the Forest."

I catch Gwynn's and Mavrik's eyes, then Thierren's, all of us exchanging a quick look of surprise.

"It is good to have you back with us, Dryad'kin," Sylvan enthuses, his usually severe tone shot through with feeling as Yulan flows lavender-flowering vines out from the soil beneath her feet to encircle Oaklyyn.

Oaklyyn grows quiet, the powerful flow of her magic seeming to collapse into troubled chaos as she looks at the Death Fae Dryad amongst us. "Hazel . . ." she starts, "I might have been wrong . . . for hating you when you saved our lives." She pauses, her mouth twisting into a trembling grimace. "True Dryad'kin fight to the end for *all* Forests. And for *every* kindred. Not just their own." She tenses, blinking back the sheen of tears in her eyes as she looks to the tree line, her voice rough when it comes. "The Forest showed me what you have done . . . and who you truly are." She stops, an overwhelming remorse overtaking her expression. "Hazel . . . I was *wrong.*"

Devastation is writ hard in her eyes, and the vast-unsaid hangs in the air between them—how she leveled the slur *halfling* at him again and again. How she reviled us *all.*

Hazel considers Oaklyyn, tendrils of his snaking Darkness shivering to life to wrap around them both as a single purple viper appears at Oaklyyn's feet then slithers up and around her form to curl around her shoulders, dark tongue flickering.

"All is forgiven," Hazel says, his voice a bone-deep thrum. His black lips lift, a devilish light entering his eyes as his Death Fae energy pulses the world Dark.

"Time to strengthen our shielding," he drawls, his wicked smile broadening, "and turn our Dryad Witch and her allies into weapons for the Forest."

Hours later, I'm covered in Dryad runes that blaze every foliage color, my body newly clothed in formfitting bark armor Oaklyyn conjured onto me that's surprisingly easy to move in. An ever-growing portion of my power flows into our shielding, our linkage to it amplified via Oaklyyn's shield runes as I wrest hold of my remaining magic and face off, once again, against the one ally among us who holds even more fire than Vogel, even with a portion of it tethered to our shielding.

My Wyvernbonded mate—the Icaral of Prophecy.

Yvan stands before me in a Dyoi Forest clearing, his similarly rune-marked body coiled. His wings are drawn in tight, and both his hands glow violet as he draws fire magic into his palms. Oaklyyn and Raz'zor are watching us from the Forest clearing's violet grass periphery, along with Sylvan, Iris, Yulan, Hazel, Wrenfir, Mavrik, and Gwynnifer.

It's a struggle to keep my focus from being scattered by the sight of Yvan's handsome face and bare chest, peak foliage amplifying our already strong draw to each other, a feverish warmth having overtaken me. Yvan gives me a slow, dangerous smile that sparks a hotter flaring of our bond, his eyes narrowing on me with an all too knowing light.

"Attack," Sylvan charges, and Yvan lunges at me in a blur, raising his palms.

I level my branch's tip at the ground, Oaklyyn's knowledge of soil spells flashing through my rootlines and fluently rolling off my lips.

A dark mass of metallic powder flies up from the ground, and I send fire into it, melting it into thick, black fibers that I whip around Yvan's wrists and ankles. Before Yvan can release his power, I arc my branch toward the earth, my conjured fibers following my motion, yanking Yvan to the ground and tethering him there.

Yvan gives me a teasing smile before deploying a punch of his heat, his body flashing violet for a split second as my lashings melt away and he springs at me once more in a blur, knocks my branch from my hand and takes hold of me from behind.

I can feel his smile against my cheek, my heart skidding from the hot contact. "You're getting better," he murmurs as I ignore the thrum of my pulse and force myself to focus, drawing on Yulan's avian knowledge to send a mental call out to the Forest's wingeds.

A sapphire hummingbird darts in from the Forest, a small twig grasped in the bird's talons. It zooms close to my hand, and I grab the twig and rapidly murmur a series of Sylvan's storm spells.

Wind bursts to life between Yvan and me, blowing him backward.

I swing around as he hits the ground, leveling my twig at him as he springs to his feet. He thrusts his glowing hands forward and blasts a wall of fire toward me while I deploy a bolt of storm shot through with prismatic lightning.

Yvan's incoming wall of flame crashes into my tempest, our power pressed tight in crackling prismatic-and-violet walls, a backdraft of static energy sizzling over my skin. I dig my heels into the soil, holding my ground, teeth gritted, twig raised, as Yvan's magic battles against mine, our bond's heat intensifying the storm, a sudden desire for him gripping hold once again. My feet skid against earth along with Yvan's as our storming walls enlarge, growing higher than the treetops, the two of us locked into a churning, roaring standoff.

A smile spreads across Yvan's lips and I sense my foliage-fueled power gaining ground, even as I hold a portion back to keep from igniting the surrounding Forest.

Yvan abruptly surrenders, my wall of power crashing into him, its edges whipping back around me and skidding me forward. Carried by my magic's momentum, I hurtle toward Yvan. He catches me and pulls me close, my prismatic lightning flashing around us as we fall to the ground.

He rolls me onto my back and brings his lips to mine, his impassioned kiss sending a charged thrill through my body, violet-hot, a triumphant energy coursing through me along with a shuddering flash of Yvan's fire.

"You did it, Dryad," he says as we break the kiss, his eyes afire, my compact storm still whipping around us. "You held your own against the Dread Icaral of Prophecy."

A laugh bursts from me, a rush of love flooding our bond as he slides off me and rises to his feet with his usual grace then holds out his hand to me. I let him help me up before glancing around to find Yulan and Gwynn beaming at me and the others giving me sly looks of approval.

I turn back to Yvan, growing serious. "I held back," I admit. "To keep from killing trees. Or kindred ones."

"I sensed as much," he confides, growing serious as he reaches up to caress the side of my face, the edge of his warm thumb trailing sparks.

"That's our great weakness," I worriedly say as I sheathe my twig through my vine belt, then turn and take in Oaklyyn's wolverines, Yulan's heron, Mavrik's and

Gwynnifer's Agolith Flame Hawks, my Errilor Ravens, and the other kindreds. Along with the beautiful, multihued Forest surrounding us.

"We *care*," I rue to Yvan, "and Vogel will show no such weakness." Unease shivers through me, and I unfurl the fingers of my branch hand, glancing at the image of III imprinted on my palm, a shimmer of the slain Tree's rich energy humming through the mark, the sensation steadily gaining potency as we near peak foliage.

"This III mark," I murmur, closing my fingers around it, before looking to Sylvan and the other Dryads, "there's what feels like growing power in it."

"I'm feeling it too," Yvan affirms, balling his fist around his mark.

"As am I," Gwynnifer concurs, to poignant nods all around.

"Perhaps it's a call III left in the mark," Yulan suggests. "Our call to unite with everyone in the East—the call that you all saw when you were inside the Forest, sent to you in visions of the peoples of every land gathered around III. We must hold on to our hope of this."

A cautionary look enters Sylvan's severe visage as he glances up at our shielding, Iris beside him, the two of them seeming increasingly inseparable. "Our shielding should hold enough power in a matter of days," he notes, "as soon as peak foliage arrives. After which, we'll be able to send it over the entire East. We'll then have, at most, three or four days to travel to the Wyvernguard and bring the entire East to our side so we can all merge power and take down Vogel's Shadow before foliage season recedes. And the Forest goes dormant along with our power."

A weighted gravity descends, the odds so firmly stacked against us.

Against the entire Forest and Natural World.

Defiance fires up inside me, and I look pointedly at Yvan. "If you and I can become Wyvernbonded mates with an *entire world* bent on us hating each other, then there's *got* to be a chance of uniting the East."

My uncle Wrenfir spits out a jaded sound, and I turn, an expression of frustrated derision on his spider-marked face. "I want to believe this, Elloren, truly I do," he says. "But do you honestly think there's a chance in all the hells that the *entire East* will immediately jump into the trees and radically change the way they think about *everything*?" He huffs out a bitter laugh. "We had quite the time of even uniting *ourselves*."

"Wren . . ." Hazel softly interjects.

"No, Hazel, no," Wrenfir snarls, rounding on him, my uncle's invisible fire-and-earth aura encircling Hazel with desperate, crackling intensity. "I'll tell you what's going to happen. The East will fracture, and you'll be pulled into a Reckoning. *All* the Death Fae will. *Everything* lost to us all *forever*. The Eastern Realm will tear itself to *shreds*, the Magedom's Shadow winter will descend, the Natural World will fall and you will be forced to devastate it and then fall with it. And there will be *nothing* left but *Shadow.*"

A fraught silence overtakes us, jagged energy shivering through Wrenfir's power, my uncle trembling now, his body stiff with rage as he stares Hazel down, the whole world briefly pulsing with Hazel's dread-stricken Darkness.

Hazel's Darkness suddenly breaks free of the dread and pulses around Wrenfir in defiant, embracing coils. Wrenfir grimaces and looks away, pain slashing through his magic as a gust of cold blows in from the Shadow net beyond our shield.

Grayed frost shimmers to life along the edges of every prismatic leaf, the temperature dipping.

Alarm flares through the Forest and everyone's power as I shiver, our kindreds growing agitated, my Errilor Ravens letting out loud *CAW*s.

"Holy gods," Mavrik exclaims, his breath puffing fog into the air, "winter's going to come faster than we thought." He turns to Sylvan. "How much foliage time have we lost?"

Sylvan shakes his head, his brow furrowing. He half closes his eyes, and I've a sense of him hooking his empathic senses into the Forest's power. "Perhaps a day?" he gravely states.

"Which now gives us only two or three days to unite the entire East once we expand our shielding over it," Wrenfir seethes, his power cast into a desperate, fitful embrace around Hazel.

I meet Yvan's fiery eyes, alarm crackling more intensely through our bond because my uncle is right—we're running out of time. And it took more time than we have left just to unite the people under this dome.

CHAPTER FIFTEEN

UNBROKEN DRAGON

Elloren Guryev

Northern Dyoi Mountain Range

I climb up to the Dyoi Forest canopy that night and surveil our surroundings with my Errilor Ravens, my flock silently soaring over the Dyoi Forest. The strengthened soles of my bare feet rest on the bumpy surface of the small woven-vine platform I've conjured, two upthrust branches supporting it.

My hand pressed to one branch's bark, I survey the Forest's canopy, my gaze sliding over our dome-shield. A line of my power is feeding directly into it via Oaklyyn's runes, the multihued, brightly charged runes she marked flooding the shield with our collective magic. My gaze narrows past the runes, snagging on the Shadow net encasing our shield. Like a soldier sizing up a disastrously worthy opponent, my gaze traces the imprisoning net's faint gray lines, exhaustion bearing down.

You're lying in wait, aren't you, Vogel? I glower. *Ready to spring on us once our power dips . . .*

The affection of the huge ash tree beneath me swoops around me in a wispy embrace. A loving ache squeezes my heart, my awareness of the Forest's fragility surging. Worry lancing through me, the feel of Yvan's incoming fire suddenly blazes through our bond. He bursts up through the Dyoi Forest canopy, violet eyes aglow, his silhouette night-darkened as he lands on the platform before me, the verdant strength-amplification rune Oaklyyn marked on us all burning bright on his chest.

He gives me a close look and brings his warm palm to my shoulder, his wings arcing around me. "Get some sleep, Elloren," he offers. "I can sense how tired you are. There are more than enough people on watch tonight."

"I'm scared, Yvan," I confide as I gesture toward the leagues upon leagues of

Shadowed land. "Wrenfir's right. Even with *this* staring us in the face, there's a good chance that the East will choose infighting rather than coming together to defeat it." Choking back my sudden rise of emotion, I hold his gaze. "When we blast this shield over the East," I say, "our power will be greatly depleted. Just when we could be faced with a *very hostile* East quickly followed by a *very hostile* Magedom."

He lets out a breath, giving me a grim look. "We're short on options, Elloren. We're just going to have to quickly convince the East to fight with us."

Frustration churns through my fireline as I look over the Shadowed land once more. "Sometimes I think of everything that's happened," I confide, "and wonder how we got here. How did so many people allow things to get so *monstrously* terrible?"

Yvan gives me a weighted look. "Not realizing the stakes," he suggests, a hard look entering eyes. "Letting ourselves be divided by *religion*."

I take in his condemning gaze, his violet eyes simmering with long-burning outrage. I've understood for some time that Yvan hates religion. Holds it squarely responsible for the majority of the world's ills and for the Shadowed wasteland before us. And I agree with some of his conclusions. To a point.

But not past that point.

Because I can't shake the feeling that he's missing something vital, the Watchers coming to mind, along with the Verdyllion Wand and III.

"Religion isn't all bad," I carefully suggest.

He huffs out a refuting breath, his hands coming to his hips. "It's a way to separate and control people."

"It can be," I agree, "but Jules Kristian had me read multiple religious texts at Verpax University and it got me thinking. Perhaps Erthia's faiths hold teachings in their center that can help us in this fight."

He gives me an incredulous look. "Elloren, I'm part of a group reviled by practically every religion in the Western Realm. Almost *every single one*. I've been hated my whole life because of one god or another's 'teachings.' Look what the Alfsigr did to Wynter. What the Gardnerians did to Ariel and Pyrgo. So, forgive me if I have a jaundiced view of religion. It can turn evil in a heartbeat—"

"When people worship their religion's flawed parts instead of the things they all have in common," I insist.

He coughs out a sound of derision. "You mean mindless prejudice and hate?"

"No. The things that lead us into connection with each other that seem to be present in all of Erthia's faiths—the Watchers. The Source Tree. The Verdyllion—"

"Elloren," he says, his fire aura whipping agitatedly around me, "the forces of division and hate are proving to be much stronger than that Wand that abandoned you."

"I've seen the Watchers, Yvan. I've seen them again and again—"

"Oh, I have too," he counters. "On the Mage flag. On their priests' robes and soldiers' uniforms."

"Yes," I concede. "But that's their image, not *them*. Did you see the Watchers when you went into III? I did. And they felt connected to something real and true. Something vital to this fight."

He blows out a harsh breath, his brow knotting as he shakes his head, giving me a conflicted look. "I saw them," he admits. "And I still don't know what to make of it."

We stare at each other for a loaded moment, our magic unsettled as his eyes spark, heat rising on my cheeks as his expression flickers from conflict to desire, our Wyvernbond heating.

Hot flame shuddering through our bond, Yvan looks away, clearly as flustered as I am by this inconvenient flare of attraction in the middle of a religious debate. He glances sidelong at me, then full on, before reaching out to take my hands in his, my pulse quickening as he strokes the sides of my thumbs.

"If anyone can bring me to religion, it's you," he says, giving me a sultry smile as his touch trails sparks.

I swallow, my breathing uneven as want scorches through our bond. "If anyone can make me doubt everything about religion, it's you," I return.

"Maybe those are both good things," he offers as he reaches up to caress my shoulder, the tension shifting as our fire bond flares hotter, an almost pained look overtaking his expression. "Elloren, I have loved you for *so long* . . ."

We draw each other close, his lips finding mine, and I let out an emotional sound as we deepen the kiss almost instantaneously. Heat sears through us both, my body arching against his. Yvan lets out a rough groan, his hold on me firming as his Wyvernfire spirals through me, flickering around every rootline in a sensual caress.

I pull him closer as his tongue twines with mine so enticingly, every troubled thought singes to ash, Yvan's power fixed on me with the directness of a sustained lightning bolt as we careen blazingly fast toward a place of pure, love-fueled *want*, my fingers knotting in his hair, then gripping one of his horns, his hands sliding to my hips, holding me relentlessly close as I luxuriate in his kiss, ready to fuse with both him and his obliterating heat . . .

Hordefire blasts through us both, rattling our magic, the energy of a cataclysmic threat in it.

We break our kiss, startled, alarm surging through our fire.

"Can you sense where that's coming from?" I gasp, the reverberating blast of horde power so potent it seems like it's coming from everywhere at once.

Breathing hard, he tenses his brow, his nostrils flaring. "I can sense its origin point in the Dyoi Forest," he says. His gaze snaps back to mine.

Unspoken agreement flashing through our bond, we grab tight hold of each other, and Yvan thrusts his wings down, soaring us both into the air before he angles us down over the Dyoi Forest canopy. The fiery burn of threat rises, my sense of our full horde's fire growing stronger and stronger as we descend through the canopy and fly into a large clearing.

Our entire horde is there, including Oaklyyn and Raz'zor, all of the Wyverns, save Naga, in dragon form.

In a semicircle around Ariel.

Ariel's wings are held stiffly out, her black-clad body crouched low to the ground. Her form is coiled with tension, a feral look on her face that I haven't seen in a very long time.

We land beside Naga. Her gold-blazing eyes are fixed on Ariel, her wings fanned out to their full breadth, the entire horde's fire simmering, low and careful. Confusion tightens my gut as I take in how Ariel's eyes are spitting fire at their edges. Off-kilter fire. Her teeth are bared in a threatening snarl, her mouth trembling around it.

My chest contracts with alarm as I register the grayed nilantyr plants spread around her, thick with dark berries.

And the multi-eyed raven perched on the branch just above her.

Outrage spasms through me as I realize this is Vogel's doing. He led her to the Shadow-infused berries via this corrupted winged. To destroy her, like he and his forces tried to destroy her with nilantyr in the Valgard prison.

In an attempt to turn her into a Shadow weapon.

I've never felt such fury and terror and desperate all-consuming desire pounding through Ariel's power as intensely as I do right now, her emotions so violent I'm almost blown back from them, the feel of her misery so acute, for a moment I can barely pull in a breath, the dangerously addictive berries the worst possible weapon anyone could deploy against her.

It all comes roaring back—how we almost lost Ariel, more than once, to nilantyr's powerful addiction. How it almost *broke* her . . .

"Ariel, *no* . . ." I rasp as both Yvan and I lurch toward her, ready to force her away from the cruel drug.

"Stay back," Naga hisses, halting our steps. "She needs to stand her ground against it and against *him*." She gestures toward Vogel's multi-eyed raven, and I understand immediately why no one is throwing fire at the raven. If Ariel is spooked, she might eat the berries, and if she eats even one, she's lost to us.

Ariel hisses viciously, a lethal growl erupting from her throat as she springs up and lunges threateningly toward Naga, who immediately shifts to dragon form, not retreating an inch.

And then it starts.

Yvan and Naga send a stream of invisible hordefire into Ariel, its flow powerfully embracing.

Ariel flinches back as if struck and falls into a teeth-snapping crouch.

But she doesn't block their flame.

Opening up a gap in the tortured blaze of her power, Ariel accepts their fire's flow, Naga's and Yvan's gold and violet power blazing around her out-of-control firestorm with encircling support. I join my fireline to theirs, gooseflesh prickling my skin as the heat of our entire horde rises and we send out our fire to her as one.

Ariel cries out, her neck craning back as she falls to her knees. Tears sting my eyes as she scrabbles to take hold of the berries surrounding her, a teeth-gritted sob choked from her throat. The sound guts me. In all the time I've known her, I have never once heard Ariel cry.

We double down, sending a roaring ocean of communal fire to her, Yvan's wings lighting up with threads of violet as they arc toward Ariel and we stream the full force of our Wyvernbonded fire into her.

Yvan tenses, pulling my fire more intensely into his then sending it out to Ariel, a shiver racing through me as our power melds and gives a potent flare, our bond amplifying our fused power as we all send the flaming support to Ariel.

For an excruciating moment, Ariel stills, crouched on the ground, head down, wings out, breathing hard. Nilantyr berries gripped in her fists.

But then, she drops every last shred of resistance and pulls on the horde's full fire.

THE DRYAD STORM

Both Yvan and I draw in shocked breaths as the full strength of our horde's alliance blazes into her. Singes into her. Sends a world-melting level of fire straight into her core.

Ariel's hands heat to gold, the berries clutched in them exploding into flame and falling away. She lets out a roaring scream, thrusts out her hands and blasts fire from both palms, incinerating the nilantyr around her before she whips around to hurl a bolt of fire at the multi-eyed raven, consuming the beast in a bright inferno.

A stifled cry of emotion bursts against my throat as Ariel rises, surrounded by fire. She snaps her wings out, lines of fire flashing to life all over their expanse, horns rising from her scalp, claws forming on her hands.

Claws made of golden fire.

She lifts her eyes and meets the gaze of every member of the horde. Her eyes luminescent. Defiant. As she lets out a sky-ripping growl.

Our entire horde growls back, power rising in the air and prickling my skin. Power coming from both Ariel and our entire horde, our joint fire fusing tighter, my Wyvernbond to Yvan suddenly shot through with so much flame when his hand finds mine, I can barely keep from leaping toward him.

And then Ariel steps forward, away from the burning carpet of berries, flaps her wings powerfully down, and launches herself into the sky.

Joy explodes through the entire horde as Wyverns take to the sky with Ariel, Oaklyyn leaping astride Raz'zor's back.

Leaving only Yvan and me in the clearing.

Tears streak down my face. Tears of pure joy, even in the midst of the Shadow bearing down, as I'm swept up in the certainty that *this* is how Vogel and the Shadow can truly be beaten.

By all of us standing together as one.

I turn to Yvan, his fire whipped up by the same wild, euphoric heat as mine, his eyes to the sky, watching our horde soar through it. My heart clenches as I remember, so many months ago, when Yvan and I left the Amaz lands after rescuing Ariel and Pyrgo, both of us certain Ariel would soon be dead. I remember how Yvan broke down in the Forest, choking out his misery for her, his glamoured wings in hiding, even from me.

To keep me safe from his dangerous destiny.

My aching love for him grips tighter hold—love for his courage and willingness to sacrifice for others, love for his fiery compassion and piercing intellect.

Love for *everything* he is.

Yvan's magic sizzles toward me even as his eyes remain fixed on our horde in the sky, the fire flashing through our bond intensifying. He turns to me, and our gazes don't so much meet as ignite, a sudden, blazing purpose in his flaming eyes, everything surrounding us burning away to a blur, my power zeroed just as completely on him.

All hesitation collapsing, we lay claim to each other, his hot hand taking hold of mine, his jaw set ruthlessly tight as he leads me into the dark of the woods at a fast, purposeful clip, the whole of Nature seeming to thrum inside us with the very fire that fuels the whole of Life.

Yvan embraces me in a blur, his hot mouth coming to mine as I grasp demanding hold of him, my back hitting the tree behind me as my fire lurches toward him in an urgent *yes*.

I open my mouth to his kiss, his tongue wrapping sinuously around mine as I grip hold of one of his horns and pull, forcing his kiss deeper. Yvan lets out a low groan as I throw my leg around him and tug his body hungrily closer, pivoting myself emphatically against his hard desire.

Violet light blasts into being, flashing through my closed lids.

I open my eyes to find fire licking at Yvan's shoulders, a sudden alarm flashing from the surrounding trees.

Yvan draws back a fraction, seeming dazed.

A lust-addled surprise overtakes me as my gaze slides over his flame-coated chest before I meet his gaze once more, finding none of his usual Keltish reticence there, only a burning Lasair-Wyvern love and lust that sends heat flashing through my lines.

As the alarm pouring off the trees intensifies.

Breathing hard, Yvan closes his eyes tight, angles his head down, and manages to pull the fire into himself and away from the Forest, the trees' palpable surge of relief shivering through the air.

Yvan is quiet for a moment, his hands now on either side of me, palms pressed to bark.

"I'm ready to be with you fully," I tell him.

Yvan nods, desire burning in his eyes. "I want you so much, I'm feverish with it. If there was no danger to this Forest . . ."

He grows silent, want burning through his power. And I know, if we could give ourselves to each other without risking harm to the Forest, he'd unleash himself on me right now.

And I'd unleash myself on him.

But this Forest is not the Zhilaan . . . it can't handle our fire.

Yvan and I stare sparks at each other, so much want and love in that stare that I feel as if we'll melt into each other.

There are not enough words. There never have been.

We're two fiery stars on a collision course, and we both know how this will end. Unless the Shadow takes us down first.

I hold back from touching Yvan, and I can sense him holding back from touching me, both of us full of the unspoken understanding that if we touch, we'll take each other fully.

"I know that . . . this has been difficult for you," I falteringly say. "I know that for our Wyvernbond to reach its full strength, we need to have sex."

Yvan exhales, his fire incandescent with longing as he pushes himself back a fraction more and reaches up to rake his fingers frustratedly through his hair. "Elloren, that word is so *wholly* inadequate. It doesn't even *begin* to describe what I want with you." His eyes take on a hotter glow, a frisson of heat coursing through our bond. "The words in the West," he says, then pauses for a moment, his crimson brow furrowing, as if he's casting about for the right explanation. "They feel all *wrong*. There are no words for what I want in the Common Tongue. I *hate* the way Westerners talk about intimacy. I always have. So base and empty."

"What is it you want, then?" I half whisper.

He takes gentle hold of my hand, his thumb caressing the edge of it, tracing heat. "I want . . . *tiev'ssssithra'ohvrasssil.*"

The sibilant Wyvern words send a line of heat through me, our bond newly alight with a palpable level of emotion just from his uttering them, a quaver kicking up along his hand and body.

"You're trembling," I marvel in a whisper. "What does it mean?"

He swallows, attempting to pull in an even breath as he looks to the heavens.

"It's almost impossible to translate. It means too much. Runs too deep."

"Try," I encourage.

He lowers his gaze to mine, the level of emotion in his eyes an unbridled, Erthia-upending thing. "It's the joining of my love for you to desire. The joining of the deepest core of our fire to the joining of our bodies."

His words bolt fire through my heart, as I realize I desperately need a new language too.

"I love you," I say, the words ripped straight from my heart, achingly raw, even as a piece of my heart shreds over the cruel finality of Lukas's death. "I love you so much."

"I know you do," he says, eyeing me meaningfully before reaching up to caress the side of my face.

And then he leads me to a mossy patch of ground, and we lie down next to each other, his arm and wing embracing me, my fire reaching for his with just as much intensity as his is reaching for mine, our eyes locked. And then Yvan raises my hand to his mouth and runs his tongue sinuously along the back of each finger, kissing each one's tip with a spiraling heat that makes my pulse trip over itself.

"I love you, Elloren," he says in Lasair, his flame pulsing hot around me. "You're in the very center of my fire."

"You're in the center of mine, as well," I say, voice hitching, the emotion I'm feeling for him suddenly so hot and tight, it's an ache against my chest.

Yvan's fire gives a harder, passionate flare toward me. "I will love you forever," he tells me in Lasair.

I nod, my fire returning the sentiment, grief and love and lust balling up tight in my chest.

And then we fall asleep, our fire power linked, hearts binding tight.

A few hours later, Yvan and I follow our horde's fire to find both them and our allies gathered around the ledge's runic bonfire, the predawn light just beginning to illuminate the sky to the East, Or'myr's line of purple moons still glowing bright to the West. It's clear that the shifters and even the non-shifters can sense the new turn of Yvan's and my relationship in our close embrace and the steady blaze of our fire around each other and through our Wyvernbond.

In the way it *burns*.

Jarod and Aislinn, Rafe and Diana, Raz'zor and the other shifters, they're all silent as I sit down and Yvan pours me mint tea and hands the stone cup to me, pausing to kiss my hair, tears glassing Soleiya's fiery eyes as she gives me a heartfelt smile that I return.

I glance past the bonfire toward Diana, who, incredibly, is sitting next to the huge Amaz Alcippe, Diana's blond brow arched all the way up as she scents Yvan and me. Jules Kristian sends me a warm smile from where he sits beside Lucretia, his arm wrapped around her, his silver kestrel perched on his shoulder.

Yvan takes a seat next to me, our joint fire aura burning hot around us as Diana's eyes narrow with an all too knowing light. But her expression holds no amusement. It's dead serious as she remains uncharacteristically silent, understanding in her amber stare. I realize that a Lupine, more than almost anyone, would comprehend the solemnity of this. What it is to lose a mate with no time to grieve, and what it feels like to be ready to fully bond to a new one.

Yvan's arm snakes around my waist, our fire power leaping so intensely toward each other that Rafe shoots me a surprised look before averting his gaze.

I'm not embarrassed by Yvan's and my blaring love and desire for each other. This thing between us is too profound. Too deep. We've turned a corner. And I realize later, during a break in battle training when Yvan pulls me aside and draws me into a kiss, keeping his feral, hungry fire firmly in check—barely—that it's only a matter of time until we take each other fully as our own.

Blue increasingly lights the eastern sky as growing numbers of Dryad'khin gather around the ledge's central bonfire for some food and drink, Yvan pausing to converse with his mother.

Spotting Ariel in an isolated corner, I approach her and take a seat beside her, a small, conjured bonfire before her, the remaining stars above our shielding and Vogel's Shadow net rapidly fading, Ariel's raven kindred perched on her shoulder.

Like Yvan and me, Ariel seems to have turned a corner.

I can sense the triumph simmering through her, sense her drawing more strongly on our horde's combined fire.

"What happened when Naga left Amazakaraan with you?" I cautiously ask.

She's quiet for a long moment, a thread of tension simmering to life on the air between us. "Naga found our Wyvern horde in the East," she finally says, succinctly, even as I sense her core of fire churning hotter. "They burned the nilantyr poison out of me." She grows silent for a moment, a lashing edge to her flame. "I fought them at first," she admits, eyes tight on the small bonfire before us. "Bit them. Cursed them up and down. But they stayed with me. And eventually horded to me." She sets her gaze on me. "I want no part of the Mage in me. I'm a dragon now."

I take in her newly slitted pupils and the obsidian horns rising from her head, as well as the dark claws she makes no move to retract.

"You always were," I agree, both respect and apology in my words.

Because, truly, she always was this fierce, beautiful being. We were just too ignorant to see it. *I* was too ignorant to see it.

Ariel smirks, narrowing her fiery eyes at me. "I can scent what you and your dragon-boy want from each other from about ten leagues away."

I flush at this and give her a sheepish look.

Ariel laughs. A full-throated laugh, and it bolsters me, prompting my own irrepressible smile. It's a laugh I would never have imagined hearing from her back in Verpacia. Back in the North Tower.

I peer at her closely, affection for her coursing through my fire and out to her through our horde bond. "Wynter will love seeing you like this," I say, the words catching with emotion. "When Naga took you away, Alder said Wynter cried for days."

Ariel tenses, and chagrin sears through me as I realize I've overstepped. Because Wynter isn't here. Wynter is likely still trapped in the Sublands of the West and in grave danger, along with her brother and Rhys and so many others.

Passion rises in Ariel's fire. "When we all deploy West," she vows in a low growl, "I'm going after her."

"You'll go with the full strength of the horde," I vow in turn.

Ariel glances toward the Forest and winces, growing quiet again for a long moment. "Resisting nilantyr is a daily fight," she murmurs, the flow of her fire strained. "I . . . struggle."

"But not alone," I promise.

I send more fire to her, and Ariel's lips slant up. She catches hold of my power and sends a searing rush of flame into me through it, strong enough to almost shudder me off my seat. But then our flames link and join, our fire power twining tight, and we grin at each other, the two of us joined in powerful Wyvern alliance.

A spark of peace burning in my center, I glance up . . . the spark instantly singed to char, shock igniting, as the Shadow net Vogel cast over our shield explodes in a flash of gray.

CHAPTER SIXTEEN

PEAK FOLIAGE RISING

Elloren Guryev

Northern Dyoi Mountain Range

Alarm blazes through Yvan's and my Wyvernbond, my Errilor Ravens and the raven on Ariel's shoulder letting out distressed *CAW*s as I catch Yvan's violet-fire eyes across the ledge, sounds of shock rising, everyone clearly searching for a reason Vogel would so abruptly free us by withdrawing his Shadow net.

With the brightening blue sky no longer obscured by the net's faint striations of gray, confusion pounds through every thudding beat of my heart. A low growl erupts from Diana's throat, the central bonfire's multihued light illuminating my sister's battle-tensed posture, her claws flicking out with a sharp *snick* just as dawn breaks.

Spectacularly.

Sunlight rays out over our world, every leaf more intensely overtaken by fall's kaleidoscopic riot of color, the Eastern Forest having tipped to near peak foliage overnight.

The Dyoi Forest's amplified light power floods my lines in a euphoric, spangling rush, sparks of color igniting across my vision. All thought momentarily scattered, I glance toward my Dryad'khin—all our eyes lit up with chromatic light. And our dome-shield's runes . . . they've all brightened and are raying out prismatic luminescence.

I look to Rivyr'el as the rainbow Elf touches his silver stylus to the expansion runes marking our shield's base, multihued dragonfly kindreds flitting around his tall frame, the contact of stylus to rune triggering a spray of chromatic sparks.

"Well, my Dryad'khin," Rivyr'el announces, caution flashing through his eyes, "it would seem our shield's expansion runes are fully charged. We're ready to expand this shield over the entire East *right now.*" The tension in the air gains ground as Rivyr'el's stylus tip hovers over the rune. "Just say the word," he states, "and I'll unleash the spells."

"I sense the energy of anticipation in Vogel's Shadow," Hazel notes, ropes of misty Darkness encircling both him and Wrenfir beside him.

"It's a trap," Ariel hisses. "Vogel *wants* us to shield the East."

"But *why?*" Ra'Ven questions as he scans our color-flashing shielding.

"There's unknown danger in this," Vang Troi succinctly levels, her swords unsheathed and flashing Noi-sapphire light.

"That might be true," Sylvan interjects, "but there's an even greater danger in not shielding the surviving Natural Matrix of the East and bringing all the people of Noilaan and Zhilaan into alliance with the Forest."

"There could be some threat from within," Queen Freyja warns, a low growl rumbling through the huge grizzly bear beside her. "Something that Vogel *wants* under an expanded dome with us."

"Whatever it is," Wrenfir bites out, scowling, his bobcat kindred emitting a low snarl, "we're running out of time."

"We have to meet the threat head-on," Soleiya insists.

"I agree," I call out, lit up with warrior determination and foliage power.

"As do I," Yvan states, his wings snapping open, his core fire flashing hot through our bond. "We expand the shield and fight through whatever Vogel throws at us."

Raz'zor's vermillion fire burgeons, scorching through our entire horde's fire, a large portion of it encircling Oaklyyn, who stands next to his human form. *"We will meet the Magelings with fire and claw and ripping teeth,"* he growls.

I sense Oaklyyn's rise of foliage-amplified elemental power, all of it streaming toward Raz'zor, sparks flashing between them.

Silence descends as Sylvan surveys us all, dawn's light gaining ground. "Prepare your weapons and your power, Dryad'khin," he commands as his flinty gaze turns lethal, brighter sparks of color flashing through it. "It's time to go to war for Erthia."

"Ready, Dryad'khin?" Sylvan asks us all from astride one of Alder's giant eagles, Iris behind him, all of us assembled on the great ledge, readying ourselves for rapid flight east.

I'm seated on Errilith, the rest of my flock gathered around me, Soleiya and other allies astride them, a living branch gripped in my hand. My Errilor are still as Death, their Darkness winding around us in misty tendrils. Yvan is poised beside Errilor and me. Rafe, Diana and the other Lupines, and the remainder of allies without flight, are carried by Wyvern-shifters and Alder's eagles.

Yvan exchanges fiery looks with me and his mother as we wait to rise as one.

Bring the war, Raz'zor growls through our horde bond, Oaklyyn astride his huge dragon form, his vermillion fire searing across my vision as he sets his red-fire eyes on Vang Troi.

Vang Troi sits atop Naga, her runic blades unsheathed, her penumbra of sapphire power gathered around her as she meets Raz'zor's vermillion gaze before turning to Rivyr'el, who is poised on giant eagleback near our shield's base, his silver stylus raised.

"Shield the East!" she calls out to him.

His silver aura surging, Rivyr'el touches his stylus to the shield's largest expansion rune and begins murmuring a series of spells.

An audible rumble rises in the air and builds like a storm, sparks of multicolored light crackling along the edges of my vision. A great, Erthia-rending *SNAP* has us all flinching, our rune-linked magic more powerfully siphoned toward our shielding.

We let out a collective gasp as bright streaks of prismatic light ray through the entire dome-shield, the shield's runes flashing every color as the eastern half of its mammoth expanse rises and punches out over the entire Eastern Realm.

A tense silence descends, my heart in my throat as I tighten my hold on my living branch, a firestorm gathering in Yvan's palms as we brace ourselves for Vogel's countermove.

But . . . *nothing.*

Just autumn's spectacular foliage spread out over the East in a carpet of glorious Life and light, the leaves rustling in the cool breeze, the energy of alliance in them.

"We fly southeast to the Wyvernguard!" Vang Troi booms, thrusting her sword up.

We launch into the air, the full power of the autumn Forest rising with us. Yvan's dark wings thrust mightily down from where he soars beside Errilor and me, his fire power and mine twined tight.

We traverse the rocky peaks of the Dyoi Mountain Range, flying from its western side to its eastern expanse. Awe widens my eyes as Trystan and Vothe's long, lightning-flashing dome-shield arcing over the Zonor River's expanse comes into view, the Vo Mountain Range just beyond. The Zonor shielding sits a distance below our mammoth Eastern Realm shielding, the river's protective barrier encasing the entire Zonor and its adjacent Forest from north to south, as far as the eye can see.

I sense an unfamiliar energy and call out to Yvan, "There's more than just Trystan and Vothe's power in this shield." My power empathy activates more fully, reading golden lightning intermingled with Trystan and Vothe's blue and white magic.

We soar down toward the Zonor River, and a bolt of my brother's power spears toward their shield from below. A broad oval opening forms, and we all fly through it, the gap crackling closed behind us, three figures coming into sharper view on the riverbank below—Trystan, Vothe, and a winged and horned white-haired female Wyvern with Vothe's same onyx hue. Golden lightning flashes through her eyes and my power empathy immediately traces the shield's gilded lightning energy to her.

"Reshield the Dyoi wilds *right now!*" Trystan bellows as we descend, and I register in a split second my brother's newly Vo-blue hair, his ears now slightly pointed like mine, and his skin's hue morphed to the same shimmering deep green. An incandescent silver half-moon mark newly blazing from the inner edge of his shoulder.

A jagged alarm strikes through me as I take in Trystan's expression, my younger brother's eyes full of urgency. Trystan is never this rattled, even in a crisis, and Vothe's and the elderly Wyvern woman's expressions are just as dire.

"We've shielded the entire East," Ra'Ven calls out to them as we land, a chorus of *thumps* sounding. "The Dyoi Forest is safe—"

"No it's *not!*" Vothe growls, blue-and-white lightning spitting through his gaze. "Throw a shield around the Dyoi wilds *immediately!*"

"We can't," Oaklyyn vehemently counters. "We linked the bulk of our power to the East's shielding. We don't hold enough additional power to fabricate another shield at the moment."

"Then contract your shielding back in around the Dyoi wilds!" Trystan insists.

"There's no contracting our shielding," Mavrik says. "It took days just to charge it with enough power to expand it!"

Vothe rounds on him. "They're going to siphon all the Dyoi Forest's power and use a portion of it to strike down our Zonor shielding and consume this River's power, as well! Then they're going to use that siphoned power to form the most powerful storm band Erthia has *ever seen!*"

Confusion ripples through my Dryad'khin allies' linked power.

"The Dyoi Forest is *safe*," Sylvan insists. "The entire East is now *shielded*."

"Have Vogel's forces gotten into the East somehow?" Yvan demands of Vothe, the fire in our bond whipped into high alert.

"It's not the Magedom that's the immediate threat to our wilds," the elderly Wyvern woman cuts in. "The threat comes from *our side!*"

I'm hit with an invisible wave of power, its electric energy raising the hairs on my skin. I glance up, my pulse leaping as a line of sapphire runes blast into being along the half-destroyed Vo Mountain Range's apex, our shield's ceiling far above it. A dark mass of storm power explodes from the runes, and we all flinch. A storm band forms and then rises along the range's apex, potent energy spitting and flashing through it.

"That's Zhilaan Wyvern power," Vang Troi murmurs as she narrows her eyes at the consolidating storm band, "shot through with Noi siphoning runes."

Vu Trin soldiers soar out of a small gap in the storm band's base to fly toward us, the Zhilaan Vu Trin Wyverns in dragon form, Noi Vu Trin soldiers astride them.

The magic of Noilaan and Zhilaan united.

Against us.

✴

PART THREE

✴

The Great Unraveling

CHAPTER ONE

FRACTURE

Olilly Emmylian

Olilly jolts to attention as a regiment of dour-looking Vu Trin soldiers march into the city-size Eastern Subland cavern. Their boots thud martially against the stone of the broad, elevated ledge before her. Wide-eyed, she looks on, along with thousands of other Western Realm refugees and Smaragdalfar as well as smatterings of Noi citizens who have taken shelter here since the Magedom's attack on Voloi.

Their surrounding tents and rough-hewn dwellings form a threadbare underground metropolis, everything lit by the green glow of countless Varg runes marked on the cavern's stone. Large roots wind around huge, black-opal stalactites hanging from high above like a sea of spears. Olilly's boyfriend, Kirin, and her friends Nym'ellia and Effrey stand beside her, along with Sagellyn Za'Nor's teenage sisters, Clover and Retta, and Nym'ellia's little sister, Tibryl.

Olilly reaches for Kirin's hand at the same moment he reaches for hers, the young teens' fingers protectively interlacing as Olilly's heart patters, hummingbird fast. She meets Kirin's dark gaze in a shared look of unspoken alarm, the sharp planes of his face illuminated by their underground world's emerald light.

The Vu Trin halt in neat rows on the huge ledge, the only sound the constant chorus of coughing from those with the Red Grippe, scattered all around. A commanding soldier strides forward, the woman's dark hair bound in ropy coils, two curved runic swords sheathed at her sides, a row of silver runic battle stars strapped across her chest. She lifts a rune-marked palm, and a sapphire voice-amplification rune blinks to life before her, suspended just beneath her chin.

"We are here to facilitate the immediate evacuation of all Noi citizens to the Noi

Sunlands," she booms, her military-stern voice echoing off the purple-veined black opal stone. "By order of the Noilaan's newly re-formed and named Vo Conclave," she continues, "we extend an offer of Noi citizenship to all Smaragdalfar Elves who pledge fealty to the Vo Conclave and the Goddess Vo on High." She scans the sea of people, her expression unforgiving. "All others who immigrated here from the West are ordered to *immediately* return to your Western Realm countries."

Distressed murmuring breaks out, then angered shouting as Olilly's stomach drops through the floor. Kirin's grip firms around hers as the hostile tension gains steam.

The newly appointed leader of the Smaragdalfar, Fyon Hawkkyn, strides past Olilly, Kirin, Nym'ellia, and Effrey, making his way toward the Vu Trin soldiers at a fast clip, anger radiating off of him in palpable waves. He halts just before the ledge, draws his emerald-glowing stylus, and swiftly conjures an amplification rune of his own.

"What is the meaning of this?" Fyon challenges, tone incensed. He jabs his emerald-patterned finger at the ground beneath his feet. "This is sovereign *Smaragdalfar* territory. And our monarch, Ra'Ven Za'Nor, has opened the Sublands to those fleeing the Western Realm's atrocities."

"Your 'monarch,'" the soldier bites back, "has proved to be a traitor to this Realm."

A sea of shocked murmuring goes up as Fyon's stance tenses, and dread ripples through Olilly's core.

"Ra'Ven Za'Nor and his Crow consort, Sagellyn Gaffney," the Vu Trin soldier continues, "have allied with the Magedom's Black Witch, Elloren Gardner Grey."

Another wave of audible shock flashes through the entire cavern.

"Your people," the Vu Trin soldier levels at Fyon, "were most graciously granted *temporary* jurisdiction over Noilaan's Sublands. Our Vo Conclave has deemed Noilaan is for the *Noi*, both the Sunlands above and the Sublands below. Which means you are standing on *sovereign Noi territory*. As Noilaan's ruling force, we *insist* on the immediate expulsion of Western Realm refugees, the creation of a Subland runic barrier to wall off the ongoing invasion of Westerners, and a pledge of fealty to Vo's Blessed Vo Conclave and the Goddess Vo on High. Or the Smaragdalfar, too, will be expelled from Noilaan."

"This is the Goddess Oo'na's sacred ground!" an enraged-looking Smaragdalfar woman near Olilly snarls. The woman levels a finger up at the thick masses of roots winding around the sea of gleaming black-opal stalactites. "These are Oo'na's roots! *Not* your dragon goddess's!"

Shouts of agreement boom out.

"The Smaragdalfar have one day to comply if they wish to be granted Noilaan's most generous offer of citizenship," the soldier stresses to Fyon, ignoring the woman's outburst and the rise of livid voices. "Defy us, and we will take military action to reclaim our sovereign land."

Fyon and the Smaragdalfar soldiers draw Varg swords as one, and the Vu Trin respond in kind, a screech rending the air as they unsheathe countless curved swords in a flash of sapphire. Olilly's alarm threatens to tilt into panic as sounds of anger surge, and she and Effrey exchange a dire glance.

Mora'lee unexpectedly leaps forward toward the Vu Trin, Ra'Ven and Sagellyn's purple-hued Icaral toddler, Fyn'ir, hugged close to her chest. She swiftly raises a stylus and conjures an amplification rune before her.

"We can't go to war with each other!" Mora'lee cries out.

Two of the Urisk children she's caring for—Sage and Ra'Ven's adopted daughter, pink-hued Fern, and Mora's recently adopted daughter, little blue-hued Ghor'li—rush forward to clutch hold of Mora's tunic's edge, stark fear on the young children's faces. "We need to stand *together*," Mora'lee insists, looking pointedly at the toddler in her arms and the two children at her sides, "and with all those fleeing the Magedom's madness!" Mora gestures all around. "Many here have fallen ill with the Grippe. They need *medicine*, not expulsion from the Realm!"

"All Noi citizens who wish to *remain* citizens," the Vu Trin Commander booms out, paying no heed to Mora'lee, "are hereby ordered to come with us. *Now.*"

Olilly watches, stunned, as most of the Noi citizens who were sheltering in the Sublands after Vogel's siege on Voloi surge forward, many dragging their fearful, crying children. Olilly is overcome by a sense of the whole world coming undone, everything spinning into dangerous chaos.

"Kirin . . ." Olilly stammers, her hand trembling in his.

Kirin pivots to face her, electrifying energy in his eyes that Olilly feels jolting straight down her spine, the spark of rebellion there stronger than anything she's yet seen in him. "I *won't leave you*," he states. "And I *won't* let them drive you back West."

"Kirin, get over here. *Now!*" Kirin's belligerent father growls.

Olilly's and Kirin's attention snaps to Kirin's father, Zosh Lyyo, the Noi man's eyes set on Olilly with an eviscerating level of hate.

Kirin makes no move to let go of Olilly's hand, his face a mask of fury. *"No,"* he growls back at his father. "This is *wrong*. They have *nowhere else to go*. Wasn't it *you* who taught me about Vo's compassion for those without shelter?"

"Vo's compassion is for Her Vo'lon followers!" his father snarls. "Not for *Western filth!*"

"Vo's compassion is for *everyone*," Kirin counters before turning to Olilly once more. "I will *not* leave you," he vows, his voice shaking with passion as boots sound and Vu Trin soldiers begin to stream down from the ledge, surrounding the cavern on all sides, other Vu Trin ushering the Noi citizens toward a tunnel leading to the Sunlands. Kirin is undaunted. "I will stay and fight with you against the Magedom's Shadow forces *and* the Vu Trin if I have to!"

"Take hold of my son," Zosh Lyyo spits out to the nearest Vu Trin, gesturing sharply toward Kirin. "He's too young to know what's at stake here."

One of the soldiers angles her sword at Kirin, and sapphire ropes fly from its runes, instantly binding him, his hand wrested from Olilly's as he's reeled in.

"*Kirin!*" Olilly cries as she lunges for him only to be held back by both Nym'ellia and Effrey as Kirin kicks and wrestles against his bindings.

"*Olilly!*" Kirin frantically yells.

"Silence yourself!" Kirin's father slashes back at him. "Noilaan is for the *Noi!*"

"Noilaan is for *all!*" Kirin defiantly levels back at him, eyes wild. He wrenches his gaze to Olilly's. "I will find you!" he vehemently promises. "And I *will* fight with you! *NOILAAN FOR ALL!*"

A sob shudders through Olilly's throat as soldiers close in around Kirin and he continues to cry out, "*Noilaan for all!*" His screams are soon muffled as he's dragged onto the ledge, then through a stony corridor, his voice becoming barely audible, then gone, along with most of the soldiers and almost all the Noi citizens.

Devastation clenching her heart, Olilly is barely aware of Effrey's and Nym'ellia's grips growing gentler around her arms as they try to convey the danger here.

Fern erupts into hysterical sobbing, the child's pain like a blade, twisting in Olilly's chest.

"I want Mamma Sage!" Fern chokes out to Mora'lee as the child grips her threadbare cloth doll, which has Fern's same pink braids and hue. "And Papa Ra'Ven! Where *are they?*"

"We'll do everything we can to get you back to them," Mora'lee croons, a forced calmness to her features as she comes down to one knee and embraces Fern while both Fyn'ir and Ghor'li break into terrified wails, as well.

Feeling like she's coming apart at the seams, Olilly shrugs off Nym'ellia and Effrey and stumbles away from her friends toward a small outcropping of onyx stalagmites rising from the floor, her gaze hooking on an outgrowth of purple crystal affixed to one of the conical formations, something deep inside her straining toward it. She shambles over and breaks it off from the stalagmite.

A tingle kicks up over Olilly's skin as she runs her thumb over it, something trapped inside her sparking to life, as it always does when she handles purple stones.

Her friends close in beside her, and Olilly catches the looks of concern in Effrey's and Nym'ellia's purple and green gazes, as well as in the eyes of gentle Retta and ferocious Clover. A trembling Tibryl hugs Nym'ellia's side, and the child's vulnerability sparks the rise of courage inside Olilly.

"I'm done crying," Olilly tells them all, her gaze fixed on the crystalline rock. "Powerless or not, they won't send me or anyone we care about back to the West without a fight. Are you with me?" She glances pointedly at Tibryl, then looks at Nym'ellia, Effrey, Clover, and Retta full on, noticing the amethyst already gripped in Effrey's hand.

"We're with you," Effrey vows, a subtle aura of violet crackling to life around the young Strafeling geomancer, Effrey's resolve mirrored in Nym'ellia's, Clover's, and even timid Retta's expressions.

Hundreds of huge Varg runes suddenly blast to life, suspended just below the huge cavern's ceiling, yanking Olilly and her friends' attention upward as shocked gasps resound. Ropes of glowing emerald blink into existence to connect the suspended runes, forming a huge net above them, the smaller Varg runes marked all over the cavern's expanse and on every Varg weapon blinking out of existence.

"What is this?" Mora calls out to Fyon as she hugs the crying children close. "And why have our weapons lost their charge?"

Fyon curses as he scans the netted ceiling. "It would appear Noilaan has taken hold of the Varg power-siphoning runes we fabricated for their defense," he grits out. He lowers his gaze, giving Mora a grim look. "They're using our own power to trap us here. To turn the entire Sublands into a prison."

CHAPTER TWO

THE EAST

Elloren Guryev

Eastern Realm

I watch with mounting horror as the Vu Trin storm band rises from the Vo Mountain Range's apex. A contingent of close to twenty Vu Trin soldiers are flying toward us, the line of blue-glowing Noi runes inside the storm band increasingly obscured as its winds gain strength.

"The Noi runes embedded in that storm band," Sylvan spits out, eyes crackling with outrage as he watches it like a mortal enemy, "they hold enough Nature-siphoning power to consume the elemental magic in our shielding *as well as* the Zonor River and Dyoi Forest, which will unshield the East and trigger a *complete Unbalancing*."

"And a full Death Reckoning," Hazel hisses, the look of alarm in his abyssal eyes terrifying to behold, my uncle Wrenfir's fiery aura whipping into a desperate embrace around the Death Fae Dryad.

My power empathy can sense, beyond a shadow of doubt, that they're right. For a moment, fear tears at me so intensely, I feel as if my heart will rip from my chest and fly into the threatened Dyoi Forest and Zonor River, sheer desperation overtaking me as I dismount from Errilith.

Yvan's hand closes protectively around my arm, his fire shuddering through the spitfire chaos of my power as I reach for the branch sheathed at my waist.

"Careful, Elloren," he warns.

Raz'zor's seething voice simmers through me, red-hot battle-fire running steadily through it. *Conserve your magic, Dryad Witch.*

"We need to strike that damned storm band from the skies," Vothe seethes, both his eyes and those of the elderly Wyvern woman beside him incandescent with lightning.

"We will not let them take *our river!*" Trystan snarls.

I'm instantly snapped into a shocked calm by my younger brother's loss of composure, a maelstrom of rebellious energy crackling through his magic. The irony hits me—Trystan has always been the cool and collected one. The last time I had to calm him down was when he was a small child, afraid of thunder, and now my brother is mated to a storm Wyvern, the two of them able to conjure their own formidable lightning and cloud-ripping tempests.

"We can't war with them," I caution Trystan, regaining my senses as peals of thunder roll through the gathering tempest. "We'll deplete our power even further. We're good as dead if we do that, with Fallon's Shadow winter looming."

"Elloren's right," Yvan grimly agrees, meeting Vothe's and Trystan's martial stares with one of his own. "We have to *align with them.*"

My gaze slides back to the incoming Vu Trin as Yvan takes my hand. His Wyvern-warm grip closing around mine fires up our bond. Our eyes meet in a flash of heat, the surge of warmth enabling me to draw in a stream of his steadying power as the incoming Vu Trin soldiers slow to a hover above the Zonor's lightning-coated shielding. Two of them, in full dragon form, break away from the rest to soar in closer. White lightning forks over the Wyverns' onyx scales, one of them carrying a spike-haired Vu Trin soldier with a sturdy build, the woman wearing the same silver dragon-horn headpiece that adorns Vang Troi's head.

Recognition hits, and I blanche.

The full attention of Yvan's fire snaps through my fire. "What's the matter, Elloren?" he presses, his violet eyes burning into mine.

"I know that sorceress," I answer. "She's the one who tried to kill me months ago in the Agolith Desert. Then again in Voloi."

"Her name is Quoi Zhon," Vang Troi states, her sapphire aura of power intensifying.

Rivyr'el spits out a bitter laugh as he shoots Vang Troi a jaded look. "Well, it seems *you've* been replaced as high commander of the Vu Trin." His prism eyes flash toward me. "And *you've* picked a rather inconvenient choice of enemy."

"That's my father, Hizar'drile, and brother, Gethindrile, with her," Vothe growls, the angst shooting through his power only increasing my concern.

"We seek an alliance with you!" Vang Troi booms out to Quoi Zhon and Vothe's father and brother before cutting a severe glare toward Trystan. "Let them in."

Trystan shoots Vang Troi a belligerent look but complies with her order. He raises his branch toward the shielding and grits out a spell, and a small hole opens.

The two Wyverns and Quoi Zhon fly in and they land before us. Quoi Zhon's compact form deftly slides off the larger Wyvern's back, her dark eyes meeting mine with a formidable flash of loathing. Vothe's father and brother swiftly morph to their human winged forms, a straight-backed older male and a younger male who looks to be close to Vothe's age. Quoi Zhon and the Wyverns all wear the same Vo'lon faith necklace that graces Trystan's neck, an image of the dragon goddess, Vo, carved into each necklace's central ivory bead. Both Wyverns' eyes pulse with furious white lightning as they take me in, and I note how strongly Vothe resembles not just them but the elderly Wyvern woman with the gold lightning-spitting eyes allied with him and Trystan, all four Wyverns possessing the same elegant features and tall, muscular builds.

"Father." Vothe greets the older male warily. His gaze swings to his brother. "Geth," he says, his tone clipped and cautious as his invisible power whorls around Trystan.

Visible threads of lightning fork from the two Wyverns' forms as Hizar'drile and Gethindrile shoot glares at Trystan, then at the elderly Wyvern woman, who bares her teeth in response.

A mist of sapphire power springs to life around Quoi Zhon, strong enough to rival the strength of Vang Troi's. "Vang Troi," Quoi Zhon snarls, pointedly omitting "Nor," the Noi title of respect, her hands gripping the hilts of the runic swords sheathed at her sides. "Why are you here with the Crow Witch? The witch you set out to *slay*."

Anger at the slur flashes through Yvan's fire, but he keeps it in check as a harder tang of sapphire power shivers into being around Vang Troi, bright as suspended flame, her expression taking a turn for the lethal. "I am here because our Dryad'khin force brings *vital news* to the East. This fight is not what we thought it was. And remaining ignorant of its true nature will ensure the downfall of the *entire Eastern Realm* along with the entirety of Erthia!"

"Wait," Quoi Zhon sharply bites out. "Your 'Dryad'khin force'? Who exactly are you aligned with?"

"With the Natural Matrix of Erthia," Vang Troi answers.

Naga morphs to human, her dark, powerful wings snapping emphatically out. "That *must* be the center of our new alliance, Unbroken Ones," she hisses, her golden wildfire eyes burning into Quoi Zhon and the Wyverns bracketing her. "Above every country and Realm."

"If you release that storm band," Sylvan adds as he levels his deep-green finger toward it, "you will bring the Natural World to the precipice of *complete annihilation*."

"What is this Fae nonsense?" Quoi Zhon demands of Vang Troi.

"You cannot send out this storm band," Vang Troi commands in turn. "It will play *right* into Vogel's hands."

"Words do not suffice to describe the danger," Queen Freyja Zyrr chimes in. "We implore you, Nor Quoi Zhon, to connect with the Forest and hear the trees out."

Quoi Zhon shoots Freyja an incredulous glare. "The *trees*? Have you all gone *mad*?" She levels a condemning finger at me. "Has the Crow Witch ensorcelled you and the Icaral both?"

Yvan's anger flashes bright through our bond. "No one has ensorcelled me," he bites out, as my own protest rises, hot and harsh.

"I'm not a Crow Witch," I emphatically level at Quoi Zhon. "I'm a *Dryad* Witch. And I fight for Erthia and everyone here, *not* the cursed Magedom."

Hate flashes in Quoi Zhon's eyes as the auras of both Vothe's father and brother crackle invisible lightning daggers at me.

Hizar'drile's gaze swings to Vothe. "You stand by and let this witch *live*?" he hisses. "Have you forgotten she nearly destroyed all of Voloi a little over a month ago?" He thrusts a damning, black-clawed finger toward Trystan. "And then, you take this Crow filth, the brother of this *witch*, as your *mate*?"

Hurt crackles through Trystan's power—hurt that I know Vothe can sense. Vothe lets out a low growl, his power flashing embracingly around Trystan.

Rivyr'el lets out an incredulous huff from beside me, then reaches up to massage his porcelain-pale temple as he shoots me a tight look. "You Gardners certainly have a penchant for Realm-upending romance."

I glance toward Rafe and Diana, then toward Wrenfir and Hazel, who are eyeing Vothe's father and brother and Quoi Zhon with deathlike calm, their arms slung defiantly over each other's shoulders along with Hazel's misty, looping Darkness, a sharp headache starting to pound against my temples.

Vothe is unmoved, threads of his power now visibly crackling around Trystan as he stares his father down. "Elloren was ensorcelled by Marcus Vogel when she attacked Voloi. *Read her*, Father. Do you sense a threat?"

Vothe's father and brother glare at me, nostrils flaring. The energy of confusion forks through their power as they struggle to unearth some shred of treachery.

And find none.

Yulan steps forward with her heron, heartbreaking concern in the graceful Tree Fae's eyes. "We Dryad'khin stand ready to fight for both the Forests and the people of the Eastern Realm."

Quoi Zhon looks Yulan disdainfully up and down. "We don't need you in our fight, Dryad. Noilaan is for the *Noi*. We're reclaiming the East and walling off what the West has wrought with our own storm power!"

Shock blasts through my bond to Yvan, as well as through my entire horde's fire and my allies' magic, in response to Quoi Zhon's xenophobic line in the sand, the ramifications dire.

"You can't wall off what's coming by yourselves!" Vang Troi insists.

Quoi Zhon shoots her a look of blistering disgust. "Don't tell us what we can and can't do, *vill'duur*."

The koi'lon rune Valasca marked behind my ear translates the Noi word—*traitor*.

The whole world briefly pulses Dark.

"Nature doesn't acknowledge your boundaries," Hazel seethes, his subterranean voice shot through with a terrifying aura of warning, a hissing viper appearing around his shoulders. "Nature *mocks* them. Death *mocks* them. You think your walls can keep me and my Deathkin out if you force a *Reckoning*? You think you can wall out the Shadow Void when it comes for you? The only way to avoid a Reckoning and defeat the Shadow is by standing together. *Right now*. Aligned with the *Forest*."

Quoi Zhon flashes Hazel a rattled look before she turns to Yvan, her expression tilting toward hesitant. "Nor Yvan Guryev," she says, "*break* with this witch and this madness. The Prophecy still speaks of your rise."

Yvan's invisible fire simply roars more passionately around me. "Elloren and I reject your Prophecy readings. We are united and bound by Wyvernfire as mates."

Shocked sounds burst from Quoi Zhon, Hizar'drile, and Gethindrile.

"She is *not* your full mate," Hizar'drile spears out. "I scent only a partial bond, not a consummated mating. Cast this witch aside! You are fated to *war* with her!"

"Fallon Bane is the Black Witch poised at the East's doorstep," Yvan hisses. "She's the witch we need to align against."

THE DRYAD STORM

"Nor Quoi Zhon," Mavrik petitions from where he stands beside Gwynn, their golden-fastmarked hands joined in a tight clasp, "you know of my work for the Vu Trin. Our stated aim to forge a unified force with the East is a *true one.*"

"*Enough,*" Quoi Zhon snaps with a venomous glare. "I suspected you were a traitor all along, Glass. A Crow never changes its feathers."

"Well, *I* am not a Crow." Yvan's mother's voice rings out.

We all turn as Soleiya makes her way forward, eyes afire. Quoi Zhon, Vothe's father and brother—their eyes all widen at the sight of her, their powerful auras rearing with shocked energy.

"Nor Soleiya Guryev," Quoi Zhon murmurs, dipping her head in a reverential greeting.

Soleiya regally lifts her chin, her invisible fire whipping around Yvan and me with a passionate, embracing force. "Nor Quoi Zhon. Nors Hizar'drile and Gethindrile Xanthile," she formally greets them. "You all know of my sacrifice at the end of the First Realm War." Her face tenses with a look of grief, a slight tremor to her words when they come. "You know how my husband, Valentin Guryev, sacrificed his life to save the East from the Black Witch's reign of fire. And how I have labored and fought with the Western Realm Resistance for *years.*"

Both Yvan's invisible fire and mine blaze around her, and Soleiya gives us both a poignant glance before turning back to Quoi Zhon, Hizar'drile, and Gethindrile. "At first," she says, "I, too, wanted nothing more than to strike Elloren down. But then I listened to my son, and I listened to the trees. And finally, I listened to Elloren. She is truly not the Black Witch we need to fight. She is now Elloren Guryev. My ally and kin. As are *all* of these Dryad'khin." She sweeps her hand toward both me and all our allies.

Quoi Zhon's and the Wyverns' reverential looks career into sheer outrage, but Soleiya remains undaunted. "If you siphon up the elemental power of the Dyoi Forest and Zonor River with your storm band," she warns, "you will bring such damage to Erthia's Natural Matrix you will not only destroy our Dryad'khin power but bring about the destruction of your own, as well. I *beg* of you, in the name of my husband, Valentin Guryev, the Great Icaral who died for the East—let us speak to the leaders of the East before you do this thing and tip Nature's Balance toward the Shadow's triumph."

I hold my breath, my pulse tripping over itself as Quoi Zhon and the Wyverns exchange conflicted glances.

Quoi Zhon straightens, her gaze shifting to Gethindrile. "Send word to our aligned forces to hold back our storm band," she orders. "We will escort Soleiya Guryev, the Great Icaral, and their allies to Noilaan's Vo Conclave. *All* of you will come, including the witch, who will travel there, unarmed, with *me*. Or we will release our storm band as planned."

Yvan's invisible flame turns incandescent as a protest rises in my throat over the thought of being brought to a hostile Wyvernguard, unarmed, but I squelch it. Given what transpired the last time I was in Voloi, this is my only way back. I sense the same line of thought warring through Yvan before settling into a low seethe.

"I'll be on Elloren's heels all the way to Voloi," Yvan states, warning in his tone. My surrounding Errilor Ravens step toward Quoi Zhon in a warning of their own.

Quoi Zhon eyes Yvan and my ravens before nodding, her gaze then swinging to Soleiya. "When we get to Voloi, you can tell the Conclave what you know of Vogel and his Shadow and the Black Witch." Her eyes briefly cut toward mine, a hard glint in them that raises my every hackle, before she turns back to Soleiya. "Make your petition, Soleiya Guryev. And see for yourself if you can get the East to align with the Crow Witch, these Westerners, and the trees."

VO CONCLAVE

Elloren Guryev

Voloi

I know something is wrong the moment we reach Voloi. As we soar over the grayed Vo Forest, a disconcertingly large number of Eastern Realm soldiers close in around us. Quoi Zhon is pressed to my back, the new Vu Trin high commander and I astride Hizar'drile's broad, scaled dragonback, my branch weapon confiscated, leaving me disturbingly unarmed.

Yvan and I exchange a wary lash of fire through our bond as he soars close to my side, every spark of his fire poised to attack if the Vu Trin make even one violent twitch against me.

Our grouping swerves toward the Vo River. The translucent shielding that Tierney, my cousin Or'myr, and their allies cast over both the river and a wide swath along its banks remains fixedly in place, their shield's long, domed surface dotted with Deathkin runes limned with what I sense to be my cousin's purple energy, the rune-work designs built to repel not only Shadow but any attempt to siphon the river's elemental power. Soaring down over the Vo Forest, we pass through the Vo shield's cloud-high eastern wall, and I'm filled with a sense of the energy of the dome-shield's two runic origin points to the far north and south of us, as well as a tidal wave of Asrai water magic.

Finding the Vo so protected floods me with profound relief, but my solace makes a rapid turn toward unease as I view the restored runic border wall lining the Vo River's western bank. It's made up of sapphire Noi runes, with emerald Varg runes interspersed throughout. Rising twice as high as it did previously, the wall is now emblazoned with a giant depiction of Noilaan's dragon goddess, Vo, in her bright white manifestation, Vo's starlight bird messengers emblazoned around her.

The religious image sends an ominous shiver through me, Gardneria's aggressive use of the Ancient One's white messenger bird leaping to mind. My disquiet intensifies as I scan the refugee camp on the border's western side, which has more than quadrupled in size. Yvan's fire shudders against mine, his equally surging concern palpable as he flies in beside me.

The Vu Trin forces usher us over the runic wall's towering pinnacle, and we soar out over the Vo River, a chilly breeze whipping at my hair as we speed toward the Wyvernguard.

It's a jarring sight, the military academy made up of just one upthrust island now, the other a charred heap poking up from the Vo's dark blue waters.

My gut clenches as I'm hit with a memory of the last time I flew over this river. Pain knifes through my heart as it all comes roaring back—being taken over by Vogel and forced to conjure a great Shadow tree to attack Voloi. Then being freed from Vogel's control by Yvan's fiery kiss, and moments later, witnessing Lukas's death, then believing Yvan to be dead as well, as I plummeted toward the river's surface only to be rescued by Ariel.

Devastation slashes through me and tears sting my eyes as my final vision of Lukas sears into my mind, my fastmate defiantly holding his wand aloft, Yvan's and my combined fire burning hot in his eyes, *I love you* on his lips.

Lukas . . .

Clearly sensing the rise of my lacerating grief, Yvan pulses a consoling rush of fire through me, the depth of feeling in both his power and his eyes burning so blazingly strong that I'm able to force back an edge of the grief, knowing Lukas would want me to move past it and persevere despite the impossible odds.

I'll fight to the end, Lukas, I vow as we all soar toward the stone terrace encircling the Wyvernguard island's base and land on its polished, obsidian stone.

Quoi Zhon and I dismount from Hizar'drile, and Vothe's father morphs into his human form. Yvan closes in beside me, his hand pressed to the small of my back and one of his wings arcing around me as we survey our surroundings.

A huge bas relief sculpture of the Dragon Goddess Vo is marked on the stone wall before us, and Vo necklaces adorn the necks of every surrounding Vu Trin soldier, white dragon goddess and starlight-bird-messenger pendants in the center of each. An uncomfortable tension grips hold, the religious jewelry and omnipresent Vo images triggering a resurgent remembrance of the Gardnerians' silver Erthia orb necklaces and the Watcher bird images emblazoned on every Mage flag and uniform.

Several Vu Trin soldiers appear inside an arching doorway, the uniform of the tall, spiky-haired Noi soldier in the lead bearing the silver-dragon insignia of the Wyvernguard commander on her shoulder, the woman's expression stern.

"Nor Ung Li," Trystan calls to her, my brother's rush of relief over finding this sorceress here palpable in both his tone and in the flow of his power.

Commander Ung Li gives Trystan a conflicted look as both she and the soldiers behind her halt before us. Her dark gaze slides over me with such probing force that my firelines kick up into a more fitful heat before she rigidly salutes High Commander Quoi Zhon. Quoi Zhon orders Ung Li to be at ease, and Vothe's father and brother step forward to greet her.

Beside me, I catch Diana tossing her hair over her shoulder, one hand on her hip, my Lupine sister's intimidating amber eyes staring Ung Li down as Ung Li scans our varied yet unified force. Her expression takes on a questioning air, perhaps over how altered so many of us are by our linkage to the Forest, our winged kindreds massed around us.

"I am Wyvernguard Commander Ung Li," she announces, calmly meeting Diana's intimidating stare. "Noilaan's Vo Conclave will hear your petition for alliance in the Wyvernguard's Conclave Hall."

My concern resurfaces as my mind lights on the Conclave's new religious name.

Ung Li sets her gaze on me with probing force. "Before we allow you to enter, you must be marked with a Noi tracking rune."

Yvan and I exchange a grave look, both of us aware of why she's demanding this. And aware that we *have* to forge an alliance with these people fast, despite the risks.

Ung Li draws a dark rune stone glowing with a single sapphire Noi rune from her tunic's pocket and holds out her hand for mine.

Reluctance sizzling through me, I extend my hand.

She grips my wrist and turns my hand palm up, then presses the rune stone to my forearm. A sting ignites that has me wincing before she draws it away, a small sapphire rune identical to the stone's now glowing on my skin.

Ung Li releases my arm and scans my Dryad'khin. "We will need to confiscate your weapons." She waves a hand toward a weapons rack beside the doorway. "You may reclaim them after your meeting. And your ravens and eagles must remain *here*."

Unease ripples through my allies' magic. We exchange wary looks as my ravens let out low, protesting *caws*, an angry light in the fiery eyes of Alder's giant eagles. Our gazes flit pointedly toward the Wyverns and Lupines amongst us, who have no need of weapons, as well as to Mavrik and Gwynn, who can summon runes to their hands using only their twinned magic. Unspoken agreement simmering between us, those with runic blades and wands and styluses release their weapons to the Vu Trin.

High Commander Quoi Zhon thrusts her hand toward Trystan. "We'll need to confiscate your Vo'lon necklace before you enter," she snaps, scowling.

Both Trystan's and Vothe's invisible lightning bursts into crackling disarray, blue and white forks of it flashing through my brother's eyes.

"I'm a citizen of Noilaan and a convert to the Vo'lon faith," Trystan calmly outlines, his tone belying none of the fitful rise of his power.

Quoi Zhon's face twists with offense. "Your citizenship has been *revoked*. All Westerners have had their citizenship rescinded by our new ruling Conclave. As well as their acceptance into our Vo'lon faith."

"What?" Bleddyn blurts out, her emerald eyes tight with outrage.

"Have you forgotten that my *husband* was a Westerner?" Soleiya snarls, Yvan's fire running as hot as his mother's.

I notice that Ung Li's expression is one of intense disapproval as she glares at Quoi Zhon, Ung Li's dislike of her new high commander seeming to vibrate on the air.

"Pay no heed to this, Trystan," Ra'Ven cuts in, his livid gaze fixed on Quoi Zhon. "I grant you, and anyone else so cast out of Noilaan, full citizenship in the Sublands."

"The Sublands are no longer yours to command," Quoi Zhon shoots back. "They are part of Vo's Sacred Land and runically walled off until your people accept our sovereign power over Noilaan's Subland Territory."

Ra'Ven's aura of verdant power gains an incendiary brightness. "So, you've imprisoned my people?" he challenges Quoi Zhon. "Like the Alfsigr did in the Sublands of Alfsigroth?"

Sage levels a damning finger at Quoi Zhon. "You've trapped our *children* and my younger *sisters* there, amongst *thousands*!"

"And Effrey!" Thierren exclaims, condemnation firing in his eyes. "A child I swore to keep safe!"

"This is unforgivable!" Vothe's great-aunt Sithendrile hisses.

"You're turning into the West," Yvan snarls, the flow of his fire and mine echoing Sithendrile's outrage.

"What of our pack?" Rafe levels at the high commander, his tone low and dangerous, an intimidating energy flowing off both my eldest brother and Diana beside him.

"The Gerwulf pack is currently in the Vo Forest north of Voloi with the Amaz and the Kelts," Quoi Zhon snaps, "engaged in a military standoff with our forces. Which we *will* win."

Angered murmurs rise as Rivyr'el spits out an Alfsigr curse.

"You do not want a war with my people," Freya Zyrr cautions Quoi Zhon, her gaze lethally narrowed. "We will tear you apart and deplete both sides' magic in the battle, allowing Vogel to *sweep right in*."

Quoi Zhon glares back at her, unmoved. "We have given the Lupines, Amaz, and Kelts a day to agree to our plan for their repatriation back to the Western Realm before we *force* them from Vo's sovereign land."

A low growl works its way from Diana's throat and is quickly taken up by Naga and the rest of my horde, claws forming on Rafe and Diana's fingers.

Several surrounding Vu Trin draw swords, while Quoi Zhon unflinchingly stands her ground. "These are Conclave matters," she bites out. "You'd best take it up with them."

"What of the Fae Wyvernguard units?" Vang Troi demands. "What of all those Westerners who risked their lives during the Magedom's attack on Voloi?"

Quoi Zhon rounds on her. "Noilaan is for the *Noi*, as is the Wyvernguard." She casts a violent look at me, as if she'd strike me down right then and there if Noilaan's Vo Conclave granted her leave to, before she reaches toward Trystan once more. "Hand over the necklace, *Gardnerian*."

Trystan yanks off his Vo'lon necklace and thrusts it toward her, his invisible lightning crackling with angry power as she swipes it from him.

"Vo doesn't reside in that necklace," Trystan calmly levels. "Or your flags." He turns to Ung Li, his expression shifting to one of raw worry. "Where is Priest Wyn Juun? Did he survive the Magedom's attack on Voloi?"

"He did," Ung Li states, a flash of conflict in her eyes as she gestures west. "He's on the other side of the border wall."

Trystan's eyes widen. "Has the Conclave *deported* him?"

"No," Ung Li returns with a stiff shake of her head. "He's aiding Western refugees trapped there, many of them sick with the Red Grippe." She glares at Quoi Zhon. "He told us, 'That's where Vo resides now. Not here.'" Ung Li looks to

Vang Troi, her expression tightening with what seems like an edge of reluctance. "Vanglira, you've been relieved of all rank and dishonorably discharged from the Vu Trin."

Without hesitation, Vang Troi swipes off her horned headpiece and lets it drop to the terrace's stone with an emphatic clatter, her violet eyes afire. "Rank means *nothing* compared to the threat the East is faced with if you destroy the Dyoi Forest and Zonor River." Her piercing gaze falls on Quoi Zhon. "No more talk. Let us through."

Quoi Zhon stares Vang Troi down for a protracted moment before she brusquely gestures us forward. Yvan, Soleiya, and I exchange intense glances before my allies and I follow Quoi Zhon through an arching stone entranceway and into the Wyvernguard, Vu Trin soldiers filing in at our sides.

We enter the Conclave's huge circular hall. A colossal Noi flag hangs there, Vo's white dragon form emblazoned on sapphire. Noilaan's sapphire-robed Conclave sits behind a curved, obsidian table on a slightly raised dais, white dragons embroidered on every robe encircled by sewn images of Vo's white bird messengers. I count twenty Conclave members as their eyes zero in on me with palpable hostility. We still before them, Yvan's hand gripping mine, one wing arcing around me as he gathers defensive fire.

Introductions ensue, Quoi Zhon stiffly naming Conclave members before introducing, with a reverential dip of her head, the Vo Conclave's majority leader, Niko Luun.

As I take in his yellow eyes, black hair and angular features, Bleddyn spits out a curse from behind me. I angle my head toward her in question and am caught off guard by the haunted look in her eyes.

"Remember when I told you about Noilaan's Vo'nyl movement?" she whispers. "Well, Niko Luun is their leader."

The blow connects, hammer hard—the Vo'nyl responsible for all those signs in Voloi when I was in hiding in Mora'lee's rune ship—*Noilaan for the Noi.*

"Damn them," Rivyr'el mutters under his breath from beside Bleddyn. "Damn them *all*. They're truly turning Noilaan into the West."

Every nerve alight with tension, I note that only Noi are serving on the Conclave now. The Noi people are varied in skin and hair tones, but they share similar dress, hair, and makeup styles, kohl lining every man's eyes. And each Conclave member wears the Vo'lon religious necklace with its twelve multicolored beads and central white Vo-dragon bead, a white bird pendant hanging from it.

Vang Troi steps toward the Conclave, her shoulders squared, her aura shivering to powerful, sapphire life. "Nor hyoi'lir Noi'khin," she formally greets them. "We bring urgent news of the Magedom's strike on Erthia's wilds and an offer of emergency alliance. Alliance not only with the Icaral of Prophecy, Yvan Guryev, but also with his revered mother, Soleiya Guryev. Along with our entire Dryad'khin force and the transformed Dryad'kin Witch, Elloren Guryev."

Harsh murmurs break out amongst the Conclave members at the announcement of my new name. Except for Niko Luun, who remains still and silent, his hands clasped before him, his penetrating, pale yellow eyes fixed unwaveringly on me.

Naga steps toward the Conclave in human form, her movements full of powerful, serpentine grace. She gestures toward Yvan and me with a black-clawed hand. "The Icaral and Dryad Witch are united as Wyvernbonded mates," she states with formal import. "They are bound to our horde, by blood and by fire, and we can read their noble intent."

The Conclave's looks of hatred remain unchanged, the ensuing silence volatile.

"The last time we saw you, witch," Niko Luun smoothly states, breaking the silence, "you were leading an invasion of our lands that almost destroyed Voloi. And now, here you are again."

I will myself to remain calm, Yvan's fire and that of my entire horde blazing through me. "I was *forced* to move against the East," I clarify, remorse tightening my throat as I convey the full story of how Marcus Vogel took hold of me with his Shadow Wand before I was freed by the Great Tree of the Northern Forest and transformed into Dryad'kin. "And now," I tell him, "my allies and I seek to stand with you against the Magedom's Shadow."

"Yet you and your army would keep us from sending a storm band west to wall that very same Shadow out," Niko Luun counters.

"Have you listened to *nothing* Elloren just said?" Soleiya cries, her invisible fire rearing.

"The storm band you're preparing," Sylvan interjects. "It is *imperative* that you *do not* send it out over the Dyoi Forest and Zonor River."

"If you do," Yulan adds, the floral magic coursing through her lines shivering with tension, "you're as good as placing a powerful weapon right in the Magedom's hands."

"Tell us, then, Tree Fae," Niko Luun stonily offers both Yulan and Sylvan, "how could it possibly work against us to send out the strongest storm band we have ever conjured to blast Vogel's forces and corrupted storm bands back West, destroying them en route?"

Tension crackles through Sylvan's power. "For centuries," he growls, "all your power has come from Nature's Matrix. Because a critical mass of Forest has always existed, you have taken this wellspring for granted. You used the Natural World's elemental gifts to fight your Forest-destroying wars as well as to gut the Forest's root-supporting Sublands with your lumenstone mines. So much of our Forest remained as a buffer to your ignorant destruction that the Continent's Natural Matrix survived."

Sylvan's piercing gaze sweeps over the Conclave. "But now, Vogel has murdered III, the Life-anchoring Heart Tree of the Forest, only its Verdyllion branch remaining. His Magedom has razed our kindred Northern Forest, along with most of the Forests of the West and the South. He has killed and poisoned *too much*." Sylvan's elemental power burgeons, rising to storming heights within him. "If you destroy the Dyoi Forest and the Zonor River," he warns, "your power, as well as ours, will be decimated as the Matrix comes undone. You will tip the Natural World into an Unbalancing that will unleash the greatest Death Reckoning Erthia has *ever seen*."

Troubled murmurs rise among the Conclave members, the sapphire-robed officials leaning toward each other, their faces tense with agitated concern.

All except for Niko Luun

"Which will do *what*?" he presses.

"Your weather will come unhinged," Hazel answers as he slides forward, his eerie voice shot through with the weight of a nightmare foretelling. "Your seasons, *unmoored*. And a storm of Death will follow."

Vothe's father lets out a scoffing huff. "You stand in the *East*, Death Fae. *We* control the weather here."

Sylvan's gaze swings to Hizar'drile, his expression like the slash of a sword. "No," he sharply counters. "You merely amplify or suppress natural cycles. If your storm band obliterates the Dyoi and the Zonor, even the Zhilonile Wyverns of the East will be unequal to the chaos you'll unleash."

"Your crops will wither and *die*," Yulan warns, her melodic voice trembling. "Your seas, rivers, and air will spin into mayhem." She glances mournfully at the bedraggled heron hugging her side. "And our animal and plant kindreds—their worlds and lives will be *torn apart*."

All the light in the room pulses Dark, mist in the shape of silver-glowing snakes rising around Hazel's dark-clad form. "Death will come in ways that surpass your greatest nightmares," he warns, his subterranean voice vibrating through my bones. "Disease. Famine. Swarms of insects. Plagues of *every kind*."

Hazel takes a menacing step toward the Conclave, his Darkness pulsing through the room, harder this time. "We Deathlings will do what we can to hold off Nature's Great Unraveling, but if you tip the Balance too far, we will not be able to stop what will come. And then the Shadow will pour into the chaos to consume *everything*."

"All we are asking," Yulan pleads, arms outstretched, "is that you come to the Forest with us and listen to the trees to gain understanding. If the East joins with the Forest before its foliage power goes dormant, we can merge and amplify our collective might and swiftly move against the Magedom *together*."

Another tense silence descends before Niko Luun almost imperceptibly raises his palm.

Two Vu Trin sorceresses, one on each side of the Conclave dais, raise sapphire-glowing styluses. I flinch as a translucent dome snaps into being over the Conclave, cutting out all sound.

Yvan and I exchange a wary glance as the Conclave members speak to each other with emphatic gestures, Niko Luun's expression stern as he confers with them all.

After a prolonged moment, Niko Luun nods to the Vu Trin stationed beside the dais, and they raise their styluses once more. The silencing dome vanishes, and my heartbeat accelerates as we await their decision.

"We are not guided by trees," Niko Luun calmly states.

His words set off an explosion of energy through our combined Dryad'khin power, sounds of alarm and outrage rising as Hazel hisses, his Darkness strobing through the hall.

"We're not asking you to bind to the Forest as we have," Yvan snarls, anger scorching through his power.

"Just to hear the Forest out!" Oaklyyn growls, just as furious.

"You plot the East's doom," Vang Troi levels at them all.

"*Silence!*" Niko Luun booms back, his gaze fixing on Vang Troi. "You *forget* who you are, Vanglira! True Noi'khin put their trust in *Vo on High*!" He jabs his finger at the white dragon marked on the huge flag at his back. "*Not* in *trees*!"

"You will bring Death to your people," Hazel hisses, his voice ratcheting in from every direction, my gut clenching as I take in the belligerence in every Conclave member's eyes.

"Then bring your Death Reckoning, Fae'kin," Niko Luun snarls back at Hazel. "Vo will lead us *straight through it*. And then, she will restore this land with her Blessed Awakening after you have all been *struck down*!"

"I have seen Vo's Watchers inside the trees," Vang Troi rasps at Niko Luun, her tone shot through with ballistic urgency. "They stand with the *Forest*!"

Niko Luun spits out a furious sound. "You imagine yourself a Vo'lon *priest*?"

"Vo does not require the priestdom," Vang Troi snarls back. "Vo cannot be controlled. Just like Vo's Ahxhil Watcher birds cannot be controlled."

The Lupines and Naga's horde close protectively in around my allies and me, low growls rising, and I tense against the seismic power building in the room.

Yulan suddenly launches herself toward the Conclave, falling to her knees before them. "Do not do this thing," she begs, her kindred heron rushing to her side, the bird's wings agitatedly flapping. "Please, I beg of you, Honored Noi'khin," she raggedly implores, "*do not send this storm band out over our Forest and Water'kin*."

"It is already done," Niko Luun quietly responds. "The order has been sent."

My Dryad'khin and I are caught in a split second of frozen shock as every Vu Trin soldier in the hall draws their weapons, the entrance doors behind us snapping shut, the click of locks sounding.

Our communal Dryad'khin power ignites like a multitude of wildfires, my horde's firestorm exploding through it. Naga's hissing voice singes through our horde flame as she morphs to dragon form—*We will fight our way out to that storm band and destroy it!*

I catch my brother Rafe's wild amber gaze, then Diana's, unspoken understanding passing through us all as Mavrik and Gwynnifer draw twinned might into their palms, forming battle runes there, and Yvan gathers a cataclysmic level of fire power.

Naga whips her head back, opens her mouth and roars out a blast of fire at the hall's ceiling at the same moment that Mavrik and Gwynn thrust their rune-marked palms forward.

A translucent golden dome-shield blinks into being around us, a gold rune marked on it that allows our magic to pass through.

Stone and wood rain down and Vu Trin snarl out commands from every direction, rapidly conjuring thick, sapphire-glowing beams to stabilize the portion of ceiling Naga incinerated.

Seizing on their distraction, Yvan thrusts his violet-glowing palms forward, a snarl bursting from his throat as he hurls two fireballs through our shielding and into the hall's huge, locked doors, instantly exploding them.

Yvan grabs my arm, and we lunge through the flames, our shield moving with us as we rush into a curved hall, while Mavrik and Gwynn force back Vu Trin with wind power. Yvan blasts through the door before us, and we race out onto the Wyvernguard's terrace, wind now buffeting our forms, the mighty Vo River coursing past us. Mavrik and Gwynn bind the Vu Trin stationed there with golden vines as my allies swiftly retrieve their weapons, Sylvan tossing me one of his branches while Ra'Ven conjures a shimmering emerald Varg barrier inside the terrace doorway's decimated entrance, walling off the Vu Trin inside the Wyvernguard.

"The storm band has yet to be released!" Vang Troi cries, pointing west.

The killing storm band is poised over the half-decimated Vo Mountain Range. I tighten my grip around my living branch, the chromatic power of the Dyoi Forest flooding my lines.

Errilith lets out an ear-splitting *CAW* as he rushes to me, a call that's soon echoed by my other Errilor Death Ravens and joined by the rasping cry of Alder's giant eagles as the Wyverns among us in human shape morph into dragon form.

I leap onto my kindred raven's back, lift my living branch and murmur spells along with my fellow Dryad'khin to hold our shielding around us as we swiftly take to the air as one on raven-, Wyvern-, and eagleback, Yvan soaring beside me.

A blast detonates behind us, and my head whips around to see Vu Trin soldiers streaming from the Wyvernguard, the non-shifters amongst them taking to the air on Wyvernback, all in hot pursuit.

Clutching Errilith's stiff black feathers, I duck down against the wind as we accelerate west over the Vo, making a beeline toward the killing storm band.

Naga roars a warning as Vu Trin on Wyverns and military skiffs soar toward us from all sides and we fly toward Noilaan's runic border. Rapidly approaching the border wall, I join my allies in hurling out wind spells to force back the incoming Vu Trin as well as those guarding the border's apex.

We soar over the border and the crowded refugee encampment, horror rising in my throat as the lightning spitting through the storm band takes on a cataclysmic energy, the power churning in its internal line of siphoning runes intensifying as the terrified Vo and Dyoi Forests begin to rustle spells through my mind.

I raise the branch in my hand and murmur the words to the storm-blasting spells the Forests are sending me, readying every last shred of my foliage-amplified power, the static tang of magic mounting on the air.

"Release your power!" Vang Troi bellows.

Together, we release our Dryad'khin storm.

Multiple bolts of our magic blast toward the storm band, our assault holding enough power to sweep up the storm band, reroute it into the sky and explode it to smithereens.

A split second before our power slams into the storm band, a sapphire Noi rune blinks into being, hovering in front of it, cathedral huge.

Horror punches through me.

"It's a reflection rune!" Mavrik, Gwynn, and I scream in unison, our magic about to hit the rune and double back toward us.

"Conjure a shield!" Ra'Ven bellows.

I frantically murmur spells, all of us throwing out every ounce of shielding energy we can muster, multihued magic bolting from my outstretched branch. A prismatic, arcing shield-wall blasts into being before us, and our entire horde throws fortifying fire into it, Hazel and my Errilor Ravens sending ropes of Deathling Darkness to pulse through its expanse.

Our initial bolts of magic collide with the storm band in an explosion of raying, prismatic foliage light magic before it's boomeranged back, our collective might now spearing toward our shield-wall in thick bolts of multihued light and storm and fire.

The storm band's roar turns deafening as our collective might collides with our shield.

The collision slams pain through my branch hand, and I cry out, my ravens caw, Alder's eagles shriek, and Wyverns and Lupines growl as our shield explodes out of existence and we're hit by our own magic. A groan forced from my throat, I'm hurled off Errilith's back and pinwheel into a free fall through the air.

Yvan's snarl splits the air as his arms slap around me, halting my descent, while the storm band gains roaring power and releases, its apex dropping as it barrels down the western face of what remains of the Vo Mountain Range.

"Noooooooooo!" Yulan screams, her petite form gripped in Naga's talons as gravity itself seems to tilt.

THE DRYAD STORM

The scene before me blinks out of sight, replaced by what the Dyoi Forest is experiencing from every terrible angle at once—trees screaming as they're ripped out of the ground; kindred animals shrieking and fleeing as they're swept up in funneling winds or incinerated by Wyvern-crafted lightning; the Vu Trin storm band siphoning up the Forest's elemental energy as it goes, my heart shredding with agony.

The storm band collides with the Zonor River's shield and siphons up its power before taking hold of the Zonor itself. The river's water power is rapidly sucked up into the churning storm, the river and its kindred creatures sending out combined wails of anguish as Trystan, Vothe, and Sithindrile scream out their agony and the Zonor is destroyed.

I flail against Yvan's hold, pain knifing through my every rootline as millions upon millions of plants and animals—along with scattered refugees making their way East—are whipped into the Vu Trin storm band's tornado of force.

A scream bursts from my throat as the scene around me snaps back into focus, our shielding over the East blasting out rays of chromatic light as it's consumed by the storm band's mounting power.

The clouds above us shift into chaos, building unnaturally, lightning bursting fitfully through them in strange shapes.

I scream as Yvan fights the killing wind, his wings battling against it, a curse erupting from his throat. Hazel's wrenching, all-encompassing cry sounds, followed by Wrenfir's wail of anguish, and then the defiant, distant growls of Viger Maul and Tierney's kelpies, and my ravens' tortured *CAW*s as all the Deathkin explode into black mist and vanish.

The world pulses Dark and my connection to the Dyoi Forest severs, pain screaming through my rootlines as my vision cuts out and Erthia's Natural Matrix comes undone.

CHAPTER FOUR

THE GREAT UNRAVELING

Elloren Guryev

Eastern Realm

I'm half-conscious and lost in darkness. My rootlines seize, grasping for a Forest connection, my bond to the Dyoi Forest obliterated.

Yvan's mouth comes down on mine, sweeping me into a kiss, the heat of it blazing a spiral of Wyvern-strong fire through my body. I arch into him and grab desperate hold of one of his horns to pull his mouth harder against mine, my bonded connection to his fire drawing me into a stronger link to his kindred Zhilaan Forest.

His warrior fire Forest.

A Forest I can sense fighting against the Natural Matrix's complete undoing with a ferocity I did not imagine could come from trees, its violet fire aura radiating out toward the newly untethered root systems of Erthia with single-minded grit.

Consciousness floods back in a rush, deep violet light bursting through my vision as a line of the Zhilaan Forest's fire power sears through my withered rootlines.

Dryad Witch, the Forest rumbles, like a roll of thunder.

My vision returns, the purple blaze fading, and I break our kiss, breathing hard as I meet Yvan's violet-hot gaze.

"Elloren," he breathes, his expression wild with concern, his fire lashing through our bond. Soleiya is crouched beside Yvan, her gold-blazing eyes fixed on me.

I glance frantically around, desperate to locate my friends and loved ones amidst the tight crowd of allies.

We're in a large cavern. Its purple-veined black stone is lit sapphire by a suspended Noi rune. Outside the narrow mouth of our cavern, the skies are churning gray, wind blasting so violently that visibility is reduced to an arm's length. Vang

THE DRYAD STORM

Troi stands sentry beside the opening, along with Diana and Freyja Zyrr.

"Where are we?" I ask Yvan and Soleiya.

"Near the top of the Voloi Mountain Range," Yvan answers, cradling me.

"Is anything left of our shielding over the East?" I press, forcing myself into a sitting position, Yvan's embrace helping me upright.

He shakes his head, frustration burning in his eyes. "The Vu Trin storm band absorbed it. The East is unshielded."

"Ancient One," I gasp. "Vogel can invade at any moment."

A deeper fright grips hold. I look to my Dryad'kin, many of them slumped down, like Gwynn and Mavrik, their backs against the cavern's walls, their Forest-fueled power dangerously depleted, so many kindreds murdered once again. A half-conscious Lucretia is cradled in Jules's arms, his silver falcon perched on his shoulder, wings worriedly flapping. Sylvan is doubled over, bracing himself against the dark stone, his skin grayed, his pine branch hair dropping needles. Iris is holding on to him, a desperate golden fire flickering in her eyes.

Yulan is weeping uncontrollably, her flower tresses morphed to dead, shriveled vines, the deep green of her skin rapidly fading to ash gray. Her unconscious heron kindred lies crumpled at her side. Ariel is on her knees beside the bird, expression dire, her hands pressed to the heron's breast.

Oaklyyn appears to be in shock. She's on her knees, her green eyes wide as she stares into nothing, murmuring, "My kindred ones, my kindred ones," over and over. Raz'zor is crouched in human form beside her, his fire aura blazing around and through her withering rootlines with desperate, impassioned heat. A slumped, semiconscious Thierren rasps "Sparrow" over and over through grayed lips, and Alder is weeping next to the motionless form of one of her giant eagles, the rest of her battered flock gathered around her green, purple-branch-marked form, her bonded Vo Forest clearly still hanging on. But for how long?

I turn, and another jolt of fear spears through me as I spot Vothe cradling Trystan's limp form. Aislinn, Diana, Andras, Jarod, and Vothe's great-aunt Sithendrile are grouped around them, Trystan's half-lidded eyes blearily meeting mine.

"He's all right," Vothe calls to me, clearly reading the desperation flaring through my fireline, the Zonor blue stripped from the tips of his hair and his power. "Our bond is keeping his rootlines from completely withering," Vothe gravely states, and when I look further on, a limp Fain seems to be similarly anchored by Sholin.

I turn back to Yvan and Soleiya, my tenuous connection to the Zhilaan through

Yvan holding my rootlines together, its faint purple branching patterns emblazoned on my grayed skin. "Did we lose anyone to the storms?" I frantically ask them.

"No," Yvan assures me. "Mavrik and Gwynn used the last of their power to pull everyone through the Void storms by creating a loose tether to the shield-linkage runes Oaklyyn marked on us. But the tethers they created . . . their twinned binding power is so strong, if any of us tries to leave the group, we'll be yanked back. We're trapped here together until the binding fades."

I gape at him, the ramifications staggering.

"The storms outside," Soleiya adds, her tone laced with dread as she glances toward the whipping maelstrom just past our cavern's mouth, "they're stronger than the strongest of cyclones."

The three of us exchange a blazingly dire look, the unspoken raging between us—what's just swept in outside is merely the opening salvo of a nightmare of environmental undoing, the Magedom's Shadow about to infiltrate the chaos and poison *everything.*

"We've got to get to the Sublands!" Sage is raging to Ra'Ven near the cavern's mouth, her violet hair whipped about by the wind. Ra'Ven is keeping tight hold of her, as if he's preventing her from hurling herself straight into the storms outside, her purple eyes full of a wild urgency. The Wyvernfire blazing through Sage's fireline, gained when she was pregnant with their Icaral child, is keeping her somewhat magically moored, even as her shriveling rootlines flail about for purchase.

"We have to get to Fyn'ir and Fern and my sisters," she snarls at Ra'Ven as she struggles to pull her arms from his grip.

"They're in the Sublands," Ra'Ven adamantly reassures her. "With Fyon and Mora. Likely a damned sight safer there than here—"

"Nowhere is safe!" Oaklyyn cries as she desperately pulls on Raz'zor's fire.

"We've got to get out of here!" Ariel hisses from where she's crouched by Yulan's heron, more fear in her expression than I've ever witnessed. "We can't let Vogel advance *any farther*! He'll gain enough power to blast through the Sublands and come for *Wynter!*"

"Valasca is there, as well!" Ni Vin lashes out at everyone, the level of emotion in the young sorceress's voice a hard blow to my gut as Freyja paces nearby, Freyja's concern for her people writ deep in her hazel tattooed features, an agonized sorrow in her eyes, her kindred bear likely destroyed, like so many other kindreds . . .

"My people have talented sorceresses amongst them," Freyja tells us, voice rough.

"They'll likely be able to shield my Amaz'kin and their allies from the storm, but we all know that Shadow terror is about to strike the East because the Realm has left itself *wide open* to attack."

My attention pivots to my tenuous link to the Zhilaan, a slim line of its power simmering battle-fire hot through my unmoored lines.

The idea hits, like a bolt of light.

"We need to connect everyone to the Zhilaan Forest," I say to Yvan in a rush of resolve, desperate for a way forward. "The Zhilaan wants to make a stand against this, I can *feel* it."

Sylvan spits out a devastated sound, his limp body braced against both Iris and the cavern's wall as he sets his gaze on me. "You don't understand." He swipes his free hand out at all of us, tears sheening his eyes. "None of you do. You don't get an infinite number of chances to destroy the Natural World and rebound from it. It's *over*."

His words are a harsher assault than the pummeling storms outside as he slashes his hand toward the cavern's storming mouth. "What you see there?" he levels. "That's the *beginning* of *the end*."

A deeper alarm ignites as I turn to Wrenfir. "Were Hazel and my ravens pulled into a Reckoning?" I shakily ask, able to feel the trace of Darkness still connecting me to them.

"They're trying to hold off the Reckoning," Wrenfir chokes out. "They've sacrificed themselves for our cruel stupidity and dissolved themselves into Nature." He says this with devastating finality, his power a heart-shattering mess. He's slumped on the cavern's floor, his fists knotted in his dark hair. He lifts his spider-marked gaze, his cheeks streaked with tears, his eyes pierced through with violent grief. "Hazel didn't want to leave me," he gruffly forces out. "I could sense his emotions through our mating bond. But he had no choice. He pulled himself into Nature's Death energy to try and keep it from sliding into a Reckoning. But he won't be able to hold off the release of that Reckoning forever."

An ominous quiet descends, save for the violent winds battering the mountain-top around us, grief swelling in my heart for both Hazel and Wrenfir and for my Errilor Ravens, kindreds I barely had a chance to get to know and love.

And Tierney's Death Fae and the other Deathkin who were here in Noilaan—did they dissolve themselves into the Natural World as well to hold off the Reckoning as I sensed? And what of the refugees trapped past the border wall? Will any of them survive the raging storms?

Aislinn lets out a shivering breath, tears pooling in her eyes, Jarod's arm wrapped tight around her shoulder. "I never imagined it would all end like this," she rasps.

"It's not the end yet," I snarl back, rebellion rising as I battle back the despair attempting to tear a hole through my heart. "There are *still trees*," I insist. "It's not over while there is *still living Forest*."

Sylvan huffs out a harsh sound. "It's not enough, Elloren," he says. "A few scattered Forests are not enough to hold a shattered Matrix together."

"Maybe not," Yvan harshly returns, "but the Zhilaan Forest wants to keep fighting. I can feel it though our kindred bond. And I plan on fighting to the end, as well."

"*How?*" Sylvan demands. His stark challenge sizzles in the air, and we're all powerless against it, the nightmare bearing down.

"We go forward on faith," Gwynn shakily suggests, her green hue also faded to a sickly gray, but a trace of prismatic light still burning at the edges of her golden eyes. "It's all we have left."

"Faith in *what*?" Wrenfir bites back.

Gwynn levels her golden stare on him. "In the Verdyllion," she insists. "It's still out there. And, maybe . . . in the power that's at the center of all of Erthia's faiths. We've seen the Watchers inside the trees . . ."

"You honestly think *religion* can save us?" Wrenfir furiously spits out.

Gwynn shakes her head, her jaw set in a defiant line. "I don't know. But, maybe all the faiths taken together . . . maybe they could point a way forward. For however long we have left in this fight."

"We *have* to keep fighting with everything in us," Andras snarls, urgency in his gaze. "I don't have the luxury of giving up! I have a *child*!"

"As do I!" Alcippe growls, a large amethyst gripped in her fist.

Andras's and Alcippe's outbursts strike deep, a remembrance of Valasca's words like a bell rung straight through my heart—

You will lose every last thing that's important to you.

But you'll lose those things so that others won't have to.

I realize in one, great swoop that Andras and Valasca are right. We have to keep fighting for a future for all the surviving children, everywhere. And for every last surviving tree.

"Gwynn might be on to something," I say on impulse, grasping for a path forward. "There might be something in all the faiths that can show us how to fight

498

back. They all have the Watchers. And the Verdyllion, in one form or another—"

"And the Source Tree," Gwynn adds.

"And the Reaping Times," Wrenfir growls. "And *five million other stories* detailing Erthia's razing followed by the ascendancy of the 'One True Faith'!"

"You're right," I agree, "but, it's like Gwynn said . . . we've all *seen* the Watchers. And everyone who has been a Bearer of the Verdyllion Wand . . . we've all seen them *outside* of the trees." I force myself slightly up, the rebellion inside me gaining ground. "Even though the Magedom tries to pin the Watchers down on their flags and banners and clothing, and now the Noi are hell-bent on doing the same . . . they *can't* be pinned down. *That's* the faith Gwynn is talking about. Faith in *them*. And how they led us to each other. And maybe they'll lead us toward a way to *fight back*."

I look to Yvan, my love for him searing through our bond.

"I can go forward on that type of faith," Yvan offers with the force of a vow, his arms and wings wrapped around me, his unextinguishable love blazing through our bond. "I love you, Elloren," he passionately states, the level of feeling in his tone bringing tears to my eyes. "And even if Erthia is coming undone, I'll fight for you until my last breath." He sets his gaze on his mother, violet fire burning bright in his eyes. "And for you, Mav'ya." He glances around. "For *all* of you."

"I can go forward on love," Oaklyyn seconds as the violent storms blur the world outside, her gaze locking on Raz'zor's crimson-fire eyes. "I've fallen in love with you, Raz'zor the Unbroken." She glances toward the storms, tears misting her graying eyes as she chokes out a sob. "There's no sense in not saying it now, with so little time left. I've known you for such a short time . . . but your love . . . it hit me like a bolt of red lightning." Lips trembling, she shrugs. "Even though it goes against everything I ever thought I'd feel for anyone. I *love* you. And I'll fight with you till the end."

Raz'zor's fire rears. His pale wings flick dramatically out to arc around her, his eyes taking on such a fiery glow that their heat cuts straight through the storm's chill. "Be my mate, Magnificent Tree One," he hisses, his flame shot through with such a ferocious level of feeling, I can feel it blazing through our horde bond as he holds one pale, clawed hand out to her.

Emotion surging through the last traces of her power, Oaklyyn takes his hand and, in a blur, Raz'zor pulls her into a kiss, the edges of his fire blasting through our entire horde, Yvan and I both shuddering against the back-blow of vermillion flame.

Oaklyyn lets out an ecstatic cry against Raz'zor's mouth, looking dazed when they finally break their kiss, his vermillion fire now burning in her eyes. And then, for the first time since I've been hurled into Oaklyyn's orbit, she smiles at Raz'zor, wide and beaming, in beautiful defiance of the end of the world. Raz'zor grins back at her, teeth gleaming as his invisible fire whips around her with wild, protective abandon.

"It's true that the odds stacked against us are impossible," I say to everyone. "Erthia may truly be coming to an end. So, how do we want our last chapter to be written?"

"Together," Soleiya answers, her voice and fire full of fierce love. "Not apart."

"Forever unbroken!" Naga hisses.

"Vo's priest, Wyn Juun . . . he taught me a Vo'lon saying," Trystan rasps out in a battered voice. "'Way Will Open.' It means . . . to trust that if you go forward in love and faith, a path *will* open. Even when all hope is lost." He looks to the storms. "*Especially* then."

"This is all so easy for you," Wrenfir snarls, his infuriated voice shattering clear through our tenuous grasp on hope. "To *delude* yourself with all these *fantasy stories.* To *hell* with the Watchers. The love of my *life* has been *ripped away from me*! Because the world is *ending*! It's *over*! There is no hope! And I'll never see Hazel again! Unless he's forced by the Reckoning to come back and *kill* me. To kill us *all*! And soon after, there will be only *one power* at play in the world! The *Shadow.* Your love," he sneers at all of us, his lips twisting with combative devastation, "it comes *too late*! The Shadow has *WON*—"

A roar cuts through my uncle's words, a blast of white lightning detonating outside as two winged figures soar into the cavern, everyone freezing . . .

. . . as Vothe's father, Hizar'drile, and his brother, Gethindrile, land inside the cavern's mouth.

"We believe you!" Hizar'drile cries out, his eyes flashing lightning as they find Vothendrile's, a devastated expression slashed across his face. "We're here to align with you!"

A beat of wordless shock rips through the room before Vothe's aura of power catapults into an explosion of storm-hurling rage. With a snarl Vothe launches himself at his father and brother, fast as a blur, just as Rafe and Raz'zor surge toward Vothe and grab restraining hold of him, Vothe's lightning power rearing so hard, visible threads crackle out to bolt toward his kin.

THE DRYAD STORM

"You believe us *now*?" Vothe cries. "Now that everything is *destroyed*? Now that the entire Natural Matrix of Erthia is *obliterated*?" He tears himself from Rafe's and Raz'zor's restraining grips, facing his father and brother down, his power blasting toward them with spitting fury. "Do you have any idea what you've *DONE*?"

Hizar'drile's onyx face is a mask of devastation. "You were right, my son. Everything you warned us of—"

"If you had simply *listened to the trees*," Vothe rages, "*none of this* would have happened!"

"There is no putting the Forest back together again!" Sylvan levels as he forces himself up and takes a staggering step toward Hizar'drile, his fists balled. "The Dyoi Forest was *old growth Forest*! That Matrix took *thousands of years* to form!"

"Wait," I interject, realizing, in a flash, that a large swath of the sky outside the cavern is visible, the violent storm pushed away. I look to Hizar'drile. "How did you push back the weather? And how did you find us?"

Hizar'drile blinks at me. "A large portion of our Wyvern Vu Trin force and half of the remaining Vu Trin forces are outside," he answers, "holding the unmoored weather around this mountaintop at bay. Commander Ung Li is with them. We tracked you here via the rune she marked you with. We've all broken with Noilaan. And we're aligning with you. We'll listen to your trees. We'll do more than listen. We'll fight with you for Erthia."

I exchange a shocked look with Yvan, our rebellion gaining ground. Yvan rises, his gaze burning into Hizar'drile. "Do you have enough power to fly us all through the violent weather and get us to the nearest military portal to Zhilaan?"

"We do," he affirms.

Our rebellion digs in deeper, a rush of battle-fire flowing into Yvan and me from the Zhilaan Forest as the depleted power of everyone surrounding me is flooded by a renewed desire to rise and fight.

"Looks like the story is not yet over," Ariel says as she and Bleddyn toss me sly looks, Ariel's wings snapping out along with her small raven's, Bleddyn's grip tightening around the malachite stylus in her hand.

I turn my gaze back to Hizar'drile as the distant Zhilaan Forest's warrior energy rises inside Yvan and me, my words shot through with Dryad resolve when they come. "Get us to the Zhilaan Forest."

CHAPTER FIVE

THE ZHILAAN FOREST

Elloren Guryev

Zhilaan

The power radiating from the dome-shield over Zhilaan is a shock to my rootlines.

As Yvan soars us toward the Forest alongside our Dryad'khin and newfound Eastern Realm allies, the Forest's warrior energy surges through our bond, our hold on each other reflexively tightening.

The Zhilon'ile Wyverns are holding back the unmoored weather whipping around us with their own storming power, the dome-shield's blurred expanse becoming increasingly visible, spitting purple lightning and a curious blue mist coursing over its entirety. Somehow, I realize, the people of Zhilaan have found a way to channel the Zhilaan Forest's power straight into it.

I tense my brow and focus my power empathy on the colossal amount of magic at play in this shield. There's a strong framework of Eastern Wyvern storm power present in it, but that underpinning magic is dwarfed by both the Zhilaan Forest's energy and another line of magic that fills me with surprise.

Blue Urisk *geomancy*.

Somehow intimately fused to the Forest's power.

But how?

My surprise notches higher as I read how the geomancy is actively *channeling* the Zhilaan Forest's power into the dome-shield to wall off the violent weather.

"Yvan," I say, my lips brushing his warm ear. He pulls me nearer, the close contact sending an unbidden rush of heat through us both. "We've an unexpected Urisk ally," I tell him, striving to be heard over the thunderous mayhem. "Zhilaan's dome-shield is shot full of blue geomancy—"

THE DRYAD STORM

My words cut off as the Zhilaan Wyvern soldiers flying before us raise their palms and blast bright white lightning toward Zhilaan's dome-shield. An oval opening forms in its surface, and we soar through the gap into storm-free Zhilaan . . .

. . . and gain our first clear glimpse of the mighty Zhilaan Forest.

My lips part in awe.

The Zhilaan Nightwood Pine Forest is a majestic carpet of midnight purple reaching into the distance, its rich hue dotted by groves of deciduous trees bursting with autumn's every prismatic color, the fabled rocky Spikelands of Zhilaan arced around the Forest's northern edge. I can sense the Forest latching on to Yvan's and my sudden presence, its fire-fueled power embracing us both, our Wyvernbond flooded with purple flame.

"The Forest . . . it's amplifying our bond," I marvel, my awareness of Yvan's strong body intensifying as the Forest blazes what feels like an intentional pull toward each other through us.

"Gods, Elloren," Yvan murmurs as he spears us forward. "It's intensifying my draw to you. I didn't think that was possible."

An invisible trace of his fire shivers over my lips, Yvan's aura blazing around me with such impassioned energy, its motion sparks my own returning heat, his hold on me firming.

We close in on the Forest's edge, my pulse hammering against Yvan's, as we take in the gargantuan Zhilaan Nightwood Pine Trees, their spear-like apexes rising so high they almost touch the dome-shield above them. I shiver from the Forest's intensifying aura, power running blisteringly hot through its expanse.

A colossal firestorm of might.

Witch'kin, the Forest thunders through me, raising every hair on my skin as we follow the Zhilon'ile Wyverns down, the pine trees seeming to rise higher and higher as we descend. Yvan lands in a field of lavender grass in front of the Zhilaan Forest's tree line, our allies alighting all around us, Raz'zor and the other Wyverns morphing to winged-human form.

I gape at the huge Nightwood Pines before us, the girth of their trunks larger than the largest of Valgard's buildings, the trees' massive forms blazing out their invisible fire power toward the shield above through that mysterious channel of blue Urisk geomancy.

Desperate to fully restore my Dryad rootlines, I surge toward the nearest Nightwood Pine and throw my III-marked palm onto its wall-size trunk.

Errilor's onyx raven head flashes through my vision, the rest of my flock surrounding him, all of them dissolved into a mist of Dark that swirls around me with palpable love and support before flowing back down into Erthia. Tears sting my eyes, my connection to my kindreds blessedly still there for as long as they can hold off the Reckoning.

The Zhilaan Forest's violet fire blazes into me via that kindred connection with such sudden force that my body begins to vibrate. I fall to my knees, Yvan catching me from behind, his touch an anchoring force as the Zhilaan Forest fully links to my rootlines and sears into them, flooding them with its full spectrum of elemental power.

Light, earth, water, air.

And purple fire.

All of it swirling around and intensifying my bond to Yvan.

My vision clearing, I turn and meet Yvan's gaze. He's giving me a wildfire look, our love and Forest-amplified desire for each other pulsing hard through our bond, the yearning to throw myself at him almost impossible to resist.

"Your green hue has returned," he tells me, looking both relieved and a bit feral, his eyes burning.

Dazed, I glance down, grateful to find my skin's deep-green coloration and shimmer restored, the dark purple branching pattern strengthened, the Zhilaan Forest's energy running hot through me.

Yvan and I both rise and find Sylvan and my other Dryad'kin down on their knees pressing III-marked palms to the Nightwood Pines' black trunks, Raz'zor at Oaklyyn's side, Mavrik and Gwynn hanging on to each other as they make contact with the huge tree before them. Alder and Soleiya help Thierren stay upright as he lurches for one of the trees, his falcon lighting on his shoulder, Sholin aiding Fain, their dove and tailorbird kindreds flitting around them. I draw in a hard breath, my empathy filling with the heady sensation of this martial Forest flooding my Dryad'kins' rootlines with elemental power, their green hues rapidly returning, the Zhilaan's purple branching pattern overlaying it.

A flock of black Noi Fire Hawks fly out of the trees and light on the shoulders of every Dryad'khin in need of a kindred, the rest of the hawks perching on branches around us, as if waiting for their new kin.

Yulan is on her knees before one of the trees, palms to midnight bark, her injured heron beside her, and emotion tightens my throat as black clematis vines sprout to life all over her head, rapidly forming viney tresses dotted with deep-purple blooms, her Tricolor Heron's feathers shedding the gray and morphing back to their beautiful lavender, white, and blue hues as the bird fully revives. Trumpet vines flow out from the Zhilaan's tree line and twine embracingly around Yulan, lavender flowers opening as she begins to weep.

My brother Trystan has his palms pressed to the huge tree beside me, his green hue restored and marked now with the same dark violet branching pattern, his breathing labored, Vothe, Sithendrile, and Rafe holding on to him.

"I've lived in Zhilaan most of my life," Vothe tells us as he peers up at the trees' cloud-high apexes, "and I've never stepped foot inside this Forest."

"Why not?" Trystan asks as his breathing steadies.

"It doesn't permit intruders," Vothe answers.

"It's a lethal Forest," Vothe's father, Hizar'drile, interjects, a warning light in his eyes. Wyvernguard commander Ung Li and Vothe's brother, Gethindrile, bracket him, all of them standing a few paces back from the tree line, all of them eyeing it warily. "It doesn't allow anyone to enter except Dryad Fae," Hizar'drile continues. "If I attempt to step over its threshold, it will slay me."

To illustrate his point, Hizar'drile carefully steps toward the tree line and pushes his hand between two of its trunks. He yanks his hand back just as a wall of purple branches spears downward in a lethal blur, knifing into the soil with a muffled *thud*. Most of us flinch, my heart jumping into a faster rhythm as Hizar'drile takes a step back and the branches pull from the soil and slowly draw back into their original position.

Yvan and I exchange a look of surprise, as I'm hit by a wave of the blue Urisk geomancy coursing through Zhilaan's dome-shield, the aura of geopower sweeping out from the Forest.

A rustling sounds, and two silver-haired Zhilaan Mountain Goats with crystal-line horns step out of the trees at the same time that a familiar figure leaps into view on one of the branches overhead.

My heart leaps clear into my throat as Valasca Xanthrir meets my gaze, her sky blue skin surrounded by the same blue aura mist as Zhilaan's dome-shield. She's clothed in armor fashioned from thin plates of cobalt stone, countless runic blades made from blue gems sheathed all over her along with the powerful Ash'rion blade, a crystalline-blue stylus gripped in her hand.

A grin overtakes her face as she drops to the ground before us.

"Valasca!" Ni Vin cries as she staggers forward, her legs almost giving way beneath her as she bursts into tears.

The grin vanishes from Valasca's face, swiftly replaced by a look of pure ardor. She surges toward Ni Vin and sweeps her up into her arms. "My love," Valasca passionately murmurs in Noi as Ni Vin sobs and Valasca hugs her tight. "My beautiful, forever love," she continues, voice hitching. And then Valasca draws Ni Vin into a loving kiss that floods my vision with tears, Yvan's hand wrapping around mine as we surge toward her.

Valasca murmurs something to Ni Vin, kissing her once more before they draw back from each other, a number of us, including Alder, Freyja, and Kam Vin, converging around them.

"My queen," Valasca says, lowering herself to one knee before Freyja, head bowed.

Freyja draws in a deep breath before motioning Valasca up. "Rise, Warrior of the Goddess," she charges.

Valasca obeys, the two of them making the complicated goddess symbol on their chests, eyes locked. Valasca turns to me, her eyes sheening with emotion as we pull each other into a close embrace. "You're looking pointy around the ears, Elloren," she jests through her tears as we draw back from each other, a more heartfelt look overtaking her angular, blue face.

"I'm so glad to see you," I say as more of her crystal-horned goat kindreds filter out of the Forest and flock affectionately around her.

Valasca glances around at our allies, her brow knotting as her gaze lights on Thierren. "Where's Sparrow?" she presses.

A pained look tightens Thierren's severe features. "She's caught in Vogel's Shadow."

Valasca's dark eyes widen before her expression hardens. "Well, we'll simply have to find a way to free her." Thierren nods, stiffly, before Valasca looks to me. "The Great Tree, III," she tells me, "it drew me through its rootline network all the way to this Forest." She raises the stylus in her hand, a martial light in her eyes. "III freed up my geomancy. Then tasked me with the strengthening of Zhilaan's shielding."

It all falls into place, Valasca's combined Noi and Urisk heritage giving her the ability to use both runic systems to fortify Zhilaan's dome-shield with the Forest's own might.

THE DRYAD STORM

A look of sorrow tightens Valasca's features. "I know what happened to Lukas, Elloren. The trees . . . they showed me *everything*. I'm sorry. I'm *so sorry*. Lukas made this moment possible for us all."

I struggle against the ache suddenly gripping at my heart, because even though so many of us are here, finally allied, Lukas is gone. And these allies and loved ones that remain . . . we all might be lost to this fight.

Valasca raises her III-marked hand and looks toward the non-Dryad'khin amongst us. "You need to bind to the Forest *now*," she charges. "The Zhilaan will permit you to make contact with the trunks facing us. This Forest is ready to amplify and merge your elemental power, but only if you become its Dryad'khin. The Zhilaan showed me its history here. The Dryads who once lived here, they were decimated during the ancient Elfin Wars, and the Zhilaan turned against all non-Tree'kin as a result."

"I can read what transpired," Alder affirms, one of her palms pressed to the huge trunk before her. "The Alfsigr Elves not only killed this Forest's kindred Dryads, they clear-cut a huge section of the Forest's territory and came close to triggering an Unbalancing."

Hizar'drile nods. "Our legends have it that this Forest fought back and drove the Alfsigr out." He gives us all a grim look. "For centuries now, if anyone who is not Fae Dryad'kin tries to step into its depths, they're fought off with every means possible—spearing branches, Zhilaan Fire Ants, Lightning Salamanders, Fire Hawks—the trespassers promptly set aflame and exploded."

Witch'kin. The Forest shudders through me, the frequency of the word bone-deep and embracingly hot around my lines, fire to fire. Erthia's last sizable stand of old-growth Forest.

Our last stand.

"Vogel will be coming for this Forest," I warn, taking in the trees' towering potency. "Valasca's right. Everyone needs to bind to it and link to its power before foliage season ends."

Yvan takes my hand and draws me toward the tree line until we're just inside it, an instant realization of his intent dawning. He turns to the non-Dryad'khin massed before us and gives them a fervid look. "I'm bonded to this Forest," he calls out, holding up his III-marked hand. "It accepted me and named me Guardian even though I am a Keltish-Lasair Wyvern."

Vothe turns to his father, a thread of his invisible lightning crackling out toward Hizar'drile. "This is the moment we go on faith, Fav'vyar," he offers, his arm and the rest of his power tight around Trystan. "We need to show this Forest that we can be its allies instead of its destroyers."

Trystan suddenly breaks away from Vothe and strides toward Hizar'drile and Gethindrile, stilling before them and holding out his III-marked hand to Vothe's father. "Join with us," he stridently offers, his eyes alight with purple-and-white lightning.

Vothe's father stills as he holds Trystan's forthright stare, seeming as if he's struggling with a rise of powerful emotion, lightning spitting through his dark eyes. "I'm sorry," he finally manages, his expression tightening with obvious remorse. "I can scent your sincerity, Trystan Gardner." He briefly glances at me, then Rafe. "And I can sense the sincerity of your kin. I should have gotten to know you first, Trystan Gardner, before shunning you based on your lineage."

"I'm sorry, as well," Vothe's brother offers, a tortured look on Gethindrile's face.

Trystan and Vothe exchange a quick look, and Vothe draws up to my younger brother's side.

"We forgive you," Trystan says to Hizar'drile and Gethindrile, an emphatic strength crackling through his power.

"We forgive you both," Vothe seconds before they draw both Hizar'drile and Gethindrile into embraces and the potent truth strikes home—there's no time left for anything but forgiveness and alliance.

"Welcome to the family," Rafe comments wryly, grinning at Vothe's father and brother, his arm slung around Diana, Hizar'drile and Gethindrile looking a bit dazed by the turn of events.

"You'll soon have the Icaral of Prophecy as your full kin, as well," Ariel teases, shooting Yvan and me a sly look, a welcome glint of amusement in her fiery eyes.

"A few Lupines, as well," Diana adds, grinning wolfishly at Vothe's father and brother as she casts a pointed glance at Jarod, Aislinn, and the rest of our extended kin, my heart filling with so much love for my family and friends, even in the face of what's bearing down on us all.

"It's time to break down *all* the barriers," Valasca offers, growing serious. "And unite as one Dryad'khin people."

Yulan rises, her tresses now made up entirely of deep-purple blooms. There's renewed strength in her stance, the power of the Zhilaan Forest rising with her,

her heron ruffling its multihued feathers. "Come," Yulan says, beckoning all of the non-Dryad'khin toward the tree line, "let's bring you *all* to the Forest."

The entirety of our accompanying Vu Trin forces, both Zhilon'ile and Noi, along with our entire horde, enter into the trees and join with them, the Zhilaan Forest able to handle our horde's fire, Naga, Raz'zor, Ariel, and the others gaining smatterings of purple leaves and slim branches amidst their wing feathers along with the III mark on their palms.

A transformed Hizar'drile immediately sends soldier envoys out to beckon all of Zhilaan to come to the Zhilaan Forest's trees simply to listen. And then, if they freely choose a Dryad'khin bond, to enter into the Zhilaan Forest for the first time in their lives, embraced and strengthened by the combative Forest as its newfound allies and army.

Hours later, Yvan and I pause, just above the Zhilaan Forest's canopy, my feet supported by one of the Nightwood Pine's uppermost huge, dark branches as I search for any trace of Vogel's incoming power. Unbalanced storms boom against the dome-shield above, held back by Valasca's geo-channeling of the Forest's purple-hued might.

"Peak foliage is almost here," I say, light power flooding my lines as I turn to Yvan. "We have just a few days, at most, to gather power and move against the Magedom."

Yvan nods as we both turn our sights toward the slender, conical mountain that rises from the Zhilaan Forest's center, a Vu Trin military base built into the obsidian stone of the mountain's pinnacle, all of us to convene there once everyone emerges from the trees.

"I'm not picking up any trace of Shadow power," I say, giving him a sober look. "Not yet."

Yvan's violet-fire eyes hold mine, courage blazing through our bonded fire. Because we both know it's coming—Fallon's wintry Shadow cold rising against Yvan's Forest-linked fire.

"It turns out this was your fight, all along," I say, my voice hitching. "And I never was the Black Witch. But the Prophecy . . . it will likely prove to be true. Alder is still reading it in the trees."

Yvan's jaw tightens as he glances back toward the West. "If I'm meant to be Erthia's Icaral of Prophecy, then so be it. I'm ready to fight for all of you."

A rush of love burns through his fire, so much emotion in its incandescent blaze that for a moment I can barely pull in an even breath.

"I love you," he says, turning to me, a hotter band of his invisible fire sweeping in around me.

"I love you too," I say, tears sheening my eyes as I'm swept up into a longing for him that's so intense I can barely get the words out. "What happens . . . when a Wyvernbonded couple fully pair?" I venture. "I've seen the bite marks. Trystan has one. So does your mother."

Yvan's eyes spark, ardent energy crackling through his power. "Our initial kiss was like a wandfasting in some ways. Connecting us and our fire magic. When we pair, it's like a Sealing in that we'll gain a more intimate grasp on each other's magic." He hesitates, swallowing, as his gaze briefly flicks toward the base of my neck, the yearning in it so obvious it makes my skin tingle. "The bite opens up a full sharing of fire power between two Wyverns—to the point where they can deploy each other's fire. But, Elloren, I don't know what the Wyvern bite would do to our balance of magic, since we're both so uniquely powerful and you're not Wyvern'kin."

I can sense him warring against his desire for this link even as his note of caution strikes home. Because we can't risk upending our power in unknown ways, not with this war against the Magedom looming.

"Then we wait on the bite," I offer, steeling myself for what's to come. "But I don't want to wait any longer to fully belong to each other."

"I don't either," he passionately returns, wildfire in his eyes.

"Be with me tonight," I offer. "I want you as my full mate before this fight comes."

In answer, Yvan wraps his arms and wings around me and pulls me into a kiss that quickly turns explosive, both defiance and love in the hot press of his mouth, the covetous motion of his tongue, the molten feel of his hands claiming my body, the two of us letting ourselves burn for each other in this brief moment at the top of the Zhilaan Forest.

Before Yvan takes up the mantle of the prophesied Icaral, and we all go to war.

SHADOW CLAWS

Fallon Bane

Shadow wasteland west of Noilaan

Fallon Bane watches as the Eastern Realm's distant storm band barrels toward her and Marcus Vogel. Barbed frost ices through her lines along with an infuriating confusion, her hair increasingly blown back by the mammoth storm band's mounting winds, thunder booming through it as it rapidly traverses the Central Continent's Shadowed land.

Marcus has portaled just the two of them here, their joint power formidable, to be sure, but not able to strike down this incoming storm band without seriously weakening them both.

She turns to Marcus Vogel to find him watching the incoming chaos with unnerving calm and even more unnerving inaction, the Magedom's Shadow storm bands lining the horizon to their backs instead of moving *before them*, where they *should be*, ready to smash into the East's attack and siphon up all that elemental *power.*

"Why are you not sending our storm bands forward?" Fallon demands of Vogel, the incoming storm band's bursts of blue and white lightning flashing over the planes of his green-glimmering face.

In answer, Vogel turns, sets his silver-fire-rimmed eyes on hers and smiles.

Fallon can't suppress her shiver of excitement—it's the most predatory smile she's ever seen. Every nerve in her body grows deliciously cold as Vogel turns back toward the incoming storm band then inexplicably strides toward it without a trace of intimidation, Shadow Wand in hand.

Both confused and aroused, Fallon watches as Vogel halts, thrusts his Wand forward, then lifts it in a strong arc, as if summoning something from the Shadow-smoking ground.

Huge storm spiders suddenly burst up from the sand in a line as long as the attacking storm band, their thoraxes marked with Shadow runes. As one, the spiders dig their legs into the earth to keep from being blown back by the storm band's increasingly violent wind as they face it down. Then they still.

Fallon's confusion ices back to life as the storm band rises like a tidal wave, the wind growing so fierce that she has to lean into it to remain upright.

What is Marcus playing at? she rages. *Storm spiders aren't powerful enough to keep this storm band from crashing through their defensive line and straight into us.*

As if hearing her internal protest, Vogel shoots her a sly look over his shoulder before angling his Wand downward and blasting a thin bolt of Shadow into the distant ground.

"Rise!" he commands, and the Shadow fans into a circle of gray, pooling mist.

Fallon's eyes widen as huge, pale gray horns appear in the misty circle, followed by an egg-flat face, nothing on it but a slash of open mouth holding row upon row of sharp, gnashing teeth. A slim Shadow tether extends from Vogel's Wand to the huge thing's neck, like a smoking leash.

The V'yexwraith, Fallon realizes, eyes wide—the Shadow Wand's corporeal form that her brother, Damion, described to her in vivid detail.

The V'yexwraith's slender body continues to rise, pale gray spikes flowing back from its shoulders and the edges of its form. Bubbles appear on the creature's flat face and morph into one Shadow eye after another until there's a whole teeming mass of them. The beast is now taller than the Valgard Cathedral, a mist of silvery Shadow power haloing its frame.

The creature barely sways, impressively strong against the incoming storm band barreling toward its back. Fallon's fingers twitch around her wand, her pulse ratcheting into a faster rhythm as she bites back a howl of alarm.

"Tether and consume!" Vogel roars, silencing Fallon's burgeoning protest as he thrusts the Wand toward the demon.

The V'yexwraith rounds on the storm band. It lets out a shriek that spikes pain through Fallon's ears, then throws out its slender arms and flicks its long, pale fingers toward the storm spiders at its sides.

Multiple lines of Shadow spear from the V'yexwraith's fingertips and collide with the spiders, tethering them to the demon like insectile marionettes as the storm band darkens the sky, its western facing wall only paces away.

The V'yexwraith demon thrusts its palms toward the approaching storm band and lets out another ear-splicing shriek.

The roaring, lightning-spitting storm band stills before the V'yexwraith, its winds pulling into its center. The storm spiders click into a forward-leaning stance, raising their huge thoraxes toward the wall of storm.

Fallon sucks in a harsh breath of surprise as lightning-flashing columns of storm fly toward the spiders and are sucked into their forms, the blue-and-white lightning morphing to steel black just before it's consumed.

The V'yexwraith lets out another ground-shuddering shriek and opens its mouth unnaturally wide, row upon row of teeth telescoping outward.

A larger column of storm flies from the storm band and bolts into the V'yexwraith's most extended maw.

The giant demon lets out a screeching *ATCH ATCH ATCH* as both it and the spiders eat the East's storm band, siphoning up its power.

Fallon watches, every nerve lit up, as Vogel maintains his hold on the leashed demon, steely lightning crackling through the beast's tether to Vogel as the storm band's energy is drawn right into Marcus via his Shadow Wand. Marcus briefly glances back at her, his eyes filling with spitting gray lightning.

As he's transformed into a living Mage storm.

Electricity crackling off him, he holds up his Shadow Wand, the Wand of Power encircled by a spiral of gray storm, threads of dark, curving lightning flashing through it.

Fallon can't suppress her smug smile.

The East is finished.

And so is Elloren Gardner Grey and her Icaral demon.

Vogel snaps his fingers, and his Shadow tethers to the V'yexwraith and spiders snap out of view, but Fallon imagines the bindings are still very much there. Vogel lowers his lightning-flashing Wand and sheathes it as the demon and storm spiders turn toward him as if waiting for direction.

Smiling, Vogel meets Fallon's awed gaze once more.

A shock of want races through her power. She's suddenly unsteady on her feet, overcome by the ferocious desire to throw ice power through his fireline to find out if it triggers the achingly pleasurable rush of hot steam that she's felt only once before—when she kissed Lukas Grey.

But Vogel's Shadow fire and storm . . .

The entire East's power is *nothing* in the face of it.

Lukas's power was *nothing* in the face of it.

"Come with me, my Black Witch," Vogel croons, that spine-tingling static practically leaping off his skin. "It's time to fully join."

Breathless, Fallon bares her teeth at him in a vicious, excited smile because she can guess what he's alluding to.

A fasting and Sealing to each other.

Vogel gestures toward the multi-eyed, multilegged dragon that flew them through the portal, the Shadow beast standing several paces away. Fallon eagerly strides toward it and mounts the beast before Vogel lithely slides in behind her, his body enthrallingly hot against her chilly frame. Vogel hisses out a command, and they take to the skies, soaring toward the Shadow portal that will speed them back to the Magedom's Central Desert military base.

Toward her true and rightful destiny.

Reveling in her incoming position of power, Fallon strides beside Vogel through the Magedom's sprawling military base that used to be Issaan's capitol. Gray Shadow skies churn overhead, everything stripped of color save for the Magedom's shimmering green hue.

Erthia's ruling hue.

Hot static courses from Vogel's lines to batter against Fallon's aura of icy wind, their magic crackling against each other's in the most exciting way possible. Vogel has come away from his consumption of the East's storm band with a breathtaking level of power, and Fallon is beyond ready to merge with all that power through a Shadowed fasting spell that will tether his lines to hers.

Her excitement surges as she realizes Vogel is headed in the direction of the base's newly constructed Church of the First Children. White-bearded Priest Sedric stands in the church's huge, arching doorway, grayed trees devoid of life set into the entrance's bracketing walls.

"Shall I accompany you, Excellency?" Priest Sedric inquires of Vogel, a hopeful look in the priest's eyes as they flick toward Fallon, a grayed wand clutched in his hand.

Fallon's smug smile broadens. It's clear the priest is eager to be the one to fast them. But Vogel doesn't answer him. Instead, he swipes his hand sideward in a gesture of succinct dismissal. Dipping his head, Priest Sedric deferentially opens the door, and Vogel strides through it.

Fallon follows, confusion twisting to brutal life inside her as the church's door shuts behind them, her outrage rising.

She wants a fasting, and she wants it *now*. *She's* the Magedom's Black Witch—its true Black Witch all along—and she deserves access to Marcus's full, unbridled *storm*. Which will cement her status as the most powerful Black Witch the Magedom has ever seen.

So why is she following Vogel like a dog brought to heel?

Her resentment mounts as she trails him through the dead-tree-bracketed interior of the church then into a back corridor, Vogel dismissing the few soldiers stationed there as they pass.

Fallon has to bite back her snarl of protest as they descend into the church's lower levels via a spiraling staircase cut into grayed stone and Vogel opens the door to a former wine cellar, the heathen spirits removed and likely smashed to pieces, only empty shelves cut into rock remaining.

Fallon's anger breaks loose, brittle hoarfrost coating the room as Vogel shuts the door, throws the lock and faces her down. His pale green eyes are rimmed with silvery fire that quickly deepens, igniting to darker flame, a blast of his heat pulsing toward her.

Fallon gasps at the sensation, all her hoarfrost instantly melting, Vogel's radiating aura of heat forcing so much steam through her lines that her angered protest singes away in her throat.

"I thought you sought a fasting," she demands, dizzy from his fiery draw, but angling to regain a position of strength with him.

And wanting him more than she's ever wanted anyone.

Smoothly, Marcus closes the distance between them, slides a hand around her waist and draws her against him. Fallon's pulse quickens as he brings his mouth toward the base of her neck, a more wanton desire shivering through her. His mouth is so thrillingly hot against her skin, his body radiating heat straight through his silken uniform.

An incredible amount of heat.

"Do you want a full binding to me?" Vogel croons, his hot lips tracing her skin.

Fallon's skin prickles against his touch, hunger igniting low in her body, everything in her ready for a full fasting to him . . . and more.

Ready for a full *Sealing*.

"Fast to me, Marcus, and *Seal* it," she growls, ready to feel him unleashed.

Ready to feel his full storm inside her.

So she can wrest hold of it.

"My Black Witch," he croons as he runs his tongue along the nape of her neck in such a shockingly serpentine motion, an excited tremor tingles through her. "I want your ice," Vogel murmurs, and she can *hear* that bite of want in his tone. "I want your purifying *storm*."

"It's yours, Marcus," she breathes.

He draws back slightly, the side of his mouth curling into an enticing smile as he holds out his free hand. "Give me your hands."

An icy thrill coursing through her, Fallon places both her hands in his, and Vogel's fingers close around them. In one deft movement, he presses his Shadow Wand to her skin and murmurs the fasting and Sealing spells.

Fallon draws in a tremulous breath as steel gray lines tendril out from Vogel's Wand and loop around their hands, the lines undulating, then pulling in to fuse with their skin in an identical gray smoking pattern.

Vogel's power winds around her lines in a warm rush before seizing tight hold of them in a shock of burning heat.

Before she can protest, Vogel brings his mouth to hers with bruising force.

Fallon gasps against the kiss as a more painful blast of fire shocks down her throat and sears through every line, her body trembling against Vogel's as the sudden bite of claws pierces through her tunic at the same moment that unnaturally sharp teeth slice into her lips.

Her shocked fury turns seismic.

Yanking her bloodied lips from his, she lurches back, just as a tearing sound rips through the air. Pieces of Vogel's shredded tunic flutter to the ground, and she freezes in horror as she finds Vogel before her, terrifyingly transformed.

Her whole world tilting into chaos, she reaches for her wand at the same moment that Vogel flicks his Shadow Wand toward her.

Fallon cries out as bindings snare tight around her wrists, ankles, and wand, the wand yanked away and her arms pulled behind her back and bound, her ankles tethered to the floor.

She meets Vogel's merciless stare, feeling as if the ground is giving way beneath her.

"Release me," she demands in a quavering voice, realizing, even as she makes the demand, that it's over. It's all over. "Release me, or I'll tell the entire Magedom what you are."

Vogel smiles. "You'll tell them what I want you to tell them." His smile morphs into a burning look of hunger as his gray-fire eyes rake over her form. "And your ice will be my salvation."

Fallon screams as he lunges toward her, his mouth clamping down on the base of her neck. She cries out as teeth bite through her skin, Shadowfire races through her lines . . . and the whole world turns gray.

CHAPTER SEVEN

DRYAD'KHIN ARMY

Elloren Guryev

Zhilaan Forest Vu Trin military base

"Vogel has absorbed the storm band the Eastern forces sent against him," Vothe's father, Hizar'drile, grimly informs us. His lightning-limned onyx face is stern, his black Noi Fire Hawk kindred perched on his shoulder. "We just received word of this from our most elite unit of Wyvern-shifters, who followed the East's storm band west."

Troubled murmurs rise amongst our Dryad'khin, all of us assembled on the Zhilaan Forest military base's huge terrace. It's built into the apex of the spiky mountain it sits on, a panoramic twilight view of the Nightwood Pine Forest surrounding us, knots of multicolored deciduous trees scattered throughout its expanse. Torches set on black metal stands spit white lightning, the East's storms a distant roar against Valasca and the Zhilaan Forest's shielding of the country of Zhilaan.

Hizar'drile, Sylvan, Yulan, Oaklyyn, and Alder are grouped in the center of a curved obsidian command table, Iris beside Sylvan, and Raz'zor in his pale human form by Oaklyyn's side, their invisible power blazing around each other. Multiple high-ranking Vu Trin Dryad'khin soldiers, including Vang Troi and Ung Li, bracket the group.

Yvan and I are seated beside each other at one end of the table, a large crowd of our Dryad'khin forces massed on the expansive terrace before us. Yvan's restless energy mirrors my own, his fingers interlaced with mine under the table's stone edge, our invisible fire powers embracing with a mounting fervor that has us palpably fighting off the wild urge to take tighter hold of each other.

I can still feel the hot brand of Yvan's kiss in the Zhilaan Forest's canopy. The tingle of his tongue's hungered motion lingers on my own, like a scorching tether set down between us. The Zhilaan Forest's fiery energy encircles us both in a warm rush, as if the Forest itself is drawing us together.

"Our combined magic will never be stronger than it will be in two days' time," Sylvan warns, expression severe, his link to some unknown kindred reestablished, like an invisible elemental cord I can track toward a spot deep in the Zhilaan Forest. "Peak foliage will be *here*," Sylvan stresses, glancing toward a large section of decidous trees, their mosaic of color evident even in twilight's deep blue dimness.

"After the color falls," Yulan chimes in, "our magic will rapidly slide into dormancy. After which, the Magedom will likely sweep into the Unbalanced East with their Shadow winter, blast down our last remaining shields, and overtake the rest of Erthia."

Yvan's fire rears. "So we deploy against the Magedom before it comes to that," he charges, molten steel in his tone.

Yvan meets my gaze in a look of ardent alliance, sparks igniting through our bond with such force that my thoughts scatter, the Forest's fire aura coursing around us intensifying, enhancing our pull to each other, as if our claiming each other as full mates holds some vital importance to the trees themselves, both Yvan's gaze and mine drawn in question toward the surrounding Nightwood Pines.

I'm suddenly overly aware of the strength of Yvan's grip, the feel of his warm wrist and forearm pressed against mine, the sustained contact sending a swirling blaze of heat through my body that's so fervid I don't dare look at him again, and he makes no move to look at me, eye contact having triggered too much *want*.

When we need to be focused on the battle at hand—our coming war with the Magedom.

And Yvan's prophesied battle with the Black Witch.

Fear for Yvan is suddenly lancing through me, and I have to stamp it back. The possibility of never having an extended chance to build a life with Yvan . . . it's almost too much to bear. And I can tell, by the way his grip is firming around mine, that we're both stamping down that fear while fiercely holding on to our love for each other.

Both of us ready to fight.

"The way Vogel gained power from our storm band is of dire concern," Vang Troi warns. "He siphoned it into an army of storm spiders and a creature we've encountered only in myth. A primordial V'yexwraith demon."

Rivyr'el and others let out sounds of shock, and I blink at Vang Troi, a hard dart of fear jabbing into me. I've read about this demon in Jules Kristian's books on religious lore. I glance toward the table's other end, where Jules and Lucretia are seated, and meet Jules's gaze, the dire light in his brown eyes mirrored by both Lucretia and the silver kestrel perched on Jules's shoulder.

"I never imagined that demon could be real," Rivyr'el blurts out, his prismatic eyes two beacons of dread. "When it comes into its full power, its horror is world-ending. It was last seen during the ancient Elfin Wars."

"The V'yexwraith was the most feared demon-weapon of the Elfin Conflict," Jules grimly interjects. "The Alfsigr religious texts speak about it as a vicious parasite, able to consume limitless amounts of elemental power and transform it into Shadow might. It is said to be an actual physical manifestion of the Shadow Wand-Stylus."

More dread-filled murmuring rises as my thoughts spin.

"Does the Verdyllion Wand-Stylus have a manifestation?" I ask.

Everyone quiets as we all look to the Dryads.

"A tree," Yulan quietly states.

An explosion of protest breaks out.

"It's not enough!" the Noi soldier Hee Muur cries.

"How can a tree stand against a world-consuming demon?" my uncle Wrenfir exclaims, and I curse, for maybe the hundredth time, the East's foolish decision to send out their storm band despite our strident warning. I look toward Sylvan, Oaklyyn, Yulan, and Alder. They're a single silent unit, Sylvan's gaze fixed with piercing gravity on us all, our alliance too little, too late.

Hizar'drile turns to the Dryads, remorse writ deep in his night-dark features. "You were right about everything," he admits. He moves his lightning-flashing gaze over us all. "Who here agrees it's time for us to follow the Dryad Fae as our leaders in this fight?"

Sylvan spits out a disgusted sound, and Iris gives him a tortured look, her invisible fire whipping around him, a mournful expression overtaking Yulan's deep-green features.

"You seek to follow us?" Oaklyyn snarls, her gaze a lance. "Then follow *them*." She slashes a finger toward the Zhilaan Forest's cloud-high canopy. "Place them above *everything*. Cede *not one more inch of Forest*."

The Forest's agreement rumbles through my rootlines—through all our rootlines—in a bone-deep rush, and Raz'zor growls his support, red fire burning in his eyes, his aura lashing protectively around Oaklyyn.

"There is one heartening development," Vang Troi informs us. "The Water Fae Tierney Calix and the geomancer Mage Or'myr Syllvir have managed to reshield the Vo River and its bracketing Forest."

Renewed sounds of surprise break out as Yvan and I dare one quick look at each other.

Both Vang Troi and the Noi Fire Hawk kindred perched on her shoulder narrow their violet and midnight gazes on me. "It seems your geomancer cousin has been quite active," Vang Troi comments, a sly edge to her tone. "We've received word that Mage unity is breaking down in Gardneria. A new Resistance has sprung up with the purple Xishlon moon as its symbol. All thanks to Or'myr Syll'vir."

More murmurs of surprise.

"It seems Or'myr fought Vogel's V'yexwraith when the demon's power was fledgling," Vang Troi continues. "He marked the beast with a Xishlon moon before the creature was drawn back west through some type of Shadow tether. Apparently, the moon marking was embedded with concentrated geomancy spells that partially detonated before Vogel could destroy them all."

"What did they do?" Diana demands.

Vang Troi's shrewd gaze swings to my Lupine sister, Rafe beside her. "They caused suspended purple moons to appear in the sky all over the Western Realm. Including one large moon suspended straight over Valgard."

A shocked laugh bursts from Rivyr'el, stunned looks traded all around.

Vang Troi's expression hardens. "Vogel's rapid destruction of the Forests of the West has thrown the Natural World there into dangerous disarray. The already stormy autumn weather of the West has been whipped into constant tempests, causing increasing numbers of Mage farmers and fishermen to sour on Vogel. A group of fishermen went so far as to lodge a protest against the Shadow sea weapon Vogel created, which had the unfortunate side effect of poisoning and disfiguring huge numbers of fish."

"Vogel will kill anyone who dissents," Queen Freyja Zyrr points out.

"He has," Hizar'drile affirms. "Which is why the protests have taken a stealthy turn. Not only have dissenting Mages taken up Or'myr Syll'vir's purple moon as their symbol of Resistance, but they've also adopted the forbidden color purple itself as a sign of rebellion. Paintings of Xishlon moons have begun to turn up on Gardnerian buildings and on the street's cobblestones, and purple ribbons have been tied around doorknobs on Mage Council and military buildings."

"It's infuriating Vogel," Vang Troi adds. "He's made the possession of anything purple or bearing the image of a moon punishable by death."

"I hate to rain on your Resistance parade," Mavrik interjects from where he and Gwynnifer sit beside Jules and Lucretia. Mavrik holds up his fastmarked hand. "As Vogel's Shadow power increases, he'll gain the ability to tether more and more of the Magedom to himself via their fasting spells. Including *everyone* in this purple Resistance as well as the whole of Alfsigroth via their Zalyn'or necklaces."

Wrenfir huffs out a sound of blistering frustration as he glares at us all. "Vogel has access to primordial demonic magic that we don't have a good understanding of. He's always one step ahead. Who knows what other horrors he's accessing with that Shadow Wand of his."

"The question is," Ra'Ven adds, "how do we access that knowledge, as well?"

"We have a way," a masculine voice calls from beyond the Dryad'khin massed before us.

We all turn, unsettled sounds rising as the thick crowd parts and four figures stride toward us.

Astonishment shocks through Yvan and my Wyvernbond as I blink at them, not quite believing my eyes.

The lead figure is a slender Mage about the age of my uncle Wrenfir. He's clearly joined with the Forest, his ears pointed, his green hue deepened and heightened, a streak of violet through his short black hair . . . and there are *gills* on the sides of his neck. He's dressed in purple leaf armor and is holding hands with a Selkie woman garbed in the same purple Dryad'khin leaf armor. The Selkie's dark blue feet are bare, her long, silver tresses violet streaked, a silver sealskin wrapped around her shoulders.

And behind them stride Gareth Keeler and Marina the Selkie.

A sound of surprise bursts from my throat as a sense of Marina's prismatic light and water auras, that flash every color on Erthia, shimmer through my vision. The image of the Verdyllion Wand-Stylus pulses through my mind as my power empathy picks up a new Dryad line of light power inside both her and the other Selkie.

Gareth's and Marina's hands are tightly clasped, Gareth's powerful water aura swirling around her. A small octopus is looped over Marina's shoulders, its hide flashing every bright color, water magicked into being around the tentacled kindred. My Dryad'kin senses identify purple mangrove roots sheathed at both their sides, Marina's silver sealskin secured around her shoulders, both of them garbed in purple leaf armor.

There's a shock of dark purple through Gareth's black hair, its silver streaks now blazingly prominent, gills marked on the sides of his neck, as well. His ears have gained subtle points, and streaks of violet decorate Marina's waterfalling silver tresses.

"*Gareth . . . Marina . . .*" The words escape my lips as Yvan and I both rise, along with my brothers, Ariel, Valasca, Ni Vin, Andras, Alder, Queen Freyja, and my other Dryad'khin family, friends and allies who worked to liberate the Selkies what feels like a lifetime ago.

Marina's and Gareth's eyes light up with looks of deep emotion and even deeper alliance as they draw up beside the other Mage and Selkie couple and take in our equally Forest-altered appearances.

"I'm Alaric Fynnes," the Mage with them announces as he holds up his palm, marked with III's image. "I'm a former priest-apprentice to Marcus Vogel. We've been led here, by the power in the center of all Erthia's faiths, to bring you knowledge that can help you fight the Shadow Wand."

CHAPTER EIGHT

THE CENTER

Elloren Guryev

Zhilaan Forest military base

Gareth and Marina, then Alaric and the Selkie Nerissa tell us their extraordinary tales.

How, through Gareth's joining with the mangrove forests of the Southeast and their power-joining as Selkie mates, they drove off an invasion of Vogel's Shadow sea and cast warded protection over the northern Salish Ocean and southernmost Vo River, then convinced an invading army of Selkies and other Ocean'kin to align as allies against Vogel's forces.

"We've held our protection over the Vo and the Salish," Gareth tells us all, "even as Vogel kept hold of his Shadow net imprisoning us under our own protective dome." The lightning torchlight's illumination flickers over Gareth's face and hair, night closing in on the military base's mountaintop terrace. "And trapped there," Gareth continues, "in the Shadow's darkness, we pled with everyone, Noi'khin and Ocean'kin alike, to align with each other and join with the mangrove forests of the South. At the time of our leaving, many had."

A prickle sweeps over my skin, Yvan's echoing rise of emotion sending a juddering flare of heat through our bond. Because it feels like we're riding right up to the edge of sweeping, transformational change throughout Erthia, with the growing Shadow power increasingly able to blot it all out before it can truly take root.

"Birds of light beckoned us here . . . in dreams," Marina haltingly conveys, gills flaring, her ocean eyes holding an emphatic light. "You know them as Watchers and Ahxhils, and by other names. We Selkies know them as the Blessed Winged of Light, kindreds of our Ocean Goddess. Gareth's Storm Whale kindreds managed to punch a small hole in Vogel's Shadow net that allowed us quick passage through our Southern Voloi shielding, along with Zephyr Quillen . . ."

Fain Quillen and his sister, Lucretia, bolt to their feet. "You were with Zephyr?" Fain calls out, both Fain's power and Lucretia's cast into tempestuous whorls at the mention of their adopted daughter.

Marina nods, gills ruffling. "It was Zephyr and an Asrai Fae named Fyordin Lir who helped us requisition a Vu Trin portal to travel here while they stayed behind to help hold Southern Voloi's shielding. And now, before you we stand. To join our knowledge and power to yours."

"We were almost apprehended by Vu Trin," Gareth interjects. "There was no convincing them of the Ocean Peoples' newfound desire for an alliance with the East, since the Ocean People initially came here as an invading force."

"But are now starting to realize there is only one true enemy of us all," Alaric firmly states. "The Shadow."

Alaric launches into his story—how as a Mage priest-apprentice, several years past, he was there when Vogel first found the Shadow Wand after a treacherous, kraken-infested sea journey to the Lost Continent of the West.

"A Death Fae who had lived through a Reckoning there tried to warn us what the Shadow power had done to the Lost Continent," Alaric conveys, a haunted look in his green eyes. "After the Shadow consumed everything, there was nothing left alive save that single Death Fae, who did not need food and water to survive."

Alaric describes how Vogel sensed his trepidation over Vogel's possession of the Shadow Wand and promptly hurled Alaric overboard to die. Instead, Alaric was rescued by the Selkie here with him now, her translated name, Nerissa, meaning "of the Sea."

"Nerissa brought me to a small island," Alaric reveals, casting her a poignant look. "She helped me forage for food along the coast and brought me fish. We communicated via the sign language known to ocean dwellers and mariners alike and told each other the story of our lives." His invisible aura of light magery intensifies, its sunset hues swirling around Nerissa's deep-blue, silver-haired form and answered by her own water aura and, surprisingly, a slim line of light power flashing from Nerissa to embrace Alaric's form.

"We were . . . drawn to each other . . . from the start," Nerissa states, her gills flaring as she speaks, the column of her neck tensing, the effort needed to make air speech clearly formidable. "We could not fight . . . the pull," she admits, her blue hand sliding over Alaric's green one, their fingers interlacing as his light aura shimmers more intensely around her, a sympathetic heat crackling through my bond with Yvan. "Even though my people rejected Alaric as a 'land devil,'" Nerissa says, "and I knew his people considered my Selkie'kin dangerous animals to be abused or disposed of, we felt an instantaneous kinship."

"I told Nerissa of my upbringing in Valgard," Alaric says. "How sheltered I was. Kept from every other group on Erthia save my family's strict Styvian sect. How I'd been taught to hate everyone who wasn't Styvian. And Nerissa told me of her rich, happy upbringing on the Western Ocean's floor."

Nerissa continues their story, conveying how one night, under a rose-blush sunset, their lips first met. And then on another night, not long after, how more than their lips touched under the ocean's warm current. In the way of Selkie'kin, their powers *merged*, shocking them both, Alaric gaining gills and the ability to breathe underwater and Nerissa gaining a connection to Alaric's Level Five light magery, which granted her numerous new ocean abilities, such as the ability to color-shift like octopi and draw on the electric power of moray eels.

"We decided to approach my people to seek acceptance as both mates and Selkie'khin," Nerissa continues. "And to warn them of the Shadow Wand. We traveled together to my city on the ocean's floor, only to be met with revulsion and damnation from our Naiad priestesses." A look of pain tenses Nerissa's features. "I was cast out and shunned." She glances at Alaric. "And all the while, there was always this terrible knowledge hanging over us that Vogel and the Mages would use the Shadow Wand to do to the Waters what they did to the Lost Continent, its coastline Shadow-poisoned beyond repair."

"We journeyed back to the Lost Continent," Alaric says. "And tracked down the slain Death Fae's journals to read the entire story of what happened there. And now, we come to you with the weapon of that Death Fae's knowledge." He glances around at us all, his green eyes weighted with urgency. "The Shadow Wand is adept at unearthing fracture points in societies so it can parasitically *feed* on that division." A sly light enters his gaze. "But it has its weaknesses and can be fought."

"How?" Vang Troi presses. "Its magic is primordial. Predating all our grimoires."

Alaric's shrewd gaze slides to her. "You have primordial texts at your fingertips, as well. Your religions."

Discord erupts, and I feel Yvan stiffen beside me. I'm suddenly on edge, too, remembering our heated debates about religious faiths.

"Religion is an agent of *fracture*," Yvan levels.

"I agree," Wrenfir scathingly chimes in. "Vogel tracked down the Shadow Wand to use against every other group on Erthia because of *religion*." My uncle slices his hand emphatically across the air. "All these competing faiths are the greatest scourge Erthia has ever known."

"They can be," Alaric agrees, nodding. "When their flawed edges are worshipped instead of the true things at their center. But, if you look to that center, you'll find power there, and tools to help you defeat the Shadow Wand. But you must bring all your faiths *together*."

Wrenfir spits out an incredulous laugh. "Erthia has *never* been able to do that."

"Erthia has never been staring down the imminent destruction of the Natural World," Alaric counters. "The paths of division have landed us *here*. On the precipice of the Shadow overrunning *everything*, the Natural World ready to collapse around us. Pool your faiths. Pool your cultures and their strengths. Keeping them separate and shutting each other out is *not working*. You'll have runic border walls for your final monuments."

"The Shadow is at our doorstep," Gareth agrees. "The Natural World is about to irrevocably *fall*."

The Dryads are silent beside us, as if waiting for us to come to our senses, urgency coursing through their magic, the acute awareness inescapable—they're one of the only groups who consistently, throughout Erthia's history, put the Natural World first. But then, I remember that the Dryads were also a group that drove the Mages away from the Forest when my people begged them for help in the face of cruelty and oppression, my people longing for both Forest linkage and refuge.

I realize we all shoulder some of the blame for what's come to pass on Erthia. Some so much more than others, but it doesn't change the fact that we have to forge a new path forward.

Together.

With the Forest.

"The Great Source Tree appears in every one of your faiths," Alaric says, holding up his III-marked palm. "Along with stories of messenger birds made of starlight. And everyone has stories of the sacred Verdyllion Wand-Stylus. And the Shadow Wand-Stylus. *Use* those common threads as your central rallying point. Then mine each other's faiths and cultures for *every primordial weapon* you can use to bring the

Shadow down. It's *all there*." He levels a grim stare at us all. "Or remain separate and divided. And *fall*."

"The Errilor Ravens spoken about in *The Book of the Ancients*," I tell Alaric, an ache constricting my heart over Errilith and my other ravens' noble sacrifice. "They came to me, and have drawn themselves into Nature to try and hold off a Reckoning."

"My Saffron Eagles," Alder puts forth, glancing toward the flock of orange birds perched all around us, "they're known as the Goddess's Fire Eagles in Issani myths, harbingers that the Shadow Times are at hand."

"The V'yexwraith demon shows up in Alfsigr religious lore," Rivyr'el adds. "I thought it was simply a mythical monster. But here we are, faced with it."

"And Ironflowers," I say, my mind whirling with everything I've read in the mythology and religious texts Professor Jules Kristian gave to me to read, as well as the religious myths I grew up hearing. "They're used in *The Book of the Ancients* as a tool to fight the demonic."

Jules nods thoughtfully. "Both Keltish and Mage religious myths include their use in fighting back primordial Shadow power."

"Back in Verpacia," I say, "Tierney Calix and I used the concentrated essence of Ironflowers to block Mage spells. Perhaps they can block much more than that."

"I can manifest Ironflowers," Yulan tells us. She snaps her fingers, and the flowers on her head morph to tresses of thick, glowing blue Ironflowers. "I can manifest them in large numbers."

"I am a professor of theology at Noilaan's Voshir University," Fain Quillen's partner, the Wyvern-shifter Sholindrile, says from where he stands beside Fain. "I have studied the many faiths and myths of Erthia. Read all the major holy books and mythological texts. The Shadow Wand-Stylus is a parasitical force in *all* of them and employs a branching Shadow net that consumes the elemental power of everything it binds to, eventually drawing it *all* into its Void."

"Vogel will link that Shadow net to every Mage fasting spell and Alfsigr Zalyn'or necklace," Mavrik cuts in, warning blazing in both his and Gwynn's eyes. "He almost took control of Gwynn and me through our former fastlines. He's tethered to most Mage and Alfsigr soldiers and increasing numbers of civilians. He'll soon control all of them."

A dread-filled silence descends.

"Your twinned magic is a formidable weapon," Alaric says, breaking the quiet, a calculating glint in his eyes. "There's a possibility that if you get hold of both the Verdyllion and the Shadow Wand, as well as enough prismatic light power, you can use your twinned power to take over Vogel's Shadow network. You might then be able to divert everyone's fastings and Zalyn'or spell-linkages to join them to the Forest instead of the Shadow, so that the Mages and the Alfsigr can hear the Forest out, en masse, as we all have done."

Alaric's words are like the detonation of a runic explosive. Intense conversation rises, the path forward suddenly clear, the surrounding Forest's palpable rise in energy emboldening our joint Dryad'khin aura of purpose and power.

"The Smaragdalfar religion speaks of what Alaric has conveyed," Sholindrile says, lightning leaping through his eyes. "The ability of multihued light power to overtake Shadow."

"Mavrik and I can track the Verdyllion," Gwynn offers, "then connect every shred of our shared light power to it. I've seen visions of this path forward."

Yvan's eyes meet mine, our fire bond searing through us, and I know, as much as he mistrusts religion and all its lore, there's a spark of agreement in his eyes that this bold plan to use the Verdyllion to link *everyone* to the Forest may be the only hope for Erthia.

"It will be nearly impossible to bring Noilaan's Vo Conclave to the Forest," Ung Li puts forth, a scowl twisting the former Wyvernguard commander's mouth. "My people have fallen into religious rigidity. They're clinging to stories about the Great Ending Times when the Goddess Vo will swoop down on a broken world and set everything right."

Both Jules and Sholindrile nod at this. "Most faiths teach the same thing," Jules offers. "The Gardnerians have their Reaping Times."

"The Amaz have the Goddess's Time of Reckoning," Alder grimly adds.

"Perhaps," Sholindrile quietly puts forth, "these 'end times' stories are imperfect metaphors for this very time we're living in."

Wrenfir spits out a sound of disgust and glares at Sholindrile, my uncle's power burning white-hot. "So, we're supposed to sit around and wait to be saved by some god or goddess," he snaps, "while the entirety of Erthia falls apart and the Death Fae are pulled straight into the Reckoning they've risked their lives to *stave off*?"

"No," Sholindrile calmly counters. "I believe these stories are misread. I think they are about an inevitable worldwide crisis that will force us all to choose between radical unity or radical fracture. And that time is upon us."

Wrenfir bares his teeth at Sholin in a mocking smile. "If you're going to find weapons against the Shadow in your faiths, do it *quickly*. The Death Fae saw what was coming better than anything in your religious texts did. They are holding off nature's *vengeance*." A look of pain slashes through my uncle's spider-marked features. "Hazel warned me, again and again—we're *running out of time*."

"What of the Great Prophecy?" one of our new Zhilon'ile Dryad'khin calls out, murmurs of agreement rising around him.

Tension flares hot through Yvan's and my Wyvernbond as his mother's invisible fire explodes into being to lash protectively around him. I glance toward Soleiya, her fiery eyes streaked with pain.

Yvan sends out a tendril of consoling fire to embrace his mother before he looks pointedly at Alder, his jaw set tight. "You hold the clearest reading from the Forest."

Tension tightens Alder's forest green features as she nods and rises. "I am Alder Xanthos," she greets everyone in that timber-steady voice of hers. "I am a Dryad'kin Seer and have been gifted with scrying abilities from multiple lines of lineage. The Prophecy is still embedded in the trees. A battle that determines the future of Erthia is still foretold." She meets Yvan's gaze once more, her expression unwaveringly intense. "The Great Icaral against the Black Witch—Fallon Bane."

My heart constricts as Yvan rises, his invisible fire flowing out to keep tight hold of me. "I'm ready to fight for you all," he states, violet flame crackling in his eyes.

I can barely pull in a breath, every muscle taut.

"You will not fight alone, Wyvern'kin," Naga vows, rising along with Ariel, Raz'zor, and the rest of our horde, the power of the Forest's last stand rising with them. "You will fight this battle alongside an army of your Dryad'khin and with our horde's full fire."

Yvan nods and sends out a bolt of invisible fire to them all.

"We go to war in two days' time," Sylvan states, "when foliage power reaches its peak and our joint power will be strongest." He narrows his gaze on Hizar'drile and Vang Troi. "Charge a sky portal to bring us West toward the location of the Verdyllion. And send Dryad'khin envoys to Noilaan and the entirety of Zhilaan to bring as many people as possible to the Forest as quickly as you can. If you're able, send envoys to *both sides* of Noilaan's runic border wall and to the Sublands below. And send word to Or'myr Syll'vir and Tierney Calix to *hold the Vo*."

"In the meantime," Vang Troi puts forth, "we need to gather everyone here who holds an in-depth understanding of Erthia's faiths and mythologies to aid us in developing a plan of magical attack so we can get hold of the Shadow and Verdyllion Wands of Power." She pointedly looks at Oaklyyn and me, Mavrik and Gwynn, Ra'Ven and Sage and Rivyr'el and others. "Those with powerful sorcery need to runically amplify the power of every weapon and place iron wards on every susceptible Dryad'khin."

We all voice assent before Hizar'drile's gaze zeroes in on Yvan. "We deploy the evening after next. As your army, Yvan Guryev. To aid you in bringing down the Magedom's Black Witch." He turns to the Dryads, lightning streaking through his eyes. "And then, we fight as the Forest's own army. To get hold of both the Verdyllion and Vogel's Wand, and take back all of Erthia from the Shadow."

Emphatic cries of approval rise, the Zhilaan Forest's martial energy flooding through us all, the Dryads' collective power joining the magical surge, my throat cinching tight as I struggle against my surging fear of losing Yvan.

"Elloren," Yvan says, his hand finding my shoulder.

I look up at him, his gaze locking hold of mine, blazing resolve in it. And love. A love for me that has defied all the odds stacked against us. A love so heatedly potent it fuels the rise of my own defiant love for him, a sudden yearning crackling through the air between us.

My heart in my throat, I stand and press my hand to his chest, right over his strong heartbeat, and he folds his hand protectively over mine. Blinking against the rising sting of emotion in my eyes, I hold his scorching stare, no words sufficing. We've been on a collision course since we first met at Verpax University, his love, once he fell into it, like a fixed, burning star.

Yvan's fire aura breaks loose to brush against my lips in an impassioned kiss and I give in to the bond-pull as well, my fire flowing unreservedly around his, the whole world momentarily fading save for his heat on my mouth and the molten pillar of Wyvernfire connecting his heart to mine.

CHAPTER NINE

WYVERN FIREKISS

Elloren Guryev

Zhilaan Forest military base

An incandescent flash of heat pulses through me, sparks searing across my vision as, several hours later, I catch Yvan's eye across the Zhilaan base's lightning-torch-lit terrace, his heat now tracing my mouth in an almost constant kiss.

Our bond's pull no longer something either one of us wants to restrain in any way.

Open desire blazes through the thread of power he just sent to me, the feel of it like lightning through my veins, stealing my breath and igniting our fire thrall to volcanic heights, the surrounding Forest's fire power feeding into and amplifying our draw.

Yvan is surrounded by Vothe and two other Wyvern-shifters. The military base terrace is rapidly emptying, the Vu Trin I was conferring with having just departed, our battle plans solidified and lodging doled out, deep night closing in. Torch lightning flickers over Yvan and the Wyverns, illuminating Yvan's crimson hair and heart-stopping features.

His fiery gaze holds mine, and everything else fades away. We're suddenly the only two people on Erthia, my surge of emotion feeding into our heated draw as I send out a returning flare of beckoning fire, ready to take him as my own before we go to war.

Yvan's eyes flash violet as he bids goodbye to Vothe and the others, a knowing look on their faces as he strides purposefully toward me and every nerve ending in my body sparks.

Kam Vin and Lucretia intercept him, and his shoulders stiffen, the caress of his fire around me now so all-encompassing it's hard to know where the edge of his power ends and mine begins, every speck of our fire magic lightning-focused on each other.

Yvan listens to Kam Vin and Lucretia, his lip ticking up when Jules and Valasca join them, his fire continuing to stream toward me and over my lips in a fiercely hot tide.

A quick, stolen meeting of our eyes, and we both smile, the two of us seeming to register the outrageous gallows humor of our situation—the Icaral of Prophecy, ready to stand at the leading edge of a Dryad'khin army as we deploy, together, against Vogel's vast forces, and yet unable to break away from this damned terrace.

The amusement helps me beat back my ever-present fear of losing him. Emboldened, I send another tendril of flame toward him, and Yvan shoots me a look so charged that it curls my toes as Lucretia says something to Valasca, Jules, and Kam Vin. There's a challenge burning in Yvan's eyes as he gives me a slow smile and pulses another enticing flush of heat over my skin and mouth.

Desire sears a prickling line down my spine.

Clear I'm literally playing with fire—monumental, scorching Wyvernfire—I recklessly send out a hotter rush of heat to brush Yvan's neck and slide under his clothing.

Yvan's eyes widen, and he turns to face me fully, his smile gone, his eyes narrowing. His full aura hits me in a shimmer of heat, cascading over my body like rain made of tingling embers.

My breath hitches against the wildly arousing sensation as I latch hold of his daring look and send out a dare of my own—a rush of spiraling fire that cascades over his chest.

Yvan's head arcs back a fraction, his jaw and neck tensing. My breathing quickens as I ripple invisible heat over his hard stomach, his hip bones, lower . . .

Yvan's arm lashes out in a quick arc, deftly capturing my invisible prismatic fire before drawing it into his palm and tethering it there, his hand glowing as he tenses it into a fist, and I thrill to his display of mastery over both my power and his.

No longer playing, he bids a quick farewell to Kam Vin and the others and strides toward me, horns up, wings fanning out, his eyes aflame. The powerful beauty of his lithe, muscular grace sends my heartbeat into a faster rhythm as I make my way toward him as well, the two of us rapidly closing the distance between us.

He reaches me and arcs his wings around us, a more fervid hunger entering his gaze as his hot hand slides around my waist, trailing sparks. "I can't control the draw of our bond any longer," he murmurs, tugging me closer.

I smile. "I noticed. Your fire has been on my lips for hours."

His mouth ticks up as he gives me a look so knowing, a flush blooms on my face.

"The Zhilaan Forest," he says, glancing at it, "it wants us to be fully together, as well. I know you can feel its pull through our bond."

I nod, swallowing. "It's as if there's something essential about us taking each other as full mates. Something we don't yet understand. Something important to this fight." A tremor kicks through me, suffused with desire for him I have no wish to suppress.

Yvan draws me into a close embrace, his warm breath brushing my cheek. "I want to give you my fire, Elloren," he murmurs in Lasair. "*All* of it."

My flush sears into a pleasurable burn, every tendril of my magic straining toward him as I nod in breathless assent.

"Do you have Sanjire root?' he whispers.

I nod again. "I found some in the Forest. Where should we go?"

Amusement sparks in his eyes. "Somewhere fireproof," he suggests, his voice a silken thrum.

Oh, my.

I can't suppress a returning, teasing smile, excited and intimidated and amused all at the same time. "You're a bit stoked up, Wyvern."

He doesn't blink. "After that fire you just sent me? I'm about two seconds away from burning all your clothes off. And mine."

Sweet holy gods on high.

"Well, we better go somewhere fireproof *and* private," I manage, throat dry.

"We'd better."

"The room I was given?" I suggest.

He nods, and we depart without hesitation, hand in hand, toward the section of unoccupied barracks Hizar'drile offered us all for rest this night and the next, the key to my room hanging from a cord looped around my wrist. Yvan's fire aura burns hotter and hotter, my body lit up by the sheer strength of the love and desire blazing through us both.

We reach my room, and I unwind the cord around my wrist before taking hold of the brass key, my hand quivering slightly as I insert it in the lock, which refuses to give. Yvan gently takes hold of my hand, his fingers a warm caress as he guides it away then proceeds to thrust out his palm and blast a violet-hot bolt of flame at the lock, melting it to glowing liquid before firmly pushing the door open.

Overtaken with want, I step inside then turn to find him inside as well, melting the door's metal edging shut before he fixes his eyes and fire on me with such volcanic intensity, it elicits a dizzying rush of warmth through my lines.

In a blur he closes the distance between us and catches me in an embrace.

I thrill to the feel of his warm body against mine as I pull him close and he pushes me against the room's stone wall, his wings arcing around us, his lips meeting mine with a sudden jolt of flame that lights up my entire body, every one of my lines catching glorious fire.

I grab one of Yvan's horns and urge him nearer, unable to hold back my moan as he deepens the kiss and I open my mouth to his, our tongues brazenly stroking each other while I send a sizzling rush of flame over his entire body.

Yvan groans and presses himself against me, hard sparks of want flaring at the most brazen point of contact. A ravenous heat surging, I wrap a leg around him to draw him tighter against me, desperate to meld straight into him.

"I can conjure more clothing if you burn it off," I say.

"Is that an invitation?" he teases before sliding his hot mouth to the base of my neck and swirling his tongue in a tight spiral against my skin, heat radiating from the motion and rippling toe-curling sparks through my every line.

"That is *absolutely* an invitation," I gasp.

Yvan stills, a more explosive energy suddenly coursing through his fire. "I'm going to take you with more fire than you could ever imagine," he says as he raises his flaming gaze to mine, deadly serious, but with a spark of hesitation, as if he's waiting for my full consent.

"I want you to," I prod as I teasingly trace my fingers along his lower back then up along the base of his wings.

Yvan shivers, his mouth opening in a harsh exhale, his fire pulsing *hard*.

"You like being touched there?" I ask, lit up by his feverish response.

"*Yes*," he barely manages, his whole body rigid, his breathing taking on a rough, uneven cadence.

Wicked delight surging, I run my fingers up along his wings' silken edges.

Yvan's fire explodes through our Wyvernbond as he grabs tighter hold of me. The room shifts and spins, and I'm suddenly on the bed, Yvan on top of me, desperately unfastening my clothing. I reach down to help him, just as desperate, his claws snapping to life and shredding through the fused leaves of my tunic and pants as we tear the remnants off. Then he's wresting hold of his own clothing and rapidly yanking it off his lean frame

Shocked delight sears through me, my breath catching as I gain a brief glimpse of his body before he captures my mouth in another intoxicating kiss, his body pressing on mine once more, his skin blazing hot.

The whole scene cuts out as flame streaks across my vision, as if the room surrounding us has caught fire, Yvan's power flowing through me, searing away all thought. I wrap my legs around him, thrilling to the feel of his desire pressed hard against me.

"Elloren," he rasps, eyes incendiary with blistering heat, waiting for me to give him full leave to release it.

In answer I take hold of his hips and pull him insistently closer, capturing his mouth with mine as I send my fire straight through him then snake a hand between us. Yvan lets out a tight gasp as I grip hold of him, our eyes meeting in a sweep of fiery intention as I breathlessly guide him, both of us hurtling toward a molten precipice.

Yvan joins with me in a rush of fire so hot my body arches against him, a hard groan escaping his lips as his body trembles against mine.

"My love . . ." he gasps in Lasair, every muscle tensed as he forcibly stills himself, his fire coursing through us, the pressure of our connection sending hot, pulsing sparks of pleasure through me.

The sensations are so surprisingly intense, it's almost unbearable as we fall into a slow then confident rhythm, the pulsing force of it growing tighter and hotter as I sense him reading my fire, finding just the right motion, an explosive rush of heat building.

With one strengthening wave of ecstasy after another, our bodies grow slick with fiery want. The hot pleasure builds, unbearably intense, then crests and explodes into an inferno of flame, sun rivaling in its intensity. I cry out, overtaken, melding and fusing into Yvan's fire as he lets out a guttural groan, flame erupting around us as I'm flooded with the full force of his heat.

Yvan stills inside me, the two of us breathing hard, his rough exhalation hot against my shoulder as we clutch tight hold of each other and the flames die down around us.

Love floods through me and is instantly met with a returning rush of love from him, the emotion in it so vivid it's almost painful. Overcome, I kiss his slick shoulder as it dawns on me—this was his first time.

The thought is bittersweet, another rush of feeling edging into the swirling haze of pleasure that's overtaken me along with his fire.

Yvan pushes himself slightly up and looks deep into my eyes. He's still breathing hard, his angular face flushed. He makes no move to separate us as his grip on my hip loosens into a caress, my legs still wrapped around him, my breathing ragged. His gaze turns slightly questioning, a stunned awe in it, as if he's been rendered speechless, all the words burned out of him.

"You were a bit pent-up," I finally manage, giving him a small, awestruck smile.

He huffs out a breath. "A bit," he agrees. His lips lift into a slight, knowing smile as he glances toward where we're still quite joined before his gaze returns to mine, serious now, an ardent heat in his eyes. "Was that all right, Elloren?" he asks, his powerful body glistening, his naked form a thrill to behold. "I threw out . . . quite a lot of fire."

I lick my still-hot lips, wanting his kiss and fire back on them, his hot tongue in my mouth. "That was *incredible*, Yvan."

He lets out what sounds like a breath of relief, then leans in to tenderly kiss my neck, lingering at the base of it before kissing my temple and my lips, slow and sensual, and I surrender to his instinctual Wyvern finesse. Or maybe, I fervidly consider, he's just naturally, stunningly good at this.

"I love you," he says with ragged passion.

"I love you too," I respond, my voice breaking around the emotion. Around everything we had to go through to finally get to this place. To finally be this to each other.

To finally be *everything* to each other.

"I love you in every possible way," he says in passionate Lasair, his forehead coming to mine, his wings fanned out around us. "I'll love you forever, ti'a'lore." And then he's kissing me again between murmuring Lasair endearments.

Before long, the kissing grows more heated, and the tips of his claws brush gently against my sides.

He stills, and I can feel his desire rising once more.

"Elloren," he says, almost hesitant, while his Icaral body is anything but. "Can I take you again?" His voice is throaty, and my own scorching need rises in a fiery tide alongside his.

I press my palms to his chest and gently push. He follows my lead, letting me roll us both over until I'm straddling him, my hands now pressing his wrists into the bed, his fiery eyes widening then narrowing with wicked surprise.

I give him a sultry smile as my gaze rakes his slick form, his wings spread out beneath us. "No, Yvan," I croon. "This time I'll take *you*."

I'm awakened by Yvan's kiss on my shoulder, the view from the room's small window still night dark. Drowsily I stir, heat kindling then surging through my root-lines as I find myself wrapped in Yvan's embrace, his chest to my back, his arms around my waist, his breath warm on my neck.

He's awake.

So very much *awake*.

His body feverish with desire, his fire power churning with want.

I draw in a quavering breath and run my hand along the arms he has wrapped around me, my own fire quickly kicking up to burn as bright as his.

His hot fingertips trace down my abdomen, then over my hip, trailing flame. He pauses, his fire reading the rapid-fire rise of my desire, my heartbeat tripping over itself as he slides his hand around my thigh and coaxes my leg up.

I'm instantly caught up in the heart-thuddingly exciting feeling that we're thieves, stealing something forbidden from the night, as I press myself back against him and he lets out a groan against my neck, his muscles tensing, his power growing incandescently hot. My mouth falls open in surprise as he smoothly joins us, a cry of astonished pleasure escaping my lips, his heat overwhelming.

I can't hold back the moan as his fire spirals through me, one of his wings flicking forward to arc around me as he pulls me insistently closer.

"Elloren . . ."

My head arches back, my mouth falling open with another moan as he thrusts his body and fire into me again, then again, heat building, the two of us lost to this deep-night haze of pleasure and flame.

A harder surge of his fire flashes through me, the power and force of his want intensifying. The motion of his flame grows unbridled, his grip on my hips firming as he presses his mouth to the arch of my neck and I push back against him, wanting more of the delirious flame and pleasure, wanting to merge with Yvan so completely we'll turn liquid and *fuse*.

I reach up and run my fingers along his wing's edge.

Yvan's fire ignites into an inferno, a low hiss torn from his mouth before he regains a semblance of control, his rhythm increasingly powerful. His hand slides down my waist, my stomach, tentatively trailing lower as I sense his fire intently reading mine, guiding him toward my most sensitive spot.

Pressing lightly down, he spirals fire through it.

Ecstasy arcs through my body, bowstring tight, the pleasure so intense, it's almost shattering. "Gods, *Yvan* . . ."

Another blast of pleasurable heat scorches through me as his core fire rides my lines. I gasp and hurtle over our power's blazing edge, lit up like a star as Yvan sends every bit of his flame through my body in a volcanic surge and gives in to his own explosive release. Quivering, I bask in his overwhelming heat and maleness, my whole body arching against his.

We still, and I pull in a shuddering breath, his arms tight around me, his chin pressed to my shoulder, his breath coming in a harsh, uneven cadence, one gasp after another.

After a long moment, our grip on each other loosens as we lie there, seeming stunned anew by each other.

"Ancient One," I half whisper, half gasp. "*Yvan* . . ."

He kisses my shoulder. "My beautiful fire mate. My flame. My true flame," he murmurs in Lasair as his fire aura whips ardently around me,

Love for him fluttering through my heart, I slide forward slightly, and he pivots himself back, breaking our connection. I roll over to face him, and he takes my hand in his, caressing it lovingly before raising it to kiss the image of III on my palm.

We exchange a look of sheer adoration, his fire a reverberating pulse through my body, a tingling pleasure still coursing through my every line. I huff out a sound of astonishment, and he gives me an almost abashed look before he rolls onto his back, fingers threaded through mine, and runs his free hand through his tousled, crimson hair, absently grabbing hold of the base of one of his horns.

"You're . . . *fiery*," is all I can manage.

His lips slant up as he turns to face me, humor glinting in his gaze. "I'm dragon'kin, Elloren."

"I know but . . . you're so reserved on the surface, and you're *incredible* at . . . this." I can't get enough of him. I want to join with him without ceasing.

"Wyverns can be a bit . . . insatiable," he admits, searching my eyes for a reaction. "Or so I'm told. And . . . our *bond* . . ." His gaze rakes over me, and I raise a brow at the lust still swimming in his eyes. He lets out a long breath and gives me a shy smile. "Don't worry, Elloren. I'll let you get some sleep." His gaze roves over me once more. "Even though I could keep you up all night."

I swallow, a spark of hunger igniting. "That was . . . what you just did . . . you behind me . . . that was . . . *interesting*. I never knew that position was even . . ."

He cocks a brow as I trail off.

"I'm wondering . . ." I say, flustered by his effect on me. By how he is, in this. "I'm wondering if you have any other . . . tricks up your sleeve."

"My sleeve?" Amusement dances in his eyes.

"Or . . . other places."

He narrows his eyes and smiles, and a shiver races down my spine at the sultry warmth in it.

"It's not like you've done this . . . quite a lot . . ." I note.

"Elloren, you're my first."

"So, how did you know about . . . *that* . . ."

Mischief lights his expression. "I have an active imagination."

"Well, you should run with it."

Yvan laughs, and I grin at him, his fire ramping up hotter. His smile widens.

"What?" I ask, sensing his deeper flicker of amusement.

"We're such . . . Westerners."

A laugh escapes me. "I know."

"We just . . . joined," he says, "and we can barely speak of it."

He pulls me into a loving embrace, his fire flaring. His *desire* flaring.

Holy all the gods.

"I love you, Elloren," he says, heartfelt. And I realize, Yvan is reserved in so many ways, but not in this. His heart is wide open. Wide open to me.

"I love you too," I tell him, my heart equally open to him.

The two of us fully bonded, in every way, save for the Wyvern bite.

Yvan moves back a fraction and traces his fingertip down the center of my body, stopping just below my stomach, his touch hovering between my hips.

"I can't get enough of you," he murmurs, his gaze lifting to meet mine. "Tell me if you want me to stop."

I reach up, thread my fingers through his hair, grab hold of a horn, and pull him toward me, kissing him deeply in answer.

In a flash he's over me, wings fanning out. "You truly want me to run with it?" he asks, eyes flaring hot.

I bare my teeth in a cheeky grin. "Get creative, Wyvern."

The lascivious heat in his gaze ignites hotter.

"Go ahead, Yvan," I prod, "make up for lost time."

"Just lie back," he offers as he pushes himself up a fraction, the assured heat in his voice sending a shiver down my spine. "The Zhilon'ile Wyverns told me about something called the Wyvern Firekiss. I'm going to show you what that is." He opens his mouth slightly to reveal his tongue heating to glowing violet at its tip.

I clutch the bedcovers, my heart quickening, as Yvan kisses the center of my chest then slides his tongue down the length of my body, trailing fire. He traces kisses lower and lower, that serpentine tongue flickering intimately over me as an inferno of pleasure detonates, I call out his name, and my vision cuts to fire as hot as a star.

We're summoned to wakefulness by a military horn.

I turn to Yvan, his face awash in predawn's pale blue light. He turns toward me, a steady, grave simmer to his fire.

Emotion grips my throat, and I swallow it back, holding his intense stare, the feel of our joined fire conveying more than words ever could.

Yvan takes my hand, and we tighten our fingers around each other at the same time, our breathing momentarily unsteady as the invisible flames of our bond surge covetously toward each other and I struggle to force down the sudden surge of emotion. Yes, we might lose each other in the looming fight. We might lose *everything*. But Erthia needs us if there's to be any future worth having.

"I was drawn to you the first moment I saw you," Yvan quietly admits as his fire gives an impassioned surge.

A thick laugh escapes me through my brimming tears as I give him a wry look. "You looked at me like you hated me."

His expression tenses with obvious remorse. "I had such a strong reaction to you I didn't know how to handle it. The instant attraction . . . it was *seismic*."

I lift a brow at this, a flush sizzling over my neck as I realize I felt an instant draw to him too.

"I felt guilty about it," he admits. "*Wildly* guilty. It just got worse when you started working in the kitchens, and I scented how sincere you were. How truly ignorant you were about the world you'd landed in . . . and what your people were doing. I tried to keep my distance from you. But not only did I *want* you—" flame kicks up in his eyes "—I could scent how drawn you were to me, as well. I'm truly sorry for how I treated you, Elloren."

I shake my head, refuting his need for an apology as I wince internally at the memory of my own ignorant self and my unknowingly cruel actions.

"You're the Icaral of Prophecy," I say, "and I'm the granddaughter of the Black Witch. This was always going to be . . . *complicated*."

He gives me a poignant smile as his fire power lovingly encircles me. "We were on a collision course from day one."

I nod at this, sending my fire out to fan over his back. He pulls in a tight breath, his smile sharpening as he gently ripples his invisible fire over my shoulders and the back of my neck.

"I think I was first drawn to you," I tell him, "that very first day I came to the kitchens in Verpacia. I looked through the storeroom window, into the main kitchen . . . and little Fern, she was running around laughing and blowing bubbles. She spilled her bottle of bubble soap all over you. And instead of getting upset at her . . . you *smiled*." I pause, overcome by so much emotion I'm rendered momentarily speechless. "Something in me lit up in that moment," I finally manage, giving him a wavering smile. I shrug. "And I started to have feelings for you. I didn't realize it fully in that moment, but I realize it now."

Yvan pulls in a long, emotional breath and slides his arm around my waist, his wing arcing over me, his hand gently tracing a caressing spiral against my lower back, a shiver of sparks chasing his touch. "I think about Fern often," he says, voice low and serious as his touch stills. "I haven't seen her in a long time. But it's a comfort to know that Fyon and Mora'lee are taking care of her in the Sublands."

"Fernyllia asked me to fight for a better world for Fern," I confide, a tear escaping my eye at the remembrance of courageous, kind Fernyllia.

Yvan nods, reaching up to gently brush away my tear. "Fernyllia took me aside the last time I saw her," he says. "Asked me to do the same. I always got the sense she knew I was hiding something from her. From *everyone*. I think she guessed what I am."

We grow quiet for a moment as I think of Fern and all the other young children currently being sheltered in the Eastern Realm Sublands—Sage and Ra'Ven's baby, Fyn'ir; fierce Nym'ellia's little sister, Tibryl; and the fiery Icaral-child, Pyrgomanche, whom Yvan and I rescued from Valgard's Icaral prison. And many more.

I send up a silent prayer to whatever god or goddess will listen to help them survive what's to come . . . if they've even survived what's already come to pass.

Tension weighing down the air between us, Yvan and I exchange a somber look. I can feel us both mindfully putting all these children first—putting Erthia first— but refusing to let go just yet as we pull each other into one more close hug.

We embrace for a moment in wordless, ardent alliance and unextinguishable love before we share one last kiss . . . and get up to face the world.

The predawn sky has lightened to a deep blue through Zhilaan's dome-shield when Yvan and I step onto the broad, torchlit terrace hand in hand, our Wyvernbond whipping around us with a steady new intensity. Row upon row of charged weapons line the entire terrace, their multicolored runes glowing bright. Suspended, prismatic Dryad runes hang above them, feeding foliage power into their wards, and a steadily charging sky portal slashes across the sky directly above us.

Set for the West.

The terrace is already populated, a series of long tables set up, plates, mugs, and utensils stacked in their centers. I catch Rafe's eye, and he waves me over. Diana, Andras, Aislinn, and Jarod are standing around him amidst scattered Vu Trin Dryad'khin as Zhilon'ile Dryad'khin soldiers bring out bowls of food. Valasca and Ni Vin are standing to one side near the terrace's edge, their arms looped around each other as they converse in low tones with Trystan and Kam Vin.

I glance through the suspended runes over the dark carpet of trees, a low rumble shivering through my rootlines as the Zhilaan Forest notes Yvan's and my presence and flows a rippling line of its fire power through our Wyvernbond, as if searching for something.

Diana raises her chin and cocks a blond brow as Yvan and I approach, her nostrils flaring.

I can spot the other Lupines doing a quick double take as well, their eyes widening slightly, and realize they're reading what's transpired between us. Taking obvious note of their reaction, Valasca narrows her gaze on me, one black brow rising. A sly spark dances to life in her dark eyes that warms my cheeks as Trystan surveys everyone in that quiet, insightful way of his.

Diana rushes toward us, an overjoyed light overtaking her expression that pushes back the serious energy suffusing our world.

"You two have mated! *Finally!*" she enthuses, so brazenly that a hot rush of heat sizzles over my face and through Yvan's fire. She throws her arms around me with gusto, then embraces Yvan, joyously kissing us both on our cheeks before drawing back, grinning widely.

Yvan and I exchange a brief look of surrender to the huge, slightly mortifying cultural chasm.

Unfazed by our wall of silence, Diana's nostrils flare once more as she gives Yvan a look of shrewd appraisal. "Ah, he is virile!" she announces, sounding deeply pleased.

Yvan's crimson brows fly up as Diana grins at her own pronouncement, my lips parting as I cast about for some response to her outrageous statement.

Diana nods at me in smug approval. "I can scent him in you. Scent the power in your draw to each other." She claps Yvan on the shoulder, a tremor of deeper emotion passing through her gaze. "You are well mated," she declares, amber eyes sheened with feeling. "I'm so glad of it."

She glances around expectantly, as if waiting for everyone else to mirror her vocal enthusiasm for this *quite private* thing. Diana's blond brow knots as she finds Aislinn flushing and averting her eyes, Rafe grinning and looking to the sky while Trystan wryly takes us all in and Jarod suppresses a bemused smile.

Diana narrows her eyes further and tosses her blond hair haughtily over her shoulder. "You are all *ridiculous*."

Rafe laughs as he steps toward her and pulls her into his arms. "We most certainly are. But we're not without our charms."

Diana snorts and mock-scowls at him as he nuzzles her neck, her annoyed stance returning as she mock-glares at Jarod and swipes her hand toward Yvan and me. "Well, aren't you going to at least congratulate them?" She looks at Yvan, and something serious and heartfelt flickers through her eyes.

My throat tightens as Yvan holds Diana's stare, a returning warmth in his gaze as Jarod and Aislinn approach, affection lighting their amber eyes.

"I know your Keltish traditions are more reserved," Jarod says to Yvan. "So, I'll simply say, I'm honored to call you brother."

Yvan's fire gives a potent flare toward Jarod and Aislinn both. "I, as well," Yvan responds as he and Jarod draw each other into an embrace, and then Trystan joins us, everyone offering congratulations and hugging us.

"Welcome to the family, Yvan," Aislinn says as she draws back from his embrace, beaming at him with tears in her eyes.

"I always wanted a sister," Yvan confides, returning her wavering smile.

"Well now you have *two*!" Diana crows, and Yvan and I laugh before we all grow somber once more, the very air shifting toward what's to come. And how much there is to lose.

This miracle of time together, all too brief.

Overcome, I turn to find Valasca giving Ni Vin a quick kiss before sauntering toward us, a knowing gleam in her eyes. I sense the jaunty flare of Valasca's sapphire geo-magic as well as her welcome desire to lighten the mood.

"Well, don't you look worn-out," she drawls at me before cocking a brow at Yvan. "But you seem positively lit up, Icaral."

Yvan grins. "I have limitless fire," he shoots back, surprising me as he throws his reserve to the wind and a private line of flame to me, an amused light sparking in his eyes as they meet mine.

Both of Valasca's brows fly up before she chuckles and claps him on the arm. She turns her probing gaze back to me as I stand there, shaking my head and blushing over her outrageous level of openness.

"Wyvern'kin!" Vothendrile's voice booms to us from across the terrace as a knot of Wyvern males stride onto it, Vothe's brother, Gethindrile, amongst them, their lightning-flashing eyes pinned on Yvan, a broad grin forming on all their faces. "You've mated!" Vothe enthuses.

Yvan gives me a look of resigned good humor, and I motion for him to go ahead and join them, sure my blush will incinerate my face if I have to endure the brazen congratulations of this entire crowd of men.

As Vothe pulls Yvan into a hearty embrace and they welcome each other as brothers, the contrast between this scene and my experience with Gardnerian culture triggers a memory that prompts a sudden upswell of aching grief.

My Sealing night with Lukas.

Men congratulating him while belittling and excluding me—and Lukas secretly and aggressively railing against that.

Tears are suddenly welling in my eyes, a knot forming in my throat. Because Lukas never had the chance to be embraced by a more open and accepting culture.

And he deserved that chance.

"Rescue me," I plead with Valasca.

Peering at me with searching intensity, she takes hold of my arm and walks with me to the terrace's deserted far end. She leans back against the terrace's railing, a drop of what seems like a million feet to the Forest floor just beyond her, a small cloud wafting by below like a silent ship.

"Diana's right," Valasca notes as she raises a brow, a kind smile on her sky blue lips as she glances at Yvan then back to me. "Your reserve around pairing is ridiculous."

I roll my eyes at her and turn, leaning my forearms against the railing, the painful grief tightening inside my chest. I stare over the Zhilaan Forest toward the shielding's storming edge.

Toward the chaos of the West.

An image of Lukas holding up his wand just before he exploded the upper half of the Vo Mountain Range and a large portion of Vogel's army with it resonates through my mind.

The pain in my chest becomes nearly unbearable.

"Elloren," Valasca says, nudging my arm with hers, "I jest, but I'm happy for you and Yvan. Truly. So happy for you both."

I swallow, my throat constricting. "I love Yvan, Valasca. With all my heart. But . . . I can't help but think about Lukas in this moment."

The dam breaks, my hand flying to my mouth as tears pool and I shudder against them.

Valasca nods and pivots to lean over the railing beside me, the two of us gazing toward the West. "Then think about him," she says, and she sets her dark gaze back on me. "You loved him. You're not betraying any of us by being honest about that. And you're not betraying Yvan."

Struggling, I blink back the tears. "It's been difficult to reconcile my feelings for them both."

She nods at this. "You loved Lukas. And he was cruelly taken from you. But his love *wasn't*." She reaches over to gently tap my breastbone, right over my heart. "It's forever there. Alongside your love for Yvan." She gives me a deeply significant look. "Elloren, it's important to keep your heart open in this world and embrace all the love you feel."

I nod, bottom lip quivering, as Valasca straightens and draws me into a hearty hug.

"My faith in you was well-placed, Dryad," she says as we hold each other tight and, for a moment, I let the tears flow. And surrender to my vast grief for Lukas while embracing my expansive love for Yvan.

"My faith in you was well-placed as well, Amaz," I whisper, heartfelt, as I draw back from her.

Valasca grins. "Then let's get to work." Her expression turns lethally serious.

"Tomorrow, we bring the full weight of the Prophecy down on the Magedom's heads."

I nod, a warrior energy suddenly rising around us both. I look toward Yvan and the Wyverns just as Gethindrile lifts his arm. The heavily Varg-warded Noi Fire Hawk perched on it takes wing and streaks across the sky, a translucent green, bubble-like shield bursting to life around it.

As it wings southwest to bring word of our battle plan to Tierney and Or'myr.

I say a quick prayer that the courageous hawk will find them before I turn back to Yvan and freeze as I find him giving me an unsettled look, the Zhilaan Forest's equally disquieted energy suddenly blazing around our bond in a searching flow. A slim strand of Yvan's invisible fire whips out toward the edge of my shoulder with what feels like a surge of longing before it yanks back, as if of its own volition.

Concern and confusion ignite through our bond as Yvan holds my gaze, a growing conflict in his eyes as my empathy picks up on a deeper well of his power I've never felt the extent of before, straining toward me but blocked from our bond, the flow of my own fire abruptly guttering toward his to no avail.

Our magical auras, locked into a desperate flow toward each other, unable to connect.

CHAPTER TEN

THE GARDEN

Tierney Calix

Northern Vo River

"Open the shielding!" Tierney cries, her gaze pinned on the black Noi Fire Hawk hurtling through the Unbalanced storms toward the Vo River's dome-shield, which she and Or'myr are struggling to hold over the Vo. The hawk's wings beat the air, its form lit up in the night by the emerald light emanating from the ring of Varg runes orbiting it, a bubble-like translucent green shield coursing out from them.

Wasting no time, Or'myr slides his wand over the series of purple geo-runes marked on the wall before them.

A small opening snaps into being just in front of the bird, the roar of the surrounding storms suddenly battering Tierney's sensitive ears.

The hawk soars through, and Or'myr swipes his wand over the runes before him. The shield's hole snaps shut, and the sound of the battering storms is once again muffled.

Tierney sprints toward the hawk as it lands on the riverbank in a flurry of midnight feathers, its shielding blinking out of existence. The hawk sets its violet eyes on her, a scroll cylinder strapped to its leg. Wasting no time, Tierney retrieves the cylinder and pulls out a small missive. She rapidly scans it, struggling mightily against an almost violent upsurge of grief that has her gut heaving.

"Tierney," Or'myr murmurs as he lowers himself beside her, holding out his palm for the missive.

Furious tears welling in her eyes, Tierney thrusts the missive toward Or'myr, and he takes it, her River's increasingly frightened energy ramping up her distress as she rises.

"It confirms some of what I've already read in the Waters," Tierney snarls, angry tears falling, but she doesn't care as the salty tears slick her lips, her rage and grief overwhelming all other possible emotion. "The Zonor has been *destroyed*," she rages. "The Natural Matrix of the East has been *destroyed*. The Dyoi Forest has been *destroyed*. We're holding on to Erthia's *last uncorrupted major Waterway*."

"This is Trystan's writing," Or'myr notes, voice tight, purple eyes grave. His Strafeling aura is pulsing violet-hot around him as Trystan's leading words blare out from the page—*HOLD THE VO.*

"So," Tierney roughly spits out, "there's one day left before they go to war with Vogel. And possibly only a few days before my River is *consumed* by Shadow."

Or'myr's jaw ticks with tension as he gently strokes the hawk then prods it forward, the exhausted-looking bird taking flight and alighting on a nearby branch. Or'myr stands and turns to face Tierney, purple lightning flashing through his eyes. "It's not over yet," he insists. "Your river still *lives*."

Static from Or'myr's lightning aura crackles around Tierney, and she looks toward the beautiful jade-hued dragonflies flitting across her River, hundreds of animals and plants sheltered near and under its surface. Or'myr's lightning embrace intensifies, challenging her to hold firm, the palpable love in it only provoking her internal storm to more painful, chaotic heights.

"Everything good in this world is about to be *lost*," she rages. "And Vogel hasn't even sent his own storms in yet." She thrusts her hand toward the maelstrom lashing above. "All this, the East's own doing! Fools, all of them! Cruel and unthinking fools! East and West alike!"

Her magic breaks loose, a storm cloud forming above her head, her tempestuous grief and fury triggering a peal of thunder and a sheet of rain that soaks them both.

"I can sense Deathkin energy rippling through my River," Tierney grits out. "I can feel Viger and my kelpies and the other Deathkin holding back a Reckoning. *Barely* . . ."

"Your river still *lives*," Or'myr insists again, ignoring his increasingly rain-drenched form. The lightning flashing through his eyes is so intense that Tierney is stopped short, an upswell of answering warrior resolve surging through her power like a lifeline.

"Then we *hold* it," Tierney vows, wiping the tears from her cheeks, every fiber of her Asrai being filling with the terrified Vo's As'lorion call for protection.

Against all odds.

Tierney gets ahold of herself and her storm, strikes the water from her and Or'myr's forms and they wordlessly set back to work, feeding power into the Vo River's shielding in concert with distant Fyordin, his power shot through with the same determination as theirs, all of them intimately linked.

Tierney pulls in a deep breath as she keeps her left hand pressed to one of Or'myr's shield-amplification wards that's marked on the stone embankment before them. She concentrates, brow knotted tight, and flows the Vo's powerful energy into the wards in a rippling rush while Or'myr feeds his formidable geomancy and Magery into the wards, as well.

Both they and Fyordin holding back the East's untethered storms and fortifying their shielding for the Magedom's inevitable onslaught.

"We're so strong together," Or'myr marvels from beside her, his eyes meeting hers as he holds his geo-wand to the rune before him. "We can hold this shielding, Tierney. We can hold the Vo. And if our allies win the coming battle, we can *keep* hold of it."

The passion in Or'myr's tone catches Tierney in an upsurge of emotion. She studies him as he focuses back on the violet rune he's pressing his wand to. The wand is lit up phosphorescent purple, a luminous net of violet energy coursing out from the ward to ray clear over the huge dome-shield above them while Or'myr's invisible lightning continues to envelop her in a crackling embrace that's been building throughout the day.

"I can sense, through your power . . . that what you feel for me has gotten . . . stronger." Her words break off, both the draw of their bond and her fatigue making it far too easy to speak with blistering honesty, Or'myr's proximity and the pull of their Deathkin binding filling her with the increasingly hard-to-control desire to blast through their incompatible magic and pull him into a desperate embrace.

Or'myr shakes his head, his jaw tensing. "I really love being linked to you in a way that makes it possible for you to read my every emotion." He casts her a beleaguered yet affectionate look that immediately softens the unbearable stress and loosens Tierney's shoulders. She *loves* this about him—how his humor is able to cut through her intensity and help her keep hold of her internal storm. His personality, his affection, and even his magic, able to so powerfully *ground* her.

"At least this mind-scattering bond provides a distraction from the possible end of the world," Tierney returns, attempting to be wry in turn. And failing miserably. She looks at him, her mouth trembling, struggling to tamp down her terror for her Vo.

Their gazes snag, and Or'myr studies her closely, a glint of understanding passing through his eyes before his lip ticks up once more. "So, it's a distraction you're looking for?" He gives her a rakish look, eyes sparking, and Tierney feels that blastedly strong flare of attraction firing between them like it always does now. Every damned time their eyes meet.

She realizes her flare of longing for him has briefly cut through her fear, steadying her nerves.

"I'm in sore need of a distraction," she admits as the Vo's energy flows more easily through her and into their shield. "I'll go mad if I continue to dwell on what could happen if Vogel and his forces win the battle ahead. Distract me, Or'myr."

"All right," he agrees as he tinkers with the amplification rune, swiftly linking an additional rune to it. He shoots her a knowing smile. "Have you given any more thought as to where you stand in 'the garden'?"

Surprise darts through Tierney. She shoots him an exasperated look, which prompts a short laugh that's so enticingly wicked, Tierney's water aura gives a chaotic leap toward him, a flush blooming on her face.

"I *see*," Or'myr notes.

Tierney bristles as she keeps her palm pressed to the runes. "I really love being linked to you in a way that allows you to read *my* every feeling."

Or'myr laughs. "You *asked* me to distract you."

She opens her mouth, closes it. Then shakes her head, glaring at him. "You know I have a hard time talking about such things."

He cocks a purple brow.

She purses her lips at him. "You don't understand. You're from the East." She waves her free hand loosely around in the air. "You're all so brazen and unfettered. With your Xishlon 'finding the moon' all over each other."

Or'myr laughs again, and the runes before them flash a brighter, fully charged violet. He lowers his wand, and Tierney draws her hand away from the stone wall, the break in tension allowing their power to flow without touch into the charged runes.

"Use *your* euphemisms, then," Or'myr prods. "That's sure to be a good distraction for us both." He glances up through their shield at the surrounding, lightning-pulsing storms. "Clearly, I could use one, as well."

Tierney gapes at him. "*My* euphemisms?"

He shoots her a dry look. "You mentioned one before. They must have quite a few in the West. Every culture does."

"Well," Tierney hedges with a shrug. She gives him a sheepish look, suddenly all too aware of his dauntingly attractive, very *male* form. "Swords and so forth."

Or'myr's eyes widen. *"Swords?"* he sputters, seeming instantly scandalized.

"You *know* . . ." Tierney prods, rolling her hand in the air, her embarrassment reaching epic proportions.

"No, I really don't," Or'myr states, emphatic.

She loosely motions toward his groin, barely able to look at him. "Your . . . your 'sword of manhood.'"

"My '*sword* of manhood'?" Or'myr sputters. "Like . . . for fencing? That's bringing an incredibly bizarre picture to mind."

"Not like *that*."

"You use *weapons* for sex metaphors? That's horrifying. No wonder none of you Westerners can speak of this."

"Well, what do *you* call it?" Tierney asks, growing exasperated. "Your 'magic wand'?"

Or'myr flashes her a wicked grin. "See, you're good at this."

"Okay," Tierney sharply returns. "You're completely mortifying me, but go ahead." She swipes out a hand in invitation. "Tell me your Eastern Realm metaphors."

"Well," he says, growing thoughtful, "we have the 'staff of delight.' You must have seen one or two on Xishlon. People dancing around them and trying to land wreaths of violet seashells atop their pinnacles."

Tierney coughs out a laugh. "Staff of delight? Like a *runic staff*?"

Or'myr throws her a look of mock censure. "Not like a *weapon*. You don't *joust* with it. Sweet Holy Vo, you probably would in the West."

"Likely," Tierney concedes.

Their eyes meet and they both burst into much-needed laughter.

"You know, it's good luck on Xishlon," Or'myr says, wiping the mirthful tears from his eyes, "to send a wish out to the Goddess Vo for your beloved. You send the wish into the shell wreath and toss it onto the Vo'vish'luure staff. You can just about imagine what the wreaths represent." He waggles his brow suggestively.

Tierney can barely bite back the laugh. "Did you toss a seashell wreath onto the staff for Xishlon?" she jests, barely believing she's daring to joke like this.

Or'myr shrugs, tossing her a grin. "I might have thought of you and laid one."

"To get hold of my seashell?" Tierney asks, grinning, unable to contain the laughter that's bubbling up once more.

Or'myr's grin widens. "With my 'staff of delight.'" They break into uproarious laughter once more. But then Or'myr's laughter fades, his gaze on her suddenly serious. Pained almost. "I really like you," he says. "We're poised before what actually could be the end of the world, and all I can think about in this moment is how much I like you."

Tierney gives him an answering smile, joviality still dancing in it. "I like you too."

"No," he says, firm, as he motions between them. "I *really* like you. This is hard. Because I want to be your closest friend. I want to be the first person you want to come to with . . . with *anything*. And yes, Tierney, I *want* you. I'm so in love with you, it's tearing me apart. And the fact that these could be our last days together . . ."

A knot of emotion forms in Tierney's throat, his words striking way too close to home. "These won't be our last days together," she doggedly insists, knowing, as her inner storm strains to break free and fly toward him, that it's her turn to be strong. "Our allies are going to drive Vogel back."

Or'myr nods stiffly, shooting her an impassioned look, and Tierney senses, through the flow of their magic around each other, how she's bolstering *him* in this moment. Grounding *him*.

Which makes her frustrated urge to embrace him even stronger.

"And even if we had hundreds more days together," she says, attempting to suppress her growing want, "it wouldn't matter. Our magic won't allow us to be together, and there's no sense pining for what can never be."

Or'myr brings his hands to his hips and looks out over the River, jaw rigid, his lightning aura a crackling, forking mess, flashing around and through her. "It's so easy for you, then?" he raggedly levels.

Her feelings surge, her storm cloud breaking loose to churn above them. "You *know* it isn't! But it doesn't *matter* if it's easy or hard. We *can't* have each other. Even if, by some miracle, we survive all this!" She shocks herself with the harshness of her own tone, everything in her suddenly wanting to drive him away, to stamp down this uncomfortable whirl of emotion that's tightening her chest. "Let this go, Or'myr," she insists, glaring at him even as her feelings for him tear at her heart and she curses the fact that she can't keep her lips from trembling around the words. "If we survive this, find another 'garden.' Not every woman in the East is unable to handle your lightning."

Or'myr looks away, rigid. He swallows as if holding back a fierce wave of emotion, the hurt crackling through his power sending a shard of glass-like pain through Tierney's heart.

"We've thrown as much power into the shield as we can for the moment," he says, his tone clipped, not looking at her. "When the runes dim a bit, we'll anchor more power to them. Get some rest. I'll stand sentry."

He gets up and walks away, and Tierney feels his absence like a knife strike straight through her heart.

The second he's out of earshot, the tears come, fast and furious. Great, heaving sobs that Tierney struggles to keep quiet—grief for this thing building between them that they can never have. Then, an even bigger grief rushes in on the heels of it.

Grief for the Natural World.

Her near-debilitating fear for her River rushes in, so hard Tierney feels crushed by it. She stays there for a long time, watching the Vo, trying not to let its lapping waves of affection completely shatter her heart, as night digs in deeper and she reads, in the steady, relentless flow of both Or'myr's power and hers toward the shielding above, that despite their pain, they *will* hold the Vo.

Or die trying.

A few hours later, Tierney finds Or'myr by the rune-marked embankment wall. She watches as he steadily reorients geopower from the purple crystal veins in the bank's stone to their shielding's northern focal rune, puffs of purple light trailing his wand's motions.

Her throat tight with emotion, Tierney takes a seat on one of the benches Or'myr carved in the embankment's stone.

"You should really get some rest," he comments without looking at her.

"I can't sleep," Tierney stiffly responds, her cursed feelings for him surging.

After a moment, Or'myr sheathes his wand and quietly sits down next to her, the two of them staring over the night-dark River, the Xishlon moon Or'myr conjured still stubbornly suspended above the Vo.

Tierney glances at him sidelong. "Your Eastern Realm metaphors were a bit overwhelming," she stiltedly jests, realizing, almost instantly, that she's picking at the wound running between them.

Or'myr's lips lift. "You prefer your weapons metaphors?" he jests back, glancing warmly at her. Their eyes lock, and Tierney feels that spark of attraction race straight down her spine, her magic heating with it.

"Maybe something in the middle that isn't so ridiculous?" she ventures, suddenly hyperaware of how close they are.

Or'myr cocks a brow. "The sword thing is pretty ridiculous. And frightening."

They share small, knowing smiles as a more intense warmth slides through Tierney that's only heightened by the affection crackling out to her from Or'myr's lines of magic. They reach for each other's hands at the same time, fingers interlacing, the static of Or'myr's power prickling over Tierney's skin.

Her breathing turns erratic, a flush warming her face and neck. She notices that Or'myr's breathing has deepened too.

"I love you," she states raggedly, unable to hold back honesty in this moment, the words streaming from her as her storm cloud forms above them and rain begins to patter down on their heads, warm tears escaping her eyes.

"I love you too," he says, his voice tight with feeling as her rain falls. He meets her tear- and rain-slicked gaze. "I would kiss away your tears if I could do it without hurting you," he roughly states, a mournful look in his eyes.

"I know you would," Tierney responds as her rain strengthens, saturating them both.

"So, we love each other from a distance," he offers. "And fight the war for the Natural World together. A war that allows others to love. That allows children to live."

Tierney nods. Steeling herself, she gets hold of her storm, drawing it in, her rain ceasing. "We'll fight it together," she staunchly agrees. "So that others may love and Waters can flow clean and children can live."

Or'myr's lips twist into a heartbroken smile. "Let our hearts break, then, Tierney'a'lin. It will be our tribute to the world."

"A cruel tribute," she spits out, giving him a tear-soaked, loving smile.

Or'myr nods, eyes flashing jagged purple lightning. "If we survive this," he says, a harsher edge to his tone, "find someone else. As horrible as never being able to have you is, the thought of you alone and unhappy is even more terrible. Luckily, there are many, many gardens."

"None like yours, I'd imagine," Tierney says with a trembling attempt at a smile, her rush of affection for him slicing into her heart anew.

Or'myr grins. "It's a rather nice garden," he concedes, glancing teasingly down his frame before his smile dampens once more.

Tierney brings her palm to his shoulder, braving the sting of lightning crackling through her palm, a momentous sorrow shivering through the bond between them. Ignoring the hurt, she sends a bolstering wave of water power out to him at the same time that he sends a supporting wave of geopower out to her.

"C'mon," she says, caressing his shoulder, "let's get back to work. We have a River to hold."

WYVERN AND FOREST BONDED

Elloren Guryev

Zhilaan Forest military base

Yvan's hand is clasped around mine, our fire power straining toward each other with chaotic force, but unable to connect like it could before *we* connected.

The sensation has been building throughout the day and into this night, leaving us barely able to focus in on Hizar'drile, who stands with us at the center of the torchlit terrace's command table, our allies massed before us. A small blue voice amplification rune glows in the air just in front of Hizar'drile's chin, Vang Troi, Sylvan, and the other Dryads beside him.

"Tomorrow eve, we deploy West," Hizar'drile charges. "We will have, at most, three days to track down the Verdyllion and wage war on Vogel's forces before Forest power begins its slide into dormancy and Vogel gains the advantage."

An uneasy energy gutters through Yvan's and my fire. As it does through the magical auras of the legion of our Dryad'khin on the terrace and perched all over the surrounding Zhilaan Forest canopy like a sea of Tree'khin, the huge sky portal above us due to be fully charged for passage to the West by this time tomorrow.

Amplification runes from every tradition are suspended above the Zhilaan Forest's canopy to feed the Forest's power into our Tree'khin linkage, the runes thrumming with the prismatic might of the Zhilaan's scattered groves of multicolored deciduous trees.

All my foliage-amplified magic straining toward Yvan.

He sends out a potent lash of fire power toward me, as he has throughout the day, testing our Wyvernbond's blockage, his aura struggling to embrace me while my fire reflexively reaches for him. As it has every time, our magic slams to an abrupt, sparking halt in the center of our bond, unable to traverse it.

Yvan tenses and huffs out a breath as he meets my gaze sidelong, the two of us exchanging a concerned look.

Because our lack of fire-connection is not our only linkage that's veering off course.

Throughout the day, the Zhilaan Forest has been whipping elemental energy around our Wyvernbond, as if sounding an alarm while tugging us toward the Forest's floor.

Vang Troi swipes her stylus, the sharp motion breaking into our disquiet as the voice amplification rune suspended in front of Hizar'drile flies to her.

"With twinned Mages Gwynnifer and Mavrik Glass as our tracking guides to the Verdyllion," she states, staring our forces down, "we will portal to the continent's Central Lands, just above where they sense the Verdyllion's location. Once there, we will break through Vogel's Shadow net, enter the Sublands, and take hold of the Verdyllion while freeing Wynter Eirllyn and her forces, joining them to ours."

At the mention of Wynter, an impassioned rush of Ariel's golden fire streaks through our horde's bond, Ariel's eyes glowing sun bright, a look of ferocious determination on her face.

Vang Troi flicks her stylus, and the voice amplification rune streaks to Yvan and me.

I straighten and look out at the sea of Dryad'khin. "Using the Verdyllion," I roughly state, struggling to focus past my power's mounting desperation to get to Yvan, "I'll draw on our combined magic to strike down Vogel's storm bands, which will likely draw him, the Black Witch, and his forces to us." I look to Yvan, our eyes meeting in a blaze of frustrated heat before he turns to our Dryad'khin.

"I'll then face down Fallon Bane, fire to ice," he says, steel in his tone. "While Elloren and our horde, along with you, our Dryad'khin army, strike down Vogel and take possession of his Shadow Wand."

Vang Troi swipes the amplification toward Mavrik and Gwynn.

"Once we have both the Shadow Wand and the Verdyllion in hand," Mavrik says, "Gwynn and I will use our twinned magic to link at least seven Dryad'khin with light power to the Verdyllion, overtake the Shadow Wand's tether to every bound Mage and Alfsigr, and link the entire tethered West, en masse, to the trees."

Mavrik, along with all of us, looks to the Dryads at the mention of trees. The voice amplification rune slides to Sylvan.

THE DRYAD STORM

"Tonight," Sylvan calmly states, a lethal light in his pine-green eyes, "we will finish charging our weapons, our sky portal, and the storm-shield runes that will surround us when we deploy—runes that will drive back both the Eastern Realm's weather chaos and Vogel's Shadow storm bands." He scans everyone assembled. "Rest well, Dryad'khin. Tomorrow eve we deploy as one united force, fueled by foliage might."

A wave of thunderous calls of alliance rises from all sides, echoing into the sky at the same moment that a powerfully unsettled current surges through Yvan's power and I turn to him, shock flashing through me. Because his *eyes* . . . his pupils have lost their vertical Wyvern shape and have snapped into a non-Wyvern roundness.

Vothe, Naga, and our horde mates send us looks of alarm.

As the meeting breaks and everyone disperses to continue runic work, further planning, or to get a few hours of vital sleep, Yvan pulls me aside. His eyes are twin points of violet fire against the evening's dark, his horns draw in along with his wings, his crimson hair morphing to glamoured brown. "Elloren," he says as his fire sears against the barrier solidifying between us, "we need to talk. *Now.*"

We stride into my room, his hand tight around mine, the contact prompting surge after surge of our fire magic toward each other.

Only to have it slam up against the newly impenetrable barrier.

Yvan sweeps his hand through the air, and the night-darkened room's three lanterns instantly light. He firmly closes the door and fuses it shut.

"What's happening to our magic?" I prod, tension simmering to life between us as my magic strains toward him, the memories of what we did here last night still pulsing over my body like a hot imprint. "And why are you glamouring yourself?"

"It's the lack of a bond mark," he says, his gaze a fiery brand as he brings his hands to his hips. "Setting down that mark . . . it's a strong Wyvern instinct. More intense than I imagined. I had a hard time controlling the impulse last night . . . and it keeps getting stronger, like the bond's magic is struggling to come into its fullness. Glamouring helps to tamp it down a fraction, but I can't go up against Fallon and Vogel's forces glamoured with my power straining toward you. But, it's like we discussed . . . since you're not Wyvern'kin and we have a unique level of power . . . I don't know what will happen to your magic if I set the mark on you and completely fuse our fire power. You and I—" he motions between us "—we're *unprecedented.*"

"That's an understatement," I huff out, struggling to suppress the ridiculously strong urge to kiss him.

A charged silence descends, Yvan's fire aura leaping toward my magic in ardent flares, hungry to break through, certainty suddenly burning inside me.

"We take a leap of faith, then," I offer, "the risks be damned. Yvan, we can't hold any aspect of our true selves back from each other any longer. Come what may."

"I don't want to hold anything back from you," he agrees, eyes afire.

"Then tell me what we need to do about this."

The flame in his eyes deepens. "I need to claim you, Elloren."

"You mean the bite?"

He swallows, his gaze sliding to the inner edge of my shoulder, his eyes going a bit molten before they meet mine once more. "It *involves* a bite."

"Here?" I ask, running my fingertips along the spot near the base of my neck where his mouth lingered last night, again and again.

He nods, a ruddy flush forming on his face, a more heated look entering his gaze. I can sense how worked up he's getting just from the thought of this, his fire sizzling toward me in rampant flares.

"How much of a bite?" I ask, tension sparking in the air between us.

"A small one," he clarifies, clearly ill at ease with the strength of this Wyvern urge. "Just enough to connect with your blood and send fire through it."

I hold his intent stare—his non-Wyvern, *round*-pupiled stare. Unsettled, I remember how he had to hide himself in the West. How he had to hide his wings. His eyes. Even his language. And that's not what I want for him ever again. That's not what I want for *us*.

"Take down the glamour," I urge, my fire straining toward him.

Yvan gives me a molten look, then tenses and fully releases his glamour, his pupils contracting, hair morphing from brown to crimson, horns rising and wings fanning out as his fire surges so hot that it races across my skin and warms the entire room.

My pulse quickening, I step closer to him, then reach up and pull down my tunic's collar, exposing the skin near my neck's base.

Yvan draws in a wavering breath, his nostrils flaring along with his fervid aura.

"Go ahead," I offer, heart thudding. "Claim me."

He shakes his head, dragging his fiery gaze from my shoulder with obvious effort. "Not . . . at this moment," he says, his eyes and power taking on a hungrier tension. "In . . . *bed*."

THE DRYAD STORM

Heat shoots down my spine as I fully grasp what this is—a true *mating* bond.

Nerves firing, I move to the bed and sit down, unable to stifle a slight smile as Yvan tracks me with his eyes but holds himself back, the energy in his conflagration of power like a tensed bowstring ready to snap, everything in him longing to hurl himself at me.

Holy all the gods.

"You gave me a Wyvern Firekiss last night and you're suddenly *shy*?" I tease.

Yvan flashes me a sultry look. "Say the word and I'll do it again."

My amusement instantly shifts to toe-curling surprise, our magic rising like storm static between us.

"You're such a mix," I breathlessly observe. "You're so Keltish and Lasair *and* Wyvern."

He steps toward me and lifts his hand to caress the side of my face. "Elloren, let me make you part Wyvern too."

A hard ache grips my heart as sparks trail his touch, tears filling my eyes as the intuitive realization hits me. This thing that he wants . . . it's more than a Wyvern Sealing.

It's a marriage of equals, a complete fusing of fire.

I stand up to face him, fire for fire, and take his hands in mine. Yvan inhales a shaky breath, his wildfire gaze riveted to mine.

"Do Wyverns have some type of ceremony?" I venture. "Is there anything else that's important here?"

"After," he manages, the word tight as his fire takes over, a surge of it breaking free to give me a fuller, wordless answer, his flame shot through with bottomless passion. "After this war is over, I want that."

A tear falls as I consider how, outside this room, the Natural World is in terrible peril. Even if we survive, there are no guarantees of any type of decent future. But there is something unshakable *here*. In our bonding. In spite of every last thing the world has thrown at us all. *The story is not yet over*, Ill promised, and the idea lights in my heart that maybe this moment is an important part of that story—to love, against all the odds.

Maybe that's the important part of everyone's story right now.

Surrendering to that love, I bring my palm to the center of Yvan's chest, bottomless affection filling me in response to the rise and fall of his breaths, his heartbeat strong and steady.

"Claim me," I breathlessly offer. "But not here. Claim me not only like a true Wyvern'kin would, but as a true Dryad'khin would as well—in the arms of our fire-powered Forest."

Yvan flies us deep into the heart of the Zhilaan Forest, our bodies wrapped around each other.

The Forest welcomes us with a pulse of heat as Yvan soars us down into a deserted clearing lit solely by the violet fire blazing in his eyes, the runes marked on our bodies and the golden horde stars emblazoned on the bases of our necks.

Yvan draws me into an embrace and kisses me, slow and sensual, taking his time as our breathing deepens and his fire crackles with suppressed power and desire.

I draw him closer, leaning back against the trunk behind me, wanting to feel the full pressure of Yvan against me amplified by the Forest connection at my back, my own fire ramping up, struggling to reach him.

Yvan holds himself in check, though the press of his body's arousal is unmistakable. Instead, we kiss for a long while as he murmurs Lasair endearments that send an emotional ache through my heart, before he falls into the Wyvern language I don't understand and don't need to, hissing the words against my lips as he opens his dragon heart to me, losing all reserve. *Finally* showing me his complete self, his fire starting to flow into a freer, hotter stream.

Straight toward me.

His kisses gain an edge of urgency before he sets about removing my clothing with loving deliberation. There's no aggressive shredding like last night, the slight tremble in his hands prompting a warm swell of affection through me. I gently run my fingers through his silken, crimson hair, over his pointed ears as he stills, his gaze skimming my unclothed form.

Keeping tight hold of his fire, he gives me a besotted look before bringing his mouth to mine once more and pressing me against the tree, his kiss long and hot and deliciously thorough as my hand slides up and around one of his horns.

"I love your horns," I breathe against his mouth, and his smile arcs against my lips.

"I can sense it in the flow of your fire," he murmurs, amused.

He draws back a fraction and looks closely at me before taking his garb off, a hot flush racing over my skin as I take in his naked body.

Then he's embracing me once more, kissing and caressing me, following the trail of what I want through his sense of my fire. I let out a surprised gasp in response to the intimacy of his hot touch, slow and tentative at first as he reads what I like, then bolder.

Much bolder.

A rush of pleasure grips hold, building like a fiery tide, my head arching back as Yvan slides both hands around my upper thighs and hoists me up, bracing me against the trunk behind me.

"Are you ready?" he asks, low in his throat, eyes burning.

I nod, lips parted with need, and Yvan pushes forward, a hard breath escaping us both as he sheathes himself inside me, his body rigid as his fire surges, his breathing staggered as his mouth comes to my shoulder.

He begins to move with urgency and power, the hot pulse of his fire gaining momentum. I tighten my thighs around him, gripping his hair, his horns. My neck arches back, his fire surging through mine as he takes me more intensely, waves of hot pleasure radiating through us both, a cry escaping my lips. I can feel his fire power mounting in potency, sense his own hot, rhythmic rushes of intense pleasure, building into an inferno.

His wings slam down to either side of me, stealing my breath as his mouth clamps down on the inner edge of my shoulder and his canines pierce my skin.

A rush of fiery power detonates, wave after wave of it, as our fires *merge*, the pleasure so intense I lose all sense of self, both of us hurtling into his inferno as I cry out his name and we release ourselves into each other.

There's only his fire.

Only *him*.

Only his body merged with mine. Both of us one being of flame.

Fully Wyvernbonded.

As our merged fire settles, Yvan stills, holding me suspended and pressed to the tree, his skin slick against mine as our chests rise and fall against each other, the sting along the inner edge of my shoulder rapidly shifting to a pleasurable, fiery blaze.

I glance down to find a half-moon of violet flame marked there, a stunned delight igniting.

Yvan gives me an impassioned look, emotion lashing through our now fully linked fire. He lowers his head and tenderly kisses the mark, then runs his tongue over it as tears of joy blur my vision.

I send my own fire out to him, astonished to be so fully connected with his power. I pull on it, and his flame slides right through my rootlines. A shiver of astonishment flashes through him as he does the same, drawing my fire into his own, our fire magic fully melding into a shimmering, blazing caress.

Yvan murmurs a stream of words in the deeply sibilant language of Western Wyvern'kin, and I'm stunned anew to be able to fully comprehend his ardent words.

My beautiful mate.

My fire.

My Wyvernbonded love.

CHAPTER
TWELVE

SHADOW DRAGON RISING

Elloren Guryev

Zhilaan Forest

I'm wrapped around Yvan, lying on the mossy soil of the Zhilaan Forest's western edge, our limbs entangled. In his sleep, Yvan's fire flows through mine with steady force, more intimately than I could have ever imagined, his wing draped over my shoulder, his strong arms embracing me.

His love for me burning bright through our merged fire power.

I glance at the Wyvernbond mark emblazoned on the inner edge of my shoulder. It burns violet bright against the night, the Forest's approving affection swirling through it.

Love swelling in my breast, my gaze slides over Yvan, tracing his handsome face, his normally serious angular features softened by sleep. He put his pants back on at some point, and his crimson hair is tousled charmingly around his dark horns, his chest rising and falling against mine, his heartbeat reassuringly strong, the Varg iron-protection rune marked in the center of his chest glowing emerald bright.

My smile wavers, and tears warm my eyes, the real world intruding on my idyllic moment. The battle with the Magedom looms tomorrow eve. I slide a protective arm around Yvan, wanting to hold on to this precious, suspended moment.

Yvan smiles slightly in response to my caress, his eyelids fluttering in sleep as he nestles me closer. My heart twists with a surge of feeling for him, just as a knot of glowing milk white flowers past him in the distance snag my attention.

Norfure blossoms.

My heartbeat quickens.

The essential ingredient in Norfure tincture, one of the only formulations able to cure the vicious Red Grippe, and desperately needed by the refugees streaming into the East. I look past the small knot of blossoms and can just make out a larger patch of hazy glowing white. My pulse jumps into an even faster rhythm. Norfure blossoms are a touchy night-blooming flower, exceedingly rare and difficult to grow in captivity.

And there just might be enough here to cure hundreds of people.

I gently disentangle myself from Yvan.

"Elloren," he murmurs, his voice thick with sleep, eyes half opening. His gaze zeroes in on my Wyvernbond mark, glowing as bright as the violet fire overtaking his eyes.

"I've spotted Norfure flowers," I tell him as I pull on my melded-leaf garb. "I think there's a larger patch of blossoms just ahead. They're difficult to spot during the day because they curl into themselves."

"Stay close," he urges.

"I will," I promise, pointedly lifting my living branch and giving Yvan a significant look as I sheathe it at my side. He nods, caressing me with an encircling rush of heat before he closes his eyes once more.

Darkness washes over the world, save for the green glimmer of my skin, my Wyvernbond mark, horde mark, and the edges of a few runes, which prove to be enough to illuminate the area surrounding me.

I step around brush and move toward the blossoms' dim white glow, the air chilly, several Winter Dark Fireflies zooming in to encircle me in their constellation of butter yellow light.

I can sense these autumn-loving fireflies' activity throughout the Forest, the other species of fireflies already settled in for the coming winter, burrowed underground or nestled under tree bark, only these fiery ones able to withstand autumn's cooling temperatures.

I huff out an elated breath as the Norfure patch comes into sharper view, anticipation sparking, a larger carpet of the blossoms spread out before me than I had anticipated.

Enough to make *thousands* of vials of medicine.

A low animal groan sounds somewhere farther ahead, drawing my focus, a sense of the Zhilaan Forest's call to the sound filling the air.

Taking hold of the branch sheathed at my side, I make a mental note of the Norfure flowers' location before pushing forward through a dense thicket. I emerge in a small clearing beside a sizable bog, the fireflies swirling out to whirl over the wetland and a deep-purple bull moose that looks to be struggling to free himself from the bog's dense mud, the rear half of his body submerged.

The large animal's eyes meet mine, a pleading fear in them that sets my Dryad heart lurching into a faster rhythm.

"I'll help you," I vow, raising my branch hand. I murmur the Dryadin words drawn from Oaklyyn's spell-link rune and thrust my branch forward.

A thick vine bursts from the branch's tip and bolts past the moose before lashing around one of the huge Zhilaan Cypress trees edging the bog. The vine slingshots around the cypress's slender trunk then whips around the moose's body, creating a magic-wrought pulley.

"Draw him out," I murmur in Dryadin, digging my heels into the soil. I pull in a deep breath, keeping my wand aloft as I'm filled with a sense of the Zhilaan Forest's elemental force rippling in to work with me. The vine tethered to my branch draws back into its tip with mighty power, snapping tight around the distant trunk and yanking the moose forward.

The bog groans, a pop of released suction snapping through the air as the moose springs free of the mud and shambles onto denser soil. Euphoric triumph leaps in my breast as the huge creature pauses and sets its gaze on me, a rush of palpable gratitude overtaking me before the moose lollops away. I watch him go, expecting the tension shivering on the Forest air to evaporate.

But it lingers.

Strengthens.

Growing uneasy, I turn to make my way back to Yvan as a raven I recognize lights on a nearby branch—Ariel's raven.

"Hello there," I say, then glance around for Ariel.

"Elloren."

I turn and find Yvan behind me, his fire contained, a concerning tension in his voice, his eyes cooled to green.

"What's wrong?" I ask, gripping my branch, the tension on the Forest's air turning so pungent I can scent its pine-sharp unease.

"I don't know," Yvan says, glancing around at the trees as Ariel's raven takes flight, soaring toward the West. "Something's . . . *off*," he says, an odd tightness to his voice.

"I'm picking up a sense of warning and confusion," I tell him, "coming from the Forest."

"We should take to the air," he offers. "And see what's spooking the trees. If we need to, we can alert everyone."

I nod and step toward him, then throw my arms around his neck, his power disquietingly constrained. Before I can comment on it, he throws down his powerful wings, and we shoot into the air, his chest Wyvern hot against mine.

The Forest's aura of tension abruptly surges to ballistic heights—*Danger! Danger! Danger!* riding on the air.

"There's an incoming threat," I warn Yvan as we soar southwest, my gaze darting everywhere for some sign of it. "The Forest's sense of danger . . . it just exploded into what feels like *panic*."

"I can read it too," he grimly agrees.

We approach the western edge of the Zhilaan Mountain Range and soar out of the Forest and over its peaks, the Shadow- and storm-decimated land just beyond Zhilaan's dome-shield a punch to the gut.

The East's Unbalanced storms have moved southward, and I can just make out Vogel's huge stormwall looming in the distant West. Unnaturally deep thunder rumbles through the gigantic band, curling black lightning crackling through it. But there's no sign of Vogel's forces.

So, what is the Zhilaan Forest trying to warn us about?

Yvan lands on a broad, stony ledge recessed between two peaks, a panoramic view surrounding us of both the Zhilaan to the East and the Shadowed lands to the West. He sets me down, and it takes me a moment to fully find my balance, an odd tension pulling at our Wyvernbond.

"Our bond," I say. "It's yanking us back toward the Zhilaan Forest."

"I feel it too," he says, seeming equally thrown as he peers in the direction from which we came. "It's as if the Forest holds our bond instead of us." He sets his gaze back on me. "Are you armed?"

I hold up the branch in my hand. "I am."

"Do you have any other weapons?" he presses.

"No," I say, confused. "Why?"

Yvan darts forward in a blur, wrests the branch from my hand and hurls it away. Before I can fully register my shock, he pulls swiftly back, a dark wand suddenly in his hand. He thrusts it toward me.

Confusion explodes into alarm as vines shoot from his wand's tip and slap around my wrists and ankles, binding them tight and yanking me to the ground, my back colliding painfully with stone. Yvan's eyes erupt into silver flame, his fire aura releasing from his tight hold on it.

A shock of terror lances through me as a dark Void tree punches into the back of my mind, an aura of steel-bright flame burning against my rootlines. I've felt this fire before. In a horrific binding kiss . . .

My horror turns cataclysmic as Ariel's raven lights on Yvan's shoulder and morphs into a Shadow-rune-marked raven with multiple eyes. Yvan's silver-burning eyes narrow on me as he draws a rune-marked stone from his tunic's pocket, murmurs a spell . . . and his glamour drops away.

Revealing Vogel's green-glimmering, black-haired, shockingly shirtless form.

The Shadow Wand is gripped in his hand, *dark wings* fanning out from his back and black horns rising from his head, unfamiliar Shadow fastlines marking his hands and wrists.

The world-upending truth slams through me with planetary force.

"You're an *Icaral*," I gasp.

Vogel hisses and lunges for me, the multi-eyed raven winging away as he falls on me. Dark-clawed fingers slap onto the stone beside my arms as he bares sharpened teeth and snaps them close to my face.

"I'm a *Mage*," he snarls. "Not an Icaral demon. And my *true* Black Witch is going to *freeze* this winged corruption *out of me*."

My heart thunders against my ribs, the whole Forest echoing my overwhelming alarm.

He's mad. He's completely and utterly mad.

Straddling me, Vogel leers at my Wyvernbond mark before he bares elongating teeth and grabs cruel hold of my jaw. "I'm going to draw your power out of you, *Fae whore*," he growls, eyes burning, "and siphon it *all* into my Black Witch. And then the Magedom's prophesied Black Witch will *rise* and your cursed Fae Wilds and Icaral beast will *fall*!"

I gape at him in horror as the shattering comprehension slams down.

Yvan was never the Icaral of Prophecy.

Vogel is.

And Fallon isn't the Black Witch, no matter how much Vogel wants to try to turn her into one.

I am.

It all falls into horrifying place—the Void tree image that assaulted my mind when I first met Vogel, the two of us on a Forest-prophesied collision course from that very first moment onward. My eyes flick toward the Wand in his hand—the Shadow counterforce to the Verdyllion. The Wand that took down III.

Panic rising, I grit my teeth and summon every ounce of magical aura in my Wyvernbond, horde bond, and rootlines. Letting loose a rage-filled scream, I blast my aura out toward Yvan and my entire horde.

Vogel snarls and flicks the Shadow Wand's tip forward. A gag flies around my mouth just as I'm hit by the sudden, burning sense of not only Yvan's fire scalding through our bond, but my entire horde's fire blasting toward me, a blaze of returning alarm in it.

"Oh, I can feel their fire too," Vogel sneers with a vicious grin as he rises and steps away from me, drawing his wings in tight behind his back. He grabs hold of a military tunic lying on a boulder beside us and throws it on, hiding his wings, before thrusting his hand into the tunic's pocket. Withdrawing it, he drops a rune-marked stone to the ground.

A line of rotating Shadow runes fly up from the stone then arc down to form a portal arch, its interior rippling silvery black.

Holy Ancient One, no. I gasp, my alarm sliding into primal horror.

I blast urgency through my bonds once more, Yvan's fire blazing searing-hot through our Wyvernbond as he bursts into view in the distance, soaring toward us, my entire horde flying behind him, including Raz'zor's pale dragon form. Yvan's full storm of fire power is zeroed in on Vogel, a feral rage slashing through it.

Vogel grabs hold of my bindings and yanks me up as I struggle violently against them to no avail, a vicious smile on his lips as the multi-eyed raven lands on his shoulder.

"Elloren!" Yvan snarls, speeding toward me and lifting a violet-glowing hand as Vogel hurls me at the portal.

"Vogel's the Icaral of Prophecy and I'm the Black Witch!" I struggle to scream out against my gag, my words muffled into incoherence as Yvan and my horde release their fire, the portal's Shadow power closes in around me and I'm swallowed up by Vogel's silvery Void.

PART FOUR

The Battle for Erthia

CHAPTER ONE

THE BLACK WITCH

Elloren

Shadow wasteland

I'm the Black Witch of Prophecy.

The will to fight pounds through me as Vogel drags my vine-bound and gagged form out of the rippling Void darkness of his Shadow portal. We emerge into a deserted steel gray cavern. Shadowfire torches are set into its walls, flickering pewter light.

One of his arms slung around my torso, Vogel drags me into a narrow stone tunnel with effortless Icaral strength.

I glance around with the caginess of a prey animal, searching for weapons, my feet futilely scudding against stone for purchase. Vogel's grotesque multi-eyed raven follows us, its wings beating the air as it flies from one stony outcropping to another, my heart ratcheting into a thunderous beat.

I'm the Black Witch.

And Vogel *is the Icaral of Prophecy.*

Yvan's fire burns with volcanic heat through our bond, rife with wild, snarling energy.

My gut clenches, viselike.

Because I can sense that Vogel's silvery Shadowfire is stronger than Yvan's. And stronger, now, than mine, a whole burning abyss of Void fire churning inside him, ready to finish consuming *everything*.

We round a corner, and an arching entrance comes into view, an iron door set into it, heavily studded.

Two burly, blank-faced Level Five Mage soldiers bracket the door, their gray eyes glowing, and I can sense their completed tether to Vogel's Shadow, invisible

THE DRYAD STORM

Void power curling out from the Shadow Wand toward the grayed fastlines marking the soldiers' hands and wrists. I trace how the malignant power winds through their every Mageline and wraps demonic fog through their minds, their auras of Level Five earth magery being siphoned into the Shadow Wand.

I zero in on the gray-smoking wands sheathed at their sides, every nerve in my body coming alive.

Wood.

I clench my branch hand, my heart a battle axe against my ribs even as I remember that these deadwood wands are no longer any use to me. I have to get hold of *living* wood. I focus inward, a distant sense of the Zhilaan Forest struggling to send fire to me over the great expanse between us sizzling against my rootlines, tenuously anchoring my foliage-amplified magic.

"Unlock the door," Vogel commands.

One of the soldiers grabs the ring of keys attached to his belt and sets about unlocking the door's three locks. I take note of the Shadow locking rune emblazoned in the door's center as the soldier steps back.

My feet skid against stone as Vogel drags me forward with a vicious yank then presses the Shadow Wand's tip into the center of the locking rune, which erupts into tendrils of undulating smoke.

Seeming satisfied, Vogel shoves the door open and drags me into a cell.

As he slams the iron door shut behind us, I take in two black canvas military cots before me and surprise bolts through me.

Fallon Bane is lying on one of them.

She's bound by Shadow vines, her eyes glowing a churning gray, as if Vogel trapped two thunderheads in her irises. Shadow fastlines identical to Vogel's mark her hands and wrists.

Forcing even breaths, I try to calm the disgust roiling through me, even as the urge to retch tightens my gut.

Did he take her after wresting control of her mind?

Fallon's eyes meet mine. The air dips to ice, her lips curling back into an animalistic snarl, my alarm intensifying as Vogel drags me toward the empty cot.

Living wood . . . I need living wood . . . pounds every slamming beat of my heart, my heels battering against stone in a futile attempt to fight Vogel's pull. I sense Yvan reading the urgent flare of my internal fire, heat searing through me as he floods my lines with a formidable surge of his Wyvernfire.

Fire I can't access without a living branch.

Vogel hurls me onto the empty cot, then steps back in a blur and levels the Shadow Wand at me.

I growl against my gag and thrash as he binds me to the cot, Yvan's fire scorching through our bond so intensely that I begin to vibrate from the pulsing heat.

Vogel lurches forward, a wild look in his eyes as silver fire overtakes them. Dark horns rise from his head, and his pupils contract to vertical slits. He grabs one of my ears, and I snarl my protest against my gag as his sharp claws dig in then pierce clear through my ear's Dryad point.

An explosion of agony bursts through the side of my head as Vogel rips off the pointed top of my ear. "Aughhhhh!" I cry out against my gag, my body arching from the pain, warm blood trickling through my hair, Yvan's fury blazing through me.

"You Fae *bitch*!" Vogel snarls, drawing back his bloodied hand and shaking off my torn flesh. He levels the Shadow Wand at me once more, the Wand I'm desperate to get away from him.

Yvan's fire flashes violet at the edges of my vision as Vogel murmurs what sounds like an Issani spell. A slim line of Shadow mist bursts out to encircle me, the misty rope slithering around my body before dissolving into it. Ear throbbing, I tense as the Shadow twines tight around my rootlines then flows toward Fallon and ropes around her prone form.

Before dissolving into her and around her lines of power, as well.

"I'm connecting you and my Black Witch with a Shadow twinning spell," Vogel hisses, giving me a fanged smile.

Terror strikes through me as he casts another line of misty Shadow from my lines to Fallon's. Then another. And another. Weaving us together with a corrupted version of the spell linking Gwynn and Mavrik.

Weaving together Fallon's Magelines and my Forest-bound Dryad rootlines with one of the strongest spells on Erthia.

A connection to Fallon's power takes hold, her corrupted ice and wind powers suddenly invading my rootlines and painfully chilling my skin as a portion of my magic starts to stream toward Fallon's dormant fire-, earth-, and lightlines.

My power graying as it's pulled into her.

I bite into my gag, forcing back panic. Fallon's dormant earth-, fire-, and lightlines slowly awaken, like demons rising.

THE DRYAD STORM

"You don't deserve your power, Fae whore," Vogel sneers as he weaves his spell, his horrible raven motionless as it watches from a stony outcropping. "It belongs to my Black Witch," he hisses. "The Magedom's *true* Black Witch."

I growl against my gag, tensing every muscle and line as I fight to hold on to my fireline's power and my bond to Yvan while I struggle to think of some way to free myself, get hold of the Shadow Wand, and take Vogel down. Ignoring the pain hammering through my ear and the poisonous draw on my power, I cast my Dryad senses about, frantically searching for some sense of surviving Forest creatures, some remaining speck of the Living World, that I can draw on for aid in this Shadowed hellscape, but there's *nothing*.

Only the terrible, lifeless Shadow Void for leagues and leagues. No living wood. No surviving animal or plant kindreds. Yvan and my allies too far away.

Vogel's green-glimmering lips lift into a smug smile, as if he's reading my thoughts, his utter victory sliding into place.

He leans in close. "After I've drawn every drop of your power into my Black Witch," he croons as he presses the Wand's tip into my throat, "I will *rip* your Fae heart out of your chest as your Icaral demon flies in to rescue you. And then I will watch as your death shrivels his power to nothing and your whore-bond to him is *destroyed*."

An image of Fallon striking down a powerless Yvan and Vogel falling on him, claws out, as he rips the wings from Yvan's back and Fallon spears ice through his body assaults my mind.

Growing desperate, I blaze the energy of warning through our bond, but Yvan's furious fire only intensifies, moving closer every second.

A heavy, reverberating knock sounds on the metal door, drawing Vogel's and my attention, a sense of vicious gray fire whooshing through the door to burn around us.

Vogel straightens and sheathes his Wand, his eyes cooling to pale green, pupils rounding and horns retracting. "Enter," he commands.

The door opens to reveal a pyrr-demon standing between the two guards with a glamour I can see through. His eyes glow sulfuric red, Shadow-smoke horns tendriling up from his head. "Excellency," the demon says, baring sharp, black teeth. "Damion Bane has arrived at the base's Central Hall. He's demanding to see his sister."

Vogel straightens, his inferno of Shadowed Wyvernfire held tight in his core. He glances at the two soldiers bracketing the door. "Remain at your posts while I meet with him," he orders, casting me a chillingly brutal smile. "Damion Bane will see his sister soon enough."

With that, Vogel strides out of the cell and slams the door with a soul-crushing clang. The door's Shadow locking rune's glow brightens, tendrils of gray mist snaking through the complicated locks as they click into place.

CHAPTER TWO

BLACK WITCH RISING

Elloren Guryev

Shadow wasteland

Silence descends in the cramped cavern, only Fallon's occasional feral snarl breaking through the silver torchlight guttering over our bound forms.

My heart thuds, the sound of my pulse whooshing through my ears as I strain against my bindings.

I sense Yvan drawing nearer with what must be portal-speed, the painful stretch of our bond relaxing, his fire increasingly roaring through me along with that of my entire horde, assuring me that they are on their way.

But sweat breaks out over my skin. The Shadowed twinning spell striving to fully connect my rootlines with Fallon's has taken on a parasitical life of its own, my gut clenching against the feel of my magic being siphoned out of me and into Fallon, the Shadow mist slithering around our lines winding tighter and tighter . . .

. . . then pulling excruciatingly tight.

I scream against my Shadow gag at the same moment Fallon lets out a throaty growl, every one of my muscles tensed bowstring tight as Yvan and my horde's Wyvernfire is punched back, cold invades my rootlines, and my power starts to funnel more intensely toward Fallon.

I tense every rootline, struggling to hold my magic back from the evil linkage. I manage to tenuously slow its flow, but the effort is torturous, like knives being dragged along my rootlines.

Another surge of Yvan's fire hits me, searing through our mating mark and bond before streaking through my arms to my hands and concentrating there as if Yvan is trying to send his might into my palms.

Wood, I agonize. *If I had one single sliver of living* wood.

I'm trembling now, my power like a roaring tide battering against a dam that's about to break and send every last ounce of my magic straight into Fallon, my mating mark and palms burning hotter and hotter . . .

A memory of something Yvan said suddenly connects—

The bite opens up a full sharing of fire power.

The revelation of what Yvan is trying to convey strikes home with the force of stars colliding, my heart striking into a rib-battering rhythm.

I don't need living wood to get free, I breathlessly consider, a brutal ruthlessness descending. *I have access to* Icaral *fire.*

I draw in a harsh breath, pull on Yvan's power . . . and draw his Icaral inferno toward my palms.

The scene around me tints to flickering violet, a hotter scald overtaking my palms.

Snarling against my gag, I splay my fingers open, tense every line and roar out the inferno of Icaral fire.

Heat blasts from my palms in an explosion of violet flame, every Shadow vine restraining me igniting.

Fallon shrieks as my gag and other bindings sizzle away, freeing me.

My gaze jerks to her as I sit up, a new jolt of panic spearing through me as I realize her bindings are burning to ash as well, the guards outside shouting and pounding on the rune-sealed iron door.

The split-second realization hits. *They can't get in. Only Vogel can . . .*

I spring to my feet at the same moment that Fallon does, her movements unnaturally quick, her whole being seeming transformed into an animalistic state by the Shadow coursing through her lines. Her glowing gray eyes lock with mine, her lips pulling back in a bloodcurdling hiss.

Before I can attack, she lunges and knocks me to the ground.

My back collides with stone, the breath knocked from my lungs as Fallon's hands close around my throat. I'm unable to breathe, Fallon's grip clenching so tight that I fear her fingers will puncture my skin, her ice spearing into my lines. My eyes bulge as I struggle to both pull in air and draw more of Yvan's fire into my palms. Thrashing against Fallon's hold, I punch her to no avail and she hisses and bears down. Dark stars explode through my vision, and I begin to black out,

Yvan's fire power taking on a feral, lashing force as it burns through wave upon wave of ice.

Seizing on my final shred of consciousness, I reach up, grasp Fallon's shoulder, and blast Wyvernfire straight into her.

Fallon screams, her hands flying off my throat as she erupts into violet flames.

Breath floods back into my lungs, and I force myself up, wheezing. Wasting no time, I whip my palms forward with a snarl and blast more fire at Fallon. She screams, writhing and burning, her Shadow-destroyed form soon stilling inside the inferno.

Her power's hold on me fully releases, the twinned spell fading to steam and ash.

Shock grips hold, devastation riding in close on its heels.

I killed her.

My stomach heaves, a jolt of remorse lancing through me over having killed someone. But there's no time to dwell on it. There's no time for anything but taking down this entire Shadow world before it's too late.

Swallowing back the urge to retch, I raise my palms to the iron door and blast Wyvernfire into it.

The door heats to a glowing purple and liquefies to the ground in a molten puddle, a hot, metallic tang on the air. Before the guards outside can respond, I snarl a battle cry and thrust my palms forward, then blast out a wall of fire and hurl myself through the door, my vision briefly overtaken by my violet firestorm.

I spin in a semicircle, whipping out fire, soldiers screaming as they burn, my flames clearing as they grow silent.

Panting, I take in six charred bodies littering the ground before I set off at a sprint down one stone tunnel then another and another, soon reaching another locked iron door.

Raising my palms, I blast out twin shots of fire and incinerate the door's bolt, lock, and hinges, then kick it open.

It falls to the stone ground with a deafening *clang*, revealing the outside world.

Two Level Five Mage soldiers wheel around to face me. Their green eyes are grayed only at the edges, their free will not yet overtaken. They're standing on an elevated ledge, a gigantic military base spread out behind them, the view panoramic from this vantage point. Broken multi-eyed and multilimbed Shadow dragons screech through the air, Mages astride them. There's a vast encampment of dark tents, a sea of Mage troops astride Shadow dragons aligned in neat formation to the south of them. A chill races down my spine. I recognize the central stone buildings from pictures in the history texts Jules Kristian gave me.

Issyl.

The capital of Issaan.

But completely stripped of color. Shadow clouds roil overhead, a poisonous tang on the air. Shadow storm bands line every horizon, leagues of charred land before them.

The Natural World decimated.

Rage sparks within me and heats into a vengeful inferno.

"State your name!" one of the soldiers demands as they both level wands at me.

"The Black Witch," I snarl, and blast bolts of violet fire straight at their chests. The soldiers burst into flame and crumple to the ground just as alarm horns begin to sound.

Pulse skyrocketing, I look up and see a legion of Mage soldiers on dragonback wheeling around in the sky and soaring directly toward me.

I focus on drawing power to my hands, quickly realizing that the Shadowed landscape is siphoning away Yvan's Wyvernfire as fast as he's feeding it into me—I don't have enough to take down an army.

Spitting out a curse, I turn and set off at a sprint up the stony hillock behind me, climbing toward its rounded pinnacle as I draw in more of Yvan's Wyvernfire.

I leap over the hillock's apex, and my heart plummets as I come face-to-face with the colossally long and high storm band rising a short distance from the hillock's base. Thunder crashes through it with emphatic force, curved, dark lightning flashing through its expanse.

A *crack* sounds, and I flinch as the storm band expands, its front rising higher and higher into the sky.

Vogel knows, I realize. *He knows I'm free, and he's attempting to trap me here.*

Rebellion fires through every nerve as I spare a glance over my shoulder to find Vogel's forces soaring over the hillock, straight toward me.

I lurch toward the hillock's base, my feet skidding as I slide and sprint down it, then launch into a sprint toward the storm band. Dragons shriek as they traverse the hillock, and I raise both palms and blast out as much of Yvan's violet fire as I can summon, conjuring a flaming shield around myself before I run straight into Vogel's wall of storm.

CHAPTER THREE

PROPHECY RISING

Elloren Guryev

Issani wasteland

Surrounded by my shield of violet Wyvernfire, I surge through the Shadow storm band, the roar of black-gray churning chaos surrounding me and pummeling against my fire-shield, which rapidly thins as Vogel's Shadow storm siphons off its energy.

I accelerate, racing for what feels like forever to outrun the storm band's consumption of Yvan's magic. Eventually, I sense a lessoning of the maelstrom just ahead. Heart in my throat, I leap toward the storm band's farthest edge at the same moment the surrounding storm crashes through my fire-shield.

A lung-punching gust hits my back, its Shadow slithering straight through me and around my rootlines as I'm blown clear off my feet and out of the storm band's eastern-facing side.

I cry out, hurtling through the air and then colliding with the ground. My palms slam down onto charred, smoking soil, an acid tang in the corrupted air.

Heart thundering, I force myself up, nothing but the blackened shapes of dead trees all around as I'm overtaken by the rootline-clutching feel of the Shadow tendrils curling up from the ground parasitically linking into my power.

The shrieks of broken dragons sound over the roaring storm band's expanse, so loud their collective rage shakes the ground. Breath shudders through my lungs as my empathy senses Vogel's forces gathering on the other side of the storm band. Possibly waiting for Vogel to arrive and open a path through it, or for the bulk of my Wyvern power to be siphoned off by the leaching Shadow tendrils before they strike.

Or both.

A chill streaks down my spine as I launch into a sprint away from the storm band, the Shadow tendrils drawing more intently on my power, the Wyvernfire Yvan is flooding into me soon struggling to even reach my lines.

I need to find living wood, or it's all over.

I zigzag around grayed, smoking corpses of trees, frantically searching for some sliver of surviving wood until a cramp screams in my side. My steps falter, fire power sapped from my rootlines and into the Shadow as I begin to severely weaken.

I catch sight of a sliver of pale brown bark.

My eyes widen at the slash of rich color in the center of the charred trunk just ahead.

Pulse quickening into a gallop, I lurch forward and fall to my knees before it. Lifting my hands, I frantically scratch back the small slash of uncharred bark with my Dryad nails and uncover a surviving sliver of tawny, living wood, my breathing becoming labored as my rootlines begin to shrivel.

I pry the sliver of wood from the charred tree just as my glimmering Dryad-green hue fades to gray, my Zhilaan Forest linkage too distant to fight off this much Shadow. A cry escapes me, the rapidly diminishing thread of my Wyvernbond to Yvan the only thing keeping me from collapsing into gray oblivion.

A pulse of monumental Shadowed Wyvern-Mage power hits my back, stealing my breath, silver sparks streaking across my vision.

Vogel.

His strengthening aura of corrupted fire approaching from the storm band's western side.

Desperation ripples through me, my access to magic decimated, Yvan still leagues away, Vogel and his forces poised to advance through their storm band and take hold of me.

Clear that my chances of survival are dwindling, I do the last thing left to me.

Pray.

"Ancient One," I implore, clutching at the living wood as tears blur my eyes, "Blessed Vo. Mai'ya. Oo'na. *Anyone* who can hear me. Please, *help me.* I will give my *life* for Erthia if you do. I'm *begging* you. *Please. Don't let Vogel win.*"

Elloren.

I freeze, the voice seeming to come from deep inside of me as well as from the tiny piece of living wood. A familiar, masculine voice I thought I'd never hear again.

Stunned, I glance up to find Lukas sitting on a charred branch just above me, a Watcher perched on his shoulder.

An explosive surge of emotion shears straight through my heart.

"Lukas!" I cry, choking on his name, my tears giving way.

Because he's as transparent as the Watcher.

And utterly transfigured.

His skin is a deep, glimmering Dryad green, his ears pointed and his *eyes . . .* they're full of verdant fire. More Watchers shiver into view on the charred branches around him.

"Are you dead?" I rasp out. "Please, Lukas, don't be dead."

He smiles.

I'm transformed, he says from inside me, from inside the wood.

My gaze darts toward the distant storm band, my empathic sense of Vogel's approach intensifying, another pulse of Vogel's silver-fire power coursing through me.

I look back at Lukas, the world surrounding us blurring, time seeming to pause, a tidal wave of emotion rushing in. "I miss you," I choke out. "I love you, Lukas. I'm *sorry.*"

Don't be, he says, the words shot through with compassion. And love. Love I can feel searing straight through my heart, tears now streaming down my face.

"I never wanted you to end up alone," I roughly choke out.

His loving smile is undimmed. *I'm not, Elloren,* he says from inside my heart as he gestures toward the East. *I'm part of* everything *now.*

My anguish burgeons. "Lukas, everything is about to be *destroyed.*"

His expression turns blazingly serious. *Then don't let it be.*

"How," I cry, holding up my grayed hand. "Lukas, *how?*"

He raises his palm, the image of III marked on it, passion in his burning gaze. *Everything you ever needed, Elloren, it's all inside you. It always has been.*

And then he and the Watchers vanish.

"No!" I cry, reaching toward where he just was and finding only air. The sliver of living wood turns gray, and the nightmare rushes back in.

"Lukas, *don't leave me!*" I cry, despair crashing through me.

A slight sting on my palm has my gaze jerking downward.

Trembling, I turn my grayed palm up, and the image of III briefly seems to shimmer with Lukas's verdant light just as the leading edge of the Mage forces on dragonback burst through the distant storm band.

Terror threatens to overwhelm me, but I battle it back, comprehension igniting,

Lukas's words striking through me with the force of a war hammer.

It's all inside you.

On reckless instinct, I force my nails into the charred, smoking soil and swiftly dig a small hole then thrust my branch hand into it, burying the image of III.

A hard sting races over my palm. Rays of green light flare through the loosened soil, and the tendrils of Shadow disappear in a sizable circle around me, as if pushed back by a superior force.

I turn my submerged palm upward, and my eyes widen as a seedling breaks through the soil, springing from III's mark, the small Ironwood sapling branching as it grows and sprouts vividly green leaves, its roots pushing my hand aside.

Stunned, I withdraw my hand from the soil as the small tree rises and branches, its love and support flooding through me in a brilliant green rush as its canopy thickens just above my head.

Dryad, the sapling sends through me as it drops one of its living branches into my lap.

"Bless you," I gasp, grabbing hold of the living branch, resolve flooding through me as my rootlines link into the branch and the tree.

Glimmering Dryad green ripples over my skin's grayed hue, the tree's elemental power flooding through me as my rootlines shimmer back to strength with Black Witch *Dryad* power.

"Dryad Witch!" a man's voice bellows, his tone unnaturally deep.

I bolt to my feet, about twenty soldiers soaring toward me, their wands raised, their broken dragons shrieking.

The sapling sends a series of spells to me, and I ready my branch, the two of us our own small Dryad army.

Our own small Dryad *storm.*

Snarling out a battle cry, I thrust my branch forward.

A maelstrom of green magic blasts from my branch and forms a wall of pulsing green power, shot through with verdant lightning that rapidly fans out and rises as the wall barrels forward.

My stormwall slams into the Mage forces, and dragons and Mages scream as they're lanced through with Dryad lightning and explode into churning masses of green fire. The wall continues to push forward until it slams into Vogel's storm band, blasting a Forest of green-lightning trees into being throughout its expanse— trees filled with enough elemental might to blow up any Mage or dragon or Shadow creature on contact, the storm band now pulsing with green light.

I start to draw up more of my sapling-ally's power, just as I'm overtaken by a surge of incoming violet and then gold and vermillion Wyvernfire shot through with purple sparks, both my bond with Yvan and my horde bond surging to scorching life.

I wheel around and let out a strangled gasp as the dark slash of a sky portal bursts into being in the grayed heavens. Yvan soars through it and speeds toward me over the forest of charred trees, his gaze incandescent.

A powerful wave of aching relief and love hits me so hard that I almost lose my footing. I cry out Yvan's name as he, and then Ariel and Raz'zor, fly out of the portal and toward me, followed by Naga and our Wyvern horde in dragon form.

Dryad Witch! Raz'zor snarls through our bond, martial heat shuddering through his red fire.

Yvan, Naga, Raz'zor, Ariel, and the horde, save Oaklyyn, touch down in front of the storm band I've overtaken, the protective runes marked on Yvan's chest glowing bright. Yvan thrusts his palms forward and, as one, they blast out roaring streams of fire to rapidly form their own stormwall of Wyvernflame in front of the storm band.

Naga and our horde hold the wall of fire as Yvan runs to me, Ariel at his heels. Yvan takes me in desperately, the violet fire in his eyes turning white-hot as he notices my torn, bloodied ear. Volcanic rage on my behalf roars through our bond.

His hand slides up to cradle my ear as I grip hold of him. "Did Vogel do this to you?" he hisses.

I nod, but there's no time to dwell on my mutilated ear. "Vogel's an Icaral," I rasp.

Yvan's eyes widen, shock blasting through his fire as he blazes out a fiery image of Vogel with wings through our entire horde's bond.

Naga's head whips toward us, the fire in her eyes giving a stunned flare as Ariel hisses out a string of shocked curses.

"It was never you," I say to Yvan. "Never you all along. *Vogel's* the Icaral of Prophecy. And, Yvan, *I'm* the Black Witch."

"But . . . Fallon," Yvan says as I watch him working to piece it all together.

"She's dead," I tell him, voice harsh. "I killed her. And Vogel's coming. Along with his army. They're massed just past their storm band. His forces might not be able to easily get through the Shadow storm band and the lightning forest I've conjured, but *he* can."

"Our forces might not arrive for some time," Yvan tells me, glancing toward the fading sky portal. "We came through once the portal held enough charge for a few, but the whole portal might take close to another hour before it can transport our entire army."

"That's *too long*," I counter.

Silver-hot fire knifes into me, and Vogel's Void tree punches into my mind with staggering force. I cry out, a huge concentration of Vogel's magic suddenly advancing through the storm band.

"Vogel's coming," I warn, pulse thundering as I hold up my hand, revealing my III mark. "Throw your palms in the soil," I urge Yvan and Ariel. "III put seeds in our tree marks. We can manifest saplings to push back the Shadow and replenish our elemental power—"

Multiple bolts of steely Shadow wind blast from the storm band and smash into us, the ground giving way as we're all hurled through the air away from each other. I grab hold of my sapling as I'm blown past it, my wind-buffeted trajectory halted as the small tree's pain and defiance shiver through me. Frantically searching through the maelstrom, I catch sight of Yvan's blurred form to my far left.

Shadowed storm spiders burst out of the earth, charred soil spraying. In a split second, their legs slam down, encasing Yvan and my horde mates in leg-cages, gray power blasting from raised holes in their thoraxes to whip around the cages. Yvan and my horde mates blaze a mammoth amount of Wyvern power at the spiders, only to find it being siphoned off by the largest spider amongst them—

The gigantic queen imprisoning Yvan.

I watch with horror as Yvan and my horde mates stagger then fall to the ground, the fire in their eyes snapping out.

"*Yvan!*" I cry, outrage sizzling through our rapidly weakening bond.

I lurch toward him just as a bolt of silver-gray Wyvernfire streaks through my horde's fiery stormwall and blasts into my sapling ally.

The small tree explodes into Shadowfire.

"*No!*" I roar, my sapling kindred's scream of agony tearing through me, my source of Dryad power whisked away, tendrils of Shadow flowing in around my lines.

Vogel's Void tree strobes painfully against my mind, as I sense the storm band I overtook graying, my lightning trees sizzling to nothing as Vogel strides through the wall of Wyvernfire. He's bare-chested, his grayed wings fanned out. His Shadow horns are up, his slit-pupiled eyes alight with hate-bright silver flame as they meet mine.

He lifts the Shadow Wand.

I flinch as my horde's entire Wyvernfire stormwall morphs to gray mist and falls to the ground before surging forward to snake around my ankles.

The entirety of Vogel's cataclysmically superior Shadow power zeroed in on *me*.

CHAPTER FOUR

PROPHECY WAR

Elloren Guryev

Shadow wasteland

"The Magedom is stronger than a thousand hordes," Vogel hisses.

He advances toward me over the Void wasteland, the Shadow Wand raised. I can feel Yvan's rage and desperate fight to regain hold of his power from the giant Shadow spiders imprisoning both him and my horde mates.

Shadow mist is now thick on the ground, obscuring my feet, the body of the colossal queen spider poised over Yvan increasingly lit up with pulsing gray lightning as she consumes his vast power.

Slumped on the ground, Shadow fog swirling around him, Yvan blazes a line of fire to me, only to have it siphoned into the giant spider before I can latch hold of even a cinder of it.

"Elloren," Yvan calls in a strangled voice as he raises his quivering, III-marked palm, giving me an urgent look before thrusting his hand down through the mist, the motion quickly followed by the rest of my horde.

My heartbeat quickens as I realize what they're doing—pushing their III marks under the Shadowed soil in an attempt to manifest trees to empower me.

Desperate, I drop to the Shadow-fogged ground, transfer my sapling branch to my non-marked hand and thrust my III-marked palm into the soil as well, hoping against hope that we'll be able to manifest a small grove of saplings through the thickened Shadow to restore my power.

But . . . *nothing.*

Only a slight tingle along my III mark as thick Shadow slithers over it, Vogel's power too strong for Life to break through.

Vogel stops before my lowered form, a smile on his lips as he stares contemptuously at the branch gripped in my left hand.

I transfer my branch back to my III-marked hand, immediately filled with a sense of the distant Zhilaan Forest desperately hurling elemental power into my rootlines via our linkage, only to have that power consumed by the Shadow.

Vogel glances around pointedly, as if daring me to take in his triumph. To take in the Magedom's domination of the entire world.

"You're an *Icaral*," I grit out, rage rising. "How can you think the way you do?"

Vogel's silvery eyes ignite with hatred. "I'm *not* an Icaral," he seethes, baring unnaturally sharp teeth. "I'm the Ancient One's conduit. Soon to be purified once the Fae corruption of Erthia is swept away."

My mind frantically casts about for a way to defeat him as I tighten my grip around my sapling's branch, a speck of life still thrumming in it, but enough for only a single weak spell—perhaps enough to light a candle or send out a single vine, but no more.

Black Witch, the distant Zhilaan Forest booms through our bond from leagues away.

Too far away.

Vogel's cruel smile returns as he gestures toward my branch. "You can't best me with your speck of Fae energy. I'm a power empath, just like you. I sense that you're *stripped bare*." His smile turns leering. "I will instantly incinerate any attack you conjure. Your *filthy* Fae power never had a chance against the Holy Magedom."

Something inside me breaks, and I rise, hand clenched tight around my branch.

I level it at him and Vogel gives me a bemused look, clearly savoring this moment as he draws his wings in tight.

"Let your army through your storm band," I challenge, taking a confrontational step toward him, nothing in the world left to lose. "I know you have the power to create a path through it. Let them see your *wings*, Marcus. And see if any of them want to follow an Icaral."

A look of malignant hate distorts Vogel's features. "Our war ends *here*, Dryad Witch," he hisses with terrible finality, raising the Shadow Wand.

I sense him drawing up a world-ending level of power, siphoning Yvan's and my horde's corrupted Wyvernfire from his tethered storm spiders straight into the Shadow Wand. "When my Wand's power hits you," he snarls, "it won't just kill *you*. It will flow its full storm right through your bond to the Zhilaan Forest. And explode it to *ash*."

A shock of cold terror slashes down my spine, freezing my branch hand, the world seeming to tilt on its axis as Vogel furiously draws up more power.

Further depleting mine.

My knees buckle, and I sink toward the ground, gasping.

Black Witch! the Zhilaan Forest growls to me, my kindred Forest's warrior defiance so strong I can feel it pulsing out over the leagues and leagues of Void land between us, urging me to hold the line.

In a slash of brutal reckoning, I realize there's only one way to fight back. Only one way to give the Zhilaan Forest another day to live. Only one way to give our incoming Dryad'khin army a chance to hold on to their Zhilaan-anchored power and *fight back*.

"I love you, Yvan!" I cry out as I bring my branch's terminal point to my chest and draw on my last trace of magic as I prepare the vine strike.

"Elloren, NO!" Yvan roars out over the Shadowed expanse between us, my entire horde taking up the protest with spitting growls. Every spark Yvan can still wrest hold of crackles toward me, the ferocious love in it searing through me even as the bulk of his power is consumed by Vogel's Shadow. Tears glassing my eyes, I begin to murmur the words to the spell that will impale my heart.

Dark wings flash into being in the back of my mind, and I freeze. A spark of unfamiliar, prismatic flame ignites low in my belly, its heat *volcanic*.

My eyes widen, astonishment overtaking me for a split second as the dark wings pulse powerfully through my mind. Prismatic light sears through my vision, my firelines and bond to Yvan filling with multicolored flame, my body shuddering against it. And it's not just flame . . .

It's prismatic *Wyvernfire*.

Black Witch, comes the Zhilaan Forest's triumphant cry, its voice startlingly clear, the Zhilaan's full elemental power suddenly flooding my lines and my branch via the prismatic flame in my center, as if I'm standing in the middle of the Great Nightwood Pine Forest instead of leagues away in a Shadowed wasteland.

Stunned exultation overtakes me, Erthia's full, creative power of Life flooding my body, the fiery power of my bond to Yvan surging, the mating mark on my shoulder igniting with glorious potency.

As the miracle conceived in the Zhilaan Forest blazes to more intense life inside me.

Gaining *fire*.

THE DRYAD STORM

The dark wings strobe against my mind once more, Vogel's look of smug victory sliding into one of confusion, then shock as he takes in the gaze I have pinned on him, prismatic fire flashing through my sight as a tingle races over my skin, my deep-green, purple-branch-patterned hue returning in a rush.

Murmuring spells, I thrust my living branch forward at the same time Vogel levels the Shadow Wand at me, the full power of the Zhilaan Forest along with the surging prismatic Wyvern power in my core exploding through me.

A storm of elemental might blasts from my branch at the same time that Vogel sends out a countering stormwall of Void power. Our storms slam into each other, his curving lightning crackling against my riot of chromatic lightning.

Vogel's wings beat against air, and he skids backward. The will to fight surging, I press forward and snarl out another series of spells the Zhilaan Forest is sending to me, while sensing Yvan drawing up a huge amount of fire power from our bond.

My gaze briefly flicks toward Yvan just as he springs to his feet and thrusts his palms outward.

The queen spider imprisoning him explodes in a huge ball of churning prismatic flame, his renewed fire blazing through our entire horde.

Naga's roar splits the air as my horde mates blast the remaining spiders into churning balls of multihued Wyvernfire. Power roars through my bond to Yvan as I battle Vogel, the mating mark on my shoulder burning hotter as my wall of power gains potency. Yvan and the rest of the horde surge toward me as my storm blasts clear through Vogel's in a spray of multicolored lightning, the air between Vogel and me rapidly clearing.

Vogel snarls at me, teeth elongated, a wild, silver-fire look in his eyes as he lifts the Shadow Wand and draws on the full force of his demonic power, and I murmur the spells the Zhilaan Forest is hurling out to me. We thrust our weapons forward, my spells clicking into place a split second before Vogel's can engage.

Living purple branches spear from my wand and slam into Vogel, impaling him at multiple points. He's punched backward, the Shadow Wand flying from his hand.

I lunge toward him and ready another spell, drawing from both the burgeoning chromatic fire in my core and the Zhilaan Forest's power as Vogel lurches toward the Shadow Wand, gasping and clutching his chest, snatching the Wand from the Shadow-misted ground before I can reach him.

He levels the Wand at me, a cruel gleam in his pale eyes. "The Holy Magedom will rise against you," he snarls.

"Then they'll face our Dryad storm," I snarl back as Yvan and our horde bolt out strikes of multicolored fire at Vogel, blasting the Shadow Wand far from his hand as I spear a large vine straight through his chest.

Vogel screams, his wings beating against the ground then stilling as his body begins to disintegrate, rapidly reduced to Shadow ash in the shape of a horned, winged figure singed into the ground.

I'm frozen in place, locked into stunned silence, the Prophecy finally come to pass. The Shadow fog closes in over Vogel's charred remains, and I immediately cast my empathy out, picking up no sense of Vogel's army advancing.

Yvan reaches me and throws his arms desperately around me, pulling me tight.

"Yvan," I barely manage, trembling as I reach around to grip tight hold of him in turn. "Oh, my gods . . . *Yvan*."

Emotion surging through us both, he draws slightly back to give me a searing look before his lips meet mine in an impassioned flash of fire that I eagerly return, clinging to him as our mating bond's flame surges to new heights, black wings flashing through my mind again and again with heart-swelling vibrancy.

"How are you manifesting so much power?" Yvan asks once we break the kiss, that spark of prismatic fire within me burning through our Wyvernbond with the force of a star, our power merging with the Zhilaan-bonded new life taking root inside me.

Tears sheen my eyes as I hold Yvan's gaze, love for him expanding my heart to the point where the surge of joy is almost too painful to endure as the rest of our horde draws in around us. "I'm pregnant," I tell him, my hand sliding over my abdomen, "with our baby, who happens to be an Icaral *and* an incredibly powerful Light Mage."

Yvan's eyes widen, and I watch everything falling into place in his astonished gaze. A blaze of echoing joy shudders through his power, our multihued flame now whipping around not only each other but the new life growing inside me—new life so intimately linked to the Zhilaan Forest, it was able to anchor Yvan's and my power with enough strength to hold fast against the Shadow.

Concern cuts through our joy as I remember our need to unite the Shadow Wand to the Verdyllion so we can free everyone imprisoned by Shadow power.

My gaze darts toward the Shadow Wand, my concern surging into wildfire alarm as I catch its fog-obscured form sinking into the ground.

"The Wand!" I cry just as Ariel and Raz'zor pounce on the area in a blur only to find the Wand disappeared into the poisoned earth.

Ariel and Raz'zor scrabble at the soil with their claws as I'm filled with the awful sense of the Wand *moving*.

"It's going toward the storm band!" I cry as I leap toward it, but my words come too late.

A crack of Erthia-cleaving thunder punches through my ears, just before a demon I've seen only in mythological texts rapidly emerges from the ground—a demon my allies warned us about.

Dark lightning flashes around the V'yexwraith's pale gray, stretched-out form as it unfurls up from the Shadowed ground, rising higher and higher. Spiky horns emerge from its flat head and bubbling eyes form all over its upper face, gray mist cycloning around where its legs should be.

In its long-fingered hand, it holds the Shadow Wand, their poisonous energy one and the same.

With a screeching cry the V'yexwraith thrusts the Wand upward and absorbs Vogel's entire storm band, the demon growing tall as the clouds as it does so.

Vogel's huge army revealed, massed in the far distance.

I realize, in a devastating jolt, that Vogel and the Magedom have been pawns of a larger battle all along, and this evil we're still facing has taken on a life of its own.

The *Shadow Wand* has gained enough power to take on a life of its own.

The V'yexwraith opens its sharp-toothed maw, lets out a bone-jarring, continent-shaking *ATCH ATCH ATCH*, and surges toward us, along with its Shadow-possessed army, every Mage's skin morphed to gray.

CHAPTER FIVE

VOID MOONS

Elloren Guryev

Shadow wasteland

I level my branch at the advancing V'yexwraith demon and incoming Shadow army as Yvan raises his palms, both of us drawing on the power of the Zhilaan Forest via the spark of our child in my womb.

By land and air, the distant army surges toward us in a huge gray tide, their thunderous chorus of snarls and shrieks building as they near, while our horde readies the fire Yvan has blazed out to them.

The V'yexwraith grows even taller than the clouds, its slender legs taking form. It booms forward, each step rattling the earth, then sets its many-eyed gaze on me with a terrible focus, my heart striking into a wilder rhythm. New eyes are bubbling to life on the demon's upper face, the Shadow Wand gripped in its long-fingered hand, the Wand's Void tree pulsing into my mind with disastrously burgeoning power.

Arm draped protectively over my womb, I thrust my branch forward at the same time that Yvan deploys power from his glowing palms.

Bolts of multihued flame blast from both Yvan's palms and my branch at the same moment that Naga and my horde mates blaze chromatic fire at the V'yexwraith, while the demon thrusts the Shadow Wand straight up into the air.

A pulse of translucent gray power bursts from the Wand's tip and snaps outward to form a translucent Shadow orb shield around the demon's torso.

Our fiery attack collides with the V'yexwraith's protective orb and splits into unfocused chaos, swirling around the demon's shielding in a chromatic, spark-spitting tempest before our magic grays and the Shadow Wand begins to siphon it up.

THE DRYAD STORM

The image of my kindred raven, Errilith, flashes through my mind. The world seems to pulse Dark as a spell whispers through my mind, through my very bones, the whispers soon joined by leafy-utterances of complementary spells sent out by the Zhilaan, the path forward crystallizing.

"Form another wall of Wyvernfire between the V'yexwraith and its forces!" I cry out to Yvan and our horde, galvanized.

"The demon will just consume it!" Ariel hisses as the V'yexwraith siphons up the last of our grayed fire into the Wand and the Shadow army roars closer.

"Just *do it*!" I cry.

Yvan and I exchange an urgent glance before he and my horde blast another Wyvernfire stormwall into being, cutting the incoming army from sight even as their oceanic roar builds.

The V'yexwraith lets out an earsplitting shriek, and I blast a dark purple line of earth magic toward the huge creature, my vines whipping around the V'yexwraith's unshielded lower legs. Sounding out the Zhilaan Forest's force-amplifying spell, I yank my branch back, *hard*.

The V'yexwraith arches its head back, screeching as it falls, its cavernous slash of a mouth gaping open with fury. Another mouth telescopes out of its maw, then another, all of the mouths gnashing sharp gray together with enough force to split the sky.

The demon's towering body slams onto the Shadow-smoking earth with a ground-shaking *BOOM*, and I tether it there with thick purple vines.

Narrowing its multiple eyes at me, the demon swerves the Shadow Wand's point toward my horde's wall of Wyvernfire and blasts siphoning fog toward it, just as I lift my branch and grit out Errilith's spell and pull on the power of Natural *Death*.

A line of Deathkin deflection runes flash into existence inside the wall of Wyvernfire, their suspended forms rippling with midnight Darkness that turns the flames black, the shield-wall's upper edge enlarging high into the sky.

The V'yexwraith's vaporous gray magic hits our runic wall, flashes to black then streams back toward the demon in a midnight tide, blasting its orb shield into Dark mist.

The V'yexwraith snarls out its fury and swipes the Wand toward us.

Before we can stage a counterattack, a rippling, gray half orb of Void power bursts from the V'yexwraith's Shadow Wand and surges outward to monstrous size.

The pulse of power slams into us with bone-jarring force, the breath punched from my lungs as my feet leave the ground and we're all hurled into the air once more, my branch torn from my hand.

My back hits the ground, and I hug my abdomen, desperate to keep my baby safe.

Yvan growls and quickly rights himself, then leaps between me and the demon.

I lunge for my branch and grab it just as the V'yexwraith thrusts the Shadow Wand toward Yvan and deploys another half orb of gray magic at the same moment Yvan and the rest of my horde blast huge bolts of chromatic lightning at the demon.

My horde's lightning slams into the demon's half orb, which rapidly crackles away to dark gray smoke. The smoke drifts to the ground and darkens to steel, snakelike portions of veiny gray power darting out toward Yvan, our horde and me, frightfully fast.

I let out a protesting cry as one of the steel-hued segments collides with my foot and slithers around my ankle, morphing into a smoking bracelet. The taste of poisonous tin coats the back of my tongue, and I sense my power, along with Yvan's and my horde's, being drawn into the Shadowed earth and toward the parasitical V'yexwraith. Fear snaps through my blood as I'm filled with the line-stretching sense of the V'yexwraith rerouting the bulk of our power's flow to *itself*, our magic graying as it's absorbed.

Yvan thrusts his palms toward the unshielded demon once more, while I force myself to my feet, my alarm compounding as I sense most of Yvan's power doubling back from his palms and being yanked down into the earth and toward the V'yexwraith before he can release it.

Teeth gritted, I futilely attempt to deploy a Zhilaan spell, horror surging as I find my magic's flow also rerouted toward the demon.

Yvan shoots me an urgent look over his shoulder, the fire in his eyes guttering. "Can you access your power, Elloren?"

"Only a trace," I shout back, struggling to stave off burgeoning dread. "The V'yexwraith has rerouted our magic's flow!"

The V'yexwraith gnashes its teeth as it takes a parasitical hit of our power, its stretched-out form enlarging even more. It snaps free of my graying bindings, and Yvan protectively backs up toward me as the demon rises to new, impossible heights, far larger than III.

The Void tree punches harder into my mind, and a clearer sense of the Shadow tree's size and scope overtake me, triggering a gut-clenching alarm.

THE DRYAD STORM

Yvan fans out his wings to shield me as my growling horde readies tooth and claw.

The V'yexwraith lets out a sky-shattering cry that has me recoiling as it lashes the Shadow Wand toward the heavens.

Glowing metallic gray spheres blast into being throughout the entire expanse of visible sky, suspended high above us like hundreds upon hundreds of Shadow moons. The metallic tang of sorcery overtakes the air, Yvan's and my power, along with the power of our horde mates, now swooping upward as it's siphoned toward the sky.

The V'yexwraith hisses, fanged smiles forming on all its mouths, spite glinting in its multiple eyes as it narrows them all on me. The image of the Void tree assaults my vision once more in a painful pulse, and I freeze, a stifling fright gripping hold. As I'm filled with the awful realization that the V'yexwraith is fully sentient and purposefully making a mockery of the East's sacred Xishlon moons by conjuring these Shadow orbs, just like Vogel did on Xishlon.

A lethal mockery.

There's Fae-killing iron power in these orbs. I can sense it. And it's not natural iron. It's some type of Void iron, its leaching force on our elemental power increasing, like the pull of hundreds of magnets.

Explosive Shadowfire forming in the moons' cores.

"Those spheres," I rasp out to Yvan, "they're Shadow-iron explosives. Your iron-protective rune isn't strong enough to survive them!"

Heightened horror slashes through us both as it hits me that the Void iron in these moons has the power to take out not only part-Lasair-Fae Yvan, but our part-Lasair unborn child. Along with every one of our incoming Fae allies, save the Mage-Dryad'kin—our Keltish heritage conferring iron-resistance. But the rest of us will be destroyed by the moons' explosive power, which feels strong enough to destroy even the strongest foliage-amplified weapons and shielding, our stormwall of Deathkin-warded Wyvernfire beginning to gray.

Vogel's army is about to descend on us along with the Shadow Wand demon before the moons fall.

As if sensing my thoughts, the V'yexwraith lets out an explosive shriek and lunges toward me.

In a blur, Yvan takes to the air, soaring toward the demon at the same moment that Naga, Raz'zor, Ariel, and the rest of my horde launch themselves toward the V'yexwraith.

"*No!*" I cry out, fear streaking through me, clear that, sapped of their power, Yvan and my horde mates are no match for this Shadow creature.

The V'yexwraith opens its great maws and lets out a reverberating battle cry, powerful enough to shake the heavens. It thrusts the Shadow Wand forward, and multiple Shadow trees burst from it, their spear-like canopies knifing toward Yvan and me and my attacking horde mates.

Yvan dodges impalement via sheer speed as he arcs through the air and punches away the tree hurtling toward me. Shadow trees collide with my horde mates, and my heart constricts as they're slammed to the ground, their wings and limbs impaled, the insect-like trees pinning them to Shadowed earth while the V'yexwraith continues to siphon our power into the Void moons above.

Naga, Raz'zor, and the others let out furious snarls, as Ariel falls to a heap to my right, screaming with rage, the edges of her wings pinioned. The V'yexwraith deploys another tree toward Yvan that he shifts away from, but the tree's glancing blow to his side hurls him a great distance sideways.

Outrage bolts through me, and I lift my branch, teeth gritted, tensing every line to the breaking point to wrest back my power, the moons' pull on my magic too cursedly strong for me to send even a trace of magic through my branch.

Seeming to sense my frustrated will to fight, the V'yexwraith's huge head swivels toward me. I stumble backward, hugging my abdomen, as the demon stalks toward me, teeth bared, and raises the Shadow Wand.

"*Elloren!*" Yvan snarls desperately as he soars toward me from too far away, and panic tears through me, our child and I about to meet our ends.

Ariel suddenly rips herself away from the impaling branches in a spray of blood. Letting out an unearthly growl, she launches herself toward the V'yexwraith, and her form *explodes*.

Astonishment lances through me as Ariel's body enlarges, her wings expanding as she morphs into a *huge, black dragon*.

The V'yexwraith rears back and Ariel blasts into the sky, slamming into the demon's chest with such force that the V'yexwraith drops the Shadow Wand and falls thunderously to the ground.

Seizing my chance, I dash toward the Wand, but Yvan is there in an instant, grabbing hold of it first.

The V'yexwraith lets out a bloodcurdling scream that's quickly taken up by the army beyond our shielding as Ariel slashes claws at the demon's chest in a vicious blur, the V'yexwraith's long arms straining toward the Shadow Wand as if a limb has been torn from its body and flown away.

Yvan soars toward me, Shadow Wand in hand, his flight pattern suddenly chaotic, his prismatic eyes flashing a glowing gray. He hurls the Shadow Wand to the ground, as if ridding himself of something that was burning through his hands, and careens to the earth.

The Wand falls to the gray-misted land at my feet just before Yvan lands.

"Don't touch it!" Yvan cries as I move to take the evil Wand in hand and the V'yexwraith growls and thrusts Ariel's dragon form away.

The demon leaps up and barrels toward the Wand with a shriek that seems to split the heavens from every direction. Yvan takes flight once more just as Ariel bolts back into the sky and soars toward the incoming demon, the two of them battling it back with brute force.

Desperate to keep hold of the Shadow Wand, I tear off the leafy hem of my tunic, and drop to one knee before the evil tool. I throw the ripped hem over it and take it into my non-III-marked hand at the same moment I'm hit by an incoming wall of elemental power so strong that it rattles my teeth, all of it blasting toward me from high in the eastern sky.

I whip my gaze east just as a Vu Trin portal splits the sky and our Dryad'khin army soars out of it on wings and eagle- and Wyvernback, flying in like an incoming tide under the ceiling of iron Void moons.

Void moons about to rain down Shadow-iron explosives on us all.

CHAPTER SIX

PRISMATIC POWER

Elloren Guryev

Shadow wasteland

"Portal out of here!" I shout, striving to wave off our incoming forces to no avail, my screams swallowed by the mounting roar of Vogel's forces battling to get through to us. Gray-fire explosions flash against our runic fire-shield with ever-increasing intensity, Yvan and Ariel fighting against the V'yexwraith with brute force.

While the leafy-cloth-wrapped Shadow Wand grows heavier in my hand as it continues to feed power into the ripening Void moons above.

The full nightmare of the situation hits like a fist to the gut as I'm flooded by the empathic sense of all my loved ones' incoming magic—Trystan's and Vothe's, Sage's and Soleiya's, Sylvan's, Yulan's, Wrenfir's, and everyone else's as they soar through the sky portal, a multitude of winged kindreds flying in with them.

A knot of my allies swerve toward me, and Vang Troi and Hizar'drile land and immediately begin booming out orders. The bulk of our forces fans out and masses in front of my horde's wall of Wyvernfire, Trystan, Vothe, Fain, and Sholindrile amongst them. Rafe, Diana, and the rest of our Lupine Dryad'khin dismount from eagleback and speed toward the V'yexwraith in a blur, along with Freyja, Valasca, and other Amaz, to aid Yvan and Ariel in battling the colossal demon.

Dryad of my heart! Raz'zor snarls to Oaklyyn through the horde bond.

Oaklyyn lets out a battle cry and launches herself toward Raz'zor's Shadow tree–impaled form, while Sylvan, Iris, Bleddyn, and Alder, accompanied by several Lasair, including Soleiya, rush forward and set about freeing and healing Naga and our other impaled horde mates while I fight to keep hold of the increasingly leaden Shadow Wand.

Rafe, Diana, and Andras get to the V'yexwraith first, all of them joining Yvan and Ariel to leap at the V'yexwraith with vicious growls, claws slashing. Yvan strikes the demon to the ground, and it goes strangely limp, its form growing as transparent as a specter, my allies' attacks passing right through it.

My eyes widen as the creature turns and fixes its multiple churning gray eyes on me, its Void tree blasting through my mind once more with painful force.

"Elloren!" Gwynn and Mavrik call out.

I tear my gaze from the demon to find the twinned Dryad'kin sprinting toward me, their Agolith Flame Hawks winging in behind them. Rivyr'el, Ra'Ven, Sage, and Yulan and her heron, along with Jules and Lucretia and Jules's Noi Kestrel are close on their heels.

"I have the Shadow Wand!" I cry out to them.

The Void tree hammers into my mind with shattering force and I wince against the pain. It's as if the wretched Wand wants to crack my skull apart and wrest itself from my grip, its increasing weight pulling my hand to the Shadowed earth while the magical tension of the orbs above us begins to feel like a thousand tightly wound springs, soon to be released to rain hell down on us all.

"The moons," I force out, gritting my teeth against the Void tree's assault as my allies draw near. I gesture skyward. "They're Shadow-iron explosives! They're going to fall once they siphon up enough of our power!"

My fear notches higher as I'm overtaken by the sense of the orbs hooking into all the incoming allies' magic with invisible Shadow tethers, latching tight. Threads of my Dryad'khin's power begin to stream toward the evil orbs, graying as it goes.

Rivyr'el stiffens, staring up at the moons. "Well, that's not good," he drawls.

"Portal us all back to the East, *now*!" I insist.

"We *can't*," Sage counters, voice hard. "That portal will take hours to recharge for the return trip."

"We have to stand our ground and fight," Lucretia grits out, her water aura being siphoned upward as she speaks.

"Fight *fast*," I urge as the roar of Vogel's army beyond our shield intensifies, Yvan now standing sentry around the prone V'yexwraith with our allies, our larger force assembled just beyond them. "Vogel is dead," I inform my companions as the Wand weighs down my hand, "but his army is positioned just past our stormwall of Wyvernfire. A much bigger army than we can defeat with our power being siphoned away. And the Deathkin runes marked through our shield won't hold it forever."

"Can you get a reading on a way to defeat those moons?" Sage asks Gwynn and Mavrik as my uncle Wrenfir, Marina, Gareth, and Thierren Stone join us, along with Alaric and Nerissa.

In answer, Mavrik and Gwynn take each other's hands and thrust their branches toward the sky. Misty ropes of gold streak toward the moons and blast over the orbs' surfaces in a flash of golden light that rapidly morphs to gray, their gilded power swiftly absorbed.

"We can't destroy them," Mavrik grimly states as he lowers his branch, both his hawk and Gwynn's agitatedly ruffling their feathers where they perch on their shoulders. "A Shadow-geomancy locking spell surrounds each of them."

Gwynn nods, expression grave. "Only a Strafeling geomancer could destroy those moons before they fall."

Frustration spikes through me. *Or'myr. I need you, cousin. But you're with Tierney, guarding the Vo. Leagues away . . .*

The Void tree impales my mind once more, forcing a cry from my throat, the evil Wand in my hand bolting pain through my temples that's so intense, my knees start to buckle. Wrenfir grips hold of my arm, steadying me, and I glare at the Shadow Wand, filled with the sense of it drawing up power for another mind attack, possibly strong enough to knock me unconscious.

"What is it, Elloren?" Wrenfir insists.

"The Wand," I huff, gray streaking through my vision. "It's attacking my *mind—*"

Color suddenly explodes through my sight, the vision of a prismatic tree materializing into being. The gray clears from my vision as the prismatic tree's branches lock hold of the Void tree, the multihued tree's chromatic light power flashing through my rootlines as the two trees begin to wage war, their limbs locking like buck antlers.

"The Verdyllion," Gwynn gasps, gesturing toward the Sublands to our north.

"It's coming in beneath us," Mavrik finishes.

My sense of prismatic power intensifies, silver Wyvernfire wrapped around it. An image of the multicolored Verdyllion shimmers into my mind, superimposed over the prismatic tree.

The Shadow Wand's Void tree sends an ear-splicing shriek through my skull, lashing gray branches against both the Verdyllion and its tree, as if seeking to beat the images into submission. Dazed, I glance down at my free hand and find glowing color streaking through my III mark at the same moment that my surrounding allies hold up their palms, revealing the same.

"Unshield these Sublands!" Rivyr'el urges Gwynn and Mavrik. "While you still can!"

Wasting no time, they point their branches in the direction of the Verdyllion and murmur a spell in unison, wresting hold of what power they still can from the Void moons' relentless pull.

A gigantic circle filled with golden runes blinks into being on the distant, Shadow-smoking earth, Vogel's net of Shadow visible just under it, Mavrik and Gwynnifer's multicolored net of shielding layered beneath both runic circle and Shadow net, the encircled portion of their shield rapidly shivering away.

Mavrik spits out a curse and exchanges a grim look with Gwynn.

"We've removed our Subland shielding," Gwynn tells us, sweat beading both her and Mavrik's brows, "but we can't get through Vogel's!"

The Shadow Wand's fury pours through me, the war raging inside my head ramping up to agonizing heights as the Void tree clamps its branches down around both the Verdyllion and its tree at the same moment our runic firewall holding back Vogel's army explodes into gray steam along with its Deathkin runes.

A terrible, thundering roar goes up, and the sea of Vogel's forces launches toward us by land and air, Vogel's four pyrr-demons leading the charge and morphing out of their glamours to reveal their fiery forms, smoke horns and lower halves made of spiraling grayed flame. Our Dryad'khin army strengthens our defensive line, the Eastern Wyverns wresting hold of the last of their unsiphoned power to blast a shield-wall made of crackling white lightning into existence before them, gray-fire explosions detonating against it, the demons ramming solidifying horns into it, sparks flying as the white lightning begins to gray. Yvan and other allies fall in with our forces while Ariel and Andras remain behind to guard the prone V'yexwraith. Ra'Ven, Gareth, Thierren, Wrenfir, and Lucretia draw weapons and sprint out to join the incoming battle.

My stomach drops as I meet the misty V'yexwraith's multitude of eyes, its great maw pulling into a sickening smile as it looks at the Wand in my hand, the siphoning pull of the demon's moons intensifying as the lightning wall turns completely gray.

The specter-like V'yexwraith lets out a ratcheting, earsplitting laugh that cuts straight through the magical explosions of battle and echoes off the moons above as our final defense falls, horror fires through my every line and the Shadow army rushes at our forces—

—just as Gwynn and Mavrik's runic circle flashes with starbright light.

Startled, I turn toward it as an explosion of silver-green fire bursts into being inside its expanse.

I blink at it, surprise wresting hold. Because I can sense it's not just any fire.

It's a world-bending inferno of *Wyvernfire*.

Vogel's circle of Shadow net scorches away, and I flinch back as a green dragon blasts through the fire, leaves amassed on its wings, branches for horns, bright silver lightning crackling around its body.

The Verdyllion Wand-Stylus gripped in the dragon's silvery talons.

The circle of fire gutters out, and a new battle roar rises as scores of Smaragdalfar soldiers and freed Wyverns stream from the runic Subland opening, all of them wielding emerald-glowing Varg weaponry.

The Smaragdalfar soldiers rush toward our forces as they blast out a huge line of suspended emerald runes.

The runes fly over us and slam down in front of the bulk of Vogel's army, tenuously walling them off as our forces make quick work of those soldiers, dragons, and Shadow beasts remaining on our side of the Varg wall, while other Smaragdalfar conjure a compact Varg shield to contain the V'yexwraith and pyrr-demons.

The green dragon lands before me and rapidly contracts into a slender female figure, her leafy wings flashing with forking silver light, urgency crackling in her eyes.

"Wynter!" I choke out, relief slashing through me that's so staggering it feels like vertigo as the Void tree lets out a skull-rattling snarl through my mind.

Wynter is garbed in Smaragdalfar battle armor, her newly green-tinted face and form surrounded by a swirling, verdant aura—the same aura, I sense, that swirled around the Great Tree III. Her silver eyes are edged with starbright fire, and lightning horns rise from her alabaster hair, a translucent Watcher kindred perched on her shoulder.

The prismatic Verdyllion Wand-Stylus gripped in her hand.

Wynter's blazing eyes immediately find first the Shadow Wand in my hand, then Ariel in dragon form, her eyes widening as she obviously recognizes Ariel's lightning. Ariel is pacing near the V'yexwraith's newly Varg-bound form as our collective power continues to diminish, the Void moons swiftly locking hold of the Smaragdalfar army's power.

Their Varg wall rippling gray.

A shocked breath pulls through Wynter's throat as her gaze darts from Ariel to the moons and back again, a streak of Wynter's aura blazing fervidly out to encircle Ariel.

"Can you take out those moons with the Verdyllion?" I press Wynter.

Before Wynter can answer, a severe-faced Smaragdalfar woman with a half-shaved head sprints toward us, Wynter's now green-tinted brother, Cael, and his equally greened Second, Rhys, running in behind the woman along with a willowy, long-tressed Smaragdalfar woman and two young male Subland soldiers.

"Yyzz'ra!" Mavrik calls to the severe-faced woman.

"Gather your light sorcerers around the Verdyllion Shard!" Yyzz'ra bellows. "It needs seven lines of light! *Now!*"

Time seems to pause as my power empathy desperately searches for seven allies still holding on to some semblance of their light power. I can sense unbound reserves of light power remaining inside Wynter, Sage, Gwynn and Mavrik, Rivyr'el, Marina, and myself, everyone else's light magic being swept into the Void moons, including every trace of Alaric's and Nerissa's powers.

"We only have six conduits of light power," I tell Yyzz'ra. "Gwynn and Mavrik's magic flows as *one*."

"You need *seven* to balance your magic and fully connect it to Oó'na's Shard!" Yyzz'ra insists.

The Zhilaan Forest tugs on my lines, pulling my attention inward as dark wings flash through my mind, a bud of prismatic color pulsing in my center.

"We have seven!" I cry, lifting my free hand to cradle my abdomen. "I'm pregnant with a light sorcerer!"

Everyone's eyes widen, surprise crackling through their remaining traces of power. Wasting no time, Wynter reaches for my free hand and I give it to her, her pale fingers closing in around mine as she reads both me and my spark of a child.

The silver Wyvernfire in Wynter's eyes flashes brighter as she releases my hand and reverentially holds the Verdyllion out to me. "Your child is strongly anchored in both Forest power and every hue of light," she says. "The Verdyllion wants to return to you, Elloren."

A vortex of urgency balling in my throat, I take hold of the Verdyllion's spiraling, multicolored form, feeling the arc of my whole destiny cycling down, the arc of *all* our destinies cycling down, the Verdyllion's prismatic tree expanding in my mind, holding firm against the Void.

Wynter holds out her hand. "Elloren," she says, the flame in her eyes blazing, "give me the Shadow Wand."

I make no move to give it to her, suddenly overtaken by the realization that the Shadow Wand has ceased its attacks on my mind. It's gone strangely silent and is now light in my hand, the sensation of a sly, siphoning line connecting its gray, spiraling form to the Void moons above taking hold.

My pulse skyrockets, and I yank the Shadow Wand farther away from Wynter to keep her from making contact with the evil tool as the Varg barriers flash a darker, all-encompassing gray. "Don't touch it!" I cry. "It wants to tether your magic to the Void moons and turn you into a creature of Shadow!"

"I have to touch it, Elloren," Wynter insists. "I need to link the Shadow Wand's tethering Void tree with my empathy so we can take control of it."

My mind races for some way to block the Shadow Wand's siphoning power . . .

. . . and lights on a time that seems like a million years ago.

Tierney and I, in the Verpax University lab. Blocking magic with a distillate of concentrated Ironflower oil and vivid blue color.

My thoughts careen toward the stories in *The Book of the Ancients*—how the prophetess Galliana used Ironflowers to fight demonic power, the myths all converging in *this* moment . . .

My eyes swing toward Yulan. "We need Ironflowers. Can you latch hold of whatever remaining power you have to cover Wynter with them?"

A light sparks in Yulan's eyes and she nods, the petite Dryad's face tensing with an expression of great effort. She points her branch toward Wynter and wrests hold of the thread of power still under her control.

A flash of deep-blue light detonates around Wynter. Woven strands of glowing blue Ironflowers twine around her legs, torso, and arms, casting her in a penumbra of blue light.

Without further pause, Wynter holds out her hand for the Shadow Wand.

Pulse galloping, I hand it to her and she takes hold of the evil thing. Unwinding its leaf-cloth wrapping, she takes it directly in hand.

Wynter gasps and falls to her knees, her eyelids fluttering as the glow of the Ironflowers flash defensively bright, and I'm filled with the sense of her empathy touching down on the Shadow's huge, branching Void tree.

Invisible Void branches knife toward Wynter's core of silver fire but are stopped up short by the Ironflowers' blue aura, which is weaving protection around her magic. A whirling gray mist briefly slashes around Wynter's form with surging might, but it's unable to penetrate the blue.

Her delicate jaw set tight, Wynter rises with what appears to be great effort, the Shadow Wand held doggedly tight in her fist.

"The Seven need to make contact with the Verdyllion," Wynter rasps out.

My allies huddle close, my heart pounding as I keep tight hold of the Verdyllion, and Marina, Sage, Gwynn, Mavrik, and Rivyr'el reach out to loop fingers around its spiraling form.

"Touch the Verdyllion to the Shadow Wand!" Wynter vehemently prods as she joins us in looping a finger around the Verdyllion, completing the seven points of power.

The full prism of color explodes across my vision, brighter than ever before, the Verdyllion's power coursing around us all in a rainbow spray of sparks.

Wynter drags the Shadow Wand's tip toward the Verdyllion, and the Wand *screams*, its Void tree exploding into being inside me, impaling my mind with brutal force.

A cry escapes my lips, my legs buckling as Jules and Yulan grab hold of me and keep me upright, every color in the world around us pulsing to iron gray.

Heart hammering, I grit my teeth and fight through the pain as, together, we force the Verdyllion's tip to the Shadow Wand's.

The Wands make contact, and the V'yexwraith's ratcheting shriek tears through both the air and my mind, the sound world-cleaving as I'm flooded with an empathic awareness of the Void tree's entire branching network of control.

Monumentally strengthened.

"I can sense the Shadow's linkage to every fasted Mage and Zalyn'or-controlled Alfsigr!" Wynter cries.

"Connect them *all* to our Forest," Yulan urges as she and Jules keep hold of me, Yulan's melodic voice shot through with the Forest's own steel. "Connect them to the living *trees*."

"More than that," Jules Kristian insists, his hand closing in around ours, around the Verdyllion, "connect them to the power of Erthia's *entire history*."

"And the power the Watchers have woven through it," Wynter rasps as the Watcher on her shoulder bursts into bright light that swirls around our hands.

Our lines and cores of power contract toward the Verdyllion, my lungs seizing as the Verdyllion pulls on our seven conduits of light power, Jules's link to Erthia's history, and the Watchers' ethereal might, the Verdyllion's power amplifying with the full force of III.

Light explodes through my vision once more as the Verdyllion's amplified power whorls around the Shadow's Void tree, coming close to breaking into its network of control before being stopped up short.

My urgency sliding toward desperation, I search for the weak link in our connection and quickly locate it.

The Verdyllion is unable to fully connect with the Zhilaan-anchored light power growing inside me.

The Verdyllion Wand flashes an image of Yvan through my mind at the same moment that every Varg barrier falls, and a cacophony of shrieks and roars rise, the Shadow army and its pyrr-demons launching into an attack of our frontline forces once more.

Alarm spikes as Yvan and the rest of my horde close in around us in a blur, facing outward, claws extended, the few sparks of Yvan's power that remain under his control burning hot around our bond with the furious urge to protect.

Our eyes meet over my shoulder, his gaze a lethal green, alarmingly stripped of violet fire.

"Touch me!" I urge Yvan. "The Verdyllion needs to connect with both of us to fully engage with our child!"

Without hesitation, Yvan embraces me from behind, his arms wrapping around my waist, his hot form pressed tight against my back. As if on instinct, he presses his heated lips to the half-moon mating mark on my shoulder's upper edge, sparks igniting through my lines.

Wings strobe against my vision, the contact with him instantly amplifying our threefold link to Zhilaan power, the magic streaming out into the Verdyllion, like water through a burst dam.

A dazzling flash of prismatic light momentarily cuts out my vision as the Verdyllion draws on all seven lines of power along with a line of Zhilaan might and overtakes the giant Void tree, clamping down on gray limbs with renewed force, the Shadow branches withering beneath the onslaught of chromatic might. I shudder against Yvan as the Verdyllion wrests hold of the branching Void network, sending a prismatic link through every fastline and Zalyn'or necklace, forming a connection with every fasted Mage and every Zalyn'or-imprinted

Alfsigr, flooding them all with the Forest's message and history, the Watchers' light swirling around it all . . .

. . . gifting everyone with an invitation to abandon the Shadow and join with the surviving Natural World.

As one, united Dryad'khin.

The sea of Mage and Marfoir soldiers still and fall to their knees, those on multilimbed Shadow dragons slumping down.

My vision clearing, I spot a Mage in the distance who resembles Damion Bane, but it's difficult to know for certain, my attention drawn skyward as the airborne Shadow dragons and wraith bats are pulled to the ground and bound there by prismatic lines of power, along with scorpios, other Shadowed beasts, and the pyrr-demons, their screaming chorus of snarls a transient disturbance as chromatic energy wraps around their mouths, the roar of battle vanishing.

"Stand down!" Vang Troi booms out to our forces, her voice echoing out across the Shadowed land's expanse.

A weighted silence descends, my heart drumming against my chest.

The V'yexwraith's screeching laugh bursts forth, echoing across the smoking wasteland and up to the sea of moons.

My gaze snaps skyward as the moons abruptly burgeon then blink to midnight gray, darkness swallowing the world, even the glow of Wynter's Ironflowers dimming as the moons surge with power.

A swoop of light-headed horror threatens to overwhelm me.

The moons . . . they're about to kill us all. And then, the V'yexwraith will rise and retake the Shadow Wand, wielding it to siphon every remaining speck of Life from Erthia.

My horror careens into defiant, white-hot fury.

"NO!" I scream as I force the Verdyllion toward the heavens, pulling everyone's grips on it with my motion, as I blast what's left of our merged power toward the moons.

A sky-flashing bolt of our prismatic light power detonates, spearing upward to glance harmlessly off the orbs before the moons' gray darkness overtakes the world once more, our remaining magic siphoned out of our grasp to flow up toward the moons.

"Holy gods," Gwynn stammers as my allies release their hold on the Verdyllion and panic threatens to choke me.

Yvan's embrace around my trembling form tightens. "I love you, Elloren," he says against my cheek, his tone shot through with defiance as he slides his hand down over my womb. "I will love you forever."

"I love you too," I say through my pooling tears, grief splintering my voice as dark wings gently flutter through my mind and Yvan and I send a blaze of love to our Icaral Light Mage child.

Our child who will never see the light of day.

"Yvan! Elloren!" Soleiya cries over the distance between us as the moons' attack magic fully snaps into place and I flinch, my hand closing around Yvan's wrist.

"I love you," Yvan cries out to his mother, as the moons fall, a cry escaping me as they rapidly enlarge to terrifying size. Holding desperately tight to Yvan's strong arms, I tremble against him, bracing myself for impact.

A sudden earthquake rumbles to life, the ground beneath my feet shaking, my balance giving way.

Yvan abruptly takes flight, lifting us just off the ground as my allies are knocked off their feet, a great fissure forming beside the V'yexwraith, a magnificent purple light raying up from its depths in brilliant purple rays.

The huge demon screams against the sudden color-assault, which feels like a pulse of powerful geomancy.

Strafeling-level geomancy.

The purple light fills the sky and wraps around the moons, bringing them to a screeching halt only a few handspans above us.

I gasp, the ground continuing to shiver as the moons slowly recede upward, all of them taking on a bright violet glow as they're filled with the incoming geopower.

Appearing now like a sky full of Xishlon moons.

"It's geomancy," I rasp to Yvan as the V'yexwraith lets out a bloodcurdling shriek and teeters, cracks beginning to appear all over its solidifying and crystallizing form, its huge body shot through with reflected violet color as the ground continues to shake.

A bolt of what looks like purple crystal spears up from the fissure and rapidly expands into a huge, crystalline tree. My eyes widen as a smaller explosion of violet light detonates along the violet geo-tree's base, forming a passage.

Sparrow Trillium steps out. She's gripping a purple stylus in her hand, a diffuse halo of violet energy surrounding her body—the telltale aura of an Urisk Strafeling.

Erthia's most powerful class of geomancer.

"Sparrow!" Thierren cries as she thrusts her geo-stylus toward the V'yexwraith and calls out an Urisk spell.

A bolt of pure purple light blasts from her stylus and into the demon.

The V'yexwraith lets out a ground-vibrating scream, its violet glow heightening as its limbs flail and its body begins to crack apart.

"You'll never be rid of me!" the V'yexwraith screeches as Sparrow angles her stylus down, another fissure opening in the earth beneath the demon. *"I will re-form around your conflicts and CONSUME EVERYTHING!"* the demon shrieks before its fragmenting body drops into the crevice.

As it falls, I'm hit by the sensation of the demon's poisonous essence streaming back into the Shadow Wand gripped in Wynter's hand, a shiver coursing through me.

Sparrow looks to the sky and slashes her amethyst stylus upward.

The suspended moons liquefy into a suspended sea of molten purple before Sparrow swipes the amethyst down toward the fissure she's just crafted.

The purple sea follows her motion, waterfalling into the fissure's abyss before Sparrow murmurs another Urisk spell and the ground closes up and stops shaking, the moons now gone from the Shadow-poisoned sky as Yvan's magic and mine surge and snap back under our control.

Yvan lands, and my feet touch ground, a cry of stunned relief bursting from me as I catch sight of Rafe and Trystan, Diana, Aislinn, and so many other loved ones.

Still alive . . . all of us still alive.

Euphoria surging through me, I whirl around, and Yvan sweeps me into an embrace, the two of us clutching each other, his hot lips now pressed to my temple, his tears warm against my cheek. "My love," he hisses in Wyvern. "My beautiful, Dryad love."

My hand slides between us and over my womb, my own tears suddenly falling.

We'll live. We'll live to meet our child.

After a moment, I step back from Yvan and turn to face the Forest-linked Mages and smatterings of Marfoir Elves, Verdyllion in hand. They're all still down on their knees, eyes closed.

So many Mages.

A stunned shock rolls through me, an upsurge of grief close on its heels as I take in the poisoned landscape all around us and our scattered dead at the front lines, my blood beginning to boil as anger rises like a tide.

They *did* this.

The Mages *did* this.

"Elloren," Yvan says, a cautionary weight to his tone that I ignore as power floods me—*Black Witch* power. I step toward Vogel's forces, overwhelmed by the vicious Black Witch urge to slay them all and watch them burn.

To make every last Mage *pay*.

Ignoring Yvan's cautioning flow of fire, I draw up magic, knowing I now hold enough Zhilaan-fortified power to incinerate them *all*.

The Verdyllion tingles against my palm, its urgent energy halting my steps.

A flash of verdant color blasts over the sea of Mages and Marfoir, and I startle, surprise coursing through Yvan's and my restored fire as the vast majority of Vogel's Mage soldiers take on a deep, Dryad-green shimmer and the Marfoir transform back into Alfsigr men, their salt-white hue gaining a greenish tint, the bound Shadow creatures falling into gray dust.

A flash of the Verdyllion's light shocks through me, and the scene before me cuts out.

I'm overtaken by visions of my entire story, from my first sighting of a Watcher in Halfix to my time at Verpax University, initially mistrusting every non-Mage . . . to where I stand right now.

In a split second, I relive it all.

The Verdyllion shifts the vision, images flashing through my mind of what I might have been, had I cast Ariel out when I had the chance, had my uncle Edwin not hidden my power from the Magedom, had I not listened and learned from my former adversaries who are now my allies.

Including a rebellious Icaral who became the father of my spark of a child.

Pain courses through me, remorse shearing through my heart. Because I know what I might have been had I chosen differently.

I'd be one of the Mages massed before us.

But I wouldn't be down on my knees, listening to the Forest.

I'd stand at their gray, leading edge, the Shadow Wand clutched in my hand.

And I wouldn't have needed Vogel's control to put me there.

With one inescapable bolt of reckoning, I'm struck by the realization that we all hold the possibility of being drawn to the Shadow or the Verdyllion. We all hold both the pull toward hatred and cruel fracture and the opposing pull toward the loving, unifying path of the Watchers deep inside us.

And it's up to each of us to choose which pull to follow.

Trembling and painfully chastened, I lower the Verdyllion at the same moment

Ariel, morphed into Icaral form, takes to the sky and arrows toward Wynter while Thierren sprints toward Sparrow.

I scan the Mages, distantly registering that the Mage who seemed to resemble Damion is nowhere in sight as our forces set about taking those few Mages who haven't joined with the Forest into military custody.

"Dryad'kin!" Sylvan shouts as he runs toward the opening to the Sublands.

My empathy picks up a sizable mass of depleted Dryads sheltering just beneath us, Alder and Oaklyyn rushing toward the opening as well, as Dryads begin to filter out of it. Yulan pauses to lash out a bolt of sapphire power at the bound pyrr-demons, the creatures shrieking as Ironflowers suddenly wind around them and the demons sizzle away to gray stream.

Dazed, I watch the Dryads embrace their kin and Thierren and Sparrow fall into each other's arms, their powers swirling around each other with ardent force, while Ariel zooms in and lands in front of Wynter, dropping to one knee before her, her horned head lowering in supplication, wings fanning out.

"My beloved one," Ariel says, in a clearer voice than I've ever heard from her. "Ealaiontora of Alfsigroth and Dryad'khin warrior. I give myself up to you as your Second. To protect you and ally with you. *Forever.*"

Tears spill from Wynter's silver-fire eyes as she tears a strip of cloth from the emerald tunic under her armor and carefully wraps the Shadow Wand in the fabric then slides it into her tunic's pocket, only a trace of the Shadow Wand's power remaining. Wynter then lowers herself to Ariel's level and cups her face in her hands. "No, my beloved one," she says, her voice suffused with affection. "You are not my Second. You are my Great Love. My Forever Love."

Ariel's head rises, moisture sheening her gold-fire eyes. She chokes out a strangled sound of emotion before she and Wynter pull each other into an embrace, then into an impassioned kiss. Emotion tightens my heart as they burst into gold and silver-green flame, love burning bright in it.

And then the flames die down and Wynter rises and steps back, the Ironflowers singed away. Silvery lightning limns the edges of Wynter's branch wings, and a beatific smile lifts her lips as she holds out her hand to Ariel. Ariel takes it and rises, as well.

As the surrounding Mages and Alfsigr awaken.

Appearing dazed, the Mages feel the points on their ears and stare at their hands, clearly marveling at their skin's heightened green glow and the absence of fastlines around their hands and wrists. The Alfsigr Elf soldiers look around blankly, seeming stunned by the sudden freeing of their minds from the Zalyn'or's cruel hold, all of them—the whole sea of them—seeming shocked into silence. And then, as one, they all look to us.

Almost every single Mage and Alfsigr holds up a III-marked palm, pain slashed across their faces. And remorse. Fierce remorse.

Remorse I feel burning in my own chest, tears stinging my eyes.

I meet the green gaze of one of the Mages kneeling only a few paces away, and realize I know him—Curren Dell, a fellow Mage scholar at Verpax University who was kind to me what seems like years ago.

"Elloren," he stammers. "The Forest showed us . . . *everything*."

I nod through my tears. Complicated tears. Because Curren willingly gave himself up to be part of this *nightmare*.

"Shane!" Sage cries, rushing over the battlefield to her older brother. They fall into each other's arms, sobbing, other allies calling out to transformed Mages and Alfsigr.

Curren blinks at the Shadow-destroyed land, a tortured look in his eyes, as if he's remembering everything the Forest likely showed him. Tears slip down his cheeks as he meets my gaze once more with a stricken look of horror. "What have we done?" he rasps.

The same expression appears on almost every Mage and Alfsigr face, all of them in the process of waking up from a decades-long nightmare—a nightmare that might have permanently destroyed Erthia.

Watchers blink into view, perched on the shoulders of every Dryad'khin, including the newly III-bonded Mages and Alfsigr, and a collective gasp rises.

"Do you see them?" I breathe out to Yvan.

His hand comes to my shoulder, as Wynter and the others close in around us and I glance at the Watcher on my own shoulder, then his.

Yvan and Wynter nod, an astonished look on Yvan's face as he takes in the ethereal birds, the Watchers' message clear—

Align.

The Watchers blink out of sight, and the Verdyllion's prismatic energy gives a pull toward Wynter.

I hold the glowing Wand out to her. "It wants to return to you."

"What can the Verdyllion do?" I ask her as she takes reverent hold of it, wanting to know, once and for all, what this Wand-Stylus I thought was so weak is truly capable of.

"It can break bonds," Wynter answers. "It can link magic for the good. Create connections and portals via the path of love. And work to restore the Balance. Its power . . . it amplifies as more of us join with the power of Life." Wynter breathes in deeply as she hugs the Verdyllion to her chest and closes her eyes, her green-tinted brow knotting. "I can sense a portion of its amplified magic breaking free." She opens her eyes, meeting my gaze with a look of astonishment then determination as she murmurs several spells and thrusts the Wand upward.

Light rays out in every direction, a tingle racing down my spine.

"It sent me images of a large flow of Mages and Alfsigr . . ." Wynter falteringly says ". . . and others . . . fleeing from the Shadow destruction and famine in the Western Realm. The Verdyllion . . . it's using our light power to conjure portals as we speak, to help the Mages and Alfsigr and other survivors in the West flee to the East. Including those trapped on the Fae and Pyrran Islands."

"We need to aid everyone escaping from those islands," Sparrow says as she and Thierren approach, hand in hand, Sparrow's violet Strafeling aura intensifying with an urgent glow, and I remember that she and Effrey were once imprisoned on the Fae Islands.

"I agree," Thierren seconds, exchanging a decisive look with her.

I sense a pulse of gray stirring inside the Shadow Wand in Wynter's pocket, and my every nerve springs alert.

"Wynter," I caution. "The Shadow Wand . . ."

Wynter slides her hand toward her pocket, a stark expression tightening her gaze as she makes a sliver of contact with the evil thing's hilt. "The Shadow Wand is waiting to renew its power," she warns, "from the discord this huge migration of people will bring."

Yvan's power blazes to hotter life through our bond. "Which means we need to go east quickly to try to head off that conflict."

I glance warily at Wynter's pocket where the Shadow Wand is stirring. "The cycle of fracture throughout history has to end *now*," I agree as I lift my gaze to meet Wynter's, gesturing toward the Shadow tool. "What can we do to subdue that Wand?"

Wynter tilts her head, her finger still touching the Shadow Wand's hilt as she reads it once more. "We can't destroy it outright. We can keep its power at bay only by being something much greater than we have ever been. *Together.*"

"Which means we need to unite the surviving people of Erthia," Jules says from beside Lucretia, giving me a meaningful look, "messy as that might prove to be."

I glance around at the transformed Mages and Alfsigr, my gaze zeroing in on my Mage Dryad'kin, realizing, in a flash of emotion, that my prophesied role as the Black Witch was true all along. Yes, part of my task was to help take down Vogel and his Shadow. But I can sense the call to lead my people out of the horror we all became.

Alfsigr voices rise, calling out to Wynter in their language, "Ealaiontora" echoing again and again as they emphatically make a sign on their chests that has the feel of an Alfsigr religious symbol.

Wynter fans out her wings, Ariel staunchly beside her, and looks lovingly toward her people. She raises her hand and flicks out a finger, and a suspended silver amplification rune blinks into existence before her.

"I speak as your Ealaiontora," she calls out, her voice like a bell, reverberating over the Shadowed wasteland. "The Shining Ones are calling us onto the path of united Dryad'khin. It is time to cast off the Zalyn'or's lies of division and take our place as what we must all become—Guardians of Erthia's Balance and Guardians of *all* Erthia's children."

And then Wynter turns, lifts the Verdyllion, and blasts out a line of runic portals, all of them a glowing prism-edged green.

III green.

Wynter hands the Verdyllion back to me, a slight, emotional smile on her lips.

I hesitate, then take hold of the ever-living Wand once more. Its spiraling form feels so right as my fingers wrap around it. Like a circle finally closing. I straighten and look out at all the Mages. And all the Alfsigr. At *everyone.*

Stepping forward, I feel myself rising, finally, as the true Black Witch. But not as some central figure in this story. Because it's clear this fight requires not just me, but every one of us to rise as restorers of the Balance.

So, instead, I rise as a messenger and catalyst amongst many, many messengers and catalysts, each of us ready to lose everything so that others won't have to.

So that the children of Erthia won't have to.

"Dryad'khin," I say, looking to all my Tree'khin as I gesture with the Verdyllion toward the line of portals. "We need to go to the East as one unified Tree'khin." I glance at the Shadow-destroyed sky and land, pain lancing through my heart. "And work to save our world *together.*"

CHAPTER SEVEN

DRYAD'KHIN

Elloren Guryev

Noilaan

Yvan and I hold tight to each other. His fire sparks tempestuously against mine through our bond as we approach the portal's exit into the East, unsure of what level of chaos we might find there.

We emerge from one of the Verdyllion's line of portals along with Soleiya and our other family members and allies.

Including the new Dryad'khin soldiers of Gardneria and Alfsigroth.

We pour out onto a hugely expansive, elevated ledge near the base of the half-decimated Vo Mountain Range, just west of Voloi. I glance around, morbid unease shuddering through everyone's power as we collectively assess the situation we're met with. The eastern bank of the Vo River is spread out before us, Erthia's violent, unmoored weather tentatively held back by the dome Tierney and her allies cast over the Vo and its bracketing land, a dome that they've managed to enlarge, its translucent western side only a few paces behind us, their magic purpling the Vo's waters.

"They did it," Vothe marvels from where he stands in human form by Trystan, Wrenfir and his great-aunt Sithendrile bracketing them. Vothe's nostrils flare as he tilts his head. "I sense Tierney, Or'myr, and Viger's power . . . and Fyordin Lir's power coming in from the far south . . . they managed to hold the Vo and its surrounding land."

I nod then wince, a twinge of pain streaking through my injured ear. The throb along my torn ear's apex is greatly reduced after Yvan's healing ministrations, but there's no time for further healing, the trees surrounding us almost completely grayed, the air chill and dank.

The Verdyllion is sheathed at my side, thrumming with the amplified energy from the rapid increase in Forest-linked Dryad'khin. The Shadow Wand is wrapped in several layers of buffering cloth and secured in Wynter's tunic pocket.

But I'm tense, every nerve on high alert. Because the Shadow Wand's subtle frisson of slithering energy is completely gone.

As if it's *hiding* itself from us.

Wynter frowns down at her pocket, her eyes tinged with worry. "The Shadow Wand . . ." she says from beside Ariel ". . . its power is strangely silent. It feels like it's sunk into some type of evil dormancy."

"I sense it too," I respond as Sylvan, Yulan, Oaklyyn, Raz'zor, and Alder and many others, including Valasca and Ni Vin, set about helping the severely weakened Dryad Fae who emerged from the Sublands. The Dryads stagger toward trees, seeking to bind rapidly to the Vo Forest, kindreds rushing in to link to them, the Verdyllion's energy having barely sustained the Tree Fae when their Northern Forest was destroyed along with their kindreds.

I study the runic dome above us. Steel-hued knots of clouds churn violently just beyond it, dark, curving Shadow lightning crackling through the tempest.

"Vogel's Shadow corruption has slithered into the East's unmoored weather," Vang Troi states, glaring at the storm along with Hizar'drile and Queen Freyja Zyrr.

I nod once more, ignoring my ear's twinge. "The power holding up the Vo's shielding . . . it's wavering," I warn, sensing the great effort it's taking Tierney and Or'myr to flow so much power into their shield from the far north, while Fyordin Lir's current of Asrai Fae power struggles to flow magic into it from the river's far south.

A ripple of Deathkin Darkness eddies through my rootlines, and I tense, swept up in the fleeting sense of my Errilor Ravens' auras coursing through me in a warning shudder, as I'm caught up in an awareness of the Deathkin collectively struggling to hold Erthia's Reckoning at bay.

"If the Vo River's shield falls," Wynter cautions, "the Shadow Wand will feed on the corruption flowing into the weather here and amplify the chaos."

"And a Reckoning will sweep over the entirety of Erthia," Wrenfir bites out, his aura a lash of fire, fear edging into his tone. "I can sense Hazel throwing every ounce of his power against it. But he'll soon lose that fight."

The awful truth of both Wynter's and Wrenfir's warnings lances through me, fear for my spark of a child resurfacing, both Yvan and Soleiya protectively reaching out to me.

Soleiya was overjoyed to the point of breaking into tears when Yvan and I told her of the child taking root inside me, her fire aura steadily blazing around us both with a loving heat rivaled only by Yvan's.

Large tendrils of Shadow curling through the storms catch my eye, my concern mushrooming. "I'm picking up what feels like a line of Level Five wind magery *amplifying* the storms," I warn. "Someone is actively pulling Shadow *east*."

"I sense it too," Vothendrile affirms.

Bleddyn curses, as I exchange a fraught glance with fellow power empath Vothe.

"Can you identify the power at play?" Andras asks.

Vothe and I shake our heads in frustration as we struggle to parse out who this remaining Mage enemy could be, a look of dogged concentration tightening Vothe's features.

Angry *booms* suddenly sound against the Vo's shield, wresting our attention, clusters of Shadowed clouds turning ghoulishly dark as their curved, dark lightning strikes against the shield like a barrage of knives.

"Holy Vo," Trystan breathes out just before three sick-looking Noi Herons fly out of the surrounding Vo Forest. They land around Yulan and her heron kindred, traumatized looks in the graceful birds' eyes, their lilac feathers and eyes edged in gray.

Anguish brimming in her gaze, Yulan drops down and gently makes contact with the frightened herons, her expression tensing before she lifts her gaze to meet ours. "This land has no chance of recovering if the weather cannot be rebalanced and stripped of Shadow."

"We need a mass planting of trees to drive off the Shadow," Sylvan states from beside Iris. He pointedly holds up his III-marked palm, the black Noi Fire Falcon kindred perched on Iris's shoulder fluffing out its feathers, as if heralding their agreement. "Our numbers have grown," Sylvan says, "but we need the help of more Dryad'khin to have a chance of achieving this. *Many, many* more."

He's right, I empathically sense. But it will be an almost impossible challenge to quickly align the East with the Forest. I zero in on the desperate chaos of the riverbank spread out before us in the distance. It's covered, just *covered*, with a refugee tent city, Noilaan's towering runic border just beyond, a large Vu Trin military presence visible before it.

Luminous runic portals the Verdyllion crafted are scattered throughout the refugee encampment, and I can just make out the lines of Western refugees streaming out of them, new portals popping into existence faster than the knots of Vu Trin military can explode them into sapphire mist. I draw in a harsh breath, hit by the daunting reality of such huge numbers of people fleeing the Shadow horrors of the West, only to find themselves in the hostile East.

There's a stark look in Gwynn's golden eyes as she grips Mavrik's arm. "Ancient One, Mavrik. Do you think my parents could be amongst those people portaling in?"

Mavrik's invisible lines of twinned magic embrace her more intently. "If they are," he responds, "we'll find them."

"That refugee encampment," Yvan says, exchanging a charged look with me, "it's already at least ten times larger than it was last time we were here."

"It's about to get a *lot* larger," Jules interjects, a troubled current flowing through the water aura Lucretia is streaming around him.

Vang Troi's aura gives a visible sapphire flare. "Well, it's time to stir up the chaos a bit more." Vang Troi turns to Hizar'drile and Queen Freyja. The three of them conjure voice amplification runes and set about directing the bulk of our forces— along with the Smaragdalfar army—to remain here to protect the recovering Dryad Fae and other rescued Subland civilians. They direct the Mage and Alfsigr Dry-ad'khin who have abandoned the Shadow to remain here, as well, to avoid giving the appearance of a military invasion when a segment of our forces portal into Noilaan.

With that accomplished, Vang Troi recharges her voice-amplification rune and succinctly commands a small portion of our original army forward.

We make our way off the ledge and through the Vo Forest, eventually emerging from the tree line to stride into the tent city.

Gasps rise all around us as we enter the encampment, people recoiling with evident fear as we follow Vang Troi through the sea of emaciated-looking refugees, many of the surrounding Kelt, Urisk, Elfhollen, Ishkart, and Verpacian people clearly thrown by the point-eared Dryad-Fae appearance of myself and the other Mages among us, as well as the astonishing purple Strafeling aura encircling Sparrow and flowing out to embrace Thierren beside her, Thierren's arm defiantly wrapped around Sparrow's shoulders.

Naga leads our horde of Western Wyverns in her onyx-scaled human form, the wounds on my horde mates' wings splinted and stitched with Lasair healing fire, their cores of fire rapidly strengthening. Oaklyyn remains staunchly by Raz'zor's side, his pale arm wrapped around her for support, his left wing dragging.

A spark of worry for him ignites through my fireline, and he turns to me.

I will rise again in strength, he hisses through me, eyes burning red-hot, *as will Erthia*. He bares his teeth, and some of my worry dampens.

The refugees' disquieted murmuring gains momentum as we move, en masse, toward Noilaan's enormous runic border, which runs along the edge of the Vo's western bank, the Goddess Vo's starbright dragon form emblazoned on its expanse.

I glance up toward the border wall's high apex with trepidation that I feel mirrored in the flow of Yvan's fire around mine.

"That wall is twice as high as it was before," Yvan hisses in Wyvern.

A hard blaze of concern sizzles through our bond. We take in the Vu Trin military ships and skiffs darting along the runic border wall's upper edge, a thick band of soldiers lining the wall's base. How will we peacefully get past *this* and bring the East into alliance with the Natural World before the brewing Shadow attack breaks through?

"Wyn Juun!" Trystan calls out, breaking into my dire thoughts.

Following my brother's line of sight, I spot an elderly Noi priest approaching, a purple Noi Starling perched on his shoulder. The priest clearly recognizes Trystan, a palpable warmth entering his dark eyes. Wyn Juun is garbed in the holy garments of the Eastern Realm's Vo'lon faith, his tunic's worn, sapphire fabric embroidered with Vo's twelve dragon manifestations, each dragon a different color. His long, snow-hued beard is tied in a knot below his chin, a cloth marked with a purple Xishlon moon tied around his arm.

My heart twists as I take in the gravely ill Mage baby Wyn Juun is cradling in his arms. Yvan and his mother immediately launch forward to lay their hands on the baby, but I know his Lasair healing power is not equal to the vicious Grippe, even Yvan's immense Lasair might holding only enough magic to slightly alleviate the Grippe's cruel symptoms.

The baby's eyes and mouth are encrusted with sores, the child struggling for breath through dangerously congested lungs. Wyn Juun looks pointedly down at the baby, then back at us, determination on his face as he raises his palm to us, displaying the mark of III.

The energy of alliance shocks through both Yvan's and my fire as well as Trystan's and Soleiya's and through the power of my Dryad'khin surrounding us as we raise

III-marked palms to the priest in instant, mutual recognition. The motion is echoed by a number of refugees moving toward us, a multitude of kindreds closing in with them. I cast Hizar'drile an appreciative look.

"Well done, Hizar'drile," Queen Freyja Zyrr says. "Those Wyverns you sent out to bring people to the Forest seem to have made inroads."

A deeper astonishment takes hold as I notice how many of these new Dryad'khin refugees are *Mages* and now possess the pointed ears and deeper forest green hue of Dryad Fae. A large number of them are also wearing the same Xishlon moon–marked armband that Wyn Juun sports. And the scattered Alfsigr refugees I can make out all possess a pale green Dryad'khin tint to their alabaster coloration.

The Forest's call for everyone to align being taken up by so many new allies.

But my tenuous spark of hope is doused as I notice how many of the refugees are sick, many quite ill with the Grippe, Dryad'khin and non-Dryad'khin alike.

Bleddyn shoots me an alarmed look. "Holy hells," she exclaims, "Elloren . . . these people need care. *Immediately.*"

My own concern gains traction as a chorus of congested coughing sounds all around us, our newly established Dryad'khin bonds with the surviving Natural World not able to heal the Grippe on their own.

A remembrance of the huge expanse of Norfure flowers I came upon in the Zhilaan Forest surfaces, just before Vogel captured me, my urgency sliding into a heated rebellion. There's no reason for anyone to suffer from this sickness. We know how to treat it. All we lack is the will.

And that needs to change.

Now.

"You have joined with us, Wyn Juun," Vang Troi somberly greets the priest as my uncle Wrenfir draws up beside us and glances around at the sick people with an expression of abject horror.

"It is true that I have become Dryad'khin," Wyn Juun affirms. "As have so many here. More each passing hour . . ."

"These people need *medicine*," Wrenfir snarls, cutting him off, fire blazing through my uncle's rootlines and practically spitting off his skin. "They need Norfure tincture *immediately.*"

Wyn Juun turns his dark eyes toward my uncle. "They do," he agrees before both he and the purple starling on his shoulder glance up at the border wall. Wyn Juun's gaze narrows, as if he's sizing up a potent and insurmountable enemy. "But our new Vo Conclave wants all those here to return to the West."

A growl bursts from Diana's throat. "The West would be a death sentence!" she snarls, my Lupine sister's amber eyes ablaze as she takes in the sick baby, the look of misery in the Mage child's bloodshot eyes positively heartbreaking.

"Access to medicine could cure this child in a *day*," Wrenfir stresses.

"We need to get these children and the others who need help to the Sublands," Ra'Ven urges as a crack of Shadow thunder booms overhead, the dank air growing chillier. "They shouldn't be exposed to the elements like this, especially with the power of the shielding above us dissipating."

Wyn Juun gives Ra'Ven a hard look. "The Vo Conclave has magically walled off the Sublands with the Smaragdalfar Elves' own Varg magic. There's no getting in or out."

A lethal glint enters Ra'Ven's gaze. "They're *still* warring with my people? With the Shadow about to break into the East and destroy *everything*?"

"Holy gods," Sage says to Ra'Ven, alarm flashing through her eyes and power, "Fyn'ir and Fern . . . and so many others . . . they're all imprisoned there."

"Effrey's likely trapped underground, as well," Sparrow cuts in, giving Thierren a tortured look, her violet aura taking on a static, martial energy.

"Elloren."

Aislinn's shocked voice beside me draws my attention, my Lupine sister's hand clamping around my arm. I turn and take in Aislinn's stunned, amber gaze as she stares into the crowd before us, her concern mirrored in Jarod's gaze. "My *family* . . ." she stammers.

"Linnie!" a stout, conservatively dressed young Mage woman calls out as she rushes toward Aislinn.

Recognition hits.

Aislinn's sister, Auralie. Utterly transformed. I remember her beaten-down appearance when I met her at Verpax University on Founder's Day. But now, her green eyes blaze with purpose, and she wears a Xishlon Moon Resistance band tied around her black sleeve, a gravely ill child who looks to be about six years old in her arms.

It's Erin, I realize, my heart painfully clenching. Aislinn's niece. So bubbly and full of life when I last saw her, excited about a new kitten and her marble collection. Now, there are Grippe sores all over Erin's face, her black hair dirty and matted, her pale green face scarily gaunt as she struggles to breathe.

"Ancient One," Aislinn cries, lurching toward them. *"Erin . . ."*

Erin takes one look at Aislinn and lets out a congested whimper, then recoils when her bloodshot eyes turn toward Jarod. "He turned you into a *wolf monster!*" Erin cries.

Aislinn gives Jarod a devastated look, and he immediately takes a careful step back so as not to further spook the child.

"Don't be afraid, sweet one," Aislinn insists in a gentle, fractured tone as she turns back to the child. "I'm still Auntie Aislinn. And Jarod—" she motions to him "—he's my mate. We want to help you."

Erin only cries harder and shakes her head in emphatic refute, choking on tears that quickly devolve into hacking coughs.

Aislinn looks imploringly to Auralie, her tone turning desperate. "Where's Liesbeth? And the rest of the children? Are they ill too?"

Auralie's face hardens. "I had to practically throw them into the escape portals. The West has become a nightmare. The weather's gone wild, skies so gray it's like a stormy night all the time. The crops have all failed. There's no food, Linnie. Or medicine. And Shadow monsters . . . they're *everywhere*. All manner of multi-eyed creatures. But Liesbeth is still terrified to be *here*. She's convinced we've fallen into one of the Ancient One's hells and will be massacred at any moment by the Evil Ones, you included. Our children—almost all of them are sick. Erin's got the worst of it. Linnie, we need your help."

"I'll help these children," Wrenfir offers, stepping forward. "I'm an apothecary. I have a few vials of the medicine they need in my laboratory in Voloi—"

"Get away from my child!"

We all turn as Aislinn's sister Liesbeth pushes through the crowd, making for us like the Ancient One's own avenger. Her transformation is as shocking as Auralie's. Gone is Liesbeth's perfectly put-together, zealous, Styvian poise. Her form is skeletal, her hue a pale, sickly green, fear stark in her eyes as she takes in Aislinn, Jarod, and Wrenfir, and then me and Yvan.

Liesbeth grabs desperate hold of Erin and moves to flee from us.

"Stop!" Wrenfir implores, and Liesbeth startles and turns, terror and rage in her eyes. Wrenfir takes a step toward her, his fire aura turning fiercely protective, great, glowing strands of it flowing out to encircle both Erin and the baby in Wyn Juun's arms. *"Please,"* Wrenfir begs, my uncle's usually caustic tone more impassioned than I've ever heard it. "I had this disease as a child," he says, voice splintering. "I *know*

what it's like to struggle for breath. We are *not* what you think we are. We are this child's *last chance*. I'm an apothecary. A good one. Let me *help her*."

A tortured expression overtakes Liesbeth's face as her eyes lock with my uncle's, conflict warring in them. And then, shockingly, she gives him a quick nod of assent before her eyes flutter closed and she collapses.

Yvan, Wrenfir, Aislinn, Soleiya, and Jarod all spring forward to catch both Liesbeth and a sobbing, coughing Erin. A semiconscious Liesbeth winds up in Jarod's arms, Yvan's hands pressed to her temples, and a terrified Erin in Wrenfir's arms while Aislinn murmurs soothingly to the child.

Wrenfir glares at us all, his power striking to wildfire heights through his rootlines as he cradles Erin, looking as if he'd walk through hell's own fury to save her. "I need to get to my lab in Voloi. *Right now!*"

Bootsteps sound, and we turn to find a contingent of Vu Trin marching toward us, swords drawn. Their eyes scan us before zeroing in on me, then Yvan, and then Soleiya with evident surprise before narrowing on Vang Troi.

"The Black Witch and her allies are wanted by the Vo Conclave," the lead soldier firmly declares, the expression on her angular face severe as she glares at us all.

"Good," Vang Troi shoots back, her aura pulsing with lethal sapphire light, both her hands around the hilts of her sheathed swords. "We need to speak with them."

"And we're taking these children and this ill woman with us," Soleiya insists, her gaze spitting fire.

"I'm ready to blast right through your border wall to get them the help they need," Yvan warns as he draws back from a tenuously stabilized Liesbeth and fans his wings combatively out. There's a vehement glow in Yvan's narrowed eyes, his internal fire ratcheting hotter.

"We'll join you in that inferno," Naga hisses, her golden gaze burning bright as my horde moves in around us.

Vang Troi gives Yvan, Naga, and Soleiya a look of agreement before pinning her steely gaze once more on the Vu Trin. "We stand with Yvan and Soleiya Guryev and Naga the Unbroken's horde in this demand," she states, her lips lifting in a slight smile. "So, you'd best lead the way, Noi'khin."

CHAPTER EIGHT

CYCLE OF HISTORY

Elloren Guryev

Noilaan

"We seek to align with you to save Erthia," Vang Troi declares as she finishes her petition to Noilaan's Vo Conclave.

Niko Luun, the golden-eyed Vo Conclave leader, stands on the riverbank before us just past the Eastern-facing wall of Noilaan's runic border, the white-capped Vo River spread out before us, Yvan and Soleiya flanking me. Several members of the Conclave bracket Niko, including a heavy Vu Trin military presence. They've let only a small number of us through, including Aislinn's sick relatives and Priest Wyn Juun and the ill baby.

Studying the corrupted skies, Bleddyn bites out an epithet under her breath from beside me. The Shadow storm has grown more violent, crashing against Tierney's and her allies' shielding.

Vang Troi holds up her III-marked palm and glances pointedly up at the battering storms. "We will ask, once more" she says, "for you to simply *hear our Forest out*. Before enough Shadow streams in from the West to break through the shielding above, and Nature's Reckoning *descends*."

"Heralding the destruction of every last surviving shred of the Natural World," Sylvan passionately adds.

Niko Luun gives Vang Troi a blisteringly hard look. "Oh, we listened to 'your Forest,'" he sneers. His scornful gaze flicks toward me before he levels it back at Vang Troi with enough venom to burn a hole straight through her. "We listened to the *lies* ensorcelled into your trees. Lies that put Vogel's Shadow tool in your hands.

And lies that would enable you to infiltrate our country once more and *destroy what remains of it.*"

"This land is already being destroyed!" Oaklyyn cries, Raz'zor's vermillion-coal eyes fixed murderously on Niko Luun as Raz'zor blazes an image through our hordefire of the Conclave leader bursting into an explosion of flame.

Yvan stiffens, hissing, *Steady, Wyvern,* through our horde bond.

Sylvan points a deep-green finger up at the storms. "Do you not have eyes to see? The Shadow is about to come crashing through!"

"Silence, Fae!" Niko Luun hurls back. "Noilaan is for the Vo-worshipping *Noi.* And none of this would have happened if it had *stayed that way!*"

Now it's Yvan's turn to blaze combative fire through our horde bond, a low hiss rising in his throat as Naga urges us all, *Hold your fire!*

Distress strikes through me as I take in the sapphire armbands around every Conclave member's arm, Vo's white dragon manifestation imprinted on them. So much like the white Gardnerian armbands.

"There are many types of Noi'khin, Nikovir," Vang Troi says with forced calm as an earsplitting explosion of Shadow thunder breaks, strands of Shadow pulsing into the Vo's shielding.

"No, *Vanglira,*" Niko Luun knifes back, "there is but *one* type of Noi'khin. And you are no longer one of them." He swipes a hand toward me. "The Crow Witch dares to bring an army of Mages and Alfsigr not once but *twice* into the Realm." He levels a finger toward Wynter's pocket. "Along with Vogel's Shadow tool. Yet you stand with the Black Witch still!"

Vang Troi's aura flares brighter. "It is as we have told you—Elloren Guryev has *slain* Marcus Vogel. And those Mages and Alfsigr who portaled here with us are Vogel's army *no longer.* They have become our Dryad'khin allies." Vang Troi looks pointedly toward Mavrik and Gwynn beside her. "They have been freed of their Shadow tether by light spells sent through the Verdyllion, the Zhilin Stylus of our religious lore. Nikovir, the war is *over.*"

Niko Luun gapes at her. "This war will *never* be over." He turns to his military's new high commander, Quoi Zhon, as more of Noilaan's Vu Trin forces stream in on runic vessels, by land and by air.

But there are other forces closing in, I note with mounting dread. Hundreds of civilian rune ships streaming in on the Vo River or soaring through the air toward us. Along with a multitude of Vu Trin Wyverns, who morph into human form as soon as they touch down on the riverbank's soil.

And a fleet of Vu Trin naval vessels, speeding in from the South.

Closing in to take me and my loved ones down.

My baby's dark wings flutter against my mind, and I place a hand defensively over my abdomen and take hold of the Verdyllion, a feral urge to fight rising as I draw Zhilaan- and foliage-fueled power into my lines—enough power to usher in a new war.

Yvan places a cautioning hand on my arm, and my gaze snaps to him to find his eyes fixed on the sea of Vu Trin forces and Noi civilians closing in around us. My confusion burgeons as our entire horde, save Raz'zor, floods my lines with a cautioning line of fire, the flow of its energy urging calm, Raz'zor's power cast into as much churning confusion as mine as he combatively eyes the incoming forces.

Heart hammering, I shoot Yvan a demanding look, which he fervidly meets, sending out a more intense blaze of his cautioning fire. "Wait," he urges, nostrils flaring.

Protest rises in my throat as Nike Luun bellows, "Vu Trin! I command you to *strike down these enemies of Noilaan!*"

Throwing caution to the wind, I grit my teeth and draw a huge volume of power into the Verdyllion. The Vu Trin surrounding Niko Luun draw swords, metallic screeches knifing through the air, their sapphire power rising.

Dryad Witch, hold your fire! Raz'zor hisses through our bond, his vermillion flame outrageously taking on Yvan's, Naga's, and my entire horde's cautioning motion.

"*No!*" I hiss at Yvan and my horde in Wyvern. "I won't let them—"

"Elloren," Yvan cuts in, his fire blazing around mine with impassioned heat. "*Look.*"

Thrown, I scan the Vu Trin . . . and that's when I notice it, a dart of shock spiking through me. The large mass of Vu Trin soldiers closing in around us have made no move to draw their weapons or even pull on their power, High Commander Ung Li and the small force surrounding Niko Luun eyeing them with open confusion.

"I ordered you to attack!" Niko Luun bellows again, his face reddening with fury.

My pulse spikes as the surrounding mass of soldiers and civilians streaming in behind them all raise their palms to us in unison.

III's mark on all of them.

"Holy Ancient One," I gasp, my shock blasted into renewed confusion as I'm hit by an incoming wave of purple geo-aura, pulsing up through the ground.

"What are you sensing?" Yvan hisses.

"Geopower . . ." I barely manage to answer before purple lines blink into being all over the riverbank. The net extends in every direction, including down over the Vo River's entire bed, the Waters lighting up a more vivid, ripping purple. Large violet geo-runes explode into existence across the geo-net's land-based expanse, openings appearing in their centers.

My eyes widen.

These are passages leading out of the Sublands.

Varg-shielded Subland Elves are suddenly streaming out of the passages. I spot Fyon Hawkkyn, Clive Soren, and Andras's former love, Sorcha Xanthippe, in the lead. An army of Smaragdalfar, then Rafe and Diana's Lupine pack, and Amaz and Keltish soldiers stream in behind them, including Andras's heavily tattooed mother, Astrid Volya, with Andras's son in her arms.

"Konnor!" Andras calls out to the child at the same time that Freyja roughly cries out "Clive!"

My heart leaps as Freyja strides out to meet Clive, and Andras sets off at a sprint toward his son. Effrey and Olilly run in behind Fyon, and an emotional sound bursts from Sparrow's throat as she and Thierren set out toward them.

Both Effrey and Olilly are gripping glowing violet geo-styluses, Effrey's purple Strafeling aura burning visibly bright. And Olilly . . . her aura might not be strong enough to be visible, but it still holds a formidable level of might, both youths' power connected to the purple geo-magic that blasted through Noilaan's imprisoning Subland barrier.

"Holy hells," Bleddyn exclaims. "Did Effrey and Olilly just free the Sublands?"

Gareth surges forward, a euphoric smile on his face as he passes us and raises his hand to the Vo River, lightning coursing over his skin.

Renewed shock blasts through everyone's power as whales breach the surface of the Vo in explosive sprays of water. Their seismic current of storm energy hits me, and frissons of lightning crackle around my lines. Deep-blue Selkie soldiers and other Oceanic peoples sit astride them, more Ocean-shifter soldiers streaming off the Vu Trin naval ships, along with Vu Trin soldiers, and swiftly carried to shore by small skiffs and more ocean creatures.

All of the incoming forces raise III-marked palms as a host of kindred animals close in alongside them, a large purple grizzly bear kindred lumbering behind Clive as he and Freyja sweep each other into a passionate embrace and Andras gathers his son into his muscular arms.

"They're *all* allied with us," Yvan marvels in Wyvern as we grip each other's hands, a powerful bolt of emotion blazing through our bond.

"My brother!" Marina cries and signs out to the Selkie male in the lead at the same moment that Fain and Lucretia call out "Zephyr!"

I realize Zephyr must be the steel-hued Sylphan Vu Trin soldier running in beside Marina's tall, formidable-looking brother. The unlikely couple's intermingled water-and-air magic flows around each other in an ardent caress as my Dryad'khin call out to incoming friends and loved ones.

"Stand down!" High Commander Quoi Zhon calls out to her knot of non-Dryad'khin soldiers, clearly realizing they're grievously outnumbered, all of them pointedly resheathing their swords.

Tears sting my eyes as Niko Luun shoots Quoi Zhon a look of pure fury, his hate no longer holding any bite. Because I know, deep in my heart, as Sage and Ra'Ven reach Mora'lee and take their baby Fyn'ir and young Fern into their loving arms while Dryad'khin embrace and press their III-marked palms together, their fingers twining tight, that right now, in this moment, the war is truly over.

"You are no longer the majority leader, Niko Luun," Vang Troi calls out, glancing up at the monstrous storms gaining ground above. "Which is a good thing. Erthia can't withstand this type of division any longer."

Vang Troi's words strike deep, as Shadow flashes through the Vo's shielding with intensifying force—a Death Reckoning ready to snap its leash. Hazel, Viger, my ravens, and all the other Deathkin have bought us time . . . but will it prove to be enough?

Can we swiftly use that time to repair enough of the damage we've wrought to have any future at all?

A tingle races across my palm, and my eyes widen as the Verdyllion pulses a revolutionary directive through the Forest link I share with all my Dryad'khin. The Wand erupts into a prism-edged glow that's brighter than anything I've ever seen emanating from it, as it pulses out a subversive image to us all, our next, world-changing step crystal clear. My gaze pivots to Yvan's then toward my fellow Tree'khin, the same stunned look on everyone's face quickly morphing into expressions of fierce, collective resolve.

Pulse quickening, I turn to Bleddyn as the momentous crossroads bears down. "You once told me," I say to her, "that your religion was *no children dying of curable things on the other side of a wall.*"

Bleddyn's lip tics up even as a look of dead-serious awe overtakes her gem-green eyes. "I did, in fact, say that."

"Is that still your religion," I press, "even if a good number of those children are Mages and Alfsigr Elves?"

Bleddyn glances toward Aislinn's sick niece, Erin, and the baby cradled in Wyn Juun's arms, clearly remembering, as I am, all the desperate people trapped on the other side of the runic border beside us.

Bleddyn nods, a fierce light shining in her emerald eyes. "Yeah," she says with a broad grin. "It's still my religion."

And I can see in her gaze that she senses the potential ramifications of this moment as potently as me. *Here. Right here.*

This is how the cycle of history ends.

And how hope begins.

Vang Troi climbs onto a large, flat boulder along with Sylvan and Yulan. "Dryad'khin!" she calls out to everyone assembled, her voice amplified by the rune she's swept into existence before herself and the two Dryad Fae, the word holding its own against the mounting Shadow storms. Vang Troi quiets as if searching for her next words in the vision the surviving Forest is streaming out to every Tree'khin.

"For too long," she finally says, "we have let ourselves be divided, forgetting the source of all our magic and forgetting our connections to each other."

Yulan, Vang Troi, and Sylvan exchange looks of staunch alliance.

"We stand on a threshold," Yulan calls out in her melodic voice, her Ironflower tresses glowing bright, the three grayed herons flying in and alighting on the stone beside her and her healed heron kindred. She casts a worried look toward the skies as Shadow lightning cracks against the graying shield. "The old ways of division and fracture are about to bring the destruction of the entire Natural World."

"Our only hope," Sylvan booms, "is to forge a new path, and come together as Dryad'khin to fight for each other. And to fight for the trees."

Sylvan raises his III-marked palm and looks at me as a flood of magic breaks loose and streams toward the Verdyllion from all sides.

I draw in a hard breath and stiffen, the entire surviving Forest and every Dryad'khin suddenly pouring their power into my rootlines via our Dryad'khin linkage to the Forest in a potent, gathering tide, and I join my own power to it all, like rapids converging.

The Verdyllion warms in my hand, its spiral green form flashing prismatic light before settling into a luminous green burn, as bright as a verdant star. As if it was meant for this moment. As if *I'm* coming into the best use of my Black Witch power at this moment.

Heart expanding with so much communal love it aches, I stride toward the runic wall.

Silence descends, save for the strengthening storms above us as Dryad'khin part to allow me passage to the wall's interlocking sapphire runes. And then I raise the Verdyllion, murmur the spell the Forest is whispering through us all, and press the tip of the Verdyllion to the border wall's surface.

Our collective power shocks through me, and my pulse leaps as the border wall's sapphire runes blast into every prismatic color on Erthia, bright as a million stars, and we watch, together, as the runic wall harmlessly explodes in a flash of shimmering multicolored light.

And falls.

IV

Elloren Guryev

Noilaan

Together, my Dryad'khin and I fan out through the city and the adjacent shielded lands, a group of us assembling in Voloi's war-battered Voling Plaza, where an expansive Wisteria Forest and gardens once stood, the Forest's huge, central Wisteria tree almost completely grayed. But it's still standing, a trace of prismatic fall foliage color shining in the centers of scattered leaves.

I can sense the Wisteria's cry of relief, feel its embracing energy as we touch down beside it and join our Dryad'khin in pressing our III-marked palms into the soil.

Saplings rise all around, our joint magic surging with each newly established grove.

Throughout the day and into the night, we manifest trees and channel their energy into the Vo River's shielding, keeping the Shadow storms at bay while my allies set up an extensive field hospital on the plaza's rough ground, Dryad'khin of every background streaming in to help.

Cabinets, storerooms, and what remains of cropland are gleaned to secure ingredients to fabricate Norfure tincture and locate food to share with the refugees streaming into Voloi from the West.

The former Noi Vo Conclave has been disbanded, and a temporary new Noi Conclave formed under Sylvan's and Vang Troi's leadership. And the Shadow Wand is newly encased in a stone box and kept under heavy Dryad'khin military guard, no trace of its power detectable, its continued dormancy unnerving.

"What will happen to her?" Aislinn's sister Liesbeth frantically presses Wrenfir as night descends. Pale and sickly, Liesbeth keeps fierce hold of her child's hand as Erin struggles to pull in each breath. A number of my loved ones and allies are gathered with Liesbeth, Aislinn, and their sister, Auralie, beside Erin's cot in a tent under the battered and grayed Wisteria tree, Jarod standing a discreet distance behind Aislinn.

My uncle Wrenfir cradles Erin's back, and she wheezes, her eyes bugged out and locked on his in a silent, panicked plea for breath he gently murmurs to her and brings the vial of Norfure tincture he just finished concocting to her lips, coaxing her to drink it.

Erin downs the medicine and goes frighteningly still, a shiver coursing through her. My own breath catches tight in my throat, and the entire world seems to pause. Suddenly, the child lets out a series of rattling coughs then draws in a long, hard breath.

Shock blooms on Erin's expression as well as Liesbeth's, and a broad smile overtakes my uncle's normally dour face.

Wrenfir gently lowers Erin to her pillow before turning to a frozen, wide-eyed Liesbeth and holding out another vial of Norfure tincture to her. "She'll sleep," he assures Liesbeth, eyes brimming with compassion as he nods toward both Erin and the newly medicated Mage baby who slumbers in a cradle beside her, small spots of pink returning to the baby's cheeks, the little one's breathing growing less labored by the minute. "And then," Wrenfir assures Liesbeth as she shakily accepts the vial, "she'll heal. And so will you."

An emotional sound erupts from Liesbeth's throat before she devolves into heaving sobs. *"Thank you, thank you, thank you,"* she weeps to Wrenfir again and again, teetering a bit, seeming on the verge of collapse.

Wrenfir rises and takes hold of her, gently coaxing her to take the medicine while assuring her that she's very welcome. Liesbeth downs the medicine, and Aislinn draws her into an embrace that she returns, murmuring through her tears, "I'm sorry, Linnie. I'm *so sorry.* Can you ever forgive me, my sister?" Liesbeth turns and looks at Jarod. "Can any of you ever forgive me?"

"I can," Jarod says, pain and compassion shining in his amber eyes.

Tears misting my gaze, I turn and look at the multitude of makeshift beds. Yvan sends an embracing line of fire through our bond, warming my every line and drawing my gaze to him where he's working with Soleiya, Iris, and other Lasair to heal injuries and other maladies as the Norfure tincture begins to turn a portion of the Red Grippe tide. His mother glances up at me as Yvan sends a warmer rush of fire straight through me.

I smile at their tear-blurred forms, their gazes lit up, love burning bright in them.

Twilight descends, and I pause with Yvan, Wynter, and Ariel in the center of Voling Plaza, where a black opalescent statue used to stand. The larger-than-life Icaral slaying the Black Witch has been reduced to rubble, but I catch a glimpse of a disembodied face strikingly similar to my own lying next to the remnants of a broken Icaral wing.

"It's time for something new there," I say to Yvan as we survey the wreckage.

"It's time for something new practically *everywhere*," Yvan agrees, the love blazing through our bond in full defiance of statues like the one that once stood here.

The Verdyllion tingles against my side, and I turn to Wynter, my heart kicking up into a fast, anticipatory rhythm as a vision of the Verdyllion's intent once more suffuses me. Breathless, I reach out and offer the Verdyllion to Wynter.

Wynter smiles as she takes it, her Wyvernfire aura rising, silver flame igniting in her eyes as her III-green aura brightens. "Come, then," Wynter says. "We need to gather the seven Bearers of the Verdyllion."

Peak foliage arrives that night, and my light power surges as Yvan and I gather before the rubble of the Icaral and Black Witch statue with my fellow Bearers and other allies with powerful light and amplification magic. Prismatic orbs that Mavrik and Gwynnifer suspended in the air cast a rainbow of light over the gathered crowd of my family and fellow Dryad'khin.

Tension mounts in the air as Mavrik and Gwynn's twinned power rises in a golden wave before they point their living branches toward the destroyed statue, murmuring a spell in unison.

Bolts of prismatic light blast from their branches and collide with the rubble in an ear-splicing *boom* that rivals the Shadow storms above, blasting clear through to the living soil beneath, the Deathkin energy pulsing through it staving off the Natural World's Reckoning.

Yvan and I, along with the rest of my fellow Wand Bearers, step toward the soil.

Gripped in Wynter's pale green hand, the Verdyllion pulses with every hue. "Are you ready, Dryad'khin?" Wynter asks, Ariel standing protectively beside her.

We nod, peak foliage suffusing us all. Oaklyyn's, Sylvan's, Yulan's, and Alder's foliage-amplified auras are all so strong the magic tingles over my skin. Sage is practically glowing with violet power, and Mavrik and Gwynn's gilded lines of magic have become visible, embracing us all with their twinned might. And Marina . . . her single lightline is surging, a portion of it channeling into the color-pulsing octopus wrapped around her shoulders, her ocean kindred bathed in a swirling, magicked ball of salt water. Just below her octopus, her silver sealskin is tied around her neck, and Gareth is caressing her fur-draped shoulder with a gentle hand.

I raise my own gentle hand to my abdomen, my Icaral-Dryad baby's light power blazing through my color-drenched rootlines with fiery Zhilaan might.

Yvan kisses the mating mark on my shoulder as he slides his arms around me from behind while Gwynn and Mavrik, Sage, Rivyr'el, Marina, and I link our fingers around the Verdyllion in Wynter's hand.

A shudder passes through me as our combined light magic floods my rootlines in a spangling rush at the same moment the surrounding Dryad Fae cast a power-amplifying spell. A line of prismatic energy appears in the air, connecting our III marks, and our joint power surges.

Following the vision the Verdyllion is sending to us all, we lower ourselves to the soil as one and thrust the Verdyllion's spiraling hilt straight into it.

Sun-strong prismatic rays blast from the Verdyllion. We release it and step back, retreating farther and farther as the Verdyllion's green form darkens to black and slim roots surrounded by verdant mist suddenly flow out from its lower half and weave into the soil.

A frisson of awe shudders through Yvan's and my joined fire as both the Verdyllion and its roots rapidly enlarge and morph into an Ironwood sapling. The tree keeps enlarging, its branches rising as additional roots fan out through the plaza's battered stone. I can sense the Verdyllion's roots burrowing under all of Voloi, then lower still, flowing out to support the Sublands beneath us as they link to Erthia's surviving web of roots, a portion of the root network leading all the way to the Zhilaan Forest.

A heightened awe shimmers through my bond to Yvan as the Verdyllion expands into a III-size Ironwood Tree surrounded by verdant mist, its canopy stretching all the way up to the shield's cloud-high edge. Its leaves, colored in every hue of the rainbow, rustle in the breeze, its canopy expanding to shelter a large portion of Voloi, its benevolent power joining with all of our magic.

As IV roots itself to both us and the world.

THE DRYAD STORM

A green pulse of IV's energy blasts through the shielding above us and punches away a portion of the Shadow storms just above the Great Tree. Stars become visible overhead, and it feels like a miracle, my breath catching tight as the circle of stars begins to slowly expand, the sky opening up north and south along the shielding, and I realize IV's power will eventually reach Tierney and Or'myr and Fyordin Lir.

Wynter steps toward the Great Tree as if she's answering a summons. Reaching it, she places her palms to its trunk and inclines her head down, her wings pulling in tight. The flow of her magic turns troubled, then chaotically alarmed, and Ariel rushes toward it.

"What is it, Wynter?" Ariel demands, her invisible Wyvernfire crackling protectively hot around Wynter.

Wynter shivers and turns to Ariel as unnatural thunder cracks and the Shadow storms roll back over our shielding from the West, blotting out the stars.

I stare at the churning, darkening sky, overcome, once again, by the sense of Level Five magery drawing Shadow power to the East, the Shadow storms suddenly gaining might almost as fast as our Great Tree–amplified magic.

"It's as Elloren sensed," Wynter says. "There's a remaining threat rising. A Mage here in the East . . . actively pulling in Shadow might from the West. The Shadow Wand is still linked to his fastlines. And it's channeling all of its remaining power into him."

Fear shudders through Wynter's power, as I focus on the storms.

I stiffen as it all clicks into place—where I've sensed this power before.

"Damion Bane survived," I call out, meeting Wynter's widened gaze, then Aislinn's, a horrified look tensing my Lupine sister's face. I turn back to Wynter. "Can you track him through IV?"

Wynter nods, the silver fire in her eyes intensifying. "I can. I know *exactly* where he is."

CHAPTER TEN

SHADOW MAGE

Damion Bane

Vo Forest

Damion Bane glances at the smoking fastlines on his hands and wrists as he strides out of the Shadow portal he conjured into a foggy, grayed stretch of Noilaan's Vo Forest, following the pull of the Shadow Wand.

A pull toward Voloi.

Shadowed thunder *booms* overhead, and Damion glances up at the Shadow storms battering against the shielding the heathens cast over the Vo River and its bracketing land. Shadow storms he wrested hold of and drew East, more rolling in, ready to crash through the shield's northern and southern focal points.

His Shadow attack on the East just beginning.

The heathen's shielding is about to *fall*, regardless of the rise of a new Tree of Power.

Pausing, Damion draws in a deep breath, lifts his wand hand and runs a finger over the steely fastmarks on it, a tendril of gray smoke emanating from them curling around his finger. Concentrating on the Shadow Wand's directional pull on his fastlines, he senses the Wand closing off its power from heathen detection while it floods its gray might into him, its magic *thrumming* with the desire for him to recapture the Wand and take it firmly in hand.

Rising as the Magedom's *true* ruler.

A Magedom that will rise again and prevail against every vile enemy.

Anger ices through Damion's lines and quickly barrels into vengeful rage. Because he's seen, through his brief, forced, fastline-connection to the Fae Wilds, what Vogel truly was all along—a cursed Icaral demon.

THE DRYAD STORM

The whole Magedom led disastrously astray.

Damion balls his fastmarked hands, savoring how he used the Forest's brief link-age to his fastlines to find out as much as he could about the Magedom's enemies, leaving him with the information he needs to retake the Shadow Wand, gather the small army of true Mages who resisted the heathen Forest's pull, wrest hold of the continent's Shadow power, then take down the Dryad whore and her allies *once and for all*.

Oh, yes, he'll finish what he started with Elloren Gardner on that Valgard bal-cony so many months ago.

Damion's magic whips into a frenzy, battering against his lines for release, Shadow-amplified wind and water storming through him. The desire to avenge his slain sister, Fallon, and their brother, Sylus, surging.

He'll hunt down his fastmate, Aislinn, as well. The little wolf bitch *belongs* to him. His to do with as he pleases, Lupine freak that she is. Arousal takes root just thinking about it. Oh, he'll fully break her this time. And get his fill of her animal-istic corruption before killing her *slowly*.

Leaving him free to fast to another.

The certainty of his impending triumph floods Damion with resolve. He launches back into motion, striding toward the Shadow Wand, reveling in its guid-ing pull, a sense of destiny filling him.

A slim, cloaked figure suddenly slips in front of him, so fast it's as if she's appeared out of nowhere.

He halts, startled, and reflexively unsheathes his wand, his Shadow-amplified power brewing to life.

Killing life.

The slim figure raises her gaze to meet his, her cloaked face cast in darkness.

But her *eyes*.

Wild and glowing with amber ferocity.

Concern sparks inside Damion, but then he looks closer and his concern evap-orates.

Aislinn.

His little bitch of a fastmate.

He flashes her a congenial smile as he begins to murmur the binding spell in the back of his throat.

"Hello, Damion," Aislinn says.

Her tone catches him off guard. It's so lacking in inflection. Devoid of the tremor it used to hold when she was under his control. *But she'll be under my control in a moment*, he considers as binding power fills his wand. Because Lupines might be immune to Mage magic, but they aren't immune to *Shadow* magic. And she's so *very* alone.

Damion's blood heats.

Oh, he's going to savor breaking her once more.

"My fastmate," he croons before subtly flicking his wand, Shadow vines lashing toward her . . .

. . . to flick against nothing as she's gone in a blur, his wand suddenly wrested from his hand and his vines colliding with the tree Aislinn is no longer in front of, binding tight to its trunk.

Every nerve sparking, Damion spins as a blur races around him and Aislinn appears, once more, where she previously stood, his wand now in her hand. Those wild amber eyes pinned unblinkingly on him.

A sudden creeping tingle coils through Damion's spine, and his skin bristles with a sense of the situation shifting . . .

But then he remembers how weak she is. How pathetic. How easily browbeaten.

"You can't wield it," he chides as he stares her down, gesturing with a flick of his fingers toward the wand. He grins at her, the sheer force of his domineering aura always enough to gain the upper hand. "Which means you'll have to *fight* me."

But that stare of hers. That unnerving, amber *stare*.

"I promised myself that I would never touch you nor be touched by you again," Aislinn states, calm and cold as deep winter.

Some of Damion's fear uncoils. "Good, good," he says, his throat thick, relief loosening his lungs as he plans his attack . . .

"But *they* made no such promise," Aislinn says as several black dragons slide into view from every side, moving as silently as Aislinn did through the Void Forest's dense fog.

Damion's breath catches in his chest.

Because the nearest dragon . . . he *remembers* this one. The giant black one that he couldn't break. Even after he smashed her wing and leg. Even after he tore off her ear and ate it in front of her.

The huge dragon snarls, the sound rumbling straight down Damion's spine as his eyes snag on the piercing green gaze of a leaf-hued Amaz carried on the back of another incoming dragon. Damion's alarm intensifies.

Alder Xanthos . . . the Dryad Amaz.

A purple eagle with a charred wing perched on her shoulder.

"Do you remember me?" Alder asks, tone harsh. A flock of giant eagles with saffron feathers emerge from the dense Forest, their golden eyes all pinned on him with looks of keen, predatory interest. "Do you remember Azion, my eagle kindred, whom you murdered?" Alder inquires.

Damion takes a step back. "Aislinn," he says, cursing the tremor that's entered his voice, his throat tightening against it as something new blurs in from the fog.

Diana Ulrich appears before him, standing beside Aislinn. Diana's stance is casually powerful as she surveys his entire form, head to toe, with merciless Lupine eyes.

Like she's sizing up a meal.

"So," Diana says as she raises her hand and flexes it. "I was told you hurt my sister." She flicks her claws out with audible *snicks* as she gives Damion a smile that's so chilling, his insides turn to liquid.

"Aislinn," he pleads, taking another step back, "you can't let them do this . . ."

Aislinn turns and walks away as Diana's growl tears through the Forest, Naga's roars shake the world, a ripping, slashing noise sounds . . . and Damion Bane begins to scream.

GEOMANCER DRYAD

Or'myr Syll'vir

Northern Vo River

Or'myr's stylus and Tierney's palms are pressed to their Vo shield's ever-thinning surface, this Western-facing wall of their shielding set down inside the Forest bracketing the Vo's Western bank. Their arms tremble against the Shadow storm's relentless assault, lethal winds battering their entire shield, the storm a roar in Or'myr's ears, every Xishlon moon he's conjured sizzled away, Fyordin's distant power rapidly dissipating.

"My power's almost tapped out," Tierney cries over the din, her voice strained with an agony that shears straight through Or'myr's heart.

They won't be able to hold their shield much longer.

Or'myr meets Tierney's gaze in a mutual look of terrible knowing as he readies himself to pull Tierney into a protective embrace when the last reserves of their power run out. Through their Deathkin bond, he can sense her preparing to do the same, a strand of her magic spiraling ever tighter around his.

Tierney's look of devastation turns to one of impassioned rebellion. "I love you," she declares with the force of an Erthia-tilting vow.

A shred of Or'myr's rapidly diminishing lightning forks through their bond. "I love you too," he says, passion for her pounding through every vein as he prepares to sweep her up before the Shadow crashes through the shield, so they can, at least, die in each other's arms. "I will love you forever, Tierney'lin."

"Kiss me as we meet our end," Tierney rasps, voice splintering. "Your lightning be damned. I want this to end with your lips on mine."

Or'myr nods tightly, defiant love flashing through their bond, both of them ready, he knows, to let this last kiss be their final cry of rebellion against the Shadow's triumph.

Another punch of Shadow crashes against their shield, forcing it inward, their heels skidding against soil, another crack of thunder booming, the storm relentlessly advancing toward the Vo River at their backs, ready to siphon up its elemental power.

Growling out a curse, Or'myr digs in his heels, ready to send the very last shred of his power into the shielding, when a blast of natural magic suddenly shocks through its expanse.

Flashing in from the South.

Its force expands outward, the current of power colliding with Or'myr's front like a wall of hot static, his feet skidding against earth as both he and Tierney are blasted backward.

Or'myr's back hits a tree trunk, the breath knocked from his lungs, his remaining shred of lightning cast into forking chaos. Concern for Tierney coursing through him, he turns to find her slumped on the ground. He lunges toward her, drops to his knees, and brings his hand protectively to her shoulder. She holds up a reassuring palm, appearing dazed as she takes in the shield-wall before them, which is now pulsing with every hue of prismatic color as it slowly pushes outward, battering against the Shadow storm to encompass more and more of the Vo River's adjacent Forest.

"What's happening?" Tierney gasps.

A huge CRACK sounds above, and they both flinch. Their heads jerk up just as chromatic lightning sizzles through the shield and it punches outward in every direction, forcing back the storms, blue sky opening overhead.

They give each other a quick, wide-eyed look, a surge of shock flashing through their bond. Tierney springs up and sets off toward her River at a sprint and Or'myr jolts up to race after her, the two of them darting out of the Forest and onto the Vo's western bank.

The whole world flashes violet, so bright that Or'myr skids to a halt and yanks up his forearm to protect his eyes. The flash rapidly recedes to reveal a purple moon shimmering into being just above their shielding.

All the breath stutters from Or'myr's chest. "Someone's sending us a message," he barely manages, not daring to hope.

Tierney rushes into the River and falls to her knees in the Vo's shallow edge, throwing her palms down through the water to its bed.

She gasps and turns to him. "Holy gods, Or'myr. There's a new Great Tree. Its image flashed into my mind the moment my palms touched the Waters. Its power is *flooding* the Vo shielding." Tears are suddenly streaking down her cheeks, powerful feeling rushing through their bond. "The entire Vo," she says, forcing the words out through a strangled sob, "it's been reshielded. But not just my River. The *entire surviving East* has been reshielded."

Movement in the sky to the south catches their attention, and they both turn as a pale dragon soars toward them. Two Mages with gold-flashing eyes are carried on the dragon's back, a young man and a young woman, two flame-hued hawks flying behind them, purple branches and leaves marking the dragon's pale wings.

"Raz'zor," Or'myr murmurs as the dragon, Mages, and hawks soar closer.

"I sense incoming Asrai power," Tierney rasps, pointing at the Vo.

Or'myr follows her gaze to the River just as four Asrai Fae burst up from the Waters and launch into a sprint toward them, quickly followed by six more. Raz'zor lands beside them with a heavy *thump*.

Thrown, Or'myr meets Raz'zor's crimson gaze before surveying the curiously golden-eyed couple on Raz'zor's back—Mages, yet not Mages. Or'myr's brow knits in confusion over their deeper-than-usual green hue, the rainbow streaks in their hair and the chromatic light flashing at the edges of their irises.

"Vogel is dead," the male Mage announces as he approaches, a series of branches instead of wands sheathed at his sides, one of the hawks perched on his shoulder. "Slain by your cousin, Elloren Guryev."

Or'myr exchanges a shocked look with Tierney, not only in response to the news of Vogel's death, but to hear that Elloren now bears Yvan Guryev's name.

Well, it's about damned time, he thinks, unable to suppress a shocked smile.

"The Magedom has been defeated," the golden-eyed woman adds. Or'myr's gaze flicks over the glowing gold fastlines marked on both her hands and wrists and the man's, his heartbeat a hammer.

"Asrai!" one of the Water Fae calls to Tierney as she approaches, tears glassing the willowy, deep-blue woman's eyes.

Recognition lights inside Or'myr. This is Asra'leen—Tierney's gentle, foam-haired Wyvernguard roommate. Asra'leen pulls Tierney into an embrace as Tierney begins to sob in earnest, a surge of violent relief coursing through her and Or'myr's joined power.

THE DRYAD STORM

Attempting to blink away his own tears, Or'myr watches as Raz'zor's tear-blurred figure suddenly contracts into the form of a young man with alabaster scales and horns, glowing crimson eyes, and pale, leaf-speckled wings.

A joyful laugh escapes Or'myr. "Hello, Shifter," he says, only slightly surprised by Raz'zor having gained the ability to morph into human form.

Ready for the miraculous everywhere.

Raz'zor shoots Or'myr a sharp-toothed smile and snaps his pale wings out to their full breadth. "Greetings, my Runic Liberator," Raz'zor growls, the red fire in his eyes burning hotter. "We have need of your geomancy."

"I'm Mavrik Glass," the male Mage says to Or'myr, holding up a palm marked with the image of an Ironwood tree. "We've been sent on behalf of the Eastern Realm's new Dryad'khin forces to bring you to Voloi. Your Strafeling geomancy and Mage powers are needed there, *urgently*."

Or'myr and Tierney exchange looks of confusion. Reluctance to part is suddenly roaring through their bond, its strength tidal.

"What do you need me for?" Or'myr asks Mavrik Glass, a momentous tension circling down as he takes in the grave look in everyone's eyes.

"Our Dryad'khin forces have taken hold of the Shadow Wand," the golden-eyed young woman tells them, tone urgent. "We need you to go to war with it."

Hunched low on Raz'zor's back, Or'myr speeds south over the Vo, the twinned Dryads, Mavrik and Gwynnifer Glass, pressed in behind him. The damage the East's magic visited upon the briefly unshielded Forest bracketing the Vo is hard to take in, large tracts of trees decimated by the East's Unbalanced storms, but here and there, defiant groves hold on to prismatic color, still standing.

Vogel wasn't able to destroy it all, Or'myr rebelliously considers.

The spots of color whiz by as Mavrik and Gwynnifer fill Or'myr in on everything that's happened, while Raz'zor flies them south fast as a sustained crossbow shot, his speed accelerated by Gwynn and Mavrik's layered wind spells.

A sudden ache twists at Or'myr's heart, triggered by his separation from Tierney, his beloved having remained behind to help anchor Asrai'kin water magic to the Vo shield's northern focal rune. He can feel Tierney's ache for him as well, swirling through their bond, a raw longing suffusing it that's a struggle for them both to suppress.

✴

Or'myr and his companions reach Voloi the next evening, Or'myr's magic nearly fully restored by the amplification runes marked on him by Gwynn during their journey, purple lightning now crackling through his lines and out toward Tierney through their bond in potent flashes.

They round a bend in the Vo River . . . and a gigantic tree comes into view.

Astonishment forks through Or'myr as he realizes that this is the Great Tree IV that Tierney sensed and that Mavrik and Gwynn described—the Tree whose power is now anchored to their shielding—a resurgence of III, the Great Tree emblazoned on Gwynn's, Mavrik's, and Raz'zor's palms.

Raz'zor soars past the Great Tree, and Or'myr notes, with a quickly cast detection spell, that his glamoured mountaintop Vonor refuge is still blessedly intact, everything in him longing to bring Tierney to it.

The sunset has deepened to indigo hues by the time they're descending toward the base of the Voloi Mountain Range just past Voloi's southernmost edge, where a small, surviving Vu Trin military base is located.

Or'myr takes in the large military presence assembling on the base's central sapphire-torchlit courtyard, Vang Troi in its center, many Urisk and what appear to be Dryad Fae among them. Beside Vang Troi stands a young woman with deep-green shimmering skin, a shock of green in her long black hair, a crimson-haired Icaral beside her.

Emotion seizes hold of Or'myr's chest.

Elloren. And Yvan Guryev.

And . . . his mother, Li'ra, beside them.

Or'myr's heart leaps as he meets his mother's gaze, a look of profound relief and love on her lilac face, a lilac-quartz stylus in her hand. Or'myr thrills to the sight, overjoyed at hearing that the women of Uriskan have regained their geopower.

He wishes with everything in him that Tierney was here, but is heartened by the sight of so many other friends and loved ones—Effrey and Bleddyn Arterra, Sparrow Trillium and Thierren Stone, and a whole host of his other Urisk'kin, friends and family members from all backgrounds, along with a few tattooed Amaz Urisk, one a blue woman with short black hair surrounded by silvery goats and an Icaral Elf who must be Wynter Eirllyn, holding something wrapped in cloth in her pale, green-tinted hands.

A cold dread rises inside Or'myr because he knows what that must be.

The remaining threat that could destroy them all.

That could destroy his beloved Tierney, the love of his life, as well as her bonded river.

Or'myr's hands loosen from Raz'zor's shoulder horns, and he quickly climbs off his friend's back along with Mavrik and Gwynn and strides toward his mother.

"You've regained your geomancy, Maam'yir," he says to her, raw emotion crackling through his power as he embraces her.

"I have, my son," she says through joyful tears.

They draw back from each other, and Or'myr turns and drops to one knee to hug young Effrey who promptly bursts into tears, clutching at him.

"I thought you *died!*" Effrey chokes out.

Tears sting Or'myr's eyes as he hugs his gentle, bespectacled geo-apprentice close. He draws back, smiling. "You think I'm so easy to kill?"

Lips trembling, Effrey shakes his head and messily swipes away his tears as Or'myr scrutinizes the intensified aura mist of violet Strafeling power gathered around the child, almost as intense as Or'myr's own aura.

His power has grown, Or'myr notes with deep satisfaction.

"You did well," he tells Effrey, "breaking the bonds of the Sublands."

Effrey nods as he continues to sob, choking on his tears.

"Effrey," Or'myr says, warm but firm as he brings his hand to the child's shoulder. Effrey meets Or'myr's purple eyes with a look of grave trust. "We need to be strong now and I know you can be," Or'myr encourages. "We're powerful and we're needed by the entire Realm. By the entirety of *Erthia.* Do you understand?"

Effrey nods again and straightens, his jaw tensing with a look of resolve as he swallows back his tears.

Or'myr shoots him a look of approval before patting his shoulder, rising to his feet and turning to Elloren. "Cousin," he says, another upswell of feeling overtaking him that's mirrored in her eyes.

"It's so very good to see you, cousin," Elloren says as they draw each other into a heartfelt embrace.

Drawing back, Or'myr smiles slightly and motions toward Elloren's newly pointed ear, concern surging as he takes in the jagged scar where her left ear's point must have been.

"Who did that to you?" he asks, motioning toward it.

"Vogel," she flatly replies. "Yvan healed it as best he could."

Or'myr nods, forcing back the rise of rage over Vogel's cruelty as he takes in the pained look tensing Elloren's features. "Well, we still look even more alike, now," he gently teases, gesturing toward his own pointed ears.

Elloren laughs, wiping away her tears. "That we do, my cousin."

"I'd wager your child will join our point-eared club, as well," Or'myr says with a wink, his throat catching with emotion as he briefly looks at Yvan, all three of them growing serious.

So very much at stake.

Steeling himself, Or'myr turns to Vang Troi. "I was told you have urgent need of my power." He takes in the large Urisk presence surrounding them, kindred gems and geo-styluses in all of their hands.

"As you know," Vang Troi says, her violet eyes grave, "we have the Shadow Wand in our possession. We need as much geomancy as possible to encase it in layers of the strongest stone that can be conjured."

"Time to put that Strafeling level of power to work," Bleddyn chimes in, a lethal light in her emerald eyes. Or'myr can sense the verdant geomancy radiating off the tall Urisk woman, her green glow almost Strafeling strong.

"That Wand is incredibly dangerous," Vang Troi tells him as his eyes flick toward the cloth-wrapped Wand gripped in Wynter Eirllyn's hand.

Another chill skitters down Or'myr's spine. It's one thing to hear of the evil tool, quite another to come face-to-face with it—the Wor Shadow Stylus spoken about in his Vo'lon faith's sacred texts. And in every holy text of every land, fear of it echoing down through the ages.

The people of Erthia falling prey to it again and again and again.

"Our magical efforts support what all of Erthia's myths describe," Vang Troi states, her tone clipped. "The Wor can't be destroyed. And it seems to have a mind of its own. A mind that feeds on fracture. It's sending out dreams to try and escape our hold on it."

Or'myr's eyes widen.

"It came to me in a dream," Bleddyn explains, a haunted light entering her gaze. "It showed me visions of myself in possession of it. Killing every Urisk belonging to every class above my Urol status to avenge the Urol and Uuril for centuries of oppression. Followed by visions of the Wand striking down every last non-Urol or Uuril person on Erthia. It filled me with this . . . *feeling* . . . that if I wielded it and wiped out every group that has ever oppressed my people . . . that a new, perfect age would come."

"It came to me in a dream, as well," Vang Troi interjects, warning in her violet eyes. "It urged me to cleanse Noilaan of everyone who has refused a link to the Forest. I could feel the Wand's rage when I fought its pull."

"We believe it was leading Damion Bane to attempt to reclaim it for the Magedom," Elloren confides. "Wynter read Damion's intent through her empathic link to IV, which showed her visions of his tree-witnessed actions."

Or'myr meets Wynter Eirllyn's silver-fire eyes.

"It's a dangerous balance at the moment," Wynter admits, her brow knotting. "IV's power is growing as more and more people join with the Forest and come together as Dryad'khin to heal Erthia. But discord still exists. And the corruption that's taken over so much of the continent . . . the Shadow Wand is still able to siphon magic from it, so the Wand remains a threat."

"Especially since it's actively searching for someone to take hold of it so that it can rise again," Sparrow chimes in.

"So, we'll encase it leagues-deep in stone," Or'myr vehemently offers.

"We need to read it before we do, cousin," Elloren says, "to gauge its every weakness."

Or'myr gives Elloren a wary look. "Read it?"

She nods, a battle-hardened light entering her gaze. "It's likely that you and I will be able to get the clearest of readings from it, since we're both wood empaths. Wynter can read intent, but we'll likely be able to read the very quality of the Shadow Wand's wood, possibly getting more concrete information about how to contain it. Remember when we touched wood together in your Vonor? We could see its source all the more clearly working *together*."

Or'myr looks toward the Wor, eyeing it like the monster that it is. Drawing in a harsh breath, he turns back to Elloren. "All right, cousin. We read it together."

A thick tension descends as a graceful Dryad Fae with glowing Ironflower tresses steps toward him and introduces herself as Yulan, a Tricolor Heron nervously hugging her side. Yulan proceeds to conjure wreaths of protective Ironflowers around Or'myr and Elloren, Or'myr's violet Strafeling aura suffusing the flowers' blue glow.

He eyes the Shadow Wand with extreme caution as Wynter hands it to Elloren and Elloren carefully draws back its cloth wrapping, exposing the Wor's gray upper half. Then, exchanging one quick, determined look at each other, they take direct hold of the Wor.

The surrounding world snaps out of sight, Or'myr's pulse quickening, as he and

Elloren are hurled into a Shadowed wasteland—gray sky, gray earth, tendrils of Shadow mist rising from the charred ground.

And there, in the center of it all, stands a leafless tree as big as IV. The Great Void Tree is made entirely of wavering gray Shadow, a palpable sea of malice swirling around it.

A branch drops from the Void tree and lands on the ground before their feet, and Or'myr immediately intuits what this is.

The Shadow Wor.

A dreamy thrall, soft as velvet, begins to wind around Or'myr. Lulled, his shoulders slacken as a gentle pull tugs on his wand hand, the Wor's slither of power, reaching out to seductively caress his lines. *Reading* him.

A vision snakes into Or'myr's mind—the Wor in his hand, his amplified-lightning turned to glorious gray. As he uses it to subdue every last person in the East who ever spat at him or hurled a slur at him for being the grandson of the Black Witch.

The Wor shivers a new scene into being around him—he's inside his Vonor, the unglamoured refuge now taking up the entire Voloi Mountain Range, the city below under his complete control. He turns to find Tierney there, bound to his Vonor's wall with Shadow vines, as if the Wor is offering her up to him, her power leached to gray, her eyes aglow with the dead color, their magic no longer at odds, the Wor's spiraling form on a shelf just behind her, both Tierney and the Wor ripe for the taking . . .

Outrage explodes through Or'myr, a whole purple galaxy of it. With a brutal snarl, he thrusts his palm forward and throws out as much of his Strafeling lightning at the Shadow Wor as he can, his power suffused and strengthened by his fierce love for Tierney.

A terrifying scream strafes through Or'myr's mind as the Wor erupts into purple fire, its scream of rage knifing through every line. He stiffens his shoulders against the brutal pain as the scene is wrenched from sight and he's thrust back into the Void Forest, as if the Wor, realizing its mistake, is suddenly desperate to cleanse his mind of thoughts of Tierney.

A stunned certainty hits as Or'myr realizes that the Wor is reacting not only to his lightning . . . but to his powerful love for Tierney.

He whips his gaze toward Elloren, finding her gone rigid and doubled over on the Shadow-misted ground. Her teeth are gritted, her breathing labored, her eyes wide and pinned to the Wor now suspended in the air before them, beckoningly within reach. Elloren is gripping her wand hand's wrist, as if battling the urge to reach for the evil thing.

"Take my hand!" Or'myr insists, leaping toward her and grabbing her wrist. Elloren's eyes snap to his, primal terror in them. "It fears *love!*" Or'myr cries out.

Elloren grabs him as Or'myr sweeps out his wand and draws up a crackling, invisible shield of violet lightning around them, blazing his full love for Tierney into it, as well as his love for Elloren, his mother, and the rest of his family and friends— for everyone and everything truly worth fighting for—as he realizes that the stone he and the other geomancers are about to conjure around this Shadow beast isn't the greatest weapon they all possess against it.

Ultimately, it's the love they all have for one another.

The Wor's shriek reaches world-trembling levels and its form morphs to that of its V'yexwraith manifestation, multiple mouths full of teeth wide open as it screams, leaning close, ready to consume them both. Or'myr and Elloren shudder against the force of the Wor's scream, its battering assault on their shield and their lines kicking up their trembling to the point Or'myr fears their very lines will be ripped apart, but he holds on to the shield and to his love.

The scene abruptly snaps out of sight with such whiplashing force, gravity gives way.

Dizzy and disoriented, Or'myr finds himself crumpled onto the Voloi ground with Elloren, both of them struggling to regain breath and gripping each other's hands, Yvan's arms wrapped around his cousin, keeping her upright, Or'myr's mother's arms encircling him, both Yvan and his mother's faces filled with looks of blazing relief.

The Wor once more cloth-wrapped and gripped in Wynter's hands, unharmed.

"It tried to draw you in as well, didn't it?" Sparrow urgently questions.

Or'myr and Elloren both nod and shoot each other looks of warm alliance while they catch their breath, clear they possess the power to create a strong bulwark against the Wor, more powerful than all the geomancy around them combined.

By building connection and community.

By building a world for *everyone.*

"I suspect it's as all the holy books and myths say," Or'myr flatly states. "I don't think it can be destroyed. But its thrall can, via the love we hold for each other."

Surprised murmuring kicks up as he and Elloren reveal what their moment inside the Wor's wood showed them. Yes, Or'myr considers, as he narrows his eyes on the cloth-wrapped Wor gripped in Wynter's hands, they can fight the wretched tool with love and connection. But it's also not a bad idea to encase the evil thing in as much stone as possible.

To give the world time to build on what love there is.

"Let's imprison the damned thing," Or'myr says, tightening his grip on his gem-encrusted geo-wand as he looks to his fellow Urisk and rises along with Elloren, all of them staring the Wor down.

"I'm ready," Bleddyn says, lifting her malachite stylus. "Let's begin."

Or'myr works with his Urisk'kin straight through the night and through the entirety of the next day to encase the Shadow Wor deep in the earth surrounded with layer upon layer of their strongest, most impenetrable encasings of stone.

Once it's done, powerful Dryad'khin from Erthia's every group and magical tradition send multiple bands of defensive magic around the stone-encased Wor, and Vang Troi posts a constantly changing guard from every cultural group in Noilaan to monitor the site, the Ironflower-tressed Dryad, Yulan, casting a dense field of demon-repelling Ironflowers over the Wor's location.

Because they all know that the Shadow Wand will remain ever-waiting. Sending out dreams and visions to its guards and others. Dreams of power and glory and domination. Seductive dreams hooking into every impulse for fracture and vengeance. But finding no firm purchase.

Because, for the moment, a critical mass of the people of the East are aligned with IV and with each other as Dryad'khin.

Ready to work to heal Erthia.

"Come to the Forest, cousin," Elloren prods Or'myr as the two of them stand before the Great Tree IV the next evening, along with a constantly changing crowd of Dryad'khin streaming in to make contact with IV's embracing mist. Elloren turns to him, her green eyes alight with affection. "Come out of your Dryad dormancy."

Or'myr smiles wryly as he peers up at the gigantic tree, stars twinkling through the gaps in its cloud-high canopy.

"You know," he says, turning to his cousin, "I never fully related to the Mage side of myself."

Elloren smirks at him. "Even as you were drawn to collect every piece of wood you came across, like me? And set trees into the walls of your Vonor?"

Or'myr lets out a short laugh, ever heartened by her kindred understanding. "I have a complicated relationship with my Gardnerian lineage."

"Your *Dryad* lineage," Elloren insists, growing serious. "Or'myr, let the Forest heal the fracture inside you."

He huffs out a breath, peering up at the huge tree. "I don't think the Forest can heal all the fracture inside me." He grows silent for a moment, knowing it can't touch the worst fracture of all.

His inability to fully be with Tierney.

A look of pained understanding crosses Elloren's features, her hand coming gently to his arm. "Then let it heal *some* of it. You've sacrificed so much for all of us. You inspired a Western Mage Resistance. Did you know that? Do you have any idea how many Mages arrived here with Resistance bands marked with purple moons on their arms?"

Or'myr blinks at her in surprise.

"Cousin," Elloren says, with great import, "you sparked a rebellion in the West."

Or'myr lets out a hard exhale, looking toward the pale white moon above. "Vo sparked it."

"We *all* did," Elloren insists, before smiling at him. "Maybe Vo did too."

Or'myr looks closely at Elloren, suddenly wanting the sense of connection she and the other Dryad'khin seem to have found with the Forest, even if the connection he's most longing for can never be his.

"All right, cousin," he says, his mouth slanting up as emotion mists his eyes, "bring me to your Forest."

Elloren takes his hand, and he lets her lead him to IV's enormous mass of a trunk. He lifts his palms and presses them through the green mist to the trunk's night-black bark.

Purple rays flash out around his hands, and gravity gives way, and then he's suddenly falling, falling straight into the Tree and enveloped in a swirl of darkness, then liquid purple light as IV's energy connects to the Vo River and he's swept up in a sudden, heart-expanding sense of Tierney's Asrai aura all around him, swirling through the streaming power.

And he's certain that somehow, she's fallen into the trees, as well.

Tierney, he calls out, and can feel her answering leap of shock as well as the joy-filled surge of her power in response to finding him there. And Or'myr knows, stunned joy tightening his heart, that Tierney is *right there*, somehow, in the Natural Matrix alongside him, a vision of one of the Eastern Cypress groves that grow straight up from the edges of the Northern Vo River suffusing his mind.

A new connection begins to form between them both, stone and water power uniting, their love for each other weaving the magic ever tighter. As Or'myr says yes to IV's invitation and feels himself being named Guardian of the stone and soil that make up the Vo's entire riverbed and banks, Tierney's Water kindreds cradled within it.

And then new rootlines of magic are surging through Or'myr, winding around his blazingly strengthened violet lightline, his powerful geomancy and fire power, IV's gift of awakened rootlines of wind gusting magic through his power and filling his lungs.

Closely followed by the rushing might of a powerful rootline of water.

CHAPTER TWELVE

THE PURPLE GARDEN

Tierney Calix

Eastern bank of the Vo River

Tierney arrives in Voloi a few nights later, flowing through her Vo River in water form.

Flowing eagerly toward Or'myr.

It shocked her, how much she missed him when he left with Raz'zor for Voloi. Her water aura reflexively reached for him, again and again, as she went about showing her Asrai'kin how to flow their power into the northern focal point of what's become the entire Eastern Realm's shielding, the liquid swirl of Tierney's aura flowing out in yearning to caress Or'myr's beloved form only to find him gone, her center seeming unmoored without his wry, ridiculously intelligent, charmingly domestic self in her life.

Everything in her yearning for his anchoring love.

She misses his physical presence too. A flush heats her water form just thinking about their shared dream and their attempts at kissing before his lightning shocked her.

Running her eyes over Or'myr's tall physique was a constant—albeit wildly frustrating—thrill, even though they can never act on their attraction to each other. And beyond all that, just having him near never failed to strike a deep emotional chord inside her, being with him increasingly like coming home.

A home she's ready to find.

Especially after being drawn by her River to the cypress roots growing through its Waters and being pulled into the center of the Natural World and enveloped by Or'myr's magical aura . . . as if he were *right there*. And then, after accepting the Forest's invitation to join with Nature as a Dryad'khin Asrai with the Vo as her kindred, a sense blossomed of Or'myr and herself more intimately joined via their all-encompassing connection to both her River's Life-filled Waters and its supporting bed.

"Go," Asra'leen gently prodded Tierney the morning she left, her Asrai friend's rainbow-sparkling blue eyes full of a knowing light, a poignant smile on Asra'leen's deep-blue lips. "Go find him, Tierney'lin. You saved our Waters. Now find your love."

Even the Vo River seemed to echo Asra'leen's sentiment, its embracing flow tugging Tierney joyfully south with a stronger and stronger current.

And so, with the Realm's shielding Asrai-strengthened and stabilized, Tierney gave in to the call of her River and the call of her heart, letting her Waters pull her south all the way to Voloi.

Tierney'lin.

As night falls and she reaches the Vo's central Waters, the sound of Or'myr's voice triggers a leap of surprise through Tierney. Or'myr's magical aura is suddenly *right there*, his geomancy suffusing the entire riverbed. Purple light strobes through Tierney's vision, the image of a young Eastern Cypress grove just south of Voloi filling her mind, the night sky splashed with stars above it.

Tierney makes a beeline for it, flushed through with anticipation, flowing fast as spring rapids.

Back to *him*.

Soon, Tierney senses the geography of the Vo just below Voloi all around her and she slows and coalesces from liquid to corporeal form, garbing herself in clothing made from the delicate, melded leaves of violet river plants. Heart in her throat, she takes in the underwater, deep-purple Cypress trunks anchored to the riverbed before her, the trees intimately connected to her River.

Or'myr's aura now intimately connected to her River and these trees, the solidity of his magic and personality a riverbed to her turbulent stream.

Her heartbeat quickens.

She can *feel* him here, somewhere in this very grove.

Anticipation welling in a strong tide, she swims through the grove's underwater roots and surfaces, breaking through into the starlit world, her gaze immediately drawn north toward the city of Voloi.

Tierney gasps as she's met with the sight of the huge Ironwood Tree IV, rising from the Voling Gardens' center, a luminous verdant mist swirling around the Great

Tree, its display of prismatic foliage breathtaking.

A ripple of awe courses through Tierney. IV's chromatic canopy shelters a huge portion of the battered tiered city, casting its faint green glow over a wide swath.

A rush of Or'myr's purple energy flowing through the Waters connects with her power in an ardent current, doubling her heart's speed. She starts toward the source of its flow, waist-deep in water now as she moves past the city and reaches the deserted wilds, swimming toward the cypress trees.

Tierney rounds a thick copse of trees and catches sight of Or'myr, waist-deep in the water, a rush of yearning eddying through her power.

Or'myr's eyes zero in on hers, so much violet lightning crackling in them that she can feel it sizzling through her water magic, her skin prickling from the sensation as she holds up her IV-marked hand to him. Or'myr moves toward her like a purple storm, and she notes the change in him. His purple skin . . . its hue is deepened and covered with a glowing violet sheen, his Strafeling aura intensified.

And his power . . . she can sense through their bond how two new sets of Magelines have awakened to Level Five power in him now, joining with his earth and fire magic.

She draws in a quick, shocked breath.

Water. And air.

"Or'myr," she greets him as he closes the remaining distance between them and brings his IV-marked palm to hers. "You're *altered*," she marvels. "Am I sensing . . . water- and airlines?"

"You are," he responds, voice fraught with passion, his body tense, as if it's taking everything in him not to sweep her into his arms. So much electricity is crackling off him and forking to her that Tierney feels lit up by it.

"I want to kiss you, Tierney," he declares, voice pained, eyes flashing. "I have control over my power now. *Complete* control. Say yes, Tierney. Just say yes and I'm *yours*."

Tierney's eyes widen.

She has a sense of it through their bond—that his control over his power truly and fundamentally changed when he bonded to this very Forest as both its kindred and the kindred of the entire riverbed, a new focus to the magic coursing through his lines.

Her heart swelling with so much love for him she fears she might burst, Tierney nods. "Yes, Or'myr," she affirms, tears misting her eyes. "I want you, and I love you."

A wide smile overtaking Or'myr's mouth, he sweeps her into an embrace, an emotional sound escaping Tierney as she thrills to the sizzle of lightning pulsing over his skin.

And then he's drawing them both down below the water's surface, and Tierney gives a start as the surrounding Waters shiver to crystalline violet, a besotted delight coursing through her.

As Or'myr draws her close and brings his lips to hers.

Lightning shocks through Tierney's water magic the moment their lips meet, and a moan escapes her, not of pain but of intense, crackling *pleasure*, her water power enhancing their electrified draw, her body eagerly arching against his. Or'myr's new control over his lightning steals her breath, small threads of it tingling over her skin while swirls of his fire power suffuse her magic with a delicious warmth.

Or'myr's lips and body are hungry against hers, and Tierney responds to him fully, opening her mouth to his deepening kiss—the kiss she always wanted from him—so much love and desire in it, her heart open wide to his, Or'myr's full purple garden there for the taking.

The Vo's Waters swirl around them with joyful encouragement, the River's energy shot through with the Natural World's relentless, glorious pull toward *Life*.

A sliver of rational thought cuts through Tierney's haze of desire, and she breaks the kiss, gaping at Or'myr before drawing them both back above the water's surface. Water streaming off his face and body, Or'myr gives her a wolfish, ebullient grin, bright anticipation in his eyes. The sizzle of his desire still tingles on her lips and sparks over every place they touched as he waits for her to voice the realization overtaking her.

"Sweet holy gods . . ." Tierney manages breathlessly, barely able to fight off the urge to spring at him. "You can breathe underwater."

Or'myr's grin widens. "When I bonded to this Forest along with the Vo's bed," he affirms, "my waterline was awakened. The trees pulled my airline out of dormancy as well and granted me some of their water linkage. So, yes, Tierney, I can breathe underwater now." A rakish gleam enters his gaze as he slides it over her damp form. "I could pull you down to the very bottom of your River and—"

"Do it, then, Or'myr," Tierney enthusiastically cuts in. "Give me *everything*."

A more serious light overtakes Or'myr's expression before his mouth claims hers once more, a stronger pulse of his lightning shooting through Tierney, the press of his body under the water's surface hard with want.

Emotion crackles through Or'myr's power, and he draws back a fraction to look closely at her, his breathing uneven, his heart thudding against hers. "My beautiful Xishlon Rose," he enthuses in Asrai, his tone rife with feeling. "My one and only garden."

Surprise courses through Tierney to hear her Water Fae tongue so fluidly sliding from Or'myr's purple lips. "Have you been practicing that?" she asks, deeply touched.

"For *days*," he answers, some of that wry amusement she missed so much breaking through. "I had to enlist Asrai help with the pronunciation. *Garden* is dauntingly hard to pronounce. I kept saying 'my one and only hipbone' until quite recently."

Tierney laughs, swamped by so much happiness, she fears her heart might burst from it. "Or'myr," she says, her smile wavering as a knot of emotion forms in her throat. "As you know, I'm to have two lifetimes. And in this Asrai life, I want only one garden. I want *you*." Her lips tick up, tears full of deep love for him misting her eyes. So much love. "Besides," she ventures, daring a glance toward the lower half of his form, his obvious show of desire obscured by the rippling violet of the water. "You're garden enough."

A laugh escapes Or'myr as he shoots her another smile, love to rival her River's in it, a wicked glint entering his gaze. "Oh . . . you haven't even begun to explore my garden." His eyes rake playfully over her. "Shall I shift to bizarrely oblique terms regarding the pleasure I'm about to rain down on you if you simply say the word?"

Tierney can't suppress her besotted smile. "And what word would that be?"

"Oak tree?" he offers.

Tierney laughs and gives him a brazenly suggestive smile, her cheeks heating. "That's two words. And I don't want the oak tree. I want the Purple Birch."

Or'myr grins and draws her tightly against his toe-curlingly aroused form. "That could be arranged," he croons into her ear. "Repeatedly. I'd like a taste of the whirlpool of delight."

Tierney's eyes widen, her flush deepening.

Another laugh escapes Or'myr as he cocks a purple brow at her. "You can't even handle the bizarrely oblique metaphors?"

Tierney gives him a bashful look. "Apparently not."

Or'myr shakes his head and mock-frowns. *"Westerners."*

Biting her lip, Tierney runs a finger straight down the center of his chest, stopping just below the water's upper edge. "Do we have to speak?" she teases.

Or'myr shivers, his gaze growing liquid as the water. "Gods no. You gorgeous Xishlon—"

Tierney cuts him off with an impassioned kiss that shocks his lightning through them both. Then another kiss. And another.

"You're not going to let me get another metaphor out are you," Or'myr manages when they finally come up for air.

"Be quiet, Or'myr," Tierney says, raining kisses along the length of his neck. "And ready that great arrow of stone."

Or'myr huffs out an amused breath. "Oh, it's long nocked . . ."

And then his mouth slants down on hers in a shock of power, and Tierney gasps against his lips, her body shuddering in response to the magic in Or'myr's kiss as he pulls her underwater and the whole world explodes into swirls of purple and lightning-pulsing delight.

Later, Tierney takes in her reflection in the Vo's shimmering water, which has returned to its blue hue. Dawn's first light has begun to tint Voloi's Eastern horizon cerulean through gaps in the cypress grove, the dark, cool sands of the Vo's eastern bank beneath her feet. Seeking to make sure her reflection isn't deceiving her, she raises her hand and studies it, a shocked flush heating her cheeks.

She's still purple.

Completely purple, with threads of purple lightning crackling over her skin.

She whirls around to face Or'myr, holding up her quite purple hand to him. "Did you know about this?" she demands as he pulls his tunic back on over his tattooed chest, unable to keep from noticing that his other rather impressive attributes are still . . . well, rather impressive under the cloth of his pants.

"Um, no," he says, barely able to suppress his delighted smile. His face is flushed, violet lightning dancing over his lips and skin, as well. "How would I have known about it?" he ventures, grinning as he envelops her in a caress. "That was my first time too."

Tierney purses her lips at him, even as she thrills to the sinuous feel of his arms encircling her, barely able to think around her lingering delight over how good his body and magic can make her feel. She gives him a narrow look. "You're full of surprises."

He shoots her a returning sultry look, scanning her purpled form with obvious relish. "Apparently so."

Tierney glances at her hand again, the purple coloration beginning to fade, some of her Vo blue returning. But still, she remains very much purple. "So, every time we pair," she presses, "I'm going to light up *purple*?"

Or'myr's grin widens before his expression turns reflective. "I think it's happening because you're supposed to get over the Western Realm ridiculousness around this particular pastime."

Tierney mock-frowns at him. "You're just feeling smug because you're ridiculously good at this."

An eager light sparks in his eyes. "Am I?"

"Do you really need me to stroke your ego?" Tierney sputters. "You turned me *purple*!"

Or'myr flashes a wicked grin. "You could stroke other things . . ."

A throaty laugh escapes Tierney. "You just want to see if you can make me erupt into lilac fireworks."

"I am up for the challenge," he valiantly offers.

Tierney shakes her head and blows out a breath, her flush intensifying. "This is a mortifying conversation."

"I'm not going to lie," Or'myr says as he reaches up to trace the skin just above her tunic's collar. "My ego is doing cartwheels. I just turned the most desirable woman in the entire Eastern Realm *purple*."

Tierney shoots him another derisive glare, but she can't maintain it. Her mouth twitches into a smile, her heart so warm and full of him.

Smiling, Or'myr lifts her hand and kisses it. "I love you, Asrai."

The ardent sincerity in his words catches Tierney up short, her throat tightening with emotion, affectionate amusement riding in close on its heels. "I love you, too, you ridiculously smug Dryad-y person."

"I also love being able to stay underwater with you," he enthuses. "To breathe in the whole River." A devious gleam enters his gaze. "You know, my lightning gives me quite a bit of . . . energy. I could pull you down to the very bottom of the Vo and—"

"No metaphors this time," Tierney insists.

Or'myr pauses, a heartfelt gravity entering his expression. "And make love to you with the arms of the Vo around us."

Tears are suddenly glistening in Tierney's eyes, her voice rough with feeling when it comes. "Spoken like a true Asrai'khin."

"No," Or'myr gently but firmly rejoins. "Spoken like a man deeply in love with an Asrai. And ready to love and defend her River too."

And then he catches her in a kiss that Tierney eagerly returns, giving herself up to the bright, purple love in it.

That night, Tierney falls asleep at the bottom of the Vo River, Or'myr's arms and body wrapped around her.

As she spirals into a dream.

She's suddenly perched on a ledge jutting out from what she quickly realizes is the pinnacle of the Dyoi Mountain Range, a shocking nightmare scene laid out before her, dream-wavy at its edges.

Viger sitting beside her.

Tierney's heart lurches toward Viger, emotion surging. His full-Dark eyes are looking out over the Shadow wasteland that covers more than half the continent, the distant Unbalancing Void storms spitting dark lightning as they gather power.

A reflexive terror for her River rising, Tierney turns and glances back east.

She can just make out the prismatic glint of the dome cast over the East, just past the destroyed Zonor River, a strip of muddy gray filth where the majestic River once flowed, and her heart twists at the sight. The Great Tree IV's canopy juts out above the clouds, the surviving East a tenuous stretch of Natural Life amidst leagues and leagues of Shadow corruption.

She turns back toward the West, toward the dense storms that churn steel gray in the distance, Viger's Death thrall reaching out to encircle her in floating, ropy tendrils.

His bone-deep stillness descends.

Viger is still staring west with those abyss eyes of his. Horns out, claws in, his two black vipers draped around his shoulders.

He turns and sets his night-deep eyes on her. "Fight this with him," he says. His words have the feel of a solemn charge, shot through with both Deathkin rebellion and grief.

Tierney's heart constricts, everything left unsaid between them rushing in.

"I will," she promises, voice catching, knowing he can feel her every emotion in her magic's flow through their bond. "Viger, I want you to know that . . . I love Or'myr. But I love you too."

A dart of pain lashes through their linkage. "I know," he says.

"But you were right," she admits. "It's not our time."

He draws in a deep breath, his eyes and thrall locked on her. "Someday," he says in that subterranean voice that's always sent a tight trill through Tierney's power.

They go quiet as unnatural Shadow thunder churns in the distance.

Finally, Viger speaks without moving, his voice seeming to emanate from her very core.

I'll be there in the soil. In Nature's Darkness. Waiting for you. Heal the Balance, Asrai'kin. And someday, I'll come back to claim you.

Her heart in her throat, Tierney wrenches her gaze from his, and studies the vast, gathering Shadow power, barely held back. She's all too aware, via the tension filling her Deathkin line, that the Great Death Reckoning is still struggling to break free if a Rebalancing does not take solid root.

And soon.

Viger, Sylla, her kelpies, and all the other Deathkin the only things holding back the horrors of the Reckoning.

Tierney's words burst free in a tangled rush. "I'm scared we won't be able to do it, Viger. Feeling the immensity of what's been destroyed . . . I'm scared the Waters will fall. I'm scared that it's all too late. Viger, I'm *scared*."

Her lips tremble, tears pooling in her eyes. Tierney turns toward him once more to find Viger's Dark eyes still fixed on her, an uncharacteristic smile on his black lips, such vast love in it her heart tightens with a deep, stunned ache.

"Your fears are beautiful, Tierney Calix," he murmurs, pain tightening his gaze. "They always have been."

"What now, Viger?" she asks, voice tremulous as a tear streaks down her face. She gestures toward the Shadow world ahead. "How can we prevail against *that*?"

Viger's thrall embraces her, the dreamscape pulsing with his Natural Dark.

Follow your fears, he croons, his voice seeming to come from everywhere at once. *Follow them, Asrai, and face them fully. Then work to heal the world.*

A dart of panic lights as she senses he's about to dissolve into the Natural Matrix more fully to stave off the Reckoning.

Buying Erthia time.

She slips into his fears and tunnels down the line of them, through his own fear for the Natural World toward the three words still reverberating at the base of all his fears. Her eyes widen. Because those words . . . there's less terror wrapped around them than there was before. And something new. Something unexpected.

A silvery thread of *hope*.

An answering hope ripples through Tierney's magic as the dream fades, and she sends those words back to him, to Or'myr, to her River, and to the entire Natural World, as Viger lets himself be fully absorbed into Nature's Darkness.

I love you.

PART FIVE

Xishlon Rising

CHAPTER ONE

XISHLON RENAISSANCE

Andras Volya

Voloi, Noilaan
Xishlon night, close to a year later

Andras glances out over the violet-washed Vo River then up past Noilaan's translucent dome. His gaze narrows in on the purple Xishlon moon hanging above it all like a lantern, his entire chest tight with painful longing.

He hugs his three-year-old son, Konnor, close, knowing he should have nothing but joy in his heart. Because they've survived. His son is safe in his arms, and Andras's mother, Astrid, stands beside them on the rebuilt dock of Voloi, all of them watching the purple fireworks sent up by Dryad'khin sorceresses and geomancers, the bursts of light shimmering in the sky over the Vo.

Yes, he's grateful for so many things. For the survival of the East. For the fragile hope for his son's future, and for the future of *all* Erthia's children.

Now that almost the entire population has united as Dryad'khin.

And Andras has rewarding work here as one of the East's most knowledgeable animal healers, working not only with Ariel Haven to heal animals, but also with his entire Lupine pack to aid in the reintroduction of species into land that's slowly being reclaimed from the Shadow, a whole herd of wild purple Noi horses amongst his kindreds.

"Papa, *look*," Konnor breathes as he points toward the sky.

Andras's aching heart lifts a fraction as he takes in the dazzled wonder in his son's crimson Lupine eyes. His child's spiky blue-and-purple-streaked black hair picks up flashes of the fireworks' light as they form incandescent designs reflected in the Vo River . . . great, shimmering irises; deep violet roses that gorgeously sizzle to sparks; a constellation of stars; then a giant purple dragon—Vo's purple manifestation of love.

THE DRYAD STORM

Tears sheen Andras's eyes, the tight longing in his chest intensifying even as he smiles warmly at his son. He's grateful, truly he is, to see his small family and other Dryad'khin taking a moment to celebrate love in this magical moment, after so much devastating loss followed by strenuous work to regain some of Nature's Balance. But the pull of the East's lavender moon and the torment of its thrall grow ever more acute as the moon's purple light deepens.

Because he's still in love with her.

Sorcha.

Andras's heart twists. His undimmed longing for Sorcha . . . it's worse, so much worse, under this moon.

"You were right, my son," his mother says, drawing his attention.

He turns and meets his mother's dark gaze, her face, decorated with its Amaz runic tattoos. She's turned toward him with a look of both deep love and remorse. "You were right to push me toward being open to new ways," Astrid admits. "This festival . . . it's a good one."

His eyes widen a fraction over the Xishlon moon's ability to loosen his rigidly reserved mother's tongue and help her speak from her heart . . . and offer what he knows is a difficult apology.

"The Amaz have many admirable ways, as well," he suggests.

"They do," Astrid agrees, her voice tight with emotion, the black metallic beads decorating her braided black-and-purple hair glinting in the Xishlon light. "But Queen Alkaia knew . . . she *knew* that the path forward is diverse. And that it was time to change more than a few traditions."

Andras considers this. "Will you join Queen Freyja's Amaz faction now?"

Queen Freyja Zyrr has set up a new Amaz homeland, with close to three-quarters of the Amaz, in the Northern Vo Forest, establishing a new, more liberal approach toward having men in their midst, including the queen's love, Clive Soren. The remaining Amaz faction has split off under a new queen and is readying to journey to the continent's harsh northern reaches.

Away from all men.

"Freyja's faction will allow you to embrace both me and your grandson without being cast out," Andras offers, clear how painful this separation from her people has always been for his mother—a separation caused by her wildly rebellious decision to let her son live.

And to love him.

Astrid peers back up at the moon, a slight, melancholy smile on her lips as a huge firework detonates into the shape of a purple Xishlon rose. "I love my people, it's true," she says, "and I always will. But I've decided to join the Lupines."

Andras pulls in a harsh breath while Konnor lets out a delighted gasp at the display, fireworks now exploding into the shapes of two herons flying joyfully around the moon. But Andras is only half-aware of the Xishlon display. Because . . . his mother joining the Lupines isn't just a breaking of boundaries. It's a *flat-out rebellion*. A rebellion of the best kind.

In defense of love.

Andras's thoughts careen back to Sorcha, his beautiful Amaz love, and his breathing grows uneven and tight.

When he and his Dryad'khin allies returned to the Eastern Realm last fall and Andras first caught sight of Sorcha in the front lines of a combined Amaz, Smaragdalfar, Lupine, and Keltish force, his heart had leaped in his chest, hope rising that there was some chance Sorcha's rigid adherence to Amaz ways had softened.

Days later, as she retreated into a closed-off area north of Voloi claimed by the traditional faction of Amaz resistant to working with men or joining with the Forest, he tried to seek her out only to be harshly rebuffed by a line of battle-hardened Amaz soldiers. They'd informed him that Sorcha was planning to travel north with them where Andras could never follow.

Devastated, Andras struggled to hold on to the shred of hope Valasca had given him after her own visit to those same Amaz, during which she sought out Sorcha.

"Don't lose faith," Valasca urged him the evening she returned as he battled a wave of longing so acute, he wondered if his heart would fully shatter from its force. "Sorcha needs time," Valasca insisted. "She loves you still. I'm sure of it. But every single member of her family, save her son, is going *north*. The type of break with family, religion, and culture that being with you would require of her . . . it's more than most people can withstand."

"Yet you say to have faith," Andras spat out, glaring at her.

Valasca's forthright stare didn't waver for a second. "There are no guarantees for any of us," she responded, a pained look tensing her brow. "But if you're going to hitch your wagon to some heavenly body, Andras, I'd go with the Xishlon moon. Choose love every time. Even if it breaks your heart."

Andras chews over the memory of her words as more fireworks burst and sizzle into the shapes of hundreds of small Xishlon moons, and Konnor lets out a delighted shriek.

His longing for Sorcha surging to unbearable heights, Andras turns away from the sparkling moons and the large Xishlon moon hanging bright over them all.

Because he can't take one more moment of the damned moon's pull.

And then, his gaze caught by an approaching figure, he blinks and stares, then blinks again, not quite sure what he's seeing is real. As if summoned by the Xishlon light, Sorcha is walking toward him through the purple-clad crowds, eyes full of what looks like a distraught yearning, strong enough to match his own.

Their gazes meet, and Andras's heart explodes into a pounding rhythm. Everything surrounding Sorcha's scarlet-clad form fades into a violet blur, her lake-blue skin tinted purple by the moonlight, her long, sapphire hair swishing behind her. Her pointed ears are rimmed with cascading silver hoops that flash the Xishlon moon's light, the dark Amaz runic tattoos swirling over her lovely face accentuating her dazzling golden eyes.

Andras's pulse grows even stronger, a million emotions firing in him all at once with more power than every firework in existence.

"Sorcha," he rasps, his voice hitching around her name, and she pauses a respectful distance away.

Tears pool in her eyes as she stares at Konnor, a look of agony tensing her features, her lips starting to tremble.

"Who is she, Papa?" Konnor asks, clearly sensing the heightened emotions riding the air, worry in his child's crimson eyes. Sorcha gives Konnor a wavering smile, tears spilling over her cheeks while her lips part then close again.

"She's your mother," Andras answers, firm, so much pain and yearning and remorse in those words that he feels his heart may break around them.

Sorcha looks at Astrid, and Andras does, as well. His mother is eyeing Sorcha with those shrewd, piercing eyes of hers, but there's no censure there, just a look overflowing with compassion.

Andras's mother turns to him. "Go," she prods, gesturing toward Sorcha as she holds her arms out for Konnor. She glances up at the Xishlon moon and takes hold of the child before giving both Andras and Sorcha a slight smile. "The Goddess works in mysterious ways," she says. "Who knows, perhaps the Lupines are correct, and the deity at the heart of everything is a shape-shifter. Maybe sometimes She's an

Amaz goddess with snake and deer and white bird familiars." Astrid glances wryly up at the moon. "And maybe sometimes She's a Xishlon dragon who sends down purple light from the sky."

And then, Astrid Volya gives Andras and Sorcha an exuberant smile before she turns and walks away, hugging Konnor and murmuring happily to him as she points toward the purple moon, fireworks shaped like giant dragonflies now winging by it.

Andras turns to Sorcha, a storm of emotion upending him as he gestures toward a narrow path leading away from the dock and down toward the river's edge. Sorcha falls in beside him, and Andras's heart crowds his throat as they stride silently down to an isolated rocky outcropping, the purple-tinged waters of the Vo lapping at the stone where they pause.

Face-to-face.

Sorcha holds up a quivering hand, the image of IV imprinted there. "I was *wrong*, Andras," she says, voice cracking as a purple-tinted tear streaks down her face. "I love you. I have *always* loved you." She chokes on her tears, her chest heaving as she breaks into sobs. "And I love our child. I *never* stopped thinking about you. And I *never* stopped thinking about him."

And then she drops her face into her hands, sobbing into them as Andras feels the warm slide of tears down his own face and tastes the salt on his lips.

Love for her breaking through the years of pent-up anguish, Andras steps toward her then reaches up to caress her heaving shoulder. He draws her into an embrace, and she inhales a great breath, her arms coming tight around him as she sobs against his chest. "Shhh," he says, the pain in his heart overwhelmingly dwarfed by the fierce love rushing in.

"The trees showed me *so much*," Sorcha tells him in a broken voice. She lifts her tear-streaked golden eyes. "I was *so wrong* to put *anything* above my love for you and our son."

"The trees showed me so much, as well," Andras tells her, her beautiful face wavering through his tears. "They showed me the history of the Amaz and what led them to band together." He grimaces from the remembrance. "The *horrors* inflicted on womankind by men. The trees revealed to me how men's cruelty fueled this division. I understand more of your struggle, now, and the struggle of the women of your family. I forgive you, Sorcha. And I have *never* stopped loving you."

Sorcha's lips tremble as she gazes up at him, vulnerability in her eyes, twin Xishlon moons reflected in them. "I'm not going north." She motions toward the crystalline-blue stylus sheathed at her hip. "The Forest . . . it's given me back my Urisk geomancy. I'm staying right here, as part of Queen Freyja's circle of geo-sorcerers. And I would give *anything* for another chance to be with you and our child."

Andras smiles, all the love of Xishlon flooding through him. He glances up at the moon. "Xishlon night is a good night for new beginnings," he says before stepping back and holding out his hand. "Come. Let's go spend time with our son."

CHAPTER TWO

XISHLON TEA

Tierney Calix

Western bank of the Vo River, Noilaan
Xishlon night

Waist-deep in the violet-marbled waters, Tierney stares over the purple-moonlit Vo River, the city of Voloi just beyond. Xishlon-amplified love for her River courses through her as fireworks sparkle overhead and small, silver-flecked minnows happily swirl around her.

Her River's love for her eddying straight through her heart.

Joy bubbling up inside her, Tierney turns, reaches out and lovingly strokes the purple, striated bark of the Eastern Cypress tree rising from the shallow water beside her, the tree's aura of affection rippling through her magic along with her River's love, this newly established Cypress Forest, like Gareth and Marina's expanding Mangrove Forests, all working to anchor the coasts and bring Balance to the weather above and the land below.

Fighting back against the Shadow chaos massed in the West, *increment by hard-won increment* . . .

Tierney draws in a deep breath and glances south, toward Voloi. IV's great purple canopy is spread out over the entire city with sheltering might, its usual verdant mist turned Xishlon purple as it winds around the huge Balance-anchoring tree. Her beloved younger brother and newly Dryad'khin adoptive family are out there somewhere, enjoying the holiday festivities, her Asrai'kin having opened up water tunnels under the Vo to allow everyone to experience the beauty of the underwater Natural World.

Xishlon fireworks shimmer into being over the water, drawing Tierney's attention as they fleetingly form the luminous image of hundreds of Xishlon moons before coalescing into the sizzling shape of a giant, violet dragon.

Tierney smiles at the hopeful show, reveling in the company of her river-loving tree kindreds and in the feel of her River's sheer Matrix-anchoring *power*. Wry amusement lights as she lifts her free hand from the water and notices, not for the first time this eve, that her hue this night is a bright, swirling Xishlon purple.

She can imagine Or'myr's reaction to her overwhelming *purpleness*. She's eager to finally take him as her Xishlon'vir, after he finishes his work reinforcing the geomancy imprisoning the always-straining-to-escape Shadow Wand, everyone set on keeping this Xishlon safe from the Shadow's cruel grip.

And Tierney holds out hope that it will be.

Even the Vo seems caught up in the Xishlon moon's pull, its waters lapping affectionately against her purple-kelp-clad form. A trace of melancholy edges in as her thoughts slide to last Xishlon, not far from this spot, deep in the Forest with Viger and deep in his Deathkin *kiss* when Vogel's Shadow hell rained down upon the East.

Vogel's demonic tide slithering across her beloved River.

Emotion shudders through her. It was such a close call for the Vo. And for the whole of Erthia.

But the world has *changed*.

Almost everyone is now united in the Dryad'khin goal to bring the Balance back to the Natural World of the East. Through her River's flow, Tierney can feel the East's Natural Matrix slowly knitting itself back together, the gray corruption gradually being cleansed from the land. It's a huge, daunting undertaking, to be sure, so much harder to replenish Nature than it was to destroy it, but with enough Dryad'khin setting their will to the task, Tierney can't help but think there's a sliver of hope on the horizon.

But only because of the sacrifice of the Deathkin, which bought them all *time*, staving off Nature's Reckoning.

Her heart tightens, a pang of longing overtaking her as her thoughts turn to Or'myr and Viger both, these two men destined to be the Great Loves of her Asrai and Deathkin lives. She scans her world before her, knowing Viger is out there somewhere, embedded in Nature, along with Sylla and Vesper, Hazel, her kelpies, and Elloren's Errilor Ravens, their combined auras of Darkness suffusing the surviving Natural World with the rejuvenating power of Death, all of them a bulwark.

To give us all a chance for a future.

Her heart twists tighter as she remembers the mind-expanding feel of Viger's kiss on last year's Xishlon night. And what he revealed to her about the power of Death to seed Life.

The beginning, not the end.

She pulls in another breath and draws on her own fledgling line of Death Fae Darkness, sliding her fingertips through the water's surface as she sends a ripple of her power, infused with Xishlon love, out to Viger, anchoring it to her line of fear.

She watches her swirling Darkness radiate in concentric circles through the River's bright Xishlon purple, then she freezes as what seems like an answering ripple flows back toward hers. Her vision pulses Dark as the circles in the water intermingle before giving way to the purple reflection of the Xishlon moon.

Tears mist Tierney's eyes.

Someday, she thinks out to Viger, sending the thought through her line of fears. *We'll meet again someday.*

Blinking back the tears, she withdraws her hands from her Waters and presses the Vo's dampness over her heart, giddy anticipation welling. Because what she's about to attempt might have the power to bring even more hope to Erthia. But she needs a certain Dryad'khin to help her carry out her outrageous plan—her geomancer-Dryad love, who feels like home. Whose power now runs through the Vo's entire base, cradling it.

Supporting it.

Embracing it.

Crackling energy forks up from the Vo's bed to sizzle teasingly along the edge of Tierney's magic. Her heartbeat quickens as Or'myr strides from the riverbank's dense Forest dressed in his IV-marked, purple-tinted Vu Trin military uniform.

They were wed several months ago, in a joint Asrai and Vo'lon service officiated by Priest Wyn Juun, a huge crowd of loved ones in attendance, including Elloren, Yvan, and Fyordin along with his new love, the fierce shark-shifter Vizz'la, both Fyordin and Vizz'la part of a new Vu Trin–Ocean'kin force protecting the span of water where the Vo River meets the Salish Ocean.

Both Land and Ocean People working to restore the estuary's health and keep it safe from Vogel's Shadow sea.

Or'myr flashes Tierney a smile that's so warm, her thoughts scatter as he sheaths his geo-wand and throws off his tunic to reveal his elaborate Xishlon moon and Vo dragon tattoo emblazoned on his muscular chest, Tierney's breath hitching at the sight. He steps into the water and wades to her, her swirling attraction to him bubbling up with ardent force, making her feel a bit breathless.

He's like my own Xishlon moon, she ponders, amused, admiring his vivid violet hue as they drink each other in for a protracted moment, not touching.

Yet.

"You beckoned me here?" he drawls.

Heart pattering, Tierney slides her hand into her tunic's pocket and withdraws the dark portal stone inside it, multiple interlocking runes from a number of traditions marking its surface.

"I need your help, Or'myr," she says as purple fireworks continue to flash above, their violet light dancing over the scene.

Or'myr's eyes take on a glazed look as he scans her form, his power crackling around her with more heated force. "It's a bit difficult for me to maintain any semblance of coherent thought around you," he murmurs. "Seeing as how you're not only *purple*, but you're flashing purple light." He grins. "I'll make a valiant effort not to hurl myself at you. What is it you need, my love?"

Tierney holds up the portal stone. "I think I might have found a way to charge this stone with enough power to create our river portal. *Tonight*."

Or'myr's eyes widen, and Tierney can tell that, as strong as the moon's thrall is, her words have managed to cut clear through it.

The East's destruction of the Zonor River was a major victory for the Shadow, unbalancing in the extreme. She and Or'myr have worked for months alongside Trystan, Vothe, Sithendrile, Fyordin, and a whole host of sorcerers, Asrai and Ocean'kin, to try to find a way to create a complicated underwater portal strong enough to flow a portion of the Vo River's healthy water into the Zonor's bed of gray filth. It's the only plan they've come up with that might work to restore the Zonor, all other magical attempts at rejuvenation swallowed by the Zonor's infestation of Shadow pollution. Up until now, they and their allies have lacked the power needed to fully charge the water portal.

But herein lies a potential way to turn the tide.

"I've been told by Noi'khin," Tierney says, "that if you and I . . . 'connect' . . . under the light of the Xishlon moon, our love-bonded power will be amplified to new heights, giving us a shot at success."

Or'myr blinks at her. "That's brilliant," he enthuses, rapt. "*You're* brilliant."

Tierney's face heats as Or'myr's rise of affection crackles over her in a static embrace, her own affection for him streaming warm through their bond.

Or'myr's expression takes a turn for the mischievous. "So, you'll need to spell out exactly what type of 'connection' you're looking for."

Instantly flustered, Tierney side-eyes him. "You *know* . . ."

Grinning now, Or'myr crosses his arms. "Describe it for me. *In detail.*"

"Have you met me?" Tierney sputters. "You know I can't do that!"

Or'myr's grin doesn't budge. "I think you're going to have to try."

And then he gives her a look so full of love, her giddy desire for him rises, love for him and his embracing sense of humor welling in her power. She shoots him a sultry look. "Wonderful Or'myr, help me rescue the Zonor River, and I'll 'dance around your oak tree.'"

He laughs, casting her a look of heated mischief. "Oh, you'll dance around it regardless." He leans close, his voice pitched low when it comes. "I know you're feeling this moon's crazy pull just like I am. And I know what you like. You just can't bring yourself to ask for it."

"That is true," Tierney staunchly agrees as that familiar, strong spark of heat lights between them. "I cannot."

"Just say it," Or'myr coaxes. "'Sweet Or'myr, I want to have sex with you under the Xishlon moon.'"

Tierney gapes at him as her tingling desire gathers in her power, everything in her lit up by the promise of a Xishlon evening spent in his arms. His glorious body wrapped around hers, along with his purple *fire*.

Holy ever-loving Vo on High.

Or'myr laughs as he studies her, giving her a slightly incredulous look. "We have been wed for *months*. You really can't just out-and-out ask for this? *Still?*"

Tierney purses her lips, her thoughts scrambling into mortification over the idea of asking for what she can picture all to clearly, her water aura now rushing wantonly around his tall form.

Or'myr's grin widens. "You are bonded to the greatest River in all of Erthia. You hold *monumental* power. Yet you cannot even say the word *sex*." He shakes his head and mutters "The power of culture" under his breath.

"Sex," Tierney throws out defiantly as the temptation to fling herself at him mounts.

Or'myr's eyes spark with friendly challenge. "What about it?"

Tierney blows out an exasperated breath, her flush heating to a scald. "You're *impossible*."

"And you're turning an even more enticing shade of purple. Which only makes me want to sex you up and down even more thoroughly."

"*Or'myr!*"

"Would you like to have a cup of Xishlon tea instead?"

Tierney's overheated water aura breaks free and storms around him in a grasping caress. "Get over here, you tease."

Or'myr steps back. "Tell me what you want, my beautiful, wonderful Asrai."

Lit up by the compliment, Tierney draws a long, measured breath. "Sweet, magnificent Or'myr," she formally states, unable to suppress her smile, "please bequeath me with your attentions."

He gives a short laugh. "My *attentions?*"

She mock-glares at him, even as her heart picks up speed. "Your wand of stone?"

Lightning crackles through his eyes. "Better."

"Your glorious rod of geopower?"

"Getting there."

Tierney bites her lip, both so heatedly turned on and so mortified, she can feel her tongue tying itself into more and more intricate knotwork.

Or'myr's look of amusement turns adoring. "You are a verbally repressed enchantress, do you know that?"

Tierney straightens. "I simply uphold the mystery."

He flashes her a wicked grin. "I'd rather you uphold my glorious rod of geopower."

"Oh, you'd like that, would you?"

"Metaphorically speaking."

"Stop teasing me and take me down to the bottom of the River and do that focused lightning thing!"

"Ah, so now you *like* my lightning."

Tierney rolls her eyes. "You're a big purple tease, do you know that?"

Or'myr pulls her into his arms and leans down to nuzzle her neck, sending a shiver of controlled lightning out to dance just under her skin. Tierney's breath hitches, her body thrilling to the sensation, Or'myr's voice a caress when it comes. "I'm going to take you this evening in a way that will flash that river portal right into existence and make you spark violet. For *days*."

"Promise?" Tierney asks, growing even more breathless.

Or'myr kisses the base of her neck, toe-tingling sparks radiating from his mouth, and Tierney shivers against him.

His lips curve into a smile against her skin. "You can tell everyone we had 'tea.'"

CHAPTER THREE

XISHLON KISS

Olilly Emmylian and Kir Lyyo

Voloi, Noilaan
Xishlon night

Across one of Voloi's many newly crafted sky bridges, Olilly and Kir Lyyo spot each other for the first time since they were so cruelly torn away from each other in the Sublands many months ago.

They close in from opposite directions, Olilly's steps fleet as a deer's as the distance between them narrows on this highest bridge where Kirin's runic-hawk missive said he'd be, the purple light from Xishlon fireworks flashing over the scene.

As the bridge gently sways, Olilly glances past its vine railings, the woven-vine pathways magicked into being by the Dryad Fae refugees that Wynter Eirllyn and the Smaragdalfar forces liberated. The Tree Fae have guided the crafting of so many of the city's new structures, sharing their techniques for building in harmony with the Natural World, spherical gall dwellings now hugging so many Ironwood trees' upper reaches. This isolated, river-facing bridge is placed high up in IV's branches, above one of the larger gall dwellings and near the top of the Great Tree's cloud-high canopy.

Allowing a breathtaking panoramic view of the Xishlon-moonlit Vo River.

Olilly's heart trips into a faster rhythm as she takes in Kirin's slender, black-cloaked figure. Her steps slow on the woven purple vines as throngs of Xishlon revelers stream across the large vine bridges that crisscross the air below them, more Xishlon throngs swirling through the gardens at IV's base and over every one of the city's forested tiers, music and drumbeats joyful on the air.

Reaching her, Kirin stills before Olilly, and the festive purple world recedes into the background, nothing left but the two of them and the Xishlon moon overhead.

A smile tugs at Olilly's lips as she's overcome by a sense of the moon smiling down on them both, a memory lighting of how she and Kirin lingered on the dock last Xishlon near the river's edge for one brief, magic moment before the Shadow War descended.

Blushing, she remembers their first tentative and thoroughly exciting kiss. Remembers how they felt like thieves, stealing all the purple gems in the world.

Before the world turned gray.

Kirin cocks his head, concern in his beautiful dark kohl-lined eyes as he seems to read Olilly's brief flare of pain.

Her heart warms, the affection in his gaze pushing away all troubled thoughts. She looks down and notices a glowing purple lily in his hand, just like he had last Xishlon night, her flush pleasurably heating.

Kirin glances at the luminous lily in his hand, clearly noticing her noticing it, before a look of ardent purpose overtakes his angular features. He holds up his free hand, palm out, revealing the image of IV imprinted there, then tilts his head to the side, revealing a new streak of purple in his dark, spiky hair. A lavender Eastern Realm Cottontail Rabbit kindred pokes its head out of his cloak's edge to peer up at her.

Olilly's heart lifts so fast that all the breath whooshes from her lungs. She feels as if she's floated straight off the ground into the moonlit air as she lifts her own palm, revealing the same Dryad'khin image emblazoned there.

Kirin's face breaks into the most dazzling smile Olilly has ever seen on any face *ever*.

This levity is a welcome change, smiles rare during the Shadowed times they've so recently been through, the two of them huddled in the Sublands during the worst of it, listening as violent explosions then storms battered the city above. And watching, with mounting horror, as the different groups around them threatened to tear each other apart, a faction of Subland Smaragdalfar fighting with Fyon's faction over who should be allowed shelter there while Noilaan above fought to keep the entire Eastern Realm just for the Noi.

Olilly unwelcome both aboveground and below.

And then, Kirin was cruelly ripped away from her as his father returned him to Noilaan to attempt to force him to take up the cause of Noilaan for the Noi.

But now, as more and more people join with the Forest, everything is changing.

THE DRYAD STORM

An excited tension snaps between them as Kirin holds the beautiful lily out and Olilly eagerly accepts it, both of them so thoroughly lit up purple by the moonlight, her kindred Urisk color.

"You've joined us," Olilly notes, heart fluttering, the two of them transformed by more than the moonlight, Olilly now wearing a Wyvernguard uniform, its fabric tinted purple by her burgeoning geomancy, a lavender amethyst stylus worn proudly at her side and more of her kindred purple stones adorning her wrists and ankles and neck.

Kirin's gaze flits intently over her uniform. "I heard you joined the Wyvernguard's Geomancer Division."

Olilly nods. "We're training with Dryad Fae and older Urisk geomancers and Earth Mage Dryad'kin," she enthuses, "to rebuild Erthia's cities and towns in a whole new way. In harmony with the Natural World."

She details for him how her life has been filled with bright purpose these past few months, her division's special project the creation of more towering islands rising from the Vo River to serve as great, spiraling marvels of vertical agriculture that will help meet the food needs of the East's growing population.

The Wyvernguard now an Erthia force under Dryad Fae and Ung Li's leadership, dedicated to the restoration of the Natural World.

"We've geo-crafted vertical landmasses throughout the city, as well," she joyfully relays, gesturing toward a few she worked on with other Urisk and the magically brilliant botanist Yulan. "We've carved hundreds of small homes into many of them, interspersed with tree seedlings, crops, and other plant life."

A delighted shiver courses through Olilly over what she and her fellow Dryad'khin have wrought so far, their magical efforts slowly turning Voloi's tiered city into a weather-stabilizing forest that coexists, side by side, with Voloi's dense population of mostly Dryad'khin.

Olilly's love of food and cooking has lent itself seamlessly to her new passion for agriculture in harmony with the Forest. It's been a challenge, increasing food production for so many on so little Unshadowed land, while rewilding more and more of the Shadowed East to help the Natural World restore itself . . . a challenge that's demanded the effort of every Dryad'khin.

Luckily, there is an ever-growing number of Dryad'khin.

Like her.

And wonderful Kirin.

"And you?" she asks, curiosity fizzing through her. "What brought you to Voloi?"

A slight smile edges Kirin's lips, even as his eyes take on a serious light. "I've just joined the Wyvernguard's Agricultural Division."

Surprise rays through Olilly, sunlight strong. She knows Kirin is conveying so much more than those calmly spoken words, revealing that he's broken with his father *completely*.

Forging a new path forward at the Wyvernguard.

With *her*.

Kirin undoes the clasps of his cloak and lets its edges fall to the side.

Stunned, Olilly takes in his brand-new Wyvernguard uniform. Hers has morphed to purple due to her geomancy affinity for violet stone. His is the traditional sapphire, and imprinted, as is hers, with the new Noi design of IV rendered in shining onyx thread.

"How did you get your father to let you leave?" Olilly asks, dazed, having heard that Kirin and his father relocated north of Voloi, where a community of Noi who refuse to join with the Forest still live, all of them set on ridding the Eastern Realm of every non-Noi person.

Kirin's jaw hardens as he glances toward the purple-shimmering Vo. He sets his dark gaze back on her, immovable decision in his eyes. "I love my father. But the way he thinks . . . it's a terrible path forward, fueled by hate. Erthia can't survive it, and it's not what I want. It never was. My father's way isn't the future." Kirin holds up his IV-marked palm. "*This* is the future."

He pauses, as if all his words are suddenly caught in his throat, but Olilly can read the unspoken in the intensity firing in his eyes, her pulse tripping over itself.

"I've left home for good," he announces, tone final. "I petitioned the Dryad'khin Conclave for entry into the Wyveryguard, and . . . as you can see, my request was granted."

Olilly pulls in a wavering breath, her heart flooded with a sense of revolution and new beginnings.

"I . . . I remember the last time we were here together," she stammers, needing to look away for a moment, but also needing to show him her heart. As she remembers the feel of Kirin's lips on hers.

Before the upper half of the Vo Mountain Range exploded, mid-kiss.

His cheeks reddening, Kirin glances at the ground, the moon, the river, clearly as flustered as she is and swept up in the same heated remembrance. But then, he seems to gather himself, his gaze meeting then firming on hers. "We never got a chance to finish that kiss," he ventures, a slight tremor to his voice as fireworks in the shape of hundreds of Xishlon moons detonate over the river to a chorus of delighted cheers.

Olilly is barely aware of the show, Kirin's words hanging in the air between them, lit up by the fireworks' rush of shimmering light.

And by the Xishlon moon's aura of infinite possibility.

Olilly glances at one of the vertical islands that she helped to craft, a plethora of vegetables already planted and flourishing in the island's rich, geo-magicked soil. Enough food to feed hundreds. Thousands.

Her geomancy's mark on Noilaan just beginning.

She turns back to Kirin, emboldened. No longer the scared, timid thing she once was. She's even wearing her scarred ears proudly. Defiantly. No more pretend points.

Because she's beautiful just the way she is.

And she's still here. Defiantly *still here.*

Working for a better future.

She peers meaningfully up at the moon, hope for the future, solid as her amethyst stylus, crystallizing in her heart, her lips trembling with emotion. "I feel like I'm truly part of Xishlon now," she says, adamant. "I've found not just my magic, but my place here in this purple-moon world."

She dares a glance at Kirin to find him giving her a look of pure emotion.

"Xishlon is so much the better for it," he insists, moving slightly closer, his rabbit kindred venturing forward to press affectionately against her.

"Kir Lyyo," Olilly says with giddy formality, her smile bright, her heart pattering, "would you be my Xishlon'vir . . . again?"

Kirin laughs, his own beaming smile turning as bright as the moon above. And then they both lean in, and Kirin brings his lips to hers in a shy, second kiss for them both. Then less shy as they bring their arms lightly around each other.

Then fully embracing.

As love blooms in both their hearts, along with rock-solid hope for the future.

CHAPTER FOUR

XISHLON FIRE

Iris Morgaine

Zhilaan Forest
Xishlon night

Iris holds up her III-marked palm to the Zhilaan Forest's Eastern tree line, waiting to be allowed entrance, her Noi Fire Falcon kindred perched on her shoulder. Iris's heartbeat patters against her chest in a nervous rhythm over her bold quest, her fire power a hot, blazing mess. The Zhilaan's gigantic Nightwood Pines loom over her, high as the purple-tinted clouds above, the whole Eastern Realm suffused with the Xishlon moon's purple light.

She can sense the fiery Forest's welcoming energy whooshing through her, her Lasair spirits lifting in response to the sensation even as her trepidation intensifies. Blazingly determined, she steps through the tree line into the Forest's Dryad'khin territory then pauses, overcome by the hair-prickling sensation of being watched.

The Forest's wash of purple moonlight embraces her, its loving aura suffusing her Lasair might and tinting her fire aura purple. Her tightly guarded hold on her emotions is suddenly wrenched open, every pent-up, impassioned feeling rushing forth, as her kindred falcon lets out a joyful cry and flies up and alights on a branch overhead.

"What if he feels nothing for me?" she asks the fire-loving Forest as she brings her palms to the rough trunk before her, the tree's fierce love instantly encircling her. "What if I give in to the moon's pull to honesty, and he says he could never love a Fire Fae?"

Insecurity rises, potent enough to cut through the Xishlon moon's thrall, a feeling of overwhelming loneliness overtaking Iris, her gut clenching from the sheer strength of it.

THE DRYAD STORM

You utter fool, she roughly chastises herself. *What are you thinking? Yes, there seemed to be a strong attraction between the two of you, but he clearly fought it. He could never want you for his Xishlon'vir.*

A jaded laugh bursts from Iris's throat, bitterness rising over her deluded idea that Dryad Sylvan would want to entertain the non-Dryad Xishlon'vir tradition, his own peoples and their traditions almost completely wiped out several times over.

She knows that the Dryad Fae have established a growing community here, naming Sylvan as the leader of their Tree Council. She's heard they've built elaborately crafted canopy homes here, set inside huge burls that cling to the top of the Nightwood Pines' enormous trunks, the Dryads' elevated dwellings connected by vine bridges, everything lit by phosphorescent fungi, the Dryads' knowledge of building and farming in Balance with Nature transforming the entire Realm.

Several months ago, when Sylvan left with most of the Dryad Fae for their new Zhilaan Forest territory, Iris thought she sensed reluctance on his end to be parted from her, his strong fireline keeping tight hold of hers as they clung to each other's hands, the surrounding Dryad refugees eyeing them with everything from knowing curiosity to open concern.

Iris could read their unspoken thoughts simmering on the air—a powerful Dryad like Sylvan was clearly meant to find a mate from those of his own kind.

And then, Sylvan wrangled his magic away from hers with what felt like great effort before bidding her a strained goodbye, and Iris wondered, as raw longing for him gripped hold, if she'd ever feel that closeness between them again.

Certain that the answer was a firm *no.*

But then, his letters started arriving.

A trickle of them at first, carried southeast by a Fire Hawk, the trickle strengthening to a letter almost every day, the walnut-ink missives matter-of-factly detailing Sylvan's work to reestablish a Dryad homeland and bring their Balance-minded ways to the entire Eastern Realm.

Ensconced in her small Fire Fae community to the north of Voloi, Iris pored over every letter, her pulse never failing to quicken as she read each one multiple times. Her aura flared white-hot when he sent his shortest letter yet, inviting her to travel to Zhilaan so he could show her what they were building there.

Yet, his prose was so succinct, Iris agonized over whether she was reading too much into his correspondence, suffusing it with her own longing for him.

Wrestling with her feelings, Iris decided to give in to her yearning to see Sylvan again, forgetting that the trip would coincide with Xishlon, the damned moon turning her into a lovesick mess, unable to approach him with any semblance of hidden feelings.

Get a hold of yourself! she gruffly urges as she withdraws her palms from the tree before her and bunches them into fists. *Admit it—coming here was a mistake. Even if he has feelings for you, he'll never give in to them. Let him go before he breaks your heart.*

Her emotions bottoming out, Iris roughly swipes away the tears pooling in her eyes and turns to leave, to get as far away as she can from the man who will never, ever want a Fire Fae.

Rancid misery simmering through her power, she moves to turn back toward the tree line, but freezes in her tracks.

A majestic, deep-purple stag is watching her.

The breathtakingly handsome creature is standing, stock-still, between two Nightwood Pines, its silvery rack seeming to possess hundreds upon hundreds of points, its eyes flashing like violet gems.

Iris's heartbeat quickens, her magic roaring into sudden, hotter life as the certainty sweeps through her—

This is Sylvan's hidden kindred.

Staring straight at her, as if at a treasure found.

Emotion grips Iris's throat, hot and raw.

Could he be searching for me this Xishlon like I'm searching for him?

After they parted, Iris tried to fall back in with her fellow Lasair Fae, settling with them in Eastern Noilaan, where the Lasair had taken up residence near the Eastern Realm's sole active volcano, the fire power there a marvel to behold.

She tried to forget Sylvan. Truly she did. Tried to fit in with a solely Lasair community once more. But the xenophobic views still held by some of the non-Dryad'khin Lasair felt like clothing Iris no longer fit into, and she found herself arguing against such thinking as passionately as she used to argue *for* it, her thoughts and dreams increasingly drawn back to Sylvan.

Night after night, she revisited the time when she'd emerged from the Dyoi Forest's innermost being and experienced that first awareness of her fire powers and Sylvan's flashing around each other . . . and how he'd grabbed hold of her when she almost fell to her knees, his embrace igniting something powerful between them. They'd sought each other out from that point on, their late-night conversations under the stars a sometimes painful illumination as they told each other about their lives and confronted the difficult history of both their people, the Lasair and the Dryads having always existed on the mistrusted periphery of the Sidhe Fae'kin. Both groups almost wiped clear off the face of Erthia during the Fae wars.

But it's not just Sylvan's fierce personality she misses.

Increasingly, he's part of the hottest fire of her dreams. For so many years, she'd thought she was meant to pair with Yvan. But *this* attraction . . . it's like all the lightning bolts in the world colliding in a firestorm of sparks. There were moments she was sure that Sylvan felt it, too, as she caught a few of his sidelong glances before he'd quickly look away, his face tense with conflict. He seemed, in those moments, to be struggling as mightily against their draw as she was, the two of them hells-bent on holding to their own Fae ways. Both of them voicing, as if in an attempt to ward off this thing growing between them, how they planned to seek out their own kind after the Realm War.

If the Natural World survived.

And now, here they are in a world that *has*, against all the odds, survived—tenuously—the opportunity to seek out their own Fae kind suddenly before them like a path unscrolled at their feet.

But the Xishlon moon seems to have other plans, Iris thinks as she peers up through the Zhilaan canopy. As does her aching heart. An ember of hope ignites as Iris moves toward the stag, only to have that ember snuffed out as the stag turns and strides away.

The pain of rejection clutches Iris's heart with surprising force, just as the buck pauses once more, turns and gives her an unmistakably beckoning look, her falcon kindred landing on the buck's majestic rack.

Startled, Iris's fire magic blazes into a swirling, sparking anticipation. Emboldened, she finds her footing and follows the silent, stately kindred and her falcon through the Forest, caught up in a sense of the whole Forest eagerly watching.

And breathlessly waiting.

Eventually, the buck stills, and both kindreds set their gazes on her. Iris stills as well, her heart thudding as the kindred gives her one long, last look then darts away, disappearing into some dense brush set around a raised hillock, her falcon taking flight toward the canopy above.

Confusion flooding her, Iris lets out a hard sigh, tracking her kindred's flight path. Her fire aura leaps when she finds Sylvan there, sitting on a branch just above her, washed in the Xishlon moon's purple light, her falcon perched on his shoulder.

Iris's heart lurches toward Sylvan, her fire magic warming every vein as her falcon takes flight once more and Sylvan drops down before her, branch horns rising from his pine hair, his piercing eyes intent.

Those beautiful pine eyes of his.

"Your kindred," Iris marvels, entranced by him. "It's . . . *beautiful.*" Her vulnerability rises, fear swamping her emotions as she looks away, overcome by intimidation. She pulls in a deep breath, draws on her fire to fuel her courage . . . and meets his eyes.

"I . . . I thought . . ." Iris starts, tripping over the words as the Xishlon moon coaxes her every feeling for Sylvan to the surface, "I thought that maybe . . . there's a chance that a Lasair might be welcome as a permanent addition to your fire-loving Forest." Her pulse beats hot against the sides of her neck as he studies her, his rooted steadiness such a contrast to her often out-of-control flame, her intense passion, which she has so much trouble keeping hold of.

"It's not *my* Forest, Dryad'khin," he offers, his deep voice thrumming right down Iris's spine. "It's *our* Forest." A slight, amused smile tilts his green lips. "And the Forest isn't the only fire-loving thing here."

Heat shoots straight down Iris's spine.

"I want you as my Xishlon'vir," she blurts out with a quick glance toward the purple moon above, this moon that's throwing her heart as well as every tendril of her fire *wide open.*

An emotional look overtakes Sylvan's expression before his lips slant upward once more and he takes a step toward her, his hands moving lightly to her waist, her magic flaring around that touch. "You've a mind for melding traditions tonight it seems," he says, serious now, "as do I."

Iris nods, remorse coursing through her for briefly losing her way. Only to be shown a better path forward by the Forest. And by her blossoming love for Sylvan. A path that embraces diversity and love, the Forest itself expanding the circle of Dryad'khin.

"I feel like you truly see me," Iris says, the words flowing off her tongue, every heartfelt thing eased into existence by the moonlight. "Even though . . . even though you're Dryad and I'm Lasair."

Sylvan reaches up and threads his fingers through her hair, an almost pained look on his severe face that sends Iris's heart into a faster rhythm. "We were wrong to fight this," he murmurs as she reaches up to place her hand over his heart. Sylvan's breath hitches as he gives her a deeply besotted look and draws her closer, his scent such a deep, rich pine. "This entire Forest," he murmurs as he caresses her back, "is fueled by fire. Which means you would be a *most welcome* permanent addition to it."

Tears mist Iris's eyes, the subtext in his words clear, his touch and his love singe-ing away every barrier between them.

"I want you, Sylvan," Iris admits.

Sylvan gives her an impassioned look, the surge of Iris's fire echoing his intensity because she knows the two of them have found something in each other strong as wildfire. Strong as the surrounding Zhilaan Forest.

Strong as the Xishlon moon above.

"I want you too," Sylvan says, his warm lips brushing her temple. "Let's meld all the traditions this eve, my beautiful Lasair-Dryad'khin."

And then he draws back slightly, reaches out to run his fingertips along the sta-mens of a moon-blooming Xishlon Lily twined around the nearest trunk, its petals glowing violet along with the pollen now gracing Sylvan's fingertips.

He brings his fingertips to her skin, and Iris shivers as he traces a line of the pol-len down the side of her neck, over her inner shoulder, then down her bare lower arms.

"What are you doing?" she breathlessly asks.

"Showing you the Forest," he says before bringing his lips to hers.

Iris ignites against his impassioned kiss, heated tendrils of pleasure coursing over her skin where he traced the pollen, entrancingly flame-hot.

"What was that?" she breathlessly stammers.

Sylvan smiles. "Fire pollen," he answers, voice low and husky with want. "It holds the Forest's fire-embrace in it."

Iris gapes at him, stunned. "What else can this Forest do?"

Sylvan's smile turns sultry. "Oh, so much more."

Iris can't suppress her own besotted smile as she grips Sylvan's leafy tunic and pulls him into another fiery and thoroughly claiming kiss, the two of them sur-rendering themselves without reservation to the moonlight. As Sylvan draws her down to the mossy Forest floor and reveals the full, Xishlon-fueled wonders of the Zhilaan Forest's embracing love.

CHAPTER FIVE

XISHLON LIGHT

Wrenfir Harrow

Voloi
Xishlon night

Wrenfir glares at the purple moon.

The moon that's wrenching his heart from his chest as he strides through the Mage-refugee encampment on the northern edge of Voloi's docks. A bag containing his apothecary supplies is slung over his shoulder, IV's great canopy spread high above it all.

Day after day, a steady stream of sickly, half-starved Gardnerian refugees stumble out of Verdyllion portals, haunted looks in their eyes. All of them seeming thunderstruck to have made it to the East before they either collapsed from illness or were slain by Shadow creatures.

The Red Grippe has been as cruel to them as their own Shadowed Magedom, all medical care in Gardneria having broken down, along with the Natural World.

Two of Wrenfir's rescued cats flank him, a gentle purple calico and a sleek silver shorthair. A sickly fluffy black kitten rides in his pocket, but his kindred bobcat hangs back in the Forest just north of here so as not to frighten the Mage children and the skittish adult Gardnerians who have yet to embrace the Forest.

Music kicks up not far ahead, its origin seeming to be one of the pockets of Forest that have been established throughout the city, trees planted in every available space to fight the Shadow and help stabilize the East's devasted weather system.

Wrenfir scowls and glares at Voloi's purple-laden tiers as purple fireworks flash over the city. Because he has no use for Xishlon love and romance. No use for the sliver of hope that arises with every new link to the Forest.

Because it's too damned late.

The weather beyond Noilaan's protective Great Tree and dome-shield is out of control, much of the continent a Shadowed wasteland.

Wrenfir blinks back the sting of emotion in his eyes, every muscle tensing against his firestorm of anger. Because Hazel is forever lost to him, all the Death Fae absorbed into Nature to hold off a Reckoning, their sacrifice having made this whole gods-damned purple idiocy possible.

Wrenfir experienced Nature's terror firsthand as a child, almost lost to the cursed Red Grippe. His throat tightens at the memories of those wildly frightening nights when he briefly lost the ability to pull in even a single, rasping breath.

His turmoil blazing hotter, he glares at the city once more and snarls an epithet under his breath. They're deluding themselves with this asinine revelry. Forgetting what the Death Fae did for them all. What Hazel and Viger, Sylla and Vesper, and all the Death Fae creatures staved off.

A nightmare as terrible as anything Vogel could have ever rained down.

And it's highly likely that their sacrifice will have been for naught. Just like the terrible deaths of his sister Tessla, his brother-in-law Vale, and Edwin Gardner were for naught.

Because the Dryad'khin have sorely underestimated the power of fracture.

That will usher in the eventual triumph of the Shadow.

The sound of a child's hacking cough snaps through Wrenfir's tortured thoughts, yanking his attention back to the task at hand. Forcing aside his grief, he strides toward the tent the sound is coming from, a painfully thin Gardnerian woman standing in front of the tent's entrance.

"Are . . . are you the medic?" she stammers as he approaches, clearly scared of his Death Fae spider tattoos, his pointed ears and deep-green hue. Her look of fright takes a turn toward confusion as her eyes slide to the midnight-hued kitten peeking out of his pocket.

Her gaze slides back to his with a look of wary concern, as if he's planning on eating the kitten whole. A kitten he's spent most of last night nursing and crooning to. A kitten now glued to his side after Wrenfir empathically read, with his new Dryad'kin abilities, images of the little feline's terror and grief, memories of its mother and littermates being murdered by grayed Shadowfire, this small one consumed with a trauma that Wrenfir understands on a bone-deep level.

He's all too acquainted with soul-shearing grief, having lost Tessla, Vale, and Edwin to the Magedom's cruelty, as well as his beloved childhood pet, a cat named Patches.

He's named the kitten in his pocket Deathling as tribute to the Death Fae, in an attempt to infuse the little animal with some of the strength and courage that managed to fight off a Reckoning.

Wrenfir draws a bottle of Norfure tincture from his sack and holds it out to the Mage woman. "This will cure your child," he offers tersely as his eyes flick over her conservative garb, her unchanged fastmarks.

She's likely stubbornly glued to Mage dogma, even after connecting with the Forest.

Anger rises in Wrenfir as he and the woman stare each other down and she makes no move to accept the medicine. He struggles to bite back the harsh words burning for release.

"Mamma," a small, constricted voice chirps from behind the woman, drawing both his attention and the woman's. A little boy slips into view from behind her skirts and looks worriedly up at Wrenfir before breaking into a spasming cough.

Wrenfir's gut tightens as he notes that the child's entire mouth is ringed with red sores, his eyes reddened to a flame hue by the cruel disease.

The end stages of the Grippe.

He can feel it in his own lungs once more, a muscle memory of those childhood nights gasping for breath, his sister, Tessla, and his grandfather too poor to afford expensive medicine, until Vale Gardner and Fain Quillen intervened . . .

"Here," he says, adamantly holding out the Norfure tincture to the woman— medicine he spent the entire night fabricating from the flowers Elloren had sourced from the distant Zhilaan Forest, his eyes bleary with fatigue.

The woman finally relents and takes the bottle, a deeply conflicted look in her eyes. Wrenfir catches the child studying him with similarly wary eyes before the little one's eyes light on the kitten, then on the cats affectionately rubbing against Wrenfir's ankles.

"I had a cat," the child blurts out, tears brimming in his eyes as he starts to cry and cough at the same time. "We . . . we had to *leave* her."

Pain strikes through Wrenfir's heart.

He drops to one knee before the boy. "I lost my cat too," he tells him. "During the last Realm War." And suddenly the damned Xishlon moon is causing a tear to spill down Wrenfir's cheek as he and the child take each other in. "Would you like to visit my cats when you get better?" Wrenfir offers. "I'm a medic for them too."

"Thank you, but *no*," the woman hastily intervenes as she edges between her child and Wrenfir, gripping the medicine to her chest and tugging the boy protectively behind her long black skirt.

Keeping him safe from *me*, Wrenfir bitterly notes.

"Isil needs to conserve his strength," she tightly explains.

And Wrenfir can see it in her eyes. Her rejection of him as a Heathen Evil One. He realizes she'll likely spend all her days here in the East with a few other militantly dormant Mages, walling herself off from non-Mages and Dryad'khin Mages. Clinging to the same madness that ripped Hazel away from him. That almost destroyed *everything*.

But then he meets the boy's eyes again and the realization hits him . . .

The child won't forget this kindness.

And Wrenfir will find a way to get a cat to him. A kitten just conveniently wandering by, perhaps. Accepted by the child's rigid mother as a gift from the Ancient One on high, instead of coming from a thoroughly Deathkin-corrupted, point-eared Dryad'khin Mage.

And so Wrenfir perseveres, spending Xishlon eve handing out medicine and tending to the sick until he can't take the agony the moon is coaxing to life in his chest for one minute more.

He flees the refugee tent city and Voloi's cursed purple revelry, veering north until he's in the denser Forest bracketing this higher stretch of the Vo River, surrounded by Noi Maple and Noi Birch trees. Until he feels himself to be truly alone.

And then, he falls to his knees and weeps for Tessla, for Vale, for Edwin, and for Hazel, feeling as if his grief will scour his lungs straight out of his chest. He and Hazel had so little time together . . . but that smidgen was enough to show them both that they had found their great True Love in each other. The type of love that never comes again.

The purple-moonlit world pulses Dark, tendrils of black mist swirling around Wrenfir.

He startles, shock catching the sob tight in his chest as a figure made entirely of the mist appears before him, down on one knee, his features solidifying slightly into . . .

". . . Hazel," Wrenfir rasps, lurching toward him only to have his hands pass right through Hazel's misty form. Frustration burns through Wrenfir like wildfire as he meets Hazel's night-Dark eyes.

Eyes he could get lost in.

Forever.

"I'll come back to you," Hazel's voice murmurs from everywhere at once, yearning in those beloved, full-Dark eyes.

"When?" Wrenfir agonizes. *"How?"*

"My link to the Forest," Hazel explains. "The full Deathkin . . . if the Balance is restored, they'll reemerge after being bound for a full hundred years. But me . . . I'll be bound for only a portion of that time, because I'm Dryad Fae, as well." A slash of intense emotion sharpens his features. "Wrenfir. *Wait for me.*"

"I will," Wrenfir promises, his throat closing in around the words. "I'd wait for you *forever.*"

Hazel's misty form leans forward, and Wrenfir can feel the brush of a kiss against his mouth all the way down his spine, the moon's purple light seeming to swirl around them both, straight through Hazel's tendrils of Darkness.

As they take each other as Xishlon'virs with that one, ethereal kiss.

And then, Hazel vanishes into the pulsing Darkness, leaving Wrenfir on his knees, alone in the Forest, the tears coming fast and furious. Then lessening as a small black snake winds over his lap. Then another. And another. Before they slither into the wilderness, turning back once, tongues flickering, as if conveying a strange, loving farewell.

Deathling lets out a small meow, and Wrenfir looks to the tiny animal. He swallows his grief and strokes the kitten's furry back, equal parts affection and trauma emanating from the small feline that takes a slide toward love as Deathling's purr vibrates against Wrenfir's hand. He looks up at the Xishlon moon, wondering if its magic had a hand in allowing Hazel to come to him on this Xishlon night.

So that Wrenfir could take him as his Xishlon'vir.

Deep in Wrenfir's chest, hope blooms that, if the Natural World survives, somewhere in the near future, maybe even by the next Xishlon . . . Hazel will re-form and come back to him.

"All right, you damned orb," Wrenfir spits out at the moon as he cradles

Deathling and wipes his tears brusquely away. "I accept your light." His throat tenses with emotion. "Bring him back to me. Bring him back to me with your light."

A small ember of purple-hued hope now lit deep in his chest, Wrenfir stands, his kitten in his pocket, his other two cats trailing behind him, and makes his way back to the complicated, awful, beautiful purple chaos of Voloi.

CHAPTER SIX

XISHLON HOPE

Elloren Guryev

Noilaan
Xishlon night

The purple moon above shines its light down on me as I stare past the Eastern Realm's translucent dome into its luminous depths. My heart is so full of love that it feels like an ache, my sleeping baby, Tessla, wrapped in my arms, my child named for my late mother. The two of us are poised by the railing that lines the edge of Voloi's newly restored Voling Gardens, the city's docks and Tierney and Or'myr's beloved Vo River spread out before us, suffused with every shade of violet.

The Great Tree, IV, sheltering it all.

Tessla shifts in her slumber, her velvety soft wings wrapped around her, and I can't suppress my besotted smile. I stroke her midnight-black hair, admiring the small horn nubs nestled amidst her tousled curls, her hue my same shimmering, Dryad green. She stirs and opens her eyes then breaks into an adoring smile, and my heart swells as it always does. Because her coloring might reflect mine, but her features are all Yvan, the vivid Lasair green of her eyes ringed with purple fire. I breathe deeply, filled with a sense of the rootlines strengthening inside her, including her powerful line of prismatic light.

Amidst a potent core of Icaral fire.

Two young girls beside us giggle, drawing my attention to the golden-haired Issani girl as she breaks her purple moon cookie and hands half to her Dryad Fae friend before the two of them happily stride off, hand in hand, as they munch on the traditional sweets meant for sharing with those you love.

Emotion cinches my throat. It feels like an eternity ago that I was a naive girl breaking wings off Icaral cookies and believing everything that my culture fed me, these moon cookies such a *vast* improvement.

Hugging Tessla close, I look at the Xishlon moon once more and send up a small prayer of thanks that my naivete was smashed to pieces, following that with a prayer of gratitude for everyone who challenged me along the way, my heart filling with a fiery love for Yvan, Lukas, and so many others.

Tears pooling in my eyes, I feel Tessla snuggling back into sleep, and I kiss her warm head. The smell of loamy, upturned soil is rich in the surrounding air as a vastly diverse crowd of people continue with the tree plantings that have been happening all day, the surviving Xishlon Wisterias and the new saplings raining down glowing lavender tresses of flowers.

For months now, Dryad'khin have planted trees and other plants in every spare space throughout the cities and villages of Noilaan, their soil and weather-stabilizing effect incrementally weaving a slice of Erthia's Natural Matrix back together.

It's a start.

A start in rebuilding the fragile Natural Balance, enough to aid the Deathkin in holding off the Reckoning.

But grief tightens my gut when I consider what's been lost, not even the Xishlon moon above able to blot it out. The majority of the continent has been stripped of Forest and riddled with Shadow-polluted waters and poisoned air, demonic creatures roaming the destroyed land.

I glance West, toward the Vo Mountain Range that was blown up to half its former height last Xishlon, memories of Lukas constricting my heart—his sacrifice making every good thing now surrounding Tessla and me possible.

Even the Vo Mountain Range Lukas had to explode is making a comeback, Or'myr, Sparrow, and a host of other geomancers working with Dryad Fae and Gwynn and Mavrik to rebuild and rewild the mountaintop. An obsidian statue Wynter crafted of a piece of music Lukas wrote for me marks the mountain range's base in honor of what he did for us all. I've journeyed there, to the mountain's newly Snow Oak–forested side, a Noi violin in hand, to play the stone-carved notes of the song we played together so long ago, swept up in a sense of Lukas smiling down on me as I caught a brief flash of Watchers in the trees, a bittersweet memory of the Snow Oak pendant he once gave me suffusing my mind.

Resurgent tears burn in my eyes, my chest crushed in a love- and grief-constricted vise. I press my palm to the bark of the Wisteria beside me and am engulfed in a swirl of the tree's affection and a wispy, dreamlike sense of Lukas's love embracing me, as I so often am when I share a quiet moment with the Forest. His Dryad energy infuses *everything*, along with that of my Errilor kindreds.

"Thank you, Lukas," I whisper through quivering lips, a tear streaking my cheek. *And thank you, my Deathkin. For giving us a chance.*

I peer up at IV's distant canopy, Noilaan's protective dome just beyond. Sliding my gaze west, I'm acutely aware of the Shadow pollution ceaselessly pressing against the western side of our shielding, threatening my daughter's future.

Threatening every child's future.

Valasca, Ni Vin, and Alder have ventured to the West with a small pioneering army and Alder's flock of giant eagles, all of them intent on fighting their way through the Shadow filth and its multi-eyed creatures to regenerate what used to be Amazakaraan's Caledonian Mountain Range—Alder's first kindred Forest.

To wrest it back from the Shadow and reclaim Amazakaraan for the Natural World.

"I *will* see you again, Black Witch," Valasca insisted after we bade each other a tearful farewell and I promised to care for her goat kindreds while Andras took in Ni Vin's midnight-hued mare.

I send up another prayer for their safety as I gently rock Tessla, hoping against hope that we'll all see each other again someday.

Someone steps up beside me, and I glance over and see Jules Kristian leaning on the railing and studying the Xishlon moon, his silver kestrel perched on his shoulder. It's clear he's pausing in the planting of trees, a soil-encrusted shovel in his hand. Noilaan's surviving Vo mystics have declared the rewilding of land a new sacred Xishlon tradition, like so many other traditions being created or rewritten to support the Natural World, along with love and connection and Life. It's a welcome change.

But why did it have to come so late?

"Do you think there's hope for the Natural World?" I ask Jules as purple fireworks detonate over the river, sizzling into the shapes of hundreds of Xishlon moons.

Jules frowns and draws in a deep breath. "I don't know if there's as much hope as we would like." He meets my gaze. "A slim ecological chance, perhaps? Erthia is not what it was, Elloren." He holds up his hand, unfurling his fingers to reveal the imprint of III on his palm. "I think a lot depends on us staying connected to the Forest and letting it change us. Truly *being* with the Forest." His kestrel ruffles her feathers, and Jules reaches up to absently stroke the bird's side, tension knotting his brow. "It's a new paradigm. A whole new way."

He's right, I consider. A whole new, often difficult, Dryad'khin way of life.
Living simply.

Counting riches in trees planted and wilds restored and protected, not in wealth
or power accrued. Embracing sustainability.

Embracing *Life*.

"There's so much discord," I say, casting him a worried look, thinking of the
infighting going on among the new Dryad'khin Conclave, of which he's an elected
member along with Vang Troi, Soleiya, Lucretia, Naga, and Ra'Ven, among others.
"I know a great many people here think we made a mistake in striking down the
runic border and letting the Mage and Alfsigr refugees in," I rue. "Especially since
so many Mages have refused to join with the Forest. There are arguments over such
a multitude of things, it's . . . daunting."

Jules tilts his head. "There *is* debate and conflict. But that's what the road to a
better world looks like—everyone finally getting their say, especially the recently
oppressed. Full disagreement and reckoning. Difficult dialogue."

"Confusion?" I venture, shooting him a fraught look as I remember our conversations in Valgard.

He laughs, a knowing gleam in his eyes. "*Especially* confusion." His expression
grows serious. "But then, a healing of the fracture. The old cycles can't stand. They
brought this Shadow to our gates and almost destroyed everything."

III's promise comes to mind, an ethereal thing, fragile and gleaming.

The story is not yet over.

Jules's hand comes to my arm in gentle support. "Elloren . . . I believe time will
prove beyond a doubt that breaking the cycle of hate and letting the Mage and Alfsigr refugees in amongst the others was the *right thing to do*."

I nod, clinging to a thread of hope that the vision III sent to me in its depths was
right—that the unexpected can come when division is healed.

"Ah, my beautiful daughter and granddaughter," a familiar voice says from just
behind us. "We've found you."

Jules and I turn as Soleiya and Lucretia make a beeline for us, the two of them
meeting me here as promised, to care for little Tessla for part of Xishlon eve.

They're crowned in wreaths of purple flowers and wearing clothing dyed violet
for the festival, like Jules's and mine. Their arms are jauntily linked as they beam
at us, Soleiya's eyes like Xishlon beacons, burning Zhilaan-violet bright. I grin,

pleased that the two of them surprised Yvan and me by becoming fast friends over these past few chaotic months.

Soleiya coos at Tessla, and I transfer my sleepy babe into her arms along with a cloth sack of baby-care items while Jules sweeps Lucretia into an embrace and kisses her with a Xishlon fervor that heats my cheeks and has me glancing away, her water aura swirling ardently around him.

Tessla settles against Soleiya's chest, and Soleiya smiles at me as I'm struck, once more, by the heartwarming awareness of how much Tessla is going to look like her and Yvan.

She'll be *beautiful* like them both.

Another thought strikes home, and I still. The face of the Black Witch potentially ends with me.

Could it be that the Gardnerian line of Great Mages is finally, truly over?

With that momentous thought reverberating through my mind, I nod farewell to Jules, Lucretia, and Soleiya and silently walk through the gardens and throngs of revelers. Eventually I step into the grassy, moonlit clearing that used to be the Voling Gardens' largest plaza. IV's great trunk rises from its center, right where the old statue of the Great Icaral slaying the Black Witch used to stand.

IV's purple mist envelops me, the Great Tree's embracing love pulsing through my rootlines, and I smile at IV. Xishlon moonlight caresses the Great Tree's every leaf, and a multitude of revelers continuously stop by to press IV-marked hands to the trunk and spend time in IV's loving presence.

I reach into my tunic pocket and pull out the wrapped gift Wynter gave me earlier, telling me, with a shy smile, *It's for you. And Yvan. And Baby Tessla. Open it near IV on the night of the purple moon.*

Walking to a more isolated edge of IV's vast trunk, I study the present's wrapping—a swath of lavender cloth on which Wynter painted a glowing Xishlon moon, the package bound with artfully tied purple string.

Warm arms slide around my waist, and Yvan's fiery aura encircles me. I smile, the feel of his body pressed against my back immediately tugging on our mating bond. Warmth races over my skin, our melded fire power giving a hard flare.

"Happy Xishlon, my beautiful Dryad Witch," he hisses in Wyvern, then kisses my neck with an affectionate slowness that sends hot shivers of delight straight through my rootlines.

I pivot to face him, my heart tripping into a faster rhythm at the sight of his beloved, angular face, sultry affection burning in his eyes, his wings arcing around me.

His crimson hair is tinted reddish-purple by the moonlight, the Xishlon moon's thrall swiftly revving our mating bond up to such molten heights that I can feel the flush blooming on my skin. Yvan cocks a brow and smiles, his knowing look quickening my pulse as he draws me into a slow, deep kiss, a more intense desire for him firing through my every line as I surrender to his enthralling heat.

"You said you had something to show me," he murmurs against my lips as he lightly presses his forehead to mine, his fingertips trailing sparks over my skin.

My breathing erratic, I nod and lift the cloth-wrapped gift. "Wynter made this for us. She wanted us to open it here."

Curiosity lights in Yvan's eyes as I untie the purple string and fold back the cloth.

We both draw in emotional breaths as we take in what Wynter has crafted for us. It's a small statue, carved from purple stone. A statue I envisioned during Shadowed times—a revolutionary reimagining that Wynter read from a single touch of my wrist. A new Prophecy to replace all the others.

An Icaral and a Dryad Witch embracing, Watchers perched on their shoulders.

A trace of peace settles in my heart as I take in the impassioned nonmartial vision. Because Erthia can't take any more martial visions. Erthia can't take any more Realm Wars. We need a future free of that type of conflict, if there's going to be any future at all.

It's time for new visions and new statues.

Yvan lifts his hand and wraps his palm around the statue's edge, running his thumb over my stone form in a way that mirrors the mesmerizingly deft way he runs those hands over *me*.

His mouth slants into a smile as he lets out a short laugh. "Well, that's an incredible improvement." We exchange an intense look, this statue feeling like the turning of a corner. Like a story ending and a new, better one just beginning.

Pocketing the statue, I reach up and trace a teasing line of heat down the center of Yvan's bare chest. He shivers, giving me an inviting look, the violet fire in his eyes glowing hotter.

"It's our last night in Noilaan for a while," he comments, his eyes and fire suddenly full of so much love that my heart can barely hold it. Drawing me closer, he leans in and gives me another heated kiss. "Be my Xishlon'vir, Elloren Guryev."

I laugh, grinning at him. "I think I'm already your Xishlon'vir about two hundred times over. Maybe more."

Yvan shoots me a wicked look that quickly takes a turn for the adoring, affection for him warming my every rootline.

"I'm ready for us to return to Zhilaan tomorrow with Tessla and your mother," I say, our bonded fire-Forest always tugging on our Wyvernbond, beckoning us home. "I'm ready to build our home there and raise our daughter. And take up my work as an apothecary and luthier, while we work to safeguard our Forest." A tingle races through me, so much possibility opening up with the lifting of war, so many former goals reasserting themselves. I glance toward the West, growing serious, even the Xishlon moonlight unable to dampen our awareness of the urgent Forest-saving work ahead. "And you?" I ask, turning back to him.

"Physician," he states without hesitation, his gaze taking on a meaningful light. "Along with raising Tessla and building our home together. And safeguarding our Forest with our Dryad'khin." The fire in his eyes intensifies, brighter than the moon above. "I never want to be parted from you again, Elloren," he hisses in Wyvern, as everything we've been through circles around us and tears sheen my eyes.

"I love you, Yvan," I say in Wyvern, the hissed words sliding easily off my tongue.

"I love you too," he says in Dryadin, smiling as he draws me into another rootline-heating, toe-curling kiss that leaves me wanting and breathless. He trails his lips along my neck, then runs the hot tip of his tongue along the edge of my ear before kissing me there, his fingertips tracing a spiral of sparks along my waist, desire firing through our bond.

"Are you looking to 'find the moon'?" I tease.

He flashes me a smile that's feral and loving at the same time. "Oh, I've already found it." His wings fan out to their full breadth, his lips brushing mine once more before he lifts me into his arms, eyes aflame. "Now, let's fly out of here, my Dryad Witch, find a mountaintop cavern . . . and set each other on fire."

EPILOGUE

The Next Great Mage
Valen

Almost a year ago

Six-year-old Valen falls out of his mother's arms and to the Valgard ground, tendrils of Shadow curling around him as panicked Mages rush by.

"My son!" his mother cries, as she's whisked from his sight by the press of fleeing Mages. "Help me get back to my son!" he can just make out her screaming. "He's our *next Great Mage!*"

"Mamma!" Valen screams as the booted foot of a fleeing Mage connects with his shoulder, his leg. The poisoned sky overhead is full of low-hanging, nightmarish Shadow clouds spitting curling black lightning, Valen's Level Five Magelines sizzling terrified fire through his whole body. Roughly jostled on every side, Valen breaks into heaving sobs just as a Gardnerian woman grabs rough hold of him and yanks him into her arms.

The terrifying scene surrounding them comes back into full view as Valen and the stranger-Mage are swept forward by the sea of black-clad Gardnerians, all in desperate flight toward a series of glowing arches made from prismatic runes situated at the plaza's far end, the interiors rippling silver.

Valen glances around frantically, no sign of his mother anywhere. *"Mamma!"* he screams again and again as shrieks split the air. Valen's eyes widen in horror as Mage soldiers with multitudes of glowing gray eyes fly in on dragonback, their multi-eyed dragons possessing six or even eight limbs, huge gray wraith bats soaring in beside them.

One dragon lands a few paces away from Valen with a ground-shaking *thump*, crushing an old woman under its huge body. The multi-eyed Mage astride it dismounts, fast as a blur, then grabs a screaming woman and latches his elongating teeth into her throat. Valen's gut clenches with terror as tendrils of Shadow course from the Mage-thing's body, and the woman goes limp in his Shadow-clawed hands.

"*MAMMA!*" Valen screams again, as the woman holding him suddenly throws him straight into one of the prismatic arches.

The scene cuts out, and a vision of a starlight bird flashes through Valen's panicked vision as he hurtles, limbs flailing, through the silvery mist.

Valen lands with a thud and vomits onto brushy soil. His gaze whips around, the surrounding Forest bizarrely prismatic, some of the mostly gray-tinged leaves colored blue and purple along with the more familiar colors of fall. A cold rain batters his skinny frame and thunder rumbles, drawing his gaze skyward. Far overhead, he can make out a translucent dome marked with faintly visible prismatic runes.

So terrified he can barely pull a breath, Valen breaks into heaving sobs, all alone in the oddly colored forest.

"Mamma!" he chokes out.

An onyx-hued woman with *horns!* and *wings!* and *dragon eyes!* bursts from the woods and runs toward him, a Lupine wolf-monster woman with wild amber eyes and flaxen hair racing beside her, a rush of terror shooting down his spine.

A Wyvern monster and Lupine monster! Just like his scariest toys!

Out to kill and eat Mage children!

Valen screams, fright turning him into a wild thing. He grabs hold of the closest branch, struggling to remember the words to the candle-lighting spell his mamma taught him to use if Evil Ones got hold of him—the same spell he learned for his wand-testing, when he blasted out a huge column of fire and blew a burning hole through the room's wall. The priests' eyes had widened, all the surrounding adults murmuring and exclaiming as the wand was wrested from his hand and they'd grouped around the wall's smoking wreckage, eyeing him in a strange way that made Valen feel scared.

Calling him "the next Great Mage."

Faced with the incoming Wyvern and Lupine monsters, Valen shrieks out the candle-lighting spell once more, screaming his vengeance at the monsters, along with his fear over not being able to find his mamma, his wand hand trembling.

A huge bolt of fire explodes from the branch and blasts toward the Evil Ones.

The Lupine monster throws up her forearm, and the firebolt glances off it, the flames quickly pulled toward the Wyvern monster and sucked into her outstretched palm.

Before Valen can blast out another column of Magefire, the Lupine monster reaches him in a blur, wrests the branch from his grip, and grabs him in her frightfully strong arms. Valen thrashes against her, snarling, his fire power searing through him, his ferocious magic desperate for release.

The Wyvern monster narrows her slit-pupiled eyes at him, her nostrils flaring. "Kill him, Diana," she urges.

The scary wolf woman keeps an iron hold on Valen's writhing, screaming form as she growls at the Wyvern monster, low in her throat. "No, Voor'nile. He's a *child*."

"Do you sense the level of power coming off that *child*?" the Wyvern monster growls back. "That's no normal Mage child. That child is at least a Level Five, with the potential for Great Mage power. He should be destroyed before he can grow into it."

Another growl cuts through the woods, low and scarily resonant.

Valen freezes as another Lupine monster, a tall male, strides out of the forest. Confusion rips through Valen. Because this Lupine monster is a *Mage*, with the same green-hued skin and night-black hair as Valen's own.

"Diana's right," the Lupine Mage man states, his stance powerful. "We're placing him under the pack's protection."

The Wyvern monster spits out what sounds like a hissing curse as Valen devolves into wailing misery, screaming, *"Mamma, Mamma, Mamma!"*

And then he's in motion, the forest around him a blur as he screams and screams and is carried through the trees by the Lupine monster woman, the scary Lupine Mage man keeping pace at her side.

Eventually, Valen's earsplitting wails slow then stop, exhaustion overtaking him. A tremor kicks up as he finds himself able to manage only an exhausted, soul-destroyed whimper. The Wolf monsters reduce their tree-blurring pace, the Lupine woman gently shushing Valen as she rubs his back.

He goes limp in her arms. There's something so warmly kind in her tone . . . something that seems, as her voice catches with what feels like kindred grief, like she understands on some heart-deep level his rageful, slashing grief and terror. And so, completely spent, Valen allows the Lupine monster to hug his limp form. Allows her to talk and murmur softly to him. And later, after they reach a small dwelling in the purple woods, he allows her to tuck a blanket around him before enveloping him in her strong arms and gently murmuring him to sleep.

Valen spends the next night falling asleep beside the Wolf monster woman.

And the night after that.

But days are a different thing.

Valen screams and rages and tries to hit and bite any of the Evil Ones who come near. He finds wood in an attempt to hurt them with fire. As he screams for his family. Screams out his terror and pain and trauma.

"He's no good," passing monsters say. Elf monsters and Noi monsters and Fae monsters and others.

"That Crow child has too much power," they say.

"You're playing with fire, there, Diana."

"Rafe, he's another Great Mage. Get rid of him."

But the wolf woman and the wolf man calmly refute all of it.

Time passes, and Valen starts to remain calm around Diana, the wolf woman, only Diana able to approach him without provoking an attack. He bites or punches anyone else who tries to come near. Finds a multitude of sticks and sets a multitude of things on fire.

But Diana and Rafe refuse to give up on him.

More time passes, and new monsters come to visit, those who are completely immune to his fits of fire because they have so much fire of their own. Elloren, a Dryad Mage monster who has as much fire as he does. And the Icaral monster, Yvan, who offers to fly Valen into the sky when he's ready.

But still, when he's not careening into outright hostility, Valen turns increasingly despondent, lapsing into dull silence when he's not lashing out.

Until Ariel comes.

Valen hisses at Ariel, and she hisses back. Then she gives him a wide smile, her fire eyes full of fierce understanding. Thrust into a whirlwind of confusion, Valen lashes out at her. Tries to set her wings on fire. But she meets it all with narrow-eyed calm.

And comes back every day.

Soon, out of sheer confusion, Valen stops trying to set fire to her wings. Stops trying to set fire to everything in sight.

And before long, he's going off with Ariel. Then with the Wyvern Raz'zor. Up, up, up into the sky, the three of them throwing fire out at the heavens. Great lashes of it across the sky, turning the night gold and crimson.

Good, they say, Ariel and Raz'zor both.

Be angry, they say.

Set the damned sky on fire.

And so he does. Sensing that Ariel and Raz'zor need to do this, too, from time to time.

And, as more time passes and Valen is surrounded by so many who are so kind, who understand and accept him, somehow, his fear and rage begin to lessen.

Before long, step by step, little by little, so incrementally he almost doesn't notice the changes happening, he's letting Ariel and Raz'zor fly him up so high that he touches the clouds.

Letting Trystan and his mate, Vothendrile, teach him to hone his fire into lightning bolts so he can light up the heavens with forking electricity through the dark of night.

Then, as more time passes and he grows taller and taller, Valen lets spider-marked Wrenfir teach him to care for injured cats and use his fire power to speed Wrenfir's apothecary spells as they work together to fabricate medicines for both people and Wrenfir's rescued felines, Wrenfir gifting him with a purple kitten of his own.

Interests build and build, and before long, Valen's love of cats branches into a love of horses, and he's letting Andras teach him how to treat injured equines. Letting Ariel teach him how to set a bird's broken wing. Letting Wynter teach him how to sculpt a small statue of the bird he and Ariel just healed and released back into the wilds.

The Great, Blessed Forest.

More time passes, and before long, twelve-year-old Valen is letting patient Or'myr teach him how to throw power through crystals and charge them to heat a home, to power a ship. Then how to grow mushrooms and brew them into tea. How to play the violin.

And letting Elloren, Yvan, Oaklyyn, and Yulan show him the meaning of the Balance, and the Nature-balancing magic of the Zhilaan Forest.

Year upon year passes, with so much love and attention enfolding Valen, his heart has trouble holding it all sometimes. It's so gradual that it's impossible to pinpoint the day it fully and irrevocably happens—the day he fully lays down his Mage defenses. The day the desire to draw a branch, rage out a spell, and set someone on fire truly abates.

The day he heals enough to stop fighting and lets in their collective love.

THIRTEEN YEARS LATER . . .

For All of Us
Valen Ulrich

Lupine Territory, Northern Vo Forest
Xishlon night

Fern Hawthorne-Za'Nor has never looked as heart-expandingly lovely as she does right now. For a moment, nineteen-year-old Valen Ulrich can barely pull in a steady breath, his wits thoroughly scattered, his heart on purple-moon *fire* for her as he meets Fern's gorgeous pink-amethyst gaze.

She's hanging back at the edge of the large, lilac-grassed Forest clearing with her friends, her eyes boldly fixed on Valen where he stands in the clearing's center facing Rafe and Diana. The whole Realm is awash in purple from Vo's Xishlon moon, a sizable crowd of family and friends surrounding Valen.

On this momentous day.

His Lupine Change Day.

Fern is eyeing him with that entrancing mix of flirtatious mischief and shyness that never fails to quicken Valen's heartbeat, dizzying love spiraling through him when he considers his outrageous luck to have had her as his Xishlon'vir for a full year now.

He'll never forget that first intoxicating kiss under last year's purple moon.

And another kiss, only a few days past, in the darkest, stillest hours in the Voloi kitchen of Mora'lee's rune-ship restaurant, Fern's back pressed against the counter, Valen's tongue twining with hers, their bodies fitted so enticingly *tight* against each other.

His desire for her pressed so heatedly against her warm, curvaceous figure.

And oh, she noticed. Shyly and then boldly running a hand over him as he fought the urge to peel off her clothes and take her right then and there.

"Xishlon is only a week away," she'd managed that night, her breathing as uneven as his as he ran his lips down her rose-hued neck, pressed himself more urgently against her, wanting to get closer than ever before.

Wanting *all* of her.

But Fern drew herself back a fraction, her hands coming up to cup his cheeks, her face flushed a wild rose. Valen could barely stand the beauty of her, the two of them best friends since they were twelve.

And then, years later . . . *more*.

Their friendship blossoming into a connection that suffused his dreams and caused him to wake in heated sweats, murmuring her name, his desire as stiff as steel.

"It's a great blessing to take each other fully on Xishlon," she offered, swallowing, her gorgeous amethyst eyes bright with desire, the two of them so enticingly *alone*.

Valen grew serious as he took what felt like a leap off a cliff, swept up in their shared intimacy. Swept up in his love for her. "I'm going to Change on Xishlon," he confided.

Fern's breath caught on a surprised inhale, her hands on his cheeks stilling.

"What does that mean for us?" she finally managed, a quaver in her voice.

Valen leaned in and kissed her with great care before resting his forehead lightly against hers. "It means," he said, a tremor now coursing through *him*, "that I'll want to take you to be my mate on that same night under the Xishlon moon."

Fern drew back a fraction, her gaze wide as she looked closely at him, and Valen knew she understood what he was asking. They had enough Lupine friends and family for it to be clear.

He was asking for a forever bond.

"You know that I don't want to become Lupine," she reminded him, an emotional vibration in her tone, both of them poised on the edge of a beautiful precipice. One they'd been headed toward for years with reckless abandon.

He nodded. Of course he knew that. He knew Fern was attached to the Natural World in a different way, through her geomancy and affinity for rose-hued crystals and stones. Her love of cooking dovetailed with her attraction to agro-geology, his beloved widely sought after for her intuitive grasp on which rock powders could best replenish the Eastern Realm's Shadow-depleted soil with vital minerals, enhancing crop yields.

Fern held out her palm to him, displaying the image of IV emblazoned there, and Valen calmly took the gesture in, his own palms bare, since he'd decided on a different type of bond to the Natural World.

The Lupine bond to Erthia's Great Wilds.

"I love you, Fern," he responded in her Uriskal tongue, his heartbeat thundering. "I want to take you to mate under Vo's moon as your beautiful geomancer self. And my pack is ready to accept you as family just as you are."

Fern blinked, tears glimmering in her eyes, before she gave him a dazzling smile.

A whoosh of joy swept through Valen, everything in him bowled over by the happiness in her smile. Hard-won happiness. He knows this, all too well, from their countless late-night conversations when he held a weeping Fern close as she confided her struggles as a young child in the East, orphaned at a young age when her parents were killed by the Mages. Tears flowing, she told him how she was raised by her beloved grandmother, Fernyllia, who was eventually executed by the Mages for a feat of heroism that ultimately allowed Fern to escape from the Western Realm, along with so many of their friends and family. Like Valen, Fern became a child refugee in the war-decimated Eastern Realm.

Decimated by what happens when so many groups are bent on hating each other and have forgotten their tether to the Forest and to Vo's love.

"All right, Wolf Boy," Fern tossed out in the Common Tongue, beaming at him as tears streaked down her cheeks, her grin filling with flirtatious mischief. "Accept the Xishlon moon as a Lupine. Then bring it to me."

And now, one week later, Xishlon has returned to the Eastern Realm.

Vo's purple moonlight streams into the huge Forest clearing, anticipation and love quickening Valen's heartbeat. A large crowd of family and friends are gathered around him, including the whole Eastern Gerwulf pack.

"You ready for this?" his close friend Konnor Volya asks from beside him.

A broad grin breaks out over Konnor's deep-brown face, warm merriment in his crimson Lupine eyes. Valen grins back at Konnor, his strapping purple-and-black-haired friend a good head taller than him and as steady and warm as his horse-healer father, Andras. Konnor's solid manner is always such a balm to Valen's tempestuous emotions and even more tempestuous Mage magic, Valen's Level Five fire power often casting his emotions into turmoil.

But in a few moments, he'll be free of his Magelines and linked to a whole new power.

His pack.

And bonded to the Forest in a whole new way.

"I'm ready," Valen assures Konnor, beaming back at him and his two other closest male friends, who are standing beside him on this momentous day—bookish and bespectacled Effrey and young Fyn'ir Za'nor. A penumbra of purple Strafeling mist surrounds Effrey's straight-backed form, and purple-patterned Fyn'ir's silver-green eyes are twinkling with his ever-present look of mischief, his Icaral wings pulled in tight behind him, his violet squirrel kindred hugging his arm.

Valen is bolstered by their presence, ready to be reborn as a wolf-shifter and take to the woods for his first run with his family and friends, as Lupine custom encourages.

Before taking Fern soundly to mate.

His eyes seek out Fern again, a thrill coursing through him as their gazes meet and they smile besottedly at each other. Fern's good friends also bracket her—fiery, forest-hued Pyrgo, the purple-hued geomancer-Dryad Tibryl, Smaragdalfar sorceress Nil'ya, and artistic Ghor'li, along with geomancers Bloom'ilya and graceful Ee'vee, all of the young women regarding Fern and Valen with looks of open amusement. Valen's attention slides back to Fern, his gaze wandering appreciatively over his love's formfitting Xishlon tunic and pants, her lavender garb embroidered with Xishlon's fabled purple blossoms, that lovely figure of hers never failing to set his blood and fire burning hotter.

Fern shifts slightly, cocking her hip enticingly and raising her bosom in bold invitation, and Valen has to look away, all too aware of his body's overenthusiastic response to her sultry flirtation, a hot flush suffusing his neck as Pyrgo lets out a bark of a laugh.

"Easy now," Fyn'ir teases, nostrils flaring, his wings pulling in tight. "I'm not sure my sister's ready for you."

Valen returns Fyn'ir's ribald smile, knowing full well that both Fyn'ir and Pyrgo, along with all the shifters and power empaths here, can scent the desire practically leaping in the air between himself and Fern.

"If anyone can handle Lupine Valen, it's Fern," Effrey laughs as he pushes up his spectacles. "She's managed to handle his out-of-control Level Five fire quite admirably."

Fyn'ir's grin widens, his squirrel on his head now, like a jaunty cap. "Of course, you're right," he agrees. "She'll quickly bring Valen to heel."

"I can't wait to see your eyes change!" eight-year-old Kendra enthuses, breaking into his friends' teasing.

Valen looks down to find his sister suddenly beside him and hugging his arm as she beams up at him with a warm, wide smile. Kendra confidently tosses her long raven-hued hair over her shoulder, one hand coming to her hip with rakish bravado, her stance dominant. Her ever-present twin, the equally raven-haired, green-hued, and ultraconfident Edwin, lopes up beside her, mirroring her cheerful grin, both twins strongly resembling their mother, Diana, in both facial features and unflappable charisma, their Dryad hue a mirror of their father, Rafe.

"We won't just be your 'dopted brother and sister after this," Edwin adds as Valen brings his hand to his brother's shoulder. "We'll be full packmates and look even more alike!"

"You don't have to look alike to be family," Diana good-naturedly chides.

And Valen knows this to be oh so very blessedly true.

He glances around at his huge extended family, their collective love washing over him, and his love for them heart-expandingly drawn to the surface by the Xishlon moon.

His aunt Aislinn and uncle Jarod approach, Uncle Jarod's arm looped around her waist, the both of them Voloi University archivists.

"For you on your Change Day," his aunt Aislinn enthuses as she hands him a slim violet tome.

Valen glances down at the book. *Lupine Forest Dream* by Aislinn and Jarod Ulrich. He smiles—it's their new book of poetry.

Touched, Valen embraces them both, shooting a smile as Aislinn and Jarod's seven-year-old daughter, Daciana, peeks out from behind them. The black-haired, amber-eyed child smiles back at Valen, her arms wrapped around a slim stack of books as usual, the whimsical, gentle child always bringing "three book friends" with her everywhere she goes.

Daciana's best friend, the equally bookish and bespectacled eight-year-old Fernyllia, hugs Daciana's side, a book bag slung over her shoulder. Three branches are sheathed at Fernyllia's hip, and her small owl kindred sits solemnly on her shoulder. Her black hair is woven into braids and secured with purple ribbon, her parents, university professor Jules Kristian and naval Dryad'kin Lucretia Quillen, hovering nearby.

THE DRYAD STORM

Fernyllia's glimmering green-hued face is turned expectantly toward Valen, the girls obviously curious about all his Change Day gifts. He can't help but remember when Fernyllia and Daciana were tiny babes with comical tufts of black hair, and he finds himself unable to suppress a swell of delight to have grown up alongside so many of the children here.

"A joyous Change Day," his aunt Elloren enthuses as she and his uncle Yvan step forward, and Elloren holds out their Change Day gift, tears brimming in her Forest green eyes.

Valen's throat tightens as he accepts the violin case. Yvan and Elloren's adopted ten-year-old son, Lukas, hugs Yvan's side, the war orphan's wings flapping. It's a blessing to see Lukas so settled in here, the Icaral child originally a feral, uncontrollable, and heartbreakingly unnamed three-year-old when first brought to Elloren and Yvan.

Lukas is still fiery and high-strung, but blossoming in the circle of fiery love coming not only from fire-resistant Elloren and Yvan and their daughter, Tessla, but from so many friends and family who are gathered here now—his aunts Ariel and Wynter as well as Naga's expansive horde, along with Grandma Soleiya's community of Fire Fae friends and loved ones.

"I helped make the violin," Tessla crows with an emphatic flap of her wings and a cheeky smile, the thirteen-year-old flame-eyed and fiery, her black horns glinting purple in the moonlight, her garb, which is usually every shade of the rainbow, glowing purple instead, lines of Xishlon moons printed along every hem. A powerful Icaral and Light Mage, Tessla is the spitting image of both her father and equally fiery grandmother, Soleiya, who hovers nearby. But Tessla's black hair and green coloring are all Elloren, a rainbow parakeet kindred perched on her shoulder.

Valen opens the violin case, heart leaping when he finds the instrument made of purple wood and handcrafted by Elloren and Tessla nestled inside, two lacquered purple moons shining bright from its surface. For a moment his throat is too knotted with emotion to allow speech.

"It's beautiful," he finally manages as he's enveloped in a hug by Yvan, Elloren, and Tessla, wiry Lukas reaching out to tentatively bump Valen on the arm. Valen ruffles Lukas's hair and is rewarded by a quick flash of a smile.

"Welcome to an even fuller bond to our very strange family," his uncle Wrenfir drawls as he approaches with his partner, the Death Fae–Dryad Hazel, their arms wrapped loosely around each other, tendrils of Hazel's Darkness encircling them

713

both as Wrenfir's bobcat hugs his side. There's a huge smile on Wrenfir's dark lips as he holds out a small vial filled with midnight-black liquid, a swirl of Dark mist encircling it. "A potion," Hazel explains. "To further enhance the night vision you're about to develop along with those amber eyes."

Valen thanks them both and takes the vial, the Dark mist winding around his hand. He considers how different Wrenfir has been since Hazel emerged from his melding with Natural Death several months earlier.

It's as if a heavy misery lifted from Wrenfir, their renewed pairing resulting in the most unexpected of outcomes. Their magic infusing each other's rootlines, they promptly set about pooling their Deathkin and Dryad magic to create a net of magic able to hunt down and kill the microbes responsible for the Red Grippe, rapidly clearing the cruel pathogen from the East entirely.

Forever wiping out the deadly disease.

Emotion constricting his chest, Valen considers how so many Dryad'khin couples have merged power through their love pairings. He wonders, as he pockets the vial and anticipation tingles over his skin, what revelations the pairing of his soon-to-be Lupine self with geomancer Fern will bring.

A flood of Change Day gifts follow—a small statue of Vo's purple Xishlon dragon manifestation, gifted to him by his uncles Trystan and Vothe, who are partially responsible for the restoration of the mighty Zonor River; a piece of rare purple lumenstone shaped like a Xishlon moon, given to him by Fern and Fyn'ir's parents, Sage and Ra'Ven; a pale-white moon orchid gifted to him by Yulan and her Alfsigr love, Rhysindor; and a green Caledonian pine seedling brought back East for him by Valasca, her love, Ni Vin, and their good friend Alder, along with an invitation to visit their fledgling Amazakaraan colony in the Western Realm, where they've recovered seeds under the Shadow filth and are fighting back the gray with rewilded land.

Valen can barely keep up with the flood of gifts and love. He accepts an emerald tin covered with Smaragdalfar script from Mora'lee and Fyon.

"Smaragdalfar courting tea," Mora'lee saucily reveals with a wink and a sly glance toward Fern as he accepts the tin.

"Enough for thirty cups," Fyon adds, grinning.

Next comes a conch shell holding whale song from Gareth and Marina; a violet reed basket that Or'myr, Tierney, and their fifteen-year-old daughter, Li'ra, crafted for him, purple gems sewn into the basket's intricate design, tins of mushroom tea inside; then a portal stone from Gwynn, Mavrik, and Gwynn's Dryad'khin parents, containing enough charge for several journeys to visit distant friends and family; and a whole host of other presents, including an Amaz blessing pendant depicting the Goddess's starlight deer form from Queen Freyja and her partner, Clive, and a statue of a purple crystalline geo-tree crafted by Thierren and Sparrow, the geo-tree having become a potent symbol of victory over the Shadow.

Finally, all the Change Day gifts have been received, Valen's friends carrying them off to create a sizable pile at the clearing's edge, but Valen knows he'd be content if there were no gifts at all. Because he's rich in the most important things he could ever hope to possess.

Connection . . . and love.

And soon I'll be even richer, he muses, looking to the Forest's canopy.

Rafe steps forward, smiling with vast affection. His father's unfailing paternal love washes over Valen, filling him with the fierce desire to do his family proud.

"Are you ready, son?" Rafe asks, glancing up at the Xishlon moon, Vo's benevolent light shining down on them all.

Valen straightens, thrilling to the muscular, energetic feel of his body, vitalized by the moon, his emotions swept up in anticipation of joining fully to his pack then to his love, Fern.

"I'm ready," he answers, clear and sure as the moon above.

The throngs around them grow reverentially quiet, anticipation crackling in the air, as he and Rafe speak the traditional words of consent and Rafe grips hold of Valen's upper arm and moves to lower his elongated canines to the base of Valen's neck, Valen's heart quickening to a pounding rhythm.

"WAIT!"

A woman's urgent, desperate plea sounds out through the clearing.

Everyone pauses, and Rafe straightens as they all look toward the Gardnerian woman rushing out of the purple tree line, her hue a pale, dormant green, her ears rounded.

Four other Mages accompany her, their pale green faces tensed with dour expressions, all of them garbed in conservative Styvian Mage blacks. White birds are embroidered over their chests, wands sheathed at the male Mages' sides, all of them around Jules Kristian's age.

"What is it you seek, friends?" Rafe inquires calmly, as Diana gives a subtle flick of her hand, claws snicking out, the pack tensing as one—an army facing possibly hostile invaders.

The Mage woman's narrowed gaze darts around the gathered crowd, as if sizing up an enemy, and Valen is struck by her resemblance to . . . *himself*, the two of them possessing the same sharp features, vividly green eyes and curve to their lips.

The Mage woman is now peering at him strangely, as if he's the focal point of the entire world, the family and friends surrounding him mere chaff—something to be swept clear away.

"I am Magda, your aunt—your only surviving relative," she states, shooting Rafe and Diana a look of barely concealed loathing before fixing her intense gaze back on Valen. "We have spent *years* trying to find you. We guessed you were here when we heard of this gathering. Valen, *please*. We need to talk before you do this irrevocable thing."

Valen blinks in surprise at the desperation in all the Mages' eyes. Deeply thrown, he looks to Fern. Her rose-hued brow is high with surprise, her gaze narrowing into a look of concern. He turns to Diana, who seems to be swallowing a growl, her nostrils flared, her forearms now covered in golden fur. A tortured question in his eyes, Valen meets Rafe's amber gaze as some of that turmoil from his younger years floods back, a shard of it forever lodged in his core.

"Rafe . . ." Valen starts.

Rafe brings his hand to Valen's shoulder, his grip firm and reassuring. "This Change," Rafe says, adamant, "is freely chosen." He flits his gaze toward the Mages before it slides back to Valen. "It's *never* forced. Hear them out if you need to, my son."

Valen pulls in a deep breath, bolstered by Rafe's unyielding acceptance as he's filled with the sudden desire to hear what his Mage'kin have to say. And so Valen nods once at the woman and follows the Mages out of the clearing and into the Forest.

He pauses when they're a few paces in, overcome by the feeling that these Mages would lead him far away, if they could.

And he has no intention of being led away.

They stop and turn to him, their urgency burning through the air.

"Valen, you are not just my kin," the desperate woman states, bringing her hand to his arm, eyes ferocious, as if she's *willing* him to understand her earnestness via her stare alone. "You are the Magedom's last, great hope. Valen, you are our people's *next Great Mage*."

Valen stiffens. He's studied history. Read books given to him by Jules and

Lucretia. He's clear on what came of the Magedom having ultimate power.

And he knows that the power in him is beyond Level Five.

"The last time the Mages had power," Valen says to her, "Marcus Vogel took apart the world."

"An *Icaral demon* took apart the world," the woman seethes before pausing, as if she's casting about to find the right words to make him *see*. She swipes her hand toward the clearing. "You've been *tricked* and *fooled*. Brainwashed into believing those heathens and demons should not be slain. Like that demon Marcus Vogel should have been slain. The Magedom itself was led astray. But, Valen, you can change all that for us. You can bring about the true Reaping Times and *fully cleanse Erthia*."

She is staring at him with an expression of such hopeful rapture that a chill shivers down Valen's spine, his emotions rapidly overtaken by a rush of shocked anger.

But then, something else floods in to replace it.

A mixture of pity and gratitude. Pity for these Mages and their life-limiting hatred and delusions. And vast gratitude that they are no longer in power. That they have no power over *him*.

"The Reaping Times won't save Erthia," he insists, quiet and certain.

An expression of pained compassion floods the woman's severe face. "Oh, my nephew, you've been *misled*—"

"No." Valen cuts her off, revulsion for her destructive ignorance shuddering through him. "Stabilizing the weather. Rewilding the land and safeguarding the Waters. Protecting the mangroves. Planting trees. All of us, working together. *That's* what's going to save Erthia. And if you join with us, the Forest will welcome you."

The woman's expression turns vicious. "Don't do this, Valen," she hisses. "Don't let yourself be led down a heathen path. We won't let you throw your life away. We won't let you throw away the Magedom's *only chance to rise again*. You can't let that bastard Urisk's daughter become the next Black Witch!"

For a moment, Valen's mind spins with confusion.

That bastard Urisk's daughter . . .

Comprehension lights, quickly followed by sheer incredulity.

They're speaking of Or'myr and Tierney's teenage daughter, Li'ra, a Level Five Mage-geomancer, who is Fyn'ir's secret crush. Li'ra, who is named for Or'myr's mother and looks *exactly* like a purple-hued Elloren and holds Black Witch level power, only Valen's own power able to best hers.

Li'ra's face an *exact replica* of the Black Witch's.

A purple Black Witch.

Amusement bubbles up inside Valen.

Yes, he thinks, *if anyone should be the next Great Mage, it should be Li'ra. And she's welcome to it.* Time for a Xishlon-bright violet branch on the Black Witch family tree.

The sheer outrageousness of the situation sends laughter breaking through Valen's throat, which seems to cast the Mage woman into near spasming anger.

"You cannot fight the Ancient One's Holy Will!" she shrieks at him.

Valen jumps back as two of the male Mages draw wands, viper fast, but Valen is faster, his wand unsheathed as he recites a spell and deploys it.

Quick as a flash, the Mages' wands are charred to flame while several Lupines, Sylvan and Iris, a portion of Naga's horde—including Raz'zor, Oaklyyn, and Ariel—and a whole host of his former-Mage Dryad'kin friends emerge from the Forest and surround them all. His friends Erin and Isil level branches at the Mages, the small black cat gifted to Isil by Wrenfir perched on his shoulder. Three Noi panthers prowl in with Isil, growls rumbling in their throats, and Erin's lavender-spotted leopard kindred slinks in beside the panthers alongside a large purple moose kindred with impressive antlers, two bears, and several raptors, all of the animals poised for attack.

The Mages' gazes dart around, taking in the Forest allies and kindreds.

"I've made my choice," Valen says to his Mage'kin, staring his aunt straight in the eye. "I've chosen both my family and what I want to do with my life and my power. Your way is *over*."

And then he turns and strides away, headed back toward his family.

"Wait, Valen . . . stop!" the woman cries.

Valen glances back and sees the Lupines, Wyverns, and Dryad'kin close in behind him, keeping the Mages at bay. He walks back into the clearing and strides up to Rafe, then stills before him and emphatically draws his tunic's edge back from his shoulder.

Rafe studies him closely before nodding. And then Rafe straightens, his voice booming out over the clearing once more. "Valen Ulrich. Do you seek this Change of your own free will?"

A sense of anticipation builds in the air more intensely than before, and Valen's heartbeat quickens.

"I seek this Change of my own free will," Valen affirms.

Rafe draws nearer but pauses, Valen knows, to allow him time. To grant him this one last chance to step away.

But Valen is ready.

Surer than he's ever been in his entire life.

Rafe's smile broadens with parental pride as he takes firm hold of Valen's upper arm once more, then lowers his teeth to the nape of Valen's neck. Valen stiffens as his adoptive father's canines puncture his skin, a sting chasing the motion.

He gasps as amber light bursts across his vision, his gaze drawn upward in a swooping rush that almost buckles his knees, the Xishlon moon seeming to enlarge above, his whole self drawn toward it. His chest expands with the deepest breath of his life as the entire Forest contracts inward to greet him in a euphoric tide. As the energy of the entire pack floods in and bonds to him, steel solid, connecting to his very core.

Rafe draws away, smiling, and the entire crowd bursts into cheers and applause as Valen's internal Magelines and magic fade away and a new power rushes in, strengthening his already strong limbs, drawing the very Forest into his heart.

Suddenly the whole world is brighter, the moon's glow more vivid as his every muscle is suffused with a tingling sensation that heralds his incoming shifter powers—power that will soon give him the ability to fully morph to wolf. The feel of Fern's love for him rides out over the clearing in heady waves that he can newly scent on the very air, her flower-sweet aroma wafting toward him in an intoxicating rush that almost sweeps him off his feet.

And then he's running to Fern and sweeping *her* into his arms, the Forest's love swooping in around them both.

Fern breaks into a delighted laugh before he kisses her ravenously, *wolfishly*, and she returns the kiss in kind. Valen draws back to look to her, his heart feeling moon bright, as he scents her heightened certainty.

Taking hold of her hand, he turns toward the rest of his loved ones. "I have an announcement!"

The raucous cheers die down, the scent of love and support rich in the air, Rafe and Diana beaming at him and Fern. Tears are running down both Elloren's and his geomancer-aunt Bleddyn's faces, the two friends clinging to each other as if joyfully waiting for what everyone likely anticipates is about to happen next.

Tears sheen Valen's eyes as he takes them in. He knows how close Elloren and

Bleddyn were to Fern's grandmother Fernyllia, Jules and Lucretia's daughter's name-sake. And he knows what they all sacrificed to get Fern out of the Western Realm.

Hand in hand, Valen and Fern stride to the center of the clearing, everything washed in the loving light of Vo's purple moon, and for a moment, Valen swears he can spot translucent white birds dotting the surrounding tree canopy. Swears he can feel the Ancient One's and Vo's and Oo'na's and the Lupine Goddess Maiya's combined light shining down on them all.

Clearing his throat, he launches into a recitation of his entire adopted lineage to all assembled, a look of grief briefly tensing Rafe's, Elloren's, and Trystan's features when he gets to the names of the adoptive grandparents he'll never meet—Vale and Tessla. And then Fern, in a voice clear as bell, recites her own lineage as well, Bleddyn and Aunt Elloren and others breaking into more intense tears as Fern gets to Fernillya's name.

"Before my entire pack," Valen announces, his heart thudding as he holds tight to Fern's hand, "I take Fern to be my forever mate."

A sound of joy escapes Fern, happy tears streaming down her cheeks, the entire crowd and even the moon above seeming to hold their breath.

"Before this entire pack," Fern chimes in, "soon to be my own pack as well, I take Valen to be my forever mate."

A roar of cheers rises as Valen pulls Fern into an enthusiastic hug, his beloved laughing and crying at the same time as he kisses her tear-slicked lips, the instinctual desire to set down a full mating bond surging and heating his blood.

But first, there is something he must do.

Something the Forest and the moon are calling him to do.

First, he must run.

"C'mon, cousin!" Li'ra calls to him from the tree line, where all his friends are gathering with eager anticipation. Ready to take that first Lupine run with him. The twins, Kendra and Edwin, look fair ready to burst out of their skin if he doesn't launch into a wolfish streak through the woods with them soon.

Joy and love for his family and friends rushing inside him, Valen sweeps a shocked and delighted Fern into his arms and launches into a run toward the Forest.

His Forest.

Everyone's Forest.

The trees speed past in a blur, his friends laughing and boisterously calling out to him as they run by his side, the Xishlon moon shining down on them all as they merge into the wilds. Into the magical, gloriously complex, blessedly still here Natural World.

It's all out here, Valen's blood sings with joy as he runs.

The Whole of Life.

Here and spread out like a loving banquet. Welcoming and ever waiting.

For all of us.

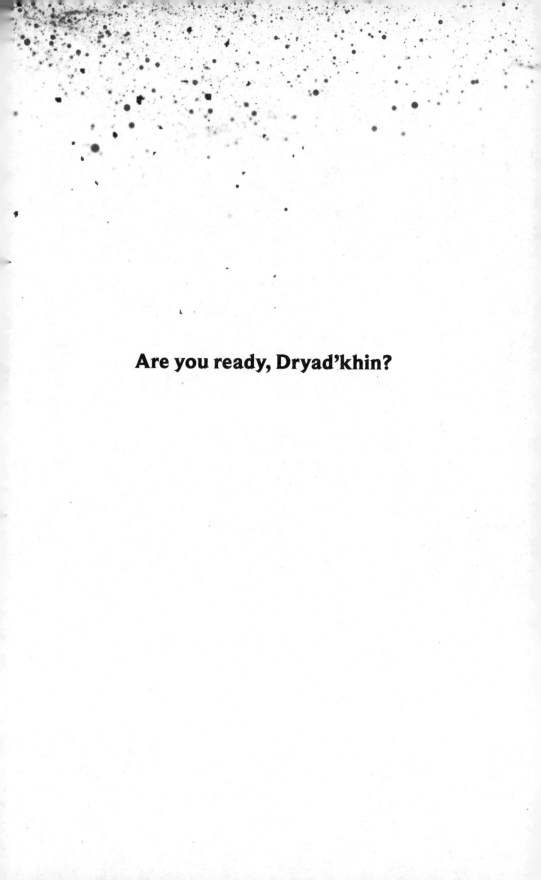

Are you ready, Dryad'khin?

The Shadow Times are here.

And the Forest's Wand is calling to you.

**The center
of all the religions
is calling to you.**

Come to the Forest.

Come to the trees.

**Pick up
the
Verdyllion.**

The Beginning

ACKNOWLEDGMENTS

It's hard to believe that the series has reached its Dryad-y completion—what a magical, arduous, incredible journey! It takes a village to put a fantasy series out into the world, and my village is the best in all the realms.

First of all and above all—bottomless gratitude and all the purple Xishlon moonlight going out to my brilliant, witty, incomparable series editor, Natashya Wilson. Tashya, there would be no series without you. Thank you for giving *The Black Witch* a chance and for bringing your Level Five Mage editing skills to all my messy, adverb-laden manuscripts. It has been a gift to get to work with an editor of your caliber. It has been an even greater gift to get to count you as my friend.

To my wonderful agent, Carrie Hannigan, and to everyone at HG Literary (aka Best Agency in All the Realms). Carrie, it's been an absolute joy and privilege to work with you. Thank you for your unflinching support for this series and all the behind-the-scenes efforts required to bring these books to readers all over the globe. Thank you also to Ellen Goff and Soumeya B. Roberts for all your hard work and for helping to make these books international bestsellers.

To Lauren Miller, magical editor—thank you for the high level of editing talent you brought to the early books in this series, as well as your patience with a fledgling author who had never taken any writing classes, and for your unflinching support and wonderful sense of humor. I'm so grateful I had the chance to work with you.

To the HarperCollins and Harlequin teams—Erica Sussman, Caitlin Lonning, Chris Kwon, Gina Macedo, Ingrid Dolan, Eleanor Elliott, Larissa Walker, Monika Rola, Olivia Gissing, Marianna Ricciuto, and Brendan Flattery.

To my incredible cover artists, Kathleen Oudit and Mary Luna. And to Steve Stone, who designed the cover for *The Dryad Storm*.

To my fantastic audio readers: Julia Whelan (main series), Jesse Vilinsky

(*Wandfasted*), and Amy McFadden (*Light Mage*). Thank you for bringing these books to life in new and exciting ways.

To my village of sensitivity readers—especially the "purple person"—your ideas have made every book in the series miles better. I'm grateful to you all.

Thank you to Reka Rubin, Christine Tsai, Gabrielle Vicedomini, Laura Gianino, Evan Brown, Amy Jones, Bryn Collier, Aurora Ruiz, Krista Mitchell, Gillian Wise, Connolly Bottum, Brittany Mitchell, Bess Braswell, and Siena Koncsol for all your hard work and support.

To my international publishers, editors, audio readers, etc., thank you for turning this series into an international bestseller in a growing number of languages.

To my Epic Writing Group members—Cam M. Sato and Kimberly Ann Hunt—it's been a deep privilege to be on this author journey with both of you. And thank you, Cam, for your beautiful edits—the books are all so much stronger because of your talent.

To favorite fantasy author and friend Selene Kallan—Selene, thank you for all the beta reading and for letting me be part of your author journey as well. And for creating Nox, who is now mine (lol). And thank you to Selene's hilarious mother—my series' premier reviewer *biting nails as I wait to find out if she likes this book.*

To favorite author Nancy Richardson Fischer—your friendship and books have been one of the shining gems of this journey.

To my good friends Betty King and Liz Zundel—I couldn't have done it without you; so much love going out to you both. And thank you to my college buddy Sue for all the support.

To author and dark academia goddess Lia Keyes for being so generous with her talent and friendship, and for helping me design my author website.

To my many author friends—particularly Cerece Rennie Murphy, Zoya Cochran, Erin Beaty, Shaila Patel, Kelly deVos, Tricia Levenseller, McCall Hoyle, Ira Bloom, Abigail Johnson, Jon, Keira, Joel, Meg, and countless others. And to Gini Koch for being so incredibly kind to a nervous fledgling author during my first book tour.

To my late mom, Mary Sexton, and to my deceased friend Diane Dexter—your feisty early support has fueled this series to its completion.

To all my Vermont author/reader friends—Eva Gumprecht, Dian, George S., the members of the Burlington Writers Workshop past and present, Leslie W., and countless others.

Thank you, Seth H. Frisbie, PhD, and Erika Mitchell for help with the science ideas that appear in the series with a fantasy spin on them (distillation, soil science, magnetism, etc.)—I'm grateful to count such brilliant, kind, wonderful people as friends.

A special thanks to Linette Kim and Shara Alexander for support during the sometimes challenging beginning of my author journey—so grateful for the awesomeness you put out into the world.

To Vermont bookstores Phoenix Books, Next Chapter Bookstore, and the South Burlington Barnes & Noble (where quite a bit of the early books in the series was written)—your ongoing support has meant the world to me. A special shout-out to Tod Gross for his kindness toward new and aspiring authors.

To all the librarians and libraries across the globe who have supported this series—thank you. Getting to know so many of you has been a highlight of this journey.

To favorite authors Tamora Pierce and Robin Hobb for all the inspiration, encouragement, and for writing such wonderful blurbs for *The Black Witch*—your support has meant the world to me.

To my Sweeto and awesome daughters—thank you for your support of this writing thing and for always having my back. I love you all very much.

To my brother, the Famous Beanbag, for being the Best Bro in All the Realms, even though I'm STILL waiting for you to write a book with a dragon in it! ☺

To my sister-in-law, Jessica Bowers, who helped me to find my epic agent—thank you! And to my mother-in-law, Gail Kamaras, for her friendship and support.

To my recently deceased elderly cats Bings (Lord Charles of Bingley) and Sammy—thank you for being my faithful, sweet, and epic feline companions during the years it took to write this series. You were the best furry friends an author could ever wish for.

And, most important, to my incredible readers across the globe. Thank you for the countless notes, wonderful conversations, artwork, and friendship, as well as for your inspiration, encouragement, and support of the themes of these books. Whenever I start to feel daunted by the terrible challenges of our times, I think of all of you and hold on to a spark of hope. This series is a Xishlon-moonlight-infused love letter to every last one of you.